Praise for Laurie Forest and *The Black Witch*

"I absolutely loved *The Black Witch* and will have a very hard time waiting for the second book! Maximum suspense, unusual magic— a whole new, thrilling approach to fantasy!"
—Tamora Pierce, #1 *New York Times* bestselling author

"This briskly paced, tightly plotted novel enacts the transformative power of education, creating engaging characters set in a rich alternative universe with a complicated history that can help us better understand our own. A massive page-turner that leaves readers longing for more."
—*Kirkus Reviews*, starred review

"Forest uses a richly imagined magical world to offer an uncompromising condemnation of prejudice and injustice.... With strong feminist messages, lively secondary characters, and an especially nasty rival (imagine a female Draco Malfoy), fans of Harry Potter and Tamora Pierce will gobble down the 600-plus pages and demand the sequel."
—*Booklist*, starred review

"*The Black Witch* is a refreshing, powerful young adult fantasy. This strong debut offers an uncompromising glimpse of world-altering politics amplified by a magical setting in which prejudice and discrimination cut both ways."
—Robin Hobb, *New York Times* bestselling author

"Exquisite character work, an elaborate mythology, and a spectacularly rendered universe make this a noteworthy debut, which argues passionately against fascism and xenophobia.... [The] thrilling conclusion will leave readers eager for the next book in this series."
—*Publishers Weekly*, starred review

"We fell under the spell of this rich, (world! Characters that come alive of swoon-worthy romance! Love the fr Prepare to fangirl!"

D1431332

ce.

ne

The Black Witch Chronicles

The Black Witch
The Iron Flower
The Shadow Wand
The Demon Tide
Wandfasted (ebook novella)*
Light Mage (ebook novella)*

*Also available in print in *The Rebel Mages* anthology

LAURIE FOREST

THE IRON FLOWER

inkyard PRESS

Recycling programs
for this product may
not exist in your area.

ISBN-13: 978-1-335-99582-7

The Iron Flower

First published in 2018. This edition published in 2020 with revised text.

For questions and comments about the quality of this book, please contact us at
CustomerService@Harlequin.com.

Inkyard Press
22 Adelaide St. West, 40th Floor
Toronto, Ontario M5H 4E3, Canada
www.InkyardPress.com

Printed in Italy by Grafica Veneta

To Walter—for everything.

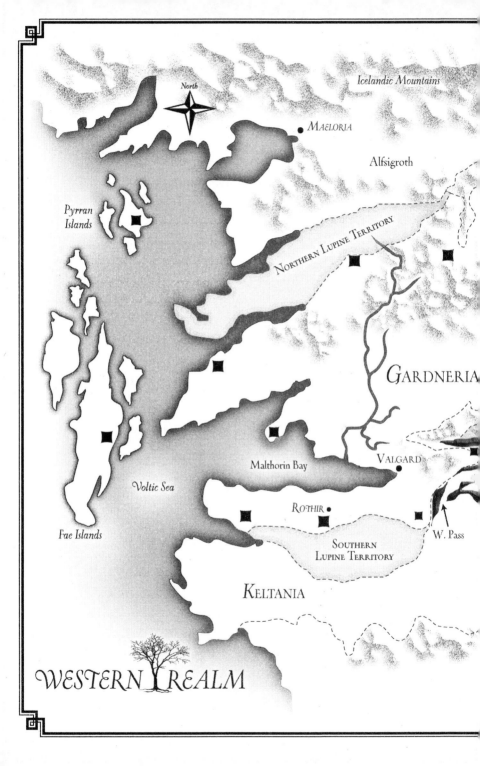

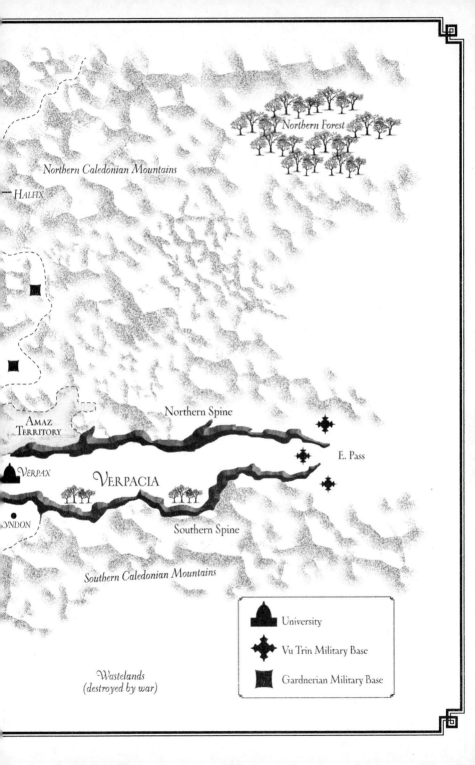

PART ONE

PROLOGUE

Welcome to the Resistance.

Vice Chancellor Quillen's words echo in my mind as I bow my head against the driving wind and hurry through the torchlit University streets. I pull my cloak taut, no longer daunted by the wanted posters nailed up all over the city. Instead, I'm overcome by a renewed sense of urgency and purpose.

I need to find Yvan.

I have to tell him that Professor Kristian and Vice Chancellor Quillen are going to help my friend Tierney and her family escape to the Eastern Realm. Yvan was the one who suggested that I go to our history teacher, so Yvan must know about Professor Kristian's connection to the Resistance.

And like Tierney, Yvan clearly has Fae blood. He needs to get out of the Western Realm, too.

A sudden rush of emotion swamps over me at the thought of Yvan leaving for good. My steps slow, and tears sting at my eyes as I come to a halt beside a torch post and brace myself against it. Pellets of snow fall from the pitch-black sky, their icy points needling the exposed skin of my face and hands as the torch spits crackling sparks into the frozen air.

I struggle to catch my breath, the full force of Gardneria suddenly pressing down, threatening to engulf everyone I love.

A cluster of Alfsigr Elfin scholars silently pass by without even a cursory glance my way, their ivory cloaks wrapped tight as they glide like phantoms through the gauzy veil of falling snow. I watch their pale forms blur, then blend into the misty white as I force myself to take deep breaths and beat back the tears.

Urging myself into motion, I resume my advance down the snow-slicked streets. Eventually, I come to the winding path that leads to the rear entrance of the main kitchen, and a wave of blessed warmth envelops me the moment I step inside. I glance around hopefully for Yvan, but find only Fernyllia, the Kitchen Mistress, scouring the remnants of sticky bread dough off one of the long tables.

"Ah, Elloren." Fernyllia greets me with a warm smile, her pale rose face beaming, strands of white hair escaping her bun. "What brings you here at this late hour?"

Her calm demeanor is so at odds with my roiling emotions that my thoughts scramble for a moment. "I'm looking for Yvan."

Fernyllia gestures toward the back door with her bristled brush. "I asked him to bring some waste to the pigs. There's a few more buckets to go out. I suppose if you and I were to both grab one or two, we could finish the task, save him a couple trips?"

"Of course," I agree eagerly.

"You go on ahead. I'll be right behind you."

I hoist two of the heavy buckets, the muscles in my arms

easily absorbing the weight after months of kitchen work. I shoulder open the back door and make my way up the hill toward the livestock barn, a frosty wind swirling the glittering snow up around me.

As I step inside the barn's door, the sound of muffled conversation reaches my ears. Cautiously, I move toward the voices and peer through the wooden handles of propped-up rakes and hoes and shovels. Two familiar faces come into view, and I freeze.

Yvan and Iris.

Yvan's expression is serious, as is hers, their eyes intent on each other. And they're standing close together—*too* close.

"They're going to start iron-testing everyone," Iris says to Yvan in a quavering voice. "You know they will. I have to get out. I have to get out *now.*"

My thoughts spin into confusion as the meaning of her words sweeps through me.

Iris Morgaine is... Fae?

I struggle to remember even one time I've seen Iris touch iron in the kitchen and realize that, unlike Yvan, she never goes near the iron pots or the stove. She's always preparing pastries and bread.

Always.

If she's so afraid of being iron-tested... Iris might be full-blooded Fae. Glamoured, just like Tierney.

Iris begins to cry as she looks up at Yvan imploringly. He pulls her into a gentle embrace, murmuring softly to her as his strong arms hold her close, bending his head down over her shoulder, his tousled brown hair mingling with strands of her golden locks.

A stinging ache rushes through me, along with the unbidden and thoroughly selfish desire to be the one encircled by Yvan's arms—and the sudden, fierce wish to not look exactly like my cursed grandmother. Maybe then Yvan would want me instead.

You've no right to feel this way, I rage against myself. *He's not yours.*

Iris tilts her head and kisses Yvan's neck, nuzzling against him with a soft moan.

Yvan stiffens, his eyes widening as his lips part in evident surprise. "Iris..." He moves slightly away from her as a frustrated longing for him, so raw that it hurts, explodes inside me.

Suddenly, as if sensing my torrent of emotion, Yvan looks straight at me, his fiery green eyes locking hard on to mine with blazing recognition. And I know, beyond a shadow of a doubt, that somehow, he can read the full intensity of my feelings for him.

Horror and humiliation cut through me. I drop the scrap buckets and run from the barn, out into the snowy night, nearly knocking over a very surprised Fernyllia as I sprint past, almost losing my footing on the snowy hill.

Tears stream down my face as I race into the kitchen and out through the empty dining hall, my breath coming in ragged gasps as I run down corridors and finally duck into a deserted lecture room, collapsing onto one of the many chairs in the dark space and crumpling onto the desk before me. I bury my head in my arms and break down into great, shuddering sobs that strain painfully at my ribs and choke the air from my lungs.

I've let myself fall for him. And he'll never want me.

The pain of Yvan's continued rejection is like a thundering ache, and I'm wholly unprepared for the force of it.

Lost in misery, I'm not aware of Fernyllia's quiet presence until I glimpse her out of the corner of my eye and feel her calloused hand on my shoulder. The chair next to mine scrapes against the stone floor as she sits down beside me.

"You care for him, don't you, child?" Fernyllia asks, her voice kind.

I squeeze my eyes tightly together and nod stiffly. She rubs my back gently, murmuring softly in Uriskal.

"I don't want to be Gardnerian," I finally manage, internally raging, not wanting to wear my black Gardnerian garb ever again. Not wanting the heinous white armband, an unspoken gesture of support for High Mage Marcus Vogel, around my arm. Not wanting any part of the cruel tyranny my people have inflicted on others.

Wanting to be free of all of it.

Wanting Yvan.

Fernyllia is quiet for a moment. "We don't get to choose what we are," she says finally, her voice low. "But we do get to choose *who* we are."

I look up to find her staring at me intently. "Did you know I was married once?" Fernyllia asks with a slight, nostalgic smile. "Before the Realm War, that is." Her face grows troubled, the wrinkles around her eyes tightening. "Then your people came and killed all our men. After it was over, they rounded up the survivors and put us to work for the Gardnerians."

Fernyllia grows quiet for a moment. Then, in a whisper, she adds, "They took my young son down, as well."

My breath catches in my throat.

"Life can be very unfair," she says, her voice strained.

Shame ripples through me. My problems pale in comparison to Fernyllia's. She's been through so much, yet she's still strong, still working to help others. And here I am, feeling sorry for myself. Chastened, I swallow back my tears, straighten and struggle to pull myself together.

"That's it, Elloren Gardner," Fernyllia says, her expression steely, but not unkind. "Buck up. My granddaughter, Fern... I want something more for her. More than being a servant to the Gardnerians and told she's worth less than nothing. I want her to be free of mind and free of body, the former being the hardest part for any of us. They don't have your mind, though—do they, Elloren?"

I meet her gaze squarely and shake my head.

"Good," she says, pleased. "You make sure it stays that way. There's much work to be done. A lot needs to change so that my Fern can have a good life."

MAGE COUNCIL RULING

#103

Any information regarding the seizure of an
unbroken military dragon from the
Gardnerian Fourth Division Base must be
immediately reported to the Mage Council.
Involvement in the theft of military dragons
is punishable by execution.

CHAPTER ONE

OUTSIDER

"Vogel's closed the Gardnerian border tight."

Silence fills the kitchen's sizable storeroom as Professor Kristian's words sink in. He meets each of our eyes in turn, his hands clasped on the broad table before him.

Tierney and I exchange an anxious glance. Part of our Resistance group surrounds the wooden table, our exhausted faces lit by the guttering lamps. Yvan sits across from me, next to Iris, a tight line of tension between his eyes, and I struggle to resist the pull of my gaze toward him. Behind Yvan, Fernyllia leans against shelves stocked with preserves, her rose-hued eyes locked on Jules Kristian, her arms crossed in front of her stout body. Bleddyn Arterra hangs back in the shadows, glowering, her face cast deep green in the lambent light. Vice Chancellor Lucretia Quillen is perched primly beside Jules, her sharp face cool and composed.

There's only a few of us here—we can't often meet in large groups without rousing suspicion. So, it's become our responsibility to relay messages to the other small Resistance groups throughout Verpacia, including my brothers and the friends who helped us rescue Naga, the unbroken military dragon Yvan had befriended.

"The Mage Guard is patrolling their border day and night," Jules continues gravely. He hesitates for a moment. "And now they're using trained hydreenas to hunt down Fae."

"Hydreenas?" Tierney echoes fearfully. She's sitting beside me, her face tight as a bowstring. Her terror is understandable—the huge, boar-shaped beasts are both horrifyingly vicious and able to track scents over long distances.

"Vogel's got the help of the local Gardnerian population, too," Lucretia says ominously. "He's placed a hefty price on the heads of any glamoured Fae." The black silk of her Gardnerian tunic glistens in the lamplight. She's camouflaged just like Tierney, and like I usually am when I'm not working in the kitchens—in a black Gardnerian tunic over a long ebony skirt, a white band of fabric cinched tightly around her upper arm. The white band worn by supporters of High Mage Marcus Vogel.

It's imperative that our fellow Gardnerians believe we're on their side, in order to protect the Resistance. Still, I can't help feeling sick every time I have to don one of those armbands.

I'm only days into working for the Verpacian Resistance, but I know that it's led by Jules, Lucretia and Fernyllia. There's a Keltic arm of the Resistance that carries out acts of sabotage against the Gardnerian and Alfsigr forces, but the Verpacian group mainly works to evacuate refugees through Verpacia and out of the Western Realm.

Fear of both the Gardnerian and Alfsigr militaries runs high everywhere, so the Verpacian Resistance is small, under-armed and overwhelmed. Our only potential advantage is an unbroken military dragon with catastrophically shattered legs and wings.

The situation is daunting, to say the least.

I massage my temple in an attempt to soothe my unrelenting headache. The yeasty aroma of rising dough and the leafy smell of dried herbs waft in from the kitchen, along with an embrace of warmth that provides only slim comfort. I've been in foul spirits all day.

I bolted awake at dawn in a cold sweat, my blankets roped tight around my limbs as my mind shook off yet another terrible nightmare. The same nightmare that's been haunting me for days.

Disoriented, I grasped for details of the frightening dream as they started to fly away, faint as wisps of smoke.

A battlefield beneath a reddened sky, a malefic hooded figure roaming toward me as I cowered behind a blackened dead tree, a pale, spiraling wand gripped in my hand.

Now, many hours later, all that remains of the nightmare is a lingering sense of dread and the vague, unsettling feeling that something shadowed is searching for me.

"Any word on the Verpacian Council election?" Bleddyn asks.

Fernyllia gives her a somber look. "The Gardnerians are now the vast majority."

"Ancient One," I breathe out in dismay as Iris huffs angrily, her lovely hazel eyes filling with outrage.

And fear.

Yvan places his hand comfortingly on her arm, and I shake off the prick of envy that rises in me.

"We all knew that was coming." Tierney's words are acerbic, her mouth twisted into a half sneer. "The Verpacian Council has been a lost cause for a while now."

But it's more than just a lost cause—it's an unmitigated disaster.

Verpacia is populated by a variety of ethnic groups—mainly Verpacian, Gardnerian, Elfhollen and Keltic. Now that its ruling Council is predominantly Gardnerian, it's only a matter of time before their influence bears down on the country and begins to consume it.

Light flashes above us, and we all glance up. A dense cloud has formed near the storeroom's raftered ceiling, small veins of white lightning pulsing inside it. I look to Tierney with alarm, and she gives me an anxious glance in return. Her increasingly powerful Asrai water magic is spinning out of control. Again.

Tierney closes her eyes tightly and pulls in a long, quivering breath. The cloud begins to dissipate, then disappears entirely. Both Jules and Lucretia are studying Tierney with expressions of deep concern, but she stubbornly avoids looking at either of them.

"The Gardnerians have their flags hanging everywhere." Bleddyn punctuates her words with a slice of her hand. She fixes her eyes on me, her green lips twisting with disgust. "They're waving the vile things around, acting like they're the masters of Erthia."

I inwardly shrink back from the force of Bleddyn's glare, all too aware of my Gardnerian black hair and the deep green shimmer of my skin that's only heightened by the storeroom's dim light.

"We're only days away from Verpacia being nothing more than an extension of Gardneria." Iris's voice is shrill as she looks at Jules entreatingly. "We *cannot* be here much longer, Jules."

He nods sympathetically. "We're preparing to move as many people east as we can, but we have to wait a few months for the desert storms to clear and for winter to give way. It's too dangerous right now." Jules does his best to reassure her, outlining when a safer opportunity for escape is likely to present itself, and as much as I dislike Iris, my heart goes out to her.

Yvan's eyes meet mine for a moment, but then he quickly averts his gaze, and I feel a pang of hurt. He's been noticeably cool toward me ever since we rescued Naga and destroyed the Gardnerian military base. And he's become cooler still after my mortifying display only days ago, when I walked in on him and Iris in the barn and put my feelings for him on vivid display.

I pull in a long, shaky breath and force the biting memory to the back of my mind as Jules begins telling Fernyllia about the food supplies he needs for a group of refugees. My hand reflexively reaches for the Snow Oak necklace Lukas Grey sent me. Despite my efforts to keep him at arm's length, Lukas still seems determined to wandfast to me, if his gifts and letters are anything to judge by.

I slide my fingers over the pendant's embossed tree design, the soothing image of a pale leafed tree rustling to life in the back of my mind. Increasingly, I find myself drawn to the pendant, compelled by the comfort it offers, much like the wand Sage gave me.

As I clasp the pendant more tightly, a shimmering energy ripples through me, and I'm reminded of Wynter's words of caution when I donned the necklace for the first time. We both sensed the subtle power in it, a power that calls to some deep part of myself I can't yet name. It holds the warmth of a flickering flame, the rooted strength of an ancient tree— and a temptation I'm having trouble resisting.

I release the pendant with a sigh, glancing covertly at Yvan again. Iris is pressed so near to him that her chin is almost resting on his shoulder. A fresh wave of envy laps at me, and I fight to subdue the bitter feeling, but I'm so exhausted it seeps in anyway. Longing tangles up inside me as Iris leans even closer to him, her blond hair like honey in the lamplight as it brushes against his arm.

Did I imagine it, Yvan? How you almost kissed me that night? Why did you pull away?

As I search Yvan's beautiful, angular face, hoping to find an answer, Iris turns her head toward me. Her eyes tighten with censure, and I wrench my gaze away from them, my face heating to an uncomfortable burn. I struggle to regain my composure, but when I look back up, Iris is still glaring at me. She makes a show of gently resting her head on Yvan's shoulder and wrapping a languid hand around his arm.

Yvan absentmindedly glances at Iris, then brings his hand comfortingly over hers. The triumphant smile on her face makes me swallow hard, my throat gone coarse and dry as my dark mood deepens.

"Is there any word on amnesty for the refugees?" Tierney asks Lucretia as Jules and Fernyllia wrap up their conversation.

"We're trying," Lucretia says. "The political climate is... *difficult* at the moment. The Amaz are taking in a limited number of refugees, but only women—and with the covert understanding that the Vu Trin will eventually bring the refugees east." Seeing Tierney's anxious look, she hurriedly adds, "But that *is* significant. And quite brave of the Amaz." Then Lucretia's mouth hardens. "The Lupines and the Kelts and the Verpacians are wary of provoking Gardnerian ire."

"So, what do we do now?" Tierney asks, almost a demand.

"We continue to work to get refugees out of a Realm that is hostile to them," Jules answers. "Out of the line of Gardnerian and Alfsigr fire." He sits back, takes off his glasses and fishes a handkerchief from his pocket to clean them with. "The local Vu Trin might be able to help us. Their commander, Kam Vin, is sympathetic to the plight of the refugees."

Surprise fills me at this revelation, as I remember how harsh and intimidating Commander Vin was when she wand-tested me.

"Commander Vin is trying to maintain a careful balance, though," Jules adds. "Politically, the Noi people are on guardedly good terms with the Gardnerians. And they don't want their own Vu Trin military to inadvertently provoke a war."

"So, the Noi are appeasing the Gardnerians," Tierney spits out, disgusted. "Like the rest."

Jules flashes Tierney a jaded look. "They are, Tierney. They most certainly are. But it appears that Commander Vin sees the writing on the wall. She knows that it won't be possible to appease the Gardnerians forever, so we have a potential ally in her. Which is good, because the current situation is likely to get much worse."

"It's *already* gotten much worse," Tierney adamantly states.

"She's right," Yvan interjects, glancing around. "Some of the Gardnerian military apprentices have started cropping Urisk."

Iris pales, and Bleddyn spits out what sounds like an Uris-kal curse.

"There have been four incidents in the past two days," Yvan gravely continues. He looks to Fernyllia and Bleddyn with concern. "So be careful. Don't go anywhere alone."

"What's cropping?" I blurt out, confused.

Bleddyn glowers at me. "The Gardnerians are cutting off the points of our ears, like we're animals. And shearing the hair from our heads. *That's* what cropping means."

Holy Ancient One. Shock and nausea roil through me.

"A Gardnerian farmer here in Verpacia was attacked by some Urisk workers," Yvan says to me, his demeanor momentarily softening as his eyes meet mine, as if he can sense how much this has upset me. "The Gardnerians on the Verpacian Council are calling for retribution, and it's provoking mob violence."

"I heard about the situation on that farm," Fernyllia says, her expression hard as a plank. "The Gardnerian farmer was abusing his workers mercilessly. Beating them to within an inch of their lives." She hesitates, her expression darkening. "And much worse."

"Grandma? What's going on?"

All eyes dart to little Fern, who has just slipped into the room. Her arms are wrapped around her favorite cloth doll, Mee'na—the doll lovingly stitched by her grandmother, Fernyllia. Mee'na has blush-white skin, rose braids and sweeping pointed ears, just like Fern.

I pray that she didn't hear a word of this horrible conversation, but I can tell from her wide, frightened eyes that she's heard quite a bit.

Fernyllia clicks her tongue and goes to her granddaughter. She creakily lowers herself to Fern's level, hugs the child close and murmurs to her gently in Uriskal.

Olilly slips in shyly behind Fern. The lavender-hued Urisk kitchen girl gives us all a slight, faltering smile.

"Run along with Olilly now," Fernyllia says in a reassuring tone. "I'll come tell you a story in a bit, *shush'onin*."

Fern gets a hug and kiss from her grandmother and leaves with Olilly, the wooden storeroom door clicking shut behind them.

We're all grimly quiet for a moment.

"Keep Fern hidden," Yvan says to Fernyllia, stark warning in his eyes. "*Well* hidden."

A wave of horror sweeps over me. The thought of someone grabbing up little Fern, shearing off her rosy braids and cutting off the points of her ears—it's so ghastly, I can barely wrap my mind around it. A few months ago, I never would have believed that even the threat of such cruelty could exist in the world.

Now I know better. And it sickens me.

"One last terrible announcement." Jules turns to face Tierney and me. "The mandatory wandfasting age for Gardnerians has been lowered to sixteen. All Gardnerians over the age of sixteen not fasted by the end of the fifth month will be *forced* into a fasting by the Mage Council."

I glance down at my hands, nails chipped and skin stained blue and green by medicinal herbs. Blessedly unmarked. *But not for long.*

I shudder as I imagine black fasting marks creeping across my hands, forever binding me to someone I barely know. My aunt Vyvian has started sending threatening letters in the last few weeks, hinting that she might need to cut back on the expensive medical care for my sick uncle if I don't fast to Lukas Grey soon.

Ire rises in me at the thought, along with a burgeoning sense of desperation. Who will I fast to, if not Lukas? There might not be any way to avoid fasting, even if I stay in Verpacia and refuse to return to Gardneria. There's enough of a Gardnerian presence here that my aunt could easily enforce the new fasting mandate.

Tierney's face has grown rigid with anxiety over the looming threat of wandfasting—and the iron-testing that Vogel has ordered to precede each ceremony. A test that would not only reveal who Tierney really is, but potentially kill her.

"We're trying to negotiate with both the Lupines and the Vu Trin to get you and your family and the rest of the hidden Fae out," Lucretia tells Tierney as Jules rolls out a map of Verpacia, flattens it on the table and leans over to examine the handwritten notes.

Escape routes. For Urisk and Smaragdalfar Elves and the Fae-blooded fleeing east.

"Have Rafe and the Lupine twins come see me, Elloren," Jules says, looking up from the map. "We need trackers to scout out new trails for refugees. The Verpacian military has shut down most of the northern routes."

I nod, heartened by the contributions my family and friends are making toward the Resistance efforts. My brother Trystan has enthusiastically fallen in as well, fashioning weapons on the sly for the refugees and their guides.

Everyone in the room knows about all of this.

But Iris and Bleddyn have no idea who was really behind the destruction of the nearby Gardnerian military base and the theft of an unbroken dragon.

And of the people here, only Tierney and Yvan know about Marina, the Selkie hidden in my lodging.

"We're going to need help from you and Tierney, as well," Lucretia puts in. "There's a bad outbreak of the Red Grippe among the refugees streaming into Verpacia, especially the children."

"And instead of showing one shred of compassion," Jules interjects, disgust edging his tone, "the Verpacian Council is using their illness as a reason to bear down on anyone who's here without working papers, making it impossible for the refugees to seek help from physicians and apothecaries."

Tierney and I exchange a resolved glance, but we have no illusions about the difficulty of what we're being asked to do. *Norfure* tincture is tricky and expensive to make, and the ingredients are difficult to procure. But we're the only ones in our small Resistance group who have the necessary skills to prepare it.

"We'll make the medicine," Tierney promises, her voice shot through with rebellion.

"Thank you," Jules says gratefully, then turns to me again. "And Elloren, let your brother Trystan know that we've found someone who can train him in the use of combat spells. His name is Mavrik Glass. He's the head wandmaster at the Fourth Division Base, but he's come over to our side. He's been holding back in his training of the Gardnerian soldiers and saving the best instruction for our people. He's also secretly working flaws into the Mage Guard's wands."

Trepidation flashes through me. I'm sure this was easy to hide when Damion Bane was in charge, but the base has a new commander now. And there's no fooling Lukas Grey.

"Tell him not to hold back on his training anymore," I insist. "And he should stop making flawed wands."

Yvan's eyes fly to mine with surprise, and the others immediately look suspicious "Why?" Jules asks.

I meet Jules's gaze evenly. "Because Lukas will know."

He shakes his head. "Damion never did—"

"Maybe not," I cut in vehemently, "but Lukas *will.*"

Iris's lip curls up in contempt. Her eyes flick to Jules. "Is *she* giving the orders now?"

I hold my hands out defensively. "You need to trust me on this."

"Trust *you?*" Iris asks scathingly.

"You're still in touch with Lukas Grey, then?" Bleddyn's eyes are hard on mine.

I swallow the dry lump in my throat. Lukas's tree pendant thrums enticingly beneath my tunic, and an uncomfortable warmth slides down my neck. "He's...friendly with me. Which could be of use to us."

Yvan's gaze flashes with rancor, and I swear I feel heat surge through the air between us. His mouth sets in a hard, unforgiving line that sends a palpable sting through me.

Jules's and Lucretia's expressions have turned calculating as they coolly appraise me, as if suddenly seeing me in a new light.

Iris stands abruptly, gesturing angrily in my direction. "She shouldn't be here!" she cries. "We shouldn't be working with *any* Gardnerians. Or Alfsigr."

I bristle at this as Lucretia considers Iris calmly, seeming unfazed by her pronouncement. I know Iris doesn't like working with Gardnerian Lucretia, either, but she doesn't have much of a choice in that regard, since Lucretia is one of our leaders.

Tierney throws Iris a caustic look. "I understand where you're coming from, Iris. I really do. But what you're suggesting would put my entire Gardnerian family in danger."

Iris ignores Tierney as she rounds on me, outrage blazing in her eyes. "Are you planning to have Lukas Grey come back to threaten us again? To threaten Fern?"

I remember how Lukas terrorized Fernyllia's granddaughter, and for a moment, I can't even look at Iris. Or Fernyllia. *Especially* not Fernyllia.

"No," I counter, my voice breaking with shame, "of course not—"

"And why does she dress in our clothes?" Iris demands of Jules.

I shift uncomfortably in my dark brown tunic and skirt from home. I've taken to wearing the simple garb again when working in the kitchens, saving Aunt Vyvian's elaborate silks for classes and events.

"Iris, Elloren is one of us," Jules says firmly. "You know how I feel about this."

Iris glares at me. "You're not one of us. You'll *never* be one of us. You're simply bringing attention to yourself. And that places *us* at risk."

Yvan places a hand on her arm. "She's on our side, Iris."

"No, Yvan. You're *wrong*." Iris wrenches away from him and sends me a penetrating glare, as if she can look straight into my soul and spot my grandmother's destructive power hidden there. "You forget who she is," Iris says, her voice low with a foreboding that sends a chill down my spine. "You forget who her family is. She's *dangerous*."

Then Iris gets up and storms out of the room. Bleddyn shoots me a hostile look and follows close on her heels.

Bereft, I glance toward Yvan to find his concerned gaze suddenly riveted on me, open and impassioned. And for a brief moment, the rest of the room recedes as a flare of what he once seemed to feel for me breaks through.

Then it's gone again, his open expression shuttering as the wall between us slams back down. He gives me one last tense, pained look before he gets up and follows Iris and Bleddyn out.

"Elloren, can I speak with you for a moment?" Lucretia asks as everyone else filters out of the storeroom. Tierney looks at me curiously for a moment, then offers to meet me in the apothecary lab. I nod, and she takes her leave as Lucretia quietly closes the door.

Lucretia turns to peer at me through gold-rimmed spectacles. "I don't know if you've realized this yet, but your connection to Lukas Grey could prove to be important for us," she says.

An unsettling tension spreads through me at the mention of Lukas's name.

"He's turning out to be a voice for moderation in the

Mage Guard," Lucretia explains. "He might be someone we could influence."

I look to her with surprise, thrown by this new information. Lucretia seems to register my shock and quickly adds a word of caution. "He could be an ally, but don't let your guard down around him, Elloren. He's not to be trifled with. Still, we've been watching him closely, and he's already been reprimanded several times for refusing to enforce some of Vogel's new religious strictures."

"How does he get away with defying Vogel?" I ask.

"Power. Vogel wants Lukas Grey's power on his side. So, he's overlooking his insubordination. For now, at least."

I'm suddenly wary of what she might be preparing to ask of me and draw slightly away from her, giving her a narrow, guarded look.

"You've made it clear you don't want to fast to him," Lucretia says, her tone full of import. "But...perhaps he doesn't need to know that at the moment. Do you understand?"

I consider this and give a slight nod.

"If Verpacia falls to the Gardnerians," she says, "Lukas Grey gains jurisdiction over the borders here. We need you to find out where his loyalties lie...and whether he could be convinced to make a break with the Gardnerians."

My eyes widen in astonishment. "Do you really think there's a chance of that?"

"Yes," she says, a conspiratorial gleam in her eyes.

An unsettling thought occurs to me, one I'm at first hesitant to share. "I have a strange compulsion to be honest with Lukas," I admit finally. "I can't explain why, but the feeling is...sometimes overwhelming. You should know that."

Lucretia ponders this. "You both must have strong earth affinity lines," she muses.

"I don't have strong anything," I bitterly counter. "I'm a Level One Mage."

She shakes her head at this. "Just because you can't access your power doesn't mean your affinity lines are weak. Your wand level is just a measurement of your ability to use your magic. That never changes. But the depth of power in your affinity lines—that can strengthen over time."

I've often wondered about my Mage affinities, the lines of elemental magic that course through every Gardnerian and begin to quicken as we come of age. Every Mage possesses a different balance of earth, water, air, fire and light lines— lines that I'm starting to have a vague sense of, ever since I started wearing the Snow Oak pendant. I clasp it now, a disquieting flush coursing through me.

"Can you feel your affinity lines?" I ask tentatively. I know Lucretia's a Level Four Water Mage, but being a woman, there are no silver lines marking her Gardnerian silks.

"All the time," she says. "Sometimes it's like an ocean of power rushing through me. Sometimes it feels like small streams of water rippling over the lines. I don't have much of a sense of my other affinities, though." She furrows her brow in question. "Do you have a strong pull toward earth?"

I nod. "I crave the feel of wood. And…if I touch it, I can tell what its source tree looked like."

I remember the image of the dark tree that shuddered through me when I kissed Lukas. "When I'm with Lukas, I can sense that he has a strong earth line, as well," I confess. "And…it seems to rouse mine."

"What do you know of our true lineage as Gardnerians?" Lucretia asks me carefully.

"Professor Kristian told me Gardnerians are of mixed ancestry," I brazenly answer. "We're not 'pure-blooded' at all, regardless of what our priests tell us. We're part-Dryad, part-Kelt."

She nods her head in assent, her lip twitching up in response to my enthusiastic blasphemy. "Like the Greys, your family comes from a particularly strong Dryad line. The telltale sign of that is a strong earth affinity. And powerful Dryads can't lie to each other."

"Well, that presents a significant problem, don't you think?"

Lucretia grows thoughtful. "Perhaps you can focus on what you find appealing about Lukas Grey. That could offset this compulsion and draw him in."

The unspoken suggestion is clear, and I flush as I remember Lukas's seductive kisses, the intoxicating draw of his magic flashing through me. I'm instantly cast into shamed conflict. How can I set out to draw Lukas in when I have such strong feelings for Yvan?

But you can't have Yvan, I harshly remind myself, the image of Yvan embracing Iris painfully fresh in my mind. *So, stay close to Lukas. For the protection of everyone.*

"All right," I tell her, fingering the Snow Oak pendant, a branching rush of heat pulsing through me. "I'll maintain my connection to Lukas Grey."

MAGE COUNCIL
RULING
#156

The Iron Test must be applied to anyone
crossing the border in or out of the
Blessed Magedom of Gardneria.

CHAPTER TWO

REUNION

The sharp glare of sunlight off the thin coating of snow makes my eyes smart.

I peer down the Verpax City street, past the clamoring horse and pedestrian traffic, toward the miller's warehouse and beyond, my breath misting the air. The long edge of the snowcapped Southern Spine pierces the clouds like a jagged blade.

A sense of fatalistic resignation washes over me. The political situation is so bleak, but amid it all, the heart-stoppingly beautiful Spine still rises up. It's so magnificent, it almost hurts to look at it.

I set my heavy box of medicinal vials in the crunchy snow and lean back against a tree, surveying the line of glistening white peaks. Calmed by the solidity of the tree behind me, I pull in a deep breath and rest a hand on the rough, bumpy bark, a summertime image of the glossy-leafed Lacebark Elm suffusing my mind. With my other hand, I unconsciously reach up to grasp the Snow Oak pendant.

My eyes widen with surprise as an intoxicating burst of energy twines through me, branching straight down to my toes. I inhale deeply, concentrating now, feeling a pattern of tendriling earth lines winding through me. But there's also a new sensation—a delicious, prickling heat trailing alongside those lines.

Fire.

Something stirs in the tree behind my back, like the slight ripple on a lake, and a glimmer of fear from the tree fills me with a sudden disquiet. I move away and turn to glance warily at it, releasing the pendant.

What was that?

Men call out amiably to each other, and the sound tugs my attention back toward the street. Two blond Verpacian miller's apprentices are hefting sack after sack of grain onto a broad wagon, their breath puffing smoke into the cold air. They both have white Vogel armbands around their arms, and I frown at the sight. Ever since the Gardnerians won control of Verpacia's ruling council, many non-Gardnerians have begun showing this outward gesture of support for Vogel in an effort to appease the increasingly oppressive Gardnerian majority. No one wants to become a target.

A sizable grouping of Gardnerian soldiers chats jovially off to the side, all of them wearing armbands, as well. Like the soldiers' tunics, the wagon being loaded is pitch-black and marked with a silver Erthia sphere. I scan the row of businesses and notice that Gardnerian flags are now hung from every storefront, whether they're owned by Gardnerian shopkeepers or not.

I watch the soldiers, my expression darkening. Marcus Vogel's massive restructuring of our Mage Guard is now complete, and large numbers of Fourth Division soldiers have returned to rebuild their nearby base under Lukas Grey's command. As a result, there's a marked increase in the number of soldiers present in Verpax City, since it's the closest center of commerce to the base.

The Gardnerian soldiers seem like a foreign invading force to my eyes, dotting the streets in their smart, neatly pressed uniforms, their swords gleaming, their expensive wands in full view. And all around them, the ominous wanted postings flap in the harsh winter wind, a constant reminder that my friends and I are still being sought for the blow we dealt the Gardnerian forces.

I glare at the soldiers and anxiously bite at my lip.

I remember the stories Yvan told me about how Gardnerian soldiers set their dragons on the Kelts during the Realm War. How the soldiers wiped out entire villages and burned them to the ground. As I watch the square-jawed, black-haired young men and take in their smug expressions, I don't doubt for one moment that they'll do whatever is commanded of them.

Without stopping to question any of it.

My dark reverie is abruptly broken by the unexpected brush of warm lips against my neck. I jump back in shocked surprise and whirl around, my heart racing as indignation rises within me.

I suck in a breath as I realize who's behind me.

Lukas Grey.

In all his black-haired, green-eyed military glory.

Memory never can do him justice.

He stands there grinning, handsome as sin, the edge of his dark cloak thrown rakishly over his shoulder. The hem of his uniform is marked with the five silver lines of a Level Five Mage and the additional thick silver band of a division commander. His wand rests loosely in its sheath, and the Fourth Division's dragon insignia is pinned on his chest.

"Don't sneak up on me like that," I breathlessly demand, thrown by Lukas's sudden presence and the way he's smiling at me.

Lukas laughs, leans into the tree and gives me a suggestive once-over. I glance down at myself, suddenly keenly aware of my Kelt-style work clothes, my woolen cloak thrown loosely over them.

"Interesting outfit," he says with a grin. "It won't work, you know." He leans in close. "You still look like your grandmother."

The almost magnetic compulsion to be honest with him takes hold, embittered words escaping my lips. "That's not why I'm dressed like this. I don't feel comfortable wearing clothes made by Urisk *slaves*."

"It *is* possible to have clothing made by Verpacian tailors," he calmly retorts, that ever-present feral gleam in his eyes. "*Nice* clothing."

My traitorous heart deepens its rhythm in response to his alluring tone, his nearness. I look away, desperate to maintain some semblance of coherent thought around him.

You don't know which side he's on, Elloren. Be careful.

Lukas reaches up to hook his finger under the chain of my Snow Oak necklace. I swallow nervously as he gently teases the pendant out from under my tunic.

"You're wearing it," he croons, looking pleased, his fingers skimming along the chain. A prickling warmth stirs inside me in response to his touch. I reflexively reach up to clasp the pendant, and the amorphous heat coalesces into slender lines of fire deep within me.

My eyes widen. "What exactly is this necklace, Lukas?" The fiery sensation shimmers through me in a tingling rush. "When I touch it...it seems to awaken something inside me. Things I've never felt before."

"The wood from the Snow Oak enhances magic," Lukas says, his smile slow and languid. "That's why I gave it to you. It coaxes affinity lines to life."

A sudden surge of heat has me pulling in a shuddering breath, and Lukas's smile inches wider. "Your affinities are quickening, Elloren. What have you been sensing?"

I swallow and look inward, tightening my grip on the pendant. "Lines of earth...like small branches flowing out. All over me. I've been feeling that for several days. And then today, just now...it feels like fire."

Lukas gently takes hold of my wand hand and presses his palm to mine. The branching lines inside me suddenly blaze, as if shot through with torchlight.

"And now?" Lukas asks.

"There's more of it," I breathlessly marvel. "More fire."

Lukas smiles. "Does it feel good?"

I nod in spite of myself as his supple warmth ignites all over my lines. "You're like the pendant," I say with astonished realization.

"I am," he says, his gaze enticingly dark. "I think we both are, to each other."

My heart thudding, I pull my hand away from his and release the pendant, trying to regain my balance. "So... I must have strong earth and fire lines."

"Yes, most definitely. You may sense other lines, in time."

I glance up at him, curious. "What do you have?"

His lips tilt into a suggestive smile. "I think you know."

A warm flush heats my cheeks. *Yes, I know. From kissing him.* "Almost all earth and fire."

Lukas nods.

"Like me."

"Yes. Just like you."

My thoughts whirl as I realize why he's both an enigma to me and completely familiar, all at the same time.

We're a perfect affinity match—the balance of our elemental lines exactly the same.

Suddenly, the possibility that he's not aligned with Vogel is almost as unsettling as the possibility that he is.

Men's voices cut through my turbulent thoughts and pull my eyes across the street. The soldiers' wagon is pulling away, revealing a defaced wall between two storefronts. I inwardly draw back at the sight before me, the troubles of the world crashing down. Painted on the wall in heavy black lettering is a phrase from our holy book.

BRING THE REAPING TIMES.

I cringe at the words, this vile defacement of buildings rapidly escalating over the past few days.

"Doesn't any of this bother you?" I ask Lukas, the question flying out of me. I gesture toward the words, both angered and troubled by them.

Lukas narrows his eyes at the wall, then turns back to me, serious. "Yes, that bothers me," he says, as if in challenge of my view of him. "I don't agree with the religious madness that seems to be gripping our people, if that's what you're getting at, Elloren."

"That's good, Lukas," I say, meeting his gaze squarely. "I don't think I could stomach you if you did."

It suddenly dawns on me—if he can't lie to me, and I can't lie to him, then there's a simple way to find out where he stands.

"What do you think of Vogel?" I ask, challenge in my tone.

Lukas's eyes take on a guarded cast. "Elloren, I'm in the

military. Mage Councils and High Mages come and go. We don't pick the government, we defend the Magedom."

We stare at each other for a fraught moment, tension igniting in the air between us.

A mutual standoff.

I sullenly realize that we might not be able to lie to each other, but we can hold our secrets back.

Lukas raises an eyebrow as if reading my fractious unease and considers me closely. "Are you having a bad day?"

I shoot him a frustrated look, and his lip lifts with a trace of amusment. "I could make it better." His subtle grin widens to a dazzling smile.

Oh, Holy Ancient One.

No, No, No, I warn myself. *He's trouble. Don't let yourself be so completely drawn in.*

I tense my brow pointedly at him, my eyes briefly flicking over his new commander stripe. "How goes the quest for world domination?"

Lukas gives a short laugh as he looks out over the crowded streets. "It appears that the Resistance has one small feather in their cap. Not only did our forces let them destroy half of the Fourth Division Base, they actually allowed an unbroken military dragon to slip right out from under them. Seems no one even bothered to post a guard." He smiles, a predatory gleam in his eyes. "It doesn't matter. We can be disorganized and sloppy and we'll still win. And the hunt for a missing dragon should provide for a day's amusement, don't you think?"

His sly, knowing look sends a ripple of unease through me. "So, this is all just a game to you?"

Lukas's eyes narrow. "You've become quite the little cynic, haven't you?"

"I have. And I find your twisted worldview to be completely infuriating."

In one deft motion, Lukas slides his arms around me and pulls me close.

"Miss me?" His breath is warm on my cheek. "I certainly missed you."

His scent…it's like a deep forest. And I've a new sense of the power thrumming just under his skin, my earth lines stirring in response to it. Being close to him feels temptingly good, like touching wood.

"What?" Lukas's lips brush my ear. "No kiss for the returning warrior?"

My earth lines branch toward his, pulsing with heat. "You're a plague on Erthia," I attempt, trying to steel myself against the pull of our matching affinities, but the words are caught in a gasp as he traces his lips slowly down my neck. His hands slip under my cloak and slide around my waist.

"Who turned you into the little subversive?" His voice is silken, his lips lingering against my skin.

"Why are you pursuing me, Lukas?" I demand weakly, evading the question as I thrill to the feel of his magic reaching for mine.

He laughs against my neck. "Because you're beautiful. And your draw is irresistible. The way your affinities complement mine…it's more than a bit enticing."

His pianist fingers reach up to thread through my hair, and his warmth slides straight through me, kindling my wakening lines of fire. I know I should be stronger than this, that I shouldn't fall so easily under his thrall. But a dark remembrance forms in my mind that abets the temptation to be reckless.

You need to keep your connection to Lukas. To keep everyone safe. And to draw him over to our side.

So, when Lukas leans in to kiss me, I let my lips soften, like sugar melting against his heat. I close my eyes as I fall into his seductive kiss, our affinity lines flaring around each other, his dark branches caressing mine, smooth leaves gently uncurling.

He breaks the kiss and teasingly runs his lips near the edge of my ear. "You promised you'd go to the Yule Dance with me this week's end."

"All right," I agree, far too readily. I tilt my head toward him, foolishly wanting more, wanting to feel the sinuous unfurling of the tree. And his fire.

Lukas releases me, looking smug as he backs away. "I'll come for you at sixth hour."

Panic rears, cutting through the sensual haze. *Marina.* Lukas can't come anywhere near the North Tower while she's hidden there.

"No, don't come for me..." I struggle to find a plausible excuse, but the words stick tight in my throat. It's no use. Try as I may, it's frustratingly impossible to lie to him.

Lukas cocks an eyebrow and smirks. "All right then, I'll meet you at the dance. Look for me."

I arch my brow at him. "You're kind of hard to miss."

He laughs. "So are you, Elloren. So are you."

"I might wear this tunic," I warn in a sudden blaze of defiance.

Lukas's eyes slide over me, making me shiver slightly. "I really don't care what you wear," he says wickedly. Then he turns and strides off.

Oh, sweet Ancient One in the heavens above.

How in the name of all that is holy am I going to keep my wits around him?

MAGE COUNCIL
RULING
#160

The Iron Test must be applied to anyone
applying for Guild admittance in the
Blessed Magedom of Gardneria.

CHAPTER
THREE

IRONFLOWERS

"Elloren. You're not planning on going to the Yule Dance, are you?"

Lead Apprentice Gesine Bane calls the words out lightly from the head of the apothecary lab, but I can hear the underlying threat in them.

"I hadn't planned on it," I reply evasively from the laboratory's rear, my tone softly lamenting. I know that anything I say to Gesine is likely to be repeated back to her cousin, Fallon Bane, who would be furious at the thought of me going anywhere with Lukas.

"Mmm," she says, looking up from the pile of lab papers she's correcting. Her lips pout in mock sympathy. "It seems that Lukas Grey has quite lost interest in you. Pity." Her eyes glint malevolently. "I heard he hasn't visited you once."

"Yes," I tell her, dark amusement flickering inside me. "I've felt his absence acutely."

The thought of Gesine Bane watching me arrive at the Yule Dance with Lukas Grey shatters any lingering hesitancy I might have had about attending. But my small spark of triumph is quickly extinguished as I take in the enormous Gardnerian flag hanging behind Gesine's desk.

More flags are pinned on my Gardnerian classmates' tunics and bags, and everyone in our class wears a white Vogel armband. Like Tierney, I wish I could rip my own hideous armband off, throw pyyrchloric acid on it, strike a flint and watch it burst into a churning ball of blue fire.

As if the Vogel armbands aren't bad enough, Yule Dance postings decorated with Ironflowers cover every available wall of the University. The event coincides with our sacred Ironflower Festival, and it's being openly touted as an opportunity to revel in patriotic fervor and the overwhelming power advantage we now have in the Realm.

The whole thing fills me with disgust.

Rattled, I focus back in on our lab—the distillation of Ironflower essence. It's an ingredient with a huge range of applications, but Tierney and I absolutely despise working with Ironflowers. They're exacting and complicated to handle, and almost impossible to distill without wand-power.

Which means that Tierney and I will be wrestling with this lab for hours longer than the rest of our smug classmates.

As I scan the classroom, I realize that our classmates' receiving flasks are already filled with dark azure liquid, and Gesine has begun swanning around the room to check on everyone's progress. She points her wand at each table's final product in turn, the distillations briefly turning a plum color if the experiment was done correctly.

"We need to hurry," Tierney says anxiously, glancing at the pale blue liquid in our flask. "She'll be back here in a moment."

Her frustration matches my own. If we don't have something better to show Fallon's vile cousin, she'll have an excuse to assign remedial work, which will set us back further and make it even more difficult to pass this class.

A class I need.

"They're feeding magic into the distillation to spark the reaction," Tierney says in a coarse whisper.

"I know," I say, mirroring her discontent. "Fire and water magic…"

"Wait." Tierney's eyes grow wide, as if with a sudden idea. Her gaze drops to my Snow Oak pendant. She glances warily over at Gesine, who's now just a few tables away. "Put your hand on the receiving flask," she whispers, "and hold on to that pendant of yours. If it coaxes magic into your lines like you told me, then maybe I can draw on your affinities with my water power."

I hesitate. It's an audacious idea, but risks revealing her abilities. "Are you sure, Tierney?"

She frowns, as if annoyed that I'm doubting her. "I can control my power."

Cautiously relenting, I reach one hand toward the flask and grasp hold of my pendant with the other, surreptitiously checking to make sure Gesine isn't watching us.

Tierney places her slender hands over mine. "Now, concentrate on your affinity lines."

I pull in a deep breath and tighten my fist around the Snow Oak pendant as the cool sensation of Tierney's rushing water flows through my hand. My earth lines shudder to life in response to her water power, and my fire lines spark. Tierney's water flows through my wand hand with increased force and there's a sudden, hard pull on my lines, my internal branches lacing together and streaming towards the flask, my fire trailing closely behind in a powerful swoop.

Blue fire bursts into existence in the center of the flask, the water coming to a rapid boil, steam gushing from the distillation. We both wrench our hands away from the now scalding glass, and I notice that the liquid is no longer a pale blue.

It's glowing a deep, incandescent sapphire.

Tierney and I exchange a shocked glance as Gesine Bane is suddenly before us.

"What have you two managed this time?" she asks with disdain. Gesine reaches out, murmurs a spell and touches her wand to our receiving flask.

The distillate stubbornly refuses to budge in color.

Frowning, Gesine touches her wand to the glass again and murmurs another spell. This time, there's a bright flash of violet *around* the distillate, but still no change in the color of the liquid.

Tierney and I both gape at the flask.

"It's blocking my magic," Gesine says accusingly, her brow a tight, vexed line. She shoots us a furious glare, as if we're purposely causing trouble, but then her expression turns sly. "Congratulations," she says snidely. "You've managed to fail this lab in the most spectacular fashion yet. Please complete every remedial lab in this section by next week's end."

She turns on her heel and strides away.

"What did we do?" I ask Tierney, both of us washed in blue by the distillation's intense sapphire glow.

"I don't know," she says with a stunned shake of her head. Tierney turns to me, green eyes wide. "I could feel your power, though, Elloren," she whispers. "It was almost as if I could touch it. You've got fire. A *lot* of fire."

I throw her a cautionary look, and we both set to beginning the experiment over again from scratch.

Tierney coaxes the starting solution to a boil as scholars file out of the room. Willowy Ekaterina Salls and her lab partner hang back, peering at Tierney and whispering to each other conspiratorially, both girls united in their long-standing dislike of her.

"I hear Leander's going to the dance with his new fast-mate," Ekaterina crows, her eyes sparkling with malicious humor.

I look swifly at Tierney, concerned. It's still fresh, this wound. Leander Starke has been apprenticing with her glass-maker father for several years, and I know Tierney has feelings for him. But Leander was fasted to Grasine Pelthier, a stunningly pretty young woman, just a few days ago.

Tierney grips the edge of the lab table, head bowed. Her breathing is carefully measured as our pale blue distillation bubbles and sends up steam that's redolent of Ironflower blossom perfume.

"Ignore them," I warn Tierney in an urgent whisper, worried that she'll inadvertently conjure a storm right here in the middle of the classroom.

Tierney grips the table harder. "I'm *trying.*"

"Think on something else," I urge. "Something pleasant."

She knifes a glare at me. "Tell me you're going to the Yule Dance." It's more a demand than a request, her teeth gritted. "That would be pleasant."

Ekaterina and her friend smirk at us and exit the lab, leaving Tierney and me alone in the room. Relieved, I let out a deep breath and turn back to Tierney, surprised by her choice of subject, but eager to keep her focus away from Leander. "Honestly?" I tell her. "I considered not going."

Tierney's eyes widen. "Oh, no. You're going."

I give a dismissive snort. "I told Lukas I would, but I threatened to wear my kitchen clothes."

"Oh, ho. *No.*" Tierney shakes her head emphatically. "You're writing to your aunt. *Directly* after we finish here. You're going to ask her to have a dress made for you. By the finest tailor in Verpacia." She accentuates each point with a jab of her finger. "Tell her you need the dress to be the most magnificent dress on all of Erthia. Trust me, this is language your aunt will understand."

I tense my brow at her, incredulous. "How can I go...*celebrate*," I spit out, "with a bunch of Gardnerians?"

Even though my connection to Lukas could prove to be an important one for all of us, my hatred of all things Gardnerian momentarily overtakes such cold calculation. It's too horrible, what's going on—my own people spreading such fear and cruelty over the entire Western Realm. I don't want to celebrate Yule with them. Or the Ironflower Festival. All I want to do right now is tear all the Gardnerian flags in this room to shreds.

Tierney pins her eyes on me, razor sharp. "My life is quite difficult, Elloren. And it's likely to become even more difficult." She leans in. "The one bright spot, the only one right now, is the promise of you sticking this so thoroughly to Her Evil Majesty, Mage Fallon Bane. She may have been struck down, but with her cursed good luck, she'll eventually rally. And when she does, I want the first thing she hears to be how you went to the Yule Dance with Lukas Grey in the most stunning dress ever seen on all of Erthia." She leans closer, her eyes storming. "Do *not* take this away from me, Elloren Gardner."

I give her a wry look. "You're scaring me."

"Good." A sardonic gleam lights her gaze. "You'd best listen to me on this. Fallon's not the only one who can encase you in ice."

I cough out a laugh. "Fine. I'll go. And I'll get the dress."

Tierney sits back, looking as satisfied as a well-fed cat, a wicked smile forming on her sharp face. "I hope this makes Fallon's evil head explode," she murmurs gleefully. "Into a *million tiny pieces.*"

THE IRON FLOWER

★ ★ ★

Three days later, following the instructions my aunt sent by rune-hawk, Tierney and I make our way to Mistress Roslyn's dress shop in Verpax City.

The feminine boutique is shockingly non-Gardnerian, filled with gowns in a riot of forbidden colors. The walls are papered in lavender, and vases of pink roses stand on gilded tables between the dress displays.

Mistress Roslyn looks down at me with forced politeness. She's the Verpacian version of Valgard's Mage Heloise Florel, only with plaited blond-gray hair and sharp blue eyes. Her seamstress tools are sheathed in a quilted pouch she has tied neatly round her waist. Two green-hued Urisk girls, both about fourteen years of age, hover nearby, looking nervous. The atmosphere of the shop is elegant and welcoming, complete with a steaming tea service and platter of small cakes, but the fear emanating from Mistress Roslyn and her assistants is a palpable, unsettling thing.

This clearly isn't a shop that Gardnerians often frequent. The selection of the formfitting black tunics and long skirts Gardnerians usually wear is ensconced in one small corner of the shop. It's a growing trend among my people to only patronize Gardnerian-owned shops, but I know that fashion is the one area where Aunt Vyvian values craftsmanship above ideology. And from what I've heard, the Gardnerians avoiding this shop are missing out on the work of one of the most talented dress designers in the entire Western Realm.

Tierney and I do what we can to diffuse the tension in the room, trying our best to be friendly and accommodating, as Mistress Roslyn hands me the dress wrapped in tissue paper.

"Open it," Tierney urges me, practically vibrating with anticipation.

A scarlet dress just behind her catches my eye, momentarily distracting me. All scarlet. No black.

What would it be like to wear such a thing?

The whole store, except for the small Gardnerian space, is an explosion of vibrant color. My eyes slide to another gown, this one sky blue and covered with white embroidered birds, ivory lace trimming the sleeves and collar.

"Can you imagine?" I marvel. "A *blue* dress..."

"I don't care about blue dresses." Tierney's fidgeting from foot to foot, practically jumping out of her glamoured skin. "Open it!"

Not wanting Tierney to let loose with a raging thunderstorm right here in the middle of the shop, I turn my attention back to the parcel. I fold the tissue paper carefully back, and we both gasp as the dress is revealed.

It's Gardnerian black, deep as midnight, made of the finest silk and fashioned in the usual design—a long, fitted tunic and a separate long skirt. But it's the most scandalous, decadent, outrageously beautiful Gardnerian dress I've ever seen.

Instead of the sacred Ironflowers as acceptable, discreet trim, there's an explosion of Ironflowers all over the tunic and long skirt—life-size embroidered flowers, lavishly wrought. They look vividly real, as if the dress was held under an Ironwood tree to catch the tree's blossoms as they rained down upon it. The floral design thickens along the skirt's hem, and deep blue sapphires are splashed all over the tunic and skirt in a resplendent array.

And there's more. A separate package sent to the dress shop that I quickly fumble open.

Earrings. Ironflowers made of sapphires with emerald leaves. And a box containing black satin shoes with a slim, tapering heel. Ironflowers are embroidered over the shoes so thickly that they eclipse the black and give the illusion that the shoes are actually blue.

"Wow," Tierney marvels, momentarily dumbstruck. "That is not exactly pious attire."

"She is full of horrible contradictions, my aunt," I say, my eyes riveted on the dress. "She takes a fanatically hard line on practically everything else, but don't mess with her wardrobe."

"Sweet gods," Tierney breathes. "Try it on."

"Please do, Mage Gardner." Mistress Roslyn smiles at me, clearly relieved by my reaction to the dress. She motions toward the curtained dressing room with a practiced sweep of her hand. I carefully pick up the tunic and skirt, leaving the earrings and shoes with Tierney, and slip inside.

The skirt fits perfectly around my waist and the formfitting tunic slips on like a second skin. I pull back the rose-patterned curtain and glide out, because the dress seems to demand gliding. It's as if I'm wearing a work of fine art.

All eyes widen as I approach. I turn toward the full-length mirror, the long skirt swishing, and gasp in wonder.

I'm awash in Ironflowers. Perfectly so. Not a single petal out of place.

"Oh, Mage." Mistress Roslyn's mouth falls open, dazed. She seems to have forgotten to be intimidated by me as she steps forward. With a look of intense satisfaction, she fingers one of the embroidered flowers. "This is azurelian thread," she informs me. "I've never had the privilege of working with it before—it's so expensive. They distill the Ironflower essence and work it into the thread. It takes an incredible number of flowers to create thread like this. But your aunt insisted you have the best." She swallows, her breathing heightened as she turns to the shop girls. "Orn'lia. Mor'lli. Cut the lanterns. Draw the curtains."

The Urisk girls hastily snuff out the six amber-glass lanterns and close the curtains. A reverential silence descends upon the room.

I stand utterly still, mesmerized by my reflection in the mirror. The entire dress is alight. Every Ironflower pulses a deep, glowing azure.

"Holy gods," Tierney says, the green glimmer of her face cast blue in the glistening light of the dress. She grins widely at me. "Fallon's head is *definitely* going to explode. And frankly, Elloren, so will Lukas's."

CHAPTER FOUR

THE WILDS

The icy air of full winter hits me like a punch to the teeth.

I emerge from the North Tower into the twilight of the sloping field, a pale, rusty sunset giving way to a barren gray sky.

My breath clouds the frigid air, and I pull my dark cloak tight, the hood protecting the hair that Tierney carefully styled for me. Even Ariel paused to gape when I emerged from our North Tower washroom garbed in the splendid Ironflower gown. Marina simply blinked at me, as if mesmerized by the phosphorescent glow of the dress. Only Wynter seemed uneasy, her silver eyes instantly lighting on the Snow Oak pendant around my neck, her gaze full of ominous caution.

I pick my way down the jagged, rocky path, ice crunching beneath my feet. My cloak covers most of my dress, but the skirt's iridescent hem peeks out slightly, washing the surrounding snow in a glowing, sapphire halo. The effect is lovely, but my shoulders are tense beneath the formfitting silk, and I feel jittery with apprehension, reluctant to reenter the Gardnerian fold.

Halted by the weighty silence of the immense field before me, I pause and look toward the twinking lights of the University in the distance. My gaze is drawn past the city and up the snowcapped Southern Spine, the immense mountain range looming over everything alongside its northern twin. Both Spines scythe clear through the clouds, their jagged peaks as sharp as my deepening foreboding.

So impossibly high...

A sense of dark premonition washes over me. They have the look of a trap, these mountains. Ready to close in. Just like the Gardnerians.

Black Witch.

The words whisper on the wind, light as snow.

I glance around uneasily. A creeping awareness of the wilds around me sets the hairs on my neck prickling. The tangled forest is close, not more than several feet away.

I can feel it watching me.

I peer into its gnarled darkness and find nothing but winter's emptiness and shadows. Unsettled, I glance back toward the University.

Black Witch.

I stiffen as my heart picks up speed.

"Who's there?" My voice is shrill as my eyes frantically search the shadows of the wilds' border.

There's no reply. Only the dry scratch of some tenacious brown leaves still hanging on to the branches for dear life.

A leaf breaks free on a gust of icy wind and shoots toward me. I give a small cry as it smacks into my face and is quickly followed by several more that graze my cheek, my chin, just below my eye. I bat the leaves away like biting insects as the wind dies down.

Silence.

I look toward the snow-covered ground. A scattering of brown leaves lies piled around my feet, but the rest of the snowy ground is untouched. Alarmed, I stare deep into the forest as palpable tendrils of malice creep toward me.

Black Witch.

My breath tightens, and I step back from the forest.

"I'm not the Black Witch," I whisper nervously, aware of how senseless it is to be having a conversation with the trees. "Leave me alone."

Abruptly, the shadows of the forest pulse. Everything turns black as night. In the span of one terrifying heartbeat, the trees surround me, closing in like a ring of assassins.

I gasp and stumble back, falling onto the icy snow as a red-hot vision of fire bursts into view. Leagues of forest burning. Trees screaming. Branches, thick and dark, flow in and knit together all around me to form an impenetrable cage, and I become acutely aware of the trees' overwhelming desire to strangle me. I shut my eyes and cry out.

A hand closes tight around my arm, and the roar of the fire, the screaming trees—it all falls silent.

"Elloren? What's the matter?"

I open my eyes to see my friend Jarod's amber gaze resting on me with concern. I whip my head toward the wilds.

The forest is back where it belongs, an indifferent wind whistling through it, the leaves around me disappeared.

Tense and light-headed, I let Jarod pull me to my feet and notice that the sky has darkened to the east.

"The forest," I tell him breathlessly, my heart skittering like a rabbit's. "For a moment…it was like…it was closing in on me." My eyes dart cautiously back to the forest that now seems like a sly, sinister child.

Jarod glances toward the wilds and takes a deep breath.

"Sometimes I feel confined here, too. With everything that's happened." He squints up at the Northern Spine. "Like there's no escape."

The trees, I want to tell him, *they want to kill me.* But I hold my tongue. It's bizarre to be afraid of trees.

I flex my hand instead, wishing I still had my pale, spiraling wand—the wand I gave to Trystan. I know it's impossible, and yet more and more, I imagine my wand to be the actual Wand of Myth. Increasingly, I dream about it, along with ivory birds on branches made of starlight.

The wand would take care of me. Protect me from the trees.

"Where are you going?" Jarod asks, examining my carefully made-up face, glittering jewelry and styled hair.

I glance uncertainly toward the spires of the University as my heartbeat slows to a more normal pace. "To the Yule Dance." I reach down and brush snow off the side of my cloak, my dress unharmed.

A glimmer of confusion passes across Jarod's expression. "Who are you going with?"

I hesitate to meet his gaze. "Lukas Grey."

Jarod's eyes widen. "But... I thought you and Yvan..."

"No," I cut him off sharply, a stinging flush rising along my neck, remembering his Lupine ability to read everyone's attractions. "He doesn't want me."

I can see Jarod biting back disagreement, but like my brother Trystan, he's not prone to judgment or prying. He quietly extends his arm out to me. "Come on. I'll walk you there."

I stare at him in disbelief. "You want to escort me to a Gardnerian dance? Are you sure, Jarod? You know how they're likely to react. I don't want you to get in trouble on my behalf."

Jarod gives a slight, resigned smile. "I can take care of myself. And I'm curious about your mating rituals."

I raise an eyebrow at his blunt phrasing.

Jarod's smile disappears as he glances down at his feet. "And...maybe..."

Aislinn. Maybe Aislinn will be there.

My dear friend Aislinn Greer, who yearns for Jarod as much as he does for her. Whose strictly religious Gardnerian family would never allow them to be together.

Who's promised to another.

When Jarod looks back up at me, there's undisguised longing in his eyes, and it pains me to see it.

A hard gust of wind bends the trees and flattens my skirt against my legs.

Black Witch.

Panic gives a hard flare inside me, and I whip my head toward the forest. "Did you hear that?"

"Hear what?" Jarod cocks an ear and listens.

The wind dies down, the world silent once again.

I have to be imagining this. If Jarod can't hear something with his heightened senses, then it isn't there.

I narrow my gaze on the forest. "Do you think she's out there somewhere?"

His brow tenses in question. "Who?"

"The Black Witch of Prophecy."

Please, Ancient One, don't let it be Fallon Bane.

Jarod's expression turns somber as a lone snowy owl makes its way across the darkening sky and the first stars make their showing as pinpricks of light.

"Well, I suppose if she is," Jarod finally says, "we'll have to hope that our side finds her before Vogel does." He attempts a small, comforting smile, but his eyes remain serious.

He offers his arm to me again, and this time I take it, the two of us setting off down the field together.

Jarod chats with me amiably as we walk, but I can feel the trees watching my back.

I turn once to glance uneasily back at the wilds.

CHAPTER
FIVE

THE YULE DANCE

Hoods pulled over our heads, Jarod and I move against the flow of festive Gardnerians that's streaming toward the White Hall's main entrance.

A Gardnerian soldier positioned by the door spots us and narrows his eyes at obviously Lupine Jarod, his expression rapidly turning belligerent.

I grab hold of Jarod's hand. "C'mon. If we go that way, they'll stop us."

We dodge around Gardnerian couples, stifling laughter at the astonished looks everyone gives us. Clinging to each other's hands, Jarod and I sneak in through the side entrance that only kitchen workers know about. The muffled sounds of orchestral music and lilting conversation can be heard through the wall of black velvet fabric that hangs in front of us, the curtains extending around the White Hall's entire peripheral walkway.

I pause to pull my satiny shoes out from my inner cloak

pocket and quickly slip them on, leaving my wet boots neatly propped by the edge of a wall to retrieve later.

Jarod and I exchange an anticipatory glance and pull back the edge of the velvet curtain. Both of us excitedly peek inside, like two kids about to find forbidden candy. Warm air rushes toward us, the music growing louder and clearer.

"Oh, Jarod." I draw in a sharp breath as I take in the incredible transformation the hall has undergone, my earth affinity lines shuddering to life.

Ironwood boughs are suspended above the crowd to create a low ceiling, completely hiding the White Hall's constellation-adorned dome. Earth Mages must have coaxed the boughs into full bloom, the Ironflower blossoms glowing a sublime blue. Ironwood trees planted in enormous, black-laquered containers ring the hall and are interspersed throughout it, transforming the vast assembly room into a living forest.

A dance floor at the far end of the hall is filled with twirling couples, and scores of blue glass lanterns hang from the dense, overhanging branches, their candles only heightening the ethereal glow of the Ironflowers. The sapphire light sparkles off jewelry, dress beading and the crystal flutes being waved around by celebratory, laughing Gardnerians.

I breathe in deep, the smells of expensive perfume and Ironflower blossoms seductively transforming the hall's normally dank air. Urisk and Keltic kitchen workers move through the crowd with expressions of forced pleasantry, serving food from golden trays and tending to the lamps. I briefly spot Fernyllia carrying out a selection of appetizers and search the white-aproned workers for a glimpse of Yvan, but he's nowhere in sight.

Anxious tension rises in me. *What if Yvan's working here tonight?*

Jarod and I slip into the hall and remain discreetly behind the line of potted Ironwood trees. I leave my cloak on, not wanting my phosphorescent dress to attract attention just yet, but I pull down my hood and shake out my bejeweled hair. Jarod follows suit, grinning at me, his blond hair charmingly mussed.

An orchestra performs from the hall's central dais, the music full of melancholy grandeur. The whole scene is both breathtakingly gorgeous and completely disheartening. Seeing so many Gardnerians strutting about like a flock of triumphant, predatory crows is daunting, and it's hard to look at the oppressively large Gardnerian flag hanging behind the musicians, with its silver Erthia orb on black.

They're weapons, these flags. Meant to intimidate.

"Refreshment, Mage?"

Torn from my troubled thoughts, I glance down to find an elderly Urisk servant offering up a golden platter, her eyes flitting toward Jarod with surprise, then nervous concern. I glance down at her tray, and my gut clenches at the sight of our traditional holiday cookies, cut in the shape of Icaral wings. Wings like those of my roommates, Ariel Haven and Wynter Eirllyn.

I decline the horrid things with a shake of my head, and the Urisk woman seems more than happy to flee from us.

"Wings?" Jarod inquires as he watches a group of Gardnerians pick the buttery cookies off a tray, the couples laughing as they snap the wings in two before taking a bite.

"Icaral wings," I reply ashamedly as I remember the baskets of cookies the Gaffneys would send over every Harvest and Yule. "You break them."

Jarod's brow tightens as tray after tray of the cookies are brought into the hall, the snapping of the wings sounding like pelting rain. I wince, every snap an imaginary tear at Ariel's wings. At Wynter's.

My people will conquer the Western Realm, I lament. *As easily as they break these cookies.*

"What's the significance of the Ironflowers?" Jarod asks. "They're everywhere."

"There's a story in our holy book," I distractedly reply. "A famous prophetess, Galliana, saved my people long ago. The Mages were fleeing from demonic forces and were completely outnumbered. Galliana used the demon-slaying powers of Ironflowers as well as the Sacred Wand of Myth to fight back. She's often called the Iron Flower for that reason."

"How did she do it?"

I shrug, having heard the story countless times, its drama dulled by repetition. "She rode into battle on a giant raven and struck down the demons with a river of Magefire. Then she led my people across a desert to safety. We've a holiday every year commemorating her victory, just before Yule—*Gallianalein*. The Ironflower Festival. The dance just happens to fall on it this year."

"Hmm," Jarod says thoughtfully. He looks around. "Well, if you're going to build a festival around a flower, you certainly picked a beautiful one." There's a hint of rapture in his tone, a devotion that's often there when he and his sister Diana talk about the natural world.

As he studies the Ironwood decor more closely, Jarod frowns. "They had to kill all these trees to do this." He glances at me, deep disapproval all over his face.

"I suppose they did." I survey the boughs and the potted trees cut free of their roots, abashed by the way my earth affinity is pulling toward all the dead wood.

Hungry for it.

"It's incredibly strange, all this," Jarod comments. "Why

do you Gardnerians build everything to look like fake forests, while you hate actual *living* forests and revel in burning them down?"

"It's part of our religion." I shift uncomfortably. "We're meant to subdue the wilds. They're supposedly filled with the spirit of the Evil Ones."

Offense flashes in his eyes. "Charming. Truly."

I think of the hostile trees. Whispering to me on the wind. Sensing the magic in my veins...

"And you know what's stranger still?" he asks.

I shake my head and look to him questioningly.

Jarod scans the expansive hall. "Most of the couples in this room do not want to be with each other."

My brow lifts in surprise. "Really?"

"More than half. It's awful." Jarod points out several ill-matched couples in a rare showing of his Lupine senses. Then he points out the many true attractions that run completely counter to how the couples are paired. He gestures toward a tall, slender military apprentice in a slate gray uniform marked with a silver orb. He's standing next to a pretty, young Gardnerian woman, the two of them with fastmarked hands.

"You see that man over there?" I nod. Jarod then points at another young man—a muscular mariner's apprentice, his black tunic edged with a line of Ironflower blue. "Those two men, they're madly in love with each other. I can feel it from all the way over here."

Surprise flashes through me, and I observe the two young men more closely. Soon, I can pick out a few surreptitious, heat-filled glances. It's subtle, but there. I immediately think of my brother Trystan, desperately wishing that he was able to love freely, but scared about what would happen to him if he did.

"They'd be thrown in prison if they were found out," I tell Jarod, knowing he's probably already sensed my fear for Trystan's safety.

Jarod's blond brow furrows. "I don't understand your people. You take perfectly natural and normal things and write religious laws that state they're unnatural. Which is absurd."

Surprise takes hold. "You allow this in Lupine society? Men with men?"

"Of course." He's looking at me with a mixture of pity and concern. "It's incredibly cruel to treat people this way."

"There's nothing in your religion that condemns it?" I ask, stunned. *Nothing that condemns my beloved brother? Or forces people to hide who they really are?*

Jarod studies me closely, perhaps reading my suddenly troubled emotions. "Elloren," he says with compassion, "no, there's not. At all."

Tears sting my eyes, and I have to look away from him. "So, Trystan would be completely accepted for who he is in Lupine lands?" My voice breaks around the whispered words.

Jarod hesitates, an expression of dismay knotting his brow tighter. "Yes. But…he'd have to become Lupine first."

I throw Jarod a caustic look. "Which would strip him of his Mage powers, since Lupines are immune to wand magic." I shake my head ruefully. "He's a Level Five Mage, Jarod. It's become an important part of who he is. He'd never want to lose that."

Jarod nods gravely, and anger on my brother's behalf spikes inside me. "So, there's nowhere for him to go, then. Nowhere he can be himself and not be vilified for it."

"Only the Noi lands," Jarod says quietly, but we both know that the Noi people aren't likely to welcome the grandson of the Black Witch into their lands. I inwardly curse the cage that the people of both Realms have forced my brother into.

"Do your people have dances?" I ask a tad crossly, frustrated by the wretched state of things and struggling to regain my composure.

Jarod looks out over the hall, his expression edged with contempt. "No. Not like this. Our dancing...it's more of a spontaneous thing. And the way your people dance...it's so...*stiff*. Our music has a strong rhythm to it, and when our couples dance, it's very close. Not like this. This is like a child's dance."

A flush heats my neck as a picture of Lupine couples fills my mind, twined around each other, moving sensuously to the rhythm of the music.

As I scan the crowd, my eyes land on Paige Snowden. She's nibbling on a skewer of toasted goldenfish that glint in the lantern light and standing with a knot of young Gardnerian women. A shadow falls over her expression as they're joined by her fastmate, Sylus Bane. I recoil at the sight of Sylus in his military uniform, a gleaming wand at his hip, the same charismatic, arrogant stance and cruel smile as his vicious siblings, Fallon and Damion.

"You know," I say to Jarod, intimidation pulling at me, "when Fallon recuperates and finds out I was at this dance with Lukas Grey, she's going to kill me."

"No, she won't," he counters with surprising confidence as he selects a crystal glass full of blue punch from a servant's tray. "Diana told Fallon quite a while ago that if she ever bothered you again, she'd rip her head off and display it on a post in front of the University gates."

I cough out a shocked laugh as Jarod grabs up another glass of punch and hands it to me. He lifts his glass in a toast and straightens. "To freedom," Jarod says, smiling at me. "For everyone."

"To freedom," I agree, momentarily overcome by the sentiment. I smile back at him as we clink our glasses decidedly together.

I sip at the sweet punch. Candied Ironflower petals float on the surface of the blue liquid, and the crystal glass is cool in my hand. I survey the outwardly happy-looking couples, my thoughts turning to Diana and my eldest brother. "My aunt's cut Rafe off, did you know that?"

Jarod's pleasant expression dims.

"She found out about Diana," I tell him. "Everyone knows. My aunt's sent word that she's coming to visit us in a few days, once the Mage Council adjourns. Her letter was friendly enough, but I suspect the real reason for her trip is to threaten Rafe."

Jarod cocks an eyebrow at me. "If she's cut him off, how's Rafe going to manage the University tithe?"

I can't help but smile faintly at the absurdity of it. "He's working with me now. In the kitchens. Which is funny, because kitchen work is Rafe's least favorite chore."

A collective gasp goes up near the entrance to the hall, and we both turn to see Rafe and Diana burst into the room, laughing. He's pulling her by one arm, a wide grin on his face as she jokingly resists his pull. They're dressed in rumpled brown hiking clothes, a dead rabbit tied to Diana's back and swinging behind her.

My mouth falls open as all the blood drains from my face.

Rough shouts of protest go up as Rafe leads Diana to the middle of the dance floor and takes her into his arms, twirling her around smoothly, their faces radiant with happiness.

Alarmed, I glance toward Jarod, whose face has paled.

"This is a *Gardnerian* dance," a soldier with the stripes of a Level Three Mage barks out as he stalks toward Diana and Rafe, three more soldiers close on his heels as the music falls away.

A look of white-hot defiance crosses my brother's face. He shoots the Mage a mocking smile, pulls Diana into an embrace and kisses her deeply.

Waves of shock rip through the room, followed by an angry swell of voices.

The Level Three Mage reaches for his wand. "No!" I choke out, grasping at Jarod's arm. "Rafe doesn't have any magic!"

"I know," Jarod says tightly, the hard muscles of his arm coiling beneath my hand.

Diana pulls away from Rafe, a mischievous look in her eyes. Then she exuberantly grabs my brother's hand and tugs him after her, the two of them laughing as they bound through the crowd and out of the hall. A torrent of breath releases from my lungs at their escape, the clamor of angry voices soon dissipating along with the threat of violence as the soldiers slowly blend back into the outraged crowd.

After a moment of tense silence, I turn to Jarod. "Do your parents know about them?" I wonder if all hell is about to break loose on both sides of the aisle.

Jarod's jaw grows rigid. "They do. They're coming to Founder's Day." He hesitates. "Father wants to have a talk with Rafe."

I shoot him a panicked look. I've been looking forward to Founder's Day, when parents and families traditionally flood into Verpax to visit University scholars. Uncle Edwin is finally well enough to come see us, and I've been overjoyed at the prospect of seeing him after so many months apart. He recently sent me a letter, transcribed by one of Aunt Vyvian's servants, telling me that his health is slowly improving and he's finally able to walk again with the aid of a cane.

But now, my happy anticipation dims as a sharp worry takes hold. The Lupines may be accepting of a great many things, but I imagine that acceptance does not extend to the descendants of the Black Witch.

"It's not just my parents and younger sister who are coming," Jarod worriedly says, glancing at me sidelong. "My father's entire guard will be accompanying them, as well."

I grasp my glass tighter. "Your father's not coming to threaten Rafe, is he?"

Jarod looks out over the crowd, the music tentatively stepping up to quell the collective trauma. "No," he says with a troubling lack of conviction. "At least I hope not."

Jarod's attention is caught by something across the room. He inhales sharply as his eyes fill with emotion. "Aislinn."

I follow his gaze and soon spot Aislinn's slender frame gliding through the crowd like a panicked bird in flight. Jarod and I both step forward, away from the shelter of the trees, and I motion to Aislinn with a small wave. She waves back, her eyes widening as they settle on Jarod.

Aislinn's slightly out of breath as she reaches us. "Jarod. You're here." Her openly besotted look quickly tamps down, and she looks away from Jarod, flustered. "I'm so glad I found both of you."

"I thought you were still in Valgard," I say, surprised. Aislinn was finally going to tell her father the truth—that she doesn't want to be fasted to Randall, the fastmate her parents have chosen for her. "Weren't you going home to talk to your father?"

Aislinn nods stiffly, her eyes filling with anguish. Jarod puts his glass down on a nearby table and places his hand gently on her arm. A Gardnerian woman chatting with her friends nearby catches sight of the gesture, registers that there's a Lupine in her midst and shoots us a look of deep distress. Their entire group breaks into alarmed murmurs and rapidly flees to another part of the hall.

Tears spill down Aislinn's face, and she wipes them away with the back of her arm. "Father says I have to fast to Randall. As soon as possible. He was…very angry when I disagreed. It was *horrible*." She chokes back a sob, her shoulders shaking. "He told me that a daughter who disobeys her father…is a daughter no more."

"Oh, Aislinn," I say, my heart going out to her. "I'm so sorry."

Her face tenses miserably. "I'm *trapped*. Father was going to pull me from the University. I had to apologize and beg him to let me stay, and he made me travel back here with Randall. We argued the whole way. Father has him watching me all the time now—I just escaped from him. I've *got* to get away." She wipes at her eyes again, the silk arm of her tunic streaked with dark lines of tears.

"Come away with me," Jarod says, his voice filled with calm authority.

Aislinn looks up at him, incredulous. "Jarod, I'd be cut off from my family. *Completely* cut off. You don't understand. I…*can't*."

"Yes, you can," Jarod insists, a courageous light in his amber eyes. "Aislinn, this is a mistake. Come away with me *right now*."

Aislinn peers out over the crowd, then back up at Jarod, as affection and trust wash over her face. My heartbeat speeds up, and I sense that if Aislinn goes with Jarod now, there's a chance she'll leave with him for good.

"Go," I urgently prod her with a quick glance to Jarod. "You should go with him."

"Aislinn!" Randall's arrogant voice calls out from the crowd, and my hope for her plummets. He rushes toward us, looking obnoxiously attractive in his cleanly pressed uniform. "Unhand her, right now," he orders as he approaches. When Jarod simply glares at him, Randall roughly grabs Aislinn's free arm and yanks her toward himself.

"Let her go!" I exclaim.

Aislinn makes a hurt sound and instinctively recoils.

Jarod's eyes go wild. His lips pull back over long, white teeth as a low growl emanates from his throat. He makes a slight lunge toward Randall, muscles tensed, and I flinch back.

"Get your hand off of her, Gardnerian," Jarod snarls. "Or I will *rip* it off."

Startled, Randall lets go of Aislinn and stumbles back. "Aislinn!" he insists shrilly. "Get away from him!"

Aislinn stares up at Jarod, her eyes gone wide.

A metallic screech tears through the air as four soldiers unsheathe swords and close ranks behind Randall. Emboldened, his expression turns smug. "You are seriously outnumbered here, shapeshifter," Randall says, artlessly drawing his own sword.

Jarod lunges forward, lightning fast, grabs up Randall's sword and bends it in half with one hand, casting it to the stone floor with a deafening *clank*. Randall and the other soldiers flinch back in alarm as a snarl works its way up from the base of Jarod's throat.

"I am the son of Gunther Ulrich," Jarod growls, teeth bared, as he grasps hold of her arm once more. "And I could take on every one of you. And win."

Randall's throat bobs as he swallows nervously, frozen in place. "Aislinn," he finally croaks out in a halfhearted demand.

Aislinn shakes her head, as if trying to wake from a spell, her face agonized. "Let me go, Jarod," she says hoarsely. "I have to go with him."

Jarod's head whips toward her. "No, Aislinn. You *don't*."

"Let me go, Jarod. *Please*."

Jarod stares at Aislinn for a long moment, his face violently conflicted. He releases her arm.

"Get over here!" Randall orders, a slight tremor in his voice as he thrusts his hand out at Aislinn. She takes it without a word and lets herself be led away.

Jarod stares after her and, for a moment, I fear he'll go after Randall, there's such violence in his eyes.

I'm desperate to console him. "Jarod, I..."

Before I can say anything else, he shoots me a wild-eyed look, then stalks across the hall, through the mortified crowd, and out a back door.

I hesitate for a brief, agonized moment before following him, but by the time I reach the terrace outside, Jarod is nowhere in sight. I race through a maze of potted evergreen trees and frosty ice sculptures as I rush toward the terrace's railing, spotting Jarod's dark silhouette far across a long, barren field, and I know I'll never catch up with him.

The wilds lie just beyond the flat expanse.

I call out after him, but to no avail. Despairing, I turn, and the largest of the ice sculptures catches my eye, illuminated in the terrace's blue lantern light. The sculpture looms over me, the frozen visage of my famous grandmother staring down, wand raised to slay the Icaral lying at her feet—an exact replica of the monument outside Valgard's Cathedral.

Black Witch.

The words are soft on the cold air.

I look toward the forest just as Jarod stalks into the line of trees and is quickly swallowed up by the blackness of the wilds.

CHAPTER SIX

A WORTHY GRINDSTONE

The lonely quiet settles into me as I stare out at the forest, my heart aching for Jarod and Aislinn.

I let out a long sigh and turn toward the sculpture of the Black Witch, gentle pinpricks of snow falling on my face. Glancing down, I run my fingertips along the edge of the Icaral's stingingly cold wing, wishing I could will him back to life. I glare back up at my own face, carved in ice, and silently rail against Carnissa Gardner's cruelty as the cold seeps through my silks and sets me shivering.

"It's beautiful."

I take a deep, steadying breath, recognizing Lukas's voice.

His hands slide around my waist as his long body presses lightly against my back, a luxurious warmth cutting through the chill, my fire lines stirring in response to his touch.

"Beautiful," he says, his voice silken. "Like you."

Conflict fills me. It should be a struggle to be with Lukas Grey, but it's just too easy to surrender to his pull.

Lucretia's voice echoes in my mind. *We need you to find out where his loyalties lie.*

Tenuously justified, I melt into Lukas's arms, reaching up to grasp the Snow Oak pendant. As soon as I touch it, my earth and fire lines give a warm surge, and I let out a shuddering sigh. Lukas moves closer as the dark branches of his earth lines shiver into being and slide through my wakening lines in a tantalizing rush. My breathing deepens as our affinities twine, line by line…

The wood of the forest pulses from clear across the field, like a fire flaring. A palpable spasm of fear jolts through the trees, as if the wilds are collectively flinching back from us.

Then nothing—a cowed silence, like a terrified child trying to escape the notice of monsters. I'm momentarily filled with a heady sense of strength as I survey the dark forest, Lukas's breath warm on my cheek.

Together, we're dangerous.

A reflexive alarm sounds inside me, and I pull away from Lukas, my pulse quickening as I teeter on the precipice of this new, seductive power.

"You feel it, don't you?" he asks, smooth as glass, his green eyes glinting in the sapphire lantern light.

"Something just happened," I tell him, shaken. "A surge in my affinity lines…and then…a reaction from the trees." My brow tightens with distress. "The forest has always made me slightly uneasy. But now… I have this feeling that it *hates* me."

Lukas's gaze flickers toward the wilds. "The trees sense your grandmother's power quickening inside you." His voice drops to a whisper. "And they fear us because we have Dryad blood."

I'm surprised by his bold, forbidden statement. I glance

around, relieved to find that we're still alone on the terrace. "It's not safe to talk like that, Lukas."

The side of Lukas's mouth lifts. "Ah...the Gardnerian charade of purity. I find it amusing."

His casual cynicism infuriates me. My hand bumps against the frozen edge of the Icaral's wing as I frown at him. "I don't understand you. How can you fight for them if you don't even believe any of it?"

Lukas's expression hardens. "There is no ethnic purity, Elloren. Only power, and the lack of it."

A bonfire flares at the far end of the broad field. A number of Gardnerians are gathered around the fire and sending up a celebratory Yule cheer. Blue paper lanterns rise, their glow luminescent against the black winter sky.

I'm momentarily transported by the lanterns' ethereal beauty. Absentmindedly, I lean into the ice sculpture behind me, and most of the Icaral's icy wing breaks under the weight of my hand. Aghast, I try to grab hold of it, but the wing slips through my fingers and shatters into glittering pieces at my feet. I watch, bereft, as snow gently dots the crystalline shards.

"Come," Lukas says, his gaze steady. "Come inside and dance with me."

Blue sparks of lantern light reflect in his eyes. There's nothing kind about his face—all hard lines and sharp angles. Like my own. But there's dark understanding in his eyes, and I'm drawn in by it.

I brush the melting ice off my hand and look up at him. "I haven't shown you my dress yet."

Lukas steps back expectantly, watching as I unpin my cloak and slide it off in one smooth movement.

Lukas stills, as if captivated.

Snow falls in sparse, glittering flakes all around me as the dress's embroidered Ironflowers and sapphires pick up the shimmering blue lantern light.

Lukas's gaze does a slow slide over my body as his eyes take on a sultry heat. "That dress is deliciously scandalous." His eyes meet mine. "You're stunning, Elloren." The sudden roughness in his voice belies an undercurrent of emotion that I've rarely seen in him, and it sets off an unsettled ache deep inside me.

"After tonight," he says, an ardent fire in his eyes, "they won't be calling Galliana the Iron Flower. They'll grant that title to *you*."

The snow begins to fall more quickly, and I glance up at the swirl of white against the velvet sky.

"Let's go make an entrance," I tell Lukas, suddenly decided. Even if I won't wandfast to him, I can at least give him this night.

Lukas's mouth moves into a slow smile. He holds out his arm, and I thread mine through his, my pulse quickening.

"Are you ready?" he asks, his usual feral grin returning.

I nod, and together we make our way into the White Hall.

I match Lukas's long, confident stride through the hall.

We leave a trail of gasping Gardnerians in our wake as all eyes fall on my resplendent, glowing dress. Mages give Lukas deferential bows as he passes, the soldiers and military apprentices bringing fists to their chests in formal salute.

Lukas acknowledges exactly none of it.

The crowd parts for us, and we walk, unimpeded, toward the dance floor, the music quieting. When we reach the floor, Lukas's hand slips down my arm, his fingers twining around mine as he leads me to its center.

As my heart trips against my chest, Lukas smoothly takes me into his arms. The orchestral music swells back to life as his hand tightens around my waist and he glides us both into motion with sinuous grace. We twirl across the floor as one, and a giddy thrill sings through me. Delighted sounds rise up, along with scattered applause, other couples moving forward to fill in the dance floor.

It's pure joy, dancing with Lukas Grey, his movements fluid, his lead strong and assured. I can't help but be a bit transported by the pleasure of moving so effortlessly in time with him. The surrounding lantern light streaks Lukas's hair with blue, his eyes steady on me.

"I hear things were quite dramatic here earlier," Lukas says as he deftly twirls me around, my hand loosely in his. "I seem to have missed it all."

I catch a glimpse of Paige Snowden staring at Lukas and me, her eyes saucer-wide. Sylus Bane stands beside her on the periphery of the dance floor, a glass of punch in his hand. His lips curve into a cruel smile as he raises his glass in a mock toast, and a flood of worry washes over me. Gesine Bane is with them, her black velvet dress splashed with diamonds, her gaze on me frigid.

"She's going to kill me," I tell Lukas as he glides us around with assured grace.

"Who is?" he calmly inquires.

"Fallon Bane. When she gets back on her feet. She's going to encase me in a tomb of ice. And her brothers and cousin are likely to help."

Lukas eyes me, amused. "Fallon's under heavy military guard. There was an additional attempt on her life."

I blink at him in surprise. "There was?"

"Hmm. Another band of Ishkartan merceneries. Ten of them this time."

"Holy Ancient One."

Lukas spits out a jaded sound. "Elloren, she's thought to

be the next Black Witch. That's going to draw a certain level of attention, and up until now, she's stubbornly refused to respect that fact."

"Lukas," I say, a thread of apprehension winding through me, "she can't be the Black Witch. She just can't. I think I'm her biggest enemy."

"Relax, Elloren," he says dismissively. "Fallon's not the Black Witch."

"How can you be so sure?"

"She's powerful, but Fallon has nowhere *near* the range of magic your grandmother had. Though she does have some truly impressive ice spells, I'll give her that."

"Yes, well, when she hears I came here with you, she'll freeze my blood."

Lukas smirks at this. "She won't freeze your blood. She'll just torment you a little." He leans in close. "Or a lot." He twirls me around dramatically and shoots me a wicked grin. "But it's worth it, don't you think?"

I scowl at him, but he ignores my displeasure. "Your friend Aislinn looks miserable. I passed her walking with Randall Greyson on the way here."

"She doesn't want to fast to Randall."

"I don't blame her. Randall's an idiot."

I furrow my brow at him. "I'm surprised to hear you talk that way about a fellow soldier."

"He's a talentless coward who should never have been allowed in the Mage Guard." Lukas's lips tighten with disapproval as he looks past me, surveying the scene around us. "What the Gardnerians are in dire need of is a worthy foe. One who would immediately pick off soldiers like Randall."

"I thought soldiers were bullies who wanted easy targets," I challenge him acidly.

Lukas gives a short laugh. "That's what cowards who dress up as soldiers want. Real warriors want a real foe."

"Real warriors like you?"

"Yes," he says without hesitation.

"So, what is it you want in your foe, exactly?"

"Well, speaking metaphorically, what I want is a worthy grindstone."

"To smash to pieces?"

His eyes take on a wicked gleam. "To sharpen my blade against." I gasp as he abruptly pulls me close and grins at my surprise. "I hear your brother was here with the Lupine girl."

Ire rises in me. "I really don't feel like talking about this with you, of all people."

Lukas laughs. "Why?"

"Because you probably hate their kind."

"I don't hate the Lupines."

"Yet you would kill them if ordered to."

"Yes, I would," he agrees. "Just as Gunther Ulrich's guard would kill everyone in this room if he ordered *them* to."

"It's not the same."

"It's *exactly* the same." Lukas's gaze turns serious. "Elloren, your brother needs to remember which side he's on. He's playing a dangerous game. Marcus Vogel is intent on recapturing a contested portion of the Lupines' territory. Unfriendly diplomatic relations are about to take a hostile turn."

Rebellion flares in me. "If we provoke a war with the Lupines, Rafe won't fight them."

Lukas's expression goes granite hard. He abruptly slows us to a stop and guides me just off the dance floor, into a slightly sheltered grove of Ironwood trees.

"Your brother's going to be drafted," Lukas says, his voice low and unforgiving. "He may be without magic, but he's the best tracker to come along in ages. He'll be especially useful in fighting the Lupines."

I wrench my arm free from Lukas's grip. "He won't fight them."

"Then he'll be shot."

A picture of Rafe effortlessly dodging countless arrows comes to mind. "Good luck trying to catch him," I scoff.

"Elloren, he's no match for the Mage Guard."

I glare at him. "Well, maybe he'll join the Lupines."

Lukas lets out a short, dismissive laugh. "He's the grandson of Carnissa Gardner, the only Mage ever to go up against the Lupines with some small measure of success. Don't think for a *minute* that the Lupines don't have a very long memory regarding their losses during the Realm War. Your brother could *never* be accepted by them, and Diana Ulrich is the alpha's daughter. Do you honestly think that her people will let her go off with a *Gardnerian*? They'll kill him before they allow it."

"I'm done talking about this," I say angrily. "It's not a game to me. I happen to love my brother."

"Then do everything you can to convince him to break things off with Diana Ulrich. He needs to follow his head, not his—"

"I get the gist of what you're saying," I snap.

Lukas grows quiet. "I'm sorry," he apologizes with a dip of his head. "That was in poor taste. It's just… I feel compelled to be honest with you." He looks away, momentarily frustrated, like he's admitting to some weakness. "I think it's because our affinity lines are such a close match. I've never been with a woman I feel this way about."

"Is that why you agreed to fast to me?" I wonder, frowning.

"Yes," he says, a slight smile forming on his lips. His eyes do a slow slide over me, "And the fact that I greatly enjoy kissing you."

Heat rises in my cheeks. "So, you still want to..."

"Wandfast to you? Absolutely." His grin warms to an alluring smile as he takes my hand in his. "There are a great number of things I'd like to do with you, Elloren, wandfasting being only one of them." Lukas's touch turns into a caress, his thumb tracing a line along the back of my hand.

Heat shudders through my fire lines, and I struggle to resist his pull, eyeing him with suspicion. "But...are you in love with me, Lukas?" I ask, remembering the ardent way he looked at me outside when he first saw my dress.

"Would you rather I lied to you or told you the truth?"

"Well, you can't lie to me, and I would prefer the truth."

"I don't believe in all that romantic nonsense," Lukas says, his expression hardening. "I think it's ridiculous. So, no. I'm not in love with you, Elloren."

"You're overwhelming me with sentiment," I snipe, offended by his blunt dismissal.

Lukas draws me close as the music around us slows. His voice is sultry, his breath warm on my ear. "I do, however, feel like we're becoming friends. And that is something that is of *much* greater value to me than some false emotion that I don't believe exists."

Friends. It's hard to figure out how I feel about this as my attention is slowly caught up in the feel of his hand caressing my back. His affinity lines reach for mine, the warmth of his fire sliding through me. I sigh and surrender to the heat, forgetting every reason why I should stay away from him as his lips find mine.

I know people can spot us through the greenery. I'm vaguely aware of their shocked murmuring, but I don't care. He's like the dark Asteroth wood that sends sparks through my skin. The branches of our affinity lines twine tighter, flames teasing through them as Lukas's kiss deepens in hunger.

When Lukas pulls back, his eyes are strangely intense, and I feel a delicious undercurrent of wild danger. "Do you want to go somewhere more private?" he asks, his tone nocturnal.

A spike of both fear and desire ripples through me. "I don't think that would be a good idea."

He shoots me a knowing look, then steps back, deliberately formal, his arm outstretched in an unspoken invitation to dance once more. I let him guide me back onto the dance floor and into his arms, one slow waltz leading into another. I look out over Lukas's shoulder, over the glittering couples and past them to...

Yvan.

He's leaning against an Ironwood tree, far from the other kitchen workers, his eyes fixed on me. Heat suddenly flashes through me from clear across the room, like a streak of lightning through my lines, and I struggle not to gasp, stunned by the unexpected sensation.

I look away, thrown by this new awareness of Yvan's astonishing fire, and struggle to collect myself as an echo of his heat shudders through my lines. My breathing erratic, I venture a glance back at him. He's still watching me, with the same intense expression he usually wears, but deepened and simmering with something new.

Passionate longing.

Cast into confusion, I hold his fiery gaze as I move in perfect time with Lukas, filled with a sudden, overwhelming desire to be dancing with Yvan instead. To feel *his* lips against mine. To have *his* arms around me. And to be close to *his* fire. And for a brief moment, I throw all caution aside and look back at him with equally transparent longing.

"You feel so warm," Lukas whispers in my ear as he sweeps me around, breaking my eye contact with Yvan.

"It's hot in here," I say, my flush deepening.

Lukas's laugh is low and suggestive. "Yes, it is."

He tightens his hold on me, his lips brushing my neck, and my sense of Yvan's heat abruptly flares, then fades away. When I catch sight of Yvan once more, his attention has turned to Iris. She's talking to him and smiling flirtatiously as she sets down a platter of pastries stacked in the shape of a Yule tree, then reaches up to playfully tug at his shirt.

I'm seized by a flash of jealousy so strong, I lose track of the rhythm and almost stumble.

Yvan's gaze meets mine again, his expression hardening with conflict as his green eyes narrow in on Lukas. Then Iris takes Yvan's hand in hers, and he turns away from me as she pulls him with her into the kitchen.

Of course, he's leaving with her.

I fight to regain my outward composure, but the sting of seeing them leave together reverberates.

Let him go, I roughly urge myself. *He's made it clear he won't give in to…whatever this is between us. You can't have him. So, let him go.*

Suddenly defiant, I slide my arms around Lukas and draw him closer.

Lukas responds immediately, his hands encircling my waist, pulling me in as his lips find mine.

I don't need Yvan, I console myself, swallowing back the hurt as I fall into Lukas's heated kiss.

But the palpable feel of Yvan's longing resonates and lingers inside me.

CHAPTER SEVEN

WATER HORSE

I push through the wilds, gripping the handle of a lantern and following the overlapping boot tracks in the snow. The hem of my Ironflower dress peeks out under my cloak and illuminates my steps in a circle of glowing blue light.

The dance is long since over, the hour approaching midnight. I clutch at my Snow Oak pendant, my breath sounding loud against the weighty silence of the dark forest as I glance anxiously around and wait for the trees to stage another phantom attack.

Nothing.

Just a tremor of unease, and a sense that the trees are drawing back from me. But beneath their cowed submission, there's an undercurrent of something else.

They're waiting. Waiting for something to come for me.

Stop it, Elloren, I firmly tell myself. *Don't let the trees unsettle you. They can't harm you. They're just trees.*

I glimpse firelight shining through the branches up ahead, and relief floods through me. I let out a long, shaky breath.

It's Trystan's night to stand guard as Ariel and my friend Andras tend to Naga's injuries in the cave we've been hiding the dragon in. Andras's position as the University's equine physician affords him some limited skill in caring for a dragon, as do Ariel's animal husbandry studies. I hope Jarod is there, too—worry for him has pricked at the back of my mind all evening.

But when I step into the clearing, I find only Yvan there. He's sitting on a log and staring at the impressive bonfire with searing focus, his long form stilled but seeming rigid with pent-up tension. An uncomfortable flush rises on my cheeks at the sight of him.

He doesn't look up as I hang my lantern on a branch, but I get the strong sense that his attention is wholly on me. I sit down on the side of the fire opposite him and hold up my hands to warm them, my emotions cast into turmoil. Small sparks fly out from the bonfire in every direction, like fireflies in the dead of winter, and I strive to ignore how achingly handsome he looks, washed golden in the firelight.

"I thought it was Trystan's night to stand guard over Naga," I say, breaking the tense silence, keeping my tone as casual as I can.

"It *is* Trystan's turn to watch over her," he says, his green eyes locked on the flames. "I felt like visiting her."

"But you're out here."

"She's *sleeping*," he replies tersely as his eyes meet mine, blistering heat in his gaze.

"Then why stay?" I ask, trying to hide how much it hurts when he shuts me out like this. "I'm sure you could find other things to do." *With Iris.*

"I like starting fires." His tone is caustic as his eyes flicker hot on me. "I felt like burning something."

The uncomfortable warmth in my face stings hotter, my

feelings a tumult as I remember his eyes on me while I danced with Lukas Grey. The sense of his fire.

And that look of fierce longing.

We sit there for an uncomfortably long while, privately fuming, barely acknowledging my younger brother, Trystan, when he emerges from the cave.

"Hi, Ren," Trystan says uneasily, glancing warily from me to Yvan and back toward me again, as if gauging the tension.

I murmur a barely audible response and glower at the crackling fire. "So. Ren," Trystan starts tentatively as he takes a seat by me. "You went to the dance...with Lukas Grey?"

I shrug, avoiding Yvan's intense green eyes.

Trystan is quiet for a moment. "Are you...*with* him now?"

The fire unexpectedly roars higher, sparks exploding in random patterns. Trystan eyes the flames with a raised brow, his eyes darting from Yvan to me in question.

"I went to the dance with Lukas," I sputter defensively. "That's *it*."

Except for the kissing. A great deal of kissing.

The fire flares again, almost catching my skirts alight, and I've a sense of Yvan's heat flashing turbulently through my lines. I yank the silken fabric behind my legs and look to Yvan with startled accusation, only to find him staring into the center of the fire with predatory focus.

And I wonder if, like me, his power is quickening inside him.

Fire Fae power.

The fire quiets to a normal crackle as Trystan silently pulls out my spiraling wand and starts practicing spells, the five silver stripes edging his uniform glinting in the firelight. He conjures a tight ball of water that hovers in the air just above the wand's tip, then tosses it toward the fire, watching as it bursts into a hissing cloud of steam.

THE IRON FLOWER

My affinity lines prickle to life and strain toward the pale wooden wand, my wand hand tingling as a sullen envy takes hold. I wish I could be like Trystan, able to access this burgeoning power and wield it through that wand.

Dejected, I watch my brother try out a variety of water spells as thoughts of Yvan and wands and the evening spent with Lukas gust around in my mind, upending my emotions.

A rustling in the forest catches my attention. Yvan rises, turning toward the sound. When Tierney pushes clumsily through the evergreen boughs and into our clearing, I breathe out a sigh of relief—until I see the tears glistening on her face.

I rise, as well. "Tierney, what's the matter..." My words fall away as a shadow flows in behind Tierney, first resembling an inky puddle, then like water bubbling up, up, up into the air.

I step back in alarm as the thing rapidly takes on the size and shape of a horse—a horse made of roiling black water.

"Holy Ancient One..." Trystan breathes as he bolts up, brandishing my wand.

Firelight illuminates the fantastical creature with orange-and-red undulating lines. Its head swivels toward me, obsidian eyes focusing in tight.

"It's all right," Tierney assures us, her voice coarse from crying. "This is my Kelpie, Es'tryl'lyan..."

A palpable wave of fury lashes out at me from the Kelpie as its lips pull back to reveal icicle teeth. It abruptly lunges for me, and I cry out in fright, stumbling backward to the ground.

Fast as lightning, Yvan throws himself in front of me and flings his arm toward the creature. A torrent of flame explodes from the bonfire and surges toward the water horse just as Trystan casts a line of Mage fire at the beast's side.

The Kelpie shrieks and rears back, steam hissing from its huge form.

"Control your Kelpie!" Yvan orders as Andras bursts from Naga's cave brandishing his rune-axe. Ariel hovers at the cave's entrance, her black wings flapping agitatedly, pale green eyes wide.

The water horse bucks wildly, clearly in pain, as it sends up billows of steam.

"Stop!" Tierney cries to Trystan. holding her palms out, desperation in her eyes. *"Please!"* She turns to the Kelpie and lets loose with a torrent of impassioned words in another language while the creature writhes, its watery hooves splashing against the ground, kicking up mud. As it struggles and rages, the Kelpie fixes me with a predatory look of hatred so strong I flinch back. Then its wavering form collapses into a puddle and streams back into the forest.

In an instant, Yvan is down on one knee beside me, his unnaturally hot hand grasping my arm. The contact gives me a sudden sense of his fire power, unleashed and whipping protectively around me. His normally green eyes have turned a startling fiery yellow.

"Elloren," he says, "are you all right?"

I nod stiffly and hold his searing gaze, overcome by the sensation of his fire rippling through me. Heat suffuses the very air between us, stealing my breath away.

"He won't come after her again. I'll speak to him..." Tierney's distraught voice breaks through our sudden thrall, and we both glance toward her. Yvan rises and holds his hand out to me.

Heart thudding, I take Yvan's startlingly warm hand and let him help me to my feet, my fire lines stirring chaotically in response to his touch. "Your eyes are gold," I tell him, my voice rough with emotion, my fingers still twined around his.

Yvan winces and abruptly tilts his head down. He closes his eyes tight, his sharp jaw tensing as he takes a deep, shuddering breath. When he opens his eyes again, their color has cooled to green. His hand falls away from mine, and he gives me an uneasy look, as if willing me to ignore the obvious.

Fire Fae.

"The Gardnerians are *killing* them," Tierney rages to Andras and my brother. "They've pounded iron spikes into the waterways. Five of my Kelpies are *dead.*"

"Where is the other Kelpie now?" I ask her nervously.

Tierney glances distractedly at the woods. "Gone. I spelled him down. It will take him days to reform."

"You never told me about this," I say, rattled. "You never told me you have... *Kelpies.*"

She looks back at me, contrite. "I'm sorry, Elloren. I keep so much secret... I never thought he'd attack anyone, but..." Fear fills her eyes. "He says that you're the next Black Witch, Elloren. He says the whole forest believes it."

Trystan takes a step toward her. "Tell your Kelpie my sister is powerless." His voice is calm, but deadly firm.

Tierney furrows her brow at him. "The forest doesn't believe that." She looks to me entreatingly. "Why would the forest believe this, Elloren?"

An angry, embattled frustration swells up in me. I can feel it all around me, the subtle tremor of hatred emanating from the trees. "Do you need proof that I'm not the next Black Witch?" I ask Tierney, bitterly defensive. "Do I have to show you how I can't even do a basic candle-lighting spell?"

Tierney's expression grows wildly conflicted. "No. No, of course not. It's just...your blood, Elloren. They *feel* it. It's *her* blood."

"I cannot change my blood, Tierney," I state flatly, wanting to rip it clear from my veins. "Any more than you can change your cursed glamour." Tierney casts me a resentful look, and I immediately regret saying it. I know she doesn't like her secrets voiced, even among the people who are privy to them.

She turns to Yvan. "Vogel's discovered another one of the escape routes east. Last night, his border scouts tracked down two glamoured Fae. They..." She pauses, blinking furiously. "They iron-tested them." She stops again, her voice straining tight. "And then they killed them with iron spikes." Tears of outrage slide down her face. "Es'tryl'lyan saw the whole thing, but he couldn't do anything to stop it because of all the iron."

"Tierney..." Trystan reaches for her, but she shakes her head and pulls away from him.

She looks straight at Yvan. "They'll be doing the iron test on everyone."

My heart speeds up, concern rising. "But you've touched iron," I blurt out to Yvan. "In the kitchens—"

"I touch iron because I'm a *Kelt*." He shoots me a cautionary look, and I can practically feel the angry fire blazing in him.

"We'll fly you both out," I insist. "Once Naga heals..."

Yvan shakes his head. "Elloren, Naga's wings were *decimated* by Damion Bane. She may never fly again."

"Then the Resistance will help you," I persist, fear escalating. "You'll both find amnesty. Somewhere."

"There's nowhere to go," Tierney vehemently insists. "The Resistance is *nothing* compared to Gardnerian power." She turns to Yvan with desperation. "All the escape routes will be found and shut down. There will be nowhere left for us to go."

I reach out to touch his arm. "Yvan..."

"You can't fix this, Elloren," he says. "I know you want

to, but you can't. And you'll never fully understand what we're up against."

His words sting like wasps. "How can you say that?"

"Because you're Gardnerian," he says, his voice taking on a hard edge. "Your family, you'll all be fine." His green eyes spark as the bonfire flares brightly. "Especially once you're fasted to Lukas Grey."

Numbed by Yvan's words, I gaze sullenly into the bonfire.

Ariel has retreated back into the cave with Naga, and Yvan is sitting on the other side of the fire, talking to Tierney in low tones, his arm wrapped comfortingly around her.

I'm shivering from the cold at my back, my hands stiff as I pull my cloak more tightly around me. I gently rebuff Trystan's attempts to talk to me, and he eventually gives up and focuses back on his wandwork. Fizzy lines of blue lightning periodically flow from the tip of the spiraling wand and into the fire.

My wand.

Andras sits down beside me and hands me a hot cup of tea. The Amaz runes on his tunic glow crimson, his violet hair a deep purple in the firelight and curling around his pointed ears. He's a quiet, comforting presence, Andras. He's even patient with combative Ariel as they care for the dragon, treating her with the same unwavering calm that soothes even the most skittish horses he looks after.

I sip at the tea as Andras strips bark from branches with an impressive knife. I breathe in the scent of the green wood, the smell minty and invigorating.

Yenilin. For wound closure.

He and Ariel have been laboring long hours to undo the damage Damion Bane did to Naga's wings, trying out a variety of medicinals with only limited success.

Before long, Rafe and Diana bound into the clearing and join us, practically falling over each other with laughter as they take a seat by the fire. They're their usual happy selves, basking in their annoyingly requited love.

"Why are you here?" Andras asks me, his deep voice kind. He gestures toward the luxurious fabric of my skirt. "You're dressed a bit formally for a bonfire."

"I just came from the Yule Dance, and I was looking for Jarod," I tell him quietly. "I thought he might have come here." I recount what happened at the dance. "I'm worried that he might go after Randall. I don't want him to get himself in trouble."

"This will work itself out," Diana puts in dismissively as my brother nuzzles her neck. I send her an irritated look, finding her superior hearing to be a tad invasive.

"Aislinn will come to her senses and become one of us," Diana insists with complete assurance.

I inwardly cringe. Diana's unwavering belief that everyone's love lives will follow her own happy trajectory sometimes grates at my nerves. "Not everyone wants to become Lupine," I irritatedly remind her. "Aislinn wants to remain Gardnerian."

Diana blinks at me. "That makes no sense whatsoever."

I let out a long sigh of exasperation.

Andras glances up at Diana as he continues to strip bark. "This bond between Jarod and Aislinn will end badly," he predicts. He reaches down and throws a handful of the bark into the fire. It sends out a strong, minty aroma, and I inhale deeply, feeling a surge of energy in my earth lines.

Andras pauses and gestures toward Diana with the knife. "They cannot defy culture and win."

"You've said that before," Trystan remarks as he balances a compact, rotating ball of sapphire lightning above my wand.

He throws it at the fire, and it momentarily turns the flames blue. "What happened, Andras?" There's a dismissive edge to my brother's tone. "Did you fall for some renegade Amaz goddess?"

Andras's mouth forms into a jaded smirk. "There *was* a woman."

"Was?" Diana ventures, curiosity pulling her focus away from Rafe.

Andras takes a deep breath and sheathes his knife. He leans forward and clasps his broad hands above his knees, firelight flickering over the sweeping lines of his rune-tattoos.

"Tell us," Tierney prods, drawn away from her conversation with Yvan. Andras studies her for a long moment, then stares back into the fire and relents.

"When I turned eighteen, she came to me—Sorcha Xanthippe. A young Amaz woman. I was out in the pasture with the horses. It was fall, everything ablaze with color. I felt the thoughts of an unfamiliar horse and looked up just as Sorcha rode in from the wilds, her skin as blue as the autumn sky, her hair flowing out behind her."

Andras is quiet for a moment, as if lost in the memory.

"It was a shock to see her," he continues. "None of my mother's people had ever contacted us in all the years since she left with me. She was completely rejected, shunned." His eyes momentarily tense with sadness. "Sorcha rode up to me and explained that it was the time of the fertility rites, when the Amaz honor the Great Goddess by seeking to bring new daughters into their fold. She'd heard of me, and that I had recently come of age. Given my own Amaz lineage, and my mother's reputation as a brilliant scientist and a powerful soldier, she felt that my seed would produce especially fine, strong daughters."

"So, she wanted to…" Diana interjects, looking shocked.

Andras turns to her. "Have relations with me, yes."

"With no life bond?"

Andras seems like he doesn't quite know how to respond. "That's not the way they do things."

"So, you said *no*, of course." Diana's tone is self-righteous, her arms now folded in front of herself.

"Yes, at first," Andras says. "But we spent much time together. Many nights under the stars. And in time, we paired."

Diana's eyes widen. "You took each other as mates with no formal bond?"

"Diana," Rafe puts in, "their customs differ..."

She rounds on Rafe. "But this is very shocking." She turns back to Andras, disapproval written all over her face. "I don't understand this at all. How can you mate with someone you do not love?"

A shadow falls over Andras's expression. "What happened?" I ask softly.

He lets out a deep breath and rubs his jaw before continuing. "I began to have feelings for Sorcha. And it wasn't just the way our bodies fit together, like we had been made for each other. She returned to me again and again, and after lying together, we would talk for hours. It was forbidden, what she was doing. The Amaz are only supposed to seek out men during the fertility rites. But Sorcha seemed as drawn to me as I was to her. During our last night together, I told her that I loved her. That I wanted her to stay with me and never leave."

He pauses, staring into the fire. "She broke down crying and told me that she could not love me. That she loved the Amaz. And that she could not have both. She said that she was with child and would not need to be with me any longer, and that she had come to say goodbye." He grows quiet, suppressed emotion heavy in the air. "Then she left, and I never saw her again. And now, I am left wondering if I have a daughter in the Amaz lands. Or, if the child was a boy, did she abandon him in the woods somewhere, as my mother was urged to abandon me?"

Andras's expression darkens. "A few months after Sorcha left, another Amaz woman came to me during the rites." His jaw tenses, affront flashing in his eyes. "I sent her away. And the Amaz have stayed away from me ever since."

Everyone is silent as we stare into the crackling fire.

"Do you still love her?" Tierney asks quietly, and I wonder if she's thinking of Leander. Andras makes a bitter noise, his private anguish breaking through, but he doesn't answer.

"You need a life mate," Diana states with authority. "This way of theirs is unnatural."

Andras lets out a hollow laugh. "And who will have me, Diana Ulrich? Who?" he challenges. "*No one.* I am accepted nowhere."

"Become Lupine," Diana says. "*We* would accept you."

Andras shakes his head. "I could never do that to my mother. She gave up *everything* for me. Everything she loves. It would kill her if I rejected her in that way."

"But you wouldn't be rejecting your mother," Diana persists, confused.

An incredulous look passes over Andras's face. "She would see it as such. To become Lupine would be the worst betrayal possible."

"Why?" Diana asks, looking offended. "Are we so beneath you?"

"Diana," Andras says, as if his reasoning should be obvious, "Lupine pack life is everything the Amaz despise."

"I don't know what you're talking about," Diana replies stiffly.

"Both Northern and Southern packs have *male* alphas."

"And both have had female alphas, as well."

Andras throws her a disparaging look. "Yes, but they haven't for some time."

"We will again."

"Will you?" A mirthless smile lifts his lips. "Who is next in line to be your alpha?"

Diana eyes him with impatience. "It doesn't work that way. It's not a question of politics or lineage. Only power."

"Then who of the younger Lupines is the most powerful?"

Diana grows still and looks down with a sudden, uncharacteristic gravity. When she looks back up at Andras, there's a level force to her gaze that sets the hairs on the back of my neck prickling.

"You?" Andras says with obvious surprise. He looks Diana over appraisingly. "What if I was a Lupine?" he asks, curious and slightly amused. "Could you best me?"

Diana tilts her head. Her predatory eyes flick up and down Andras's huge, muscular frame, gauging his strength. She sits back, decided. "I could take you. I'm very fast. Speed would give me the advantage."

Andras smirks. "Now I am tempted to become Lupine, Diana. If only to watch this future transition of power."

I look to Diana, stunned at the idea of a female alpha. At the idea of *her* being a female alpha. I'm so used to living in a society where the High Mage can only be a man. It's hard to wrap my mind around such a possibility.

Diana seems lost for a moment in her own thoughts, then appears to have an idea. Her eyes light back on Andras. "There is a man of Amaz ancestry in my father's guard—his beta. You should speak with him. My people found him in the forest when he was a baby, and he's lived with us all his life. He has a mate and a child. He's happy and completely accepted."

"Diana..." Andras says, shaking his head.

"No, Andras. You don't have to live like this. You *could* have a place and a family."

I catch Yvan's intent gaze through the fire, and he quickly looks away.

Trystan stands and abruptly sheathes my wand. "It's been fascinating hearing about everyone's love lives and cultures," he tells us evenly, "but I think I'll go work on some spells. Alone. Where I can concentrate. You can all stay here and figure out who is joining the Lupines."

MAGE COUNCIL
RULING
#199

Defacing the Gardnerian flag shall be
punishable by execution.

CHAPTER EIGHT

WANDS

Aunt Vyvian is already seated before a well-appointed tea table when I enter the small receiving room on tremulous legs. She doesn't rise to greet me, which sets me even more on edge.

"Ah, Elloren," she says, her voice silken. Aunt Vyvian gestures toward a chair across from her. "Join me." She has a charming smile on her lovely face, but her eyes are glacially cool. I force a cordial smile in return as I cautiously take a seat.

It's a nice room they've given her for this visit. Perhaps the nicest one in the whole Gardnerian Athenaeum. Heat radiates from a beautiful woodstove wrought in the shape of an iron tree, and flowing roots are artfully rendered on the tile work beneath us in rich browns and blacks that fan out over the floor. Stained-glass vines rim the huge, arching windows that overlook the wintry Southern Spine.

Aunt Vyvian is just as I remember her, elegant beyond belief in luxurious black silk exquisitely embroidered with tiny acorns and oak leaves. Her posture is perfectly regal as an elderly, lavender-hued Urisk servant hovers nearby, ready to tend to her every whim.

She looks like a queen holding court—a queen who'd chop your head off for the tiniest infraction.

"Would you like some tea, Elloren?" she inquires.

"Yes, that would be lovely," I say with measured politeness, even though I'm too much on my guard to be hungry or thirsty, my stomach clenched tight.

Rafe, Trystan and I have spoken at length about this impending visit, privately agreeing to placate her as much as possible, and I know Trystan has been writing friendly letters to Aunt Vyvian to keep her at bay. But it was inevitable that Rafe's very public relationship with Diana would eventually bring her down on our heads.

Aunt Vyvian gives an imperious flick of her hand, and the Urisk woman springs forward, silently pouring tea and setting out a plate of small cakes for me. My aunt's eyes remain fixed on me while she stirs her own tea with a tiny silver spoon.

As soon as the Urisk woman finishes serving us, Aunt Vyvian gets right to the point. "You need to cut off contact with Aislinn Greer," she says bluntly. "I know you're friends with the girl, but she's fallen in with the Lupine twins. She was spotted in the library with the male. Fortunately, she's open to reason and is now back under her family's protection. She *seems* to realize the danger, but one can never be sure about such things."

Aunt Vyvian takes a deep breath and shakes her head disapprovingly. "We can only hope that her family intervened in time. They could have had another Sage Gaffney on their hands."

She taps at her china plate, tiny vines painted along its edging. Her servant springs over with a tray of assorted breads, fresh from the oven. They smell nutty and sweet, but the aroma only heightens my roiling nausea as outrage swamps over me.

It's terrible what you're doing, I inwardly rail against Aunt Vyvian and Aislinn's awful family. *You're ruining my friend's life, the whole lot of you.* I want to protest Aislinn's impending fasting right then and there, but I know I would only make things worse for my friend.

My aunt selects a roll studded with gooseberries from the plate. "Perhaps the Greer girl truly *does* see reason, but for the time being, take care, Elloren."

"I will, Aunt Vyvian," I tell her with flat and completely false assurance. I clutch at the edge of my chair to hide the angry trembling of my hands.

Blackthorn wood.

A hot flash of energy blasts through my arms, clear up to my shoulders, jettisoning through my earth lines. Startled, I yank my hands away from the wood, squeezing them into tight fists on my lap, my heartbeat quickening.

What was that?

Aunt Vyvian's gaze sharpens on me. "I've heard you've been seen with the Lupine twins, as well."

I struggle to keep my expression impassive as I clench and unclench my fists under the table's edge, surprised by the sudden rush of power. "I can't avoid Diana Ulrich," I explain, forcing myself to take even, measured breaths. "She's my assigned Chemistrie research partner."

"Well, switch partners. Immediately." Her eyes flick toward me as she butters her gooseberry roll.

"Yes, Aunt Vyvian." My wand hand tingles, my fire lines sparking. I'm suddenly and acutely aware of how much wood

I'm surrounded by. Practically everything in the room is made of wood.

Aunt Vyvian purses her lips. "Lupines are unpredictable beasts. I hear the female has forsaken her lodging to live in the woods. Like the wild animal she is."

Um, no, actually. She's living with me. Along with a Selkie and two Icarals.

Aunt Vyvian cocks an eyebrow, studying me as she takes a sip of her tea. "You're doing well in your studies?"

"Yes, Aunt Vyvian." *No, I'm actually barely passing all of my classes and living on about four hours of sleep a night. And having visions of the forest attacking me.*

"It's not surprising you're doing so well," she says with an air of satisfaction. "Our family's always been a clever lot. And I hear that you and Lukas Grey attended the Yule Dance together." Her eyes beam with approval.

A stinging flush heats my cheeks at the mention of Lukas's name. I absently reach for the Snow Oak pendant around my neck, the wood of Lukas's gift pulsing against my palm with enticing warmth.

"That's a beautiful necklace, Elloren," my aunt comments, never missing a gesture. "Where did you get it?"

My blush deepens. "Lukas gave it to me."

Aunt Vyvian's mouth lifts into a shrewd smile. "It's high time you fasted to him."

"I do plan on fasting to him," I politely lie, the pendant's humming strength soothing my nerves. "But I must speak to Uncle Edwin about it first."

"Then it's a good thing you'll be seeing your uncle on Founder's Day," she says with a tight smile. "You can secure his permission then."

Time is running out. My hands will be marked by summer.

"I'm sure he'll give permission soon—"

"I want you fasted to Lukas Grey *now*," she insists, losing all vestiges of pleasantry.

"I realize that," I tell her, unable to keep the sarcasm out of my voice. "I'm living with two Icarals." I inwardly scoff over how completely my aunt's attempt at leverage has gone awry. But then a sharp apprehension spikes through me, and I immediately regret reminding her of this—I'm scared of bringing her attention to anything pertaining to my North Tower lodging. My aunt *cannot* find out that Marina is living there with us. Not when she's the lead advocate on the Mage Council for having the Selkies killed as soon as they come to shore.

Catching my air of defiance, Aunt Vyvian narrows her eyes at me. "I'm surprised you've endured living with the Icarals this long, to be quite frank. You're made of sterner stuff than I imagined. It's a shame you don't have the magical ability to match your stubborness." Aunt Vyvian shakes her head ruefully and lets out a sigh for what might have been. Her expression turns frustrated. "It's not right that the Bane girl is heir to *our* magic."

Ah, that old rivalry. I sit up straighter, glad for the distraction.

"I know you must find me harsh, Elloren," Aunt Vyvian reasons with a frown, "but I'm keeping the pressure on you. It's for your own sake, and for the sake of this family. You need to fast to Lukas quickly, before he walks away from this for good."

Before I can formulate a response, we're interrupted by the arrival of my brothers. Trystan comes in first, wearing his finest Gardnerian clothing, his smart storm-gray military apprentice uniform marked with a silver Erthia sphere and Level Five stripes. Rafe enters behind him, smiling widely, and I'm dismayed to see he's wearing our old Kelt-styled woolen clothing from home.

No, Rafe. This is not the time to challenge her.

"Ah, Trystan." Aunt Vyvian rises to meet my younger brother with a warm smile, making a sharp point of ignoring Rafe. She kisses Trystan on both cheeks. "I'm hearing such great things about you," she says proudly. "Already accepted into the Weapons Guild at such a young age—the youngest *ever*. Quite an accomplishment, dear. Your hard work and commitment to your craft deserve a reward, so I have something for you." She holds out a long package tied with stiff brown string, her voice dropping to a conspiratorial whisper. "Your uncle doesn't have to know about it."

Trystan takes the package and tugs at the string, the paper falling open.

A wand.

My heart leaps at this unexpected advantage my aunt has handed to us. *Two wands. Two weapons.* Trystan's eyes widen as he runs his fingers over the wand, testing the feel of it.

"You are a Level Five Mage," Aunt Vyvian declares. "It's high time you had your own wand, one fine enough to match your natural talents. I'm very proud of you, Trystan."

"Thank you, Aunt Vyvian." My brother acknowledges her praise with a slight, respectful bow, his face pleasantly neutral. At moments like these, I'm incredibly grateful for Trystan's ability to remain completely calm and self-contained, no matter what he's faced with.

Aunt Vyvian dips her head toward Trystan, but her smug grin fades as she turns to my older brother. "And Rafe," she says flatly.

Rafe doesn't let her pointed unfriendliness faze him, his amused smile bright as ever. Aunt Vyvian gestures to the empty chairs, and my brothers join us at the table.

"It has come to my attention," Aunt Vyvian says to Rafe, her lips tightly pursed with displeasure, "that you were...*cavorting* with the Lupine girl at the Yule Dance. It seems you made quite the spectacle of yourself."

"Diana likes to dance," Rafe says, grinning cagily.

"Does she?" Aunt Vyvian replies, cool as ice. "Well, I've sent word to her father about it—a most unpleasant task, I can assure you. I informed him that it is the unfortunate nature of some young Gardnerian men to sow their wild oats, so to speak, outside their own kind, with Selkies and the like." She turns to me, her expression apologetic. "I'm sorry to discuss this in front of you, my dear. It's shocking, I know, but this affects your fasting prospects, as well as Trystan's. Well, maybe not yours, Elloren, as Lukas Grey seems quite intent on fasting to you. Trystan, on the other hand, might have a hard time finding a suitable young woman if Rafe continues running around with the Lupine bitch."

I flinch at her casual slur, and Rafe's mouth goes tight with anger. I reach down to clasp the edge of my chair with my wand hand and a blazing heat courses through my lines. I've a sudden flash of awareness not just of all the wood in the room, but all the wood in the building. Shocked, I wrench my hand away from the wood, ball my fist and resolve to not touch the chair again.

Aunt Vyvian sips at her tea, peering over the edge of her cup at Rafe. "Both you and Trystan need fasting partners by spring," she declares. "Cut off all contact with the Lupine female immediately."

She looks to Trystan, her expression momentarily thawing. "I have a selection of fastmate possibilities lined up for you to choose from, Trystan." She frowns at Rafe. "But at this point, we may be dependent on the Council's fasting registry to find *you* a willing partner."

"What did Diana's father say about all this?" I ask my aunt nervously, noticing that Rafe's silent wrath has shifted to the aggressive baring of teeth.

Aunt Vyvian fixes him with a calculating stare. "He felt that you should stay away from his daughter. Or he'll need to pay you a visit. Am I making myself clear, Rafe?"

"Quite," he replies, biting off the word.

"Really, Rafe, what could you possibly be thinking?" Aunt Vyvian looks to the ceiling, as if praying for strength. "Even a Selkie would be a better choice of...companion, than the daughter of the *Gerwulf Pack's alpha*." Aunt Vyvian turns to Trystan and gives him a long-suffering look. "I wish all young Gardnerian men were as morally upstanding as you, Trystan. You are a *credit* to your race."

Both Rafe and I turn to Trystan, eyebrows raised.

"You are the youngest here," she goes on, "but you have shown the greatest maturity. You must guide your older siblings, Trystan."

"I will do my best to keep them on the right path, Aunt Vyvian," Trystan promises solemnly.

"And get some practice in with that wand," she says encouragingly. "A Level Five Mage and a member of the Weapons Guild—you'll be highly placed in the Mage Guard."

Trystan's serene expression doesn't budge. "I will be careful not to neglect the natural abilities the Ancient One has blessed me with."

Aunt Vyvian nods at Trystan with solemn appreciation before turning back to Rafe with a frown. "Rafe, it's time to stop being so irresponsible."

"I will try my best to follow Trystan's example," Rafe replies, his eyes steely.

Aunt Vyvian holds Rafe's gaze, neither one of them ceding for an uncomfortably long moment. Eventually, she shifts her gaze back to Trystan, her Golden Gardnerian. "Trystan, I appreciate all your letters. I can't often be away from Valgard, so I trust you to be my eyes and ears. Please continue to stay in touch, and don't hesitate to let me know if your siblings need correction."

"I won't, Aunt Vyvian," Trystan says. "I'll keep a close eye on them for you."

Trystan shows up at my North Tower room a few nights later. When I open my door, he motions for me to join him in the hall and slides my wand out of his cloak pocket. I notice he has the wand Aunt Vyvian gave him sheathed at his side. Every day, my little brother looks more and more like the powerful Mage he is.

"Here, Ren," he says, holding the spiraling wand out to me. "Take it."

My affinity lines leap covetously toward the wand, but I hold back from accepting it. "Why? I've no power."

He shakes his head against my protest. "It won't work for me anymore. It's like it's gone dormant, or..." He pauses, a ripple of trepidation passing over his expression. "Like it's gained control over itself." He studies me, as if waiting for me to mock this odd statement.

But I don't. I know very well that there's something strange about this wand.

The Wand of Myth.

I'm instantly embarrassed to once again be entertaining such an outrageous idea. It couldn't possibly be the great Wand of Myth...but it's certainly not normal.

I take the wand from Trystan, and a look of relief passes over his face. My wand hand curls around the spiraling handle, and I pull in a deep, languid breath. It feels good to hold this wand. Too good. Better than any wood.

"You know I'm not religious, Ren," Trystan says, eyeing the wand. "But... I've been having dreams. A lot of dreams, about this wand and white birds and a tree. And they always end the same way." He gives me a significant look. "With this wand in *your* hand."

My grip tightens around the wand as a shiver of power spirals through my affinity lines and out toward the wand in a heady rush.

"Trystan," I say tentatively. "When did your affinity lines quicken?"

"Around fourteen. Why?"

"I... I can sense my earth lines now. And my fire lines. They're getting stronger—every day, almost. They flare sometimes."

Trystan nods with understanding. "It can happen very suddenly. I remember one time, we were all having supper, and my water lines just...surged. For a moment, I had the bizarre sensation that the entire room was underwater."

I arch my brow. "Well, that must have been disconcerting."

Trystan's lip lifts in a small, sardonic smile. "It was a bit overwhelming, yes."

"And your fire lines?" I ask. I know that Trystan has strong water and fire lines, which makes it difficult for him to control his powerful but stormy magic.

"I didn't have a sense of my fire line until about a year ago," he tells me.

"So...there's a chance I might develop a sense of more lines of power."

"You might. Although two is the most common."

"But I won't be able to access it."

He shakes his head. "You won't ever be able to access your power, since you're a Level One. I've never known of a Level One Mage who gained access to their power."

Confusion wells up in me. "Then why would this wand be drawn to me?"

He considers this. "Are you entertaining the idea that *this* wand is the actual Wand of Myth?"

"Yes."

"Well, the legends say that the Wand of Myth sometimes lies dormant for many years. If we're pretending that the stories are all true, then perhaps your children will have great power, and you'll pass it on to them. Or perhaps you're meant to pass it to someone else."

"Like you just passed it back to me."

Trystan is silent for a moment, and I can see he's troubled by his strange dreams and the idea of straying too closely into mythological territory. "Perhaps."

"The forest is afraid of me," I tell him, laying it all out in the open. "And just before that, it was openly hostile. I'm truly not imagining this, Trystan. You heard what Tierney said the other night. Have you sensed any of this from the woods?"

"No." He tilts his head, thoughtful. "But I've heard of this type of thing. Only directed at very high-level Earth Mages, though."

"So, I might have very high levels of earth magic inside me?"

"That you have no access to."

I let out a long, frustrated sigh. "It's increasingly strange to be me."

Trystan lets out a small laugh. "Join the club, Ren."

I smile at this and look to him with affection. "I'm glad you are who you are."

Trystan gives me a slight smile. "I feel the same way about you," he says quietly.

We wordlessly stand there for a moment, bolstered by each other, but my thoughts soon take a somber turn.

"What do you think will happen with Rafe and the Lupines?" I tentatively ask him.

Trystan's gaze darkens. "I don't know, Ren." He shakes his head. "With the possibility of war with the Lupines on the horizon, I just don't know."

MAGE COUNCIL
RULING
#200

Aiding in the illegal movement of
subland Smaragdalfar Elves into the upper
Realmlands shall be punishable by execution.
Any Smaragdalfar Elves found on Gardnerian
land must be turned over to the Mage Guard
immediately for transport to Alfsigroth.

CHAPTER NINE

FOUNDER'S DAY

Dim morning light filters through the windows of the University's largest dining hall, the vast space gorgeously appointed for Founder's Day. I shift slightly as I look around, keenly aware of the spiraling wand concealed snugly in the side of my laced-up boot.

Rafe, Trystan, Wynter's brother Cael, and his Elfin-second, Rhys, survey the dining hall as well, and seem every bit as appalled as I am.

The Gardnerians have completely taken over the event.

All the decorations are Yule-themed, even though we're the only group at University that celebrates Yule. It's spectacularly elegant, to be sure, and I have to struggle not to be entranced by it all. Pine boughs create a fragrant, false ceiling and grace the centerpieces around the room, and I can't help but rapturously breathe in the cool, evergreen scent. Red glass lanterns hang from the boughs and are set on every table over scarlet tablecloths, the color representing Gardnerian blood spilled by the Evil Ones. Deep crimson curtains are draped around every diamond-paned window and spill down to the floor.

It all makes me feel deeply uncomfortable.

I've never been so painfully aware of how my people aggressively push aside the customs and beliefs of others as I am in this moment. I darkly imagine tipping over several lanterns to set the decorations on fire, certain all the pine strewn about would become a conflagration in the blink of an eye.

The morning sky is overcast, but the gloomy weather only heightens the beauty of the lanterns' scarlet glow. Small groups of Gardnerians are beginning to dot the massive dining hall, and there's a fantastic spread of food laid out on several broad tables—an entire roast boar, sliced thin, with a pronged serving fork stuck in its side; stewed fruits sprinkled with sugar-dusted flowers; a variety of hot drinks and warm breads paired with well-aged cheeses. Multiple Keltic, Verpacian, Elfhollen and Urisk workers from all the University kitchens, including Olilly and Fernyllia, are on hand to serve the many visitors.

I turn as both of the huge doors to the main dining hall abruptly swing open, hitting the walls behind them with a resounding *thud*.

The Lupines stride into the hall with bold, predatory grace, and most of the hall's occupants draw back with looks of surprise.

A huge, muscular man leads their group, and there's no doubt that he's the alpha. He has Diana's fiery amber eyes, proud chin, dominating aura and golden hair, his beard shot through with gray at the sides. He radiates the most commanding presence I've ever witnessed, his charisma dwarfing even that of Kam Vin, the intimidating military commander of the local Vu Trin.

Close behind the man is a tall, lean woman who strongly

resembles Jarod. There's a worried, intellectual cast to her expression as she looks around the hall with a guarded reluctance. Beside her strides another Lupine female, this one with dark hair intermingled with bright red strands. Her skin is deep brown, and she has the radiant crimson eyes of the Northern Lupine pack. She's holding a small boy with her same coloring and crimson eyes, but his ears are pointed and his hair is a mingling of purple and blue.

Flanking them are four strapping men in tight formation, one striding slightly ahead of the others. This man's slate gray cheeks are marked with rune-tattoos like Andras's and framed by steel-colored hair streaked with violet. I realize this must be Ferrin Sandulf—the man with Amaz ancestry Diana told all of us about. Her father's beta, which makes him second-in-command.

Orbiting them all like a kinetic moon bounces an energetic girl of about ten. She can only be Kendra, Diana and Jarod's little sister. She's Diana all over again, only younger and shorter—and with a lot more frantic energy.

The men all have short hair and close-cropped beards and Diana's mother's hair is long and blond and pulled back with a tie. And they're all dressed for movement, in loose earth-toned tunics over pants and sturdy boots—simple dress to allow for ease of the clothing's removal so they can Change.

Everyone in the thinly populated hall grows silent and stilled.

As one, the Lupines make their way down the long center aisle.

Trystan and I exchange a glance tinged with alarm.

Rafe calmly watches them approach from where we all stand at the far end of the hall, a large turkey slung over his shoulder. He's just returned from a morning hunt with Cael and Rhys, and the three of them are all still fully armed, bows slung over their shoulders and quivers strapped to their backs.

Diana enters the dining hall from a side door, her golden hair swishing behind her. She takes one look at her family and lets out a loud shriek of delight, her hands flying up as she breaks into a joyful sprint. Her father spots her, and his stern face lights up like the sun.

"Father!" Diana cries, exuberantly throwing her arms around Gunther Ulrich.

Gunther lets out a deep, rumbling laugh and hugs her tightly. "My fierce daughter! Oh, how I've missed you!"

Little Kendra jumps around them with joy-filled excitement, embracing Diana from behind.

Jarod, who's come in behind his sister, strides over to the Lupines without so much as a glance in our direction. He's been very distant since his painful encounter with Aislinn at the Yule Dance, eating most of his meals alone and spending much of his time hunting or studying by himself. Diana's been increasingly worried about him, often venting to me about how useless her efforts have been to draw him back into our circle.

Relief washes over Jarod's face as he quietly approaches his family. His mother takes his face in her hands and murmurs something before embracing him warmly, clearly overjoyed to be with all her children again.

Diana wraps an arm around her little sister's shoulders, squeezing her affectionately. "I've missed you so much, Diana!" Kendra cries. "I've so much to tell you! Did you get my letters? I got yours! Look, Diana! Look! I got a beaver tooth!" She holds up the necklace she's wearing, decorated with a variety of teeth.

Diana fingers the necklace, clearly impressed. "That's wonderful, Kendra!"

"And I got a celyrnium for my rock collection! Remember how I've been looking for one of those for *forever*?" Kendra proudly holds up the bag that's slung haphazardly over her shoulder. "I brought the whole collection to show you! And my drawings. I did about ten new ones!"

"I can't wait to see everything," Diana says, beaming at her.

"And I got a *deer*, Diana! Just a few days ago!"

"Brought it down herself, she did," Gunther crows, patting Kendra's head.

"A *big* one!" the little girl continues breathlessly. "I got it even before Stefan! He was *so* jealous!"

"She's a fine hunter, your sister," their father brags. "She may even give you a run for your money in a few years."

Diana ruffles Kendra's golden hair. "I don't doubt it," she says, smiling down at her small clone.

Her father pulls them both into a warm hug. "My strong, fierce girls," he says adoringly.

I'm struck in that moment by the things Gunther takes pride in when it comes to his daughters—most Gardnerian parents value modesty and beauty much more highly than strength or bravery in young girls, and I find myself suddenly feeling melancholy and wondering what my father would admire most about me if he was still alive.

"Where's Rafe Gardner?" asks Kendra, looking around the room. "I want to meet him! Boy, are you in *serious* trouble!"

"Kendra," Gunther chastises, his voice full of authority.

"Oh...forgot," Kendra says, abashed, lowering her voice slightly. "Not supposed to talk about it. But where is he, Diana? Does he have weird eyes? They have such *weird eyes*. I hope he doesn't smell bad. Some of them smell *really* bad!"

Diana says something to her father that I don't catch and then gestures toward us, smiling proudly.

Cael turns to Rafe, a wry look on his face. "I still can't believe you're chasing after the alpha's daughter."

Rafe grins at him.

Cael shakes his head, amused. "I do hope you survive the day, Rafe Gardner."

Diana's father fixes his eyes on my brother, as if picking up on Cael's use of his name. The alpha straightens to his full, intimidating height, the smile on his face and on the faces of the four Lupine males behind him quickly replaced by serious, forbidding expressions. Diana's mother also looks to Rafe, her face taking on a look of deep concern.

All of them, with Diana and her father in the lead, start toward Rafe, moving together with a fluid, cohesive grace.

"Are they going to come over here and kill you now?" Trystan asks Rafe, his voice low.

"Nah," Rafe says. "They seem nice."

Trystan looks at our older brother as if he's just sprouted horns. "*Nice?* Are you completely and utterly lacking the self-preservation part of your brain?"

Rafe flashes a smile, seeming oblivious to Trystan's sarcasm. He secures his hold on the turkey and confidently strides toward Diana and her family.

"Father, Mother, Kendra," Diana says with a big, happy smile. "This is Rafe Gardner." She's gazing at her family with the smug expression of someone who fully expects them to be as instantly besotted with Rafe as she is.

Her pack's unfriendly expressions remain frozen in place—all except Kendra, whose eyes flit back and forth eagerly between Rafe and her sister.

"This is the scariest 'meet the parents' moment that has ever happened in the history of Erthia," Trystan whispers to me.

"Rafe's taller than Diana's father. Have you noticed that?" I comment.

"And your point is…what, exactly? You think this gives him some type of advantage? Against *them*?"

I shrug. "It's got to count for something."

"I'm honored to meet you all," Rafe announces. He slams his turkey down on the nearest table with a dramatic flourish. "I just came from the hunt and offer my kill to you."

Everyone's faces take on looks of surprise. Diana beams at Rafe, impressed.

"I am Rafe Gardner," he continues. And then my eldest brother proceeds to recite our lineage, clearly and fluidly, all the way back to Styvius Gardner.

"He must have practiced this," I whisper to Trystan.

Trystan raises one black eyebrow at me. "It's a list of every major enemy their people have ever had."

"Rafe," Diana says as my brother finishes, gesturing toward the alpha, "this is my father, Gunther Ulrich."

Rafe extends his hand with his usual easy confidence. "It's a pleasure to meet you, sir."

Diana's father smiles and extends his own hand, his expression more feral than friendly. He gives Rafe a look of cool appraisal and shakes my brother's hand, his muscular grip seeming strong and sure, and I imagine he's gauging the strength of Rafe's handshake and searching for any sign of fear.

"I see you've researched our customs well," Gunther Ulrich comments, glancing over at the turkey, his hand still clenched tightly around Rafe's.

"I've admired your people for some time now."

"Have you, now," Gunther says, his amber eyes glowing fiercely. "Like the exotic, do you, son?"

"Sometimes," Rafe says carefully, their hands still locked firmly together.

"Is he getting ready to rip his arm off?" Trystan asks me worriedly.

"Find my daughter exotic, do you?" Diana's father asks, his lips pulling back into a menacing grin, white teeth glistening.

"On the contrary," Rafe replies evenly. "I find your daughter to be something of a kindred spirit."

Oh, smooth, Rafe. Very smooth.

This seems to surprise and please Diana's father. He releases Rafe's hand, crosses his arms in front of his broad chest and studies him with narrowed eyes and a slight grin. "My Diana seems to be quite fond of you, Rafe Gardner."

"I'm quite fond of her, as well," Rafe replies.

"I must admit, I've been very curious to meet the Gardnerian boy who dares to court the daughter of a Lupine alpha. You either have some serious balls, son, or you're incredibly stupid."

Everyone laughs a little at this, even Diana's father. Not a jolly laugh, mind you—more of an *I'm only being pleasant to you because my daughter likes you and if you so much as make her frown I will tear you into a thousand tiny pieces* kind of laugh. He continues to eye Rafe speculatively. "I'm actually willing to bet it's the former."

Rafe grins, unfazed. "I'd like to think so, sir."

Gunther laughs at his boldness.

"I think Rafe's actually enjoying this," I whisper to Trystan, shocked.

"Or maybe he's trying to hasten his own death," Trystan replies matter-of-factly.

"She's a fierce girl, my Diana," Gunther says, showing his teeth again.

"I'm well aware of that, sir."

"She tells me you're a fine hunter. And tracker."

"Not compared to Diana, but among Gardnerians and Elves, I can hold my own."

"He's being modest, Father," Diana interjects, her arm twining through Rafe's as she looks up at him like he's a prized trophy.

Gunther nods, then glances around. "Diana also tells me you have family here at University. Your sister and brother?"

"Yes, sir," Rafe replies.

"Last chance to make a run for it," Trystan says wryly.

The pack's gaze shifts in unison to rest on the two of us. Diana's father smirks, and I blush, realizing that they've heard everything Trystan and I have said to each other.

Diana's mother looks increasingly worried as Trystan and I approach the pack.

As I near, their curious expressions fade, quickly replaced by looks of shock and concern. I realize my cursed looks and maybe even the smell of my blood could very well ruin this for my brother. My face grows tight and uncomfortably warm as I glance at each Lupine in turn.

Gunther eyes me shrewdly after giving the other Lupines a brief glance. I decide to go for broke and extend my hand to him and he takes it into his firm grip.

"When most people meet me," I tell him, "they're shocked by how much I look like my grandmother."

"You look exactly like her," he comments, his gaze searching.

He releases my hand, and I take a deep breath. "I may look exactly like her," I say, my voice quavering, "but I'm very different from her, in more ways than you might imagine."

Everyone is silent for a long moment as their alpha considers me, his wild eyes probing.

"Elloren Gardner," he says finally, his voice low and commanding, but his expression kind, "it's long been my view that a person's appearance often reveals little about their true character. I am quite willing to believe there may be more to you than meets the eye. Perhaps time will tell, eh?"

I nod, feeling surprisingly touched, tears welling in my eyes. "Thank you, sir."

He places a broad hand warmly on my shoulder, and I blink back my tears. "It's a pleasure to meet all of you," I say, the words heartfelt. "We all think very highly of Diana and Jarod."

Diana's father nods, pleased, and turns to Trystan, who's wearing his usual unreadable expression. "And you must be Trystan," he says with amusement as he shakes my younger brother's hand.

"Yes, sir."

Gunther Ulrich's mouth quirks into a smile. "Trystan Gardner, I have no plans to kill your brother." He pauses, a mischievous look in his eyes. "Not today, at least."

"That's a relief, sir," Trystan replies.

A whirlwind of introductions and conversation ensue, led mainly by Diana. She introduces us to her mother, who appears reluctant to meet us and a bit dazed by the sudden turn of events. Then Diana introduces Kendra, who seems fascinated by Rafe, and then Ferrin Sandulf, her father's beta, who's mated to the crimson-eyed woman, Soraya, and father to the little Lupine boy.

Two large, blond-haired guards, Georg Leall and Kristov Varg, briefly acknowledge us, then go back to suspiciously scanning the dining hall. This is obviously not a pleasure trip for them. But the fourth member of Gunther Ulrich's guard, a red-haired young man named Brendan Faolan, seems to be particularly good friends with Diana.

"I'll spare you the lengthy introductions," Brendan tells

me, smiling as we meet. "I know it's not your custom to share lineage."

"Maybe you should clue Diana in about this," I say teasingly. His smile widens.

"Refusing to establish lineage is just rude," Diana interjects with some irritation. Then a new thought sets her grinning from ear to ear. "I heard you took Iliana Quinn to mate."

"It's true," Brendan replies, beaming.

"I'm so happy for you, Brendan!" Diana enthuses, embracing him affectionately.

I look around the room as they catch up with each other. The hall is rapidly filling with mostly Gardnerian scholars and their families. All around us, people are chatting and embracing, but there are also quite a few shocked and disapproving stares leveled in our direction.

Then, among the gathering crowd, I spot a familiar figure—a small, disheveled Gardnerian man dressed in a plain, dark brown tunic and leaning heavily on a cane, struggling to make his way through the maze of people.

"Uncle Edwin." The words come out of me in a choked whisper. Everything around me recedes, like fog exposed to sunlight. It's really him, after all this time. After all that's happened.

I stumble into a run, lurching toward him. Uncle Edwin catches sight of me, his eyes lighting up as I almost knock him over with the force of my embrace and break into tears.

"Elloren, my sweet girl," he laughs, hugging me back warmly. "Now, what's this? Don't cry. It's all right, my girl."

I laugh through my tears and brush them away with the palm of one hand. "I'm so happy you're here."

"It's been too long, my dear." His speech is slightly muffled. He pulls back to look at me, his own eyes moist. Worry momentarily threatens to overwhelm me as I notice that half of his face appears to have gone permanently slack.

"You've changed, my girl," he says, concern briefly clouding his features. "I can see it in your face. You look...older. Tougher." He considers this for a moment, brow furrowed, and his expression grows reflective, then gratified. "I'm glad of it," he says, winking at me before pushing up his glasses and looking around. "So where are those brothers of yours?"

"Over there," I say, gesturing toward Diana's pack.

Uncle Edwin squints in their direction. "Ah, yes." He smiles at me. "Shall we go over and say hello, then?"

It heartens me to see how casually willing Uncle Edwin is to meet a whole clan of shapeshifters. But that's Uncle Edwin for you. He's never been one to make judgments about others based on whether or not they're Gardnerian.

My uncle's arm threads through mine, and I slow my gait so he can keep up. Worry for him rises as I take in how much thinner and older he looks—so much frailer than I remember him.

We've all changed.

Rafe strides over with a broad, happy grin on his face and leans down to embrace Uncle Edwin. "Ah, Rafe, my boy," our uncle says, chuckling as he pats Rafe on the back. "Your aunt certainly has given me an earful about you."

Uncle Edwin pulls back from Rafe and looks around, finding Trystan, who is standing quietly off to the side. "And Trystan," he says, tottering over to him. "My goodness, you've grown tall."

"Hello, Uncle Edwin." Anyone who doesn't know Trystan would completely miss the tumult of emotion hiding behind the aloof expression on his face as our uncle pulls him into a warm hug.

"What's this?" Uncle Edwin asks, looking down at the wand attached to Trystan's belt.

"A present from Aunt Vyvian," Trystan explains, looking a bit abashed.

Uncle Edwin frowns at this, then collects himself, turning to squint up at the most intimidating man in the room. Gunther Ulrich's eyes are flickering back and forth between Rafe and Uncle Edwin, seeming surprised that my strapping, confident brother is related to my short, mild-mannered uncle.

Rafe gestures loosely toward Diana's father. "This is Gunther Ulrich, alpha to the Gerwulf Pack."

"Oh, yes. Well," my uncle says, squinting up at Gunther through his thick glasses as he takes his hand. "Edwin Gardner. Rafe has written to me about you... A pleasure."

Kendra bounces over to get a better look at my uncle. "Your beard is awfully fluffy!" she exclaims, giggling.

Uncle Edwin chuckles and pats Kendra on the head. "And you, young lady," he tells her, "have a very impressive necklace on."

"It's my tooth collection!" she enthuses, fingering it proudly. "They're all different, and I just got two new ones! Wanna see?"

Uncle Edwin adjusts his glasses again and leans over to "ooh" and "ahh" over each tooth as Kendra beams at him, delighted to have such an attentive audience.

"Where's the rest of your pack?" she asks, looking around curiously.

"Kendra," Gunther cuts in. "Remember, they have different ways."

Uncle Edwin laughs and pats her on the head again. "We're a pack of four, Kendra," he explains. "Rafe, Elloren, Trystan and me."

"That's *all*?" Kendra exclaims, clearly confounded by the idea.

"That's all."

Her face screws up in consternation. "You must be *terribly* lonely."

Uncle Edwin pauses for a moment and looks at her thoughtfully. "Yes...well. We get on just fine, the four of us."

"But it's too *small*!" Kendra insists. "I have Mother and Father and Diana and Jarod and all my cousins and four best girl friends and three best boy friends and..." After a few minutes of this, Kendra begins running out of counting fingers as she lists her favorite aunts and uncles and friends, painting a picture of a communal life rich in love and friendship.

"Wanna see my drawings?" she asks my uncle, completely changing the subject. "I know all about mushrooms. I made a book of all the different types." She pulls a stack of papers out of her bag, bound together haphazardly with twine. The pictures are all carefully rendered in ink, painted over with watercolors.

"Why, these are very well done, Kendra," my uncle praises her. "Very well done indeed." He turns to Gunther, smiling. "You have quite the young artist here."

"She's very talented, my Kendra," Gunther agrees.

Kendra bashfully kicks her feet at the floor. "That's what Uncle Hahn says, and Inger and Micah. They all think I'm really good. Do you know about mushrooms?"

"I do," my uncle tells her. "It's actually a bit of a hobby of mine. Why don't we sit down and look at what you've done—if you'll excuse us, Gunther? You have a delightful daughter."

Her father nods, but Kendra's attention is momentarily diverted by the appearance of her sister at Rafe's side. She grabs at Diana's arm. "You come, too, Diana!"

"Ah, Diana," Uncle Edwin says, reaching over to pat her

arm warmly. "Rafe has told me all about you, my girl. I can tell from his letters that he's quite smitten."

Diana's smile widens. "It's very nice to meet you, Edwin Gardner."

"Come *on!*" Kendra's tugging at them both now, wanting their attention back.

"All right, all right," my uncle says, laughing along with Diana. The two of them are clearly delighted to be around a child, both of them patient and kind. It dawns on me that Diana will probably make a good mother someday. Mother to my brother's children. It's a strange thought—and a wonderful one, I realize.

Gunther turns to Rafe. "Diana tells me you know the woods around here quite well. Why don't we take a walk, you and me? Get to know each other."

There's that teeth-bared grin again. It's wildly disconcerting.

"I'd like that, sir," Rafe says with a newly serious expression, seeming amazingly immune to Gunther Ulrich's powers of intimidation.

"I'll see you later, then," Diana says, pulling herself away from Kendra long enough to wrap her arms around Rafe. She leans in to plant a quick kiss on his lips.

Rafe's eyebrows shoot up at her boldness, and I can see the alpha's jaw harden. My brother pushes Diana gently—but firmly—away and seems to be trying to convey to her via his expression that this is *really* not the time.

Diana just grins back at him, full of mischief.

CHAPTER
TEN

TRAPPED

Gunther and Rafe leave together, and I find myself momentarily alone. Trystan has fallen into polite conversation with Diana's mother, Daciana, who seems mystified to find herself speaking to him, and the remaining Lupines are talking among themselves.

Jarod is standing apart from the others, staring across the room, his face ashen. I follow his gaze to find that Aislinn has just come in with her family—her parents and sisters, some of her sisters' children and Randall, along with a stern couple I assume are Randall's parents.

Aislinn's father, an authoritarian-looking man with a close-cropped beard and military bearing, catches sight of the Lupines. His face takes on a look of fury, his lips pulling into a tight line of abhorrence as he quickly ushers his family to a table in the corner of the hall farthest from us.

The children's eyes grow wide with fear as they spot the Lupines. Their mothers lean in to comfort them as the children pull in to cling to their mothers' skirts. All of the adults, except for Aislinn, pointedly make the holy gesture to ward off the stain of the Evil Ones.

Aislinn looks positively heartbroken as she takes a seat, silent and pale, staring down at the table in front of her. Her eldest sister, Liesbeth, seems oblivious to this as she begins chatting merrily with Randall. Aislinn's sister Auralie frantically chases her children around, her eyes fearfully darting over to the Lupines every so often, while Aislinn's mother sits quietly with Randall's parents, her expression despondent.

"Jarod," I say as I approach him.

"This is a farce," he says, his voice strained. "She doesn't want him. Look at her—she's miserable. She wants to be with *me*, yet she fights it."

"But you know why, Jarod. It's because of her family. She's worried about her mother and her sister—"

"She can't help them," he says furiously. "She won't change *anything* by fasting to Randall. They're going to just drag her down into their misery. They already have."

Randall absently puts his hand on Aislinn's arm, and Jarod's expression turns violent.

"He wants *her*, though," he grinds out, his lips pulling back to show his canines. "He wants her and practically every young woman who gets within a few feet of him. He doesn't love her—she's completely interchangeable to him. Your men are *pathetic*."

"Jarod," I say cautiously, "let's go get something to drink."

He fixes his wild eyes on me. "I'm not *thirsty*." Jarod's lips pull back farther, exposing even more of his teeth.

"I don't care," I say firmly. "Let's go anyway."

He glances back at Aislinn and her family, as if weighing the options—get a drink, or rip Randall's head off. Then his fierce gaze darts back to meet mine, and I fight the urge to shrink back from him. "You need to step away from this for a moment and collect yourself," I tell him. "Or you're going to do something you'll regret."

"I don't know that I'd regret killing him," he says evenly.

"You don't have to kill him right *now*," I say, attempting to keep my voice light.

Jarod considers this. "True." His jaw tenses, and he takes a deep breath, as if trying to calm himself. Then, to my great relief, he relents and goes with me to get something to drink from a table set up near to the kitchens.

Far away from Aislinn and her family.

Jarod and I sit, drinking hot cider, his eyes still finding their way back to Aislinn every now and then. But he seems to have calmed down a bit, the uncharacteristic violence in his amber eyes now dimmed.

"I have some concerns about Rafe and Diana," I say to Jarod, trying to draw his attention away from Aislinn.

He shoots me a slightly indignant look.

"Jarod, I like Diana, you know that," I clarify. "She's actually perfect for Rafe. And I can picture Rafe fitting in well with your people in some ways. But my brother has never been a follower. I'm not sure this is going to work. Not the way Diana wants it to."

"He wouldn't have to follow for long."

This catches me off guard. "I don't understand."

Jarod looks at me as if I should have figured this out by now. "Elloren, Rafe's alpha material."

"I thought Diana was likely to be next in line."

"Perhaps, but I suspect when Rafe becomes Lupine, he might best even her."

I start to laugh. "Oh, that's rich. My brother, the alpha of a Lupine pack. A *Gardnerian* alpha. The grandson of Carnissa Gardner, no less."

Jarod's lip lifts, and it's good to see him almost smile. But then he glances back toward Aislinn, and the smile disappears. "Every time Randall touches her, I feel like going over there and separating his arm from the rest of his body."

"Not a good idea."

"I don't know, Elloren, it seems like a better and better idea the longer I sit here." He shoots Randall a look of pure loathing before turning back to me. "I have met so many of your fasted couples who have no interest in each other. Or the males are interested, and the females feel anything from indifference to outright revulsion. Are your men so cruel and sense blind that they're content to mate with women who don't want them? And why is it your women act like mating is something shameful? It's bizarre."

"Mating is considered sinful in our religion," I try to explain. "Its sole purpose is to bring forth as many Mages as possible. Mating for any reason beyond that is considered immoral. We're supposed to rise above our base natures. Not be like wild things, like..."

"Like us? Like shapeshifters?"

I let out a dismayed sigh. "Basically."

Jarod's stare is hard and unwavering. "That's truly awful, Elloren."

I look down, swallowing hard, thinking about what my own future might look like. "You're right. It is."

"So, you wandfast people with no thought as to whether they truly love each other."

"And at younger and younger ages," I dolefully add. "My neighbor Sage Gaffney was fasted at thirteen."

Jarod's face has taken on a deeply troubled look. "The woman with the Icaral child."

I nod. "Her fastmate beat her, so she ran away from him."

Jarod winces. "I've read your sacred book, you know," he

says, his tone grim. "Trying to understand Aislinn. The first part is truly hideous. It's so full of hatred for anyone outside of your kind. I read this book, and I see why it doesn't matter how much I love Aislinn. She'll never be free of this awful religion..."

Jarod's voice trails off, and I look up to find his mother approaching us from across the room. As she nears our table, Daciana's eyes light on me, her expression turning wary. It's clear she wishes my brothers and I would go away and leave her family alone.

I focus on my cider as Daciana sits down, ignoring me, and asks a sullen Jarod about his University studies. As they talk, her concerned expression deepens. Every now and then her eyes dart over to view me suspiciously, perhaps trying to see if I'm to blame for the change in her son. Jarod tries not to look at Aislinn—I can see it in the way he holds himself, so stiff and unmoving, but he can't resist for long.

He glances over at her for a split second as his mother is telling him about a relative's new twin girls. Daciana breaks off mid-sentence. Her head jerks around to see who Jarod just glanced at, her gaze immediately zeroing in on Aislinn. Dawning horror washes over her face. "Oh, Blessed Maiya, Jarod..."

Jarod looks down at the table, his hands tightly clasped in front of him.

"Sweet Maiya...tell me it's not true."

Jarod doesn't answer her.

"Of all the girls you have met—" his mother's voice breaks "—all the beautiful, strong Lupine girls we've introduced you to—*this* is the girl you want?" For a long moment, Jarod's mother seems too stunned to speak further. "Do you know who that girl's father is?"

"I'm well aware who her father is," Jarod says stiffly.

"Does this girl… Does she know how you feel about her?"

"Yes."

"What's happened?" Daciana asks, an edge of panic to her voice.

"Nothing, Mother. Nothing's happened," Jarod spits out. "She's to be wandfasted to a Gardnerian she doesn't love, and who doesn't love or deserve her."

Daciana shakes her head in fervent regret. "Your father and I have made a grave mistake sending you both to this University. If we had known that you would both fall in love with Gardnerians…"

Jarod looks up at her, his amber eyes gone hard. "*What*, Mother? What would you have done? Perhaps the Lupines should start wandfasting, as well. It's such a wonderful tradition. Look at Aislinn Greer, Mother. Look how happy it's making her."

"Jarod—"

"No, Mother, I'm serious. You could have wandfasted Diana and me before we came of age, forced us into mating pairs with the Lupines of your choice."

"It doesn't work that way with us—"

"I'm well aware it doesn't work that way for us!" Jarod growls. "It doesn't work that way for *anyone*!"

Daciana shakes her head, distraught. "You can't have this girl, Jarod."

"I know I can't have her," Jarod says, his voice harsh and bitter. "But you shouldn't trouble yourself. It's not a concern, since she refuses to have *me*."

"My son…"

Jarod gets up abruptly. "Please, don't tell me that everything will be all right." He holds up a hand as she starts to speak. "Because *nothing* is all right. Nothing in this entire world is all right." Jarod storms out of the hall, choosing an exit far from Aislinn.

Daciana sits frozen for a moment, as if she's trapped in a bad dream. Then she shoots me a look of hatred and follows her son out.

CHAPTER
ELEVEN

LUPINE AMAZ

The crimson-eyed Lupine boy runs toward me, giggling and clutching a branch of decorative Yule pine. Flame-haired Brendan chases after him, catching him up in his strong arms as the child shrieks in delight.

The huge, rune-tattooed man, Ferrin, strides toward his son and Brendan, smiling broadly at their antics.

"So, you're beta to the pack," I say to Ferrin as Brendan sets the squirming little boy down and the child takes hold of his father's hand.

Ferrin smiles good-naturedly, towering over me. "I am."

"Diana told me a bit about you," I say. His son giggles and breaks free from Ferrin's loose grip, running back across the hall. Brendan rolls his eyes and tears after him, leaving me alone with Ferrin. "She said you were a baby when you joined the Lupines."

"I was. They found me, abandoned in the woods, nearly starved to death." He recounts this impassively, and I marvel at this hard fact. He's bigger than Andras. It's hard to picture him ever having been small and sickly.

"Gunther's sister took me in," Ferrin explains. "She raised me as her own."

Something behind me catches his attention, and I turn to see Andras and Tierney entering the hall.

The two of them have struck up an unlikely friendship since we all met Es'tryl'lyan. Andras's love of horses has easily extended to embrace Tierney's terrifying Kelpies, and the Kelpies, in turn, have become warily friendly with Andras.

I was surprised to see the two of them fall in with each other so quickly, since Tierney is usually reluctant to trust anyone, but Andras's steady nature seems to be the only thing that soothes her these days.

Andras catches sight of Ferrin and blinks in surprise, and I realize that the Lupine beta is likely the only other male Amaz Andras has ever seen.

Ferrin straightens as Andras and Tierney approach. "I am Ferrin Sandulf," he says to Andras, holding out his hand. "Beta of the Gerwulf Pack."

"I am Andras Volya," Andras introduces himself in turn, shaking Ferrin's hand, "son of Astrid Volya."

Ferrin's eyes widen. "You are *Andras*?"

Andras looks questioningly at him, seeming puzzled by the strong response to his name. "I am."

"Sorcha Xanthippe," Ferrin continues, his face serious. "You paired with her?"

"Yes, as is our custom…"

"But, Sorcha…about three years ago…you lay together?"

"Yes." Andras's brow knits together in confusion.

Ferrin's face becomes oddly grave as he looks across the dining hall. "Soraya," he calls out. "Will you come here?"

His mate nods at him and makes her way over to us, holding their little boy in her arms. Her pleasant smile falters as she takes in Ferrin's serious expression.

"This is Andras Volya," Ferrin tells her pointedly, gesturing toward Andras. "Sorcha Xanthippe's mate."

Soraya's crimson eyes take on a look of astonishment, and her gaze immediately makes its way from Andras to the child in her arms and back again. For a moment, she seems utterly dumbfounded.

"Andras Volya," Soraya finally says, her voice filled with emotion. "This is Konnor. Your son."

Tierney and I gasp, and Andras's mouth falls open in shock, his eyes riveted on the boy. Little Konnor smiles shyly at him as he clings tightly to Soraya.

"Sorcha brought him to us," Ferrin explains, laying a steadying hand on Andras's shoulder. Andras is frozen, stunned into silence.

"Would you like to hold him?" Soraya asks gently. When he fails to respond, she comes closer, offering the toddler out to Andras.

Konnor looks up at him, unafraid as Andras lifts him into his strong arms. The boy reaches up with small fingers to touch the side of Andras's face, tracing the lines of his rune-tattoos.

Andras begins to cry.

Ferrin and Soraya move to embrace him, and Konnor's eyes dart around at everyone, as if confused. He reaches up to touch the silent tears falling from Andras's eyes with a tiny fingertip.

"You are part of our family now," Soraya tells Andras, her own eyes brimming with tears.

"I never thought I would find a place for myself anywhere," Andras replies, voice rough. "I thought my mother and I would always be alone."

"There are others like you," Soraya explains. "There are four men with Amaz ancestry in the Northern pack."

Little Konnor, perhaps put off by all the strong emotion surrounding him, fidgets agitatedly and reaches for his mother. Andras kisses the top of the child's head and hands him back to Soraya.

"Come, Andras," Ferrin says, placing a hand on his arm. "There is much to discuss."

Andras turns to Tierney, his face a tumult of emotion as they exchange a weighty glance.

"Go," she says, forcing a rare smile. "I'm so happy for you."

Andras nods, then departs with the Lupines.

My eyes meet Tierney's. I can see everything she's feeling in her troubled expression—how this friend she's rapidly grown so close to will likely be absorbed into a Lupine world she is completely shut out of, because Tierney has no desire to be anything other than what she is.

Asrai Water Fae.

"I can't talk about this," she says sharply, grimacing in response to a question I haven't voiced. "Unless you want me to inadvertently summon a very fierce storm." Her eyes flick toward the ceiling. "Right here. In the middle of this blasted Yule-fest."

Before I can even attempt to say anything, Tierney turns on her heel and stalks out of the hall.

That evening, after spending a few hours with Uncle Edwin at his Verpax City lodging house, I set out to find Andras, eager to know what happened after he went off with the Lupines.

I push through the dark woods, a lantern in hand, picking my way over the icy ground toward Naga's cave. The hostility from the trees is a chafing vibration at the edge of my mind, but I'm getting better at shutting them out.

The leaping flames of a bonfire up ahead come into view, and Andras's voice filters back through the woods.

"So, you're following me now, Mother?"

Mother?

Before I can ponder this further, Yvan appears, striding quietly toward me, cast in the forest's darkness. I slow to a stop and take in Yvan's cautionary look, his finger raised to his lips. His hand comes to my arm as he gestures at the fire with a tilt of his head.

Careful to tread quietly, I move slightly closer to the clearing until I can just make out Andras and his mother, Professor Volya, through the dark branches.

I'm filled with surprise at the dramatic change in Andras's appearance. All of his Amaz rune pendants and metallic jewelry are gone, as well as his usual rune-marked scarlet tunic, replaced by simple Keltic attire. The only part of him that's unaltered are the black rune-tattoos on his face.

Professor Volya is looking at her son with an expression of complete confusion as he sits by the fire, his hands tightly clasped on his knees, his head bowed. "Why are you dressed like that?" she demands worriedly. "Why did you leave everything...even your Goddess pendant...at our home?"

Andras is quiet for a long moment. "I met my son today, Mother," he finally says.

"Your son?"

"With Sorcha Xanthippe."

Professor Volya's face fills with both censure and alarm. "The Amaz girl who flouted every rule of the fertility rites? The one you formed that unnatural attachment to?"

For a moment, Andras is speechless, as if stunned by her dismissal. "Did you hear anything I just told you? I have a *son*."

Fierce remorse washes over his mother's face. "And so my sins multiply themselves." She looks around, as if searching for something in the woods. "Where is he? This son of yours?"

Andras glares at her, his jaw set tight. "The Lupines have taken him in. He's one of them now. And I'm going to join them."

She freezes, seeming stunned.

"For two years," Andras tells her with forced calm, "they have raised my son as one of their own. And now they've invited me to become one of them, as well. I could be a father to my son. And someday, I could have a mate and a family."

His mother flinches, as if struck. "You *have* a family," she insists, her voice breaking.

"I know I do," Andras says quietly. "I love you, Mother. And I know what you've sacrificed for me. But it's not enough, living like this. Join the Lupines with me. They have already told me that, unlike your people, they would welcome you, as well."

Fire flashes in her eyes. "No. *Never.*"

"Why?" Andras demands, suddenly incensed. "What do you really know of them?"

"I know enough!" she snarls. "Their ways are evil." She makes a sweeping gesture with her arm, as if she's slicing the air in front of her with a broadsword. "They slavishly follow their male alpha—"

"They have had female alphas, too."

"Not for some time, Andras, and it is unforgivable. They are everything the Goddess despises. And after they die, it will be as if they had never existed, whereas we will go to the Goddesshaven."

Andras shakes his head. "I don't believe that. I don't believe any of it anymore."

"What do you mean you don't believe?"

"Every race—the Fae, the Lupines, the Elves, the Gardnerians, the Amaz—they all have completely different religious beliefs, but the *one thing* they all have in common is that they all believe their way is the only way, and everyone else is less worthy."

"They are wrong!"

"Oh, I know," Andras says bitterly. "Only the Amaz are right. Don't you understand? I have no place with your people. Your every tradition says that, as a male, I am inferior and dangerous and worthless, except to be used to create more female Amaz. I don't believe this. I am not vile, and I do not have some uncontrollable urge to enslave women."

"Because we have repented!"

"No. Not because we have repented. Because it's not *true!*"

"You do not know what you are doing!" Professor Volya cries, her voice taking on a desperate edge. "You will bring down the judgment of the Goddess on us both!"

"No, I won't," Andras says, adamant. "Because there is no Goddess."

His mother seems overcome with shock. She glances at the sky as if expecting a lightning bolt to descend on them both at any minute. "Beg forgiveness now," she pleads, her voice a strangled whisper.

"No," Andras says. "I will not apologize to anyone for speaking the truth."

Her face tightens with outrage. "If you continue down this cursed path, you will no longer be my son."

Andras's expression turns stony. "How convenient for you, Mother. Now you can go back to your own people, the people you really love."

Professor Volya's resolve seems to waver, her eyes tortured. "Andras..."

Andras suddenly flings his hand up, his fingers splayed

open. "Look at my hand, Mother," he demands. "I have just as many bones in my hand as you do. Contrary to the lies told in your people's story of creation."

"You will be damned by the Goddess," she cries, her voice catching as her eyes turn glassy with tears. "You will die someday and be nothing more than a handful of ashes. And I will go to the Goddesshaven all alone. Before, maybe there was some chance the Goddess would take pity on us...but if you do this thing, my son... I will never see you again."

"No, Mother," Andras says quietly. "When we die, we will both be nothing but ash, just like everyone else. No matter how many stories are invented to try and deny this fact. And if this is the only life I get, I want more from it. I want a mate and children and acceptance. Something your people will never give to either of us."

Professor Volya stands there in silence, tears streaking down her face.

"I am leaving the Amaz, Mother," Andras tells her, compassion filling his tone. "But I'm not leaving *you*. You will always be family to me. I will be living in the wilds while I finish my commitment to help you with the care of the horses until the spring. After that, I will join the Southern Lupine pack and become one of them. And I hope that someday, you will turn your back on the lies your people have forced down your throat and join us, as well."

She shakes her head, anguish streaking across her face. "Andras, no..."

"I've decided, Mother." Andras cuts her off, sounding upset. "If you cannot accept that, then you need to go."

"My son..."

"No," Andras says, emphatic. "Leave me be."

Professor Volya hesitates, looking distraught, then turns

and pushes into the woods as Andras slumps down, his head falling into his hands.

Yvan and I wait until we can't hear her anymore, and then we go to him, hesitantly approaching.

Andras doesn't move as we quietly take a seat on either side of him.

"I'm sorry… We overheard," I tell him, placing my hand lightly on his broad back. "And… I'm sorry this is all so hard."

Andras looks up at the crackling fire, his expression devastated, his cheeks slick with tears.

"I wish I could strip the runes from my skin," he finally says, his voice rough with hurt.

I rub his back, desperate to find something to bolster him. "You know, you'll have those incredible Lupine eyes soon enough," I say encouragingly. "They'll outshine the tattoos, believe me."

Andras coughs out a laugh and shoots me a wan smile.

I reach up to put my hand on his broad shoulder. "Did you notice that your son looks like you?"

Andras's small smile turns into a wider grin, but it soon falters. He looks back to the fire, his eyes tensing with conflict. "I want my mother to come with us. I don't want to leave her. But she needs to accept my child, and I fear she never will."

I let out a long sigh. "People can change, Andras. I used to be deathly afraid of Icarals. Now I steal food from the livestock barns for Ariel's pets." I spit out the trace of a laugh and stare at the glowing coals at the fire's edge. "Your mother might come around yet. Especially when she meets your son."

Andras nods tightly, but I can see him fighting back more tears. I glance past him to find Yvan watching me. I flush to find his eyes on me so intently—it's unsettling to hold on to his green-eyed stare.

I take a deep, shuddering breath and look away.

MAGE COUNCIL
RULING
#211

Defacing or defaming *The Book of the Ancients*
shall be punishable by execution.

CHAPTER TWELVE

SPIRALING DOWN

"Will that be enough to treat Naga's wing?" Tierney whispers as I peer at the small jar of *Asterbane*.

Mage Ernoff's out-of-the-way apothecary shop is a cluttered, lantern-lit disarray of bottles filled with powders and crushed leaves and tinctures and tonics. Dried lizards hang from the ceiling on rusty iron hooks, and black dragon talons fill large glass canisters that line the shelves along the back of the store.

I eyeball the vermillion powder, mentally gauging the amount. "It should be."

Naga's left wing has stubbornly refused to heal, despite the tireless efforts of Andras and Ariel. The tear in the soft tissues around her shoulder joint is too deep, but there's a slim chance that the wound-closing properties of *Asterbane* might help.

Tierney holds up a russet tangle of bloodroot for my inspection as well, conveying everything she needs to with a blazing stare.

I nod silently. Yes, we'll need that, too—to make more of the expensive *Norfure* tincture Jules requested for the refugees suffering from a vicious outbreak of the Red Grippe.

Anguish twists in me as I remember our visit to the refugees' hiding place a few nights ago, when we delivered the first batch of tincture. An exhausted Jules had opened the door a crack, just wide enough to take each box of medicinal vials, giving us a wan smile. Over his shoulder, we'd caught only a brief glimpse of the isolated circular barn's occupants.

The space was full of Smaragdalfar refugees—mostly children, with patterned emerald skin glinting in the dim light of a single lamp and green hair as mussed as their tattered clothes. Most were sitting on or collapsed against hay bales, the torn pages from *The Book of the Ancients* splayed out under their feet.

Shock and compassion rushed through me at the sight of them. They were all much too thin, marked with bloodshot eyes and a blistering, angry rash around their mouths—telltale symptoms of the Red Grippe.

Iris, Fernyllia, Bleddyn and Yvan were all there with Jules, helping care for the children alongside a few tough-looking Smaragdalfar women and my former Metallurgie professor, Fyon Hawkkyn. I was startled to see Fyon there—believing he'd fled the Western Realm weeks ago.

Muscular Bleddyn was down on one knee, consoling a child. She caught a glimpse of me and her face instantly contorted into a threatening glare with a clear message—*get out!*

I moved to close the door just as Yvan looked up from where he was sitting by a prone child, his hand on the little girl's forehead. Our eyes met for a brief moment, a flash of his heat coursing through me, before the door shut.

As Tierney and I walked away from the barn and into the blackness of a starless night, I turned once.

Three Watchers were perched on the barn's roof, like ghostly sentinels. They remained there for the span of a heart-beat, then disappeared into the cold, bleak night.

A tug on my sleeve draws me back to the present. "We should go," Tierney says in a low voice.

Shaking my head slightly to clear it, I take the blood-root from her, and together we make our way to the front of the shop.

The bearded, disheveled-looking apothecary is busy pul-verizing a dragon's talon into black powder with a mortar and pestle as we approach him nervously, hoping that he'll just assume we need the ingredients for a class project. He hardly seems to notice what we're buying as he pivots to-ward his transaction ledger, not even bothering to look up at us as he impatiently manages our purchase.

Thankful for the Mage's distracted air and lack of curios-ity, Tierney and I pack the supplies into our sacks, fasten our cloaks tightly and hastily leave the shop. The cold bites into our exposed skin and our breath fogs the air as soon as we step out into the frigid night. We hunker down against the chill wind and start back toward the University.

"Down that alley," Tierney directs as we walk, pointing across the cobbled Spine-stone street. "That's the way I al-ways take."

We move hurriedly in that direction, weaving behind a slow-moving wagon stocked with wooden barrels and step-ping around a knot of Alfsigr Elves. I hastily follow Tier-ney as she makes for the alley, eagerly anticipating a blessed break from the wind.

A single lantern hangs from a small iron hook, illuminating the alley with a welcoming golden glow. But when we step into the narrow corridor, both Tierney and I freeze, aghast.

THE IRON FLOWER

There are words scrawled all over the stone walls in dripping, bloodred paint.

REAP THE EVIL ONES
ERTHIA FOR GARDNERIANS
TAKE BACK THE WESTERN REALM

A mammoth, five-pointed blessing star is scrawled beside the last words, one point for each of the five Gardnerian affinities—earth, fire, water, air, light.

Tierney and I stare, unmoving. Ice crackles straight through my spine, and it's not from the wintry cold. I glare at the wretched words, each line a cruel, well-aimed punch thrown at all of the people I care about.

"Ancient One," I breathe, and look to Tierney, who has paled to a sickly, shimmering gray green.

Tierney swallows hard, her eyes transfixed by the bludgeoning wall of words, fear stark on her face. "It's all spiraling completely out of control. Faster than we could have imagined."

She's right. Acts like this have become more and more common as the new Gardnerian majority on the Verpacian Council has approved increasingly alarming new policies. It's had a chilling effect on the University—segregation is now formally allowed and even encouraged for housing and classes, and the archives are being purged of any texts the Council deems "hostile to Gardneria or Alfsigroth." Some University newsprintings were initially critical of the new Verpacian Council edicts, but they've now been shut down, their writers expelled from the University.

And emboldened by the rapidly shifting political landscape, nighttime mob attacks have started, making the streets increasingly dangerous after sunset.

"Just today, they caught those Urisk who attacked the Gardnerian farmer," Tierney tells me, her eyes bolted to the bloody words. "Those four young women were abused by that farmer for years. It doesn't look good for them, though. The Verpacian Council wants to make an example out of them. They decide their fate tomorrow. I think that's prompting some of this—"

There's a crash in the distance. A woman's cry. Incoherent shouting. Our heads whip toward each other, and my heart kicks like a spooked horse.

More crashing, this time at the far end of the alley.

"We have to get out of here," Tierney says, her voice quavering, but her warning comes too late.

A mob of cloaked and hooded Gardnerians sweeps into the alley, and I inhale sharply when I see that their wands are drawn. The silver stripes on their dark cloaks range from Level Two to Level Four, and they all sport white armbands that blare their support for High Mage Marcus Vogel.

Tierney and I reflexively step back. I'm closest to the approaching mob, so I grab Tierney's arm and pull her slightly out of view behind me, scared she might inadvertently reveal her Fae power.

The men's angry eyes home in on us, like raptors spotting prey. I can see them quickly assessing us, registering us as Gardnerian and taking in our white Vogel armbands. Two of the men nod to us, as if actively sparing us from grievous harm. Then the mob stomps past us, through the alley and onto the street.

More screams echo in the distance. Crashing. Shouting from both ends of the alley. Then a sudden flurry of snow.

I look up to find a dark, fitful storm cloud only a few hand spans above us. Alarm blasts through me as I swing around to face Tierney. She's backed up against the wall, her whole body trembling.

I place a bolstering hand on her arm. "Tierney. Listen to me." I glance up at the cloud. *Oh, sweet Ancient One. They cannot discover she's Water Fae.* "You *have* to get a hold of yourself. I know it's hard, but try to think about something pleasant—do you hear me?"

She nods jerkily, eyes wide as moons.

"Take a deep breath. Think about a beautiful lake in the Noi lands." I struggle to keep my voice calm and soothing. "Gentle waves lapping. No problems anywhere. Can you do that for me? Can you concentrate *only* on that?"

Tierney nods again, her breathing now forcefully measured as she closes her eyes. Soon the snow stops, and the dark cloud dissipates into a smoky, swirling mist.

"Good," I encourage her, letting out a relieved breath. A group of young, shouting Gardnerian men run past the alley.

I turn back to Tierney. "We need to get back to the University as fast as we can."

Tierney nods, angry defiance rapidly sweeping back into her gaze. We rush down the alley, out into the road, and come to an abrupt, skidding halt.

In the center of the small plaza is a Gardnerian blessing star, big as a miller's wheel, made entirely of sputtering flame. It hangs suspended in the air a few hand spans above the ground, wrought with Mage-fire and throwing off sparks in the buffeting, wintry winds.

A large crowd of Gardnerians, mostly young men, are massed around the star, all of them wearing white Vogel armbands and raucously shouting. Laughing. Some of the Mages are holding their wands aloft, torch-like red fire shooting up from the wand tips to create more fiery stars hovering around the square and singed onto storefronts.

With horror, I notice that flames are spreading over several buildings, rapidly consuming the panes of multiple storefront windows. The targeted buildings look to be owned by non-Gardnerian merchants, all of them lacking Gardnerian guild banners.

Grim-faced, Tierney and I skirt around the crowd, keeping our heads down with breathless urgency as we hug the shadows of the plaza. Cruel eyes sweep over us as we pass, assessing. Sparing us. We slip down a side street and find another yelling mob of Gardnerians pushing an elderly Keltic merchant onto the ground. One of the Mages has his wand out and is drawing a flaming blessing star on the window of the man's bookstore.

Panicked, I glance across the cobbled street and spot an Urisk woman slumped over in a deserted alley. I can just make out her green skin and long emerald hair. I gasp as I recognize the looping embroidery on the edges of her moss-colored tunic.

"Tierney," I whisper coarsely, "I think that's Bleddyn over there!"

Tierney squints across the street. "Holy gods. She can't be out here right now."

Our eyes meet in joint resolve, and we hurry toward her, dodging the Gardnerians and studiously avoiding eye contact with the rabid crowd.

Ducking into the alley, we're quickly enveloped by its shadows. Bleddyn is listing to the side, propped up against the wall behind her. There's blood all over her face, and one of her eyes is swollen completely shut. I push back my sickened outrage as Tierney and I snap into apothecary mode, drop to our knees and each take hold of one of Bleddyn's arms.

I jostle Bleddyn's arm gently in an attempt to rouse her. "Bleddyn…"

She's only semiconscious, her unswollen eye unfocused. I shake her again, a bit more firmly, and she stirs slightly this time. Sudden clarity washes over her face as her gaze zeroes in on me. She jerks her whole body violently away, her expression twisting into a desperate snarl.

"Don't touch me, you *Roach*! Get away from me!"

"Bleddyn, it's me," I plead, stubbornly holding on to her. "It's Elloren. We need to get you out of here."

A man's pained cry echoes behind us as the mob continues their jeering threats.

"Fae-blooded bastard!"

"This is *Mage* land!"

Startled, Bleddyn tries to shake us off again, but her balance gives way, and she tilts forward. Tierney and I tighten our grip on her.

"You're coming with us," Tierney insists fiercely. "Right now. Do you hear me, Bleddyn? *Right. Now.*"

Bleddyn's head seems to clear once again as she focuses on Tierney. Her gaze flickers toward me again, then back to Tierney, stark comprehension igniting in her large, emerald eye, and she stops struggling.

We take full advantage of her hesitation.

"Put this on." I hastily slide my cloak off my shoulders.

We help Bleddyn get to her feet, and Tierney supports her as I wrap my cloak around her shoulders, the frigid cold immediately seeping into me. I pull the cloak's hood down over Bleddyn's pointed ears and quickly push her long green hair underneath, then fasten the cloak from top to bottom. Then I kneel and rip down the hem at the bottom to lengthen it, so it will fully hide Bleddyn's non-Gardnerian garb.

I stand again, and Tierney and I both link arms with Bleddyn. "Keep your head *down*!" Tierney orders frantically.

Bleddyn nods, looking dazed. We hasten through the city

streets, my teeth chattering from the onslaught of cold air as the three of us try to avoid the notice of the wild-eyed Gardnerians passing by. There are flaming stars all over the city. People running. Cries in the distance.

A group of Vu Trin ride past on horseback, shouting at a fleeing mob. Elfhollen soldiers run toward Mistress Roslyn's dress shop, where a huge blessing star is steadily burning. Shock knifes through me at the sight of it, the flames rapidly consuming the storefront window and spreading to the colorful Keltic clothing inside.

When we reach the University archway, we guide a stumbling Bleddyn under it and slip into a grove of trees, hiding under their sheltering branches.

"The kitchens," Tierney says, panting. "We can bring her there. It's not much farther."

I nod grimly and send up a prayer as we trudge forward, desperately hoping that safety lies ahead.

CHAPTER THIRTEEN

NIGHTMARE

We hug the forest's dark shadows straight up toward the livestock pens and rush to the back entrance of the main kitchen.

Tierney practically kicks the door open.

Yvan and Fernyllia are standing by the broad table, Fernyllia's hands on a pile of dough. Both of their heads snap toward us as shock swiftly overtakes them.

Fernyllia cries out in Uriskal and abandons the dough she's kneading as both she and Yvan rush forward.

Yvan catches Bleddyn before she goes limp and sweeps her up into his arms. "Clear the table," he orders.

We hastily comply, grabbing piles of raw dough off the table's broad surface. Yvan lays Bleddyn down as Fernyllia places a hastily folded kitchen towel under her head. Tierney hovers beside us, her face pale with worry.

"There are mobs of Gardnerians out in the city," I breathlessly tell them, describing everything we witnessed as Yvan directs me to restrain Bleddyn's limp hands. I curl my palms firmly around her wrists.

Yvan brings his hands to Bleddyn's face and closes his eyes as if reading her wounds, his secret healing abilities a wide-open secret by now. A sudden thought spears through me, ratcheting my pulse higher, and I look to Fernyllia in panic. "Where's Fern?"

"Inside," Fernyllia says. She pauses in the act of pumping water into an iron pot and glances worriedly around.

"Are you sure?" I insist, my voice shrill. Alarm clamors in my mind. Little Fern cannot be outside in this. She *cannot* be caught by that mob.

"Grandma?" a small voice says from one of the kitchen's side doors. Fern stands there, hugging her floppy cloth doll tight. "I heard a noise. What's happening?"

"Oh, sweet Ancient One," I breathe out. A staggering relief spreads through me at the sight of tiny Fern in her long-sleeved nightgown, pink braids hanging over her shoulders.

"Where's Olilly?" Fernyllia asks Yvan, her tone urgent.

My lungs cinch in sudden panic. I spot Olilly's small basket of colorful yarn on the counter, strands tied to the rails on the back of a wooden chair and partly woven into a bracelet. Patient, gentle Olilly has been teaching little Fern how to weave bracelets all week.

Before Yvan can answer, Bleddyn pulls in a hard breath, then several more in quick succession, and starts to struggle. I hold tight to her hands, bearing down as Yvan murmurs to her, keeping his hands firmly on her face, his right hand moving over her wounded eye.

"When did you last see Olilly?" Tierney demands of Fernyllia, a tempestuous cloud kicking up around her, sputtering small threads of white lightning.

Fernyllia's voice is tight with fear. "I sent her out for nutmeg. Before the guildmarket closed."

"The markets closed over an hour ago," Tierney says, fierce worry filling her eyes.

Fernyllia seems momentarily frozen in a dawning nightmare.

"We need to get Trystan," I say, thinking quickly. "He can go look for Olilly."

"I'll do it," Tierney says. She pauses to take a deep breath, and the cloud around her slowly disappears. She seems to have pulled the storm into her eyes, her gaze practically spitting lightning. "If I can't find him, I'll go after Olilly myself."

I hold her sparking gaze for a heartbeat, fully realizing the risk she's taking. "Take care," I say, my voice cracking.

Tierney nods and leaves.

Bleddyn stirs, her eyes fluttering open, and Yvan's hands move to the sides of her head. Incredibly, the swelling around her eye is almost completely gone, her broken nose knit back into its proper shape. I release Bleddyn's wrists as Yvan helps her sit up. Fernyllia dabs at the blood all over Bleddyn's face and neck with a warm, moist rag, her expression full of anxiety.

Iris bursts through the back entrance, the door slamming shut behind her, her face wild. "They're burning things! Attacking people!" She halts and takes in Bleddyn's blood-streaked face. Then her eyes light on me, and her face twists into a vicious snarl. "Get *out*!" she cries, starting for me, her fists balled.

I step back, stopped by the table behind me.

"Iris, stop!" Bleddyn says, rising on unsteady feet to block her path.

Iris's eyes swing to Bleddyn, wild with surprise. She points at me, her hand shaking. "She caused this!"

Yvan throws Iris an incredulous look. "No, Iris. She *didn't*."

"Yes, she did! Her whole family is responsible. They're going to come for us all!"

Fern starts to cry. I turn to find her slumped on the floor nearby, hugging her doll. My heart twists, and I drop down to my knees beside her.

"Sweet one," I say, putting my hand gently on Fern's heaving back.

"Get away from her!" Iris seethes.

Rattled, I glance up to find Iris glaring at me with such hate, I wonder if she would actually attack me if we were alone.

Iris breaks down, sobbing, and Yvan goes to her. He tries to touch her arm, but she pushes his hand away, white-hot accusation in her eyes. "She's the granddaughter of a monster!" she lashes out at him. "How can you even *look* at her without retching?"

A stinging flush suffuses my neck. I immediately sense this is part of a deeper argument between them.

"*I'm* your kind!" Iris rages. "Not *her*! They're all *monsters*! *All* of them!"

A faint scream sounds outside. "What's that?" I ask nervously, rising to my feet.

The scream grows in volume. A girl's scream. Agonized and piercing. Then the door slams open, and the kitchen devolves into instant chaos.

Rafe strides in, splattered with blood and carrying Olilly in his arms. Blood is on his face, his neck, his hands. My breath stops in my throat at the sight of them. Olilly is screaming over and over, her blood-soaked hands pressed tight over her ears.

Pointed ears that used to be too large to cover with her slender hands.

Horrified tears fill my eyes as I realize what the mobs have done to her. Olilly's amethyst eyes are huge with abject terror as she wails unceasingly. Blood covers her lovely violet face, and her beautiful hair is all gone, brutally shorn off.

Trystan runs in behind Rafe and Olilly, his dark cloak streaming behind him, wand drawn, gaze raptor-sharp. Tierney trails them in last, her face stricken. A turbulent black cloud forms and circles around her as she shuts and bolts the kitchen's back door.

Yvan and Fernyllia swoop in toward Olilly as Iris looks on with horror, and Rafe gently lowers Olilly onto a table. Yvan leans down close to try and assess her wounds. Bleddyn staggers over toward Olilly, while little Fern starts to cry convulsively. Trystan begins locking doors and setting spells on them, the door before him momentarily glowing a deep blue.

Olilly is completely hysterical, her body rigid as she sits on the edge of the table, her hands tight over ears, her eyes unnaturally wide and unblinking.

"Olilly," Yvan says, his deep voice gentle, "you need to lower your hands."

"No no no no *no!*" Olilly cries, shaking her head, closing her eyes tight, recoiling back from Yvan.

Rafe moves away from them, giving Yvan space to try and help Olilly. He comes over to stand by me, his eyes lit with rage.

"They should be arrested," I tell him, my voice shaking with fury.

Rafe's whole body is bunched like a fist. "There are too many of them," he says, his voice pitched low. "There are mobs running loose all over the city. There's no way of even knowing who did this."

Yvan has finally coaxed Olilly's hands away from her mutilated ears and replaced them with his own. Bleddyn's muscular arm is around Olilly's shoulder as she holds tight to one of her hands, and Iris holds Olilly's other hand, tears streaming down her face. Fernyllia stands facing Olilly and is murmuring a stream of gentle consolation in Uriskal.

Olilly's convulsive sobbing subsides slightly, her eyes locked on Fernyllia, her chest heaving as she cries. Yvan's head remains bowed for several long minutes in concentration. Finally, he lowers his bloodstained hands.

Olilly pulls her hands away from Bleddyn and Iris and reaches up, fumbling over the tops of her ears, the points completely gone. Her expression wrenches with despair.

"My *ears!*"

Bleddyn falls down on one knee before Olilly. *"Shush'onin."*

"Donlookatmeeeee! Donlookatmeeeeee!" Olilly sobs in a keening wail, palms pressed tight again over her ears.

"Olilly—"

"I'm so *uuugly!*"

"No. You're not," Bleddyn says with ironclad firmness.

"My *eaaaaars!* They cut my *eaaars!*"

"I know, *shush'onin.* I know they did. But you are *beautiful.* They *cannot* change that. They can *never* change that."

Bleddyn pulls her into a hug, holding tight as Olilly cries and rages into her broad shoulder.

Trystan and Tierney are standing by the largest window in the kitchen, set over the pump-sink. Trystan presses his wand against the window, its tip emitting a quick flash of blue light. He quietly confers with Tierney, then nods as she lifts her palm toward the window, a heavy white frost forming around the panes.

They both step back, assessing their work. Then Trystan strides over to Rafe and me as Tierney leaves through the back door.

"I'm going to get Diana," Rafe tells us, his tone weighted with fury.

Trystan nods somberly, and Rafe takes his leave. I turn to my younger brother. "What were you and Tierney doing? To the windows and doors?"

"Warding them," he says grimly. "If anyone tries to use Mage power to get in, the spell will double back and blast a hole through them. And if someone tries to force the windows open, their hands will freeze."

I blink at him, impressed. "Well, that's good."

"I'm going outside to find Tierney," Trystan tells me, his face agitated. "To help her check the grounds."

Worry clenches my gut. "What will you do if any of the mobs come?"

Trystan gives me a look I've never seen before in my younger brother's eyes—pure, unadulterated danger.

"I'll throw bolts of lightning straight through their chests."

For a split second, I wonder what happened to the skinny little boy who was so afraid of thunder. Who would come racing into my room, clutching his toy bear, diving completely under my covers to hide from the booming sound. Now he's standing before me, all power and assurance, prepared to throw lightning to protect everyone.

"Be careful," I say, my voice rough with emotion.

Trystan's tone is slow and lethal. "Oh, Ren, I think they're the ones who need to take care, don't you?"

Trystan strides out with an air of dark purpose, his cloak rippling behind him.

Small hands grab on to my skirts, and I look down to find little Fern clutching her doll and clinging to me.

"Oh, sweet one," I say, sinking down and pulling her close, wishing I could strip the memory of this horror from her mind.

"They're gonna cut her ears," Fern sobs, her mouth pressed against her doll's head, the words muffled.

I enfold her in my arms. "We're going to protect you."

She shakes her small head against me. "They're gonna catch her and cut Mee'na's ears."

Oh, Ancient One. Her cloth doll, Mee'na. She's afraid the Gardnerians will come and mutilate her beloved toy.

The magnitude of my people's cruelty washes over me with a force that's so staggering, for a moment I can barely breathe. And suddenly, I'm longing for power like Trystan's, so I could take up the wand concealed in the side of my boot and strike down the mobs without mercy.

"No one is going to hurt you, or Mee'na, or anyone else," I promise her fiercely. "Everyone here is going to protect you."

Fernyllia comes looking for Fern. She sends me a grave glance and lowers herself to her granddaughter's level, murmuring softly to Fern as she takes the child into her stout arms.

As I rise, my eyes meet Bleddyn's from across the room, and a flash of morbid solidarity passes between us. She and Iris are helping Olilly to her feet, their arms wrapped around the girl's slender shoulders. Led by Fernyllia, they all move toward the side-door that leads to the workers' lodging just off the side of the kitchen. Fernyllia hands Fern to Yvan, and Fern wraps her small arms tightly around his neck, her fearful eyes peeking at me over his shoulder. I attempt a small, bolstering smile, but my heart is breaking into pieces.

Yvan turns to me before he walks out, his gaze holding mine with concentrated force, his silent message clear.

Wait for me.

The door leading into the kitchen shimmers blue, and Trystan reenters the room. His eyes immediately dart toward the others as they leave, and Bleddyn nods to Trystan before she exits. He somberly dips his head in return.

"I'm going to stay here overnight, Ren," Trystan tells me as he approaches, his wand clenched in his hand. "Along with Tierney." He angles his head toward the workers' lodging. "Right outside their rooms."

"Where will you sleep?"

"On the floor in front of their doors if I have to."

I nod, glancing toward their lodging. "That's probably a good idea." I turn back to my brother, my lips trembling as my tone grows savage. "I wish I had access to my magic. I want to fight back against this."

Trystan is quiet for a moment, his eyes implacable. "I'm going to find a way to get to the Noi lands, Ren. And I'm going to join the Vu Trin, whether they want me or not." His expression darkens. "And then I'm going to come back here with an army and fight the Gardnerians."

I wait alone for Yvan, the deep night closing in around me, the kitchen lit by the flickering glow of a single lantern set on the table before me.

I've made a fresh pot of mint tea in a futile attempt to calm myself, and a soothing curl of steam wafts up from both my cup and the pot's spout. The edges of the kitchen are cast in deep shadows, and Bin'gley, the gray kitchen cat, silently prowls along the dark edges of the room.

Yvan slips into the room with that silent, lithe grace of his that never fails to make my heart trip. He leans against a counter, facing me, his eyes glowing golden in the dark.

I've only seen his eyes on fire like this twice—when he saved me from a dragon attack they glowed green, and when the Kelpie came after me they blazed all the way to gold.

"Your eyes," I say haltingly. "They're golden. Again."

His hands grasp the counter's edge. "It's getting harder to control my fire," he says, and I'm stunned by his admission. His tone is tightly controlled, but fire blazes tempestuously in his eyes. He looks around, as if searching for the right words. "It's especially difficult when I'm upset, or angry, or…"

His gaze flickers over my face. The flame in his eyes intensifies, and this time, it's me who has to look away.

"I need to fight them, Elloren."

His words have the finality of a declaration. An unbreakable vow. There's an explosive quality to him right now, as if his fire is pent up almost to the point of conflagration.

"Are you going after the mobs?" I ask carefully, my heartbeat picking up.

His lips curl with ferocity. "No. I want to go after the Gardnerian and Alfsigr militaries." His voice is low and threatening. "When the inevitable war breaks out."

"Will you join the Keltic military, then?"

"No." His gaze simmers with import. "I want to go east and join the Vu Trin Wyvernguard."

We're both quiet for a long moment as the ramifications of this settle in. "My mother doesn't want me in this fight," he says. "She wants me to be a healer, and *only* a healer. She's tired of losing everyone she loves to war."

"So, what are you going to do?"

The fire in his eyes blazes hotter, the gold stoked to incandescent yellow. "I'm going to talk to my mother and tell her I'm going east."

I pull in a quavering breath. Jules has hinted that the Vu Trin might start allowing some of the hidden Fae youth into the Noi military academy—the Wyvernguard. I've seen Yvan kill a dragon with his bare hands. And I've sensed the enormity of his fire power. Of course, the Vu Trin will want him. Of course, they'll want to bring him east with the other powerful Fae.

Where he'll be leagues away over an impassible desert.

Get hold of yourself, Elloren. One way or another, he has to leave. You've known this for some time.

I look down at the table as a tumult of emotions clash inside me, and my eyes glass over with tears. When I finally speak, my voice is so low, it's almost a whisper. "I feel like... we never had a chance to..." I break off, too overcome to continue.

A wave of heat suddenly rushes out from him, suffusing my lines. "Elloren."

There's so much conveyed in that one, impassioned word and in his surprisingly palpable fire. Everything he won't allow himself to say.

And in that one word, I can feel us already saying goodbye.

That night, I dream of the mobs. An army of Gardnerians chasing after Tierney, Bleddyn, Olilly, Fern and me. All of us running and running down one dark alley after another as the Mages close in, so many they're like a dark swarm.

We run into the plaza and skid to a halt. Uplifted wands blaze crimson torchlight as the Mages fall in around us.

I kick and lash out as they grab at me, holding tight to little Fern's hand as she screams in terror. And then her hand is yanked from my grip as she's pulled into the bloodthirsty mob of Mages, and I lose sight of her. More Mages close in around me as a scream tears loose from my throat.

I bolt up in bed, sweat-soaked, blankets tangled around my limbs. Disoriented and struggling to control my panicked breathing, I glance toward the window.

The first hint of dawn colors the sky a deep blue above the jutting Spine.

I silently curse the morning. I curse the entire country of Verpacia and the terror being rained down on so many here.

Wynter is slumped against the windowsill, fast asleep, her black wings wrapped tight around her body, only the top of her white-haired head poking up. Ariel is passed out diagonally across her messy bed and dozing fitfully, her chickens roosting beside her, her raven perched on the headboard. Marina is underwater in the washroom, most likely curled up at the base of our tub. I can hear her breathing through the open door, softly bubbling up air through the water.

A fierce protectiveness rises up in me.

My family.

The thought has an edge of surprise to it, but an even bigger edge of truth. They've all become like family to me. Even Ariel. The thought of losing a single one of them feels like the fabric of my life tearing.

Rafe, Diana, Jarod and Andras will leave soon for Lupine territory. Yvan, Trystan, Tierney, the Icarals and everyone in the kitchens will need to escape to the Noi lands.

But I can't leave Uncle Edwin here alone, and he's too frail to travel anywhere. So, I'll remain behind in hellish Gardneria, trapped among people monstrous enough to do what they did last night, as everyone I love is scattered far away, save Aislinn and my uncle.

Diana is lying on her side by the fire, watching me with her wild amber eyes.

"They're going to get away with it," I tell her, my voice thick with anguish and disgust. "Those monsters who hurt Bleddyn and Olilly. There's no way of even knowing who they are."

"I went to see Bleddyn and Olilly the kitchen girl," Diana says, deadly calm. "I scented their attackers. And I tracked them all. They are Third Division military apprentices."

My eyes widen with surprise. "What did you do?"

"I have spoken with Rafe." Her tone is low and lethal. "It seems that the killing of that many apprentice soldiers by the daughter of a Lupine alpha would be considered an act of war. So, I will wait." Her eyes glow with a patient, predatory simmer. "Until I have father's permission. And then I will hunt them down, rip off their ears and slash them to shreds."

I hold her intimidating gaze for a long moment. "Good."

Diana's brow pulls tight. "The Gardnerians are making a play for dominance, Elloren Gardner. I can smell the threat of war in the air."

MAGE COUNCIL
RULING

#223

All Urisk must vacate Gardneria by the end of
the twelfth month. All workpapers extended
past that time are hereby revoked, and any
Urisk found in the Holy Magedom after that
time will be shipped to the Pyrran Islands.

CHAPTER FOURTEEN

FALLOUT

"Olilly deserves justice." I set the crate of *Norfure* tincture down on Jules's desk with a loud thunk.

Jules glances up, wire glasses slightly askew. His brown hair is its usual disheveled, his green professorial robes wrinkled and thrown on over his dark woolen clothing. Lucretia is seated on a chair next to him. They both give me a slightly guarded look as I enter, and I get the sense that I've just barged in on a private conversation.

But I don't care. I'm simply too upset.

Jules has a pile of papers by him. The stack is uncharacteristically neat and perfectly even, at odds with the usual discordant mess of his office, which is a veritable maze of books strewn about and haphazardly arranged on shelves that line the walls. Lucretia is the picture of contrast to Jules Kristian in her perfectly pressed Gardnerian silks, not a single black hair out of place. The silver Erthia orb around her neck gleams in the evening lantern light.

My voice is rough with the anger I've carried around with

me all day. "The monsters who attacked Olilly need to be arrested. Diana knows *exactly* who they are."

Jules and Lucretia exchange a quick, loaded glance. "Close the door, Elloren," Jules says quietly. "And lock it."

Almost vibrating with outrage, I do as he asks before taking a seat in front of his desk.

"Olilly is here illegally," he says calmly.

"I don't care," I shoot back, my voice shaking. "She's fourteen years old and nothing but sweet and kind to everyone. They *mutilated* her. The military apprentices who did this should be *punished*."

"If she went to the Verpacian authorities," Jules replies, his voice hardening, "she'd be deported to Gardneria."

I internally war against what he's saying. "She won't speak," I throw out, incensed. "She won't leave the kitchen. She's got a scarf wrapped around her head to hide her bald head and her scarred ears." Now my body is trembling along with my voice.

"I understand your outrage, Elloren," Lucretia says, her gaze suddenly stripped of her prim Gardnerian demeanor and glittering with rebellion. "But Verpacia is already up in arms about the Urisk workers who attacked that Gardnerian farmer here—"

"Fernyllia said he was abusing them!" I cut in.

"He was," Lucretia replies patiently. "But most Verpacians don't know about that. All they know is that the four young women are Urisk and in Verpacia illegally. And that they attacked a Gardnerian."

"Those Urisk women have been found guilty of assault and deported to Gardneria," Jules adds somberly.

"And will likely be sent to the Pyrran Islands from there," Lucretia unflinchingly puts in.

The two of them stun me with how calm they can be

right now—willing to look this thing straight in the eye without flinching, when it's withering and frightening and heartbreaking to even think about.

I struggle to fight back the sting of furious tears. "So, the Verpacian Council doesn't care that there were mobs all over the city attacking innocent people last night?"

Lucretia's answer, when it comes, is dripping with disdain. "The Verpacian Council noted this morning that some vandalism took place in response to the capture of the 'criminal Urisk.' Do you see what they're stressing here?"

"Twelve Urisk were cropped last night," Jules Kristian says gravely. "Of those twelve, nine are in Verpacia illegally. Including Olilly."

"What about the Urisk who are here legally?" I rage. "Can't they press charges?"

The line of Jules's mouth hardens, and he shakes his head. "If they ask for help from the Verpacian authorities, they will draw the mob back down on their heads like hawks to prey. And possibly have their workpapers rescinded in retribution."

"Which would result in them being forcibly returned to Gardneria," Lucretia says.

I struggle to control my breathing. "So, there's no way to fight back against this?"

Jules picks up a few papers from the top of his tidy stack and eyes me pointedly. "There are a few."

"What are those?" I ask, desperate for a solution.

"New identity papers for Olilly, Fern and Bleddyn," he tells me. "Foolproof enough to have a chance against a thorough Verpacian or Gardnerian investigation. This is the only way we can fight back for now. Keep them and others from being deported and find a way to get them out of the Western Realm."

I slump down into my chair, unbearably discouraged,

wishing I could grab the wand from my boot and set this right. Wishing I could wield my magic and force justice.

"What's going to happen?" I ask them shakily. "Do you think it's going to keep getting worse?"

"The situation is not good," Jules says. He looks briefly to Lucretia. "We're surprised by how quickly the Verpacians have buckled to Gardnerian influence."

Lucretia gives a small nod of agreement. "Both the Gardnerians and the Alfsigr Elves have too much power, and it's growing by the day."

"Will the Western Realm fall?" I ask. The question is almost too terrible to say out loud.

"There is only one thing keeping the Gardnerians out of Keltania," Lucretia says, a jaded cast to her expression. "The fragile coalition between the Lupines, the Amaz, the Vu Trin and the Kelts." She pauses, her unflappable calm cracking for a moment. "If that fails, the Gardnerians will roll clear over the Western Realm."

I turn to Jules imploringly. "Do you think that will happen?"

He holds my gaze, his whole body rigid, as if struggling to deny his answer. "Yes, Elloren," he says finally. "I believe the Western Realm will fall."

We're all silent for a long moment as icy hail pelts the curtained window, battering the glass like it's trying to break in. My sense of foreboding swells like a tide, and I'm suddenly reminded of my recurring nightmare.

A red sky. Dead trees. The Wand of Myth in my hand.

And a shadowy figure searching, searching, searching for me.

"There's another group that needs to get out," I tell them, absently reaching down to reflexively touch my wand's hilt just under the cloth of my skirt, a seditious fire sparking in the face of such insurmountable odds. "The Selkies."

Jules's lips lift into a small smile. "Are you helping Selkies now, Elloren?"

"I might be."

A fond look washes over his face, as if he's seeing someone else when he looks at me. "You're so much like your..." He abruptly cuts himself off and looks away, clearing his throat.

"Like who?" I ask, confused.

He shakes his head, still not looking at me, as if shaking away the question. He turns back to me, his composure returning. "You should know that it's very difficult to rally support for the Selkies," he says. "There's a widespread belief that they're just animals in human form—"

"They're not animals," I state emphatically. "They're weakened without their skins, but they're *people*."

"That may be true," he agrees, "but the fact that they can't speak complicates things."

I think of Marina's flute-like mutterings and the look in her ocean-colored eyes when she's trying to communicate with us. "I think they can speak. Just not in a way we understand."

"It's despicable, what goes on with the Selkies," Lucretia spits out, color rising in her face. "I've tried to encourage sympathy for them in Resistance circles but have gotten absolutely nowhere."

"You'd need an army to free the Selkies," Jules puts in. "You'd be going up against the Gardnerian black market."

I inwardly rail against the daunting barriers. "They need to get out of here before the Mage Council decides to kill them all," I passionately argue. "My aunt and Vogel are going to push that motion through. You know they will. It's only a matter of time."

"I'll speak to some people," Jules says. "I can't promise you anything, but I'll try."

"Thank you." I pull in a long, shaky breath.

Jules wordlessly pours some tea for each of us. We drink it for a moment in silence, curlicues of steam rising from our cups and the spout of the teapot that sits on Jules's desk.

I glance down at Lucretia's hand, her long fingers gracefully holding her chipped, brown teacup. She reminds me a bit of Aunt Vyvian, all refined elegance, but she wields her power in such a different way. She looks to be in her thirties, but her hands are free of fastmarks, which is unusual for a Gardnerian woman at her age.

She looks like she might be younger than Jules, but not by a lot.

Staring at Lucretia's unmarked hands, I'm abashedly reminded of what Diana told me about Lucretia and Jules—that they've one of the strongest attractions to each other that Diana has ever sensed in any couple.

But neither one of them knows about the other's feelings.

Diana has commented on this more than once—expounding that if Jules and Lucretia were Lupine, the pack would insist they pair as their fevered longing for each other would be so distracting to the rest of the pack, it would be hard to even think around them.

And Jules, to my knowledge, has never been married.

I study them surreptitiously while they talk to each other. Jules quietly lists which Mage Council seals he needs her to pilfer the next time she's in Valgard, and she matter-of-factly outlines what's possible. I can't find any outward hint of their feelings toward each other, but it's clear they're longtime friends. Fellow soldiers in this war, battle-hardened and weary.

Yet they give nothing away of their hearts.

"You're not fasted." The comment to Lucretia escapes me thoughtlessly, and my cheeks prick with heat.

Lucretia's head bobs as she lets out a cynical laugh. "No.

I've managed to dodge that particular arrow." She eyes me significantly. "Not without challenge, you can be sure."

"What are you going to do when fifth month comes?"

Lucretia gives a long sigh. "I'll have to leave before the mandatory fasting goes into effect."

Jules is silently watching her, his expression unreadable.

"Where will you go?" I ask her.

"Noi lands," she says, cradling her teacup. "My brother Fain is there. My sisters. Our adopted daughter, Zephyr."

A distant recollection surfaces. "I've heard my Uncle Edwin mention someone named Fain. Did your brother know my uncle?"

Lucretia and Jules exchange a darkly private look.

He did, I realize in a flash. *Why are they being so secretive?*

"They knew each other at University," Lucretia says, the words oddly careful.

"Did he know my parents, too?" I ask, thrown.

Lucretia's mouth twitches. "Yes."

I can sense that's all I'm going to get from either of them for now, so I back away from the subject. "Are you going to leave for the east, too?" I ask Jules.

"Eventually," he says. "I'll stay as long as I can, though, helping others get out."

I despair at the thought of yet more people I care about leaving. I can't think on it for too long—how lonely the Western Realm will be with most of them gone.

"What are you planning on doing about the mandatory fasting?" Lucretia asks me.

"I don't know yet," I say helplessly. "But I have to stay and take care of my uncle. Someone needs to, and I can't leave him alone in Valgard with my aunt."

Lucretia's gaze narrows with a silent question, and I realize the conversation has shifted without my realizing it.

"Have you found out anything more about where Lukas Grey stands?" she asks.

Yes, that he's an enigma wrapped in an enigma. "I know he doesn't care much for Vogel's policies," I tell her, "but he's pretty evasive otherwise."

"There's talk of allowing Gardnerians to be part of the Verpacian and Vu Trin border guard for the eastern and western passes through the Spine," Jules says.

"If that happens, those guards would be drawn from the Fourth Division Base," Lucretia adds, her meaning clear.

Yvan's fiery eyes light in my mind, setting off an ache deep inside me.

No. Let him go.

Because I realize that there's something of grave significance that I can do here—something of much greater use than just making medicines.

I visit the hawkery before dawn.

Rune-hawks with glossy onyx feathers rustle on wooden perches all around the circular tower room. Small iron rings encircle each bird's left leg, connected to the perches with short, delicate chains.

I hand my note, written on the lightweight parchment, to the young Gardnerian fowler. His eyes widen as he reads the name of the message's intended recipient, and his gaze flies up to meet mine, trepidation stark on his face.

Ah, Lukas, I think grimly. *How far your reach extends.*

I glance over the fowler's head at the panoramic view of Verpacia that can be seen through the tower's arching windows. The snowcapped Northern Spine is washed in blue light and watches us with cold majesty.

Yvan will be leaving soon. There's no future where we can be together. So, I need to seal up my heart and let it go cold.

THE IRON FLOWER

And I need to seize my influence where it lies. Rooted here, in the Western Realm.

"Are you sure, Mage?" the skinny fowler asks. He swallows nervously, holding my small missive like it's about to burst into flames.

"I'm sure." I'm ready to use whatever pull I have with Lukas to fight the Gardnerians.

The fowler's eyes dart toward me uneasily as he tucks my note into a small fabric bag and ties it to the leg of one of the rune-hawks. Anticipating the journey, the hawk ruffles its feathers and makes an abbreviated hop on its perch. Deep green runes are set on to iron bands that bracelet both of the hawk's legs, restricting it to travel between the hawker and the destination point marked with identical runes, each half of the spell set by the same Gardnerian Light Mage.

The intricate patterns of the small runes glow in the dim light, mesmerizing in their verdant beauty. The ability to perform rune magic is a rarity everywhere, but it's rarest among Gardnerians, as it requires a strong light affinity line. There's only one known Light Mage able to perform rune spells in the entire Magedom, and I'm fascinated to see his work up close.

The fowler winds the north-facing window open, and a gust of icy air blasts inside, ruffling my hair. Unhooking the hawk's leg chain, the fowler releases the bird from its perch, barely restraining the excited creature on his gauntleted wrist as he carries it to the window.

I watch, darkly resolved, as the fowler makes a clicking sound with his tongue. The hawk spreads its wings and launches itself into the air, flying northwest into the chill dawn.

Past the Verpacian border and over the Spine.

Winging its way to Lukas Grey.

CHAPTER
FIFTEEN

DRYADS

That evening, a luxurious black-lacquered carriage pulls up at the base of the North Tower's hill, the silver dragon insignia of the Gardnerian Fourth Division military base on its side. Two Level Three soldiers flank the carriage on horseback, and a Level Four soldier sits on the wand-guard seat.

One of the soldiers opens the door for me, and I'm surprised to find the carriage empty.

"Where's Lukas?" I ask warily.

"We have instructions to take you to him, Mage Gardner," comes the succinct reply, the soldier's handsome face rigidly devoid of emotion.

I don't budge. "Where?"

He gives a swift glance northwest. "At the edge of the Spine, Mage."

My unease spikes. *Why there? There's nothing but farmland and wilderness.*

He stands, expressionless, waiting as I glance toward the

jutting white shards of the Northern Spine, the peaks snow-capped and silvered in the moonlight.

Gauging the situation for a split second, I take a deep breath and climb into the carriage. The door clicks into place, and I have the unsettling feeling that I've just crossed a dangerous threshold.

We drive through bustling Verpax City and eventually out of it, the lights of the city receding and soon dampened to a halo of light in the distance. The stars glitter coldly over the farms and wilds of northwestern Verpacia, the full moon suspended just above the Northern Spine and glowing like a specter.

After over an hour's ride, the carriage comes to an abrupt halt by a deserted field covered with glittering, ice-encrusted snow. The wilds encircle the field, the forest sloping upward over hills that lead to the base of the ghostly white Spine.

The door opens, and I step out into the cold air. I glance around, searching for Lukas, a prickling apprehension taking hold. There's nothing but wilderness here. Lukas's Fourth Division Base is clear on the other side of the Spine.

"Where is he…" I start to ask, but the carriage is already in motion, the soldiers riding away alongside it.

"Wait!"

I run to keep up with the carriage, but it soon outpaces me, and I'm left alone, leagues away from anything. With nothing but the barren fields surrounding me and the black wilderness beyond.

Fear seeps into me. And cold. My breath curls white on the air.

What are you playing at, Lukas?

A sudden, piercing shriek sounds from the direction of the Northern Spine. I turn to see a winged creature descending over the Spine's apex, silhouetted against the ivory stone and snow. The thing shrieks again, soaring closer, and my pulse races with a mixture of fascination and apprehension.

A dragon.

I step back as a fuller realization dawns.

Lukas. Astride a military dragon.

The dragon wings over the wilds, skimming the treetops. Lukas comes into view on its back as the creature swoops down toward the field before me. The dragon lands with a piercing shriek and a dull, heavy thump that reverberates under my feet.

Lukas firmly calls out a command, and the dragon collapses flat on the snow, wings spread over the ground like colossal fans.

He smiles and holds out his hand to me.

My heart thuds against my chest as I look at the monstrous dragon with its knifelike feathers, huge talons and opaque, dead eyes. Both fear and pity rise within me.

Broken. Like they tried to break Naga.

"Why are you here on a dragon?" I call out to him, stunned.

"Dragonflight is fast. And private," Lukas calmly replies.

"You want me to ride on *that*? Over the Spine?"

Lukas arches a black brow. He glances over his shoulder at the Spine, then turns back to me, an amused tilt to his mouth. "Did you imagine us taking a carriage over it instead?"

"If that's what you've got planned, then why didn't you just fly right to the North Tower?"

His tone takes a sardonic turn. "Because doing so would be an unforgivable and outlawed incursion into Vu Trin sky domain. I wasn't in the mood for getting shot down in a churning ball of rune fire." He gives me a smoky look. "Unless that was how you wanted our evening to play out."

His suggestive look sparks a tremor of heat in my lines. "So, the Vu Trin let you come here instead?"

"I obtained permission, yes," Lukas says smoothly. "Which is why I am currently alive and not on fire."

A jittery fear pulls through me as I contemplate climbing up onto the dragon's back. "I really don't like heights, Lukas."

He seems surprised by this. His gaze sharpens on me, serious now. "I'll bolster you with my earth lines and ground you to me. It will help dampen your fear, Elloren."

I glance up at the impossibly high, jagged Spine and picture myself hurtling to my death on its knifelike edge. It rises higher than the clouds, and I imagine it would take hours to completely tumble down from its top to the base of the gargantuan landmass.

A shiver of both fear and cold ripples through me. Stubbornly ignoring both, I trudge over the crunchy snow and around the dragon's flattened wing, then reach up and take Lukas's proffered hand, bracing my foot on the dragon's scaled side as he pulls me up in front of himself.

My skirt rides clear up as I throw my leg over the dragon and slide myself down against the front of Lukas's body. Flushing, I hastily tug my skirt down as low as I can, careful to keep the spiraling wand that's pushed into the top of my boot concealed.

"I'm not exactly dressed in dragon-riding attire," I note defensively, my nerves making me jumpy, "since someone made absolutely no mention of a dragon."

Lukas gives a low laugh, and I can feel his warm breath on my ear. He pulls out his wand and gives it a casual flick. Vines fly out its tip to wrap around both us and the dragon, securing us to the beast. I beat back the claustrophobic alarm that is suddenly swelling up in me and threatening to burst into full-blown panic.

Lukas murmurs another spell and presses his wand gently to the side of my leg. Diaphanous, shimmering gold flows out of the wand and washes over both me and Lukas. Lukas sounds out another spell and the sparkling cloud fuses to our skin, replacing our verdant Gardnerian glitter with a golden sheen. My fire lines kindle, warmth surging through them in response to Lukas's magic, and just like that, the wintry chill is gone.

Lukas's arm slides around my waist and pulls me firmly against him. Then he taps his wand against the dragon's side.

The dragon rises to its feet, wings folding back, and I can feel powerful muscles at work beneath me. My fear kicks up to a jagged roar, my pulse hammering in my ears, and I fidget against Lukas in silent, panicked protest.

"Shhh." Lukas brings his lips softly to my neck, his hand splayed out over my waist, holding me to him.

I gasp as he murmurs another spell and dark branches of his earth magic curl into me, fanning out and spreading through my affinity lines in a rippling tingle, twining and spiraling tight.

I take a deep breath, my terror lessening until it's all but disappeared. "Where do you want to go, Elloren?" Lukas asks, his voice an enticing thrum.

I swallow, getting hold of myself. "Somewhere completely private."

"I have quite a few private rooms." His voice is thick with suggestion, and I can feel his smirk.

"I don't care if it's your bedroom, Lukas," I say tersely, desperate to speak freely to him. "I need to talk to you. *Alone.*"

I sense his mood shift as he nods. He grabs hold of one of the dragon's shoulder spikes and growls out a command.

The creature lurches forward and breaks into a run, the pounding motion jarring my hips. A trill of panic races through me as the dragon lets out an ear-piercing shriek, raises its wings up and out to the limit of their extension, then brings them down with a vigorous *whoosh*.

We lift up, the ground falling away beneath us, a stomach-dropping vertigo overtaking me. We gain speed rapidly, the wind whipping around us, but Lukas's shield holds the worst of the chill at bay.

Then we're above the trees, my heart in my throat as the rhythmic, powerful beating of the dragon's wings lifts us up and up and up. I breathe deeply and take in the dizzying view as we wing toward the great wall of the Northern Spine, glancing over my shoulder briefly at light-haloed Verpax City and the moonlight-washed Southern Spine as they fall away behind us.

I peer down at the wide expanse of forest streaming by below us, and my affinity lines give a sudden covetous lurch. My fire lines blaze hot, my branches shuddering against Lukas's. A heady sense of power rushes through me, and the forest palpably convulses—shock waves of awareness radiating outward for leagues and leagues, the vast expanse of trees suddenly focused on one thing, and one thing only.

The power running through my blood.

Lukas tightens his hold on me, his dark branches twining further around my lines in a seductive, supple caress. "Your affinity lines have gotten stronger, haven't they?" he whispers in my ear.

I glance back at him, flushed with heat and wildly unsettled by the flash of power. The dragon banks sharply upward, and I fall back against Lukas, my breath cinching in my lungs. The wall of the Spine rushes past beneath me, and vertigo takes over. I clutch at Lukas's arms, my affinity branches wrapping tight around his earth lines.

And then the dragon evens out, and we're abruptly flying straight over the Spine, the stars glittering like jewels as moonlit clouds drift below us.

I pull in a hard breath, overcome by the startling grandeur.

The jagged, snow-covered peaks of the Spine are breathtaking. And from this height I can see the entire length of the Northern Spine, small Elfhollen villages clinging to alcoves in the jagged stone, the dwellings hewn into the ivory rock.

As we crest the highest, knife-edged peak, the Fourth Division military base comes into view, and my stomach clenches into a tight fist at the sight.

It's huge. Much bigger than it was before.

It completely fills the valley with a murky haze of torchlight, illuminating rows upon rows of tents and dragon cages. New buildings have been carved into the Spine-stone, some up high, but most at the base of the Spine. Many are only half completed, still under construction. I realize that dedicated Level Five earth-Magery must have been utilized to reconstruct so many buildings so rapidly. And new dragons must have been brought in from somewhere.

Dread sluices through my veins.

This is only one base, I realize. *Out of twelve. And this one alone is bigger than Verpax City.*

We fly over the base and loop back around. The dragon lets out a sonorous shriek and begins a steep dive, aiming for a shadowed, cavernous hole halfway up the towering Spine. We hurtle straight toward it, my breath cinching tight in my throat as the dragon's wings pivot abruptly up, my body thrust back hard against Lukas's as our speed rapidly slows and we soar through the opening, slamming down onto the stone floor of a cave with concussive force.

The dragon collapses to the ground, wings fanned out as the creature goes still as the stone. A wall torch gutters light over Lukas and me, the dragon and the chalky cave.

I sit there, nearly hyperventilating.

Lukas unsheathes his wand and expeditiously draws the belt-like vines off us with a spell, the black straps dissolving to dark mist. Then he draws the golden shield back into his wand.

Frigid cold blasts through me, whipping into the cave, every breath like splinters of ice. My eyelashes stick together, quickly freezing.

Lukas slides off the dragon and holds his hands out for me. I hurriedly slide down the dragon's side and into his arms, shivering uncontrollably as he guides me toward a metal-studded wooden door and into the room beyond it.

The moment Lukas shuts the door, we're enveloped in a cocoon of warmth. I blink my eyes and clear the ice crystals from my lashes, struggling to find my bearings.

"Did you enjoy the flight?" Lukas asks, his dark gaze looking me over unapologetically.

I shoot him a hard look. "It was completely terrifying, and..." I pause, realizing a part of me is lit up in a heady, new way from soaring over the Spine like a raptor. "It was also...*incredible*."

"Mmm." Lukas smiles, scrutinizing me closely, as if reading something new in me that he approves of. He holds out his hand, as if he's offering up the forbidden.

My heartbeat quickens as I take it, his fingers closing in around mine.

I let Lukas lead me down a long, Ironwood-paneled hallway, increasingly aware of our solitude. We step into an expansive library with a huge, roaring woodstove, its iron tree limb pipes branching and fanning out over the room, iron leaves decorating their metal surfaces. I glance around in wonder, aware of Lukas's eyes trained on me.

Everything is fashioned in the classic Gardnerian style.

The walls, ceiling and floor are made of dark Ironwood, and all the carpets, tapestries and rugs are wrought in black and forest green. Carved trees support the roof with dark, tangling branches, and wall torches burn with a warm, buttery-yellow flame.

If I ignore the view of the base beyond the expansive glass balcony doors, I can almost imagine that we're back in Valgard, rather than encased in stone near the apex of the Northern Spine.

Lukas releases my hand and opens another door near the woodstove. He flashes a beckoning smile and gracefully gestures for me to join him.

His bedroom.

"You asked for somewhere private," Lukas says, an amused smile on his lips as a flicker of his fire affinity pulses through me, catching me off guard.

"I can feel your fire lines," I tell him, suddenly flustered.

"Oh, I know you can," he says throatily.

"No, not just when we touch," I clarify, deeply thrown. "I just sensed your fire from across the distance between us."

Lukas's eyes narrow in on me. "That's a rare skill, Elloren. To sense affinities from a distance. I've never heard of anyone below Level Five being able to do it."

"Can you sense other Mages' affinities?" I ask.

His gaze rakes over me, taking on a sultry heat. "Only yours. And only when I touch you."

"Oh." I glance through the open doorway at Lukas's bed, a heated tremor running through me. His black bedspread is quilted with the image of a large tree styled in a deeper black. Directly across from the bed, a fireplace crackles with flames. Two black velvet chairs and a table well-appointed with food and drink are set by the fire.

I hesitate. "I'm not getting into that bed with you," I tell him, making things clear.

Lukas's predatory look doesn't waver. "I wouldn't expect so, Elloren. Not on this occasion." His voice is a caress as he adds, "But if you change your mind, please feel free to let me know."

Oh, sweet Ancient One.

I can barely think around his pull. But even though he's unabashedly teasing me, I can sense he's keeping his fire and earth magic firmly in check. Emboldened, I flash him a guarded look and step inside.

The bedroom's walls are lined with bookshelves. Curious about his interests, I walk over to one of the shelves and scan the titles, running a fingertip over the smooth leather spines—military history, foreign language dictionaries, grimoires. All impeccably organized.

I turn and scan the rest of the room.

There's a piano, just past the bed, fashioned from Ironwood. A small forest of trees is carved into it, rising up to support the instrument's lid. I'm instantly intrigued. It's the only messy area of Lukas's entire dwelling, with music thrown into piles on the piano, the floor and the piano bench—most of it written in his own hand, as if he's funneling all his passion into this one area—unleashed and uncontained.

"You should have brought your violin," he says, his eyes following my gaze.

"Mmm," I distractedly agree, remembering the exhilarating joy of playing with a musician of his caliber. The memory fills me with the uneasy realization that there are aspects of Lukas's company that I deeply enjoy.

Another balcony lies just off his bedroom. Large black

curtains sweep down and are tied back to the sides of double glass doors, another expansive view of the base just beyond.

I sit down by the fireplace. There's a full tea service before me, its elegant black porcelain shot through with golden tree limbs. A tray of small sandwiches, pastries and exotic berries is set beside it, along with an ebony glass bottle and fluted crystalline glasses.

There's also a small bouquet of glowing Ironflowers set in a black-lacquered vase. I'm oddly touched by the sight of them, remembering his dazed look when he saw my dress at Yule, sure that he's hinting at that night with this gesture.

Lukas sits down across from me and leans back with casual grace, his gaze dark and inscrutable. "Would you like some tea?" he asks.

I raise a brow. "You're going to serve me tea, Lukas?"

He laughs and reaches for the teapot to pour me a cup, his eyes lit with wicked mischief. "I'll serve you anything you like, Elloren."

His fingers graze mine as I take the proffered cup, trailing an enticing line of heat. "Are you trying to court me, Lukas?" I ask as I sit back, half in jest.

An amused sound escapes his lips. "Oh, I'd do better than tea if you'd let me." He's watching me intently, and I'm momentarily much too aware of how devastatingly handsome he is.

Scrambling for a distraction from that dangerous train of thought, I glance out the nearby window toward the base below. "You've done quite the job of rebuilding," I note, unable to keep a trace of resentment from my tone.

Lukas's mouth twitches as he studies me, suddenly serious. "Elloren, what is it you want?"

I hold his abruptly formidable gaze, both of us serious now. Overcome with nervous tension, I set down my tea, rise to my feet, and walk over to the fireplace, desperate to collect my thoughts. I study the sword that hangs over the mantel, a dragon exquisitely wrought from silver curling around its hilt.

I take a deep, steadying breath and turn around to face Lukas dead-on. "What do you think of Vogel?"

There. I said it. And we can't lie to each other, so answer me this time.

Lukas's eyes take on the look of a storm gathering, his voice dagger sharp. "Vogel's unhinged."

We're both quiet for a long moment as we try to read each other. The unconcealed, almost violent antagonism toward Vogel in Lukas's gaze emboldens me.

"Our people are forming mobs, and they've started attacking non-Gardnerians in Verpax City," I tell him.

Lukas throws me a deeply cynical look. "That's unfortunate, Elloren," he says, his tone barbed, "but not at all unexpected. Do you happen to recall what the Kelts and the Urisk did when they were in power?"

Anger fills me in response to his usual, infuriating and unfeeling logic. An image of Olilly's multilated ears and shorn hair fills my mind. Bleddyn's beaten face.

"The Kelts and the Urisk formed mobs," Lukas answers for me with a potent glare. "And tormented Gardnerians. They quickly progressed to killing them. First individually, then rounding them up in barns and setting the buildings on fire."

I glare back at him, tension igniting on the air between us.

"And just prior to that," he continues acidly, "the Fae formed mobs and tormented the Kelts. And before *that*, the Urisk formed mobs and tormented the Fae."

"I know all this, Lukas," I counter, growing impassioned. "That was *them* spinning out of control, and this is *us* spinning out of control. Someone needs to stop it."

His smirk is coldly contemptuous. "You mean stop the normal course of history?"

"Yes."

His face hardens. "It doesn't work that way, Elloren. You can choose to be on the powerful side or not. That's your *only* choice in this world."

"No," I lash back. "That is *not* the only choice. I've read a fair bit of history this year, Lukas. The balance of power could be realigned to include *everyone*. Not just one group tormenting all the others."

"Then tell me," he throws back, a sarcastic curl to his lip, "in your erudite studies of the history of the Realms, when exactly was power realigned to include everyone, Elloren?"

I move toward him, ire building. I don't care that he's a Level Five Mage. I don't care that he commands this entire base. I can't fight the compulsion to be blisteringly honest with him. "I don't care if it's never been achieved, Lukas. None of us should be aligning ourselves with this nightmare, including you. Vogel needs to be *stopped*."

Lukas's face grows savage. He abruptly rises, stalks toward me and takes hold of my arm. "Come with me," he says, a demand.

I glance down at his hand, incredulous, doggedly holding my ground. "Where?"

"Just come."

I let him guide me toward the bedroom's balcony. He throws open the glass door and leads me outside, his hand firm around my arm, drawing me right up to the edge. There are torches set on metal poles along the balcony's entire periphery, sending up crimson Mage-flame, heating the entire terrace. Mage-crafted, black tree limbs twist inside the bloodred flame.

"Look carefully, Elloren," Lukas seethes, tilting his head toward the sprawling base before us. "What do you see?"

I shrug him off and glare daggers at him. "Power."

"Yes, that's right. So be careful." He sends me a piercing, significant look. "I know *exactly* what you're involved in. You're treading on very dangerous ground."

I can read it in his eyes. A warning. And I realize, with terrifying certainty, that he knows. He knows I'm wrapped up in the Resistance. The weak Resistance. The easily crushed Resistance.

And he likely knows about Naga.

"What do you know?" I rasp out, barely able to form the words.

Lukas's expression fills with a disbelief edging toward mockery. "What do you take me for? I know *everything*."

My heart pounds against my chest, my breath becoming uneven, but I force myself to meet his savage glare. "Should I be afraid, Lukas?"

"Yes, Elloren," he shoots back. "*Very* afraid." His look of fury collapses, becoming conflicted. "But not of me."

The startling realization washes over me. *He knows. Lukas knows. But he's going to overlook all of it.*

"I want to fast to you, Elloren," he snarls, emphatic, "but my protection can only go so far. There are forces much stronger than me at work. *Much.* So, you need to take *great care*."

I hold his stare, unflinching, as steel rises within me. "Lukas. You need to break from them."

He draws back, angered. "And go where, Elloren? To what end?"

"East."

His eyes harden with fury, and he turns away, looking out over the base, seeming wildly unsettled. This is not a Lukas

I've often seen. He's like a caged, feral thing. Even though he has power here, I realize, he's not truly in control.

No one controls this thing that Vogel's unleashed. No one, except Vogel himself.

"What's Vogel planning on doing, Lukas?"

He eyes me with derision. "Read the Mage Council archives, Elloren. He's quite clear about what he's planning to do." Lukas's nostrils flare, his jaw ticking as he looks back out over the base. "Elloren," he says, suddenly almost sounding hesitant. "I might have been wrong about Fallon Bane."

Shock lashes through me. "What do you mean?"

"She's healing. And her air and water powers are quickening. She's starting to be able to access her other elemental powers, as well. Which means Vogel just might have his Black Witch. And the Icaral of Prophecy is a tiny, helpless baby. So, we have Fallon. And *this*," he says, waving his hand over the base. "We have the Alfsigr Elves as our allies, and more dragons than we've ever had before."

He stares at me with stone-cold sobriety. "We're going to mow over the entire Western and Eastern Realms. I could go east tomorrow, Elloren. And I could *not change* what's coming."

Horror laps at me, but I battle against its grip. "Lukas, are you really content to be part of this nightmare?"

Lukas sets his eyes back on the base, the tree-torches guttering around us. His voice is pitched low with struggle when it comes. "I don't know, Elloren."

I'm stunned by his sudden honesty. The urge to be equally honest with him rises in me. To voice to him what I can voice to no one else.

"Lukas...there's a lot of power rising in my affinity lines. I felt it when we flew in over the wilds. We both did." I look out over the base, remembering the intoxicating thrill of the power, and clasp my fingers around the Snow Oak pendant, my fire lines rousing in response. "The power... It felt good. *Too* good. And that scares me."

I turn to face Lukas and release the pendant, and the fire recedes to a dull ember. "I don't want to be like my grandmother."

Lukas turns to face me and reaches up to caress my cheek, his touch featherlight. "Fast to me. I understand your struggle. And I don't judge you for it."

We hold each other's gaze for a brief moment, our branches reaching for each other.

Then he steps closer and pulls me gently into his arms. Light as gossamer, he kisses the base of my neck, his lips rousing my fire lines with a heated longing that tingles straight through me.

"Fast to me, Elloren," he murmurs again, coaxing me to give in to his hypnotic draw. "The world is always in conflict. We could use our power to secure a place for ourselves in it."

Our power?

A small edge of confusion cuts through his sensual spell. "How can my power be of any use?"

"I can draw on it." Lukas trails kisses along my jaw, his fire caressing my lines.

"You can...draw on my power?" I ask breathlessly.

"A bit." Lukas's fingers skim down my back, a delicious shiver chasing his caress.

I swallow hard, my mind suddenly a whirl. "Is that why you want to fast to me?"

"No," he says as his lips brush against mine, his fire rippling through me. "There's a bond between us, Elloren. I know I'm not the only one who feels it." He draws me closer and brings his lips to mine, sending his heat straight through me in a provocative rush.

I gasp as a delicious tension ignites inside me, and Lukas's kiss deepens.

"Lukas," I say as his pianist fingers knot in my hair and he kisses along my neck, "if we can combine our power... we could use it not just for ourselves...but to fight Vogel."

He draws back a fraction, his eyes full of silken darkness. "I don't know that I want to, Elloren."

A sudden clarity overtakes me.

This is it, right here. The lure of darkness.

I step back and slowly but firmly extricate myself from Lukas—from this power and its seductive spell. This isn't something to be drawn into. This is something to fight against. Both inwardly and outwardly. Even if the only other alternative is to be powerless.

"Take me back, Lukas," I tell him, shutting this down. "I think I've seen enough."

Lukas flies me back to the barren, snow-encrusted field without a word.

A military carriage is waiting for me when we arrive. Lukas helps me down from the dragon's back and gives me a reproachful look. Then he wordlessly mounts the dragon and wings away into the pitch-black winter night.

A soldier silently escorts me to the carriage. I climb inside, and we set off toward the lights of the University, the dark forest looming through the window as a cyclone of troubled emotion storms through me.

CHAPTER
SIXTEEN

IVORY WINGS

It's well past midnight when the carriage finally arrives back at the North Tower. I trudge wearily up the hill toward my lodging, hugging the edge of the wilds, acutely aware of the trees drawing back from me.

Black Witch.

I slow to a halt, suddenly distraught. So many terrible things have happened already, and now, my very blood seems to be slipping into darkness.

And I'm powerless to stop it.

I roughly pull off my Snow Oak necklace, breaking the chain, and throw it to the ground, not wanting any part of this wretched power. I reach down and pull the wand from my boot, imagining it to be the true Wand of Myth. A pure force for good, bringing hope to all of Erthia.

Despair swells inside me.

Why don't you help us? I rage at the wand, the stars, the sky. *Why are you letting all of this happen? Why are you letting cruelty win? If there really is a force for good, where are you?*

But the wand is quiet in my hand. It remains a smooth spiraling stick, nothing more, in the silence of the night. I take a long, shuddering breath, a hot tear streaking down my chilled cheek.

It's no use. We're all alone.

I listlessly turn to continue up the hill, and my gaze is drawn up, instantly transfixed.

Two Watchers are flying in lazy circles around the North Tower.

They float on the wintry night air, the iridescent birds spiraling like gently falling leaves.

And then they simply disappear.

I slow to a stop, everything dark and still and silent.

Listen.

The word crystallizes in the back of my mind, like a hidden whisper.

I rush up the spiraling stairs to the top floor of the North Tower, filled with a nonsensical, amorphous hope. Hope in the face of the insurmountable walls of darkness. Hope borne on ivory wings.

I push open the door to our room and burst inside, lit up with anticipation. I carefully scan the room, expecting to see *something*.

My senseless hope withers. Our lodging looks much the same as it always does. Marina is curled up by the fire as usual, watching me with a weary expression.

I let out a long, deflated sigh as I regard her in turn, the reflected firelight dancing in her long, silver hair.

Ariel and Wynter are gone, as they so often are lately, probably tending to Naga with Andras. Diana is most likely studying in the archives with Jarod or off with Rafe somewhere, and Ariel's chickens are quietly roosting on her bed. Her raven is absent, probably flown off to be with her.

I throw off my cloak, stalk across the room and slump down into my desk chair. Marina pads over to sit on the floor nearby, resting her shimmering head against me.

At least there's this, I consider with a long sigh. One Selkie rescued from a terrible fate. It might seem like a small thing in the face of a mountain of darkness, but her freedom is one bright spot of hope.

Oh, Marina, I agonize, stroking her beautiful hair. *What are you thinking?* I study Marina for a long moment, never tiring of admiring her liquid-silver hair. Wishing I could look inside her mind.

Letting out another sigh, I turn my thoughts to my studies, knowing I've procrastinated long enough. I open my Apothecary text to a marked spot and pull out some paper so I can take notes through the rest of the night if I have to. I have an exam in two days' time, and I'm barely passing the class as is.

I can't access my own power, I dolefully consider, *but at least I can make medicines*. It's not a lot, and it won't stop what's coming, but at least I can provide some temporary comfort and healing to the people who need it.

And maybe Lukas is wrong. Maybe the Vu Trin forces of the Eastern Realm are stronger than he thinks. Maybe they're stronger than Vogel and all his soldiers and broken dragons combined.

Bolstered by the thought, I begin reading, pausing occasionally to scratch out some notes. As I write, Marina gets up and begins fussing with my hair, her long fingers rhythmically stroking it, her touch soothing. I smile and reach up to squeeze her hand affectionately. She gives me a weak smile in return and leans down to nuzzle her cheek against mine.

Her pale arm reaches around me, her finger pointing at the small painting of my parents that's propped up on my desk. Wynter made it for me a few weeks ago, to replace the original that Ariel smashed, their images pulled from Wynter's empathic reading of Rafe's and my scant memories of them.

Marina starts talking to herself in her flute-like tones, as she's wont to do, struggling with the sounds, as if it takes great effort to make them. I'm only half listening, absorbed in the lesson in my book, so she taps my shoulder and gestures at the picture again, almost knocking it over.

Distracted, I stop what I'm doing and turn slightly to glance over my shoulder at her. Marina cocks her head to one side and forms her mouth into a circle. Looking meaningfully at the image of my parents, she blows some air out and makes a metallic humming noise. Her gills pull in almost flat on her neck, then quickly fall slack and ruffle open. Her expression fills with frustration for a moment before she repeats the action.

I smile, humoring her. Not sure why she's suddenly so taken with my painting.

"Maaaahzhurrrrr," she blows out, the sound fractured into parts, as if she's breathing it through multiple flutes. I glance over at her, puzzled by her insistence.

She tries again, and this time the disparate notes pull together.

Shock rips through me.

I drop my pen on the desk and wheel around to face her fully. Marina is staring straight at me, her storm-gray eyes determined. She touches the picture again, her finger right on my mother's face. Then she presses both palms hard against the gills on the sides of her throat. The muscles of her neck tighten, her face tensed as if with great effort.

"Maaah Thurrr," she says, this time clearly.

My heart thuds in my chest, her ability to speak unmistakable.

"That's right," I say, so stunned I'm barely able to get the words out. "My mother."

Marina's expression turns to one of shocked surprise at my finally being able to understand her. She grabs hold of my arm so tight it pinches, her gills flying open as she launches into frantic, once again unintelligible speech.

I shake my head in confusion, trying my best to make out actual words, but her flute-like tones are back, the sounds chaotic. Marina stops, distressed by my bewilderment, her breathing heavy from the effort. Then an excited light fills her eyes.

She drags me into the washroom, toward the large tub that's filled with unheated, ice-cold water. She pivots and lets herself fall backward into the water, one of her arms still gripping mine as she pulls me roughly toward the surface, her entire body now submerged. A torrent of bubbles streams up as her gills flatten against her neck.

"You hear me?"

Shock blasts through me.

The words are very faint and muffled, but completely understandable. I realize she must be yelling against the water for her words to be audible.

Marina bursts up from the water, spraying ice water all over me. Her hand is still vise-tight around my arm, her eyes blazing with determination.

"Yes," I tell her, astonished. "I can hear you."

She throws herself down into the water again, and I press my ear almost to the surface of it.

"My sister! They took her! My sister! She is very young! Younger than me! Help me! Please help me!"

She pulls her head out of the water again, pulling at me

with desperation. And then she completely breaks down. Her gills fly open wide as she closes her eyes tightly and lets out a long, flute-toned wail.

The full horror of what she's trying to tell me crashes down. Her sister. Trapped by someone like the grounds-keeper who once held Marina prisoner—or perhaps somewhere much worse.

Overcome, I throw my arms around her. Marina's slender body is violently trembling, her gills frantically opening and closing as she sobs.

"We'll help her," I promise tearfully as she struggles to regain control of her breathing.

"I swear to you, Marina," I tell her, not knowing how we'll manage it, but sick of feeling helpless. "We'll find your sister. We'll get help, and somehow, we'll get you all out."

MAGE COUNCIL
RULING
#271

Smuggling Selkies or spirits
across the Gardnerian border shall be
grounds for imprisonment.

CHAPTER SEVENTEEN

GARETH KEELER

A few nights later, I leave my kitchen shift and venture out into the frigid cold, bundled tightly in my cloak. Marina has been on my mind all day, and I'm eager to get back to the North Tower.

I've told everyone in my small circle the news of Marina's newfound ability to communicate. Jules and Lucretia are redoubling their efforts to quietly rally support for the Selkies, and my brothers tried to visit last night, hoping she might be able to share more information about where her sister and the other Selkies are being held. Marina devolved into panicked protest at the sight of them, terrified of men, and they left quickly to avoid causing her further distress.

I'm just starting down the path by the kitchen's back door when I spot a tall, stocky young man making his way toward me from the bottom of the hill. He's broad-shouldered and wearing a dark Gardnerian cloak and tunic lined with the single blue stripe of a Gardnerian mariner. The tips of his hair glint silver in the light of the walkway's sole lantern.

My heart leaps in my chest, and I break into a run down the hill. "Gareth!"

Gareth sweeps me up in his muscular arms, chuckling as I practically hurl myself at him. We envelop each other in a warm, overjoyed hug, and for a moment all my exhaustion and grief and stress fall away as I cling to my childhood friend and tears come to my eyes. I step back from him, smiling and crying and laughing all at the same time. Gareth squeezes my shoulder and gives me a warm smile and a heartening look of solidarity.

"I'm so happy to see you," I tell him, wiping away the tears as relief spreads through me. Movement at the top of the hill catches my eye.

Yvan.

He's leaving his kitchen shift, too, heading up the higher path that goes by the livestock barns, his heavy book bag slung over his shoulder. Yvan pauses, watching Gareth and me, and I can feel a surprising flash of his unsettled fire from clear across the hill. He's been remote and closed off ever since that horrible night of mob attacks, and I suppose I've been withdrawn, as well. Both of us holding back, knowing our time for goodbyes is coming soon, and that there's absolutely nothing to be done about it.

Briefly, I hold Yvan's gaze, my sudden, heated awareness of him shimmying through my fire lines.

I remember what Lukas told me about my rising ability to read affinities—a rare skill.

Even Fae affinities, I realize.

I turn back to Gareth, flustered and acutely aware of Yvan's shadowy figure disappearing into the line of woods.

Gareth's eyes flick up to follow Yvan's retreat. "Someone you know?"

A wry sound escapes me, and I nod. "Oh, Gareth, so much

has happened." I study his face in the dim light and realize how much he's changed—his jaw squarer, his sparse beard fuller. It dawns on me that my childhood friend isn't a boy anymore. "When did you get in?" I ask.

Gareth angles his head back toward the central University buildings. "I just arrived with the other maritime apprentices. The Saltisle Pass has finally iced over, so they've got us back here for a couple of weeks to take astronomy and some other classes."

The back door to the kitchen creaks open, then slams shut. I glance up and spot Iris and Bleddyn walking down the hill together.

"Have you seen Rafe and Trystan yet?" I ask Gareth. "Have they told you anything about what's going on here?"

Gareth shakes his head, his silvered hair sparkling like it's snow-dusted. "No, I came straight here. I remembered they had you working in the kitchens."

Gareth and I pause our conversation as Bleddyn and Iris pass by. I can see Bleddyn taking in Gareth's silver-tipped hair, her large emerald eyes narrowed in appraisal. She glances at me and smirks.

Iris notices the exchange. She shoots me a glare and tugs Bleddyn decidedly away. But as they near the bottom of the hill, Bleddyn lifts her hand to Gareth and me in a silent good-night.

Heartened by her gesture, I turn back to Gareth. "Have you eaten?"

"No, and I'm starving." He eyes the back door to the kitchen, a playful glint in his eyes. "I don't suppose you'd know where we could get some food?"

A few minutes later, we're ensconced in one of the storerooms, surrounded by shelves of preserves and barrels of grain. Gareth and I sit on overturned wooden crates, the top of a barrel acting as our table. Steam wafts up from a pot of mint tea, and a mountain of warm, freshly baked mushroom turnovers fills a plate next to it.

"This is a lot of food, Ren," Gareth comments with a laugh.

I grab up a turnover and take a huge bite. "It's just enough food," I say through a mouthful, grinning at him. Gareth's like a third brother to me, and I love how I don't have to be the least bit civilized around him. "I'm starving, too. And these are really good." I'm momentarily lost in the bliss of buttery mushrooms, flaky crust and caramelized onions.

Gareth digs into the food as well, his eyes lighting up. "Sweet gods, these *are* good."

I nod, a congenial warmth washing over me. I'd much rather be sitting here with Gareth, eating mushroom pastries, than dining on roast swan at some fine Valgard estate. Plus, I bet Fernyllia's cooking skills could best any of the fancy chefs employed by wealthy Gardnerians.

Gareth takes a sip of his tea. "What's happened while I've been gone?"

I let out a long sigh, relieved to be with someone I can speak freely around. Someone I can trust completely. "Settle in and eat," I say, nodding at the plate of turnovers. "This story is going to take a while to tell."

"So, you've rescued a Selkie," Gareth marvels, the tea long since cooled, the pastries rendered to crumbs on the plate. "What's she like?"

"Marina's wonderful. Kind and sweet," I reply as I stroke the kitchen cat who's curled up, purring, in my lap. "She was very sickly at first, but her health is slowly improving now that we know she eats raw fish. And she's speaking the Common Tongue quite fluently."

Information about Marina has come in thick waves since she's found a way to communicate with us, full of incredible revelations, and I relay to Gareth everything she's told me.

The Selkies live in large cities in ocean caves lit by fluorescent coral, and though they number in the thousands, their society is very communal and tight-knit.

"It took a while for her to understand our language," I tell Gareth. "Land sounds are distorted to her, and the strange tones she makes against air are clicks and musical tones underwater. She's a musician in her land, apprenticing with a bard, so I think she has an ear for language."

"That's incredible," Gareth says, an awed look on his face. "I'm glad you've been able to help her."

"We need to do more," I reply, frowning thoughtfully as I absently pet the soft cat. "Her skin is the source of her power, but we have no idea where it might be hidden. She's in a severely weakened state without it."

"So why do the Selkies come to land?" Gareth asks, curious. "It's so dangerous for them here."

"Their shifting magic can get snagged by a spell that was cast long ago. It can happen whenever the moon is full, and it inadvertently pulls them onto our shores. I don't really understand all of it, but that's what she was able to explain to us. And...well, you know the rest."

Gareth is quiet for a long moment. "Can I meet her?"

I shake my head. "I don't think that's a good idea, Gareth. We've tried introducing her to Trystan and Rafe and some of the others, but she's terrified of men."

"You need to get her out of here, Ren," he says, his voice gentle but firm. "There's serious talk in Valgard about killing all the Selkies as soon as they come to shore, and I think someone on the Council is going to make an official motion soon."

I return his grave look. "My aunt, I know." I reach up to massage my temple, a sharp headache blooming. "Marina has a sister who's probably being held in one of those...*taverns*." I spit the word out with blistering disgust. "And there are so many others. We need to find a way to free them before my aunt rallies the support she needs on the Council."

"Can the Resistance help?"

"We'd need a small army to mount a rescue, which the Verpacian Resistance doesn't have access to. They're overwhelmed just trying to help the refugees streaming through here." I shake my aching head and meet Gareth's steady gaze.

He reaches over to place his warm hand on mine. "Ren, I'm a mariner. Let me meet her."

I hold his resolute gaze, the ever-present kindness in it swaying me. Perhaps there's some slim chance that Marina won't be as intimidated by him.

"All right, Gareth." I sit back and let out a long sigh. "Come by tomorrow night."

Gareth nods and sits back as well, a troubled look passing over his expression. "Ren," he says, pausing, "have you found a fastmate yet?"

Where is this coming from?

"Lukas Grey still wants to fast to me," I tell him and catch his gray-blue eyes tightening with a glimmer of disapproval. I shake my head. "But... I can't."

"I imagine your aunt's not too thrilled about that decision."

"She doesn't exactly know yet," I admit.

Gareth considers this. "They're going to make us fast by the end of the fifth month. They're not kidding. They *will* make us."

"What about you? Do you have someone?"

Gareth coughs out a bitter laugh. "Who would have me in Gardneria? With my hair?" He hesitates, his expression suddenly bleak. "If the Mage Council has to get involved in my fasting, it will bring down an inquiry into the purity of my bloodline."

"But, Gareth," I protest, "you're *Gardnerian*."

The line of his mouth tightens. "That's what my parents say, but…" He sends me a loaded glance. "My bloodlines aren't pure, Ren. I'm sure of it."

Concern ripples through me. "So, fasting could be an actual danger for you."

"Only if it comes down to a forced fasting," he says. "If it does, I'll have to get out of the Western Realm."

My eyes widen at this. "Where would you go?"

"Noi lands."

I let out a hard breath, my gut clenching in protest at the thought of another person I love trying to get to what seems like the other side of Erthia. "Trystan is trying to find a way to get to Noi lands, as well," I tell him, my voice catching with emotion.

Gareth's eyes widen slightly in surprise, followed swiftly by understanding.

"If I can't get out in time," he says, "and if you don't find a partner…" He pauses, looking nervous, then seems to find his resolve again. "We should fast, Ren." His momentarily determined expression falters as my mouth drops open. "As friends," he hastily amends.

I stare at him for a long moment, utterly shocked. "Gareth, we can't fast just…as *friends*," I finally sputter. "You know as well as I do that the next thing the Mage Council will be mandating is the sealing ceremony for everyone of a certain age."

And the consummation of the sealing union is expected that same night, prompting the fastlines to flow down a couple's wrists as proof of that consummation.

I drop my forehead into my hands, a blush heating my face. "Could you really be with me in that way?"

I'm not the only one who's thrown by this conversation. A red flush forms high on Gareth's cheeks as he looks away, deeply flustered. "I… We've known each other for so long. It's strange to consider…" He takes a deep breath, then meets my eyes, his expression full of sincerity. "Ren, it would be an honor to be fasted to you."

I'm touched by his words. We're all being thrown into one impossible situation after another, but would it be so bad to be fasted to one of my closest friends?

Yvan's face fills my mind, and I struggle to push the beautiful image away, as well as the sharp ache that always accompanies thoughts of him.

You can't have Yvan, I remind myself. But I can't fast to Lukas, and I can't escape the Council's mandate if I stay in the Western Realm.

Gareth is right—we need to help each other.

"If it comes down to it," I say, decided, "I'll fast to you. But let's try to get you to Noi lands instead."

CHAPTER EIGHTEEN

THE SELKIE

The next night, Gareth comes to the North Tower.

He pauses just inside the doorway as Diana and I hold our collective breaths.

"Hello, Marina. I'm Gareth Keeler."

We've carefully prepped her for this, and Marina wants to get past her fears, but still, we brace ourselves for her reaction.

Marina looks up from where she sits slumped by the fire, her ocean eyes widening as they meet Gareth's. Her nostrils give a hard flare and her gills fan out as she slowly rises, bracing herself on my desk chair for balance, seeming both shocked and strangely entranced. Then, to our collective surprise, she lets loose with a stream of earsplitting, impassioned barking that terrifies Ariel's chickens and sends them aimlessly running about.

Gareth looks at me with confusion, and this seems to frustrate Marina, her brow creasing tight. She tentatively approaches him. When Gareth doesn't move, she ventures even closer, coming right up to him and pressing her nose into the base of his neck. Gareth remains completely still while Marina inhales deeply, then reaches up to carefully feel along his neck, as if searching for something.

She murmurs something in her flute-like tones, grabs Gareth firmly by the arm and drags him into the washroom. Diana and I exchange a swift, questioning look and follow.

Marina hurls herself into the large tub, splashing all of us with cold water as Gareth comes down on one knee beside her. She reaches up and slides dripping fingers up and down the sides of Gareth's neck, the frustration in her eyes growing. Gareth watches her intently, completely under Marina's thrall as she traces his skin over and over with her deft fingertips, a look of wild confusion on her face.

Gareth's throat bobs as he swallows. "I don't have gills," he says gently. "I'm a Gardnerian."

Marina throws herself under the water, curls around and looks up at Gareth from beneath the water's surface. "You are one of us." Her voice is faint, her underwater yell muffled. "Your silver hair is Selkie hair."

Gareth's words are halting when they come. "I'm not Selkie. I can't breathe underwater—"

"You smell like us," she insists. "Not bad like the others. You are Selkie."

Gareth grows very quiet, but not in the way of a person receiving outlandish news. More like a person having something they've secretly entertained confirmed beyond a shadow of a doubt.

"Did your father take a Selkie to mate?" Diana asks Gareth. I realize that if what Marina is saying is true, Gareth's father had a Selkie lover.

"It can't be…" I stammer. I know Gareth's father. His quiet mother. His two sisters. But none of them have silver in their hair, save Gareth.

"It must be so," Diana says. "He must have Selkie blood." Her nostrils flare, and she gives us all a significant look. "He smells like a shapeshifter."

Gareth has stilled, his expression tense and pensive. "There are things I've never spoken of," he tells us hesitantly. "I... I don't need my sextant to navigate."

I gape at him. "What, *never*?"

"I pretend to use it," he admits. "But I can navigate on instinct. And I don't ever need a compass. I can't explain it. It's like there's a compass in my head." He looks to Marina. "And I can hold my breath underwater for a solid hour. Sometimes longer."

Marina nods, looking at him meaningfully while massaging her gills, as if they pain her.

Gareth looks down at his hands. "No matter how long I'm in the water, my skin never gets wrinkled." He glances back up at Marina. "And I can predict the weather. I sense the pressure change." All of a sudden, his tentative approach gives way to a rushed confession. "I want to be in the ocean all the time. When I'm not there, I *long* for it. Even now, I know exactly where the ocean is and how far away. It's a pull I can't get out of my mind." His voice breaks with emotion, like he's speaking of a lover.

Marina's eyes fill with compassion. She nods, her mouth trembling. She pushes on her gills and tenses her neck. "Come in," she says, then takes hold of Gareth's arms and tugs him gently toward the water.

Gareth resists her pull, surprised. "With you?"

Marina nods, and he gives in, letting her pull him into the wide tub, water sloshing over the edge as both of them sink completely below the water's surface, crammed in beside each other. Gareth throws his head back, closes his eyes and gives a long, bubbling sigh.

After what seems like a long time, he pushes himself up, breaking through the water's surface, and Marina follows. Gareth pulls in a long breath as water streams off him, Marina's slender arm draped around his shoulder. Then Gareth's face devolves into despair, and he drops his head into his hands.

"Aren't you cold, Gareth?" I ask him gently. The water is freezing, gooseflesh broken out all over my shivering skin just from being splashed.

Gareth shakes his head against his hands. "I don't feel the cold. And the water...no matter what temperature it is, it's always better than the air. But I can't breathe in it. I can't live in it."

"Half-shapeshifter," Diana murmurs softly, compassion riding out with words.

"Oh, Gareth." I agonize, my heart going out to my friend—my friend who's carried this secret alone for all this time. "Why didn't you ever tell us?"

"My hair causes me trouble enough. I never wanted to dwell on my other...oddities. And I could always tell it was a wound to my mother." He raises his head and looks to Marina. Their eyes lock tight in mournful kinship.

Marina reaches up to gently stroke Gareth's cheek, and his eyes shine with tears. "You are one of us," Marina says with great effort, barely intelligible. "Even if you cannot come home to the water."

Gareth's whole face tenses. "I'm not. I don't know what I am. I don't fit in anywhere."

A fierce affection for Gareth swells inside me. "You fit in with us," I adamantly insist. "You're family. You always will be."

Marina is petting Gareth's hair, and her casual affection for people she's accepted seems to be creating fault lines inside Gareth, everything held back for years rushing out as tears mingle with the water on his face.

"Has there ever been anyone else like me?" he asks Marina, his voice breaking as she rhythmically strokes his hair.

Marina's brow tightens with evident confusion. She pushes in her gills and speaks with great effort. "There has never been anyone like any of us."

"I mean...someone who is Selkie, who can't go home?" Gareth stops, too choked up to continue.

Marina studies him for a long moment, a pained expression in her eyes. "I do not know."

Gareth's head drops as he brings a hand up to cover his eyes. Marina's gills fly open, and she croons a flute-toned sound as she coaxes him into an embrace. He quietly cries against her slender shoulder, his whole face bunched tight.

Diana is watching them now with one brow cocked, her expression lit with some surprise, and I wonder what she's reading in them.

Gareth eventually stills, and Marina pulls back a fraction, her slick hands coming up to caress his cheeks. She pulls her gills in. "My sister and the others," she says, struggling to make the sounds, "they need help. They will know you are Selkie. I need you, Gareth Keeler..." She stops, as if momentarily overcome, her gills fluttering. She pulls in a long, uneven breath and forces them back down. "Please...help us. Help your people..." Her voice breaks into incomprehensible tones, her face distraught.

Gareth gently takes hold of her hand. "I'll help you," he tells her with the steady, quiet force of a vow. "We'll find your sister and the others, along with your skins. We will find a way. I don't know how, but we will. And then we'll get all of you back to the ocean."

Marina practices her newfound language skills almost without ceasing, talking to herself when not in conversation with others. Her ability to speak without dunking her head underwater improves quickly as her control over her gills increases, allowing her tones to form consistently coherent words.

Gareth spends every spare moment he has with Marina, often in our North Tower washroom, both of them completely submerged in our cold tub so she can effortlessly talk and sometimes sing to him in haunting, flute-like tones until deep into the night.

CHAPTER NINETEEN

EVIL ONES

I open my violin case with reverent hands, my eyes immediately drawn to the crimson sheen of the Alfsigr spruce. It was a gift from Lukas that I've been meaning to return to him, but I can't find the will to part with it.

It's been weeks since I've played, but the bundle of sheet music that arrived this afternoon has me lifting the Maelorin violin from its bed of green velvet and setting bow to string. The music is from Lukas, written in his own hand—discordant and fractured, his usual precision giving way to something raging and turbulent, as if he's blasted the notes on to the page.

When I attempt to play the pieces, I can only make it through about half of each composition before I have to stop. It's too raw and too reminiscent of the same amorphous conflict that's mounting inside me—a struggle against a powerful current that's all too easy to get swept up in, an essential part of him trapped.

Eventually, I give up and put the instrument away, but

the disturbing music lingers in my mind and thrusts me into a troubled confusion. It's as if Lukas has embedded a hidden message for me in the notation, and in the middle of his most turbulent piece, he's written one word amid the violent crescendo.

Elloren.

Feeling suddenly restless and needing to walk, I grab up my cloak and lantern, my wand already pressed into my boot.

"Where are you going?" Marina asks me from where she sits by the fire.

"Naga's cave," I tell her.

"I want to come."

I raise my brow at her. "Are you sure? My brothers might be there. And other men."

"Gareth?" There's a heightened intensity in her ocean eyes. I know that Gareth has become one of the few solid moorings in her life.

"He might be."

Marina stands and braces herself against the bed's headboard. "You say your people want to help free my sister." Her gills ruffle, and her words momentarily devolve into incoherent tones. She tenses her throat and pulls her gills in flush with her neck. "I need to meet with the rest of them. Let me come."

"All right, then." I cede, inspired by her courage. "Come with me."

It's slow going as Marina and I cross the North Tower's field and slip into the dark forest. She's prone to stumbling, and I have to hold on tight to her as we pick our way through the woods toward Naga's cave.

The trees are remarkably subdued as Marina and I weave

around them, but I can feel their attention disconcertingly set on me.

As if they're lying in wait.

When Marina and I near the small clearing, the bonfire becomes visible through the silhouettes of the trees, the fire sending up slender, golden arms of flame. I can hear my brothers' familiar voices and Diana's laughter, and I'm able to catch small glimpses of them sitting around the bonfire in relaxed camaraderie, Trystan balancing a ball of compact white lightning over the tip of his wand.

Everyone turns as we enter the clearing. I look just past them, toward the cave, and a rush of shock bolts through me.

Naga is out in the open with Yvan slouched against her side.

I grip at Marina's arm as Naga sets her reptilian gaze on me. Trystan's ball of lightning is immediately snuffed out as both he and Gareth rise to their feet.

"Marina," Gareth says with evident astonishment, the silver tips of his hair glittering in the firelight.

Rafe's arm has fallen away from Diana's shoulder, and Tierney and Jarod sit frozen beside them, everyone's eyes riveted on Marina. Andras and Ariel blink at us, Naga's splinted back leg held slightly suspended between them.

Only Wynter seems unsurprised, her silver gaze serene, her pale arm loose around Naga's muscular neck.

Rafe gets up and smiles warmly at Marina. "Welcome." He motions loosely toward the seats around the fire. "Please, join us."

Marina's nostrils flare, and she takes a shaky step backward.

"Are you all right?" I ask her.

Marina closes her eyes tight and jostles her head, as if trying to pry loose a torturous remembrance. "The men," she rasps out. "Their *smell*..."

Diana rises, her amber gaze fierce. "You have nothing to fear," she says, emphatic. "No one here will harm you."

I glance uneasily at Naga, remembering how she tried to attack me only a few months ago, fast as lightning, stopped only by Yvan and the bars of her cage.

The dragon is still peering at me through slitted eyes that glow a burning gold, as if they've caught fire. Her mouth lifts with what looks like wry amusement in response to my discomfiture.

I glance back at Marina to find her gills ruffling out, as they're wont to when she's deeply unsettled. Still, she forces her head up, a look of stormy resolve on her face.

Seemingly pleased by Marina's obvious show of courage, Diana straightens and gestures formally toward her brother. "Marina the Selkie, this is my brother, Jarod Ulrich." Diana hesitates, appearing for a moment like she's swallowing back her tongue, her lips twitching as she visibly bites back the longer lineage introduction. Rafe watches her closely, his eyes sparkling with mirth.

"It's good to meet you, Marina," Jarod says with a dip of his head. I notice that his face is wan and stressed, but relief rushes through me to have him back in our circle again.

Diana introduces Marina to my brothers, then sweeps her hand towards Andras. "And this is Andras. He is the University's equine physician."

"I am honored to meet you," Andras says to Marina, his low voice warm and gentle.

Naga is still watching me closely, her left wing intricately splinted, a riot of firelight reflecting off her onyx scales and horns. I wince as I take in the large M branded onto Naga's front flank—the mark of the Mage Council.

Yvan is reclining back against Naga's shoulder, his arm draped casually over her front leg, quietly watching me. I've never seen him so at ease, but I hesitate to move forward, eyeing Naga with more than a small amount of trepidation.

A crooked smile forms on Yvan's lips. "Relax, Elloren. If she wanted to kill you, you'd be dead already."

I frown at him, thrown by his rakish demeanor around Naga.

"It's true. Naga means you no harm, Elloren Gardner," Wynter says, her palm flat on the scales of Naga's neck, giving voice to the dragon's thoughts. Then she looks to Marina. "And she is a friend to you as well, Marina. And to all the Selkies. Naga is a friend to all of those in captivity."

Dubious, I meet the dragon's gaze. Naga eyes me with dark humor, then cranes her serpentine neck up and blows out a stream of golden fire. I gasp as a shower of sparks rains down on our circle, Trystan expeditiously swatting at one that lands on his tunic's arm.

"Holy Ancient One," I breathe to Naga. "You've got your fire back."

Naga's reptilian expression turns smug. Yvan inclines his head toward the dragon, then lets out a short laugh, his green gaze sliding back to me, as if in response to an acerbic comment from Naga.

I shoot him a knowing look. *I know you're speaking to her with your mind. We all do.*

"We've fixed Naga's leg," Ariel crows to me, her triumphant smile blackened from the nilantyr berries, her raven perched on her shoulder. Her mouth twists into a sneer. "Soon she'll be able to kill you with all four sets of claws."

"You did a good job, Ariel," Andras says as he surveys Naga's splinted leg with deep satisfaction, overlooking Ariel's penchant for sniping at everyone. "It's a nice set, and the *Asterbane* paste you made has finally gotten her wounds to close. She should be able to put weight on it soon."

Ariel's unfriendly grin fades, and she glances over at Andras as if wildly thrown by his praise. She turns oddly reticent, her threadbare wings agitatedly flapping as she abruptly gets up and joins Wynter near Naga's head, her raven flying off to light on a branch. The dragon rubs her scaled cheek against Ariel's shoulder in a very feline gesture of affection. Ariel throws her arms around Naga's neck, and the dragon closes her eyes and lets out a rumbling purr.

Yvan's mouth lifts into a satisfied half smile, his gaze on me almost sultry, and my face warms in response to it.

Sweet Ancient One, you're beautiful.

"Come, sit with me," Gareth invites Marina, extending his hand to her.

Marina lets Gareth lead her to a seat between himself and Tierney, and I sit down beside them, intensely aware of Yvan's eyes tracking me.

Gareth's arm comes around Marina's shoulder with an ease that catches my eye. Distracted, Marina lifts her head and smells the air, her eyes carefully homing in on Rafe, like an animal assessing a potential predator.

"This one," Marina says to Diana, angling her chin toward Rafe. "He is your mate, no?"

"Not as of yet," Diana says, smiling congenially. "Soon."

Marina studies Rafe, her brow tensing. She sniffs hard. "He is not a shifter." She turns to Diana, appearing deeply perplexed. "Is he as strong as you?"

Diana huffs out an indulgent sound. "Oh, *please.* I could snap him like a twig."

Trystan coughs out a laugh and turns to Rafe, amused. "Are you intimidated by your girlfriend yet, my brother?"

Rafe's mouth twitches up. "Not at all, my brother." He grins at Trystan and throws him a mischievous look. "I happen to enjoy the company of strong women."

Marina turns and focuses in on Yvan. "You were there. The day Elloren freed me."

Yvan regards Marina with the dragon's same even, unblinking stare. "I was."

Marina's nostrils suddenly flare and she stiffens, drawing back. "What *are* you?"

Yvan's whole demeanor instantly shifts from languid ease to a darkly shielded rigidity.

"You are other," Marina whispers, hunching down as if faced with a potential threat.

"He's a man of mystery," Rafe puts in with a smirk.

"Another Evil One," Trystan idly states as he forms a rotating ball of lightning over his wand's tip. "We're all Evil Ones here."

"Evil Ones?" Marina cautiously asks, uncomprehending.

I glower at Trystan. "My brothers have a strange sense of humor."

"Well, it's true," Trystan says as he transforms the lightning ball into a roiling orb of deep blue fire. "According to the glorious and most holy *Book of the Ancients*, we're all Evil Ones. Except, maybe, for Ren here."

I bristle at Trystan's singling me out, but Andras's broad chest rocks with a deep laugh. He gives my brother a wry look. "Yes, you Gardnerians cast a wide net with your Evil Ones."

Trystan eyes Andras sidelong. "That we do. It's our special talent." He casts the fiery blue ball into the bonfire, the flames momentarily burning with a stunning variety of vivid blues.

Gareth, Marina and Tierney fall into low conversation with my brothers and Andras. Wynter pairs off with Ariel, the two of them gathering the splinting supplies and disappearing into the cave.

THE IRON FLOWER

My attention is inexorably drawn to Yvan, as it always is when he's near. He's leaning toward Naga, no longer at ease. Their eyes are set on each other with intense focus, as if they're immersed in a silent, tension-fraught conversation, and Yvan nods stiffly every so often.

Without warning, a malicious wave of unease flows in from the trees like a dark tide, and a vision of phantom branches curling around my throat invades my mind. Ire rises within me, and I survey the blackness of the forest, my fire lines instinctively kindling faster than they ever have before. I close my eyes and mentally stoke them higher, surprised when my inner fire ratchets up to an invisible, steady blaze, then a hot stream of flame. Exhilarated by this new sense of control over my lines, I tense my whole body and exhale sharply, blasting my invisible affinity fire out on all sides of me and toward the forest in a powerful wave.

The trees fall back, their blistering hatred forced down as if hit by a concussive power. I pull in a deep breath, heat pulsing through me with delicious tension.

When I open my eyes, I find Yvan staring at me with a stunned expression, his eyes edged gold with fire.

I feel instantly exposed, as if I had thrown off my clothes in front of him. Fear slashes through me—fear that he's sensed the full extent of my grandmother's magic in my lines.

And that he'll be repulsed by it.

But his gaze is the opposite of repulsed. He looks...enraptured.

An invisible tendril of his fire power reaches out for me and twines through my fire lines, heightening the blaze. I pull in a shuddering breath, my affinity lines giving a hard flare in response to his fire, an intoxicating warmth sliding through me.

Yvan's gaze remains fixed on me, discreet and darkly private. As if he's giving in to something forbidden. Emboldened by his attraction to my power and equally tempted to disregard our carefully drawn boundaries, I coax more fire into my lines and let it flow brazenly out toward him.

The smile he sends me in return is subtle, but the flame in his eyes intensifies.

I look away, wildly flustered, only to find Jarod and Naga watching Yvan and me intently. Naga's probing gaze snags mine, and I can tell by her shrewd look that she senses my fire. Jarod averts his eyes, as if he's just intruded on something intimate, and I imagine that, like Naga, he's picked up on some semblance of what just transpired between Yvan and me.

Flushing with embarrassment, I draw my fire sharply in, struggling to avoid contact with Yvan's power, and I can sense him doing the same.

"At some point, when you feel ready," Rafe is saying to Marina, leaning forward and distracting me from my combustible haze, "can you tell us everything that's happened to you? Everything you remember? We want to get your sister and the other Selkies to safety, but we'll need your help."

Marina seems to be actively fighting off her unease over Rafe's distinctly male smell. She swallows and pulls her gills in. "I will try."

"We have a pretty good idea of where they might be, but anything you can tell us would be helpful," Rafe says.

Marina nods. She opens her mouth slightly, as if about to say more, then stops, her gills ruffling. She shakes her head, her expression devolving into one of anguish.

Tierney says something to her, too quietly for me to hear, but it seems to calm Marina. She looks at Tierney gratefully, and then her expression sharpens suddenly, her eyes lighting with recognition. She leans in to sniff Tierney's neck, inhaling deeply as Tierney stiffens at the unexpected contact.

"You smell *good*," Marina marvels, pulling back to meet Tierney's eyes. "Like water. Like rain."

Tierney spits out a facetious laugh. "Really, do I?" she says, but the repartee catches in her throat, and her eyes gloss over with sudden tears. She leans forward and hides her face in her hands, her whole body going rigid.

Andras goes to Tierney and lowers himself on one knee before her, his hand coming to rest on her skinny arm. "Tierney," he prods, his deep voice kind, "look at me."

Tierney shakes her head stiffly, but Andras quietly waits. Eventually, she looks up at him, her face slick with tears. "You will not be in this glamour forever," Andras assures her.

"You're wrong," Tierney counters, her voice rough. "I'll never be free of it."

"Magic that can be set can also be undone," Trystan puts in. "Always."

"My mother told me that the Amaz are working on breaking Fae glamours, so the Fae refugees can take their true forms once again," Andras says to her, his hand still gentle on her arm, and I'm heartened to hear that he and his mother are on speaking terms again.

Tierney emphatically shakes her head. "They combined multiple glamours to make this one. It's fused to me with Asrai magic as strong as steel."

"The Amaz combine runic systems," Andras replies. "It makes their rune-sorcery very powerful. They'll find a way."

"I don't want to be in this cage anymore," Tierney says to Andras, impassioned. "I could merge with water if I could regain my true form. I could breathe in it. I want to be who I really am…" She stops, her mouth trembling as Andras pulls her into a warm embrace. Marina looks on with an expression of quiet devastation.

Overcome, I chance a look back at Yvan. His eyes have cooled to their usual green, but they're still fervidly on me. Perhaps sensing my troubled emotions, he sends out a small tendril of his fire and sets it shimmering straight through my lines.

The spiraling wand pulses against my leg, as if in response to the sudden rush of heat, and I reflexively reach down to touch it through my boot. I can sense my earth and fire lines twining toward the wand, intimately joining with it, and suddenly, I feel a rush of wind racing through me, followed by a slim, flowing trace of water.

Earth.

Fire.

Air.

Water.

Four affinities now quickening inside me, spiraling tightly around the wand.

PART TWO

THE REAPING TIMES

Gwynnifer Croft's eyes are full of excitement as she looks out over the sea of Gardnerian Mages filling Valgard Cathedral's central plaza. Everyone's skin shimmers a spellbinding green in the darkness of the evening—a mark bestowed upon the Mages by the Ancient One's own hand as undeniable proof of the Gardnerians' blessed status.

Gwynn glances down at the glowing, verdant beauty of her own slender hand, an elated rapture filling her. Like most of the other young women here, looping black fastlines swirl over Gwynn's luminous skin, creating a lovely stained-glass effect on her hands and wrists. The women all wear dark fitted tunics over long skirts, like Gwynn's own, and their sacred uniformity fills Gwynn with a heady, comforting sense of belonging to something good and powerful and pure.

The wintry night should be freezing, but Gwynn doesn't even have her cloak on. She doesn't need it. There are huge blessing stars suspended in the air around the plaza's periphery, bigger than waterwheels and crafted from golden flame. Gwynn marvels at their incandescent beauty and how they suffuse the entire plaza with their lambent glow and enveloping warmth.

Soldiers stream into the plaza and fill the cathedral's broad staircase, row by row. The entire Third Division is here, their tunics' shoulders marked with the division's Ironflower insignia. Giddy anticipation swells in Gwynn as she strains to get a glimpse of her young fastmate, Geoffrey.

Wonderful, handsome Geoffrey.

She peers over the black-clad shoulder of the young woman in front of her, then breaks into an enamored smile as she catches sight of her tall, slender fastmate. Geoffrey's close to the top of the sweeping staircase, all of the soldiers around him standing at rigid attention and facing the gigantic crowd.

Gwynn can't help but smile as Geoffrey meets her gaze. His eyes spark and the edges of his mouth lift as he beams back at her in adoration. Geoffrey quickly schools his face back into military solemnity, but he glances back at Gwynn repeatedly, and her heart flutters each time his eyes meet hers.

There's a white bird embroidered on the chest of Geoffrey's black military tunic instead of the traditional silver Erthia orb, marking him as a member of the Styvian sect, the most devout adherents to the teachings laid out in *The Book of the Ancients.*

The most blessed of all the Mages.

Geoffrey's tunic is a reflection of the new Gardnerian flag hanging from the cathedral's front—a design proposed by High Mage Marcus Vogel that replaces the heathen Erthia sphere with the Ancient One's white bird on black.

A sweeping cheer rises up from the crowd as Marcus Vogel himself steps out onto a large platform at the staircase's broad pinnacle. Gwynn is swept up in the excitement of her people, a bolt of tingling fervor flashing through her as the crowd goes wild.

Vogel is all lithe grace and power, the sharp, elegant planes of his face shining with a verdant glow, his priestly tunic emblazoned with the Ancient One's white bird.

Vogel draws up behind the Ironwood podium at the center of the platform and looks out over the crowd as if they belong to him.

Gwynn trembles as she basks in his presence. *The most righteous and blessed amongst us.*

A line of Level Five Mages stands in an arc behind Vogel, along with several priests and Mage Council members. Four young Mage Council envoys bracket him, two on each side. Their faces fill with pride as Vogel raises both arms in a gesture for silence.

The crowd abruptly quiets, excitement thrumming on the air.

The Council's elderly Light Mage steps onto the dais. He flicks his wand and three rotating, glowing deep green runes appear in the air, hovering just below Vogel's head like small planets.

"Mages," Vogel says in a booming, sonorous voice, amplified by the runes. "*Too long* have the Evil Ones been allowed to run rampant over Erthia." His eyes sweep across the rapt crowd, and Gwynn's heart strains toward him, like the tide yearning for the moon. "*Too long* have the heathens and Fae-blooded been allowed to procreate like wild beasts on Mage land and in the cursed wilds."

Vogel grows momentarily silent, and Gwynn feels her whole-self falling into that silence.

Everyone waits, the crowd of thousands hanging suspended as if by a slender thread.

Vogel's penetrating gaze fills with zealous fire. "They

thought they could destroy us. The Kelts. The Urisk. The Fae. They enslaved us. Abused us. Mocked us. They tried to crush us under their heels." His eyes flick over the crowd like a flash of lightning. "But we have quietly filled ourselves with the will of the Ancient One. And now the Magedom is set to roll over Erthia like a *mighty river of power.*"

The crowd breaks like a storm, cheering and yelling and crying out as one torrential force.

The beautiful Magedom. Holy and strong and true.

Caught up in the fervor, Gwynn sends up an impassioned cheer, tears sheening her eyes, her smile so wide she feels like joy will burst right out of her to flow over all the other Mages.

The crowd eventually quiets, and Vogel opens *The Book of the Ancients* that's set on the podium before him.

The entire crowd listens, rapt, as he begins to read the ancient story of the prophetess Galliana. His voice swells when he describes how she rescued the blessed Magedom from an army of demons, wielding both the Sacred Wand of Myth and the demon-slaying Ironflowers.

Gwynn frowns as she scans the crowd, her gaze lingering on the less strict women of the non-Styvian sect. Their tunics are close-fitting and edged with forbidden Fae colors—purple, gold, saffron, rose. Gwynn looks down at her own chaste, pure black tunic with pride. When Vogel's impending heathen purge of Gardneria was announced, some of these non-Styvian Mages actually cried and protested the idea of surrendering their Urisk workers and servants. These Mages are objects of suspicion now—unholy *staen'en* traitors, forming ties with the heathens who seek to smite Mages.

A shudder of relief passes through Gwynn, followed by deep gratitude for her strict Styvian upbringing, her family above reproach and doing business only with other Styvian Gardnerians, avoiding all heathens and their polluting ways.

Geoffrey catches Gwynn's eye and sends her a playful half smile. Sparks tingle down her spine as she remembers how he wrapped himself around her all night, and love swells in her heart.

We'll have pure, blessed Mage children, Geoffrey and me. And they'll grow up in a world free of Evil Ones.

Vogel finishes his reading and grows silent, pulling Gwynn's attention from her blissful thoughts.

"The time of the Prophecy is upon us, Mages," he says with searing import. "The heathens have their Icaral demon, but he is still a small baby, filled with depravity and easily slain."

As Vogel details how the Fifth Division Mages are tracking the babe down, guilt rises and twists inside Gwynn. Guilt she can't share with anyone.

She knows the mother of the Icaral demon.

Sage Gaffney was once her friend. They met when they were young girls of thirteen, brimming with excitement during their fasting day and caught up in Gwynn's fanciful, wildly adventurous story about the Wand of Myth.

What was I thinking? Gwynn agonizes. *How could I have stolen that wand from Father's armory? And how could I have given it to Sage?*

And now, Sage has been twisted by the Evil Ones. She's run off with a Kelt and broken her sacred fasting. And she's given birth to an abomination of a child.

The Icaral of Prophecy.

Pain and deep regret stab through Gwynn. And warning—that horrific danger waits for any Mage who strays from the Ancient One's strict path.

"Hold fast to your faith, Mages," Vogel's strident voice

charges. "Just as one point of the Prophecy rises—" he pauses, eyes blazing "—so shall another."

There's a ripple of movement behind him as a young female Mage is brought forward, carefully supported by two young soldiers. Gwynn recognizes the young woman immediately, the crowd murmuring in dismay all around her.

Fallon Bane.

Gwynn's heart falls like a stone as she takes in the young woman's weakened state. Fallon Bane was supposed to be the shining point of the Prophecy. A new Black Witch—defender of Gardneria and destroyer of Icaral demons.

But she's been struck down by the Evil Ones.

Fallon stands now at the front of the platform, propped up by the Mages beside her. With great effort, she pulls her wand from its sheath and thrusts it into the air.

Suddenly, a spinning cloud bursts up from Fallon's upturned wand, and Gwynn gasps along with the entire crowd, her eyes widening with surprise. The cyclone rapidly gains size and speed, sending an icy wind through the plaza that abruptly extinguishes the flaming blessing stars.

Cold roars in.

Gwynn wraps her arms around her uncloaked body, the sudden chill biting and severe.

Fallon raises her wand higher, and the cyclone gives way to a dazzling spiral of crystalline ice. The crystals break free of the spiral and fountain high into the night sky, long as spears, fanning out over the plaza like a scattering flock of birds.

Gwynn's teeth begin to chatter, the cold air needling her lungs as she watches the countless ice spears start their descent, whistling as they fall. The whole crowd murmurs in growing confusion, then cries out, arms raised high in a futile attempt to protect themselves from the incoming spears.

Gwynn's heart pounds against her ribs like a hammer, but she grits her teeth and faces the jagged ice shards boldly.

The Ancient One's will be done. The Ancient One's will be done.

Gwynn pulls in a hard breath as the spear that's hurtling toward her stops a hand span from her face, quivering in the air just before her forehead. Before she can exhale, the spear explodes, along with all the others, into a puff of ice that rains down on her skin.

Gwynn looks around, stunned and cold, but filled with a strange elation. Mages are silently pulling themselves up from the ground, shock and fear stark on their ice-dusted faces.

"Pray with me, Mages," Vogel says, bowing his head as Fallon is slowly led away. "Oh, most holy Ancient One," Vogel intones. "You delivered us in primordial times from the jaws of demonic forces. You prophesized the Reaping Times to come."

Vogel looks up from his prayer, a righteous fury pulsing out from him that Gwynn can sense straight through her affinity lines. "Mages, it is time to reap the unholy ones." The High Mage's voice pitches low with savage resolve. "We will flush them out of our cities. We will flush them out of the wilds. We will flush them out of this Realm and the next. We will flush them out with the full power of the Ancient One behind us."

Vogel throws his wand up, and bloodred fire explodes from its tip, slashing over the crowd like a giant, flaming whip. The fiery blessing stars blaze back to life with red fire, and a grateful moan escapes from Gwynn, echoed by the crowd as warmth rushes back over the plaza. Then Vogel directs his fire into the sky, like a giant crimson torch, up and up and up until the flame rises clear above the Valgard Cathedral.

"Bring the Reaping Times, Mages!" he cries out.

The crowd's thunderous response consolidates into one, singular chant.

"Vogel! Vogel! Vogel! Vogel!"

Tears of pure joy stream down Gwynn's cheeks as she cries out the High Mage's name. But her cheer is abruptly strangled out as a shadowy, twisted tree shudders to life in the back of her mind.

Stunned by the sudden vision, Gwynn grows silent amid the frenzied crowd. Her eyes light on the gray wand in Vogel's hand. She has an unsettling sense of its power from clear across the plaza, as if it's brushing against her affinity lines, lightly strumming them with skeletal fingers.

Then there's a sharp pull on her affinity lines from the opposite direction, holding her back from the draw of Vogel's wand. Another image forces its way into Gwynn's mind—a tree made of starlight, ivory birds nesting in its branches. The starlight tree's incandescent light winds around the shadow tree, quickly rendering it to fading smoke.

A flash of remembrance fills Gwynn's mind, and suddenly she's thirteen years old again, handing the stolen Wand of Myth over to Sage Gaffney. Helping Sage escape to isolated Halfix with the Wand in tow, the Wand now hidden and safe in the hands of the young Light Mage.

Gwynn had long ago discarded the idea that the wand she stole was the actual Sacred Wand of Myth. Over time, she had dismissed it as a foolish, childhood imagining.

But now, that childlike belief rushes back. The fierce bond of the Wand of Myth. The comfort of the living, starlight tree. The Watchers, so like the birds pictured all around…

Wildly confused, Gwynn looks toward Vogel, and a scream threatens to tear from her throat.

The four envoys surrounding him have horns of shadowy smoke curling up from their heads.

Terror brands Gwynn like a hot iron, but everyone around her is joyful and crying and cheering, their beatific faces set on Vogel.

They can't see the horns.

The air is torn from Gwynn's lungs as she remembers it all. The two envoys who came to her home so many years ago. Glamoured demons searching for the wand.

None of it was a child's game. None of it imagined.

Gwynn's mind struggles for purchase, for some way out of this dawning nightmare.

If her childhood imaginings were real. If those envoys from so many years ago were truly demons...

Then Sage Gaffney has the true Wand of Myth.

Terrified, Gwynn looks to Geoffrey. Her fastmate catches her eye and smiles at her sunnily.

High Mage Vogel needs to be warned, Gwynn realizes desperately. *He needs to be saved from the demonic things surrounding him.*

Gwynn's frantic gaze darts toward the High Mage, latching on to the wand in Vogel's hand. Shadowy smoke tendrils up from the wand's tip, and the sight of it sends her reeling back.

Sweet Ancient One, what is it? What is that thing in his hands?

The answer comes to her in a sweeping rush of certainty as her mind spins and her world falls completely apart. It's the evil tool spoken of in *The Book of the Ancients*. The counterforce to the Wand of Myth.

The Branch of Evil. The Cursed Shard.

Marcus Vogel has the Shadow Wand.

MAGE COUNCIL
MOTION

Mage Vyvian Damon moves to propose
that all Selkies coming to shore in the
Western Realm be immediately executed,
and that aiding or abetting Selkies shall be
grounds for imprisonment.

CHAPTER ONE

KELTANIA

Ice pelts our North Tower window, the rhythmic tapping nearly drowning out the quiet knock at the door. Startled that someone is visiting at this late hour, I pull myself away from the pile of Apothecary, Chemistrie and Mathematics texts on my desk to go answer it.

"Who's there?" I ask, hesitating by the door.

"Yvan," comes the tentative reply.

A wave of surprise washes through me. Yvan hardly ever comes here, and things between us have been awkward ever since we latched hold of each other's fire so wantonly back at Naga's cave.

I open the door, my heartbeat kicking up a notch. The golden glow from the hallway lantern flickers over the hard planes of Yvan's handsome face. He swallows, and I can sense his fire give a sudden flare, as if my very presence unnerves him.

"May I speak with you privately?" he asks with a measured politeness that's at odds with his chaotic fire.

"We could speak here in the hall," I offer, struggling to tamp down the heat that's suddenly kindling along my own lines. I step out of my lodging and shut the door behind me.

Flustered, I sit down on the stone bench, and he takes a seat beside me as I futilely try to ignore the effect his proximity has on me.

"I know someone who can help Marina and the other Selkies," he says, meeting my gaze.

"Who?" I ask, surprise breaking through my unsettling haze of attraction toward him. "That would involve an armed militia, and Jules told me that only the Keltic Resistance has an organized force…"

Yvan smiles wryly. "Have you forgotten where I'm from?"

I blush and return his smile. Of course. If anyone in our small group has a connection to the Keltic Resistance, it would be Yvan.

"A friend of my mother's is one of the Resistance leaders," he tells me. "I've known him since I was a boy. The Keltic Resistance was willing to help both the Fae and the Urisk during the Realm War. Perhaps they'll help the Selkies, too, once they know how horribly they're being treated. And… how they're running out of time."

"Can we send word to him?"

Yvan shakes his head. "We can't send a rune-hawk. It's too risky. They're intercepted regularly. We need to speak with him in person. He lives in Lyndon, my home village."

I'm thrown by this. "What do you mean, 'we'? You think I should come with you?"

Yvan's answering smile sends a tremor of heat shivering through me. "I don't think he'll believe the story if you don't come with me. And—" his green eyes glint with humor "—you're persuasive."

I laugh at this and eye him teasingly. "Am I? Perhaps that's my secret power."

"I think it might be," Yvan says, his tone unexpectedly flirtatious. His gaze lingers on mine, and I have to fight a sudden, restless urge to move closer to him.

"Marina would be the best person for him to talk to," I say, flustered.

Yvan shakes his head. "The trip is taxing, and Marina's not well enough to make it in the form she's in. And it would be nearly impossible to disguise her."

I lean back against the cold stone, silently contemplating. *Traveling to Keltania. With Yvan.* It's hard to wrap my mind around the idea of it.

"What's your friend's name?" I ask.

"Clive Soren. He's a surgeon. He used to work with my father, years back. I apprentice with him during the summers."

"I could get someone to cover for me in the kitchens," I consider, my mind awhirl with the bold idea. "And we have a few days off from classes for the winter break."

A troubled thought occurs to me. "Yvan, I can't leave Verpacia. There's an Icaral who attacked me back in Valgard before I came to University, and if I travel over the border—"

"I'll protect you."

His statement is so unwaveringly firm, it stops me short.

"The border crossing will be a problem," I remind him. "The Verpacian Guard is allied too closely with the Gardnerians. They'll want my aunt's permission before they'll let me through, and she'll certainly never give it."

"We won't be going through the border crossing."

I cough out a laugh. "Yvan, we'd have to. The only other way into Keltania is straight over the Southern Spine."

His lip lifts, as if he's amused that I actually think this could be an obstacle. "We can get over it."

I eye him with wry disbelief. "Are you telling me you can fly? Without wings? Or do you magically sprout them at will?"

Yvan's face tenses, his smile disappearing. "I can climb it."

"The Verpacian *Spine*?" I sputter, confused by the sudden change in his demeanor.

"It's not unheard of. Some Amaz can climb it, as well."

I regard him speculatively, remembering the immense tree he scaled the night we rescued Naga. "So, you have advanced climbing abilities, among your many other supernatural talents. I'll have to go back to my books about the Fae and find out which type can climb vertical cliff faces."

He rolls his eyes at me, amusement quirking the corners of his mouth. The sensual curve of his upper lip snags my attention for a moment, sending a warm flush prickling over my neck.

"Maybe *you* can climb it, Yvan," I point out, struggling to ignore his ridiculous beauty, "but I *can't*."

"I'll help you. Really, Elloren, it will be easy. I never travel home through the border crossing. I always go over the Spine."

"So, you'll carry me clear over the Spine."

He nods slowly, a slight smirk on his lips.

I eye him warily. "I'm not fond of heights."

Yvan looks at me patiently, as if waiting for me to finish protesting, probably knowing that my concern for Marina and the other Selkies will win out over my fear. And there's something else I think he knows—that beneath all the tumultuous feelings and fiery tension between us, I trust him.

"How long is the trip?" I ask, relenting.

"After we get over the Spine, a few hours on horseback. Andras is showing four mares at the Keltanian winter horse market, so we could meet him there and get a horse. Then we can travel to Lyndon, meet with Clive and spend the night at my home. We'll come back the next day."

I eye him skeptically. "Your mother approves of having me stay over?"

He gives me a sidelong, cagey look. "She doesn't exactly know about it."

I laugh bitterly. "Oh, I can just imagine the welcome she'll give me."

"She's fair, my mother. She'll give you a chance."

"I've never traveled outside of Gardneria before," I tell him, both nervous and excited by the prospect. "Except to come here, that is."

"Well," he says, cocking his head to one side, "here's your chance."

I arch an eyebrow at him. "To be surrounded by a whole country of people hostile to me."

He smirks a bit at this and gestures toward my tunic. "You'll need to disguise yourself a bit, but you already dress like a Kelt much of the time."

I glance down at the very un-Gardnerian brown woolen tunic and skirt I usually wear when I'm here in the evening or working in the kitchens. "I guess I do." I hold out my hand, sliding my tunic sleeve up to my elbow. "But what do we do about this?"

My skin shimmers green in the hallway's shadowy light. Yvan brushes a finger over my glittering hand, sending a shiver up my spine and a pulse of his fire through my lines. He pulls his hand back abruptly and looks away, clearing his throat. After a moment he turns back to me, eyeing me sidelong and keeping a careful distance. "You're an apothecary, Elloren," he says softly. "I'm sure you can find a way to disguise your shimmer."

I blush and pull my sleeve back down, wondering how I'm

supposed to go anywhere with him and keep my wits about me. But we have to find a way to help Marina and the other Selkies. That's all that matters right now.

"When do you want to leave?" I ask.

"At week's end, when the winter break begins."

"All right," I tell him, drawing back from my intense attraction to him. "I'll go with you."

A few days later, Yvan and I set out for Keltania before dawn. We take a transit carriage toward the southwestern Spine, then disembark at an isolated stop and hike into the Verpacian wilds while the sun creeps over the horizon.

As we move deeper into the trees, I silently coax my fire lines into a steady, threatening blaze to keep the forest at bay and hurl the fire outward. Yvan's back shudders before me, his head arcing back. He slows to a stop and turns around to cast me a feral look, his green eyes briefly flashing a fiery gold.

The very air feels charged, and for a moment, he seems to be on the verge of saying something. Then he looks away, and I can feel him holding back, struggling to rebuild the wall between us.

"We should keep moving," I say, self-consciously aware that the words come out too breathlessly.

Yvan nods, and we resume our trek through the trees, both of us banking our fire power firmly down. Contained.

We reach the Southern Spine by midmorning, and my throat goes dry as I take in the sheer face of the mountain. It's not quite as high as the Northern Spine, but it's still impossibly steep, a mixture of long stretches of vertical rock and ice scattered with stubby pine trees and low brush.

Flying over the Northern Spine with Lukas on dragon-back was terrifying enough, but I had his magic to ground me and tamp down my debilitating fear.

"Yvan," I say, unable to control the vertigo that's assaulting me as I look at the peaks. "I can't do this. It's too high."

Yvan squints up at the imposing landform, hands on his hips. "You'll be safe," he says, his voice certain.

I shake my head vehemently. "I just don't think I can do it. I'm sorry—"

"I'll be carrying you," he insists. "I'll make sure you don't fall."

I tense my brow at him, my heart slamming against my chest just from *thinking* about climbing the Spine. "Now might be a good time for you to finally explain the exact nature of your mountain-climbing abilities," I say nervously. "It would be encouraging to know that I'm not about to plummet to my death…"

I prattle on as he patiently waits for me to finish. Eventually, I grow quiet and closer to relenting. He has such an aura of calm authority about this.

"You won't fall?" I press.

"No, Elloren," he replies evenly. "I won't."

"Okay," I agree, glancing up at the Spine again. "I'll do it. For Marina."

Yvan nods in understanding.

"So, how do you want to…" I begin, my voice trailing off awkwardly.

He peers up at the mountain again, as if gauging its difficulty. "Wrap your arms…around my neck." He gestures toward his neck, his voice becoming slightly stilted.

"From…the back?" I wonder, my face warming. The dreams I've had about him flash uncomfortably through my mind.

"No," he says, "from the front."

I hesitate, then take a deep breath and step toward him, keeping a polite distance between us. I reach my arms out and rest my hands on his broad shoulders. My cheeks grow warm, my heartbeat kicking up.

I can tell he's flustered by this, as well. I've a sense of him reining his fire tightly in, but chaotic tendrils break through. "Get as close to me as you can," he directs formally. "As flat against me as you can."

I take another deep breath and move right up against him, wrapping my arms tightly around his shoulders, my cheeks burning.

His long, lanky body stiffens against me as he wraps his own arms firmly around my back.

I try desperately not to think about how warm his body is, how good he smells. Like a midnight fire.

"Now wrap your legs around my waist," he says tightly.

What? This is just too much. We're not fasted. This type of thing is completely forbidden.

"Elloren," Yvan says with effort, "I know this is...awkward. But I can't support you if your feet are dangling in the air. I need to be able to move freely. I know it's...highly improper."

"That's an understatement," I say, letting out a nervous laugh, but I move to do as he asks. I take a deep breath and pull at his neck and shoulders, hoisting myself up at the same time he reaches beneath me to support my weight. I wrap my legs around him, my thighs coming to rest just above his hip bones.

My heart is thudding with heated force against my chest, and I can feel his doing the same.

"Now, hold on tight and stay as still as you can," he tells me. "And...you might want to close your eyes."

I nod silently into his sharp shoulder and screw my eyes shut.

His grip on me tightens and his fire ripples through me, hot and strong. The skin of my back prickles with a sweeping heat that courses through my fire lines and makes me shiver.

Yvan starts to move, the muscles of his neck and shoulders tensing against my hold as he leaps up, steadily and effortlessly. I can feel his strength, his grace as his arms and legs move around me, and I quickly abandon all shyness to cling tightly to him for dear life.

I don't dare open my eyes or think about how much slick ice coats the Spine as we ascend at what feels like breakneck speed. Instead, I try to remember complicated apothecary formulas. I silently recite the names of different constellations. I think about the steps of making a violin in sequence and try to visualize them all.

After a while, an icy wind picks up, and the sounds around us are different—open and stark. I realize we must be quite high above the trees.

Then our orientation changes, and I feel Yvan's hands beneath my thighs, steadying me. "Are you okay?" he asks gently, and I nod into his shoulder.

"We're at the top," he says, keeping a tight hold on me as wind whips against us. "The view is beautiful."

I open my eyes slightly, glimpsing a dazzling blue sky above. He turns and hoists me up a fraction so I can see the view over his shoulder, and I gasp with wonder.

We're on a bare outcropping of rock, the wilds past the Southern Spine splayed out before us. The villages of Keltania are tiny and still far off, the land snow-dusted and glittering in the sunlight. It's so spectacular, and I should be freezing, but I'm not at all. Yvan's so decadently warm.

I close my eyes again when we begin the descent, an almost vertical drop. After a while, the sharp smell of pine trees grows stronger, and before I know it, Yvan's stepping onto level ground.

"We're down, Elloren." His lips brush against my neck as he says it, warm and soft.

I open my eyes to see a thick pine forest surrounding us. Yvan loosens his hold on me as I drop my feet to the ground. I untwine my arms from his neck and step back, instantly missing his warmth as the cold snakes in under my cloak.

But more than the warmth, I miss being so close to him.

"So, what are you, Yvan?" I ask, trying to keep my tone light. "Mountain Goat Fae?"

He smiles slightly at my joke, but then his expression turns pained.

"Yvan, is it really that bad?" I ask gently.

He doesn't answer, but the anguished look that momentarily passes over his face fills me with concern for him. Whatever it is, it *is* that bad, and he clearly doesn't want to talk about it.

At least not with me.

Yvan averts his eyes, his face tensing. "We should be on our way. Andras will have the horses waiting for us. And we'll want to reach Lyndon before dark."

I nod in agreement, and we continue on, side by side, winding through the trees, our arms bumping against each other every now and then. Every time it happens, a zing of heat trickles through my fire lines, and we give each other a hesitant smile, and I resist the urge to take his hand.

My mind wanders back to the night we freed Naga. I remember how Yvan touched my face; how it seemed like he wanted to kiss me. And that night by her cave, when we recklessly let our fire power rush toward each other. In those rare moments, it was as if his true self finally emerged. And for a brief moment earlier, when we were wrapped around each other climbing the Spine, it felt like that again.

Feeling reckless, I let my hand lightly bump into Yvan's and hook a finger around his. He inhales sharply, and I feel the hard flare of his fire power as he shoots me a heated look.

Then he twines his fingers wordlessly through mine.

Eventually, we come to the end of the wilds, and I can hear the sound of male voices mixed with horses snorting and whinnying up ahead.

"Make sure you hide your hair and pull down your hood," Yvan cautions me, peering out through the trees and dense brush toward the horse market, his fingers still clasped around mine.

My face is already camouflaged by a dye Tierney mixed for me, the tone a ruddy Keltic coloring to hide the green glimmer of my skin, and my hair is mostly hidden by a long white linen scarf wrapped around my head.

I let go of Yvan's hand and push every last strand of my jet-black hair under the scarf, drawing the hood of my cloak over it. Then I pull up my woolen scarf, hiding the lower half of my face.

"Do I still look like my grandmother?" I ask him, the wool of my scarf scratching against my lips as I speak.

"No," Yvan says with an affectionate smile as he assesses me. "You look Keltic. I don't think your grandmother would have been caught dead in clothing like that." He holds out his elbow, and I thread my arm through his. "Just stay close to me until we find Andras."

Activity swirls all around us as we enter the market. Multiple horse dealers show off steeds of every color and breed. Keltic men kneel next to the animals, studying them, running their hands down the animals' legs to check for defects, bargaining for a good price.

The warm smell of horse droppings, fur and hay hangs heavy in the air. The pungent scent brings back good memories of caring for our own two horses at Uncle Edwin's and happy times riding with my brothers.

Andras's horses are by far the healthiest and best-looking of all the horses there, and he's surrounded by a number of interested buyers. He catches sight of us and waves, then says something to the men around him and strides over to where we wait near the pasture's gate.

"Hello, Andras," Yvan says.

Andras nods in greeting and glances up at the Southern Spine. "I didn't expect to see you two until much later. You made good time."

"It was my extraordinary climbing abilities," I nervously joke. "It was like I owned the Spine. I was getting a little tired of having to keep rescuing Yvan from falling to his death, though. It got old *real* fast."

Andras cocks one black eyebrow at me in surprise as Yvan's mouth lifts into a wry grin.

"Sorry," I mutter. "I'm a bit on edge."

Andras laughs and goes to fetch our mount, returning a few seconds later with a beautiful ebony mare, to the evident disappointment of the man who was assessing her.

The mare is already saddled up and ready to go, and I feel grateful for Andras's attentiveness.

"You don't have to hurry," Andras tells us. "I'll be here all day tomorrow. I'll wait for you."

Yvan takes a few minutes to pat the mare's neck and mane to soothe her before easily swinging himself into the saddle. Andras helps me climb up behind Yvan before he makes his way back to his prospective buyers.

As I watch Andras's broad back recede, I wrap my arms around Yvan's waist and pull myself in tight against him. The muscles of his abdomen stiffen in response, but then he relaxes. It feels intimate, holding on to him like this. And more than a bit thrilling.

"So," Yvan says, turning his head so he can peer back at me, his lips lifting in a teasing smile. "It sounds like I can count on you to help me back over the mountain tomorrow."

"Only if you ask me very nicely," I say enticingly, wrapping my arms a little tighter around him. "And say 'please.'"

I rue the overly flirtatious words as soon as they're said, acutely aware that we're crossing too many boundaries with each other.

Yvan's banked fire gives a hard flare, his eyebrows go up, a spot of color lighting his cheek.

"I'm sorry," I backtrack. "I'm just…nervous."

"It's okay," he says, smiling slightly, his hand coming up to caress mine, and my breathing turns erratic.

Yvan stiffens, as if he's suddenly remembered himself, his hand falling away from mine. He makes a sharp clicking sound, jerks his heels in toward the horse, and we're off.

CHAPTER TWO

THE SURGEON

For the next hour we travel through small Keltanian villages and farms, and a growing feeling of shame and dismay descends upon me.

I've never seen true, widespread poverty before, and I know that my people are largely to blame for the hardship that plagues Keltania. While the Gardnerians live in ornate towns and cities, feasting on food harvested from lush, fertile fields, this country is downtrodden and worn, its people weathered and subdued.

I remember reading about what happened during the Realm War—how the Gardnerian forces drove the Kelts off the most fertile farmland, drastically shrinking the country's borders and uprooting families who had worked the same fields for generations. I can almost hear Lukas's voice in my mind, smugly reminding me that the Kelts treated the Fae in much the same fashion. But as I survey the scenes around me, I'm more certain than ever that it's past time to find a better way.

THE IRON FLOWER

Late afternoon descends, the day growing increasingly cold and overcast as dark clouds gather in the sky. Yvan and I stop briefly outside a small tavern to tend to our horse and eat. Andras has packed bread, cheese and dried fruit for our trip, and I fish the food eagerly out of one of the saddlebags as Yvan ties the mare's reins to a hitching post.

People come and go about their business, their horses blowing out steam from warm noses as they pass.

As Yvan sets some food out for our horse, a muscular, elderly man spots him from across the wide dirt road and yells his name. The man's snow-white beard pokes out from under his scarf and his warm brown eyes are full of delight.

Yvan straightens as he approaches.

"Yvan, my boy," the man beams, reaching up to squeeze Yvan's arm. "Let me have a look at you, lad. It's been a good, long while, it has. You're turning into quite the tall young fellow, aren't you now?" He looks to me with rosy-cheeked good humor. "And who's this you have here with you? A lady friend?" His eyes twinkle at Yvan, full of mischief. "And not Miss Iris, by the looks of it."

"No," Yvan says, his voice level. "This is Ren. Ren, this is Phinneas Tarrin, a longtime friend of my family."

It surprises me, his calling me Ren. That's something only my brothers and Gareth call me, but I realize immediately how smart this is. Like a fake name, but one I can easily remember.

"Ah, so it's Ren now, is it?" Phinneas chides Yvan, his tone full of suggestion.

"It never was Iris," Yvan replies evenly.

"Not if she had any say in it, lad!" Phinneas chortles, slapping Yvan on the back. "You playing hard to get all the time! Poor Miss Iris. Ah, well, such is the fickleness of youth. Pretty eyes, this one has." He leans in toward Yvan, as if about to tell him an important secret. "Better not let Miss Ren here get away."

"I won't."

His promise both surprises and warms me.

"You don't want to end up a lonely old coot like me," Phinneas jokes, eyes twinkling mischievously. His gaze turns wistful. "Exactly two years and twelve days since the missus passed away. Ah, well, I'll be joining her soon enough, if the Gardnerians have any say in the matter. All of us will, no doubt. No match for their Mages and dragons, the whole lot of us. But no matter. Better to go down fighting, I say."

Phinneas winks at Yvan, then wraps an arm around my shoulder. "Be careful of this young man, lass. Hangs with a dangerous crowd, he does. Lot of revolutionaries, every last one of 'em. Stays out of trouble these days, though, off at that University of his." He shoots Yvan a look of mock disapproval. "All that study taking the fight out of you. Ach, it's just as well. Wouldn't want to scare off your lady here. Seems a quiet one, she does."

"She avoids trouble at all costs," Yvan tells him soberly, and it takes all of my self-control to suppress a laugh.

"Best be avoidin' you, then, lad," Phinneas says, chuckling to himself.

"That's good advice, actually," Yvan says, an edge of seriousness to his tone now.

Phinneas peers at Yvan for a brief second, as if momentarily thrown by the comment, then leans in to reassure me. "I'm only joking, Miss Ren. Yvan here, he's a fine young man. Known him most of his life. You'd be hard-pressed to find anyone better." He gives my shoulder one last squeeze before releasing me and patting Yvan's arm. "I best be leaving you two to be on your way. You take good care of Miss Ren, here."

"I will," Yvan replies with conviction.

"All right then," Phinneas says, regarding us warmly. "I'll be off. Give my best to that fine mother of yours."

After Phinneas leaves, Yvan and I share the food, eating in silence. I wonder—rather unhappily—about his long history with Iris, and what Phinneas would have said if I'd removed all my wrappings to reveal I'm not only a Gardnerian, but Carnissa Gardner's granddaughter.

And I also wonder, as I surreptitiously glance at Yvan, what he meant when he told Phinneas he wouldn't let me get away.

"I'm going to get some water for all of us," Yvan says, finishing his food and wiping crumbs off his clothing. "I'll be only a minute or so. Stay with the mare. Horse thievery is pretty rampant here."

I warily scan the crowd as he disappears into the tavern, hoping there won't be any trouble. The threat of thievery is disconcerting, but I can understand how the impoverished people here could be driven to desperate acts to feed themselves and their families.

Yvan is quick about his task, but when he returns with a jug of water, he looks stunned, as if he's just seen a ghost.

"What's wrong?" I ask him.

He waves my question off, his face stricken. "Just more bad news about the Gardnerians. Sometimes there are things that are...difficult to hear."

"Did something happen?" I ask gently.

Yvan hesitates, his eyes looking far away. I notice he's paler than usual. "It's just...someone I know," he says, handing me the jug to stow in our saddlebags. "Someone who went against the Gardnerians."

It's clear Yvan doesn't want to elaborate further, and that

he's deeply upset, so I let it drop. He mounts the mare, then extends a hand to help me into the saddle, and we continue on the road toward Lyndon.

We reach Clive Soren's surgery practice a little before twilight falls, the shadows around us lengthening. It's a sturdy, whitewashed building with a sign outside that reads *Clive Soren, Master Surgeon*.

Yvan strides through the unlocked front door, seeming quite at home here. I cautiously follow, looking around curiously. The front room is filled with dark wooden bookcases containing numerous medical texts, and a row of chairs lines the only spot of wall not covered with books.

Yvan tells me to wait for him, so I take a seat and pull off my winter coverings as he crosses the room to another door, knocking before he enters. I catch a fleeting glimpse of another space much like this one, but instead of books, the shelves are packed with rows of glass jars filled with a variety of medicinal herbs and tonics.

A deep voice booms through the partially open doorway. "Yvan Guriel! What are you doing here?"

I listen as Yvan explains that he brought someone for Clive to meet.

"You seem a bit cagey, Yvan," Clive teases. "It's a woman you've brought, isn't it? Finally found someone at the University, did you? And I'm willing to bet it's not Iris. I imagine she's not too happy about that."

I'm beginning to flat-out despise Iris. I hate that she has a history with Yvan, and I don't. And I hate how everyone we meet wants to talk about it.

Yvan says something else I can't hear, and Clive laughs heartily. A chair scrapes against the wood floor and heavy footsteps make their way toward the door.

It's clear from Clive's expression as he steps into the front room that he's prepared to like me. He's a ruggedly handsome man—tall and broad-shouldered, clean-shaven, with dark brown hair and brown eyes that rival Yvan's in intensity. He also has the air of someone used to being in charge, and who it's best not to cross.

"And you would be?" he asks, his smile dampening a bit as he takes in my black hair, my infamous looks.

I extend my hand. "Elloren Gardner."

The remnants of his smile quickly darken to an expression of stunned outrage. He suddenly looks as if he's holding his breath and fighting back the urge to strike at me with both fists, which are now balled up at his sides.

"I need to speak with you, Yvan," Clive says roughly. He glares at me, strides back into the other room and slams the door.

Stung, I move toward the door, their voices carrying straight through the wood.

"What the hell are you doing? Bringing *her* here?"

"We need your help." Yvan's voice is firm.

"'*We*'? Interesting people you're aligning yourself with these days, Yvan."

"She's not what you think."

"Oh, really? She's not the granddaughter of Carnissa Gardner, then?"

"She is."

"I've never taken you for a complete idiot before, Yvan."

"I'm not."

"Are you sleeping with her? This... *Gardnerian*?" He says the word like it's the vilest insult imaginable.

"No." Yvan's voice is tight with offense.

"So, you haven't given leave of every last one of your senses, then."

"I'm *not* sleeping with her," Yvan says, his tone hard.

There's silence between them for a moment.

"What have you told her about me, Yvan?" Clive's voice is low and combative.

"That you're a friend. Someone who might be able to help us. And that you're involved in the Resistance."

Clive snarls a low oath. "Do you have any idea how dangerous it is to be mixed up with this girl?"

"Yes."

"Has she been wandtested?"

"She's a Level One. She only looks like her grandmother. She has none of her access to power, and Elloren's nothing like her."

More silence.

"What did you come here for, Yvan?"

"Elloren rescued a Selkie."

Silence again, but more prolonged this time. "A Selkie."

"Yes."

"Wait, I *know* I heard you wrong. Did you say that Vyvian Damon's niece rescued…*a Selkie?*"

"Yes."

"From who?"

"The Verpax University groundskeeper."

It's unnervingly quiet again for a long moment. Then the door abruptly opens, and I jump back, looking up to find Clive in the doorway, glaring down at me.

"I… I'm sorry…" I start to stammer.

"Get in here," he growls.

I enter the room tentatively, unsure what to do next.

"Sit down," he orders brusquely, pointing at a chair. Yvan is leaning against a windowsill, his arms crossed in front of himself, watching Clive with an intense expression.

Clive stares at me for a long moment as I sit down, as if sizing me up. "You stole a Selkie."

"*Freed* a Selkie, yes," I reply, straightening to meet his oppressive stare.

"Holy Ancient One, you look like your grandmother."

"So, I've been told," I coolly reply.

He seems momentarily thrown. "It might be advisable for you to keep your face hidden when traveling in Keltania," he warns. "Your grandmother wasn't exactly well loved here."

"I'm well aware of that."

"So, *Elloren Gardner*," Clive says, unable to say my name without contempt seeping through, "what is it you want from me?"

"The Selkies aren't what everyone thinks they are," I explain nervously. "Marina...the Selkie we rescued...she can talk."

Clive looks surprised for a moment. "Are you quite sure?"

"Yes, quite."

His expression turns suspicious. "Selkies have been around for years. The Gardnerians' dirty little secret. Why haven't they bothered talking in all this time if they're able to?"

"Because it's incredibly difficult," I explain. "Speech through air is completely alien to them, and the sounds of our land languages are hard for them to make out. They speak against the resistance of water, not air."

"So why is your Selkie so gifted, then?"

"Marina's talented with languages. And she's had the opportunity to live with people who have been kind to her," I tell him. "It gave her time to learn the Common Tongue. She can speak it fluently now. She's even picked up a fair bit of High Elvish."

"High Elvish?"

"My roommate. She's an Elf."

Clive turns to Yvan for verification.

"An Elfin Icaral," Yvan clarifies.

His eyebrows fly up, and Yvan tells him about Ariel, as well. Clive turns back to me, clearly thrown. "So...this Selkie of yours can speak."

"We could let you meet her, prove it to you," I offer.

"Why is it so important for you to prove this to me?"

This stops me dead in my tracks. I look to Yvan with confusion, so he steps in to explain. "Marina has a sister," he says. "She's been captured, as well. We want to rescue her, and the rest. All of them."

"You want to rescue all of the Selkies," Clive repeats incredulous.

"Yes," Yvan says, his expression adamant. "Before Vyvian Damon convinces the Mage Council to have them all shot."

"And you want the Resistance to help you."

"Yes."

"You want the Resistance to throw its scant resources, with the Gardnerians massing on Keltania's border, into freeing *Selkies*?"

"Not all of your resources," Yvan says stubbornly. "Some."

"The Gardnerians could invade us at any moment."

"They're beating the Selkies," I cut in, enraged. "*Raping* them!"

"I'm well aware of what goes on with the Selkies," Clive snarls.

"They're not animals," I continue, undaunted. "They're people, just like us—"

"So are the people of Keltania!" he snipes back, baring his teeth. "But if we don't hand over our entire country to Gardneria, your people are getting ready to *slaughter* us!"

"The Resistance helped the Fae in the past," I challenge

him. "They helped the Urisk. The Selkies are people. Just like them."

"For years," Clive says, eyes blazing, "I have thought that the Selkie trade is one of the most disgusting, despicable things I have ever seen in all my life." He scrubs a hand over his face, looking furious. "But your government is about to march in here and enslave my entire country! So, I'm sorry that I can't drop everything to rescue a few seal women, but unless the Selkies can help us fight the Gardnerians, they're *useless* to me."

"Yvan said you were interested in justice!" I spit out.

"I am. Justice for *my* people."

"And no one else?"

For a moment, he looks ready to strike me, and perhaps the same worry enters Yvan's mind as he steps toward me protectively.

"I am really trying to treat you like the naive, sheltered Gardnerian princess you no doubt are," Clive says coldly, "but if you push for the truth, you're going to get it."

"Fine," I snap back.

"We have something very similar here, only it's Urisk girls in addition to a few Selkies. And a fair number of our men frequent these...*establishments*." He says the word with disgust. "Most of the men working for the Resistance won't care about a bunch of Selkie whores. They don't care about the Urisk girls, either."

"And are you one of these men?" I demand, disgusted and disillusioned. "Are you off raping Urisk girls and Selkies in your free time?"

Yvan looks visibly ratttled.

"No," Clive says, his eyes full of warning. "I told you I think it's despicable. But I'm a realist, Elloren Gardner."

"So, there's no one, then," I whisper, crushed by the injustice of it all. "No one who'll help them. Only us."

Clive considers me for a moment. Yvan is peering out the window at nothing in particular, his face full of angry tension.

"There might be someone who can help you," Clive says, sounding hesitant.

Yvan and I both turn to him. "Who?" we ask, almost in unison.

"The Amaz."

Yvan and I exchange a look of surprise.

"Go petition their queen," Clive suggests. "Don't bring any men, of course, unless you want to see them beheaded by rune-axes. Ask for Freyja. Tell her I sent you. Tell her *privately*. Don't mention my name around the others."

"Who's Freyja?" I wonder.

Clive looks away, a bitter, melancholy smile on his lips. "An old friend."

She's more than a friend. It's clear from the expression that washes over his face when he says her name.

"They'll help you," he says, looking out the window toward the forest, a faraway look in his eyes. "They can't stand to see women abused in any way. It makes them *very* angry, and if there's one group you don't want to piss off, trust me, it's the Amaz."

Clive turns back to regard me, and I can see something new in his eyes. He believes Yvan—that I'm different than he thought. "If you're going to petition the Amaz," he says, "you must be very careful to observe their protocol when approaching the queen. There's no room for error on this. Do you know someone who can help you learn their customs?"

Yvan tells him about Andras, and Diana and Jarod, as well.

"Does your mother know about any of this?" Clive asks

Yvan, a smile playing on his lips. "Last I heard, she was relieved that you were holed up at the University—quietly studying, staying out of trouble, working in the kitchens and faithfully sending every last extra cent you earn home to her."

"Most of that is true," Yvan says cagily.

"Except for the staying out of trouble part."

Yvan doesn't answer him.

Clive shakes his head and shoots Yvan a sidelong glance. "I wouldn't mind being a fly on the wall when you introduce her to your mother. Are you going to see her now?"

"We're going to stay there tonight," Yvan tells him.

"Well, then. Good luck." Clive glances at me appraisingly. "This may not be...easy. For her to accept."

"My mother's fair-minded," Yvan insists.

Clive's jaw tightens, as if he wants to argue the point, but he holds back. I'm a bit stung by his doubts. I know it's going to be hard for Yvan's mother to meet me. But it was difficult for Clive, too, and he's come around fairly quickly.

Everything will be just fine.

"Yvan," Clive says, as if he's just remembered something. "A dragon was stolen from a Gardnerian military base near that University of yours. You and your friends wouldn't have had anything to do with that, would you?"

My lungs stop working for a moment, and the muscles in Yvan's neck tighten.

"Because an unbroken dragon would be a very useful weapon," Clive adds. "I'd certainly like to get my hands on it."

"That would be up to the dragon to decide," Yvan says calmly, not meeting his piercing gaze.

"Well, then," Clive says, "I would respectfully ask the dragon if it likes the idea of the Gardnerians taking over the entirety of Erthia, killing or breaking every dragon in existence."

Yvan absently eyes the medicine shelves. "If I come across any dragons, I'll relay the message."

Clive lunges forward and grabs Yvan's arm. "Be careful, Yvan. The Gardnerians are smarter than you think. You're all out of your league. I would cease to be a friend to your mother if I didn't warn you of this."

Yvan glances down at Clive's hand on his arm, then slowly looks back up at him, unintimidated. I remember the time Rafe grabbed Diana, and how she considered ripping his arm off. I'm struck by the certainty that Yvan, if he really wanted to, could do the same.

"We'll be careful," Yvan assures him.

Clive releases his arm. "Good." His brow knits together as he glances toward me. "It was interesting meeting you, Elloren Gardner. I hope you don't wind up getting yourself killed." He turns back to Yvan. "Take care of yourself, Yvan. And good luck with your mother. You're going to need it."

CHAPTER THREE

EVIL MAGIC

Yvan's home comes into view just as the last of the day's light is slipping below the horizon. The warm glow emanating from the cozy, well-kept cottage contrasts sharply with the cold dark outside.

Yvan signals to our mare, and she slows to an easy trot as we pass by his mother's expansive gardens, covered up for the winter.

We dismount and enter a small, tidy barn, stabling the mare alongside a dappled gray horse that whinnies happily when it catches sight of Yvan. As I unsaddle our horse and prepare some grain for her, Yvan makes a point of spending a few minutes with the gray gelding, an animal, he tells me, that he grew up with and raised from a foal.

Then we make our way to his house, my heart pounding in anticipation.

Things will be all right, I tell myself. *Yvan said his mother is fair-minded.*

As we approach the cottage, Yvan seems to hesitate. I hug

myself nervously, pulling my woolen cloak tight. The air is chill and damp, and it will only get colder now that the sun is down. I eye the fire-lit windows, yearning to go inside and get warm.

Yvan turns to me, looking unsure. "Perhaps you should wait here, Elloren. I'll speak to her for a moment before I introduce you."

"All right," I agree, feeling increasingly apprehensive.

Yvan walks up to the door and knocks as I stand in the shadow of a large oak tree, like some unwanted thing in hiding. A woman who is obviously Yvan's mother opens the door. She's him, only older and female. They have the same angular, beautiful face, the same riveting green eyes and the same long, lanky build. Only their hair is different, hers a rich, shockingly vibrant red to his brown.

I wonder why Yvan told me he looks just like his father. It's clear he takes after his mother completely.

Yvan's mother gives a start when she spots him, her two slender, graceful hands flying up in delight. She throws her arms around him in a warm embrace.

I push back my cloak's hood and start unwinding my scarf as I watch their joyful reunion. I shake out my hair as I prepare to introduce myself properly—my voice unmuffled by layers of fabric, my features unhidden, only the green glimmer of my skin still disguised. Yvan's mother might as well see me for what I am right off. Best to get the shock over with.

I desperately want to make a good impression on this woman, even more so than I did with Diana's family, and my stomach twists and clenches as I wait.

Yvan says something to his mother that I can't fully make out, but I hear him mention my name. Her smile fades, replaced by a look of confusion. She turns her head in my direction, as if straining to peer into the darkness.

Taking this as my cue to approach, I emerge from the shadows, my heart pounding hard against my chest. As I step closer, the light from inside their house spills over me.

Yvan's mother's expression morphs into one of stunned horror, and she steps backward, almost losing her balance. "Yvan," she gasps, one hand finding her throat, her eyes riveted on me. "What are you doing? Why is that...*thing* here with you?"

Yvan glances over at me with confusion, as if to check that he and his mother are looking at the same person, so violent is her reaction. "She's not a *thing*," he says, placing a steadying hand on his mother's arm. "She's my friend."

Her head whirls around to face him. "Your *friend*?"

"She has a name, Mother. It's Elloren."

"Yvan, I must speak with you," she says with frantic vehemence, her eyes darting toward me as if I'm an evil apparition, something terrifying back from the dead. "Alone. *Now*."

Yvan's brow is knit tight as he sends me a look of concern. "Just give us a moment, Elloren," he says kindly before following his mother into the house.

The door shuts firmly behind them, cutting off most of the light and casting me in frigid shadows once more. It's like Clive Soren all over again.

But Clive quickly came around, I attempt to console myself.

I wait for a moment, feeling cold and dejected, before summoning the courage to step onto their porch and linger by the closed door. Eavesdropping for the second time today makes me uncomfortable, but this is going badly, and I want to know how much worse it's likely to get.

"Have you given leave of your senses?" Yvan's mother hisses. "Do you know what she is?"

"I do," he replies, his voice tight.

"Do you realize how dangerous she is? How dangerous

they *all* are? Why is she with you?" Her voice is filled with grave suspicion.

"I know what you're thinking. You're mistaken."

"Please, Yvan, please tell me she's not your lover."

Yvan hesitates for a moment before answering. "No, she's not."

"Are you in love with her?"

Again, he hesitates. "She's my friend."

"Did I raise you to be such a fool? Do you have any idea what kind of evil magic flows through that girl's veins?"

I wince, all too aware of the unsettling power I feel whenever I'm around Lukas, but Yvan spits out an incredulous laugh. "She's been wandtested, Mother. She's a Level One Mage."

"You can't be friends with that girl, Yvan," she insists, her tone urgent, as if this is shaking her to the core.

"I understand your concern—" Yvan starts, trying to reassure her.

"You don't understand *anything!*" she cries with startling ferocity, her words cutting into me like a whip. "They are monsters, Yvan! *Monsters!* They will do *anything* for power! For control! You have no idea what they're capable of! You were just a child—"

"She's not anything like you think she is!"

"How could you bring that vile creature to our *home?*"

"She's not a *creature!* If you knew her—"

"What, you think *you* know her? You think she can be trusted?" She pauses for a moment, and when she speaks again, her voice is full of fear. "How much have you told her, Yvan? What does she know?"

"Nothing. I've told her nothing."

I'm thrust into a deeper confusion.

"Don't you have *any* respect for the memory of your father?" Yvan's mother rages.

"She didn't choose the family she was born into!" he vehemently counters. "I thought you, of all people, would look past her appearance and give her a chance."

"She is Carnissa Gardner's *granddaughter*!"

"She cannot help who she is! No more than I can!"

"Even if, by some unlikely freak of nature, she's not as monstrous as her relatives, her aunt sits on the Mage Council! She can't stay here, Yvan. I can't have her in my home!"

"We have *nowhere* else to stay."

"*You* have a place to stay, Yvan. You always have a place here. But not that monster you've brought to our home. She will *never* set foot under this roof."

"Then we'll find somewhere else to go." His voice has grown hard as flint.

"Yvan, send her away," his mother pleads. "I'm sure she has more than enough money—"

"No, she doesn't. She works in the kitchens with me."

Yvan's mother makes a contemptuous sound. "I find *that* hard to believe."

"When have I ever lied to you?"

"Of all the young women you go to University with, you pick Carnissa Gardner's granddaughter to be your lover—"

Yvan lets out a bitter laugh at this. "*Lover?* I already told you that's not the case. And please, tell me, Mother, exactly how am I supposed to have a lover?"

This gives her pause. "Yvan... I never..."

"I'm not a child anymore," he says firmly. "And you didn't raise me to be a fool."

"I can't have her here, Yvan. You have to understand that. This girl is a danger to us all."

"Then I'm leaving. Elloren's waiting for me out there in the cold, and it's dangerous for her to travel alone."

"Dangerous, how?"

Yvan hesitates for a long moment before answering. "There's an Icaral after her."

"An Icaral." There's an edge of bitter sarcasm in her tone. "Well, Yvan," she says acidly, "I hope that Icaral finds her."

There's the sound of furniture being pushed against the floor and footsteps approaching the door.

His mother calls out, "Wait... Yvan!"

I jump back as Yvan emerges from the house and slams the door behind him. His eyes are blazing with anger. He strides quickly toward me and takes my arm, leading me away from the house, back to the stable. He's walking so fast, it's almost impossible to keep up with him.

Once we're in the barn, I watch silently as he unhitches our horse, his jaw and neck rigid with tension, his movements clipped, the horses responding to his uneasy mood by growing restless themselves.

We walk away from the house on foot, Yvan leading the horse beside us.

"What are we going to do?" I ask, growing worried as his home disappears behind us. It's dark now, and very cold. I have very little money with me and based on what Clive said earlier about Yvan sending most of his income home, I suspect he's also low on funds. "Where will we stay?"

He doesn't answer me right away, and I can just make out his jaw ticking as he stares straight ahead. Finally, he stops, brings his free hand to his hip and looks down at the ground in frustration before looking back up at me. "I'm sorry, Elloren."

"It's not your fault."

"I didn't think..." His words trail off, replaced by a heavy sigh. Yvan motions ahead with his hand. "There's an inn about a half-hour's ride east. It's not the most luxurious place in the world, but we might be able to find lodging there for the night."

CHAPTER FOUR

LODGING FOR THE NIGHT

"How much for two rooms?" Yvan asks the innkeeper.

I survey our surroundings nervously. Yvan is right about this inn not being the most luxurious place in the world. It's downright seedy. A crowd of Keltic men linger in the small tavern, more than a few quite drunk, some of them leering shamelessly at me as we enter, as if they're trying to make out my figure under my winter wrappings.

I'm immediately and self-consciously aware that I'm the only young woman in this place. There's one other woman here, but she's a mean-looking, scowling crone who glares at me briefly before going back to angrily serving drinks and picking up the mess left by her unruly patrons.

I instinctively move closer to Yvan, threading my arm through his, and he pulls my arm protectively toward himself. The rancid smell of stale pipe smoke coupled with spirits hangs heavy in the air and makes my lungs sting.

The innkeeper, a surly-looking old man, eyes Yvan speculatively. "Forty guilders for the night."

"Forty guilders," Yvan repeats, incredulous.

He's taking advantage of us. But it's late, and cold, and there isn't another inn for miles.

"That's right," the man replies, looking away from us to flip through some disheveled papers. Yvan glares at the man for a protracted moment before turning to me.

"We don't have enough." I squeeze Yvan's arm gently. My gaze flickers toward the innkeeper, who's now peering at me with narrowed eyes. I turn back to Yvan, trying to ignore the man's stare. "We could share a room." I feel the blush spreading on my face, even as I struggle to remain impassive.

"Well, now," the innkeeper says suggestively, "I think you should take the young lady's advice, lad. Since she's so *willing*."

Yvan's intense green eyes snap back to the innkeeper, obviously furious at the implied insult to me. The man gives a little start and looks back down at his papers.

"Fine." Yvan pushes twenty guilders toward the man.

"You'll have to start your own fire," the innkeeper informs us as he snatches up the coins. "It's ten more guilders for dry wood." A greedy look fills his eyes.

"Ten guilders for *wood*," Yvan says flatly, his neck muscles growing more tense by the minute.

"Awfully cold night tonight," the innkeeper says smugly, clearly relishing having the upper hand.

Yvan glances at me, and I shrug helplessly. We don't have any more money to spare between the two of us. "We'll have to get by without it," Yvan tells him icily.

"No matter." The innkeeper leers at me before his beady eyes dart back to Yvan with some envy. "This pretty thing will keep you warm enough, no doubt." Amused by himself, the innkeeper begins to chortle and cough at the same time, his uneven teeth heavily tobacco-stained.

Quick as a flash, Yvan reaches across the bar, grabs the

innkeeper by the front of his shirt and pulls him halfway across the counter. I flinch back, startled, and the room behind us goes silent.

"Apologize now," Yvan says calmly.

"Sorry, miss," the innkeeper chokes out.

Yvan lets go of him with a rough shove, and the man staggers back. Eyeing Yvan warily, he holds up a key. "Room's at the end of the hall," he says, the words sounding strangled, "to the left."

Yvan grabs the key out of the man's grip, takes hold of my hand and we start for the room.

The room is small and cold, with one dingy bed covered in a threadbare woolen blanket. There's a dim lantern on a small table by the drafty window, and old ashes spill out of the dark, unlit fireplace.

I wrap my arms around myself, the chill creeping in. Yvan closes the door behind us and pauses, looking around uncomfortably, as if he doesn't know what to do with himself.

"It's cold in here," I say, stating the obvious just to break the silence.

Yvan nods in unspoken agreement and considers the fireplace. "I'll go out and find some wood," he offers. He turns and starts for the door.

"It'll all be soaked," I point out. A wet snow has begun to fall outside, teetering just on the edge of freezing rain.

Yvan stops to look back at me, his hand on the wrought-iron door handle, his lip curling sarcastically. "I'm pretty good at starting fires."

I throw him a knowing look. "I'm well aware."

His expression grows uneasy. "I'll be right back," he tells me, stepping out into the shadowy hall, but pausing as he moves to shut the door. "Elloren," he says, a cautionary note to his tone, "lock the door while I'm gone."

"I know. I will."

He nods, satisfied, and closes the door.

I throw the bolt.

It isn't long before Yvan returns. I'm lying on the bed, the brown woolen blanket wrapped around myself, chilled to the bone and half-asleep. Hearing his knock, I rouse myself, let him in, then sink back down onto the bed, exhausted.

Yvan kneels down by the fireplace and arranges the sticks and logs he's gathered. In mere moments, there's a roaring fire blazing in the hearth, but its warmth isn't able to fully chase away the chill in the drafty room. Yvan stands up, brushes his hands off on his trousers and looks around awkwardly. "You can sleep on the bed tonight," he offers. "I'll sleep on the floor."

I stare at him in disbelief. "Yvan, it's a muddied stone floor."

"It's all right," he assures me, looking down uncertainly.

"If you want to…" I begin hesitantly, "share the bed with me tonight…"

"No!" he says with surprising vehemence.

A sting of warmth heats my face. "I… I didn't mean…"

"I know," he says quickly, looking around the room. At anything but me.

"I only meant—"

"It's all right," he insists, his eyes shifting to his feet. Perhaps realizing how stern he sounds, Yvan sighs, and seems to make a conscious effort to soften his expression and his tone. "Thank you," he says. "I know what you meant, Elloren. But I really will be fine on the floor."

"I know that sleeping in the same bed is…inappropriate,"

I rattle on, shivering from the cold and nerves. "But no one would need to know. And…you're always so warm."

Yvan looks me over, seeming chastened as he takes in how I'm shivering. "Of course. I should have noticed how cold you are. I don't feel the cold, so…" He catches himself and eyes me sidelong.

I hold his gaze, surprised by his open admission. Yvan suddenly looks as tense and worn-out as I feel. He eyes the bed covetously. "It *would* be nice to lie down, even for a moment," he admits.

I lie down on the bed and make room for him, my heartbeat deepening. Yvan sits down on the edge of the bed and gives me a small, awkward smile over his shoulder, leaning forward to remove his boots. Then he lies down beside me and stretches his long body out on the mattress with a sigh.

His arm brushes against mine, and it's deliciously warm. Almost hot. I breathe in deeply, my shivering quickly lessening as he releases some of his fire, his heat radiating through my lines in a rippling caress. It's strange and brazen, lying there in a bed next to him, but so wonderful.

"You don't have to hold your fire back," I tell him, fatigue making me bold. "I can feel you holding it back almost all the time now, and… I sense it's a strain."

His lips turn up in a jaded smile, and then his gaze darkens. "Trust me, Elloren, I have to hold it back." His smile disappears, his fire giving a turbulent flare.

I wonder what he means by that, but he doesn't seem willing to elaborate further, so I don't ask.

The draftiness of the room has stirred up a slight breeze, and the cobwebs hanging from the rafters above sway lazily from side to side.

"Yvan?" I ask, tentative.

He turns his head to look at me. "Hmm?"

It's hard to get the words out. "When did your father die?"

"When I was three," he tells me.

"I'm sorry," I say, my voice barely a whisper. "I'm sorry that happened."

He gives a slight shake of his head and glances over at me, the normally sharp planes of his face softened by the lamplight. "It's not your fault." He considers me for a moment. "When did your parents die?"

"I was also three." *The year my grandmother died, as well.* "Do you remember your father?"

Yvan exhales sharply, his eyes tensing with sadness. "Yes." He turns to face me, a rush of his heat suffusing me. I suddenly long to move into that warmth and let it fully overtake me. To be encircled by his arms and his fire.

"I remember my parents, too," I say, basking in his heat. "Especially my mother. She used to wrap me up in the quilt she made me..."

"The one Ariel burned," he says quietly, regret in his eyes.

"Yes."

"Elloren..." he says, then hesitates. "I was very harsh with you when we first met."

I remember him scoffing at my grief over losing my quilt. I'd hated him in that moment, but it seems like such a long time ago now. Especially considering how drastically my feelings for him have changed since then.

"It's all right," I say. "I can understand why you acted that way."

"No," he counters with a tight shake of his head, "it's not all right. I'm sorry."

I nod in acknowledgment, feeling overcome with emotion, my mutinous eyes tearing up.

"And I'm sorry my mother treated you like that," he adds.

"It was a mistake to bring you there. I thought..." He lets out a frustrated breath. "I thought she'd give you a chance."

I sigh heavily, blinking back the tears. "I imagine seeing me brought back horrific memories. I look so much like my grandmother..."

"But you're not her," he insists, staring at me intently. "I was hoping she'd be able to see that."

My breath catches in my throat. "It means a lot to hear you say that."

He gives me a small, rueful smile, and I feel my lips curving upward in return.

"You know, it's funny," I muse out loud, so tired it's easy to just speak my train of thought.

"What is?"

"This situation, right now. It's so inappropriate, it's actually funny."

Yvan's eyebrows edge higher in question.

"Here we are, two unmarried, unsealed people, you a Kelt, me a Gardnerian, alone in a room in this seedy tavern, lying in bed together..." I pause for a moment. "It's just... amusing, don't you think?"

Yvan smiles slightly. "It is."

"My people teach us that men can't control themselves around women, and that's why we need to dress so conservatively, and be chaperoned everywhere we go. Fasted younger and younger. Yet here we are, you and me, all alone—"

"The idea that men can't control themselves is ridiculous," he says adamantly. "It's just an excuse."

"That's what I've always thought. I mean, I don't have any experience with, you know..." I think of Diana's impatience with me when I trail off ambiguously on this particular subject. Yvan seems to understand, though—his culture is extremely straitlaced, as well. "But I grew up with two brothers," I continue, "and I know they'd never force anyone to do anything like that."

I blush, feeling self-conscious. "I've never spoken to anyone about things like this. I suppose I shouldn't really be talking to you about it."

"I don't mind talking with you about it," Yvan says, his expression open and unguarded.

I suddenly feel very close to him, our eyes locked in understanding. The side of his hand touches mine, and without thinking, I slide my hand over his.

He turns his head from me to stare up at the ceiling, his breathing suddenly deepening. Then he turns his hand over and threads his long fingers through mine.

My breath catches, warmth flaring inside me. I focus on the rafters above us as well, too overwhelmed by the feel of his fingers clasped around mine to look directly at him.

We lie there together for a long moment, holding hands.

It's like heaven—a thousand times better than kissing Lukas. And, strangely, more intimate. Because it feels like, in this moment, he's truly letting me in for the first time.

Both his fire power and my fire lines flare at the same moment, reaching for each other. Twining at the edges, like his hand around mine.

I finally dare to glance over at him. He continues to stare at the ceiling, stone-still except for the rise and fall of his chest.

"Yvan," I breathe out, his flame lightly caressing my lines, "the fire..."

"Do you like it, Elloren?" he asks, his voice throaty as he turns to me, his eyes sparking gold.

I nod, lit up by him. "Yes."

His full lips twitch into a smile, the gold in his eyes intensifying.

I look back at the ceiling, savoring the sultry feel of his fire shivering through mine.

"Are they going to make you fast?" he asks, his voice gaining an edge.

"If I stay in the Western Realm," I meet his eyes, an ache gathering in my chest. "But I don't want to."

Yvan's fingers tighten around mine, his gaze suddenly impassioned. "I don't want you to."

The thoughts stream through me, unbidden. *I don't want to fast to Lukas. I don't want to fast to Gareth, either. Or to anyone on the Council Registry. I don't want any of them.*

"Do you see yourself married someday?" I wonder, pain infusing the question.

A shadow falls across his face, and his eyes cool to green. "No, I don't."

I want to press, to know why he says this with such terrible certainty, but there's suddenly so much conflict in his expression I hesitate. That familiar look is back again—like he wants to tell me something but can't.

"I wish you could tell me everything," I say, running my thumb over his.

"So do I," he breathes.

I think of how he healed Bleddyn and Olilly. How he spends every spare moment helping the refugees fleeing east. How readily he jumped in to help Marina.

How kind and incredibly brave he is.

I wish I could fast to you, I think as we lie there, his eyes locked on to mine.

But I can't say it out loud. So, I let the thought gather in my head, straining for release as we lie there, our hands and fire magic entwined.

Overcome with fatigue, I try to stifle a yawn and fail. "I

didn't realize how tired I was until I lay down," I tell him softly.

"Go ahead, get some sleep," he encourages.

I can barely keep my eyes open, they feel so heavy.

"Good night, Yvan," I whisper, savoring his presence, wanting him to stay here all night long, but too shy to ask him to.

"Good night, Elloren," he whispers back, his gaze touched with longing.

I drift off to sleep but am roused soon after by a slight movement beside me. I watch through the lashes of my barely opened eyes as Yvan quietly gets up to sit by the fireplace. I'm immediately aware of the chill his departure creates, of missing him and wanting him back. I pull the woolen blanket up, hugging it tightly around my body, before drifting off once more.

I'm fast asleep when I feel the bed shift again. I slowly open my eyes, my brain fuzzy from sleep.

Yvan is sitting on the bed, staring at me. The room is softly illuminated by the fire he's coaxed higher, the flames throwing out light that dances on the walls. It's much warmer now, with only a slight chill from the draft coming in around the window. I can just make out Yvan's long, lanky figure, his head tilted down toward me. His beautiful eyes glowing with vivid golden flame.

"Yvan," I say, surprised by his searing expression, the fire blazing in his eyes. I hoist myself up on one elbow and consider him questioningly.

"Can I lie down with you again?" he asks, his voice ragged with emotion.

My heart thuds against my chest, and I lift up the edge of the blanket in invitation. The bed dips as Yvan slides the length of his lean body under the blanket in one smooth motion. He languidly curls up against me, his hand finding my waist as he pulls me close. I press my hand to his chest, tracing its hard planes through his woolen shirt. His heartbeat is strong and steady under my fingers, his fire running in a hot stream.

He's so close I can feel his warm breath on my cheek. He smells like well-stoked bonfires and something distinctly masculine that makes me want to burrow my head under his jaw and inhale his scent all night long. The glow of his eyes heightens, locked on mine, blazing with a heat I can feel straight through my fire lines. I slide my fingertips along the collar of his shirt, tracing the skin just above it and along his graceful neck. His breathing deepens as I touch him like I've yearned to for so long.

"Elloren," he says, his voice breaking with intensity. "I think I'm falling in love with you."

His words light me up, like flame to dry brush, his heat sweeping through me.

Yvan leans forward and brings his lips to mine—his mouth all softness and sensuous curves, at complete odds with the sharp angles of his face.

We kiss each other slowly at first, his kiss fervent and lingering. And then his kiss deepens, my mouth parting under his as his kiss roughens with desire, his fire sizzling down my lines. We kiss each other desperately, like two people starved for air who are finally able to draw a breath. I press myself against his hard body, wanting to be as close to him as I possibly can, and he responds eagerly.

"I'm falling in love with you, too," I say breathlessly, pulling back a fraction, staring deeply into his eyes.

He brings his lips back to mine and kisses me passionately, his tongue finding mine as his fire rushes through me.

My affinity lines give a hard, white-hot flare as my breath hitches, my body arching toward his.

Yvan's fire pulses through me as he guides me gently onto my back, his long fingers stroking my hair as he rolls on top of me, the feel of him thrilling my entire body. I wrap my legs around his, his body welded to mine and moving against me with a provocative rhythm. He pushes my tunic slowly up, his fingers sliding under its edge to explore my skin underneath.

Somewhere in the background, a man's gruff voice sings loudly and off-key, slurring the words to some tavern song. My lovely world abruptly shatters around the sound, like glass fracturing into a million pieces and quickly dissolving into the air.

Holy Ancient One, I'm dreaming!

I begin to slide out of my dream state, desperately trying to pull the image back together by sheer force of will—an impossibly intricate puzzle whose pieces are falling away, soon to be lost forever.

In its place is Yvan, sitting on a wooden chair next to the bed, staring at me intently. His face is serious and deeply unsettled, his arm resting on the frame of the window that looks out onto the street. In the background, the jarring voice continues to belch out fragments of a tune.

I prop myself up on my elbow, dazed, forcing myself to adjust to a diminished reality, the intimacy I've just shared with Yvan a complete illusion. A torrent of emotions floods through me, like dye meeting cloth—utter humiliation, loneliness, and a burning longing for him.

"I heard a man singing." My voice comes out shy and groggy from sleep. "He woke me up." I pray Yvan can't decipher anything about my dream from my voice or posture.

His face tenses, and he glances toward the window. "He's drunk. Seems to be quieting down, though." Yvan looks back at me, his brow tightly furrowed.

"Did he wake you, too?" My voice is almost a whisper.

"No." Yvan glances down and shakes his head. Then he looks back up and locks his eyes on to mine. "You did."

I gulp. "I did?" The words come out faint and strained. "Was I snoring?"

"You talk in your sleep."

We're both uncomfortably quiet for a long moment.

"What did I say?" I whisper, mortified.

He averts his gaze. "You said my name a few times."

My stomach drops, the blood draining from my face. "Oh." I can hardly take a breath. "Did I say anything else?"

He's looking anywhere but at me. "I don't want to embarrass you."

"Too late."

He turns back to face me. "You said, 'I'm falling in love with you.'"

I roll onto my back and cover my face with my hands, wanting to disappear. "I'm sorry."

"Don't be." His voice is tight, but kind.

"I can't control what I dream about." I drop my hands from my face and let them rest on my abdomen. I stare up at the swaying cobwebs as a single tear falls from my eye and I reach up to wipe it away.

"I get lonely sometimes," I say simply. Another tear falls, cold on my face.

"I understand," he says, his voice low and thick with emotion.

"When I saw you that night with Iris..." He winces slightly at the hurt in my tone, and I regret the words immediately, feeling petty and vulnerable. "You have a long history with her, don't you?"

Yvan sighs deeply, his jaw tensing. "Iris has been a good friend to me, Elloren. But it's not like that between us."

But I bet she knows all your secrets. Since she's Fae, too.
And she doesn't look exactly like Carnissa Gardner.

I sit up and hug my knees to my chest, wishing I could look like anything but what I am. "She's very beautiful," I say as more tears roll down my cheeks.

"So are you."

I stop breathing for a moment, confused by his admission. "But...you told me once that you found me to be repulsive."

He winces again. "That was before I knew you. It was wrong of me to be so unkind. I'm sorry. It doesn't excuse my behavior, but at the time, I was thinking more of what your looks represented."

"My grandmother?"

"Her... All of them."

I wipe at my tears. "And now? What do you see?"

He lets out a long sigh and studies me, his green eyes blazing gold at the edges. "I think you're the most beautiful woman I've ever seen." He inhales sharply and looks away, his mouth set in a tight line, as if he's said too much and wants to prevent himself from making the same mistake again.

When he finally looks back at me, I can see my own loneliness, my own longing for him, reflected back in his eyes. I hug my knees tight, heart racing, not quite believing I've heard him correctly.

"It's late," he says, his voice sounding strained and sad. "We should get some sleep."

No, I want to say. *Come here and stay with me. I want you. Only you.*

Instead I say, "All right," my voice equally strained, equally sad, reeling from his sudden reserve.

I watch him as he stiffly moves back to his spot near the fireplace and stretches out on the floor with his back toward me. His body looks tense and uncomfortable, his head resting on his arm. An aching loneliness hangs in the air and chills the room.

"Elloren," he says as he lies very still.

"Yes?"

"Do you know what happened to the family of the Kelt that Sage Gaffney ran off with?" When I don't answer, he says, "I ran into some people I know at that tavern we stopped at earlier today. They told me."

"What happened?" I ask hesitantly, almost not wanting to know.

"They found them a few days ago. They were all killed. By Gardnerian soldiers."

"No," I whisper, shocked.

"His parents, his brother, even their animals." Yvan hesitates for a moment before continuing. "The Mage Council sanctioned it, Elloren. At the request of the Gaffneys. It was a Mage purity strike."

Nausea roils through me, and I suddenly understand the reason for Yvan's distance. Why he's on the floor right now instead of in my arms. It says right in our holy book that the loss of a Gardnerian woman's purity by a man of another race *must* be avenged. And horrific acts like this are becoming more common in the Western Realm, the Alfsigr Elves also enforcing purity in this way.

"You think being involved with me could be dangerous in that way," I say, my voice numbed.

"I *know* it would be."

"Because of my family."

"Yes. And because some very powerful people want you wandfasted to Lukas Grey. Anyone who gets in the way of that will be in danger, especially if they're not Gardnerian."

"Anyone…meaning you and your mother."

"Yes. I can't think of a way to get around it. And believe me, I've tried."

Tears prick my eyes. "What I said in my dream was true," I tell him. No longer hiding anything. Holding my heart straight out.

"There are lots of ways to care about people," he says, his voice tightened. "As friends. Allies."

"And what if that's not enough?"

"I think, in our case, that *has* to be enough, for more reasons than you know."

"We could keep it a secret."

His tone takes on a jaded cast. "These things never stay secret."

"What am I to you, Yvan?" I ask, clutching at the blanket.

He pushes himself up and turns to me. "I think we've become good friends."

"But that's it."

"That has to be it, Elloren. For my mother's safety. And for yours. And your family's safety."

My fire line gives a defiant flare, and I fight the urge to throw a rebellious streak of flame out toward him. I can sense him holding his fire back as well, gold sparking in his eyes.

I'm lost. Trapped in a cage with no way out, steel bars separating me from Yvan. But I can't ask him to make such a dangerous sacrifice. Not for me. I won't risk his life or the lives of our families.

I turn away from Yvan and lie down, pulling the threadbare blanket over myself and balling my body up tight. I close my eyes, dam up my tears and wish that I could disappear into another beautiful dream and never wake from it.

Yvan is quiet during the trip back, and so am I, the two of us wrestling with our own private thoughts. I sit behind him on the black mare, my arms wrapped around his waist, pressed tight against his warm back, yet feeling like I'm a million miles away from him—both of us forced by birth into separate worlds.

But there's nothing to be done about it. He's right. If we went off together, we'd place everyone we love in grave danger.

Hours later, after we've left the horse with Andras and trudged through the snowy wilds for what seems like an eternity, we find ourselves once again at the base of the daunting Southern Spine.

Yvan pauses to glance up at its snowcapped pinnacle as the two of us stand there awkwardly. He doesn't need to explain his discomfort—I understand completely. It's hard to be physically close and deny our feelings for each other, knowing nothing can ever come of it.

"Yvan," I say, breaking the silence, "I just want you to know that I've thought a lot about everything you said and... I understand. About the danger to your mother, I mean. And why we can't...be together. It was reckless to even consider it."

Yvan nods, his jaw growing rigid as he glances at me and then at the ground, as if he's trying to compose himself. Trying to rein in both his fire and some powerful emotion.

"Elloren," he says, his voice heavy with feeling, "if things were different..."

The words hang in the cold air between us.

"I know," I say softly.

"I *wish* things were different."

"Me, too." I swallow, my throat suddenly raw and tight. "It's strange," I tell him. "I don't really know you that well at all, and I know you have so many secrets...but I feel like you've become my closest friend."

LAURIE FOREST

His gaze turns ardent. "I feel the same way about you."

"Friends then?" I offer. "And allies?"

He nods stiffly, clearly as miserable over the unavoidable boundaries as I am. I swallow back the ache, fight back the tears. But I have to say it. I have to know. Because if we can't ever be together...

"Iris?" I look down at the ground, not able to meet his eyes, bracing myself.

"I'm not interested in Iris," he says flatly.

Relief washes over me. I know it's unfair to want him to be exclusively mine when we can never be together, but I don't feel like being fair.

"And Lukas?" he suddenly asks, obviously not of a mind to be fair, either.

I look up at him and am thrown by the severe look he's giving me. "He's not what I want." *You are.*

He nods, and some of the tension drains from his face, only a troubled resignation remaining. He glances up at the ridge, then holds out a hand to me. "Shall we?"

I walk over to him and take his hand as I wrap one arm, then two, then my entire body around him. I close my eyes as we begin our ascent and lose myself to the feel of his warmth and his strong heartbeat against mine.

MAGE COUNCIL
RULING
#319

All diplomatic relations with the Northern
and Southern Lupine packs are hereby
suspended and trade sanctions will be
vigorously enforced.
The sanctions will not be lifted and diplomatic relations will not resume until the
Lupines cede the disputed land along the
Northern and Southern border of the Holy
Magedom.

CHAPTER FIVE

NILANTYR

The day after Yvan and I return from Keltania, a fierce storm blows in from the northeast. The heavy winds and driving snow cut off all visibility and make travel to Amaz lands an impossibility for now.

As the sun begins to set and the storm takes a sharp turn for the worse, Ariel bursts into our North Tower room, slick with snow, her eyes wild, her raven flapping in behind her and cawing abrasively.

Diana, Marina, Wynter and I stare at her in confusion, startled to see her in such a panicked state.

Ariel stalks to her bed and hauls the mattress off it. She frantically feels around the mattress's edges, searching desperately for something, not even noticing her beloved chickens as they run about her feet and try in vain to get her attention. She's deathly pale and sweating, despite the chill air.

"Ariel," I ask carefully as she flings open a dresser drawer and throws the contents on to the floor, agitatedly moving from one drawer to the next, barely noticing me. "What's the matter?"

Ariel hurls one of the drawers clear out of the dresser and lets loose with a stream of profanity. She rounds on me, her eyes savage. "Naga set it on fire! She planned it this way! She waited...waited for the storm!"

I'm thrust into further bewilderment. "What are you talking about?"

"My nilantyr!" She goes back to hurling things around in desperation.

Diana rises slowly to her feet. "Stop this right now," she demands, tensing her muscles authoritatively.

Wynter has abandoned the drawing she's working on and is slowly approaching Ariel. I can tell by Wynter's grave expression that the situation is even worse than it appears.

"Ariel," Wynter says, nearing her with supreme caution, "you brought all the nilantyr with you. I watched you put it in your bag."

"No...*no*," Ariel vehemently protests, shaking her head as she frantically tears the pillow on her bed apart, feathers flying everywhere.

"It's not here," Wynter calmly insists.

Ariel continues to shake her head from side to side as she paces the room, looking through anything she can find, thrusting her arms under furniture. I notice, with mounting alarm, that she's starting to tremble.

Sweet Ancient One, she's been pulled completely off the nilantyr.

"What will happen if she stops taking the nilantyr so suddenly?" Wynter asks me, fear in her silver eyes.

I send her a troubled look, my mind racing back through all my apothecary lessons, trying to think of a way to help Ariel. To offset what's coming.

"If it's all gone," I tell Wynter, "she'll get very sick—"

"Shut up!" Ariel screams at me, her face twisted up into a mask of hatred. "It's not gone! I know there's more! I had more! Just in case! I know I had more!" She starts rummaging through my dresser now, tossing my clothes out of it. "You hid it from me, Gardnerian! You stole it!"

Diana takes a step forward. "No one stole from you."

Ariel's eyes blaze with violence, and she takes a threatening step toward Diana. But then her legs buckle, and she throws an arm out toward my dresser to keep from falling, her trembling increasing to the point where I fear she'll collapse.

Wynter and I rush to Ariel as her face turns deathly gray, and the trembling worsens to a full-body quaking. We grasp her arms just as Ariel lurches forward and vomits all over the clothing she's pulled from my drawers. Wynter and I both recoil instinctively, and Ariel falls to her knees, still retching. We follow her down to the floor, Wynter throwing her arms around Ariel to steady her.

"We need to find a physician," I tell Wynter, my voice tight with urgency. *"Now."*

"We *can't*," Wynter cautions emphatically. "The nilantyr is illegal. If they find out she has it…"

"Then we have to go get Yvan!" I insist.

"You can't get anyone right now," Diana firmly interjects. "You'll be lost as soon as you step outside. Even I couldn't find my way around in that."

We all turn toward the window and see that the world outside is a solid, impenetrable wall of white.

The following twenty-four hours are like something from a nightmare.

Ariel lies in bed vomiting until there's nothing left in her stomach as she writhes in pain and cries out for the drug. Diana somehow manages to keep Ariel from hurting the rest of us and from clawing at her own arms, her own face, while her body burns with fever. Wynter and I clean up the vomit and try to get Ariel to drink some water, which she only retches up, and Marina fetches fresh water and soap for us and helps as best she can with the laundry.

Then, after hours of struggling, Ariel can fight no more. She collapses into unconsciousness, her breathing shallow, her skin waxy and soaked with sweat. We each take a turn tending to Ariel while the others rest, bathing her forehead with cool water to try and keep her fever down.

On the second day, as soon as the snowstorm lets up slightly, Yvan comes to us, bringing medicine to help dampen Ariel's craving for the drug.

He helps me prop a semiconscious Ariel up so she can take the medicine. None of us ask Yvan how he knew to come. By now, it's unspoken but common knowledge that Yvan can talk to Naga, just like Wynter and Ariel can.

"There's nothing more I can do for her," Yvan tells me as he kneels by Ariel's bedside, his hand on her sweat-soaked forehead, her unconscious body still racked with fever and chills.

"Stop pretending," I say coarsely, sleep deprivation and desperation for Ariel making me harsh. "You were able to help Fern and Bleddyn and Olilly. And countless refugees. Now help *her*." Tears sting at my eyes. He has to save her. She can't die. She just *can't*.

"Elloren," he counters, compassion in his tone, "I'm telling you the truth. There is *nothing* I can do, save give her some comfort with the *Ittelian* tonic. She has to overcome her dependence on the nilantyr on her own. There's no other way."

A tear slides down my cheek, and I roughly wipe it away. "Will she survive it? Tell me she'll survive it, Yvan."

He places his hand, palm down, over Ariel's heart. "I think she will."

★ ★ ★

Later that night, I sit with Yvan out in the hallway on the stone bench, slumped down with exhaustion, but filled with a tenuous hope. Ariel is hanging on and shows signs of improvement—her heartbeat strengthening, her breathing no longer faint and labored.

I look down at myself. I haven't bathed in two days and stink of sweat. There are hastily washed vomit stains down the front of my tunic, and I can feel my hair sticking to my head. I lean back against the stone wall behind me.

"I'm filthy," I observe with a long sigh.

Yvan glances me over briefly.

"I've never had to take care of someone who was so horribly ill," I tell him. "My brothers and my uncle had this awful stomach sickness once, but I didn't get it, and I had to care for everyone. That was pretty bad, but this...this is much worse. It's terrible to see her suffer like this."

"It'll get easier," he assures me. "She's through the worst now."

I reach up to rub my forehead. "Did you know that they put Ariel in a cage when she was only two years old?" I squeeze my eyes tight to try and combat the ache in my head. "That's why she lashes out at cages. They fed her the nilantyr to keep her from being violent. What two-year-old wouldn't become violent, thrown into a cage?"

Yvan doesn't say anything. He just stares at Wynter's white bird tapestry opposite us, his face tense.

I slump down and breathe out a long, shuddering sigh, deeply troubled. I glance over at Yvan, suddenly of a mind to be honest. About everything.

"You know," I tell him, "I didn't speak to her for a long time...after she told you...about my dreams." My cheeks flush as I say it, but I don't care. Tears prick at my eyes. "I should have let it go. I shouldn't have shut her out. I was just…so upset."

He leans forward to consider this.

"She's going to make it, Elloren," he tells me, his voice low and assured. "You'll have a chance to make amends."

I nod stiffly, tears sliding down my face.

"And you're not the only one who has vivid dreams," he says, almost in a whisper. "You just have the unfortunate habit of talking in your sleep." He turns to look at me, his eyes searing. "I've dreamt about you."

Warmth jettisons through me, quickly followed by despair. "We shouldn't talk of these things," I whisper. "It only makes it all worse."

"I'm sorry." His jaw tightens and he looks away. "Of course, you're right."

We're both silent for a moment.

"Yvan," I venture, "what did Naga say about Ariel and the nilantyr?"

He eyes me evasively, his lips pressing into a tight line.

"You must have found out what happened from Naga," I gently persist. "There's no other way you could have known. You went to check on Naga during the snowstorm, didn't you? To make sure she was all right."

"Yes," he admits tightly.

"What did she say?"

Again, silence.

"I know you can talk to her," I press. "Just like I know you're abnormally strong…and fast. And that you can heal people and scale mountains like gravity doesn't exist. You can be honest with me, Yvan. What did she tell you?"

His whole body tenses, both his eyes and his fire reflecting the strong emotions and conflicting thoughts raging inside him. Finally, he takes a deep breath and looks straight at me.

"Naga said...that the nilantyr would destroy Ariel. So, she decided to destroy it first. She said it's stolen Ariel's strength, that it's rendered her wings useless and robbed her of her fire. She said that soon, it would also rob Ariel of her very soul, and that she'd be like the broken dragons who started out fierce and beautiful but have been destroyed." Yvan pauses, taking a haggard breath. "She said the Gardnerians started Ariel down the path of destruction, but if she keeps taking the poison, it will be the same as digging her own grave. And then they'd win. She said that Ariel gave her back her own wings, and that this was her only chance to give Ariel back hers, as well."

A pained look crosses his face. "And then she left."

Shock spears through me. "She *left*?"

Yvan nods. "She can hunt now that she has her fire back. She'll be able to fly soon, and cold isn't an issue for dragon-kind. So, she left."

"Oh, Yvan..."

"She'll be back," he assures me. "She'll never know whether she can fly again if she doesn't go off and test her wings. But she told me she'd be back to help us."

I consider all this for a long moment as Yvan searches my face. "Naga was wrong to force Ariel off the nilantyr so quickly," I finally say with grave certainty. "She could have died."

Yvan nods. "It's different for dragons. I think she underestimated how weak the human side of Ariel is."

"Naga's right about everything she said, though," I grimly concede. "The nilantyr *was* slowly destroying Ariel. I've watched her grow weaker and weaker over the past months. She can't even cast fire anymore. And her wings...they've grown thinner, frailer."

I pause for a moment as shame washes over me. "At first,

when she'd take the nilantyr, it was almost a relief. She'd stop cursing at me. When she took it, she just didn't care about anything, and she wasn't so viciously angry all the time. But after finding out what she's been through... I feel like she has good reason to be angry. She *should* be angry." Outrage wells inside me. "The Gardnerians had no right to force this poison on her. And they had no right to try and take away her anger."

Yvan's intense gaze, which used to unnerve me so, does the opposite now. In it, I can see he understands in a fierce, true way. And it feels good to be understood, especially about this.

I ponder how he can talk to Naga as I also consider how absurdly handsome his face is. I've scoured books about the Fae, trying to find out what he might be, and my exhausted mind remembers a detail—Lasair Fae are supposed to be wildly good-looking, their faces perfectly symmetrical.

Like his.

"Who's Fae in your family, Yvan?" I ask.

He remains still, holding back the answer. "You can tell me," I encourage him more gently this time.

For a moment, the only sound is the icy wind rattling the windowpanes. Yvan takes a deep breath and, to my incredible surprise, answers me. "My mother."

My breath catches in my throat, my heartbeat quickening. We're both quiet for a long moment, the silence momentous.

"So, your mother's family..."

His green eyes blaze. "Killed by the Gardnerians during the Realm War. All of them."

Oh, merciful Ancient One. Not just his father. They killed his mother's people, too. Shame and sorrow rise in me like a relentless tide.

No wonder his mother despises me so.

"Thank you for telling me," I say, my voice breaking as

the reasons for the walls between us are thrown into even sharper relief. "Your secrets are safe with me. I hope you know that."

Yvan's hand slides over mine, and his touch sends a gently rippling trail of sparks up my arm. I pull in a shuddering breath and thread my fingers through his. He sits back and stares at the wall opposite us, watching the fire from the lanterns dance over Wynter's tapestry.

"What would you do if everything was simpler?" I ask him. "If we were both Kelts, and the world wasn't on the brink of war?"

He gives a melancholy smile at the idea. "I'd be a physician like my father." He shrugs. "I'd study...and sleep a lot more than I do right now."

I nod with understanding at this. We're both surviving on very little sleep.

His expression grows serious as he considers my hand in his, his tone becoming ardent. "And...you and I... We could be together."

Our eyes find each other, and I'm seized by an overwhelming longing for him that I can see plainly reflected in the way he's looking at me.

My heart twists. *Why does it have to be so impossible?*

Defiance flares up in me, and I rest my head on his warm shoulder, our hands still clasped tightly together. His head leans onto mine, his cheek warm on my hair.

"What did you do for fun when you were growing up?" I ask him, wanting to find a way back to safer ground.

The question seems to take him off guard, but not unpleasantly so. "For fun?"

"I just wonder if there was ever a time in your life when things weren't so...difficult."

He takes a deep breath, considering the question. "I was

an only child, so my childhood was mostly quiet. My mother and I kept to ourselves. I read a lot, helped her in the garden and with the animals." He pauses, growing pensive. "I do like to cook."

"You do?" I ask, surprised.

"My mother's a very good cook. She taught me."

It seems so prosaic, it's almost funny—Yvan, with all his supernatural powers, liking to cook. And it's surprising. He's rarely cooking in the kitchen, doing the more strenuous work instead, like hauling wood for the stoves.

"I'll have to cook for you sometime," he offers, smiling.

I smile back at him, lit up. "I'd like that."

"Fernyllia's pretty strict about people playing around in her kitchen, but maybe we can sneak in there some evening."

I laugh at the thought, at the idea of doing something just for fun. It's been so long. We're all so busy with schoolwork and kitchen labor and doing what we can to aid the Resistance.

"I like to dance, too," he tells me.

"Really?" I try to picture serious Yvan whirling around a dance floor and smile with delight at the improbable thought.

"Another thing my mother taught me," he says. "Lasair dances. The dances of her people."

Her people. The Lasair Fae. He's been closed off for so long, it's a revelation to have him finally speaking so openly about being part Fire Fae.

"What are Lasair dances like?" I wonder, imagining a group of beautiful people, all with vivid green eyes and brilliant red hair, dressed in scarlet clothing and dancing inside a ring of flames.

"They're complicated," he says. "With a lot of steps. Fae dances are difficult to learn, but once you've mastered them, they're...fun."

"Are they like the Gardnerian dances?"

"No," he says with a shake of his head and a slight smile. "Your people are a bit...stiff."

I mock frown at him. He's one to talk, so incredibly reserved all the time. But it's true, I have to admit—the Gardnerians do take the prize for stiffness, along with cruelty perhaps.

"Do you think I could learn to dance like that?" I ask, hesitant.

He looks me over, as if seeing something new, something pleasing, then squeezes my hand affectionately. "I could teach you. We'd have to go somewhere very secluded, with a large, open space." His eyes light with mischief. "Perhaps the circular barn."

I consider this, the deserted barn so often a way station for fleeing refugees, its floor littered with pages that Yvan angrily tore from *The Book of the Ancients*.

"We could dance on the pages of *The Book*," I suggest with a wry smile. "A fitting gesture of defiance."

Yvan laughs at this. "It's an appealing idea, actually."

"I'd probably step on your feet more than I would on *The Book*."

Amusement sparks in Yvan's eyes. "I stepped on my mother's feet a fair bit when she was teaching me."

I look at my sock-clad feet and pick them up off the floor slightly before setting them down again. "Yvan," I wonder, "if you're Fae, why doesn't iron ever bother you?"

"It does."

"But I've watched you in the kitchen. You handle it all the time."

He narrows his eyes at me, amused. "How long have you been watching me?"

I swallow self-consciously. "A while."

"It's irritating, that's all," he says with a small shrug. "If I touch it for a long time, I break out into a rash. But I'm only a quarter Fae, Elloren. My father comes from Keltic stock, and my maternal grandmother was a Kelt, as well."

"So, your mother's father..."

"He was full-blooded Fae, yes."

"Has your mother taught you a lot about her people?"

He nods. "Their history, stories, customs...their language."

Intrigued surprise lights in me. "You can speak a whole other language?"

"I don't speak it often. It's too dangerous to speak any Fae dialect these days."

"Would you say something to me in it?" I ask shyly.

Yvan smiles at me, a sultry edge to his grin that sends warmth sliding up my spine. "What do you want me to say?" he asks, his voice a silken thrum.

"Anything. I just want to hear what it sounds like."

He stares at me thoughtfully, then starts speaking. I'm instantly entranced, the words of the Lasair tongue fluid and full of elegant sounds. It sounds like I imagine the Fae dance would be like, incredibly complicated but beautiful when mastered.

"What did you say?" I ask, mesmerized by him.

"I said...your eyes are lovely."

"Oh," I whisper, my cheeks flushing.

Yvan's face takes a turn for the serious, and he lets out a long breath. He leans in toward me, his thumb gently tracing the back of mine. "We're not doing a very good job of staying away from each other, are we?"

"No," I agree, letting my head fall back onto his shoulder. A tendril of his heat reaches out for me, and my breath tightens as the slender flame curls around my fire lines, a warm, decadent thrill flickering through me.

"What's it like?" he asks me. "To have affinity lines?"

I force out an even breath. "It's...like branching trees inside of me. If I concentrate on an affinity, I can feel that branching line. And I can pull on the power flowing through it." I glance up at him, wondering what it would be like to pull on his fire while kissing him. "Your fire," I ask him, flustered, "is it like a Mage line?"

"It's not a line," he says, an edge of bitterness curling his full lips. "It's *everywhere* in me."

Holy Ancient One.

I feel a sudden desire to send my fire magic straight out to him. To feel what's inside him. A low warmth blooms in my center, and I struggle to hold it in check.

"You've five affinity lines?" he asks, curious.

"I have strong earth lines and fire lines," I tell him. "I'm starting to have a sense of small air lines and water lines, too, but I can't sense my light lines. Most Mages can't— Light Mages are very rare." I look to him, hesitant. "Can you sense my lines?"

"Only your fire lines," he says.

"We're similar in that," I muse. "We both have a strong affinity for fire."

"I know," he says, his thumb gently stroking the back of my hand, a delicious heat trailing his touch.

"Strange, isn't it?" I say, wanting him to trail that touch all over me.

His chin moves against my hair as he nods in agreement. I can feel the edge of his mouth lift into a smile.

I never want to move. I want to stay here with my hand in his and my head on his shoulder forever.

"Your brothers," he says. "They told me that you wanted

to make violins, before you decided to become an apothecary."

I give a melancholy smile at this. "In a perfect world where a woman could join the Crafters' Guilds?" I muse. "Maybe. Maybe I'd do both. And we'd be together."

I turn my head to look up at him, the happy idea dispersing like smoke. "But we're not likely to have the quiet life we both want, are we?"

Yvan lets out a short, grim sound, as if I don't even know the half of it. "I'll never have the life I want," he says, his voice low and jaded. "There's just nothing to be done about it. And the Mage Council would never tolerate Carnissa Gardner's granddaughter being with someone who has Fae blood. And if anything ever happened to you...because of me..." His voice trails off, and he looks away, his hand rigid around mine, as if in defiance of the entire world.

But it can't be ignored. Any kind of happy future for us... it can never be. *We* can never be. Our relationship would be a danger to ourselves and everyone we love.

So, I do the only thing I can do. I pull my head away from the refuge of his shoulder, let go of his hand and stand up.

"I need to get back," I say self-consciously, motioning to the door of my lodging. "I'm behind in my studies, and they need my help with Ariel."

Yvan nods stiffly and gets to his feet, standing there for a moment in awkward silence, the air between us charged with frustrated emotion. There's so much to say that has to remain unsaid.

But it's time for both of us to walk away.

Yvan is right.

Ariel does survive being deprived of the nilantyr, and it

does get easier, everyone coming together to help Ariel in their own way.

Wynter, ever faithful, stays close by Ariel every moment she can. Every night, she wraps Ariel in a soft, winged embrace and sings to her in High Elvish, whispering to her lovingly even as Ariel mutters incoherently and wakens only sporadically, regarding us all with half-focused, bloodshot eyes while her raven perches overhead.

Diana, whom Ariel never had much affection for, keeps her distance, but goes about efficiently keeping Ariel's clothes and bedding clean, muttering darkly to herself the whole time about the inhuman Gardnerians and their bizarre religious beliefs that target children born with wings, and how you wouldn't catch the Lupines being so horribly and unforgivably cruel. Surprisingly, Diana also takes on caring for Ariel's chickens, though they flee in a panic whenever she comes near.

Marina helps Diana with the cleaning, but has grown increasingly troubled at this further proof of the Gardnerians' barbaric behavior. Her fear for her sister grows exponentially with every day that passes, but the wilds are impassible with so much snow on the ground. There's no way around it—we have to wait until the weather improves before we can visit the Amaz and implore them to help Marina's people.

Rafe and Yvan take turns bringing Ariel food from the kitchen while Tierney and I prepare medicines to help restore her energy. Wynter's brother, Cael, and his quiet second, Rhys, bring Ariel an Elfin rune-amulet to wear, telling us that its red stone inlay is supposed to toughen the skin and might work on wings, as well.

Perhaps for the first time in her life, Ariel is surrounded by people supporting her, caring for her, wanting her to heal and be strong—strong like she was before the Gardnerians forced the nilantyr on her. Before they threw her into a cage.

That evening, I sit in the flickering firelight by Ariel's bedside, gently dabbing Ariel's fevered brow with a clean, cool rag.

The worst seems to be over.

The nightmare that's held on to Ariel for close to a full week has finally released her from its merciless grasp, though she's still pale and skeletally thin. Her wings are so threadbare you can see through them, and her body is so wilted and weak that we have to spoon-feed her.

But the stench of the poison is gone, and she sleeps soundly, as if a fragile peace has settled over her.

Like so much in her life, she's survived it.

As I gently wipe the sweat from Ariel's forehead, her eyes flutter open. My brow lifts in astonishment as she looks at me in a new way—fully alert and really here. And completely aware for the first time in days.

"Why are you doing this?" she asks in a coarse voice, the question devoid of emotion.

I draw my hand away, chastened by her direct question. "Because it's wrong, what they did to you." I tentatively bring the cloth back to her forehead and expect her to stop me, but she doesn't. "And I want you to get better."

Ariel considers me for a moment before replying. "I will always hate you," she says, but there's no malice in her tone—only exhaustion and confusion at my stubborn presence.

I shrug off the sting of her words as I continue to tend to her. "I still want you to get better."

"Why?"

"Because I don't want them to win."

I stop wiping Ariel's brow and sit back, the two of us looking at each other for a moment. Eventually, her lids become heavy, and she loses herself to sleep once more.

My eyes wander past Ariel to where Marina lies in front of the fire, staring at me, her ocean eyes alert. She's been keeping a constant vigil at the window, waiting for the weather to change, waiting for the time when we can travel to meet with the Amaz and ask for their help.

When a thaw comes a few days later, pulling snow back into the earth, Marina, Diana and I make plans to leave Ariel in Wynter's care.

And then we set out for Amaz territory.

PART THREE

MAGE COUNCIL RULING

#326

All diplomatic relations with the Amazakaran Free People of the Caledonian Mountains are hereby suspended, and trade sanctions will be vigorously enforced until the Amazakaran surrender the Urisk, Smaragdalfar Elves and Fae-blooded who reside in their territory in flagrant violation of Realm Law.

CHAPTER ONE

BORDERLINE

"No men indeed," Diana huffs as she strides next to me through the wintry, snow-patched woods. "And what, pray tell, would the Amaz do if all the men were suddenly gone and they were Queens of Erthia? Would they grow trees from which would sprout new Amaz daughters?"

Diana has been on a good half-hour-long tear about the flaws in Amaz thinking and how dare they consider themselves superior to the Lupines and why the Lupines are, in fact, superior to them. My head is starting to throb with worry just listening to her. It's beginning to seem like sheer madness to bring Diana, who's pretty incapable of tact, on a diplomatic mission to implore the Amaz to help the Selkies.

But we'll need her protection. Venturing into Amaz lands without an invitation is beyond dangerous.

Walls of Spine-stone tower above the treetops to either side of us as we hike through the long, slender ribbon of forest cutting through the only break in the Northern Spine.

Straight toward the Amaz border.

Rafe follows Diana closely, listening to her impassioned, indignant speech with his usual, wry good humor. Trystan, Andras and Jarod walk silently behind them, all three of them seeming lost in their own thoughts.

Yvan strides beside me as we weave through evergreen trees cast in late-afternoon shadow. His fire power is simmering with an almost vibrating tension, the edges of it fitful and flashing out randomly. I can sense him struggling to hold it in check, but there's an aura of heat building, dangerously close to breaching all control.

Marina needs to get out of here, I worriedly consider, *but so do you. Before the wrong person discovers what you are.*

I glance over at Marina, who's walking hand in hand with Gareth, the two of them having fallen into an intense friendship—and possibly more. I've gotten used to drifting asleep to the sound of Gareth's low, kind voice and Marina's flute-like inflections emanating from the North Tower hallway as they converse late into the night.

Diana's sharply critical voice pulls me from my thoughts. "...and if my father has to hear one more time about how we've stolen their male children from them, children they've left to *die* in the woods, I think he would be quite justified in pointing out what hypocrites they truly are—"

"Diana," I cut in, perhaps a bit too forcefully. She rounds on me, her expression irked. "You're going to *have* to make an effort to keep your views to yourself when we get there."

"Or what?" Diana shoots back dismissively. "They will threaten me with one of their rune-weapons? They are no match for me."

"There it is," Andras announces as we reach a break in the forest and step out onto a snow-covered field. Andras points across the field to where a dark wall of trees lies ready to meet us. "That's the border, just up ahead."

We all slow to a stop.

The men in our group can walk across the field, but no farther. And under no circumstances can they follow us over that borderline of trees. Any men found on Amaz land are killed. There are no negotiations, no exceptions to the rule. Everyone has heard stories of hapless male travelers crossing the border by accident, only to have their heads split in two by a sharp rune-axe.

Marina, Diana and I will be entering those woods alone.

"How will we find the Amaz?" I ask Andras.

Andras smiles slightly at this. "You won't need to find them. Once you pass into their territory, they'll find you." His expression grows serious. "Remember to bow low before the queen. Don't make eye contact until she acknowledges you. And don't step on the threshold when you enter their dwellings."

Diana listens impatiently, her arms crossed tightly, as Andras reminds us of the most important etiquette points. Yvan regards me quietly, his fire flaring restlessly, as Rafe and Andras try to impress upon a stubborn Diana the importance of diplomacy here. Trystan has his wand out and is eyeing the line of trees with dark appraisal as he converses in low tones with Jarod.

I follow Trystan's gaze across the field and toward the brooding forest, reluctant to part from the men in our party. From everything I've read about the Amaz, they don't take kindly to strangers wandering into their lands—even female strangers.

And here I am, the double of the greatest enemy they've ever known.

"Are you ready, Elloren?" Yvan asks, a tendril of his fire magic breaking free and reaching for me.

I nod apprehensively, glancing toward the forest again.

"You can do this," he says encouragingly, a slim edge of gold limning his green eyes.

I look over at Marina, who is embracing Gareth, saying her goodbyes. "We have to," I tell Yvan, grimly resolved. "There's not a lot of time left. The Mage Council will be voting on my aunt's motion soon."

He nods, the gold in his eyes briefly intensifying, his fire whipping out toward me. He glances uneasily at the border, holding himself rigid, but his fire wraps around me protectively.

We both hesitate, attempting to hold ourselves back from each other as our fires build and the boundaries between us rapidly break down.

Yvan steps close and pulls me into a heated embrace. I cling to him, burrowing my face in his shoulder as our fire powers surge free to encompass each other.

"Be careful, Elloren," he whispers, his breath hot on my ear. "This is dangerous. Promise me you'll be careful."

"I will," I promise, moved by his impassioned concern.

I pull back from Yvan, a flush suffusing my cheeks, his heat sizzling through my lines.

"Ready?" Diana asks as she sidles up next to me, Marina close behind her.

I nod, tempered by Yvan's fire.

"We'll be waiting for you here tomorrow," Andras tells us. "*Respectfully* ask them to escort you back." He gives Diana a significant look, but her attention has already turned to the forest before us.

It's time.

Time to walk across the Spine-bracketed field and over the borderline of dark forest before I lose my nerve.

I hitch my travel sack high on my shoulder and say good-bye to my brothers, Andras, Jarod and Gareth. Then I take one last look at Yvan before starting across the field with Diana and Marina.

We're about halfway to the border when a line of glowing red runes suddenly bursts into view, and we all flinch back in surprise and freeze. The runes are the size of wagon wheels and hover in a line just above the border.

Diana jerks her head up, then pivots around, nostrils flaring. Her amber eyes suddenly widen and, in a blur, she grabs hold of my arm and roughly yanks me sideways.

I cry out as my back hits the icy ground, and a small, silvery flash whizzes over my head, then another, immediately followed by a volley of glowing-red arrows whistling in from the opposite direction.

Yvan is suddenly hurling his whole body over me, his hands grasping the sides of my head, his forehead pressed tightly to mine.

"Be still," he hisses, his fire unleashed and strafing through my lines.

Fear hits me with devastating force.

There's a buzz, and the air takes on a charge, as if an intense thunderstorm is about to blow through.

Heart thundering, I turn my head to see Marina huddling in a ball close to the ground. My brothers, Gareth and Andras encircle us. Trystan is holding up his wand, a translucent golden dome emanating from its tip and encasing all of us save the Lupines. Diana's crouched just outside Trystan's Mage-shield, but I don't see Jarod anywhere.

Then I realize we're not alone on the field.

Two Vu Trin sorceresses on black horses have appeared to my right. The women are staring straight at me, their eyes merciless, their arms raised and ready to throw more silver stars.

These two women's garb is different from most Vu Trin

sorceresses. Black scarves are wrapped tightly around their heads, and their clothing is deep gray instead of the usual black, marked with glowing blue Noi runes. Crossed swords are strapped to their backs, and lines of gleaming killing stars are fastened diagonally across their chests.

I'm thrust into panicked confusion.

Why are Vu Trin sorceresses firing stars at us? And who's trying to kill us with glowing arrows?

"Stand down!" a dominant female voice bellows from the direction of the woods we came from.

I whip my head around to see Commander Kam Vin riding out onto the field, coming in like a storm as she vehemently calls out a string of orders in the Noi language.

She's wearing her military uniform—a black tunic and pants marked with glowing blue runes, curved swords at her sides, a row of silver stars strapped diagonally across her chest. Her sister, Ni Vin, rides in behind her, also clad in her soldier garb.

Ni Vin meets my gaze, her face emotionless, but then her eyes widen when she spots Marina. A memory flashes through my mind of Ni Vin helping us hide Marina's presence in the North Tower, saving her from being recaptured.

"I've got everyone shielded, Yvan," Trystan says calmly. "You can let Ren go."

"Nice shield, my brother," Rafe says in grateful amazement.

"I've been practicing," Trystan replies coolly.

Yvan relaxes his grip on me, looks around, then slowly pulls himself away. He hovers by me, tense and coiled, his heat a violent frenzy.

I force myself into a sitting position and finally spot Jarod, hovering behind one of the women who attacked us with stars, his whole body tensed and ready to spring at them.

"You forget our agreement, Kam Vin," says the taller of the two gray-clad sorceresses, her eyes set unforgivingly on me. "The girl has made a move for Amaz lands."

Fear lances down my spine.

What is she talking about?

"You're going to leave my sister alone," Rafe's authoritative voice booms out. "Or you'll have to deal with every last one of us."

"Silence!" a deep voice just past the border commands.

I gasp as a line of rune-tattooed Amaz soldiers on horseback emerge from the border of dark forest and move straight through the suspended border-runes, as if the runes are as insubstantial as smoke. All of them, save one, are heavily armed with rune-marked weapons and dressed in crimson military tunics emblazoned with glowing scarlet runes, dark winter cloaks lined with black fur secured over their shoulders. All have black runes tattooed on their faces.

But the similarities end there.

Some possess the jewel-toned features of the Urisk, while others have the deep brown coloring of the southern Ishkartan. A few are pale and blonde like the northern Issani, and one Amaz soldier has emerald-patterned Smaragdalfar skin and green hair. Another bears the ivory hair and silver eyes of the Alfsigr Elves.

Amaz archers appear high in the branches of trees just behind the borderline, rune-arrows nocked in their bows, and a few of the women on horseback hold rune-spears aloft.

All of the weapons are trained on me.

My heart beats so hard it hurts, and I hear Diana begin to growl outside the shield as a young, hazel-skinned woman with black hair and pointed ears rides out ahead of the rest, a rune-axe in her hand. She appears to be the one in command, the other Amaz women's eyes now set on her.

The hazel-skinned woman points an accusing finger at me and pins stern eyes on Commander Vin. "The granddaughter of the Black Witch is poised to cross over into Amaz land. You will explain yourself *now*, Kam Vin."

"The girl is shielded," Commander Vin points out sharply as she faces down the Amaz and the gray-clad sorceresses. "Stand down, all of you, and we will discuss the situation."

"Order the Lupines to stand down first," the taller, gray-clad sorceress coldly replies. "Especially the one threatening to attack us from behind."

Jarod doesn't move. His amber eyes glow, and his lips pull back to expose formidable teeth.

"No one tells us to stand down," Diana snarls at the sorceress. "Our father is an alpha. Only *he* commands us."

"Then we respectfully ask the children of Gunther Ulrich to withdraw," the sorceress rejoins with calm diplomacy. "We have no argument with the Lupines. We wish only to kill the girl."

Terror leaps in my chest as Yvan grips my arm, his fire power mounting. Diana takes a menacing step toward the gray-clad Vu Trin, her lips pulling back into a snarl. "Make one move for Elloren Gardner, and I will rip your throat out!"

It's at that moment, amid my own debilitating fear, that I find my voice. "We need to speak to Freyja!" I choke out, rising to my feet.

Everyone turns to look at me with surprise.

The lean, hazel-skinned woman lowers her rune-axe a fraction and narrows her eyes at me. "I am Freyja."

"We were told to seek you out," I explain breathlessly. "Marina...the Selkie...she needs your help."

"The *Selkie*?"

Marina slowly raises herself from the ground, teetering a

bit as she struggles to find her balance. She reaches up and pulls her hood down, freeing her glittering silver hair.

A collective gasp goes up.

"Is this the groundskeeper's Selkie?" Commander Vin asks, incredulous.

Diana lets out a deep rumble of a growl. "She does not *belong* to him!"

Commander Vin rounds on her sister. "Did you know of this, Ni?"

Ni Vin's face remains impassive. "I chose to overlook it."

"You *chose* to overlook it?" Commander Vin's voice is steady, but it holds a knife edge of anger. "Is there anything *else* you might have chosen to overlook?"

"Who sent you to find me?" Freyja demands of me.

I hesitate to answer. Clive told me to mention his name to her *only* in private, but refusing to answer honestly seems like a bad idea right now. So, I take a deep breath and say, "Clive Soren."

The side of Freyja's mouth twitches and her posture becomes abruptly taller, her weapon higher, as if my words are a challenge.

An Urisk-featured Amaz soldier near Freyja shoots her a murderous look. This woman is easily the largest soldier here, broad and muscular, her coloring rose-white like Fernyllia's and Fern's, her rose hair short and spiked, her ears pointed. Her face is densely tattooed with small, circular runes, giving her skin the appearance of having scales.

I swallow nervously. "We went to Keltania to ask for his help in freeing the Selkies."

"You were in Keltania? Meeting with *Clive Soren*?" Commander Vin seems furious. She shoots her sister a quelling glare.

"Yes," I tell her. I turn back to Freyja. "He told us the Amaz may be willing to help us. The Mage Council is on the brink of killing all of the Selkies in the Western Realm. We need armed help to rescue them all."

Marina's musical voice rings out. "Elloren Gardner speaks the truth."

Another collective gasp.

"Avenging Goddess," Freyja breathes. "She speaks."

"Explain this, Kam Vin," the gray-clad sorceress demands, seeming stunned.

Commander Vin ignores her, focused only on me. "Elloren Gardner, explain yourself."

"Explain *myself*?" I cry. "I just did! Why don't *you* explain why you're all trying to *kill* me?"

"We cannot allow the Black Witch into Amaz lands," the gray-clad sorceress explains grimly.

"I am *not* the Black Witch!" I vehemently insist. "I've been wandtested. I'm a Level One Mage."

"She is powerless," Commander Vin affirms. "I tested her myself."

"There is one named Fallon Bane," Diana interjects, almost conversationally. "She's likely to be the next Black Witch, and you should smite her immediately."

"We know of this one," Freyja puts in somberly, her eyes flicking to Diana. "She is no Black Witch."

"They say her magic grows stronger by the day," Diana counters, "whereas Elloren Gardner has none."

The gray-clad sorceresses lower their stars in unison, and the Amaz look around at each other in bewilderment, as if trying to figure out what to do.

"What is your quest, Elloren Gardner?" Freyja asks me in a tone of confusion.

"To meet with your queen," I answer. "To petition her for help in freeing the Selkies."

Freyja motions toward Marina. "And…how, exactly, did you come upon this Selkie?"

"I freed her."

"With magic?" the gray-clad sorceress asks suspiciously.

I glower at her. "I just told you that I have no magic."

"Then how?" Freyja presses.

I shrug. "We unchained her and just…made a run for it."

"Made a run for it," Freyja repeats.

My temper flares. "Because I have *no magic*. I may look like my grandmother, but I have none of her power."

"She was despised by many," Freyja informs me gravely.

An embattled incredulity flashes through me. "Really? Was she?"

Yvan's hand finds my arm, as if cautioning me, his fire steadier now, consolidated.

The muscular, rose-skinned soldier moves forward threateningly, jutting her strong, square chin at our party. "If your men step one foot over our border, we will slay them. Especially *that* one." She points her huge rune-axe at Rafe. "*His* male energy is particularly strong."

Rafe's mouth falls open, and he stares at her, wide-eyed, as if he doesn't know whether to be offended or flattered.

"Only Diana Ulrich, Marina the Selkie and I seek to come across your border," I hastily clarify.

"I am their guard," Diana informs them with a flash of her teeth.

Commander Vin eyes me carefully before turning to her sister. "Ni, you will accompany them. And you will inform me if there are any more *surprises*."

Ni Vin inclines her head in assent. "Yes, Commander."

"And you will strike her down if she seeks to harm what is ours," the gray-clad sorceress puts in.

I'm thrust into complete confusion. *What are they afraid of me harming?*

Diana falls into a protective crouch. "Strike her down if you wish to have your face clawed to shreds, Sorceress."

"You forget, Kam Vin," Freyja interjects, "that this is *our* territory, and *we* decide who may cross over our borders."

"We implore you," Marina says to Freyja, and everyone stills, all eyes on Marina. She splays her palms out in supplication, her flute-like tones breaking through. "Please, let us enter your land for an audience with your queen."

Freyja's hostility dissipates as she looks at Marina, her expression now conflicted. Her eyes flit to me, then back to Marina as she deliberates. She lifts her chin, as if decided. "I will grant you leave to cross," she finally says. "Diana Ulrich and Ni Vin may cross with you."

Freyja cuts me a glare. "You may also accompany them, Elloren Gardner. But only under close guard." She motions toward Commander Vin and the two gray-clad sorceresses with her rune-axe. "As for you—the Vu Trin will meet us here in two weeks' time to collect what is yours. Your time is almost up. The debt stands repaid."

I'm cast into further confusion. *What debt?*

"The Wand, Elloren Gardner," the gray-clad sorceress asks, her eyes set tight on me. "Is it still in your possession?"

I swallow hard, my head spinning as everyone's eyes turn to me. *They know about Sage's wand. How do they know?*

"Yes," I croak out, acutely aware of the spiraling wand pushed into the side of my boot.

The sorceress visibly relaxes and glances toward Ni Vin. "Watch the Gardnerian closely, Ni Vin," she cautions, her eyes darting back to me. "The Wand may have sought her out, but do not forget the evil blood that flows in her veins."

"I forget nothing," Ni Vin says grimly.

"See that you don't."

With that, the gray-clad Vu Trin sorceresses prod their dark horses into motion and ride into the forest, Jarod calmly stepping aside to let them pass. Freyja watches them go before turning back to consider us. She points her rune-axe toward the ivory-skinned Alfsigr-featured Amaz. "The Selkie may ride with Thraso." Then she looks to me. "You, Elloren Gardner, will ride with Valasca."

A dark-eyed young woman in a rune-marked indigo tunic rides forward. She appears to be around my age, or perhaps just a few years older. A small rune-knife is sheathed on her belt and she carries herself with a magnetic bravado. Her features look Noi, but her ears are pointed, her skin is sky-blue and her short, spiky black hair is streaked with vivid blue highlights. Her face is marked with Amaz rune-tattoos, and a fur-lined, black cloak is draped over her shoulders.

Valasca peers at me through Trystan's shield and smiles.

"Ni Vin," Freyja continues to direct us all, "you will ride with Euryleia. And Diana Ulrich—"

"I ride with no one," Diana counters. "I will run alongside Elloren Gardner."

"We travel fast, Lupine."

Diana smirks. "Then you might have a chance of keeping up with me, Amaz."

The other soldiers go very still, as if in awe of her boldness, but Freyja smiles widely and she dips her head to Diana. "It is an honor to meet you, Diana Ulrich."

Diana smiles back—not a friendly smile, mind you, but a wild-eyed, feral grin that makes the hair on the back of my neck stand up on end.

The huge rune-scaled Amaz soldier is still glowering at me threateningly as she grips her gigantic rune-axe. Her aggressive posture gives me serious pause.

What are we doing here? These people just tried to kill me. This is a cliff, and we're about to step right over its edge.

But then I catch sight of another face: Marina's. Seeming to sense my hesitation, her expression has morphed into one of sheer desperation.

"You can drop the shield," I shakily tell Trystan. He holds my gaze for a long, questioning moment, then murmurs a spell and the shield fizzes into oblivion, the amber wash over everything fading away.

Yvan's hand falls away from my arm as I step forward toward the young Amaz, Valasca. "I'm ready," I tell her.

Valasca grins and reaches down to help pull me onto her horse with a surprisingly strong arm. I settle in behind her and wrap my arms around her waist.

"Interesting company you keep, Gardnerian," she observes, turning her head to shoot me a wide, mischievous grin. She glances over at Diana, who stands beside us and is watching me closely. "The daughter of Gunther Ulrich. A most *excellent* choice of bodyguard."

A nervous tremble kicks up inside me, and I try in vain to still it.

"Relax, Elloren Gardner," she tells me, an edge of seriousness to her tone. "I'll protect you, as well."

I eye her with distrust. "You've only just met me."

Valasca shrugs. "I'm willing to give you the benefit of the doubt, Gardnerian, but only because you freed the Selkie. For over a year now, I've been trying to convince my people that we should do something to help the Selkies. I saw one once, when traveling near the Gardnerian border." Valasca's heavily accented Common Tongue grows tight with outrage. "They had her in a cage. Her movements, her voice... it was all very seal-like. But her eyes... I only had to look into her eyes, and I knew."

Valasca looks down at her horse and pats its neck affectionately, her expression lightening. She shoots me a wry smile. "It's my belief that you have to look past the surface of things to get to the truth of the matter. Wouldn't you agree, Elloren Gardner?"

She doesn't wait for my answer, but instead rides forward through the runes and over the border until we're just past her fellow Amaz. She raises her arm up to the heavens and looks around as the Amaz fall in around her. "Hold tight," she cautions me before calling out something in another language.

Then Valasca swipes her arm down, and we set off like a bolt of lightning. I glance back over my shoulder quickly, straining for one last look at Yvan and the others. I catch only a brief glimpse of Yvan's fierce eyes, and a hard rush of his fire, before the thick pine forest closes in around us, like a massive green door slamming shut.

CHAPTER TWO

THE AMAZAKARAN

I'm not prepared for the speed at which we move, the thunderous sound of hooves kicking up soil and snow all around us. At times, it's like the trees are hurtling straight at us, set to collide. But always, we swerve just in time, like rapids zooming through the forest. It's both exhilarating and terrifying, and I hang on to Valasca's cloaked form for dear life.

We ride through the long break in the Northern Spine as the shadows lengthen, and I lose track of time. Before long, a brilliant moon hangs above us, silvery clouds dispersing to reveal brightening stars. The immense Spine rises on either side of us to tower above the black-limbed treetops, and I stare up at it in awe.

I remember riding over those same jagged peaks with Lukas, the Spine staggeringly beautiful from above. But here, below it, I've a clearer sense of its overwhelming heft, and it takes my breath away.

It's bone-achingly cold, our speed knifing the icy air into my body. My fingers are becoming stiff and difficult to bend, and I begin to grow concerned about the dropping tempera-ture, wondering if we'll all become irreparably frostbitten.

A broader path opens up before us, and suddenly, the forest gives way to a Spine-stone road that cuts through haphaz-ard piles of mammoth white boulders. There's a borderline of suspended crimson runes just ahead.

Valasca pivots to grin at me, then yells out a hearty order in another language. Everyone's horses break into a faster run, the animals' hooves pounding the stone beneath us.

Terror clamps on to me with staggering force.

We're riding at a faster and faster clip toward what looks like the edge of a cliff. Just past it, splayed out before us, are the lights of an immense city in a bowl-shaped valley, the snowcapped Caledonian Mountains just beyond.

The Amaz border city of Cyme—the largest of the six Amaz cities set throughout the Caledonian mountain range.

My fear-stricken mind absorbs all the details of the scene at once—countless buildings densely covering the central valley, their roofs streaked with illuminated red lines.

And there's green. Everywhere in the valley. *Green* in the dead of winter.

And we're going to ride straight off a cliff of Spine-stone and hurtle down into it.

I glance pleadingly at Diana, who's running beside us, her hair flowing behind her like a pennant. Diana meets my eyes and bares her teeth in an invigorated grin.

"We need to stop," I protest frantically, panic building. "Stop the horse, Valasca!"

Valasca glances back at me with a rakish smile. "Hold on to your head, Gardnerian." She snaps the reins and urges the horse faster.

A scream takes form in my throat as the cliff barrels to-ward us.

In unison, all of the Amaz thrust their arms out, palms flat, fingers splayed open. Glowing crimson runes spring to life on the backs of their hands as we race toward the line of larger runes and the precipitous drop. Valasca's palm smashes into a huge rune and blinding red light rays out from her hand. A huge, translucent dome encasing the entire valley briefly flashes into view above and around us, warm air enveloping us all.

"Auuughhhhh!" I cry out as we gallop straight for the cliff's edge.

Just as we reach the cliff, flat, circular runes burst into life at its edge and multiply out like a swarm of insects to rapidly form a crimson road suspended high in the air. I clamp my arms around Valasca as our horse seamlessly rides off the stone road and onto the rune-road.

Swept up with a dizzying vertigo and desperate relief, I take in the startling view. The rune-road continues to form ahead of us as we ride out over the city, the runes multiplying at incredible speed.

Valasca holds up an arm, and everyone slows to a canter, then to a trot.

My heart racing, my breathing staggered, I loosen my death grip on Valasca's waist, and she gives a low chuckle. I note, with pure amazement, that it's summer here, the frosty sting in my cheeks giving way to a flushed, prickling heat. Green-leafed trees, gardens and farms are spread throughout the entire valley, many of the farms set under geometric glass domes marked with huge scarlet runes.

"How is it summer?" I ask Valasca, overcome with awe.

"Advanced rune-sorcery," she says with a grin, then points up. "You might have noticed the dome."

I look up, nothing visible above but the star-strewn night

sky. "What would happen if someone tried to fly a dragon through that dome?" I wonder.

Valasca's chest jostles with laughter. "A rather large explosion. Flying limbs. A blood-streaked sky. I'd say that it's not advised."

I raise my brow at this. *Good*, I think. At least the Amaz might have a chance of withstanding a Gardnerian military assault.

Below us, Elfin-style buildings are carved into the Spine's northern face, curving like seashells and giving way to a dome-covered forest filled with strange trees. "That's our University," Valasca tells me.

"I've never seen trees like that before," I marvel.

"Those are the University research gardens," Valasca says proudly. "We have plants from all over Erthia."

The rune-road zips out before us toward a glowing red pole rising up from the center of the city. There's a large disc atop the pole, and our rune-road slams into it with a burst of red light.

As we ride out onto the enormous disc, the rune-road disappears behind us, fading back toward the Spine as fast as it formed, then blinks out of sight.

"Holy Ancient One in the heavens above," I gasp, letting out a long, shuddering breath as I watch the road disappear.

Valasca gives a hearty laugh. "It's always fun to watch people experience that for the first time."

Diana's looking around at the panoramic view with relaxed curiosity, completely unfazed. Ni Vin also seems unaffected by our death-defying entrance. Only Marina meets my gaze with a wide-eyed look of lingering fright.

"Weren't you the least bit scared?" I say to Diana rather shrilly.

She blinks at me as if I'm being a tad alarmist. "I smelled

no fear from their entire party. It was clear some sorcery would create our path."

I flinch as the disc we're standing on starts to descend down the central pole like a wheel on an axle, the horses fidgeting. The pole, close up, is as thick as a mammoth tree trunk, and formed by a long stack of glowing, rotating scarlet runes.

"How did your people build a road like this?" I ask Valasca, astonished.

Valasca shoots me a sly look. "Our rune-sorceresses bring together runic systems from all of our origin cultures. When we combine them, we can do more with them." Her smile widens. "It gives us an incredible edge."

"I thought rune-sorcery was rare."

"It is. We only have twelve rune-sorceresses," she tells me. "But they span almost every tradition in the known world. What they lack in numbers, they make up for in diversity. Which leads to enhanced power."

I look around, astonished by what they've accomplished with their rune-sorcery. Gardnerian wand magic pales in comparison to some of the things they've created here.

Countless buildings densely cover the central valley. My eyes dart around, straining to take it all in from this height. There are so many styles of architecture here, unlike the mostly uniform Spine-stone styles of Verpacia or the unvarying Ironwood forest designs of Gardneria. It's all varied and mixed—as if every type of architecture on Erthia was thrown into the valley and tossed with a mixing spoon.

Long lines of glowing red trace the angles of each roof, casting the entire city in an otherworldly, scarlet glow. I point the glowing red lines out to Valasca as we descend, asking her what they are.

"Lines of runes," she says. "They power lights and stoves

and such. When the different runic systems are melded, they turn red. Hence our rather monolithic color scheme."

The stone floor of an enormous circular plaza is gradually rising up to meet us, its tilework fashioned into a multicolored design made up of interlocking runes. The sound of female voices echoes everywhere, spread thick across the plaza and beyond—women shouting, women talking and laughing boisterously, women singing along to the melodic sound of string instruments. All women. No men.

A crowd is gathering below us, the plaza illuminated by guttering light of countless torches that send up scarlet flame.

An immense Spine-stone sculpture stands in the center of the plaza below, reminiscent of the statue of my grandmother back in Valgard. Only this monument depicts the Amaz Goddess in flowing garments, her belt a twining serpent. There's a white dove on the Goddess's shoulder, and the three First Sisters sit at her feet, gazing up at her adoringly. Below the First Sisters, a ring of small, horned deer prance.

Beyond the Goddess sculpture lies the largest structure in the valley—a massive geodesic dome with a series of smaller domes attached to its base, like offshoots.

"That's the Queenhall, home to Queen Alkaia's Council," Valasca says proudly. "That's where we're going."

The Goddess statue rises up to tower over us as we finish our descent. We smoothly connect with the ground, the runes beneath us winking out of existence, and a ring of stone-faced, heavily armed soldiers in rune-marked scarlet tunics fall in to surround us, a throng of curious onlookers just beyond them.

The Amaz all over the plaza are as varied as our own party. Urisk of every class. Alfsigr and Smaragdalfar Elves. Elfhollen, Ishkartan, Keltic, Noi—and even a few Gardnerians, their skin tinged with a green glow like mine, some of them with fastmarked hands. Many of the women seem to be of mixed heritage, like Andras and Professor Volya, and their clothing is as varied as they are.

Only the black rune-tattoos on their faces mark them as uniformly Amaz.

Every Amaz, save the young children, is heavily armed with rune-knives, swords or axes strapped to their bodies, along with many gleaming weapons I've never seen before. Even the very old women wear sly, curved knives hanging from intricately woven belts and small double-sided hatchets fastened to their arms.

I think of Andras's adept mastery in the use of so many weapons and remember what he told me about the Amaz training all children in a wide variety of weaponry and martial arts.

Freyja points sharply at me and gives what sounds like a firm order to Valasca in another language. Valasca nods, then smiles and says something jauntily in return. I gather that Valasca's response has been somewhat cheeky, as Freyja shoots her a stern look before riding up to the soldiers surrounding our party.

Freyja confers with the soldiers, then rides off with nine of them toward the Queenhall, effectively splitting our numbers in half. The rest of us set off in the same direction as well, but slowly enough that Diana can now saunter beside me.

The Queenhall is covered with a stunning mosaic design fashioned in every shade of scarlet and deep purple, its geometric surface edged with lines of glowing scarlet runes. Worked into the front of the dome is a gigantic arcing entrance framed by a carved ivory snake, its tail undulating out onto the plaza. Beyond the arch is a series of multicolored curtains, each receding layer draping slightly longer than the one before, giving the entryway the appearance of a lush, fabric tunnel.

Rune-torches affixed to black spiraling posts bracket the Queenhall entrance and wash it in a crimson glow.

A sizable crowd is assembling near the Queenhall, spilling out over half the plaza. The dense group parts as we near, and some of the women gasp as they catch sight of me, their eyes narrowing—the older ones in particular. Their hands instinctively reach for swords or axes, as the children are swiftly hidden from view or spirited away entirely.

As we draw closer to the entrance, Valasca leans down to press her face against our horse, her eyes closed, reminding me of Andras's runed-enhanced way with horses. I remember that some of the Amaz rune-tattoos confer the ability to speak to horses with one's mind, among many other skills.

Our horse slows, then stops, and Valasca dismounts. She helps me down, then gives the mare a pat and prods her to trot off with the other horses.

The crowd is thickening around us, growing increasingly threatening in their demeanor. They're rendered all the more intimidating by the crimson torchlight, the world of the plaza a menacing landscape of flickering red light and shadow.

Diana glides closer to me in a protective stance, her wild eyes darting around, and Valasca's hand comes to rest on my back. "Stay near me," she whispers in my ear, her gaze carefully scanning the women around us.

I glance over my shoulder at Marina, who shoots me an anxious look, her ocean eyes round with worry, her arm linked through Ni Vin's. Ni Vin seems to have appointed herself as Marina's bodyguard, her unscarred hand resting lightly on the hilt of the curved sword that hangs at her side, her face expressionless as she surveys the crowd.

As we approach the Queenhall, I see that the huge rune-scaled, rose-skinned soldier has positioned herself between us and the curtained entryway, her mammoth frame blocking our way, her rune-axe gripped menacingly in both fists. We slow to a stop a few feet away from her, and the crowd's belligerent muttering dies down.

"Make way, Alcippe," Valasca orders with a casual swipe of her hand. "The Gardnerian is here to speak with Queen Alkaia. You know this. And Freyja has ordered that it be so."

"No," Alcippe growls, tightening her grip on her axe.

"Alcippe, what are you doing?" Valasca asks, seeming genuinely confused. "This is Freyja's decision."

Alcippe's face takes on a look of deep disdain, and she spits out a derisive laugh. "Freyja has forgotten who she is. I am overriding her decision."

Valasca and Alcippe launch into an intense string of conversation in another language. Then, without warning—and to my immense horror—Alcippe snarls something at Valasca and starts toward me, hoisting her rune-axe.

Fear bolts through me as Diana yanks me roughly behind her and Valasca pulls out a knife, leveling it at Alcippe.

The warrior freezes midstep, eyeing the small, glinting blade.

A *very* small blade, I note, heart hammering, compared to Alcippe's terrifyingly huge weapon.

Valasca raises her palm. "Stand down, Alcippe. You are outmatched."

Alcippe laughs contemptuously and glances around at the women encircling us, the crowd mirroring her hostility. "I think not," she counters, taking another threatening step forward.

"Queen Alkaia *must* have the final say!" Valasca insists, standing her ground. She's a good deal shorter than Alcippe, slender and sinewy in her build. I wonder if she's completely given leave of her senses to take on this monster of a warrior.

Alcippe's eyes cut to mine, blazing with ferocity. "I will not have that *evil creature* defile the air Queen Alkaia breathes! Move aside, Valasca!"

"Alcippe, *please*, stand down," Valasca persists, rune-blade still out, refusing to give an inch. Alcippe's eyes dart toward the knife again as she hesitates, looking both hell-bent on murder and deeply conflicted.

Then, to my overwhelming and blessed surprise, she lowers her rune-axe and steps aside with angry reluctance.

Diana, who always amazes me with her ability to say exactly the wrong thing at the wrong time, gestures haughtily toward Alcippe's heavy weapon, her expression contemptuous. "You think you can subdue us with that toy of yours?"

"Toy?" Alcippe lurches forward and growls through gritted teeth. "You will not think it a toy when it splits your head down the middle, Lupine!"

In a flash, Diana is crouched, her eyes bright and feral, lips pulled back to expose her teeth. Claws form and fur spreads over the hand she now has arced over her head. "Take one more step, Amaz," Diana says very slowly, flexing her wickedly curving claws, "and I will add *your* head to the collection I've ripped from the necks of my former enemies."

Just as all hell seems about to break loose, Marina launches herself between Diana and Alcippe, her gills flying open. She opens her mouth and lets out one of her unearthly, flutelike tones. Everyone turns to look at her, caught off guard by the eerie sound.

Marina pulls back her hood, and the crowd gasps in surprise. She looks around worriedly, then tenses her neck and pulls her gills in flat. "We are here to beg for your help. To rescue my people."

Murmurs of "The Selkie speaks!" can be heard all around, as well as cries of astonishment in a multitude of languages.

"We need your help." Marina looks to Alcippe entreatingly. "Please. I beg of you."

Alcippe stills, then turns to glare at Diana for a good, long moment, a storm of rage in her rose-colored eyes. Diana, never one to back down from a fight, is more than happy to meet the warrior's glare, her lips curled into a scary smile.

Alcippe's mouth tenses, her hands so tight on her weapon that her knuckles have paled, but she steps back and stands down. "Out of respect for the Selkie," she announces, her eyes tight on Diana, "and *only* because of her, I will not kill you right now, Lupine."

Valasca, Marina and I breathe a collective sigh of relief.

Diana gives a disdainful snort. "And I will let you keep your head for another day, Amaz."

Alcippe's posture stiffens, and Valasca shoots Diana a look of fierce censure.

"Thank you," Marina says gratefully to Alcippe. She sends Diana a desperate glance, as if silently pleading with her to stay silent, before turning back to Alcippe once more. "Thank you for your compassion."

This showing of respect seems to mollify the rose-haired warrior. She nods curtly at Marina and storms into the Queenhall, the others in the crowd slowly filtering in after her.

I round on Diana. "Do you *really* collect the 'heads of your former enemies'?"

Diana waves a dismissive hand. "That is irrelevant."

"Irrelevant?"

"Yes, irrelevant."

"Diana, she's the biggest, scariest soldier here. And you threaten to tear her head off?"

Diana flips her long blond hair over her shoulder and brings her hand to her hip. *"She. Was. Rude."*

"You *promised* to be diplomatic!"

Diana straightens her posture and glares at me imperiously. "I am the daughter of Gunther Ulrich. There is only so much I am willing to put up with."

"Well, then," I snap, "at least let me do the talking while we're in front of the queen!"

"Fine," she replies tightly.

Valasca is looking at Diana and me like we've sprouted horns. She turns to Marina. "Are they always like this?"

Marina nods, her face solemn as Ni Vin quietly shadows Marina, ignoring the rest of us completely.

Valasca looks to the heavens and mutters a low oath to herself before sheathing her rune-blade. "Come on." She motions for us to follow her. "You came here to speak with our queen. Well, here's your chance."

Before we enter, Valasca pauses to caution us. "Do not step on the threshold. And remember to bow low before the queen—"

"We know, we know," Diana says impatiently, striding past her through the wall of curtains, forcing the rest of us to follow along in her wake.

CHAPTER
THREE

QUEEN ALKAIA

We push through the series of scarlet and deep purple curtains and enter a large foyer lined with brightly embroidered garnet rugs and tapestries. Countless pairs of shoes are lined up on one side of the room, cloaks and other garments folded up on sectioned wooden shelves on the other.

Valasca instructs us to remove our shoes and cloaks, then lifts the edge of a heavy curtain and steps over an enameled threshold that's brightly styled in the design of a multicolored snake. She turns and motions for us to follow her into the hall.

The curving walls and ceiling of the Queenhall are huge and luxuriously lined with more garnet tapestries. The embroidered designs depict various images from the Amaz religious history—the three First Women walking in a beautiful garden with the Great Goddess; the slaying of the cruel male partner by the only faithful daughter; the Goddess rewarding this faithful daughter, naming her Amaz as she places a rune-stylus made of starlight into her hand.

At the head of the Queenhall, there's an enormous tapestry flowing out over the ceiling, showing the Great Goddess surrounded by white birds. Hundreds of them, swirling toward the ceiling until they reach its apex, where they blend to form a single, gigantic ivory bird.

I'm momentarily transfixed by the Goddess's birds, which are so like the Ancient One's bird shown in the stained-glass windows of our cathedral in Valgard. So much like the white birds in Wynter's sculptures and woven into her tapestries. The birds that led me to Marina.

The Watchers.

A shiver ripples through me, and I'm instantly aware of the pale wooden wand hidden in my boot and gripped by the desire to curl my fingers around its spiraling handle.

The long, oval interior of the Queenhall is even bigger than Valgard's Cathedral and supported by multiple columns of stacked, rotating runes. A richly carpeted central walkway leads to a raised dais at the far end of the hall, and scores of women fill the rest of the space, eating, conversing and laughing together.

My gaze darts around as we start down the walkway. A circle of green-scaled, silver-eyed Smaragdalfar Elves sitting to our left catches my eye, the young women drinking tea and talking. They're all dressed in deep green tunics and pants of the subland Elves, looping black embroidery edging their garments, but their cheeks are marked with the signature Amaz rune-tattoos.

Another woman approaches their group. She has the pointed ears, bone-white skin and silver eyes of the Alfsigr Elves, but her hair is a shock of violet. She catches my gaze, and her eyes narrow. A flush stings at my cheeks, and I look quickly away, abashed to be caught staring.

Some of the Amaz are busy serving food throughout the

hall, the aromas of rich, unfamiliar spices and fresh bread wafting on the air. I watch as women accept bowls of food and notice that it seems to be the custom to bow slightly in thanks.

My eyes widen as I spot a golden-hued Urisk woman who is naked from the waist up. She's laughing and chatting with two other women while a baby suckles contentedly at her breast. I've never seen a woman nursing so brazenly, and it both shocks and fascinates me. Such a thing is completely forbidden in Gardneria—Keltania and Verpacia, too. In all of these places, women nurse privately, and even then, with the baby hidden away underneath loose tunics.

I suddenly notice that we're attracting a fair bit of attention ourselves. Women throughout the Queenhall turn to stare at us, and a cacophony of distressed conversation rises, soon encompassing the entire room. I glance around nervously as we approach the raised Queen's dais at the end of the massive hall.

In the center of the dais, reclining back against lush cushions, is a very elderly woman. Her skin is deep green, her ears swiftly pointed, and her white hair is styled in stiff, sculptured loops that grace her head like a curling crown. She's heavily adorned with black metallic piercings and tattoos that swirl all over her deeply lined face.

I realize, with surprise, that this frail-looking old woman must be the powerful Queen Alkaia.

She's flanked by an entourage of formidable warriors in uniform. The fierce-looking women are also seated on cushions, weapons affixed to their backs or propped against the base of the huge Goddess tapestry. Alcippe is among them, sitting directly to the left of the queen, her rune-axe within arm's reach behind her. She catches sight of us as we advance, glowering with open hostility.

I swallow hard as I take in Alcippe's lethal glare, my heart pounding as I pull in a deep breath to steady myself.

Valasca slows to a stop as we reach the dais, and we come to a halt behind her. Queen Alkaia's piercing gaze zeroes in on me. She raises a trembling, gnarled hand, and the troubled sounds throughout the hall die down, then disappear altogether.

"Approach, travelers," Queen Alkaia says, beckoning us forward.

We step a bit closer, and I mirror Valasca's example, dropping to my knees and bowing deeply. Marina follows suit beside me, and I catch her tense look as we press our foreheads to the carpeted floor.

Diana and Ni Vin remain stolidly on their feet.

"Well, well," the queen says, her deep voice wizened and heavily accented. "This is a night of surprises. Can it be true? The granddaughter of Carnissa Gardner has come to petition the Queen of the Amaz for help?"

"It is true, Queen Alkaia," I say into the red-patterned rug. "I am Elloren Gardner, and we seek your aid."

Angry sounds erupt, filling the dome, and I stiffen in response. Eventually, the incensed noises recede, and I realize the queen must have motioned for silence. I venture a glance up at her.

"Rise, travelers," Queen Alkaia directs, a wry note to her tone. Marina, Valasca and I straighten, but remain on our knees.

"Valasca," Queen Alkaia says with amusement, her eyes lighting on our companion, "it was kind of you to agree to act as guard to these travelers."

Valasca rises to her feet, smiling broadly, and bows gracefully to the queen with a dramatic flourish. "I am at your service, Queen Alkaia, and happy to act as chaperone to our Gardnerian guest."

Queen Alkaia smirks. "Hmm. See that you don't chaperone her *too* closely, Valasca. I do not need the entire Gardnerian military amassed on our border, intent on stealing back the granddaughter of the Black Witch."

Steal back? What is she talking about?

"Elloren Gardner," Queen Alkaia says, growing serious, "there are many here who remember what your grandmother did to our people. There is talk that you should be struck down, as your grandmother should have been, before her powers reached their zenith."

Murmurs of assent well up, and I slump down, alarmed.

"I have no power," I insist, my voice unsteady. "I'm no threat to any of you."

"And yet you have brought a most dangerous guard." The queen looks at Diana, who is in her usual confident stance, completely at ease and unintimidated.

"I am Diana Ulrich of the Gerwulf Pack." I wait to hear her entire family tree, down to the last cousin, and am amazed when she stops there. Diana shoots me a smug look before turning back to Queen Alkaia. "Elloren Gardner is soon to be a sister to me, and I have come here as her bodyguard. She rescued Marina the Selkie from a vile man who should be slain immediately, and she wishes to raise an army to free the other Selkie women."

The hall breaks out into complete confusion. Marina, perhaps seeing this as her cue, hesitantly forces herself to her feet, her silver hair glinting in the rune-light.

"Speak, Selkie," Queen Alkaia orders, a hush once again falling over the room. "If it is, in fact, true that you can."

Marina pulls her gills in flat, her face determined. "We need your help, Queen Alkaia," she says in an unsteady voice.

"My people are being held prisoner by the Gardnerians, and their Mage Council is about to rule to have us slaughtered."

Shocked whispers fill the room. "So, it is true," Queen Alkaia observes wonderingly. "The Selkie speaks."

After studying Marina for a long moment, the queen turns back to me, her eyes narrowing. "Elloren Gardner. Do you understand why the sorceress, Ni Vin, has been sent to guard you?"

"There is a fear that I'm the Black Witch of Prophecy," I say. "Since I resemble my grandmother."

"You look *exactly* like your grandmother," Queen Alkaia puts in sharply.

Vexation flares. "That may be true, but I am unlike her in many ways. And I have absolutely no access to magic." I spare a brief glance at Ni Vin. "I don't understand why you feel I need a Vu Trin guard, to tell you the truth."

More unsettled murmuring ripples through the crowd. Queen Alkaia turns to stone-still Ni Vin and considers her speculatively. "And you, Sorceress? Do you believe this Gardnerian's aims are what she says they are?"

Ni Vin regards me thoughtfully. "I do," she finally affirms. "She did a brave thing, freeing the Selkie. I believe she is like her grandmother in looks only."

The hall erupts into another wave of angry protest. Queen Alkaia waits patiently, as if carefully gauging the situation.

"And where did you get your wounds, Sorceress?" Queen Alkaia asks Ni Vin when the crowd finally stills.

Ni Vin stiffens. "At the hands of Carnissa Gardner."

There's a fresh eruption of furious voices, and Ni Vin waits for the livid protests to subside before continuing. "It was during the Realm War," she explains, devoid of emotion. "The Black Witch rained fire down on my people as she pushed east, and my sister's home was hit by one of her fireballs. I lost my entire family that day, save my sister. I was cursed to live."

A wave of shame jettisons through me. I suspected that Ni Vin was wounded during the Realm War, but to hear her state it so plainly is devastating.

"Yet you are willing to give this girl a chance?" Queen Alkaia asks.

"I am, but only because of the Selkie."

Queen Alkaia sits back and relaxes her posture. "Then perhaps," she suggests to everyone assembled, "we might follow your example, and at least give the Gardnerian an opportunity to tell her story. I, for one, am curious about how the granddaughter of the Black Witch has come to not only rescue a Selkie, but to befriend the daughter of a Lupine alpha."

Everyone's heads turn in unison to look at me, none of their eyes friendly. It's quiet as death, except for the restless cries of a few babies and small children.

"Rise, then, Elloren Gardner," the queen says, a note of challenge in her tone. "It seems as if the floor belongs to you."

I swallow hard, feeling slightly faint as my heart thunders in my chest. I take a deep breath and rise to my feet, bolstered by Marina's eyes locked encouragingly on me.

With a tremulous voice, I launch into my tale—close to the whole story, except for the parts about Naga, Sage's pale, spiraling wand and the destruction of the military base. My nerves gradually smooth out, my voice steadying as I go on.

When I've finished, I remain on my feet, with Diana, Marina, Valasca and Ni Vin beside me.

"So, I am to believe," Queen Alkaia says, "that the granddaughter of Carnissa Gardner—a girl who looks *exactly* like her grandmother—has befriended two Icarals and the children of a Lupine alpha, freed a Selkie and has a brother who is soon to become Lupine? All of this is true?"

"Yes, Queen Alkaia."

The queen studies me for a long moment, and then she does something no one seems to expect.

She breaks out into laughter.

Eventually regaining her composure, Queen Alkaia turns to the rune-scaled warrior beside her. "May I suggest, Alcippe," she says, "that if you wish to take revenge upon this girl's family, the best way to do so would be by letting her *live*."

She turns back to me and smiles widely. "You are a troublemaker, Elloren Gardner. And for that reason alone, you are *most* welcome here. Come, join us." She glances out over the crowd benevolently. "Make room for the Gardnerian and her companions." She looks back down at me. "Eat. We will set a formal time for your appeal tomorrow morn, after everyone has been well-fed and well-rested. Hopefully, at that time, cooler heads will prevail."

I feel Valasca's cautioning hand on my arm as Queen Alkaia turns her attention elsewhere, and conversation and movement break out in the large room. The looks directed at me are still hostile, but now dampened, like a fire Queen Alkaia has sprinkled water on from her savvy, ancient hands.

CHAPTER
FOUR

ALCIPPE

Valasca ushers us to a section of the room that's far away from Alcippe.

Amaz around us are being handed food by smiling servers who chat with the women as they pass around steaming bowls of fragrant stew and flat, circular bread off of large, golden trays.

Diana and I sit down on embroidered pillows as Valasca jauntily calls out to a woman serving food nearby, giving her a friendly smile and respectful nod. The blonde, Keltic-featured woman, returns the gesture and makes her way over to us, and I notice she has snake tattoos interspersed among her rune-tattoos, jewel-eyed serpent bracelets twined around her wrists and arms. Her expression turns chilly when she catches sight of Diana and me.

She hands Valasca a portion of fragrant stew, a cup of something milky and a piece of golden flatbread, then flashes Diana an unfriendly scowl and practically tosses a bowl of food at her, which Diana deftly catches. The woman then brusquely shoves another bowl into my hands, and I fumble as I accept it, the bowl dropping to the floor, stew spilling out onto the carpet.

Valasca sends the woman an exasperated look and exclaims something in another language, but the woman just snaps something back at her and glares at me before stalking off.

Marina, on the other hand, is being carefully tended to by a large group of women, who are plying her with plates of fish and peppering her with questions, their faces full of concern. I catch Marina's eyes for a moment, her expression looking overwhelmed, and I nod encouragingly, trying to ignore the spilled food on the edge of my dark skirts.

We're here for Marina, I bolster myself, noting the belligerent looks sent my way from some of the women surrounding her. How they feel about me doesn't matter, as long as they help the Selkies—and their reaction to Marina thus far is deeply heartening.

Ni Vin is sitting just behind Marina, her quiet, shadowing presence and honed frame radiating latent power as she surveys Marina's well-wishers.

Diana picks at her stew, sniffing the pieces of cooked meat disdainfully before deigning to eat it as she glowers across the room at Alcippe, fully immersed in her newfound grudge. Alcippe glares back at Diana from the Queen's dais, like a coal simmering hot, seemingly unaware of the beautiful, smiling young woman with spring-green skin who's repeatedly touching her arm, trying to snag her attention. Alcippe's companion has stiff deep green braids that frame her face in the shape of butterfly wings and are adorned with multicolored orbs of light, and her flowing attire is comprised of silken scarves of every color imaginable.

I sigh and move to clean up the spilled stew, but Valasca has already beaten me to it. She mutters to herself as she cleans, then catches the eye of a gray-haired Urisk woman hovering close by, a food tray in her hands. This older woman has the rose-white skin of the Urisk's lowest Uuril class, like Fern and Fernyllia and Alcippe. Unlike most of the women here, she's unmarked by tattoos and dressed in a simple brown tunic and pants. When Valasca waves her over with a gentle smile, she approaches us submissively, her head bowed, her eyes on the ground.

She kneels and holds out the tray of food and drink to me as if I'm royalty—and as if I might strike her down if she displeases me. I take a bowl of stew, a cup of milk and a circle of bread from the tray, my mind thrust into confusion over her behavior.

She's acting like she's a slave.

But Clive Soren said the Amaz can't abide the abuse of women. How could they have an Uuril slave?

The gray-haired woman is still kneeling before me, her head down, as if awaiting my verdict. Valasca taps my shoulder. "Touch her arm and say this…" She speaks a few words in Uriskal.

I do as Valasca directs, and the woman looks up, relief washing through eyes the color of rose quartz. She's smiling at me like a child who's just been spared the cane.

Anger starts a slow burn at the base of my neck as the woman bows to me over and over as she backs away. There are lash scars on her neck and face and arms, and there's something not quite right about her, as if she's suffered one too many blows to the head.

I turn to Valasca, my face rigid with disgust. "So. You have Uuril slaves here?"

Valasca only seems to be half listening to me as she scoops up her stew with a piece of bread. "Sala isn't a slave," she says flatly.

What kind of fool does she take me for?

My rage notches higher. "She's running around serving and bowing as if she'll be struck if she displeases any of you. It's obvious she's been beaten one too many times, and she doesn't have the markings of your people."

"She's Alcippe's mother."

"What?"

My eyes fly to the Queen's dais, seeking out scale-tattooed Alcippe. The huge warrior is watching the Uuril serving woman, the hatred of her previous expression replaced by one of deep pain.

I glance over at Sala. "But she doesn't look anything like Alcippe," I counter, shaking my head in disbelief. Alcippe is taller than Rafe and almost as muscular as Andras. This Uuril serving woman is frail and short; Alcippe's complete opposite.

"Alcippe resembles her father," Valasca explains around the food in her mouth. "Ever heard of Farg Kyul?"

Farg Kyul. One of the strongest and most ruthless Urisk commanders during the Realm War—and one of the few lower-class Urisk to be granted dragonlord status.

"He was Alcippe's father?" I ask, incredulous. "How did she wind up here?"

Valasca swallows and wipes her mouth with the back of her hand. "She came here with her mother when she was twelve. Her father was monstrously cruel, and they escaped from him."

I try to picture weak, abused Sala spiriting Alcippe away from a life with Farg Kyul. "Impossible," I counter with an emphatic shake of my head. "There's no way that woman ever rescued her daughter from a dragonlord."

Valasca fixes me with a level glance. "Sala didn't rescue her daughter. Alcippe rescued *her.*"

I gape at her, and Valasca sets her bowl down, resting her hands on her crossed legs. "It's a long story," she cautions.

"I'm not going anywhere for a while."

Valasca regards me appraisingly before relenting. "Sala was one of Farg Kyul's four wives. She never bore him a son and lost what beauty she had soon after giving birth to Alcippe, her only child. Because of this, Sala was despised and often beaten by the dragonlord. She was also badly mistreated by the other wives."

Valasca's eyes flit toward Alcippe.

"But Sala loved her daughter a great deal and did her best to shelter her from the abuse directed at her, as well. Alcippe grew quickly, and by the time she was ten, she was courageously throwing herself between her mother and father to try and protect her mother from his angry blows, some so fierce that her mother was already deaf in one ear."

Valasca's brow furrows, and her eyes briefly flick toward Sala, who is on her knees again, offering up food to another group of women across the hall. "When Alcippe was twelve, she returned from tending their livestock and found her mother unconscious on the floor. Blood was streaming out of her mother's nose and ear, and her eyes were swollen shut. Alcippe quickly gathered some food, bundled them both up, then waited until dark and left, carrying her mother over her shoulder.

"She traveled on foot for two months straight until she reached our lands, both mother and daughter half-starved. Alcippe used her last reserves of strength to gently lower her mother to the ground before us. She had one request before she herself collapsed from exhaustion."

"What was it?"

"She said, 'Turn my mother into a warrior.'"

I glance again at Alcippe's mother, hard at work serving and bowing. I watch as she places a bowl into the hands of a Smaragdalfar woman, the woman's gray hair streaked with green, her emerald-patterned skin shimmering in the rune-lamp light. The woman grasps Sala's arm affectionately, smiles at her and murmurs something kindly. Then she gently cups Sala's submissively downturned chin in her hand, raises her head and bows respectfully to her. Sala smiles sheepishly and quickly scurries away.

"But her mother never did become a warrior, did she?" I ask, rattled by Sala's obviously broken spirit.

Valasca shakes her head grimly. "Sala never completely recovered after her last beating. Our physicians tried to tell Alcippe this, but she refused to believe it, insisting that her mother would get better with time. She threw all her energy into learning our ways and becoming a warrior herself. She kept trying to teach her mother what she learned, guiding her hands around a bow, coaxing her to grasp a spear. But her mother would always grow afraid and run back to the kitchens, back to the tasks she had been required to do for the Kyul family."

Her brow furrows as she watches Sala. "Time passed, and Alcippe became one of the fiercest, most powerful soldiers we've ever had. When she was eighteen, she received her warrior marks and her new name from the queen. Then she got on her horse and rode off, rune-axe in hand."

"Where did she go?"

Valasca narrows her eyes at me. "To pay a visit to her father."

"Oh." An icy chill runs down my spine. "What happened next?"

"She returned weeks later, Farg Kyul's head tied up with some leather twine and swinging behind her. She marched into this very hall and down the aisle, in full view of the queen. She threw the head of her father on the ground at her mother's feet. I think she always believed that her mother was under the influence of some spell, and that *this* was the thing that would finally break it, freeing her mother to heal and grow strong and finally able to become a warrior."

"But she didn't," I say, my voice low.

"No," Valasca says with a grim shake of her head. "Sala did something Alcippe never expected. She fell to her knees before the head of her dead husband and grieved for him."

Shock jabs through me. "What did Alcippe do?"

"Something snapped inside her that day. She completely fell apart. She actually tried to take a knife to her own face, to cut away the resemblance to her father."

"But she didn't."

Valasca shakes her head. "No. Skyleia managed to convince her otherwise."

"Who's Skyleia?" I ask.

"Her partner. The queen's granddaughter. The woman to her right."

The beautiful woman with the scarf dress and glowing-orb-decorated hair is sitting next to Alcippe, laughing and leaning over every so often to touch her on the shoulder or hand. Every time she does this, Alcippe's expression momentarily softens.

"Skyleia," Valasca goes on, "stayed with Alcippe day and night, never wavering in her devotion. They'd been friends ever since Alcippe arrived, but after that, they became inseparable lovers. Skyleia was the one who convinced Alcippe to tattoo her face so dramatically instead of disfiguring it. Skyleia herself applied the rune markings."

I think of Ariel and her terrible struggles, and of Wynter's understanding. Ariel often seems completely unlovable as well, but Wynter's friendship and devotion never flags.

"I can imagine what you're thinking," Valasca says, smiling slightly. "How can two people who seem so different be together? I often wonder the same thing myself. But Skyleia sees something different than you and I see when she looks at Alcippe. She sees the twelve-year-old who carried her own mother for miles to safety. She sees the warrior with the heart of a mountain lion who would go through fire for her adopted people. She sees the person who, despite the fact that I have never once seen her smile, is a favorite of the children here."

I give a disbelieving laugh. "That's surprising. I'd have thought they'd run in fear from her."

Valasca grins and shakes her head. "The children wrestle with her, cling to her arms. They bring her gifts, and Alcippe's a patient weapons teacher with them. It's like I said before—sometimes you have to look beneath the surface." She gives me a sly smile.

It dawns on me that I have something in common with this huge, rune-scaled warrior woman who hates me on sight. Alcippe and I both look like cruel family members who wreaked havoc and destruction.

"What happened when the Urisk figured out that Alcippe killed one of their leaders?" I wonder.

Valasca shrugs, picking up her food bowl again. "They sent more than a few soldiers after us, but we killed them all. Their dragons, too."

I wince, thinking of Naga. But those military dragons weren't like Naga. They'd been broken.

But they were like her once.

"I can't believe I'm actually feeling sympathy for Alcippe now," I admit.

Valasca coughs out a laugh and throws me a look of caution. "Don't let sympathy lead you to let down your guard around her," she warns "She wants you dead."

Fear needles at me. "But...the queen accepted me..."

Valasca shrugs as she eats. "That won't deter Alcippe." Seeing my aghast expression, she adds, "Did you honestly think it would be *safe* for you here?"

I've probably gone a shade paler, because Valasca cocks one eyebrow as she studies me. "Don't worry," she says reassuringly. "If you stay close to me, she'll leave you alone."

"What exactly do you do here?" I ask, casting about for some semblance of a reason why I should take comfort in this.

"Mostly goat herding," she says, scooping up some more food.

I eye her dubiously, remembering how she unflinchingly faced down Alcippe. "Goat herding."

Valasca smirks as she takes a long drink from her earthenware mug. "I like goats."

"And Alcippe. What about her?"

Valasca motions toward Alcippe with her mug, as if she's toasting her. "She's a member of the Queen's Guard."

"The Queen's Guard?"

"Our most elite fighting force."

"And you think *you* can protect me from *her*?"

Valasca nods and takes another sip from her mug, smiling, as if she's enjoying my discomfiture.

"I don't want to offend you," I say, gesturing with my chin toward Alcippe, "but she looks a great deal stronger than you."

"She is."

"Then how could you possibly protect me from her?"

The side of Valasca's mouth curls up, her dark eyes twinkling with mischief.

"You may find, Gardnerian, that I have a large number

of hidden talents." She laughs and glances down at the full bowl that's in front of me. "You should eat something. You'll need all the fortification you can get."

I look down at the food, as if noticing it for the first time, and tentatively pick up a piece of the herb-flecked flatbread. The food is rich with unfamiliar spices and vegetables, but very good—some type of chicken stew in a rich, reddish curry mixed with dried berries topped with roasted squash and goat cheese, along with a cup of warm, spiced mare's milk, which is sweeter than the cow's and goat's milk I'm accustomed to.

I look around the room as I eat, and my eyes fall on a group of teenage Uuril girls, all bunched together against the far wall. Unlike most of the women here, they're unmarked by tattoos and hunched down, their expressions stressed. Three older Urisk women with Amaz rune-tattoos on their faces hover maternally around them.

"Recent arrivals," Valasca says, noticing my stare. "Refugees. More every day."

"I'm surprised there aren't a flood of Urisk women here," I say, looking around the room and finding only a scattering of tattoo-free Urisk women who seem like recent arrivals.

"Well, Queen Alkaia only lets in a certain number of refugees each month," Valasca explains. "And the Urisk aren't allowed to bring their sons." She frowns. "I think there'd be more of them if they could." Something about the way she says this leads me to believe that she might not approve of this rigidity.

I realize what an impossible situation it must be for any Urisk woman with a son in the Western Realm—the Gardnerians and Alfsigr intent on killing all Urisk boys because of their potentially powerful geosorcery.

A black-haired, green-eyed woman dressed in turquoise

woven garb catches my eye. Her face is marked with Amaz tattoos, and she has skin that shimmers Gardnerian green. She's gesturing as she speaks to another woman, and her hands are covered in bloody slash marks.

"That woman there," I say. "She must have broken her fasting." I turn to Valasca. "My friend, Sage Gaffney...her hands are like that."

Valasca eyes me speculatively. "That woman," she tells me, glancing toward her, "she's in pain all the time, but she says it's nothing compared to the pain she endured being with the man they fasted her to—the abuse, the insults, watching her three children being beaten. She left her baby son in Gardneria and escaped with her daughters. That's them, over there."

Valasca gestures across the room with her chin, and I follow her gaze toward two raven-haired girls with skin that shimmers green, Amaz tattoos on their faces. They look to be around six and fourteen. The younger girl is sitting on the lap of an elderly woman with long, snow-white hair, giggling as the woman bounces her on her knees, a large rune-axe strapped to the old woman's back. The older girl has a confident stance and is deep in conversation with three other girls around her own age, all of them dressed in the scarlet rune-marked garb of Amaz soldiers, bows and quivers strapped to their backs.

"When they first came here," Valasca tells me, "the younger one wouldn't even speak. The two of them wouldn't make eye contact. They would only cower and tremble, waiting for blows. Now look at them. The eldest is a talented archer and has the makings of a fine soldier. And the younger girl is full of life and joy."

"And the son?" I ask.

Valasca's face darkens and she shrugs, watching the two girls. "Their mother made a sacrifice."

My mind is instantly cast into conflict. Not allowing the woman to bring her baby son—it's too cruel. What if Trystan or Rafe were in a situation like that and left behind with a violent monster? It's unthinkable.

"And you think this is right?" I challenge. "Not letting the son come with them?"

Valasca hesitates before answering. "I honestly don't know."

"My friend Andras," I say to her, "he's one of your rare male infants grown up."

"He was with you today," she says, remembering. "I know of him. He was Sorcha's lover for a time. That's her over there." Valasca points at two young women who stand off to the side, engaged in private conversation. "The one with the blue hair. That's Sorcha."

I watch as Sorcha laughs at something her companion says. She's wearing the scarlet uniform of the Amaz soldier, her face rune-tattooed, black metallic hoops lining her pointed ears. Her skin is a deep lake blue and her hair a deeper, rippling sapphire, but her eyes shimmer gold like sunlight. I remember how Andras described her beauty, lost in the memory of her.

"Do you think she would talk to me?" I wonder.

Valasca lets out a jaded laugh. "Go on, Gardnerian. Why don't you find out?"

I can't decide if Valasca is serious or not. "She should know what happened to her son," I insist.

Valasca smirks and goes about finishing her bowl of stew.

I glance back at Sorcha and make a split-second decision to be reckless. I get up and step around the groupings of women, their conversations dying down as I pass, quickly replaced by contentious stares and murmuring.

Sorcha visibly stiffens at my approach, and so does the blonde soldier she's speaking with. The two of them pull themselves up to their full, intimidating heights.

"Sorcha Xanthippe," I greet her, dipping my head respectfully, "I'm Elloren Gardner—"

"I know who you are," she snaps.

I hesitate for a moment. "I was wondering if we could talk."

She stares hard at me, golden eyes ablaze. She says something in another language to her companion, and the woman spits out a contemptuous sound as she looks me over. Sorcha walks a few steps toward the edge of the hall, then motions sharply for me to follow.

She leads me to a semiprivate, heavily curtained alcove at the edge of the large room and turns to me with an impatient, hostile expression.

"I've news of your son," I tell her.

Now she's looking at me with the same expression that was on Alcippe's face—like she flat-out wants to kill me.

"I have no son," she grinds out through her teeth.

"No, you do…"

"The Lupines," she spits out venomously, "*they* have a son. I have no use for him."

"Andras Volya is a friend of mine," I explain, thinking that if I put it all into the right words, she'll soften a bit. "He's just met your little boy. He didn't even know he existed until a couple weeks ago. So now he's joining the Lupines this summer and…"

"*I. Don't. Care.*" Her golden eyes are murderous.

Confusion takes hold and I bristle on Andras's behalf. "Andras cares for you still, you know."

"Then he is a fool," she sneers. "I went to him for one reason, and one reason only. To conceive a daughter. And he *failed* me."

"It's not right," I blurt out, rapidly growing incensed, "the way you treat boys here."

Sorcha's face fills with incredulity as she looks over my black garb. "What would *you*, a Gardnerian, know about what's right? You, with your barbaric customs that enslave women."

I draw back from her, realizing I've made a mistake in trying to reason with her. She's right about Gardnerians, but she's definitely not right about Konnor and Andras.

"He's a beautiful little boy," I tell her somberly. "I just thought you might want to know he's doing well."

Her eyes light with fury. "I don't care if he lives or dies," she snarls. "He's a stain on Erthia, like all men. And like all Gardnerians." She shoulders past me and strides away.

I watch her go, fuming. How could Andras love someone like her? Where is the woman from his stories? The woman who loved to talk with him about horses and the stars? Who preferred him above all others?

When I return to my seat next to Valasca, she's gnawing on a chicken leg. She cocks one eyebrow in my direction. "Went well, then, did it?"

"She's hideous," I spit out, glaring over at Sorcha, but the menacing sound of Diana's low growl distracts both Valasca and me. Valasca appraises the situation silently, her eyes following Diana's gaze to Alcippe.

She sets down her food and springs to her feet, light as a cat. "C'mon," she says, gesturing for me to follow. "Let's get your Lupine friend as far away from Alcippe as possible before there's a brawl."

CHAPTER FIVE

WHITE BIRDS

Several small, nimble deer shyly follow us as Diana, Marina, Ni Vin and I trail Valasca through the city. I look around in fascination, drinking in the sight of small gardens in full bloom in the dead of winter, lantern-lit homes and shuttered markets. Women are making food in tavern-like alcoves on stoves glowing with heat while others sit quietly talking, eating, playing music, laughing. I breathe in the balmy air, everything around me cast in a reddish glow by the rune-torches illuminating the streets.

There's an insistent, provocative pounding of drums just up ahead, along with the sound of women chanting power-fully in unison to interspersed applause. The buildings around us open up to reveal an expansive outdoor theater surrounded by torches flaming in every color. Women dressed in mul-ticolored scarf garb and hair decorated with glowing orbs, like Skyleia, are whirling on the stage, their flowing scarves painting the air with rippling rainbows of fabric. They hold long red scarves in their hands and move them so fast that the scarlet streaks become circles and spirals and waving lines.

I pause, mesmerized by the sheer artistry of it, swept up in the seductive, pounding rhythm, only half-aware of the women beginning to stare at me, so out of place in my Gardnerian blacks, with my Black Witch face. Something cold tickles my hand and draws my attention from the unfriendly murmuring at the edge of the theater's crowd. I look down to find one of the deer nuzzling an inquisitive nose against my palm, its twisting black horns festooned with scarlet ribbons and flowers.

I pat the little deer's coarse fur, charmed by its gentleness, its snuffling nose and long-lashed eyes. Valasca stops as well, smiling at the tiny animal with delight. She doubles back toward me as Diana, Marina and Ni Vin wait patiently up ahead. I remember Valasca's affection for her horse and realize she's enamored of animals in general.

Diana's amber eyes light on the deer with obvious predatory interest, her nostrils flaring. I shoot her a quelling look— *You cannot eat the deer!*—and Diana huffs, giving both me and the tiny animal a look of supreme annoyance. Valasca leans down to pat the deer and murmurs to it affectionately, fishing in her tunic pocket for a small orange fruit that the deer eagerly gobbles up.

The theater's drumbeat intensifies as a new group of dancers takes the stage, all of them dressed in scarves of crimson. Other dancers fill in behind them, hoisting huge puppets on beribboned wooden poles—one a twisting silver snake, one a horned deer and one a white bird. Two dancers hold additional poles attached to the bird's wings so that the bird's white wings can flap across the stage.

"I see these little deer everywhere," I say to Valasca.

"*Visay'ihne* deer," she tells me, kneeling down to scratch the neck of the small animal and murmur endearments as it crunches the fruit. She flashes a grin. "Beloved by the

Goddess. They're one of her sacred animals, along with the *Visay'ithere* snake and the *Visay'un*."

"*Visay'un?*"

Valasca angles her head toward the huge bird puppet that's now flapping through the crowd to the immense delight of the little girls in the audience. "The Goddess's messenger birds," she says reverently. "Made of her light."

A young, gray-hued Elfhollen girl darts out from the shadows of the small grove of trees beside us. She has Amaz tattoos but wears the traditional stone-colored tunic and pants of the Elfhollen people. The child gives me an anxious look and grabs the ribbon tether that's loosely tied around the deer's neck, leading the small animal quickly away. When the girl returns to her gaggle of friends in the trees, I can hear her fearfully whispering something—two words that I heard muttered in the Queenhall and by some of the women here in the streets.

Ghuul Raith.

Valasca and I rejoin the rest of our group and continue our trek, winding through the torchlit streets of Cyme.

I turn to Valasca as we walk, curious. "What does *Ghuul Raith* mean?"

Valasca eyes me sidelong. "Black Witch."

I let out a long, resigned sigh, and Valasca shrugs, as if this really should not be a surprise.

We walk out of the city proper, the small residences now more spread out, with gardens and then small farms interspersed between them. The road angles gradually up, and we stroll by crops covered by geometric domed glass structures, lines of runes running along every edge and whirring industriously. The loamy aroma of soil is rich on the air.

We reach a moonlit grassy meadow bordered by the forest just beyond. There's a chorus of bleating and the muffled sound of hooves thumping through the dark meadow as a small herd of goats hop toward Valasca. They come to a stop before a fence made of small scarlet runes that are suspended knee-high in the air, the runes whirring and giving off a faint glow.

Valasca spreads her arms out wide, a besotted look coming over her face as she looks over the goats and they bleat and hop for her attention. She blurts out what sounds like a string of endearments in her language that only whips up the goats' affectionate show.

"We can pass through," Valasca tells us happily, pointing to the low runes. "But my goats can't."

Valasca presses her palm to one of the runes, and a strand of red light rays out. She shoots me a quick grin, then steps right through the fence, passing through several runes as if they're made of smoke. Valasca motions for us to follow, and we do, passing through the runes, as well. The goats fall in beside and behind Valasca as she croons to them.

I turn to look back over Cyme, a soft, scarlet glow hanging like a gentle fog over the city, the moon-washed Spine just beyond.

The Spine.

Lukas is probably somewhere right over that western ridge, I grimly consider. His Fourth Division Base getting ready to rain chaos down on the world.

Good luck trying that here, I think wryly. *Their rune shields will blast your dragons and soldiers to bits.*

We leave the goats behind as we pass through another line of rune-fence and enter the dense forest, following on Valasca's heels. For a moment, I have a subtle sense of the forest's gathering animosity, and quickly coax my fire lines into a blaze, flaring my power out at the trees. They shrink back and go silent, and I breathe a sigh of relief.

The dark woods soon open up to reveal a small clearing. In the center stands a circular dwelling with a geometric rune-edged roof. The lodging is raised up from the forest floor on a wooden platform, and the stone walls are enameled with intricate mosaics that depict the Goddess in a forest with a variety of animals. A single red lantern that holds a suspended, glowing rune hangs by the door.

This place is removed from everything, reminiscent of the isolated North Tower. A place to bring people you want to keep separated from everyone else.

I turn to find Valasca swirling a glowing rune-stylus in the air, and I flinch as a circle of large crimson runes bursts into life all around us, ringing the entire periphery of the clearing.

She's a rune-sorceress, I marvel. *One of the twelve.*

Apprehension takes root as I examine the runes more carefully. They resemble a larger version of the goat fence runes. I move to touch the closest rune and am surprised to find my hand making contact with a solid, mostly invisible barrier.

I round on Valasca. "We're not goats. Why did you just pen us in?"

A low growl starts at the base of Diana's throat, and Valasca exchanges a grim look with Ni Vin, whose hand moves to her sword hilt.

I take a step toward them. "What are they afraid of me doing?" I demand, alarmed to be suddenly imprisoned. "What's here that you don't want me to find? I mean *no harm* to anyone here."

"I believe you," Valasca says adamantly, standing her ground. Her eyes dart cautiously to Diana, her grip tight on her rune-stylus. Then she looks back at me and lets out a hard sigh. "I was instructed to erect a barrier, just until you meet with the queen. For your own protection, as well as the protection of *our* interests. It's temporary, I assure you."

"I have been in a cage before," Marina says, her eyes wide and frightened, her voice breaking. With shaking hands, she reaches up to press her gills flat. "Why would you do this thing to us?"

Ni Vin's careful and ever-present neutrality breaks, her face tightening with conflict. "You are not a prisoner," she insists to Marina staunchly. "You have my *nhivhor*. My word." Ni Vin makes a complicated gesture over her chest with her hand. "And you have my pledge of protection."

Marina nods tightly, but her face remains troubled.

"Come," Valasca says placatingly as she walks up to the dwelling and slides back the star-patterned door. "My only desire is for your comfort this evening, as the guests of the Amazakaran. I will remove the rune-barrier in the morning."

I look to Diana questioningly, wondering if she's picked up anything troubling in their scents. Diana has her eyes fixed on Valasca with lethal singularity, as if she's deliberating on the most expeditious way to take her down, and Valasca holds her stare with a surprising level of calm. Diana purses her lips and gives me a look that reads *I'll let her live for the moment*, then gives me a curt nod.

Valasca smiles at Diana, holds back the door's edge and steps to the side, welcoming us with an elegant gesture, and I follow Marina and Diana through the entryway.

It's warm and comfortable inside our lodging. Scarlet tapestries line the walls and ceiling, and richly patterned maroon rugs cover the floor. There's a small stove in the center of the room, pumping out warmth, a steaming brass teapot set on it. A low table with a purple tablecloth holds a gilded tea service and a plate of fruit. Cushions line the edges of the dwelling, and felted bedrolls have already been laid out for us.

The tapestries show more scenes of the Great Goddess

performing various feats—defeating demons and armies of men, caring for children. And again, the motif of the small white birds swirling above the Goddess, rising up toward the ceiling to join a large bird.

Valasca stands near the door and watches us as Marina sits down on a bedroll, Ni Vin quietly arranging herself beside Marina, crossing her legs and closing her eyes. Diana follows her usual bedtime routine of stripping down to nothing, then curls up on top of one of the bedrolls near Marina.

Valasca is gazing at Ni Vin, an oddly intense set to her expression. Eventually, she pulls her gaze away and sits down at the low table, picking at some grapes. She seems deep in thought as she stares at the ceiling tapestry, her eyes following the swirl of white birds woven into the pattern.

I'm not ready to settle down to sleep. I feel too restless and confined, and also rather excited to be in such an unfamiliar and fascinating place.

"I'd like to go outside for a bit," I tell Valasca, my tone tinged with resentment over needing to ask permission.

"Go ahead," Valasca says wearily with a flick of her hand toward the door.

Ni Vin's eyes fly open. She and Valasca exchange a few tension-fraught words with each other in what sounds like the Noi language.

"It's a fortified barricade, Ni," Valasca finally says, switching to the Common Tongue, her tone dismissive.

"Wait," I say, catching their easy familiarity with each other. "You two know each other?"

Both Valasca and Ni Vin shoot me a quelling glare.

"Go," Ni Vin finally says to me, her attention more focused on Valasca than on me, the two of them locked in what feels like intense, vaguely intimate communication.

I move to the door, feeling like I'm suddenly intruding on something personal, and retreat out into the night.

I linger outside, irritated by the barrier, but savoring the smell of summer in the dead of winter. I breathe in deep, reveling in the improbable leafy smells, the sound of insects chirring. I crane my head up to take in the starry sky, wondering what Yvan is doing right now.

Is he staring at the same stars?

An unsettled heat shivers through my lines at the thought of beautiful Yvan, coupled with the longing to have him here with me, right now...

A flash of white in the trees catches my eye, and my whole body goes rigid with surprise.

A Watcher. Perched on a tree limb, just beyond the rune-barrier.

My heartbeat quickens as the wand in my boot starts emitting an insistent buzz. I breathlessly fumble under my skirts for the wand, my eyes darting to the dwelling to make sure I'm alone.

I pull the wand out, my breath catching when I see that it's glowing like it's filled with starlight and pulsing with energy. On instinct, with another quick look behind me, I raise the wand and touch it to the rune-barrier.

The huge rune before me blinks out of existence.

My heart pounding against my chest, I reach out my hand toward the invisible wall and find a large portion of it gone. Glancing up at the Watcher, I slip through the barrier and breathlessly trail the white bird as it darts from tree to tree.

I follow the Watcher through the woods and to another rune-encircled clearing, this barricade formed by emerald runes of a design completely different from the scarlet Amaz runes—fewer curls and spirals, harder geometric shapes telescoping out from their centers. There's a round dwelling similar to ours in the center of this clearing, with countless small green runes suspended above and around it like arrested raindrops, everything washed in their verdant glow.

The Watcher flies straight toward the rune-barrier, a small explosion of emerald rays flashing out as the white bird passes through. It lights on an eave above the dwelling's doorway and sets its serene eyes unblinkingly on me.

Giddy with anticipation, I press the spiraling wand to the barricade rune before me, and it pops out of existence.

I step through the gap and walk through the rainfall of runes toward the dwelling.

I'm halfway across the small clearing when the door begins to open. I freeze as a figure appears in the doorway, backlit by golden lamplight.

At first, I think I'm staring at a young Urisk woman, her hue violet and her hair a riot of purple. But her skin has a glowing amethyst quality to it, much like the green shimmer of Gardnerian skin, and her ears are round, not pointed. I look closely at her features, and a sudden, light-headed rush of recognition swoops through me, my shocked surprise almost buckling my knees.

It's Sage Gaffney standing in the doorway, her Icaral baby held in her arms.

CHAPTER SIX

THE ICARAL

"Sage?" I rasp out.

She's frozen, too, her expression one of openmouthed amazement. "Elloren? Elloren Gardner?"

It *is* Sage. My childhood friend.

Her fastmark wounds are still horribly present, but she doesn't seem as pained and distressed by them as she did the last time I saw her. There are small, golden chains affixed to her hands now, looping around her fingers and palms and wrists. The chains are adorned with a series of tiny scarlet Amaz runes that glow like iridescent berries.

Sage's Gardnerian black garb is gone, replaced by a loosely woven violet tunic and pants—*pants!*—edged with purple gemstones and golden embroidery. There's also a wand sheathed at her right hip, and a rune-dagger sheathed on the left, a flowing golden rune on its hilt.

The baby in her arms watches me with wide, silvery-green eyes filled with an almost heartbreaking innocence. He looks to be about six months old, with a gemlike pattern to his skin that glitters as many shades of violet as Sage's hair. Delicately pointed ears peek out from beneath little tufts of Gardnerian black hair, and a pair of ebony wings are folded behind him like soft fans.

Beautiful, opalescent wings. Like Naga's.

Sage's plum-colored eyes light on the glowing spiraling wand in my hand. "It led you back to me."

I try to get hold of my whirling thoughts. She's so dramatically, mind-blowingly altered.

"Um, no," I say, flustered, blinking around at the runes, at the Watcher, at Sage's unexpected purple figure. "I freed a Selkie," I say absently, everything surreal. "I'm here to petition the queen to rescue all of them."

"A Selkie," Sage echoes, more a statement than a question.

"Yes."

She stares at me for a long moment, clearly astounded. Then laughter bubbles up inside her, first as an involuntary cough, then as an open bout of incredulous mirth, her mouth lifting into an irrepressible grin. "It's because of the wand. All of it."

I nod, still adjusting to her complete metamorphosis.

"Saving all the Selkies," Sage marvels, shaking her head, a glint of mischievous rebellion in her eyes. "That's just the sort of outrageous thing that wand leads you to do."

"Why are you purple?" I blurt out.

"I'm a Light Mage, Elloren," she says, growing serious. "A Level Four Light Mage. My light affinity lines are strongly oriented toward purple, so when I started casting light spells..." Sage looks down at her violet hands and shrugs. "The color stuck."

My lip twitches up. "So now you're a purple Gardnerian?"

She stiffens slightly at the word and draws up taller. "I'm a purple Light Mage."

"And...this is your baby?" I nod at her stunningly unique child.

Sage's mouth lifts into a smile filled with pride. "Yes. This is Fyn'ir."

So, this is him. This sweet, purple, winged babe. The hunted Icaral of Prophecy.

"Stop where you are!"

I turn at the sound of Ni Vin's sharp voice just as she, Diana and Valasca burst into the clearing. Valasca and Ni Vin come to a sudden halt just before the rune-barrier, their eyes immediately lighting on the translucent Watcher hovering over Sage's door and the glowing wand in my hand. Beside them, Diana immediately relaxes her stance as she calmly surveys the entire scene.

Suddenly, it all clicks into place in my mind—exactly what the Amaz and Vu Trin are so afraid of.

You will strike her down if she seeks to harm what is ours.

Incredulous anger wells up inside of me.

"You didn't seriously think I would harm her baby?" I ask Valasca and Ni Vin, feeling stunned and more than a little bit outraged. "That's why they attacked me, isn't it? They think I'm the Black Witch, here to fulfill the Prophecy."

"You have a weapon," Ni Vin weakly points out, her eyes riveted on the Watcher with reverential awe.

I look down at the glowing wand in my hand. The Wand of Myth.

The actual Wand of Myth.

Holy Ancient One.

I hold the Wand out to Sage and immediately feel the lack of it as she somberly takes it from me. I shoot Ni Vin a look of challenge. "There. Now she has two wands. *And* a rune-dagger. I'm completely unarmed."

"Leave us," Sage tells all three of them, her gaze set tight on me.

"We are charged to protect the Icaral," Ni Vin insists, her voice tinged with confusion, as if her world has been suddenly turned on its head.

Sage's expression hardens as she sets suddenly fierce eyes on Ni Vin. "He's *my* child, and I asked you to leave us. We are both bearers of the Wand, and I wish to speak to Elloren. *Alone.*"

I stare at Sage in wonderment—what happened to my timid, obedient neighbor?

Valasca gently sets a hand on Ni Vin's arm. "Do you see it, Ni?" Her eyes flick up toward the Watcher.

"I see it," Ni Vin admits shakily. "No one else will believe it, but I see it."

Valasca says something to her, too softly for me to hear, and Ni Vin nods. Valasca looks back at Sage and me. "Go," she says respectfully. "Speak with each other." She glances at the Watcher one last time, then both she and Ni Vin walk back into the forest.

Diana flashes me a wide, gleaming smile and follows them into the darkness of the trees.

I turn to Sage, feeling like I've landed in a dream as she quietly returns the Wand to me. I take it from her and slide it back into my boot, heartened by her trust.

My gaze drifts to her little boy. "Fyn'ir? That's not a Gardnerian or Keltic name."

"Fyn'ir's father is Smaragdalfar." There's a note of bold challenge in her tone.

Smaragdalfar? Her baby's father is a subland Elf? "But, I was told—"

"Ra'Ven was glamoured," Sage cuts in sharply. "To look like a Kelt."

"Ra'Ven?" My head is fair spinning with confusion.

"His Keltic name was Ciaran. His true name is Ra'Ven."

My astonishment notches higher. "But...everyone thinks your child's father has a Keltic family...and they..." I pause, disturbed and confused by the remembrance of what Yvan told me. "Sage...they were killed by the Gardnerians."

Her face tenses with pain. "I know. I heard. They were the family who took Ra'Ven in when he escaped the sublands."

The terrible ramifications of all this swamp over me. And the fact that Sage and I are intractably, completely and forever altered.

"Oh, Sage," I say, my voice breaking.

I can see it all rushing over her, too. The world-shattering improbability of this moment. The two of us. Standing here. In Amaz lands. The Icaral of Prophecy in her arms.

Tears sheening her eyes, Sage comes toward me, and we fall into an embrace, loosely sandwiching Fyn'ir, who squirms between us and stares up at me with an expression of such adorable indignation that an affectionate laugh bursts from me.

"I'm so happy to see you," Sage says through her tears.

I hold on to her, never wanting to let go of her again. "We've quite a bit to catch up on."

A laugh escapes her. "You might say that." She angles her head toward her dwelling. "Come in. I'll make you some tea."

Sage pours us steaming tea from a cobalt teapot with a golden filigree design, the cups fashioned from clear glass, set in jeweled golden holders. The interior of her cozy lodging is similar to ours, with rich scarlet-hued tapestries, a lush rug, a circular table low to the ground and cushions all around. I sip at my tea, which tastes of vanilla and spice.

"Can I see the Wand again?" Sage asks as she cradles Fyn'ir, her eyes lighting with interest.

I set down my cup, pull the Wand from the side of my boot and set it in the center of the table.

The ambient glow of the surrounding rune-lamps seems to momentarily dim in the face of it. There's a presence about this wand. As if it's another entity in the room.

"Do you really think it's the true Wand of Myth?" I ask her. "I do."

Then I notice her necklace—a small white bird hanging on a delicate silver chain. I inhale sharply, my eyes darting up to meet Sage's.

"I see the Watchers," I confess in a whisper. "Every now and then. Like the one that just led me to you. And sometimes, when I touch the Wand... I see a tree made of starlight."

"Every religion across Erthia has something like the Watchers, Ren," she tells me, serious. "Every single one. And the tree of light. And the Wand, in some form or another. It's all there, central in every holy book in both Realms."

It surprises me to hear Sage talking like this, coming from such a strictly religious family like hers. "Do you even believe that you're a First Child anymore?" I ask.

"No." She shakes her head as she slides a squirming Fyn'ir under her tunic's edge so he can nurse. "But I think I believe in those central, true things. And I believe in the Wand."

My eyes flick to her bloody fastlines. "Your hands... How are they?"

Sage takes a deep, resigned breath, her expression darkening. "They're painful. But it's not as bad now. The runes tamp down the pain." There's a glint of steely resolve in her eyes. "I'm going to destroy this spell, Elloren. I'm planning to travel to Noi lands, to join the Wyvernguard and study light magic there."

"You think the Noi will accept you?"

She nods. "Light Mages can link magic from different rune systems, and we can fabricate and charge all the different types of runes. So, yes, I think they'll accept me into their Wyvernguard." Her look of resolve intensifies. "And I swear to you, I'm going to find a way to sever the wandfasting spell."

"I can't believe you know actual light spells," I marvel. "Who ever would have imagined?"

Sage's purple eyes sparkle, a wry smile forming on her violet lips. "Would you like to see some light magic?"

I gape at her. "Yes!"

Sage pulls her wand out with a practiced air and presses it lightly to the fabric of my sleeve. "What color do you want your tunic to be?" she asks mischievously.

The thought of altering my sacred black garb sends an unexpected surge of rebellious delight straight through me. I think of the most blasphemous color imaginable, laughing when I realize what it is.

"Purple!"

Sage gives a low chuckle. She takes a deep breath, closes her eyes and lets the breath out.

A vivid amethyst streams from her wand's tip, like liquid running through the cloth, until my entire tunic is washed in the color.

I lift up a portion of my long skirt. "The skirt, too," I seditiously urge.

Sage's head bobs with another laugh, and she pushes amethyst into the skirt.

I stand up and twirl around for her, dressed in garb that could get me imprisoned in Gardneria. "How do I look?"

"Gloriously disobedient," she says, a hard, subversive light in her eyes.

"What else can you do?" I ask, eager to see more.

Sage presses her wand to her shoulder and suddenly disappears. I jump in alarm for a moment, but then I see her eyes blinking, suspended in the air and camouflaged into the colors of the tapestry behind her. Sage shimmies a bit, and I can just make out the outlines of her body. Then she stills, closing her eyes, and she's gone again.

"Holy Ancient One," I say, both amazed and spooked. "Stop that. It's eerie."

Sage laughs and blinks back into existence. She twirls her wand in the air. "I can focus light and cut things with it," she says with a grin. "Even stone."

"That's amazing." I nod, impressed and heartened by the level of her power. "That could come in handy."

"It could," she agrees, and I notice how she carries herself with a newfound sense of her own blossoming power. Gone is the meek Sage I used to know, drawn into herself protectively, as if always bracing herself for censure.

This is a new Sage before me. Sagellyn the Light Mage.

"What happened to your sisters?" I ask, remembering that they escaped with her after Sage gave me the Wand.

"They're here, too," she says. "Clover is in love with this place. She's already made a large number of soldier friends and is in weapons training." She gives a rueful smile. "I don't know how I'm ever going to get her to leave."

That doesn't surprise me. Clover was always a combative, easily stressed child. I can readily imagine her wielding a weapon. Or several. "And Retta?"

Her brow knots with tension as she considers her gentler sister. "She misses Mother Eliss. But the weavers have taken her in, and they mother her, so I think she's as happy as she can be." She lets out a deep sigh and sends me a sober look. "In any case, there was no way I could leave them in Gardneria to be fasted into that family of monsters."

Fyn'ir rustles under her tunic, and she gently pulls him out, kissing him on both cheeks before cradling him in her arms.

He's beautiful. Pudgy and drowsy and sweet. I can't help but wonder if Ariel was cute like this before they threw her into a cage.

"I can't believe the Vu Trin actually thought I was the Black Witch, here to kill your baby."

Sage frowns at me as Fyn'ir snuggles against her. "It's completely horrifying."

I look to her worriedly. "Do you think there could be any truth to the Prophecy?"

"I don't know," she says, her expression edged with an anxious fear. "Everyone seems to believe in it because so many seers have scried the same thing." Sage grows silent for a moment. "It worries me. How they don't call Fyn'ir by his name. They call him 'The Icaral of Prophecy' and discuss him like he's nothing but a weapon."

"The Gardnerians are looking at him like a weapon, too," I tell her. "And there's a Mage... Her name is Fallon Bane. She's cruel and she's growing in power. The Gardnerians think she's the other point of the Prophecy."

Sage meets my ominous stare. "The next Black Witch."

I nod. "She might be."

Sage is trying to be strong—I can see it in her stubbornly straight posture. But after hearing this, the side of her mouth quivers, and her arms tighten around Fyn'ir.

Ancient One, what a horrible state of things.

"He's a beautiful baby," I tell her softly. "Completely adorable. He looks like he's covered in gems."

Her face softens. "Would you like to hold him?"

I nod with a smile and extend my arms out for Fyn'ir. He's heavy with sleepiness, and his wings flutter nervously as I gently take him from his mother. He glances back at Sage for reassurance, and I can feel his pull toward her, like a little moon wanting to orbit his Erthia. But Sage smiles at him and coos, and he relaxes into my arms, looking up at me with drowsy curiosity.

"Fyn'ir's a lovely name," I tell her.

"It means 'freedom' in Smaragdalfar." Her smile dissipates, her eyes suddenly pained.

I cuddle little Fyn'ir close and give Sage an encouraging smile as one of his tiny hands wraps around my finger. "I'm amazed the Amaz let him in here. Since he's male."

"Some of the Amaz ways are incomprehensible to me," she says. Fyn'ir begins to fuss, reaching for Sage, so I hand him back to her. "The Amaz have been good to me, Elloren, but I just can't understand them. How can they abandon their sons in the woods?"

I shrug, finding it difficult to comprehend, as well. "Religion and culture are powerful things."

"More powerful than love?"

"If you let them be, I think so."

Fyn'ir starts to cry, and Sage pulls him under her tunic. He gurgles happily and makes a cooing sound.

"They let him in to repay a wartime debt," Sage tells me. "The Vu Trin fought alongside the Amaz during the Realm War and endured heavy losses because of it. So now the Vu Trin are calling in the debt by having the Amaz temporarily hide us here. It's...unprecedented."

"How long will you stay?" I ask.

She shakes her head. "Not long. After we leave here, we might be spending some time with the Lupines, though that's still being negotiated. The Vu Trin are constructing a rune-portal to get us to Noi lands, bypassing the desert, but it takes time to create a portal that crosses such a vast distance. When they finish, we'll travel east through it."

And just like that, she'll be gone.

A pang of loss cuts through me. It seems like practically everyone I care about is getting ready to converge on the Eastern Realm.

"Trystan wants to join the Wyvernguard, too," I tell her. "But I don't think they'll ever accept him, with our grandmother being who she was."

"Tell him to find Ra'Ven when he goes east," she says decidedly. "He's planning to carve out a subland in the Eastern Realm for his people. We'd accept him there."

To live under the earth? With the subland Elves?

It seems like wishful thinking on her part.

"Will the Smaragdalfar truly accept a Gardnerian from the Black Witch's line?" I ask her doubtfully. *Or any Gardnerian?*

Sage stiffens. "Yes. They will."

I can sense apprehension in her about this, so I don't press the issue. "What's Ra'Ven like?" I ask instead.

A ghost of a smile plays on her lips, a sudden shyness coming over her. "He's wonderful." She infuses such passion in the words, warmth prickles along my neck. "He's kind and caring and intelligent. And powerful." She pauses, as if overcome by too many strong feelings to rein them all in. "Ra'Ven's everything I've ever wanted."

There's an ardent spark in her eyes when she says his name, and it provokes an edge of melancholy envy deep inside me. My friend's life is fraught with troubles and danger, but at least she and Ra'Ven have claimed each other as their own, despite the odds.

"Remember when we were young girls?" I say, growing nostalgic. "How we'd spend mornings whiling away our time in the meadow behind my cottage, making flower necklaces and wreaths for our hair?"

Sage nods with a wistful smile. "Those were simpler times."

"I wouldn't mind having one simple day like that again." I give her a grave look. "Things are getting really bad, much more quickly than any of us ever anticipated."

"I know." She considers the luminescent Wand on the table before us. "I think we're being called by the Wand to be more than we ever imagined we could be. To do more. To risk more for the good. Elloren, I never imagined I could wield a wand. That I could escape a fasting and rescue my sisters. If someone told me when I was thirteen that all this would happen..."

Sage coughs out a sound of disbelief and shakes her head. "Yet, here I am. Here we *both* are." She reaches across the table to place her scarred hand on mine, her rune-chains cool and bumpy as they drape against my skin. "The world is very dark, Elloren. And it's growing darker. But I have Fyn'ir. And Ra'Ven. And my sisters. And good friends." She eyes me meaningfully. "Against *all* the odds. You need to hold on to your faith in the good."

Tears are suddenly stinging at my eyes, and I'm all twisted up inside. "It's so hard sometimes." I can barely get the words out.

Sage's grip tightens on my hand. "It's going to get a whole lot harder. But hold on to it anyway." Her eyes flick to the Wand, then back to me. "Vogel and the Gardnerians and the Alfsigr Elves aren't the only forces at work in this world."

I glance at the Wand, as well—a shard of wood in the face of a raging storm of darkness. "I don't know, Sage. If you saw what's going on in Verpacia..." I gesture toward the Wand. "If that's truly the Wand of Myth, then the force of good seems very, very weak."

"Then we strengthen it," she says with hard resolve. "I

think it needs us in that way." Her expression darkens, and she looks hesitant for a moment. "Elloren, there are shadow forces after that Wand."

Trepidation shudders through me. "What do you mean?"

"Shadow demons," she says ominously. "I've seen them in my dreams. Their numbers increase every day. I warded the Wand back when I was very young, but I should ward you, too."

Fright fills me. "I don't see anything like that in my dreams," I protest. "Not even in my nightmares. Shouldn't I be the one having demon dreams, if that's truly the Wand, and if demons are after me?"

"You've only had the Wand a few months," she counters. "I had it for *years*. It bonds with its bearer over time. It's like it's sleeping, and you're sleeping, and you both start to wake up together. But once you wake up, even if the Wand leaves you, you stay awake." Sage eyes the Wand intently. "It still sends me dreams. I still see the Watchers and the tree. And sometimes, I can feel the Wand calling to me. Tonight, I sensed the Watcher outside in the back of my mind. That's why I opened the door."

Sage gives me a small smile, gets up and settles a sleeping Fyn'ir into his woven cradle, tucking him under a deep green blanket embroidered with intricate emerald runes. Then she sits back down and takes her own wand in hand.

"Give me your arm," she says.

Confused, but trusting my friend, I hold my arm out to her.

Sage pulls up my tunic's sleeve, turns the base of my forearm up and sketches a small, circular rune on my skin with the tip of her wand. It takes a while for her to draw it, the glowing emerald design similar to the complex geometric style of the runes outside her dwelling.

"Those emerald runes aren't Amaz runes, are they?" I ask curiously.

"No," Sage says as she concentrates on fabricating the rune. "They're Smaragdalfar runes." She touches the tip of her wand to the rune's center, and the emerald glow pulls back into the wand, leaving me with a black rune-tattoo in the center of my forearm.

"What does it do?"

"This one is a shield-safe rune. You can pass through a rune-barrier now. *Any* rune-barrier. Without harm." She motions up with a flick of her hand. "I need you to stand up."

I move to comply, wondering what's next. "Pull up your tunic a bit," she directs, a new urgency in her gaze that sends a thread of unease worming through me. "I'm going to place a ward on you that will deflect most demonic search spells."

"*Demonic* spells?" The words burst out of me with alarm.

Sage waits, her grave expression unmoved, and my concern notches higher. Shakily relenting, I pull up my tunic and camisole, the skin of my abdomen pricking with goose bumps as she lightly traces an elaborate rune onto my stomach. The rune lines flow out from the wand in deep, glowing emerald as her deft strokes quickly form a series of interlocking patterns inside a circle.

Sage lightly jabs her wand tip into the center of the rune, and its glow flares bright. I gasp as the light sinks into my skin with a crackling sting and morphs into solid black lines.

Sage steps back and surveys her rune-work, seeming grimly satisfied. "If it lights up—and you'll feel it prickling if it does—then be wary of whoever is around you, even if they seem harmless. Remember—demons are capable of glamours." She points to the rune on my stomach. "This will make it possible for you to look demons in the eye without them sensing the presence of the Wand of Myth."

I'm struggling to take in the enormity of her words.

"Keep the Wand hidden," she says. "Speak of it no more."

Heart thudding, I lower my tunic. Sage presses her wand to my sleeve and the violet vanishes from my tunic and skirt as she changes them back to Gardnerian black.

To look like one of them again, I brood. *To look like the Black Witch herself.*

Dread ripples through me.

Sage, I'm scared. My grandmother's power flows through my veins. And it's growing stronger.

"What if I'm the wrong person for this?" I send her an anxious glance.

Sage picks up the Wand, grasping it firmly. Her brow draws tight, and she seems suddenly overcome, as if hesitant to relinquish the Wand to me once again. Then she takes a deep breath and holds it resolutely out to me. "It's yours," she says. "Take it. It's clear that it wants to go to you."

I take it from her, feeling even more conflicted than the first time she gave it to me, and slide it back into the side of my boot.

Hidden.

We say our farewells, and Sage hugs me goodbye. As we hold on to each other, I almost break down and confide in her about the power growing within me. About the forest's disturbing reaction to it. But I can't find the words—they're too tightly bound up with a growing fear. And it's time to leave.

My hand is on the door handle, and I'm about to step outside when her voice sounds behind me.

"Elloren."

I turn. Sage's violet face flickers a deep purple in the scarlet lamplight, her expression heavy with foreboding.

"The Wand knows you have her power in your blood," she says. "It chose you anyway."

CHAPTER
SEVEN

TIRAG

Diana is outside waiting for me when I arrive back to our own clearing.

"Are you all right?" she asks me, her eyes lit up by the moonlight.

No, not really, I almost say. *I'm in possession of what might actually be the Wand of Myth. And I may never see Sage again. And the Gardnerians are sending trackers and soon Fallon Bane out after an innocent little baby.*

I rub my aching forehead, the enormity of it all pressing in. "I'd just like to be alone for a moment," I tell her. "I'll stay close." I motion toward our dwelling, the rune-barrier now conspicuously absent. "You'll hear if there's a problem."

Diana studies me, then looks toward the adjacent forest, as if she's assessing all potential threats. Then she nods and leaves me alone with my thoughts.

Once she's back inside our lodging, I walk through the quiet woods and out past the edge of the forest, staring out over the city of Cyme. The silvery clouds are gone, leaving only cold, distant stars. The air is hovering on the edge of cool, as if the surrounding winter is trying to work its way through the invisible dome protecting the city.

I lean back against a blessedly dead tree, the bark rough on my shoulder, and stare up at the starry sky. The universe seems so immense, reminding me of how small and insignificant I am in the face of everything.

Sage's baby, the feared Icaral, isn't evil at all. He isn't the nightmare creature from my dreams of so many months ago. And he isn't a weapon to be wielded. He's just a baby. An innocent little baby.

And I have a wand of power. The true Wand of Myth, the fabled force for the good.

But that Wand is turning out to be as weak as the Icaral of Prophecy, sending only ghostly visions of Watchers and choosing a bearer with no access to magic.

Why?

I suddenly long for Yvan to be here, right now, under the stars with me. I want to tell him every last thing while he listens in his intense way, holding on to my hand and caressing my fire.

An ache gathers deep inside me.

Yvan, who will be leaving for the Eastern Realm.

Yvan, who I can never have.

I'm startled by a small goat wandering through a patch of pine trees. The little animal stops just in front of me and curiously tilts its horned head. It's soon followed by several other goats, and I reach down to let the nearest one sniff at my hand.

"Hello, Elloren."

I turn to find Valasca leaning against a tree, staring at me.

I straighten. "Hello, Valasca."

Her eyes dart up, searching the tree limbs. I realize she's looking for Watchers.

"They're gone," I tell her. "They do that."

Her brow creases. "You've seen the *Visay'un* before?"

I nod.

"Ni is right," she says. "No one would believe this."

She saunters over, a small goat nipping at her tunic hem. She leans down and gives the animal a pat on the behind, sending it off to join the others.

"Were you thinking of a lover?" she asks with a quick tilt of her head toward the sky. "Just now. When you were staring up into the stars." She sends me a slight grin. "There was something in your eyes that made me think you're pining for someone."

A lover. The word doesn't quite fit Yvan and me. Can you call someone a lover when you've never so much as kissed? When you can never be anything to each other but friends? When he's leaving soon for a Realm leagues away?

I shrug in response, not daring to speak, fearing I'll say too much.

"Did Sagellyn give you the Wand back?" Valasca asks.

I glance at her sidelong and nod.

Her eyes flick over me searchingly. "Where is it?"

"Hidden. And I have no idea what I'm going to do with it," I admit.

Valasca smiles. "You don't *do* anything with it. You listen to it." She looks around, her smile widening. "And here you are. Because you listened to it."

I give a short, incredulous laugh. "And here I am." I slump back against the tree, the immensity of everything washing over me. I wince as a headache spikes in my temple and reach up to massage the sudden burst of pain.

"Are you all right?" Valasca asks, seeming concerned.

I nod wearily. "I'm prone to headaches."

She studies me for a moment, then pulls a flat flask out of her tunic pocket, unstoppers it and hands it to me. "Here," she offers. "This will help. Only drink a little, though."

"What is it?" I ask as I take it from her.

"Tirag," she explains. "Fermented mare's milk. It's a common drink here."

I bring the flask up to my nose. It smells bitter and oddly medicinal, and I give her a wary look. "Are there spirits in this?"

"Oh, I forgot," Valasca says with a laugh. "You Gardnerians don't drink spirits, do you?"

I thrust the flask back toward her. "They're not allowed. It's illegal."

She makes no move to accept it. "Rescuing Selkies is, too, last I heard."

I pause to consider this. She has a point. I touch the flask to my lips and take a small sip. It's strange and bittersweet, with odd little bubbles that tickle at my cheeks and tongue. It goes down smooth and warm. Very warm—the heat spreading out slowly through my core like Yvan's fire.

My headache begins to dissipate, so I take another sip as both Valasca and I lean against trees and consider the stars.

I savor the heated feeling when it comes, the way my muscles are beginning to relax, my troubles slowly floating away on tiny little wings.

"This is actually quite nice," I say, tilting the flask back and forth in my hand.

"Easy, Gardnerian," she laughs. "It's quite strong. You should probably stop now."

I give her a mock scowl and rebelliously take a larger sip, sinking further and further into the delicious warmth. My eyes flick over to the rune-stylus sheathed in her belt. "So, you're a rune-sorceress."

"I am," she confirms with a nod.

My thoughts fly to Tierney's predicament. "My friend Andras told me that the Amaz are getting close to removing Fae glamours. Can you do that?"

She smirks. "Do you know any glamoured Fae, Elloren?"

I shoot her a cagey look. "I might."

Valasca laughs. "We've figured out how to remove Lasair glamours."

"And Asrai?"

She shakes her head. "Not yet. But soon, I think. They're trickier. The Asrai Fae layer multiple glamours, one on top of the other, so unlocking them is a bit of a puzzle, but we'll get there in time."

Hope lights in me, and an eagerness to convey this news to Tierney. I peer out over the city, just able to make out the mammoth Queenhall and the Goddess statue rising up from the center of the plaza.

"Your people confuse me," I muse, the drink freeing my tongue and making it easy to say whatever comes to mind. "You're doing so many admirable things, helping the Fae remove their glamours, defying the Gardnerians and taking in refugees. But...the way you treat males... I met Sorcha's son, did I tell you that? I told Sorcha about him. Do you know what she said?"

Valasca raises an eyebrow.

"She said she doesn't care about him at all. And my friend Andras—he loves her. But he means *nothing* to her. How can your people be so cold?"

Valasca's gaze is steady. "Not everything is as it appears on the surface."

I spit out a sound of derision and look away.

Everything is beginning to appear liquid and hazy, like a dream. The scarlet glow of the Amaz city, the moon-washed Spine beyond. It's all blending together, like streaked paint.

"After Sorcha brought her baby to the Lupines," she says, "I spent every night with her for about two weeks while she sobbed herself to sleep. She was completely distraught over giving up her baby to the Lupines. And she was heartbroken over Andras, too."

I stare at her in bewilderment. "But...it really seemed like she *hated* him. And Konnor, too."

Valasca coughs out a sound of disbelief. "Did you really expect Sorcha to break down and cry over Andras and her son in front of a hall full of Amaz soldiers? Things are *never* as simple as they seem. There are many here who love men, who agonize over the sons they've lost, who secretly visit both. You've met Clive Soren. You must know of his relationship with Freyja. Everyone does."

"I pretty much figured it out," I admit.

"She goes to see him several times a year. She says she's going to hunt. Alone. No one asks questions, and she tells no one the truth, so she is left alone."

"And if she were honest?"

"She would be thrown out of Amaz lands."

"Forever?"

Valasca nods, seeming resigned to these unforgiving ways.

"And you agree with this?"

A deeply troubled look passes over her face. "I'm not sure, Elloren." Her voice lowers as she looks away, her eyes tight with conflict. "I don't think people should be valued only because they can sire babies. And that's the way we treat men." She turns back to me. "So, no. I don't agree with this."

"What are you going to do about it?"

Valasca stares out over the city as one of her goats playfully butts her thigh. She reaches down to gently pat the animal. "I don't know. It's a dilemma."

I take another sip, the drink making me bold. "So, do you have a secret lover?"

Her lips curl into a slow, wry grin. "I've had a few."

I take another drink of the Tirag and hand the flask back to her. Valasca looks at the flask, as if deliberating. Then she lets out a sigh and takes a long swig from it, leaning languidly back against the tree.

"So, who's your secret man?" I ask her.

A husky laugh escapes her, and she smiles crookedly at me. "No men. Only women."

Surprise lights in me. "Can you openly be that way here?"

Valasca eyes me searchingly, growing serious. "Of course."

This sobers me for a moment. I know such things are forbidden in Gardneria and many other places in the Western Realm, but then I think about the Lupines' easy acceptance of people loving whomever they love, and I'm suddenly heartened that Valasca can be open about who she is here in Amaz lands, without fear.

And I wonder if the Noi lands will be like this for Trystan. As much as the thought of my brother leaving makes me feel like my heart is being twisted into a tight knot, I want this for him. I want him to find a place where he can be who he really is, freely and openly.

Valasca's eyes have grown half-lidded. She's beginning to look like I feel—liquid and relaxed, her posture slackened, like she's melting into the tree behind her. She takes another drink and peers out over the city, smiling to herself.

I reach for the flask again, and Valasca purses her lips, her head lolling toward me as she reluctantly hands it back.

"Elloren, you really shouldn't have any more." Her eyes snag on mine, and we hold each other's gaze for a long, floating moment. "You're beautiful, did you know that?" she says, a light observation, nothing flirtatious in it.

I huff out a sound of derision. "I'm not. I look like my *grandmother.*"

She gives a short laugh. "I don't know about that," she says. "I was only a child back then. I don't remember her like the others do. But...you Gardnerians...the way your skin shimmers green. It's lovely."

"It's our magic. But... I have none." For some reason, this strikes me as very funny, and I start to laugh. This drink makes everything seem so amusing. I wonder if this is how my irreverent brother Rafe feels pretty much all the time. Always in such good spirits. In good spirits from the spirits. More laughter bursts out of me. The idea is just so...*funny.*

"I really think you've had enough of that," she says, smiling. She leans in to try to clumsily reclaim the flask from me.

"Why?" I say teasingly, holding it just out of her reach. "I like the way it makes me feel." My words are strange to my ears, all melting together, slurry and light. Everything is warm and weightless all around me.

"Trust me, you'll regret it in the morning." She reaches for the flask and stumbles as I clumsily move aside, stumbling, as well. The two of us fall against each other, wildly infectious laughter bubbling up in both of us as the flask drops to the ground. I grasp her arm for support at the same time she grabs onto mine, and we both stop laughing for a moment as our eyes meet. Then we burst out into hysterics all over again.

Valasca leans back on the tree, alternately catching her breath and laughing. Eventually, we both calm down, Valasca's back against the broad tree trunk, and me propped against it on one unsteady arm.

"Have you kissed the serious Kelt boy?" she asks. "I saw the way he looked at you earlier today."

"No," I say, my smile dimming as a sudden melancholy washes over me. "I thought once...we almost did. But no. I haven't."

"Do you think you ever will?"

I shake my head lazily from side to side. "No. Not ever." The hurt is somewhat muted by the drink, but it still aches in me.

"Do you love him?"

The question hangs in the air between us, all the suppressed emotion inside me suddenly threatening to unravel. Beautiful Yvan, his intense gaze holding mine. So completely and utterly unattainable.

Tears sting at my eyes. "I think I'm falling for him. But I can never have him. Never."

And then I'm telling Valasca everything I feel for Yvan in a sudden rush. All of it.

She stares at the stars and listens intently as I pour my heart out to her. Then, utterly spent, I fall silent and wipe away my tears.

"I know what it is to have an impossible love," Valasca says quietly, her voice suddenly rough with emotion. "I'm in love with Ni."

Ni? Our guard, Ni Vin? My eyes widen with surprise, and I look to Valasca, my head feeling strangely loose on my neck. "Does she like women, too, then?"

Valasca nods mournfully. "She has feelings for me, but... she wants me to come east with her, and..." Valasca glances out over the city and waves her hand loosely toward it. "I can't leave *this*. I love my people, and I can't leave them. Not right now. Not with things as they are."

Because of what my people are doing, I consider with dismay.

Because we're bent on creating havoc for everyone in the Western Realm.

"Every time I look at Ni," Valasca says, her voice impassioned, "it's like an arrow to my heart." She dramatically thumps her fist over her chest. "She's brave and kind and the most beautiful thing I have *ever* seen. She doesn't see it, though. All she sees is her scars. She doesn't see how *perfect* she is."

I think of Ni Vin's ravaged ear and hand, the burns that cut across half her body, and shame knifes through my drunken haze.

My grandmother gave her those scars.

She seems so private, Ni Vin. So closed off. I remember her unflappable calm, her unreadable expression when she saved Marina, purposefully ignoring her presence in the North Tower when she was supposed to be conducting an investigation.

She saved Marina's life that day.

"I'd give anything to be with her," Valasca says with heartfelt longing. Tears fill her dark eyes as she focuses on the stars.

"So, here we are," I say broodingly. "The both of us. Stuck in the Western Realm."

"Yup," Valasca agrees with an exaggerated nod.

"The commander of the Fourth Division Base wants to fast to me," I tell her with absolutely no preamble.

Valasca's head pivots toward me, her brow flying up. "Lukas Grey?"

"Yes."

Her expression turns guarded. "You know him quite well, then?"

"I've kissed him."

"You've kissed *Lukas Grey*?"

"Quite thoroughly."

Valasca's expression becomes darkly cautionary. "Sweet Goddess, Elloren. Stay away from him. He's dangerous. And unpredictable."

I glance out at the western shard of the Spine, snow-capped and just past the Amaz city. *He's there, somewhere just past those peaks.*

I remember the resentful look Lukas gave me when we last parted. How final it all felt. And I wonder if there ever was any real chance of Lukas breaking from the Gardnerians.

"Don't worry. I'm staying away from him," I tell Valasca, a sullen bitterness creeping into my voice.

"Does your Kelt know about him?"

I nod, suddenly miserable. "My life is a mess."

Valasca whistles long and low. "You're right. It is."

I frown at her, and she gives me a rueful look of solidarity. "Well, you're in good company, in any case." Valasca shakes her head and looks up at the glittering stars. "Both of us with true loves who will *never* have us."

She breathes in deep and closes her eyes for a moment, then reaches down and clumsily retrieves the flask from the ground. "This drink is making us maudlin." She throws the stopper decidedly back onto the flask.

I drop my forehead into my hands. "My head is starting to *really* hurt."

"You drank way too much." When I look up at her, Valasca's eyebrow is arched, but not unkindly. "I did warn you."

"I know you did," I pathetically relent as my head is hammered over and over. Everything is a troubled whirl inside me—Yvan, Lukas, the Wand, Sage's baby, the Prophecy... my power. "I feel so confused," I tell her. "About *everything*."

"That's all right," she says, her voice pitched low with understanding. "There's nothing wrong with being confused."

A laugh bursts from me, and I hold on to Valasca's self-assured stare as the world spins sickeningly around me. "You remind me of this professor back at University. He's always talking about confusion being a good thing. He gave me all these histories to read. All from different perspectives." I slur the last word terribly and pause to try and regain control of my tongue.

"I do that," Valasca says, growing pensive. "I read everything I can get my hands on, from every possible viewpoint." She shoots me a sly grin. "Even if I have to smuggle some of the books in here. I make sure to confuse myself on a regular basis."

Valasca's brow tightens, as if her thoughts suddenly trouble her. "It makes it difficult to judge anyone, though. I think that's why I've become the perfect confidante. I am the city's unofficial keeper of secrets. Confidante of many, and the true love of none."

She says the last part with mock chivalry, but there's something pained behind her lighthearted tone. Her mouth lifts in the ghost of a smile. "I have a good many friends, though." Valasca pauses and tilts her head, considering me appraisingly. "You know, if things don't work out with the Kelt, you could come and join us. Before they force you to fast. We could make a warrior out of you. Teach you to fight. You'd never be powerless again."

The idea is so bizarre that it makes me laugh. Me. An Amaz warrior.

But the thought is also surprisingly appealing.

"I *could* teach you," she insists.

"Goat herding, too?" I wryly ask.

Valasca grins. "Of course."

I smile back. "I'll keep it in mind, then."

A wave of nausea sweeps through me, and suddenly I want

nothing more than to be lying flat so that the world will stop tilting so disconcertingly.

Valasca lets out a long sigh and catches me before I fall clear over. "C'mon, Gardnerian," she says, wrapping her arm around my shoulder to steady me. "I'll help you get back. You and I need to sleep this off."

"You smell terrible," Diana tells me as I crawl—literally crawl, as I can't walk a straight line—to my bedroll. Marina and Ni Vin are asleep, or are at least pretending to be, and Valasca has returned to her own lodging.

I fall back on the felted material, the room spinning. "Valasca gave me spirits." I bring one hand to my forehead, which is pounding uncomfortably. "We both drank way too much of it. She tried to warn me not to."

"You should have listened."

I glower at her. "Oh, don't tell me. You Lupines, perfect as you are, never partake of spirits."

She gives me a baffled look, as if this should be obvious. "Of course not. Maiya disapproves of anything that dulls the senses."

"Well, don't judge me. My situation is pretty complicated right now."

Diana cocks an eyebrow at me. "So is mine. I'm in love with a Gardnerian."

"Who never wanted to be a Gardnerian," I irritably counter. "Who spends all his free time running around in the woods hunting."

Diana's amber gaze is calm and unflinching, which makes me feel like a jangling mess in contrast. I sigh and turn over to face her, the room tilting nauseatingly as I do so. "Diana?"

"Yes?"

I hesitate for a moment. "I think I have the Wand of Myth.

The *actual* Wand of Myth. I think it's real. Not just a story."

To my surprise, her unflappable expression doesn't waver. "Do your people believe in anything like this?"

Diana nods. "The Branch of Maiya—the last surviving branch of the three Origin Trees."

"What do your people think about this... Branch?"

"It is a tool of goodness and hope. As the other Branches were. It aids those who are oppressed."

I consider this. "In my religion, it does that as well, but it only aids the First Children."

She shakes her head, emphatic. "Not in ours. Maiya sends the Branch to anyone who is oppressed. Lupine or not."

"So...maybe the Wand wants to help the Selkies."

She doesn't even pause to consider this. "Yes."

"But if my Wand is really this Branch...then why would it come to *me*, Diana? I've no power. And...the Wand doesn't, either. Not at the moment anyway. Trystan thinks it's gone dead. Or dormant, at least."

"Perhaps it's conserving its power. Perhaps there's a bigger fight yet to come." She eyes me significantly. "Or perhaps hope has its own power."

I shoot her a jaded look. "So, here we are, hoping the Amaz will help the Selkies."

She nods, her calm suddenly breached, her blond brow tensing. I know Diana wants it to be her people who save the Selkies. But I also know that Gunther Ulrich is reluctant to inflame an already turbulent relationship with the Gardnerians.

"Perhaps the Amaz *will* help them," I say, glancing toward Marina, desperate for this to be true. Marina is curled up on her bedroll, fast asleep, her glimmering hair splayed out on her pillow. She looks so frail. So wan and easily broken.

"They might," Diana says, looking to Marina as well, an

uncomfortable note of doubt in her tone. That hint of disbelief is unsettling and kicks up the nausea already welling inside me.

"I don't feel so well," I tell her, shivering slightly from the small draft that's working its way in under the door.

Diana scrutinizes me. "Are you cold?" she asks. "You look cold."

I gaze over at her, feeling pathetic. "Yes."

Diana slides under her blanket, lifts up the edge and beckons to me with an impatient wave of her hand. "Come. Come lie by me."

Feeling morose, I clumsily slide over to curl up against her. As I lie there, safe and warm with my dangerous friend, my roiling stomach starts to calm. I snuggle in closer to Diana, and she pats my back comfortingly. She's always so different in the evening, her haughty, painfully blunt air giving way to this strong, soothing presence.

"Diana?" I ask.

"Hmm?"

"What happened to Maiya's other Branches? You said there were three."

She's quiet for a moment. "They were destroyed by the Shadow."

Silence hangs over the room.

"What happened to the people who had those other Branches?"

Again, she hesitates. "They were destroyed, as well."

"So, there's only one more branch."

"Just the one."

The silence gathers and solidifies.

Ni Vin is quietly and steadily watching me from where she's lying, and her uneasy face is the last thing I see before I close my eyes and fall asleep.

CHAPTER EIGHT

QUEEN'S COUNCIL

The next morning, we assemble in the queen's council chamber, a side dome just off the main Queenhall.

Diana, Marina, Ni Vin and I are facing the council members, all of them gray-and white-haired older women. They're seated in a semicircle, talking in low tones among themselves as we patiently wait for Queen Alkaia to arrive. Behind the council, a sizable contingent of heavily armed Queen's Guard soldiers are also seated.

Valasca is standing near us, just off to the side. She arrived at dawn to bring us to the Council's chamber, her manner aloof and all business. She avoids looking in my direction, but that's quite all right with me. I'm a little mortified to be around her after telling her every last romantic secret of my life, and I imagine she feels the same way about me at the moment. Especially with Ni Vin standing right here with us.

My head feels like a village blacksmith is pounding it into a new shape, and I'm filled with a jangling apprehension, hoping against hope that Queen Alkaia will agree to help the Selkies before it's too late.

She has to help them. How could she not?

Valasca abruptly straightens, then kneels as Queen Alkaia is ushered in, the queen's frail body supported by two young soldiers. I follow Valasca's lead and get down on my knees, bowing to the floor, Marina following suit. Diana and Ni Vin both remaining stubbornly upright.

It takes a moment for Queen Alkaia to get settled, but once she does, she motions for us to rise to our knees and turns her intelligent, piercing gaze on me.

"Elloren Gardner," she says. "The Council met this morn to discuss your appeal."

Something about her expression, how her lips are curved into the very smallest of smiles, makes me feel hopeful. My heart lifts. *She's going to say yes.*

"We have made the unanimous decision to deny your request."

The words slam into me like an avalanche.

Marina lets out a shocked exclamation, her hands flying up to her gills. Valasca, Ni Vin and Diana look stunned.

Righteous anger rises inside of me like a blinding fire. I spring to my feet. "But *why?*" I sputter furiously. "How can you reject it?"

"The decision of the council is final." She sounds almost bored, and I suddenly want to hurl something at her, to wipe that blasé expression off of her face. Doesn't she realize what's at stake?

"Clive Soren told me that the Amaz *cared*," I snarl, devastated. "He said you'd help women who were being abused. He didn't tell me you're a bunch of hypocritical *cowards!*"

"Elloren!" Diana cautions me sharply, just as several soldiers in the room spring to their feet, weapons unsheathed in a blur.

I don't flinch, my hands balled into tight fists. I know that I've just directed a serious insult at the queen. Andras has told me that calling someone a coward is huge in both Amaz and Lupine societies. Worse than any curse. But at this moment, I don't care.

Queen Alkaia places a hand on the arm of the soldier closest to her in a silent command, and slowly the weapons all around are lowered and returned to their sheaths. The soldiers reluctantly take their seats again, glaring at me murderously.

"The rescue of the Selkies is a futile endeavor at this point in time," Queen Alkaia says calmly.

"So, according to you," I challenge, struggling to hold back tears, "I should have just left my friend Marina where I found her."

Queen Alkaia leans toward me, her eyes gone steely. "You are asking me to send our soldiers, likely at great risk, up against the Gardnerians. To rescue all of the Selkies. A feat that may cause the Gardnerians to declare all-out war on us. That would be seen as an unforgivable strike on their sovereign territory."

"But it's the right thing to do!"

"Let us suppose for a moment, Elloren Gardner, that we do this thing you ask of us. Suppose we rescue all of the Selkies, but the Gardnerians remain in possession of their skins. What do you think will happen next?"

Oh, Holy Ancient One. She's right. Destroy a Selkie's skin, and she becomes like the living dead, like the soulless dragons, the broken Icarals.

"Are you ready to sentence all of the Selkies to a fate much worse than death?" Queen Alkaia challenges me.

I'm outmatched, out of my league. I'm a fool.

"Then there's no hope," I say, my fire gone, my voice weak.

Queen Alkaia's face softens, and she smiles maternally. "As long as the Avenging Goddess rules this world, there is always hope."

"Where?" I ask her, defeated. "Where is there hope for the Selkies?"

Queen Alkaia sits back. "Find their skins," she tells me. "Without the skins, rescue is futile. The Gardnerians hold the ultimate weapon against the Selkies in their hands. We could bring the Selkies to the other side of Erthia, and it would all be in vain. No, you must find their skins."

"How will we find them?"

She narrows her eyes at me. "Ask those men of yours to find them. No doubt they are familiar with the places where the Selkies are held captive."

"No, that's not true," I say, shaking my head. "They've never gone to—"

"They are lying to you," she cuts in, certain.

"No, I'm sure..."

She cuts me off with a wave of her hand. "They are liars and deceivers," Queen Alkaia says. "*All* of them. Without exception. It has been so since the beginning of time. But you can make use of their vile natures to find out what we need to know."

I bristle, because she's wrong. Wrong about Rafe and Trystan. Wrong about all my other male friends and family. But I hold my tongue, because I know that in this, there will be no convincing her otherwise.

"And then what?" I ask. "If we find their skins, what good will it do? How can we free them by ourselves?"

Queen Alkaia's gaze sears into me. "Who here," she asks the room, "would agree to the raising of an army of our finest warriors for the sole purpose of invading Gardneria to free all of the Selkies, if their skins are found?"

Every single warrior in the room, as well as the entire queen's council, rises to their feet. Not a single one of them, save the queen, remains seated.

"Find their skins, Elloren Gardner," Queen Alkaia tells me, "and we will free your Selkies."

The day is still young when we reach the border, the snow-dotted forest abruptly thinning out to reveal the small field where the Vu Trin sorceresses and the Amaz attacked us.

Yvan, Rafe, Trystan, Jarod, Andras and Gareth are all there, just as they said they would be, and my heart leaps at the sight of them.

But they're also strange to my eyes.

Men.

They're like foreign beings, a whole other race, after being around so many Amaz. So many women.

And their maleness isn't the only thing strange about them. Their expressions are oddly serious, and unease rises inside me as I scan each of their faces.

The Amaz stop just before the line of border-runes and eye our men coldly—except for Valasca, who simply studies them with an air of curiousity. Our escorts wordlessly help us dismount and gather our belongings.

I look to Yvan searchingly, his fire shimmering out toward me.

"What's happened?" I ask Yvan as I pass through the border runes and approach him.

"Something good, Elloren." Yvan looks over at Gareth, who is focused intently on Marina.

"Marina," Gareth says to her gently, "yesterday, we decided to search the area around the groundskeeper's cottage again. Now that there's been a thaw."

"What did you find?" Marina asks carefully, her mouth trembling at the edges.

Gareth reaches into the leather sack hitched over his shoulder and pulls out a shimmering, silver seal skin. Marina lets out a startled cry, her hands flying over her gills.

"It was buried near the back of the cottage," Gareth tells her. "In a box made of Elfin steel. The thaw exposed its edge. I heard a bird's wings flapping—a large white bird. It startled me, and when I looked back down, there the box was—poking out of the ground. I just knew. The moment I saw it, I just knew."

Marina stares at the skin in his hands as if mesmerized. She gives Gareth a look filled with meaning, something private and charged passing between them. "I'll be completely transformed," she prepares him.

"You'll still be you."

Marina shakes her head as if he's incredibly naive. "No. I'll be much stronger than you. Power changes *everything*."

Gareth holds out the skin for her to take. "I *want* you to be powerful. And I want you to be free."

The Amaz look stunned. I realize that Gareth's actions fly in the face of every myth, every legend, every assumption they have about men. Marina drops her travel sack and pulls off her boots, then all of her clothes, unfazed by the wintry cold.

Her eyes locked on Gareth's, she reaches for her silvery skin.

The minute she makes contact with it, flashes of sapphire lightning crackle down her arm. The lightning sparks over all of her skin, and a glowing blue aura coalesces around her, Marina's form beginning to blur as it merges with the blue light. Then both Marina and her skin fade until there's nothing left but a haze of blinding illumination.

Then the blue light begins to dim, the details sharpening until Marina reappears.

In seal form.

A magnificent, predatory seal with Marina's ocean eyes and dazzling silver fur.

Just as we're all adjusting to the idea of seeing her in this form, Marina rolls over on to her back and closes her eyes. The sapphire lightning returns, streaking in a crackling line down her seal stomach. Again, her form blurs, then splits, and Marina emerges from the silver skin, human once more.

She kneels on the ground, breathing heavily, her eyes closed, as she supports herself with trembling arms. She's still recognizable as Marina—her hair silver, her features the same—but she's lost her drawn, willowy appearance. Re-united with her seal-skin, she's now deep blue from head to toe. There was always a sheen of blue just beneath her skin, but now it's on the surface. And she looks strong, her muscles lean and taut, much like Diana.

"Are you all right?" Gareth moves toward her as she struggles to catch her breath. Marina moves her head up and down, seemingly with great effort.

Eventually, her breath evens out, and she stands, her movements more like a warrior Amaz than the weak slip of a girl she once was. She retrieves her clothes and throws them on, then slings her seal-skin over one shoulder.

She walks over to Gareth and reaches up to caress his cheek. Gareth smiles at her with a look of fierce alliance. But I can see it in the tightness around his eyes—this is the beginning of goodbye for them.

Marina steps away from Gareth, one hand on his shoulder, one hand on the silver skin. "Now," she says, turning to all of us and exposing predatory teeth, "we need to save my people."

CHAPTER
NINE

EQUINOX

"Don't you have studies to catch up on?"

Diana's stern tone cuts through my fog of worry, and I look over at her from where I sit on my bed, gripping a mug of hot tea. I don't know how she can concentrate at a time like this. My mind is a whirl of tense worry. I've tried to do some reading, but the medicinal formulas keep flying right out of my head, like birds refusing to be caged.

Rafe, Trystan and Gareth are off investigating the three Gardnerian Selkie taverns located in the isolated forests just over the Verpacian border. And, in an unexpected turn of events, Clive Soren is traveling with Yvan to the sole Selkie tavern that's in Keltania.

They left yesterday before dawn, each carrying a generous supply of guilders in their pockets, courtesy of Queen Alkaia. All of them are armed with stacks of pictures Wynter drew—images of Marina, her sister and every face Marina could remember from the night she and her sister were taken. There are also pictures of Amaz rescuing the Selkies, leading them back to the ocean—a visual map of the planned escape to show any Selkies they encounter.

Ariel hovers near the roaring fireplace, thin flames flashing out from her palm. She's getting stronger every day. She still avoids me and hardly speaks to me, but she doesn't seem so angry anymore. She's more...settled. And her wings have undergone a wondrous transformation—they're smoother and shinier, and her eyes are brighter and steadier. It fills me with quiet satisfaction to see her improving so.

Marina sits patiently by Wynter as we all wait, her sealskin tied over her shoulder and glittering in the firelight along with her silver hair. Her face is tense, and I don't think she's eaten a bite all day.

Just as dawn's faint glow makes its first tentative appearance on the eastern horizon, Gareth returns.

Marina and I jump up to greet him as he shrugs off his cloak, swirls of snow falling from it, instantly turning to tiny puddles on the floor. We press a cup of hot tea into his hands and give him a seat by the fire, which he gratefully takes.

Gareth cuts right to the chase. "Your sister wasn't there, Marina. But there was a woman there who recognized her." Marina's face fills with anguish, and he places a steadying hand on her arm.

"What was it like?" I ask him softly. "What happened?"

Gareth swallows hard before answering. "It was awful. They had some women...girls, really... They looked no older than sixteen... They had them dancing for the men." He stops to shake his head, as if trying to clear away a repulsive thought.

"They were dancing?" Marina says slowly.

Gareth shoots her a concerned glance. "They were...unclothed."

Marina nods tightly in sickened understanding. Gut-heaving outrage sweeps through me.

"They kept ushering in lines of girls and young women," Gareth says. "They were clothed, though barely. They had them standing in a row for the men to look at. Like livestock at a fair. Most of them seemed scared. A few of them, especially the younger ones, looked completely traumatized."

He stops to take a breath, clearly upset. "The tavern keeper...he brought me over to them. Told me how much they cost. I chose an older woman. She had a strong, smart look to her—I thought there was a good chance she'd understand. I also picked out a very young girl who seemed deeply disturbed. I assumed she wouldn't be able to help us, but I figured I could at least buy her a few hours of peace."

Gareth pauses to rub the bridge of his nose. Marina has gone very still, her face turning a paler shade of blue. "As soon as we were ushered into a private room," Gareth continues, "the older woman started to take off her clothing. I think she was trying to divert my attention from the younger girl...protecting her the only way she could. The girl was curled up in a corner, staring at nothing, really, just trembling, terrified. The older woman went to undress me, but as soon as she got close to me, she stopped and froze."

He looks at Marina. "I could tell she was smelling me and figuring out that I was somehow...different. I pulled out the pictures, and she was very surprised. It took her a few minutes to get her bearings. I showed her all of the pictures and, at first, she was completely confused, but she seemed to catch on quickly. She grasped that I was there to help her, and that I'm...an ally."

"She knew that you are Selkie-kin," Marina says, and he nods.

"What happened next?" Diana asks.

Gareth frowns. "The woman broke down weeping. She took the picture of the ocean and kept pointing at it, looking desperate. Then she went to the girl and tried to show her the pictures, especially the one of the ocean, but the girl was too terrified to register anything. We went over each picture of the planned escape in order several times, and I really think she understood. When our time was close to being up, she made a point of messing up the bed, of unbuttoning my shirt and undressing. About two seconds later, the tavern keeper arrived and told me I had to go."

"But the skins," Marina interjects, her voice breaking into discordant tones as she momentarily loses control of her gills. She throws her palms over the sides of her neck. "What of the skins?"

"I talked to the tavern keeper for a while when I first got there. Said I was concerned for my own safety. He told me they keep the skins in a locked trunk in a storage room. All the Selkie taverns have the same system—apparently, they streamlined things after one Selkie found her skin and murdered several people. The Amaz should have no trouble retrieving the skins from the storage rooms."

Gareth pauses, as if remembering something troubling. "The Mage Council is cracking down on the ownership of Selkies, so most of them have been quietly sold to the Selkie taverns." Gareth turns to Marina. "If you were still with him...you'd be in one of those places soon, if not already."

Marina winces, and Gareth sets down his tea, taking her hand in his.

"You need to let Wynter see your memories," Marina tells him, keeping only partial control of her voice, her tones fracturing as they do when she's upset. "Show them to her while they're fresh in your mind so we can give these images to the Amaz."

Gareth nods, then gets up and goes to Wynter, sitting down on her bed in front of her. Wynter takes a deep breath, as if steeling herself, then places her hands on the sides of Gareth's face and closes her eyes. She gives a hard flinch and draws away from him for a moment, then stiffens and settles in like a soldier going into battle. After sitting with him like that for a long while, Wynter begins to draw, pausing every so often to touch Gareth's hand.

I wander out into the hallway, feeling claustrophobic in the crowded room and frustrated with all of the waiting— and deeply troubled by what Gareth told us.

I sit on the windowsill, upset and brooding, looking out at the hard blue edge of the dawn. A few cold stars still hang in the sky, and I watch the dawn's blue edge lift higher for a good half hour.

"Elloren."

I turn my head at the sound of Yvan's voice and slide off my perch. "I've been waiting for you."

My fatigue makes it easy to throw off all hesitation. I embrace him, his own hands reaching around to hold me lightly. I can feel his distress in the way he's holding himself, so stiff and coiled—all stress and troubled emotions, the fire inside of him knifing in random flares. I can tell that, like Gareth, this has taken a toll on him.

"You smell strange," I say, pulling away slightly. It's like spirits mixed with smoke and something else...like sweat.

"I smell rancid," he replies harshly. "That place was horrifying."

"Gareth's back, too," I tell him. "But Rafe and Trystan aren't. Not yet."

"I saw men I know there, Elloren. Resistance fighters. People who I thought cared about justice and freedom. But not for Marina's kind, apparently."

His brow tightens. "More than a few are married. I know some of their wives, and I wonder what they'd make of this if they knew. When the men saw me...they welcomed me, like some long-lost relative...some initiate into this club of theirs...as if I was finally a real man, like them. It was disgusting. It was all I could do not to leave. I'm not a good actor, Elloren. You know that."

I do know that. His lack of artifice, so difficult to take when I first met him, is now one of the things I love best about him.

"But Clive," he goes on, "you should have seen him. Life of the party. By the end of the evening, he had everyone there—the tavern keeper included—completely falling-down drunk. But not before he got the tavern keeper to give us a tour of the place and a view of every single Selkie there. We both paid for time with multiple women...one right after the other. We tried to pick the ones who seemed the savviest...the ones who didn't seem...broken."

"Gareth said the woman he was with..." I hesitate for a moment. "She tried to undress him."

"There was a bit of that," Yvan admits uncomfortably, "but Wynter's pictures...once they saw them, most of the women seemed to understand."

"Wynter will want to read your thoughts," I tell him. "So she can draw more pictures for the Amaz."

"Of course," he says, looking toward the door to my room, then back to me again, hesitating.

That familiar ache I feel when I'm close to him rises up in me. A longing to be closer. To escape from the world in each other's arms.

"It's equinox," he says finally.

So, it is. I'd completely forgotten. Time to gather the sweet tree sap for the maple festival—one of the few holidays celebrated by everyone in this part of Erthia. Time to make sugar and get ready for the coming spring.

Everything seems so bleak. It's hard to believe that soon the trees will bud and the robins will return.

"Happy Equinox," I tell him, my hand finding his. He clasps his fingers around mine.

"I'm also nineteen today."

"It's your birthday?"

He nods. "My mother believed I would be safe and lucky, because it's an auspicious day to be born on." He smiles jadedly at this, as if it's terribly ironic. "I think it was wishful thinking on her part. Defiance in the face of a rather unpleasant reality."

"Oh, I don't know," I tell him, swinging our hands a bit. "Maybe you *are* lucky. We wouldn't have saved Marina if I hadn't been following you that day...and Naga is free because of you..."

And... I love you.

The words are right on the tip of my tongue, and I wish I could say them out loud. Because isn't love always lucky? Even if nothing can come of it?

It has to be.

He's staring at me so intently, I find myself coloring. I take his ardent expression as an invitation and wrap my arms around him again, his own arms sliding around my waist, pulling me close, his fire ignoring the boundaries and flickering through my lines in a decadent rush that makes me shiver.

I kiss his warm cheek and whisper into his ear. "Happy birthday, Yvan."

He tilts his head and looks down at me, his eyes suddenly glowing gold. His fire gives a hard surge, and I just know.

He wants to kiss me.

Everything stops, except for the insistent rhythm of my

heart. Then Yvan forcibly banks his fire, his eyes blazing with a sudden frustration as he looks away, his mouth tensing, the moment shattering. A crushing disappointment rolls over me.

"I should go see Wynter," he says, his arms still loosely around me.

I don't say anything. I'm thrown off balance and suddenly miserable. He must sense it, since his face tightens with concern.

"Elloren... I..."

"No, stop," I tell him, gently pulling out of his embrace. "You don't need to explain. It's just so easy sometimes...to forget everything."

He reaches up to caress the side of my face, and I can see in his fiery eyes that he's tempted to ignore every danger in this. Just like I am.

"Go to Wynter," I prod, ignoring the sullen ache inside me. "Think of the Selkies. Not about us."

He nods tightly and goes to her.

Trystan returns next. He wears his usual unreadable expression, but I can see from the tension around his eyes that he's deeply upset. He echoes a similar story very matter-of-factly and takes Yvan's place in front of Wynter.

Marina is staring out the window, standing between Diana and Gareth, the three of them speaking in hushed tones. Marina's voice breaks down into grief-stricken notes, and both Gareth's and Diana's arms come up to embrace and comfort her.

Yvan settles down next to me in front of the fire and he stares into it for a long moment. The horrific images they've all described play through my mind, and I'm finding it hard to contain my anger and sadness. When a hot tear skids down my cheek, Yvan's arm slides around me, and my breath shudders. I sniff back my tears and let my head rest on his warm shoulder. We both quietly watch as Ariel makes little fireballs and hurls them into the hearth.

Another hour passes, and Rafe finally returns.

The moment I see my older brother, I know something's very wrong. Even the way he shakes off his cloak is odd, his movements stiff and uncomfortable. Diana can sense it, too. She's strangely alert as she moves toward him, studying him intently, almost sniffing the air around him.

"Rafe, what's wrong?" I ask. Yvan's arm is still draped around my shoulder, his other hand absently petting one of Ariel's sleeping chickens.

Rafe shakes his head in reply, refusing to meet my eyes. He grabs a desk chair, drags it over to the fire and sits down, still not looking at any of us.

"What happened?" Trystan asks him.

Rafe presses the bridge of his nose between his fingers and shrugs. "They've got about forty of them. I spent time with two—they seemed to understand the message. The tavern keeper knows they're not animals. He *knows* it, and he keeps them there anyway."

"How do you know that?" I ask.

"He told me he won't let the Selkies have water containers larger than a small bowl—that they can communicate if they get underwater together." A tight fury lights Rafe's eyes. "So, I said to him, 'If they can talk to each other, does that mean they're human?' He said, 'I don't give a rat's ass what they are. They sure can bring in the guilders.'"

He glances over at Marina. "Marina, your sister's there."

Marina seems to have stopped breathing. Gareth quickly takes hold of her arm to steady her.

"I didn't actually see her," Rafe tells her, "but some of

the other Selkies recognized her picture. They made it clear that she's there."

Marina nods rigidly, too overwhelmed to speak. Gareth pulls her close, murmuring to her softly as he strokes her hair and she clings to him.

"Damion Bane was there, as well," Rafe says.

Yvan stiffens at the sound of Damion's name, and my own stomach tightens with revulsion.

"He's got some nerve, that one," Rafe says. "Acted almost glad to see me. Raised his glass to me, even. I saw him again later in the evening, just as the door to his room was closing. I spotted the two Selkies in the room with him. They were... horribly altered." Rafe stops, as if he can't quite figure out how to phrase the next part. "They've destroyed their skins."

A collective gasp goes up from all of us. Marina's gills burst open, and her hand flies to her mouth. Gareth's hold tightens on her.

Rafe's face takes on a remote, haunted expression as he stares into the fire. "Their eyes... They were opaque...like they were the walking dead. That's who Damion was with. Those two Selkies. He actually smiled at me as he shut the door."

Marina starts to weep. Rafe looks away, and we're all silent for a moment, struggling with this new horror.

Eventually, my brother turns to Wynter. "I know we need to give the Amaz as many details as we can, but...if you don't want to see..."

Wynter's face is wan but determined as she answers. "I'll be all right." She pats the bed beside her. "Here, come sit by me."

Diana, Marina, Wynter and I journey for Amaz lands after we've all snatched a few hours of rest.

There's no need for Andras to guide us this time. Like a

migrating bird, Diana only has to be shown a path through the woods once to remember the way forever.

This time, we're met at the border by Freyja and two other soldiers who escort us to Cyme quickly and efficiently, bringing us straight to the Queenhall.

When we arrive, Queen Alkaia takes her time examining each of Wynter's pictures, then passes them around to the other members of her council. All of the women listen intently to Wynter's vivid descriptions of the Selkie taverns.

Alcippe stands just to the Queen's left, glowering at Diana and me, but she also appears deeply interested in what Wynter and Marina have to say. Valasca is there as well, dressed as casually and unadorned as she was the last time I saw her, silently watching the proceedings.

Our eyes meet once in unspoken solidarity.

After thoroughly looking everything over, Queen Alkaia sits back in her chair and meets the eyes of each of her councillors in turn. The other women nod to her in silent agreement.

"It is decided," Queen Alkaia announces, hands clasped before her. "We will free the Selkies just after the full moon."

"It's dangerous to wait much longer," I caution her. "It's only a matter of time before the Mage Council votes to have all the Selkies executed."

"The full moon is a few days prior to their next meeting," she tells me. "On the night of that full moon, more Selkies could be drawn up from the sea and captured. If we wait until after the full moon, we'll be able to free those Selkies along with the others and return *all of them* to their ocean home."

CHAPTER TEN

VALASCA AND ALDER

Three days before the Amaz are poised to do what will surely be seen as a declaration of war on the Gardnerians, Diana, Tierney and I are ensconced in the North Tower, staring at our books and frantically trying to catch up with our classwork.

I glance out our lodging's large window. It's late, but the western edge of evening sky is still tinted blue, the days lengthening as spring begins its tentative hold on the land, snow increasingly disappearing into earth. Soon, the Western Realm's famously stormy spring weather will move in.

I struggle to focus on the page before me. It's difficult to study, knowing what's coming, especially with Marina gone. She remained behind in Cyme, preparing for the rescue, and we all feel her absence acutely.

Diana looks up from her thick medical text, her head tilted, nostrils flaring. "Someone's coming," she says, sniffing the air. "Amaz. Two of them."

Abruptly vigilant, Tierney and I move to the large circular window and peer down. There are two horses tethered to the old hitching post at the rear of the North Tower. I recognize the black horse with the reddish mane.

It belongs to Valasca.

Heavy footsteps clomp up the stone stairs, followed by a firm knock at the door. Tierney and I exchange a glance of curiosity.

Diana opens the door.

Valasca stands in the hall, but she's completely altered from the last time we saw her. Her blue-streaked black hair is in the same short spikes, but she's clad in Amaz battle gear—thin black armor covered with scarlet runes over a dark tunic and pants, a variety of blades strapped all over her body. Multiple black metallic rings adorn her face and ears, and thick kohl lines her eyes. Glowing runes mark the hilts of her weapons and their sheaths.

Her stance is military erect, as is that of her cohort. Valasca's tall companion pulls back the hood of her cloak, and a streak of astonishment jettisons through me.

The young woman's coloring is deep forest green, but her hair is ebony and her eyes are a dark Gardnerian green. She has long, gracefully pointed ears, and her skin shimmers green—similar to Gardnerian skin, only the sheen is dramatically heightened.

Like Valasca, she's heavily armed, but oddly so. A long bow hewn from irregular River Maple is strapped to her back, along with a quiver filled with a variety of arrows that look more like sharpened tree branches than traditional arrows. A few more branches are strapped to her belt, and I pick the grain of the bark out on sight. *Rock Maple, Red Oak, Black Walnut.*

"This is Alder Xanthos," Valasca says with cool formality. "She is a friend to the Selkies and we have come to discuss their rescue."

"You're Fae," Tierney marvels as she gapes at the tall stranger, barely noticing when one of her books slides off its haphazard pile and lands on the floor with a resounding *thunk*.

"I am part Dryad," Alder confirms. The cadence of her voice is serene and otherworldly, her accent melodic. She slowly pivots her head to peer at me. There's a palpable stillness to her as she studies me for a long moment. "My forest has told me much about you, Elloren Gardner."

I frown at Alder Xanthos. "The forest mistakes me for the Black Witch," I inform her starchly. "Which I'm not."

Her level stare doesn't waver. "The trees say otherwise."

I let out a hard sigh. "If I was, in fact, the Black Witch, that would make rescuing the Selkies a fair bit easier, don't you think?"

She's as still as timber, her eyes unblinking.

Valasca curses under her breath and shoots her companion an impatient look. "Xan, unless the trees are marching out to save the Selkies anytime soon, perhaps we can ignore their opinion for the moment." She turns back to me, eyes blazing with what looks like a sudden flare of defiance. "I wish to meet with your men."

Diana, Tierney and I look to each other with open astonishment. "Our *men*?" I clarify, cocking my head.

A look of annoyance passes over Valasca's face. "Yes," she shoots back curtly. "The ones who visited the Selkie taverns."

"But I thought—"

"Yes, I know," she cuts me off. "But I think it would be useful to speak with them before we invade."

I study Valasca. She's practically vibrating with unease, and I realize that she's crossing over staunchly forbidden lines here. Alder, too. And that meeting with men could probably get them both in serious trouble.

Perhaps even cast out of Amaz society.

"We'll find them for you," I tell her. "They'll tell you whatever you need to know."

We assemble in Andras's new dwelling, an Amaz-style geometric dome lodging deep in the woods, and not far from Naga's cave. A small iron stove in the center of his home pumps out warmth.

Alder eyes the men and the logs smoldering in the iron stove with wariness as Valasca greets my brothers, Gareth and Yvan all in turn, rebellion sparking in her dark eyes. I'm stunned to see her shaking their hands—from what Amaz has told us, it's flatly forbidden for the Amaz to touch men, unless they're partaking of fertility rites, and they're not supposed to make eye contact with them if they can help it. I've a flash of unsettled remembrance—of my mostly Gardnerian Mathematics class and professor refusing to pollute themselves by looking directly at Ariel. Of the Alfsigr and Gardnerian scholars averting their eyes from Wynter whenever she passes.

This is the same kind of thing, I realize. And it's good that Valasca is casting it off.

Valasca approaches Andras last. She looks up at him, and we all still, a sense of momentous tension suddenly in the air. I'm acutely aware, as I'm sure we all are, of the fact that Valasca is a bridge to the people who have shunned Andras all his life.

Valasca holds out her hand to him. "Well met, Andras Volya," she says, her voice heavy with import.

Andras takes her hand and holds on to it. He murmurs something in another language, formal in its cadence. Valasca's head bobs in what looks like respectful acknowledgment as she repeats the phrase back to him.

I catch Yvan's eye, and a flash of mutual wonderment passes between us over this remarkable turn of events. His lips lift in a subtle smile that warms me.

Andras tells everyone to make themselves comfortable, and Diana takes a seat off to the side, studying Alder in that calm, inscrutable way she has with people she's quietly sizing up. Tierney sits down beside Andras, her eyes fixed on Alder with a palpable intensity, clearly stunned by her presence here—an unglamoured Fae in the Western Realm.

A highly dangerous thing to be.

I imagine that Valasca and Alder took a rather isolated route here to avoid Alder being summarily arrested, but I also know that the only border guards they might have encountered would be Vu Trin. And the Vu Trin stationed here in Verpacia are proving themselves to be increasingly aligned with the Fae, even though their government has ordered them to not provoke Gardnerian ire and to rigidly enforce the region's unforgiving border rules.

Yvan crosses the small, circular room and takes a seat beside me, and I'm instantly lit up by the decided nature of his action, my heartbeat deepening. He turns and our eyes meet, a quick rush of heat coursing through me. He's so close, his shoulder almost touching mine—I can feel his warmth and smell that enticing fiery scent of his. I shift slightly, and the edge of my finger bumps lightly against his hand.

A spark of heat races through my affinity lines as our smallest fingers curl around each other, both of us initiating the contact. Both of us complicit in this small rebellion.

"All right. Here's the situation," Valasca says, and I pull part of my focus toward her, even as I remain heatedly aware of Yvan's touch.

Valasca sighs and rakes her fingers agitatedly through her spiky hair. "Queen Alkaia doesn't know I'm here, and I'd be grateful if it could remain that way." She grimaces at the floor and shakes her head, as if holding some internal debate. "I love my people, but they have some customs that border on flat-out stupidity. If I'm going to lead a military expedition to rescue the Selkies, it makes sense to actually *speak* with the people who have *been* in the places that are our targets. Even if they are men."

She pauses to glance up to the ceiling and lets out a string of oaths aimed at no one in particular. Then she glares hotly at all of us. "This type of foolishness is why the Gardnerians increased the size of their territory tenfold during the Realm War."

I'm momentarily dumbfounded, my hand pulling away from Yvan's. "Did you say you're *leading* the expedition?"

She fixes me with an even stare. "Yes. I'm highly positioned in the Queen's Guard."

I look at her with astonishment. "How high?"

She considers me for a brief second before answering, one black eyebrow cocked. "I command it."

Holy Ancient One in the heavens above. "Is that why Alcippe backed down from you that night? The night she wanted to kill us?"

Valasca lets out a quick sigh. "Alcippe may be stronger than me, but I'm rather good with a rune-blade. She was seriously outmatched."

"You could have taken her down with just that one rune-blade?" I ask, my voice shrill.

Valasca's kohl-marked eyes narrow on me, glinting with amusement. "I could probably take down everyone in this room with just that one rune-blade." She gestures loosely toward Diana with her thumb. "Except maybe the Lupine."

"I'm a Level Five Mage," Trystan interjects, tapping his wand lightly. "I might give you a run for your money."

"I'm particularly good at deflecting magic with a blade," Valasca casually informs him. "Even combined elemental spells."

"Well, all right then," Trystan says, looking impressed.

Confusion roils inside me. "But...you told me you were a goat herder."

"I *am* a goat herder," Valasca says, an irritated edge to her tone. "*And* the commander of the Queen's Guard."

It all falls into place—why Freyja chose Valasca to be my guard. Why Valasca was dressed so inconspicuously in Amaz lands. They *wanted* me to underestimate her.

I frown darkly at Valasca. "They really thought I was that much of a threat?"

She stares at me for a long moment, as if deliberating. "Yes, Elloren," she finally says, an apologetic edge creeping into her tone. "They did. I should have told you of my position once I realized, beyond a shadow of a doubt, that you weren't a threat. I'm sorry for that."

Yes, you should have told me. Before we drank all that Tirag. And told each other so many private things.

But none of that matters, I realize. She's here. Breaking with her people's ways. All to help Marina and her people.

"You don't need to apologize," I tell her. "I'm grateful for what you're doing. Thank you for going out of your way to help the Selkies."

Valasca raises her brow slightly and grows serious. "You don't need to thank me, Elloren Gardner." Her voice has become low and subdued. "The chance to stand up and fight against injustice... It is the highest gift the Goddess can bestow upon any of us."

I give her a slight smile and nod in agreement. Valasca returns my smile.

"Do you want Mage backup when you set out to free the Selkies?" Trystan lightly inquires, but his gaze is steel hard. "I would be happy to accompany you. I find the idea of rendering one of those taverns into ash to be quite appealing."

Valasca's shrewd eyes flick over the Level Five stripes on my brother's military apprentice uniform. "Thank you for your offer, Trystan Gardner," she says with a respectful dip of her head. "But the Amaz will not let men accompany our military."

Trystan holds Valasca's even stare. "Well, let me know if you change your mind."

"I do need your assistance in another way, however," she tells him. "I need to know the rough layout of each tavern—where the skins are kept, how many guards there are, what kinds of weapons they have."

"The skins are in Elfin steel trunks," Yvan puts in.

"Which are locked," Gareth adds. "And stored in locked rooms."

Valasca huffs out a dismissive sound. "We can blast through all of that."

"Every tavern has two or three Level Four Mages guarding the site," Rafe tells her.

Valasca nods thoughtfully. "We can cast a rune-net to dampen their power. That's likely the first thing we'll do. Tell me where the guards were posted."

Trystan, Rafe, Gareth and Yvan spend the next hour or so detailing where the storage rooms are, the times and days of the week when the fewest patrons and guards are likely to be at the taverns, along with a host of other logistical details.

"How is Marina?" Gareth asks Valasca as their discussion draws to a close, a note of private pain in his voice. I know it's beyond difficult for him to be losing the one person who truly understands who he is.

"She is well," Valasca assures him. "We have our best rune-sorceresses working with her. They're attempting to create runes that the Selkies can use to break the spell that drags them to shore. This rescue needs to completely end the abuse of the Selkies once and for all."

"I want to fight with you," Diana says to Valasca, her body tense with a predatory eagerness, frustration blazing in her amber eyes.

"I know you do, Diana Ulrich," Valasca replies. "But this is a dangerous move for my people. You're the daughter of an alpha. Your involvement would have far-reaching political ramifications. Your father, as I understand it, is trying to avoid an all-out war for territory."

"There is no avoiding the fight to come," Diana says, almost a growl. "And that land the Mage Council wants is Lupine land. Their Black Witch stole it from us during the Realm War, and we reclaimed it. It was *never* theirs."

It's stark, hearing Diana utter the words "Black Witch," and I'm chastened and saddened by this reminder of the unjust threats leveled against her people by mine.

"Alder Xanthos," Tierney unexpectedly blurts out, desperation stark on her face, "I implore you for your help."

Alder tilts her head slightly, her owlish gaze homing in on Tierney as everyone in the room stills.

"You're *Fae*," Tierney says, her voice rough with emotion. "You understand what's happening to all of us. If you can help the Selkies, help my family. I'm glamoured Asrai. So is my brother. We're trapped here and in real danger. Please...*help us*."

Andras sets a bolstering hand on Tierney's shoulder, and

concern tightens Alder's smooth brow. "How old were you when you were glamoured?" she asks.

"I was three," Tierney forces out, a tear streaking down her cheek.

Compassion softens Valasca's expression. "Queen Alkaia has declared amnesty for many of the Fae," she tells Tierney. "We can make an appeal on your behalf to Queen Alkaia."

"But my father," Tierney insists. "My brother…"

"My father will help them," Diana puts in stubbornly.

Valasca sighs, glancing at her. "Perhaps he will. We must wait and see."

"What about the Vu Trin?" I frustratedly ask. "Why can't they take a more active role in getting the Fae out of here?"

Valasca shakes her head. "The Vu Trin, like the Lupines, are sympathetic to the plight of the Fae, but they can't defy their Eastern Realm command." She curses under her breath, then focuses back in on Tierney. "Tell me. Do you have any control over your water magic?"

Tierney nods stiffly. "Some. And I can summon Kelpies."

"Kelpies?" Valasca cocks an eyebrow. "That is most definitely in your favor." She turns to Alder, the two of them momentarily conversing in a foreign tongue. Alder nods, and Valasca looks back at Tierney, seeming resolute.

"We give you our word, Tierney Calix. Once we have freed the Selkies, Alder Xanthos and I will do everything in our power to help you and your people, the men and women both."

CHAPTER ELEVEN

FIRE FAE

Spring peepers are sending up their nighttime chirping call as we all disperse in varying directions through the forest—Valasca and Alder back to Cyme, everyone else returning to their studies and labors.

I'm just about to emerge from the trees, heading toward the main kitchen, the lights of the University twinkling from across the North Tower's broad field.

"Elloren, wait." Yvan's hand clasps hold of my arm, and I slow to a stop, turning to face him.

"I was hoping to speak with you alone."

I wait, scanning the forest and the field surrounding us as he composes his thoughts, every one of my senses heightened by his nearness.

"The way you spoke to Valasca initially," he says, "it felt like you have doubts about her ability to do this."

"No," I say, shaking my head. "I don't. She just surprised me, that's all."

He hesitates, as if in danger of revealing part of a secret. "But...there's a tension I'm sensing between the two of you."

"It's nothing."

He stands there, obviously conflicted and unconvinced.

Out with it, Elloren. Just say it and be done with it. "This... thing happened," I reluctantly tell him. "Valasca was my guard while we were in Cyme, and she saw that I was feeling out of sorts, so...she offered me spirits. I'd never had them before, and I drank too much, even though she warned me not to. And...we told each other a lot of personal things." *And I told her how much I want to kiss you.* An uncomfortable burn starts along my neck. "I told her...about my feelings for you."

Yvan's fire gives a hard flare, and he looks away, as if suddenly at war with his emotions.

"Yvan," I venture, concerned by his unease.

He shakes his head tightly, his eyes pinned on the forest.

I draw closer to him as he struggles to maintain his focus just past me and keep his fire tightly restrained.

"I'm sorry," I tell him. "I never meant to share such private thoughts with her."

"It's not that," he says, and I can sense how much holding back is costing him, his fire straining toward me like a bucking stallion.

An impassioned rebellion rises and I dare to put my hand on his arm. He swallows sharply, the muscles of his neck tensing, as I inwardly rail against our situation, against the entire Western Realm. *Why do things have to be so difficult between us?*

Seeking to comfort him, I slide my arms loosely around his waist and rest my head lightly on his shoulder, tears stinging at my eyes.

Yvan's rigid posture abruptly loosens and he wraps his arms around me in a caress, his fire shuddering into my lines. "Elloren," he says softly.

He leans down to inhale the scent of my hair, and I nuzzle my cheek against his graceful neck, his skin so hot to the touch. Unable to resist, I tilt my head and press my lips lightly against his neck.

He inhales sharply, and his fire sears over and into mine, his slow, careful touch giving way to a harder urgency as he pulls me close, his hands gripping my back, his lips on my hair.

I kiss him just below his jaw, and his breathing deepens, his fire flaring so riotously hot it raises a prickling line of heat straight down my spine.

Then I bring my lips toward his.

Yvan's hands abruptly come to my arms, muscles tensed, holding me at bay. "We can't do this." His voice is ragged.

I blink up at him, hurt and confused and completely at a loss. *"Why?"*

He swallows hard, his gaze scorching. "If I kiss you," he says, his voice low and rough, "there is no way I'll *ever* be able to let you go."

"Then don't let me go," I say fiercely, his fire grasping at mine with ardent heat.

"A kiss... It isn't a simple thing for me," Yvan says haltingly. "There's...*power* in it."

I'm thrust into a deeper confusion. "Is this a Fire Fae trait?"

"Oh, no," he says bitterly. "It's something uniquely my own."

"Yvan..."

"If I kiss you," he says, struggling to find the right words, "it will...*bind* us."

"What do you mean? Bind us how?" That secret pain again—I can see it in his eyes. "Yvan, please. You need to be honest with me."

"I can't," he agonizes, his hands rigid on my arms. "There's no happy ending for us, Elloren. There are things...things you don't know...that you can *never* know. I'm dangerous to everyone you love...to everyone I love, as well."

"I don't care that you're Fae!" I cry, trying to free my arms from his viselike grip, but he holds on tight.

"I'm *not just Fae!*" he snarls.

I'm swept up in a sudden vortex of bewilderment. "What do you mean?"

Yvan releases me abruptly and takes a step back, his fire an incandescent storm.

"Elloren," he finally says, his voice coarsened with finality. "If for nothing else but the safety of our families, we *cannot* give in to this. I know we both want to, but we can't. And I'm sorry I keep drawing you in." Golden fire lights his eyes, his expression wildly distraught. "I wish things were different, but there is no changing them. Find someone else. Anyone you want. *Anyone* but me."

And then he walks away, his pace brisk, his fire whipping back toward me in violently discordant tendrils.

My throat tightens with sorrow as I watch him stalk away from me, rebellious tears welling in my eyes.

I only want you, I want to rage at him from clear across the night-darkened field. *Tell me what you're struggling with, Yvan. Let me help you. Whatever it is.*

Tell me what you're hiding from all of us.

CHAPTER
TWELVE

BRUISED SKY

Three days later, Diana and I sit near a bonfire in the center of the Amaz military base, the flames spitting sparks that arc up through the sky. Soldiers in full battle gear fill the clearing, preparing horses and calling out directives to each other in the Urisk dialect that's common here.

The torchlit base is in the same valley as Cyme, but on the outskirts of the city, with a heavily fortified rune-barrier keeping civilians clear of the area. This mission isn't something that the Amaz will be heralding for all to hear—they're keeping it secret even from their own people. Queen Alkaia is betting that the Gardnerians won't bother to retaliate after the Selkie rescue, since the Mage Council is already gearing up to end the Selkie trade in their own horrific way.

I pray that she's right.

One of the soldiers calls out a loud command, and all the others immediately grow silent and still, a crackling tension suddenly vibrating on the air. Diana and I rise to find the focus of everyone's attention.

The soldiers to our far right quietly part as Valasca strides forward in dark armor, her controlled movements radiating a bold, dominant grace. The soldiers raise rune-marked palms out to her in silent tribute.

Marina and Alder enter the clearing behind Valasca, both of them dressed in rune-marked battle armor, like the rest of the soldiers. I'm amazed at how much Marina has changed in the short time she's spent with the Amaz. She holds her head high, radiating power and confidence. Rune-blades are strapped all over her limbs, and her silver hair throws off a scarlet shimmer in the ruby torchlight.

Marina's gaze meets mine, and a fierce look of unity passes between us as she takes her place to Valasca's left, Alder flanking Valasca on the right.

Then Queen Alkaia enters the camp, escorted by Alcippe, the huge warrior's rune-axe strapped to her back. Marina, Alder and Valasca lower themselves to one knee before the queen, and every soldier follows suit. I drop down to my knee as well, overcome with gratitude for the Amaz gathered here, and also grateful that Queen Alkaia has allowed Diana and me to be present when they leave and when they return.

Queen Alkaia places her hands on Valasca's bowed head and intones the Goddess's blessing, then motions for everyone to rise. She pulls Marina down slightly and kisses her on both cheeks.

The soldiers mount their horses, and when Valasca raises a hand, the entire world pauses, my breath suspended in my throat. Then she throws down her hand, and they're off, sounding like thunder. I catch a glimpse of a rune-road appearing in the distance, cutting straight through the base of the Spine. They ride out onto it and abruptly disappear into the stone.

★ ★ ★

Diana and I are surrounded by silence, and I feel as if a great wave has come and gone. Only a few soldiers remain, quietly seeing to the base's upkeep. The Amaz horses are rune-marked for speed, but still, it will be many hours before they return. Diana and I exchange a fraught glance, and I take a seat by the fire once more, hunkering down for the long wait.

The hours pass, Diana pacing tirelessly while I poke at the fire with a long stick. I attempt conversation with her a few times, but she simply grunts at me and keeps pacing, so I abandon the effort. I know Diana doesn't want to be stuck here with me—she wants to be out rescuing the Selkies with the Amaz, and this waiting is pure torture for her.

And so, we bide our time, Diana pacing and me worrying the fire with my stick, united in our harried silence throughout the long night.

Dawn eventually comes, clear and cool, the colors like a raw bruise dealt by the fleeing night sky. The damp morning chill wraps cold tendrils around me, working its way under my cloak, the bonfire long since died down to embers.

Marina and the Amaz finally return as the sun begins to climb higher in the sky. Everyone looks stoic and weary, the previous night's violence still echoing in their bloodstained clothing and jaded gazes. Many of the soldiers are on foot and leading their horses, most of the animals carrying two or more Selkies.

One horse carries two motionless bodies wrapped tightly in cloth. Horrified, I realize these must be the two broken Selkies—the ones whose skins had been destroyed. Marina had instructed the Amaz to put an end to their suffering, that there was no saving them now, and that death was their only hope.

It was one thing to hear of this, but quite another to be faced with the reality of it, and the barbarity of it all hits me with crippling strength.

Alcippe shoots me a look of pure, withering rage as she passes, gripping her rune-axe, and her look hollows me out, leaving me defenseless and ill-prepared for the misery about to pour in like an undertow.

Unexpectedly, Alcippe lunges for me, teeth gritted and bared. "Look at them, Gardnerian," she snarls. *"Look!"*

And I do, with mounting devastation, as silver-haired women trail into the clearing. The pain of their abuse is etched deeply on their faces in so many different ways. Some look like their anger could overwhelm them at any moment, their heads whipping around as if debating where to attack first. Many appear horribly beaten down, the light stripped from their eyes, their heads hung low, feet dragging. Others seem terrorized, their movements frantic and nervous, as if any loud sound might send them running for cover. And a few seem to be in total shock, like one very young girl guided by two older Selkies, her eyes blank and traumatized, staring out into nothingness.

The girl drops to the ground, hugs her knees to her chest and rocks herself, refusing to get up. A tall soldier kneels down in front of her and talks to her softly, her strong hand on the girl's back. The two older Selkies also kneel down to the girl's level, all of them trying in vain to comfort her as the child looks out into nothing, straight through the women around her.

"Look at *her!*" Alcippe growls at me, motioning toward the girl. I open my mouth to respond, but I can't speak. It's all too horrifying for words.

"How old does she look?" Alcippe demands. I try to speak again, to no avail. *"How old,* Gardnerian?"

"Twelve," I manage to croak out.

"You would not believe where we found her, what the men of your kind were doing to her!"

Alcippe doesn't need to hit me with her rune-axe. The weight of this slams into me mercilessly all on its own. The shame of it presses down, threatening to suffocate.

"I tell you this, Gardnerian," Alcippe grinds out, her eyes wild with rage, "if I am *ever* face-to-face with any of your men, even the ones you call your friends, the ones you call your brothers, I will slice them in two. *This* is why the Goddess tells us to cast them out at birth. To live apart from them. To be stronger than they are. Because even the most harmless male baby—*this* is what he will grow up to do! *Look* at her!"

I force myself to look again. The Amaz and the two Selkies are trying to gently cajole the now-trembling girl to her feet. Alcippe strides over to where the girl sits and, without hesitation, picks the child up in her strong, muscular arms and carries her toward the shelter of a circular, rune-covered military tent.

I want to call after Alcippe, to tell her that not all men are like this, but at this moment, surrounded by so much misery, the words feel empty and false in my throat. Then Marina enters the clearing, her arm wrapped tightly around a young girl who clings to her as they walk. Her sister—the girl from Wynter's pictures.

Marina's head turns toward me, her expression blaring outrage. Our eyes meet with quiet devastation before she and her sister disappear into a huge tent with the others.

The Amaz care for the Selkies throughout the day and into the evening, and I stumble about, trying to help as best I can.

I work well into the night, bringing food, scrubbing plates and pots. Feeling close to collapse, I feel Diana's gentle hand on my arm, and I let her lead me away to a communal sleeping tent. Once there, she leads me to a bedroll and covers me with a thick felt blanket. Then she curls up next to me and encircles me in her warm arms.

I sob into her chest, drowning in the deep, visceral disgust over what I've seen and the stories I've heard, feeling like I never want to see another man again.

"They should give them their skins," I cry. "Not make them wait until they bring them back to the ocean. They should give their skins back and let them massacre as many Gardnerians as possible."

"Shhh," Diana tells me, stroking my hair. I cry and cry, my eyes eventually so swollen it feels natural to shut out what's left of the light. And I continue to cry until sleep claims me.

"Elloren."

I feel a hand on my shoulder, rocking me.

Marina.

I sit up, startled.

"We're all leaving," she says, crouched down beside me. She takes in my swollen eyes, her brow tensing as she briefly glances toward a solemn Diana.

"So, this is goodbye?" My heart twists at the thought of never seeing her again. She gives a small, sad smile and nods. I fall into her arms, my hand stroking her water-like hair. "I'll miss you, but I'm glad you finally get to go home. I hope you find a way to stop all this forever."

"The Amaz have given us runes," she tells me as she sits back and pulls a rune-stone from her pocket. Its ebony surface is marked with a looping scarlet rune. "They believe we'll be able to use these to break the spell that pulls us to shore."

"Good," I tell her, her form wavy through my tears.

Diana and I accompany Marina outside. It's late afternoon and overcast, spitting a light rain that probably carries an icy chill outside of the rune-warmed valley. Valasca is on horseback and calling out orders as Alcippe, Freyja and a host of other women help over a hundred Selkies onto horses in front of their armed Amaz protectors. Large sacks filled with what I assume are the Selkies' skins are tied to several horses, those mounts and their riders surrounded by heavily armed guards.

I spot Queen Alkaia approaching through the crowd. Valasca rides over to the queen and leans down from her mount, listening intently and nodding repeatedly as the queen quietly speaks to her.

"Marina," Alder calls out as she strides toward us. She's in full battle gear, her posture reed straight, and she's leading two horses. A slim young Selkie girl walks beside Alder, holding tight to her arm.

Marina's sister.

I reflexively attempt a smile at the girl Marina has named Coral in the Common Tongue, but my smile falters. There's trauma in Coral's eyes, which seem almost pinned into a widened state.

Marina motions to Alder to give her a moment. Then she turns to me, and my eyes well up, my throat stitching tight. I hug her one more time, and she kisses my forehead, my tears spilling over my cheeks. She holds my gaze for a long moment, then turns to Diana and embraces her, as well. "Goodbye, Diana Ulrich."

"Goodbye, Marina the Selkie," Diana says, stepping back and grasping Marina's arms. "It has been an honor to know you."

Marina's eyes take on a look of longing as her gaze is

drawn west. "It will be good to meet with the ocean after all this time. To be home again."

"I understand," Diana says. "It is like this for us. With the forest."

Marina nods. "Goodbye, my friends." She takes one long, last look at us. "I will never forget you."

Sadness hollows me out as I watch them go, Diana standing beside me, and I'm overcome by a fierce urge to go with them. To meet with the ocean and be pulled down into its icy blackness—and disappear from the Western Realm forever.

A dark depression claims me upon my return to the North Tower, and I let it pull me under. I retreat to my bed, refusing to eat or drink, avoiding the others. I only want to lie there and cry.

"What's wrong with the Gardnerian?" Ariel asks Diana, her wings figeting.

"She's upset about what was done to the Selkies," Diana tells her, "by her own people."

Ariel snorts in response. "Should come as no surprise."

"You weren't there," Diana counters. "It was very bad."

"I didn't have to be there to know how bad it was," Ariel snipes back.

"You were right," I say to Ariel, my voice flat. "Gardnerians are evil. And I've got their evil magic pulsing through my lines. *I'm* evil. You were right to try and drive me out my first night here."

My statement is met with silence, and I continue to cry late into the night.

I'm thinking on how the Gardnerians should be completely obliterated from the face of Erthia when I feel something warm being gently placed beside me.

One of Ariel's chickens.

"Let her roost near you," Ariel says, her voice sharp and unfriendly. "It's...soothing."

The small bird is warm, and she's making a gentle cooing sound that's oddly comforting.

I turn over to find Ariel sitting beside me, her brow deeply furrowed, her black wings flapping rhythmically in agitation.

"Why are you being nice to me?" I ask her, my voice hoarse and my nose stuffed shut.

Ariel stares at me for a long moment, struggling with the answer. "I'm not," she finally snaps. She gets up and goes back to her side of the room, sitting down on her bed with her wings wrapped tight around herself. "I just want you to shut up so I can get some sleep." She lies down and angrily turns her back to me.

But I'm too stunned to cry anymore.

I reflect for a moment on how comfort sometimes comes from the oddest places, from the least likely people—like an Icaral, in spite of herself, choosing to offer comfort to the granddaughter of Carnissa Gardner.

Life is truly strange. And very confusing.

I put my arm around the soft chicken, its warmth and rhythmic breathing eventually cutting through my misery and lulling me to sleep.

PART FOUR

MAGE COUNCIL
RULING
#336

All Selkies coming to shore in the Western
Realm are to be immediately executed.
Aiding or abetting Selkies will be
grounds for imprisonment.

CHAPTER ONE

IRON

Three days pass, and amazingly, the world remains at wary peace. We're all braced for the Gardnerian military to retaliate in some way for the Selkie raid.

So, we wait for it. And wait. And wait.

But...nothing.

And then the Mage Council holds an emergency meeting.

The next day, Tierney and I watch as a Verpacian soldier nails a wanted posting to a lamppost, the edges of the parchment flapping as they're buffeted by the strong wind. Thunder rumbles in the distance, and I glance up at the churning clouds—a dark herald of the stormy weather we'll all need to get through before we have any chance of stepping into true spring.

When the soldier walks off to hang another across the street, Tierney and I tentatively approach the lamppost. My heart thuds against my chest as we read the stark warning that Selkies are running loose in the Western Realm, the vicious seal-creatures lying in wait to kill Gardnerians and Verpacians.

Tierney pales as she scans the parchment. "The Selkies are all safe," I remind her under my breath. "This doesn't matter."

She turns to me, her expression stark. "It matters," she insists in a jagged whisper. "It gives the Gardnerian and Verpacian councils yet one more justification to double down and go after anyone they want to target."

More insistent thunder cracks overhead. Out of the corner of my eye, I watch as the young Verpacian soldier nails one posting after another all the way down the street, most pedestrians having ducked into stores or restaurants to try and wait out the impending storm.

Rafe and Trystan are rattled by the Gardnerian military's mild response to the Selkie raid.

"Vogel has to know that the Amaz were involved," Rafe plainly states that night as I lean against his desk. My brothers are sitting on their beds, jumbles of books and classwork scattered around them as rain sheets against the windows and forks of lightning flash outside.

"How could he know?" I ask, dubious.

"Well, for one thing," Trystan says, "the Amaz likely used runic explosives to obliterate the taverns. That's what Valasca was planning. And that leaves a rather unique radius of destruction."

"And the Amaz probably erased their tracks to and from the taverns, to avoid being followed," Rafe adds. "Selkies wouldn't have access to Amaz track-warding runes if they escaped on their own. So, the Gardnerians must know that rune-sorcery was used."

"And the whole thing was too coordinated." Trystan throws Rafe a poignant look. "Too military efficient."

"Which means," Rafe continues, an ominous edge creeping into his tone, "there might be another reason Vogel's not threatening the Amaz."

We're all quiet for a long moment, the silence blaring.

"What reason?" I ask nervously.

Rafe's dark look is unwavering. "Maybe Vogel is conserving his power for something else."

Disquieted by my brothers' sense of amorphous foreboding, I throw myself into the busy routine of my life. Everyone else is just as preoccupied, the past few weeks having put us all much further behind in our studies. Anxious that the Mage and Verpacian councils are covertly investigating the Selkie raid, we're all careful to stay within the boundaries of what's expected, to blend in and go unnoticed.

Now that spring has arrived, Gareth leaves with the other maritime apprentices for the Valgard docks, and I miss his comforting presence, as well as Marina's.

Yvan and I hardly speak during this time, and it's difficult to see him. An ache twists inside me whenever we pass each other in Mathematics class or when we're working the same kitchen shift, but he seems determined to maintain his distance this time and not waver.

But still, there's a spark of light.

Ariel is now actually civil to me. I almost fall clear off my bed the first time she finds something interesting in one of her animal husbandry books she wants to read to me. And Jarod has started coming in from the woods more and more, showing up at the North Tower at odd hours to sit with us while he studies.

It's almost as if a new peace is descending, and a dawning hope that maybe it's possible for things to get a little bit better instead of always worse.

One evening, I'm stirring a large pot of soup in the kitchen when Yvan comes in to load the cookstoves with wood.

I notice that he hits the stove's iron lever with his foot, shoves the wood in quickly and then, uncharacteristically, closes it with his foot as well, even though his hands are now free. He's turning to go back outside when Fernyllia calls to him.

"Yvan, be a good lad and scrape the rust off those pots there, would you? They'll be fit for use again once they're free of rust and well-seasoned."

Yvan turns to look at the pile of iron pots on a nearby table. They're covered with brown splotches of rust, the scraping tools nearby.

I notice his glimmer of hesitation where Fernyllia doesn't. She's gone right back to kneading large piles of dough with Bleddyn and a dispirited Olilly, whose head is wrapped with an ever-present scarf to hide her damaged ears.

"Yvan?" I say softly.

He shoots me a quelling look, his eyes darting around at the other kitchen workers for emphasis before he sets about doing the task. With a sigh, I go back to stirring the soup, the sound of his metallic scraping hard on my ears, setting my teeth on edge.

A sudden clatter rings out.

I turn to see Yvan retrieving the tool he's dropped, which surprises me. I've never seen Yvan drop anything. He's always so graceful and deft, always so in control of any task he's doing.

No one else seems especially concerned by the noise, lost as they are in their buzz of conversation and the business of work. And no one else notices when Yvan abruptly gets up, the task not yet finished, and leaves the kitchen through the back door.

I move the soup pot to a cooler area of the stove and tell Fernyllia that I'm taking the scrap buckets out to the livestock barn. She nods absentmindedly, and I leave to find Yvan.

Once outside, I spot him leaning against a large tree, staring at his hands, his breathing ragged. Concerned, I set down the scrap buckets and go to him. "What's the matter?"

He looks around quickly, and then, satisfied that we're alone, holds his palms out for me to see.

Even in the overcast evening light, I can see how red and raw they are, with large, angry welts bubbling up all over them.

"Holy Ancient One. That's from the iron?" I ask, my concern mounting.

He nods stiffly. "It's never bothered me like this before. It...it *really* hurts."

I reach for his arm. *Boundaries be damned.* "Come with me," I tell him.

"Where?"

"To the apothecary prep room. To get some medicine."

A few minutes later, we're in the deserted prep room, sitting opposite each other in tense silence as I rub *Arnicium* gel into his hands. I can feel the turbulent flare of Yvan's fire, his defenses shattered, but I doggedly hold my fire lines in check, even as my fire strains to reach out for him.

Yvan winces sharply as I work the medication into the sores, my emotions a tangle as I touch him.

"I've never experienced a burn," he says through gritted teeth, his eyes flicking up to meet mine, "but I imagine this is what it must feel like."

"What, you've never been burned?" I ask, surprised.

"I can't be."

"You can't?"

He shakes his head, his eyes riveted on mine.

"What would happen if you stuck your hands in fire?" I ask, not quite believing his statement.

"Nothing."

"Wow."

He shrugs, as if it's no big deal.

"It's working," I say after a time, noticing the boils are flattening out, the red beginning to fade, an unsettling warmth kindling in me as I stroke the medicine into his long fingers.

"The pain's receding," he says. He's breathing more normally now, not the quick, strained breaths from before. "This isn't good," he says, looking at his hands.

"No, it's not." I frown. "Maybe it was just too much iron."

"No, I've done this job before. It's never bothered me like this...just gave me a rash." He looks at me, his expression grave. "It's getting worse. Much worse."

"Have you told your mother?"

"No."

"Maybe you should. Maybe she can help."

He looks back down at his palms and grimaces as I continue to smooth the gel over his fingers. "I can't hide what I am for much longer. I don't know what I'm going to do."

"Maybe the Lupines will give the Fae amnesty," I offer hopefully. "Jules thinks there's a chance..."

Yvan lets out a bitter laugh. "Vogel has demanded that the Lupines cede half their territory to the Gardnerians. He's threatening military action if they don't comply."

"I know, but they've threatened the Lupines before—"

He shakes his head, his tone hardening. "The Lupines won't cede their territory, which means they can't afford to do anything else that will inflame tensions with Gardneria. They will not let the Fae in. It's too provocative." Yvan flexes his hands experimentally, a shadow falling over his expression. "It's not just the iron that's a danger. It's getting harder to contain my fire." He looks to me, uncharacteristically rattled. "I'm in a lot of trouble, Elloren."

Fear grabs at me, but I shake it off. "Rescuing Naga looked like a long shot at one point, if I remember," I note as I concentrate back on his hands. I can feel his eyes intent on me. "So did rescuing all of the Selkies. What were the chances of *that* ever happening? I think Gunther Ulrich may surprise everyone." I study his palms. "Wow, that's really helping, isn't it?"

The boils are gone. Now his palms are just red and splotchy.

"It doesn't hurt at all anymore." His deepened voice sends a thrum straight through my fire lines. "Thank you."

"You're welcome," I say, my cheeks warming. I pull more gel from the long Arnici leaf next to me and continue rubbing it all along his long fingers, between them, down his palm to his wrist, the two of us quiet for a long moment.

"Yvan," I ask, wrestling with a question that's been on the tip of my tongue for a while now. "When we all met with Valasca...well, I was just wondering..."

Yvan raises his eyebrows at me, as if prodding me to just out with it.

"Can you tell what I'm feeling from your sense of my fire?"

He hesitates, his mouth tightening the way it does when he's withholding information.

"Is this another secret?" I gently press. "You just told me you can stick your hands in fire."

He smiles slightly and dips his head, acknowledging my point.

I wait.

He finally relents, his voice low. "A little. But mostly I can scent your emotions."

Surprise flares in me. "Is that something Fire Fae can do?"

He looks away cagily. "It's something *I* can do."

"*All* of my emotions?"

"Yes."

Oh, my.

"What am I feeling right now?" I haltingly challenge.

He tilts his head to one side and considers me closely. "A little upset, I think. But mostly…you're enjoying touching my hands."

I stop rubbing his fingers, my face coloring.

"It's okay," he says, his lip lifting, his gaze turning sultry. "I like it, too, especially now that it doesn't hurt."

Heat burns at my cheeks. "You're a mystery to me, you know that?"

He lets out a hard laugh. "I'm a mystery to *myself.*"

"You're not going to explain what you mean by that, are you?"

"I'd rather not."

"All right, then," I say with a sigh of resignation. "You're hurt, so I won't press you to tell me more. And I'll go back to rubbing your hands, even though it's such a tiresome chore for me."

We exchange a flirtatious smile, which sets warmth blooming in my center. Heatedly aware of him, I turn my attention back to working the medicine into his palms and I can sense his fire simmering.

After a few moments I glance up at him, disquieted by my mounting awareness of his fire—like a turbulent stream, running red-hot just under his skin. "You're even more dangerous than I know, aren't you?"

"Yes," he says, watching my fingers. "But apparently, not invincible."

He meets my eyes, both of us serious, and I have that familiar sense of him stridently holding himself back from me.

"Why do you keep shutting me out, Yvan?" There's no hurt in the question this time, only concern.

Silence.

"I will not tell your secret."

Tensing, Yvan pulls his hands away from me and holds them up for inspection, his expression darkening.

They're still red.

His gaze takes on a hard edge. "Unfortunately, Elloren, I think my secret's going to go ahead and tell itself."

MAGE COUNCIL
RULING
#338

The Northern and Southern Lupine packs
must cede the disputed land
bordering Gardneria.
They have one month to comply. Failure
to do so will result in military action.

CHAPTER TWO

102 SELKIES

"Ah, Elloren Gardner."

Jules looks up from the book he's reading as I tentatively make my way into his disheveled office, stacks of books and papers everywhere. I place the pile of history texts I'm lugging onto the only open space on his messy desk. "I figured I'd return your books," I tell him. "I've had them a long time."

"Did they confuse you?" he asks, sitting back in his desk chair and adjusting his glasses.

"Thoroughly."

"Good. Shut the door, would you? I have a few more for you."

I close his office door and take a seat by his desk as he gets up and peruses his bookshelves. He pulls out one volume after another, pushing some back in, adding others to a growing tower on his chair.

"Seems you've been putting your complete and utter powerlessness to good use, eh?" He pauses to look at me, his eyes bemused.

"Yes, sir," I agree, cocking an eyebrow. "Seems you've been quite busy yourself."

Jules gives a short laugh, then holds up a cautioning finger and waggles it at me. "You are currently winning, however. Sixteen Fae children ushered out of Gardneria this month to your 102 Selkies back in the ocean. I shall have to work harder to keep up with you."

I smile, blushing slightly. "I can't take the credit for that, honestly. I have powerful friends."

He laughs. "As do I, Elloren Gardner. As do I." He winks at me. "And thank goodness for that, eh?" He sets another book down on the pile, his expression growing earnest. "Fernyllia and Lucretia and I have been trying to convince the Resistance to take an interest in the plight of the Selkies for a long time now. But our concerns have never been taken seriously. But you finally accomplished it—and just in the nick of time, I'd say. Well done, Elloren."

"But I'm not the one who rescued them," I protest.

Jules gives me a significant look. "Sometimes pushing the wheels of change into motion is the bulk of the battle."

I consider this for a moment as he goes back to surveying his books. "Jules," I venture, emboldened by his words, "Tierney...and her brother..."

"I know," he says, cutting me off and suddenly serious. "I'm doing all that I can. It's up to Gunther Ulrich, I'm afraid. The Amaz won't budge on this matter—they will not let male refugees through their borders."

My thoughts fly to Yvan's iron-ravaged hands. "Yvan told me that you're an old friend of his family."

He looks at me questioningly. "I've known him since he was a child."

"And his mother?"

"Yes."

"So, you...know *all* about him?" *Even what he's not telling me?*

Jules's eyes narrow slightly. "Yes."

Some relief shudders through me. This is all too big to carry alone. "I'm... I'm frightened for him."

Jules comes around to the front of his desk and pushes the piles of books and papers back a bit. He perches on the edge and sets an encouraging hand on my shoulder. "I know they're part Fae," he says in a low whisper with a glance toward the door. "I've known that for a long time. Yvan told me about what's happening to him with the iron. If Gunther decides to give the Fae amnesty, I'm sure he'll let Yvan and his mother go, too. It would be a safe place for them, and a boon to the Lupines, really. By driving the hidden Fae out, the Gardnerians could be unwittingly sending the Lupines a large number of young people with a vast array of unknown magical talents. Talents that could prove to be quite useful in the defense of the Lupines' territory."

"You think Gunther will say yes because of self-interest?"

"I think he'll say yes because Gunther Ulrich is a deeply decent man, but the idea of all that Fae magic at the Lupines' disposal... It can't hurt our cause now, can it?"

Hope swells in my heart. "You really think he'll say yes?"

"I think he might."

I hesitate before continuing. "Yvan and I... We're... We've become close friends."

"He told me that," Jules says gently. He smiles ruefully at me and shakes his head. "If ever there were two star-crossed...*friends.*" He gives me a poignant look full of compassion and sighs. "Well, perhaps, with a bit of luck, even this might turn out all right in the end. You never can tell what the future holds, even in times as dark as these."

Jules rises to his feet, chuckling to himself. "Just when

you think something is impossible, over a hundred Selkies are suddenly free and swimming around in the ocean." He turns and picks up the pile of books on his chair, lugs them over and hands them to me.

I take the books and set them on my lap. *Comparative Mythology of the Western and Eastern Realms. A History of Religion.* And translations of the holy books of the Alfsigr, the Smaragdalfar, the southern Ishkartan and the Noi.

"Religion this time?" I ask, surprised.

"Essential reading," he says.

I cock an eyebrow and give him a wry smile. "So…more confusion? In this, too?"

He grins. "*Especially* in this." He gestures loosely toward the pile. "Take a look. Mull them over." He gives me a warm smile. "Let me know what you think."

I look down at the stack. "You know," I tell him, "I never thought I'd enjoy reading about all these types of things so much." I flip through the top book, intrigued by a drawing of a starlit Noi dragon goddess rising up from the ocean, a spiral of ivory birds wreathing the goddess's neck. "All I wanted to do when I first came here was learn how to be an apothecary, like my mother."

I look up at him and smile. "This is a lot more interesting than what I'm currently studying. My Apothecarium professor has us memorizing the different uses of distilled Ironflower essence in antidotes for venomous bites, mostly from desert reptiles. I will likely *never* visit a desert."

Jules returns to the chair behind his desk, eyes glinting with amusement as he sits down. "Knowledge is never wasted, my dear. No matter how obscure or difficult…or confusing. It always serves to enrich our lives, if we let it, and in ways we can rarely anticipate."

I frown dramatically at him. "So…you think remedies

for the venom of the rare Ishkartan Pitviper will deeply enrich my life?"

He smiles at this. "You know, when I was a young scholar like yourself, they had calligraphy as part of the required trivium here. *Calligraphy*, of all things. Oh, how I hated it—having to hold my hand at such odd angles, the letters having to be all at the same, unforgiving slant. I wasn't interested in calligraphy. I only wanted to study history and great literature. Look around."

I survey the messy room—books jammed into every conceivable crevice, jumbled stacks of paper on his desk.

"It's quite obvious that I'm not someone who is overly comfortable with staying inside perfectly straight, rigid lines," he says.

"So," I ask with sarcasm, "did calligraphy enrich your life in the end?"

Jules breaks out into laughter and pushes up his falling spectacles. "It provided many hours of sheer frustration and often flat-out despair."

I snort. "So much for all knowledge being so worthwhile."

He leans back, becoming reflective. "It did, however, prove to be quite useful when the need arose to falsify documents. It turns out that I happen to be especially talented at creating false birth certificates."

My eyebrows fly up at this. "So, the hidden Fae children," I say, amused by the irony of it, "they were saved by...*calligraphy*?"

He laughs, shaking his head. "So, they were. And so might a few more. Calligraphy, of all the cursed things." His face grows serious. "Learn all you can, Elloren, about everything you can. You will find that, when you're as powerless as we are, it helps to be clever."

I slump down in my chair. "It would be better to be powerful *and* clever."

Jules laughs again. "Quite so, quite so."

And as much as I want to maintain my disgruntled look, I can't help but smile back at him, and at the small flicker of hope that now seems to hover in the air all around us.

CHAPTER THREE

AMNESTY

Two nights later, I'm outside Andras's circular dwelling, deep in the woods and surrounded by family and friends, all of us sitting around a roaring fire near Naga's cave. My brothers, Yvan, the Lupines, Tierney and Andras, Wynter, Ariel, and even Valasca and Alder—we're all here. Cael and Rhys arrive last, the two Elves an ethereal white against the dark forest.

Diana insisted we all meet her here, refusing to tell us why. She stands before us now with Rafe by her side, her wide grin sparking everyone's curiosity.

"I received word this morning," Diana says, beaming at us as if she can barely contain her joy. "My father has agreed to grant the Fae and the families who sheltered them amnesty in the Lupine territories."

Tierney lets out a gasp, along with almost everyone else. My own hand reflexively comes up to cover my mouth.

Rafe grins at Diana. "It seems they were undecided," my brother says, "but then a certain daughter of the Gerwulf Pack's alpha held some sway."

"Diana," Tierney says, overcome, barely able to get the words out. "I can never thank you enough for this. *Never.*"

Diana impatiently waves away the thanks. "I simply offered some encouragement, that's all."

Yvan looks positively stunned.

Tierney starts to cry, and Andras puts his arm around her. Everyone erupts into happy conversation, embracing each other, making their way over to Tierney.

"And that's not all," Rafe says, his smile widening. "The Lupines are offering amnesty to all the Icarals and other refugees in immediate danger. And they're not requiring anyone who comes to become Lupine."

Wynter grows very still, then closes her eyes and raises a hand to her heart. Cael's head drops into his hands, as if overcome with relief, and Rhys's face radiates a sudden serene joy. Ariel is frozen, staring wide-eyed at Rafe.

"Rafe." Trystan has gone very still, his voice low. "Does this mean..."

Tears flood my eyes. *Amnesty. There will be safety there for my beloved brother.*

Diana looks to Trystan warmly. "You'll be family. Of course, you'll be welcome."

Trystan doesn't move, but his eyes belie a torrent of strong emotion.

"Uncle Edwin?" I ask Rafe and Diana, my voice catching.

"All of you," Diana affirms, smiling.

"Rafe," Yvan says. His face has gone pale.

Rafe turns to look at Yvan.

"Does this mean they'll take in *all* Fae?" Yvan asks, his voice constricted.

"Yes, Yvan. That's my understanding."

"And there's more," Valasca puts in, her eyes flicking from Yvan to Tierney. "The Amaz have agreed to allow both male and female refugees to travel around the periphery of our lands under rune-ward protection to get to the Northern Lupine territories."

"The Northern Lupines are allowing us in, too?" Tierney manages to ask Diana through her tears.

"Yes," Diana happily explains. "My father secured their protection for the refugees, as well."

Valasca glances over at me, and we break into overjoyed grins as tears slide down my cheeks.

Everyone I care about who's been in danger, in danger no more.

"Thank you," I tell Diana, my voice cracking with emotion. *"Thank you."*

"I'm just the messenger," Diana happily deflects with a wave of her hand, but I know it isn't true. I know she's worked hard to secure this.

Yvan continues to sit there, speechless for a moment. And then he looks to me, a new openness in his gaze.

"You can tell them," I encourage him. "You don't have to keep anything hidden anymore."

The conversation dies down and everyone looks to Yvan.

Yvan lets out a long breath and looks to them all. "I'm part Fae."

"Fire Fae?" Rafe asks.

A wry laugh bursts from Trystan. "Now, how did you ever guess that?"

Rafe grins. "I've seen him playing with fire on more than one occasion."

Yvan's eyes widen.

"Relax, Yvan," Rafe says. "I'm much more observant than most."

Diana and Jarod don't seem the least bit surprised.

"Did you know?" I ask Diana.

She shrugs noncommittally. "I can smell it on him. Like smoke."

"My mother is part Fae, as well," Yvan tells her. "Do you think they'll take us both?"

"Without a doubt," Diana assures him. "I'll make sure of it."

Yvan glances down at the bonfire, holding himself rigid. When he looks back up, there are tears streaming down his face. I slide my arm around him, just as Tierney comes over to embrace him in turn, all of us overwhelmed by the unexpected turn of events.

"So," I say to Yvan with a teasing smile, "you play with fire?"

"On occasion," he replies, smiling back at me, streaks of happy tears glistening on his cheeks. He looks over at Rafe and laughs. "I *thought* discreetly."

"I want to see what that means," I encourage him playfully.

Yvan hesitates as everyone surrounds him with friendly encouragement. "Fine," he relents, smiling at us. "You all might want to step back—with the exception of the Icarals, of course."

Ariel grins wickedly and moves closer to the fire.

We all grow silent as he lifts a hand, palm forward, arm extended. He curls his fingers inward like he's summoning the fire, and the flames begin to dance, then lean toward him, as if they're listening. Yvan extends his other hand behind the first and slowly moves it backward, like he's pulling on an invisible rope. The fire leans a bit more, then a long string of it flies out to Yvan's hand in a dazzling stream and pulls into his palm.

He closes his eyes and tilts his head up, his breathing deepening as he draws the fire into himself, as if it's a sensual experience for him. The bonfire's light dims and the evening's chill seeps in as more and more of the fire flows into him. And then the fire is gone, abruptly snuffed out.

Yvan drops his hands, a pleased smile on his face. When he opens his eyes and turns to me, they're glowing bright gold, as if lit by a torch from within. Brighter than I've ever seen them glow before. It startles and enthralls me all at the same time.

"What's it like?" I ask, fascinated.

"It...feels good," he says, smiling wider. "Like power."

He notices me shiver, and his brow tenses with concern. He turns and flicks his hand at the firepit. Flames shoot forth from his palm, the wood bursting into flames, warmth and light enveloping us all once again.

Yvan holds up his hand. His fingertips are on fire, like candles. He purses his lips and blows out four of them, then hesitates, his eyes flickering to mine. He brings his thumb to his lips and puts the flame out with his mouth.

His eyes lock back on to mine, still bright and smoldering.

"What does it taste like?" I ask breathlessly, completely under his spell.

His smile widens, his voice a sultry caress. "Honeyed."

Oh, Sweet Ancient One in the heavens above.

"Oh," is all I can manage.

"I brought something for you, Ren." Flustered, I turn as Rafe sets my violin case down beside me.

The violin Lukas gave me. I shrug away thoughts of him—Lukas is the last person I want to think about tonight.

"Tonight, there's finally real cause for celebration," Rafe says. "And any proper celebration needs music and dancing."

"But they don't know our dances," I protest.

"Oh, *please*," Diana scoffs, flipping her hair over her shoulder. "It takes about two seconds to learn one of your dances."

She mock bows to Rafe, and he does the same. The two of them mimic one of our very formal, stiff dances, standing exaggeratedly apart and overly rigid. Everyone laughs, and then Rafe grabs Diana close, dipping her and kissing along her neck as she squeals with laughter.

The others turn back to me, hopeful looks in their eyes.

"Oh, all right then," I say, relenting with a smile.

I pull out the crimson violin, tightening and rosining the bow as the rest of the group pushes aside some of the log seats to create space. Then I launch into the happiest tune I know—an old Gardnerian folk dance. My playing is soon accompanied by boisterous clapping and drumming on wooden stumps, my friends laughing and whooping.

Rafe quickly teaches Diana the dance that goes with the music. She only has to see it once to immediately master it, and the two of them set off, the steps perfectly executed. Quickly growing bored with it, Diana begins to embellish the dance, adding sensual movement as she presses her hips up against Rafe, her arms high above her head, weaving about like snakes. Andras offers his hand to Tierney and soon they're dancing as well, Valasca jumping in with Alder.

I play a few more tunes, everyone learning the folk dances with happy ease, changing up the steps, showing off. After I finish about the sixth song, Rafe goes over to Wynter and holds out his hand, even though he knows that she'll inadvertently read his thoughts by touching him. Wynter looks surprised, but pleased, and takes Rafe's hand. I play a formal waltz, and they whirl around the fire, joined by Jarod and Valasca, Trystan and Alder.

Diana approaches Yvan as I finish the song and holds out a hand to him. "Come on, Fire Fae. Aren't your people famous for their dancing?"

Yvan looks to the ground, smiles, then gets up. Everyone steps back for them, eager to watch.

I play one of the folk tunes from before, and they start out with the basic steps, smiling at each other, as if they find the simplicity of it funny. Then Yvan begins to stray from it, his movements fluid, almost serpentine, as he slowly adds more complicated steps, waiting to see if Diana can follow. Soon they're wound around each other, Diana's eyes bright, her face flushed. A spike of jealousy shoots through me, but also relief. Jealousy at her easy sensuality, her dancing ability, her being so close to *my* Yvan, but relief that I'm the musician and don't need to make a fool of myself by trying to dance with Yvan. I could never dance like that, and I don't want Yvan to know it.

I finish the song, Diana laughing with delight as Yvan dips her low, and Rafe comes over to claim her. "All right, Diana," he says playfully. "Step away from the Fire Fae." He mock glares at Yvan.

Yvan releases Diana and she steps back, uncharacteristically flustered.

"Thanks for showing me up, Yvan." Rafe scowls lightheartedly as he slides an arm around Diana's waist.

Yvan bows to him, grinning. "I've simply had more practice."

"Yes, well." Rafe turns to me. "Stay away from him, Elloren. He's trouble."

"I've been told that on more than one occasion," I say with a laugh.

"Set down your instrument, Elloren," Jarod prods, gesturing toward Yvan. "Dance with him."

There are murmurs of encouragement all around.

"Go on, Gardnerian," Ariel says, smirking. "Dance with the Fire Fae."

I shake my head, smiling. "No, I'm not as good as all of you."

"Don't worry, Elloren," Diana says, still flushed. "He's a *very* strong lead."

Rafe raises his eyebrows at her, to which she laughs.

Yvan holds out his hand to me. "Put the violin down, Elloren."

"I can take over for you," Trystan volunteers with a slight smile. I hesitate, then pass the instrument to my younger brother and stand up, taking Yvan's proffered hand.

"Really," I tell him as he leads me to the open space, "I don't think I can follow the steps."

"Do you know the steps to the first dance you played?" Yvan asks, ignoring my hesitation.

"Yes."

"Dance that."

"All right," I say, unconvinced, as we arrange our hands and arms around each other.

Trystan starts to play a Gardnerian folk tune, and Jarod and Valasca drum out a rhythm. We begin in the traditional way, everyone clapping along with the beat and calling out encouragement to me, and I follow along easily, the two of us perfectly in time, perfectly in sync. And then Yvan begins to change the dance, moving gradually closer, wrapping one arm around me, then unexpectedly pulling me in tight.

I stumble into him, stepping on his foot, my flushed face growing hotter. "I'm so sorry…"

Yvan just grins as the others continue to clap out the beat for us. We begin again, and this time, he eases the changes in more gradually, an extra step here, a different hold on me there. Little by little, my body loosens, the rhythm claiming me. He starts to pull me closer, until I'm pressed up against him, his fire licking deliciously toward me, but this time, I don't stumble. I soon forget there's anyone else around, aware only of him, fascinated by him—how he weaves around the rhythm, how he weaves around me, his eyes hot on mine, the feel of his hands, his body and fire moving against mine.

Then the drumming stops, and everyone breaks into applause as I stand there out of breath, encircled in his arms. Of course, he isn't the least bit winded.

"See," he says, "you're a fine dancer."

I laugh. "*You* did all the dancing."

Yvan's smile is warmly alluring. "I'm a strong lead."

I'm all too aware of my heart hammering in my chest, and not just from the exercise. "You're dangerous, is what you are."

It's his turn to laugh. "Yes, but you knew that already."

I go back to my violin as everyone else springs up—even Ariel, who relents and lets Valasca and Alder teach her a simple Amaz folk dance.

We play music and dance throughout the night, everyone learning bits of each other's dances—Amaz dances, Fae dances, Keltic folk dances, Gardnerian dances, even the prim, graceful Elfin dance, where the partners face each other but never once touch.

And after the dancing is over, I play my favorite violin piece, the one I played so many months ago in Valgard—*Winter's Dark*. But this time, I play it with a depth I've never been able to manage before. Who knew that such moving music could spring forth from so much hardship and turmoil?

At the very end, Wynter sings for us, and I sit and listen, Yvan's arm draped around my shoulder. The words are foreign to me, but the beauty of Wynter's voice seems to reach right up to touch the stars.

How can it be? How could it have happened? All of my dreams suddenly within reach?

I lean into Yvan, and his arm tightens around me. My life

isn't at all how I'd imagined it could be a year ago, but better. So much better.

The others gradually disperse, leaving Yvan and me alone by the fire, the stars bright above us.

"Elloren," he says, his voice low, his hand caressing my shoulder. "If my mother and I... If the Lupines grant us amnesty... If we join them...will you come with us?"

My face warms from something that feels like sheer joy. I know what he's asking—he doesn't need to elaborate. By now I can read his feelings almost as well as my own.

Will you come with us? To a place where you and I can finally be together?

"You know," I answer wryly, "I think it's very likely that the Lupines are in need of a good apothecary."

Yvan turns and smiles at me, looking like he can barely contain his happiness. "It's so hard to believe," he says, shaking his head. "That it might be possible..."

He lets out a deep breath, as if he's been waiting for a long time to finally exhale. His whole life, maybe. "Perhaps," he says, beaming at me, "there is some hope after all."

CHAPTER FOUR

WATCHERS

I wake up the next morning with a smile on my face, music and happiness still echoing within me.

There's an eerie glow in the room, like a deep blue dream that keeps reverberating even after it ends. I blink sleepily, trying to determine the source of the strange light, and then suddenly bolt upright.

Watchers.

They're everywhere. Scores of them, perched motionless on the rafters supporting the North Tower's stone ceiling, their wings wrapped around themselves, hiding their eyes. Like they're in mourning.

I stare at them, transfixed, as foreboding swells deep inside me.

The line of Watchers blurs, then disappears, and the room abruptly darkens.

Ariel is still sleeping, but Wynter is sitting up in bed, her eyes wide and set on the rafters.

"What does this mean?" I rasp out to her.

Her glacial calm is unnerving. "I don't know."

A flash of white wings appears in the window.

Both Wynter and I spring from our beds and rush to the window. Together, we look out into the cool, gray dawn.

Fear leaps in my chest.

Watchers dot the tops of the trees for as far as the eye can see. They're immobile as statues, their wings wrapped tight, their eyes hidden, as if the dawning reality of this day is too much for them to bear.

A morbid chill slashes through me that I can feel deep in my bones.

Something is coming.

The sea of Watchers disappears. Like a flash of dire warning.

I whip my head toward Wynter. "I need to find my brothers. And Diana. *Everyone.*"

Wynter gives an almost imperceptible nod, her eyes moon-wide.

I race to throw on my clothes as fast as I can. Then I grab the Wand from under my pillow, shove it into the side of my boot and rush through the hall and down the spiraling stairs.

Thunder rumbles to the west as I burst out of the North Tower. I race across the field toward the University, desperately scanning the trees of the surrounding wilds, searching for more Watchers as dark storm clouds boil and gather overhead.

I enter the usual morning bustle of the University streets at a sprint, dashing past clusters of scholars and professors. My eyes dart around wildly as I pass by Spine-stone buildings and run under walkways, searching for danger. For some clue as to what's happened.

Everyone's likely to be there in the dining hall, I console myself. *Having breakfast. Or working in the kitchens.*

I try to ignore the cramp in my side as I begin the trek up the long, sloping path to the kitchen that abuts the edge of the wilds, the livestock barns coming into view ahead. I've almost reached the back entrance to the kitchen when I spot a lone figure emerging from the woods. He's wearing a heavy cloak, the cloak's hood hanging low.

He lifts his head, and I meet his wild amber gaze.

I instantly recognize him. Diana's childhood friend, Brendan. The red-haired, jovial member of her father's guard who I met on Founder's Day.

Brendan's out of breath and dragging his feet, which is strange for a Lupine. And he's holding a child in his arms. I realize he must have run very long and very hard to be so out of breath, and he has a haunted look in his eyes that sets a wave of dread washing over me.

His expression speaks of disaster.

As he nears, I realize, in a flash of confusion, that he's carrying Andras's son in his arms—little Konnor.

Konnor's pointed ears stick up from his mussed purple-and-blue hair. His face is muddy and tear-streaked, his crimson eyes thrown open too wide, as if in shock.

"What's happened?" I ask, my voice tight with fear as Brendan stumbles to a halt before me. For a moment, he looks as if he's about to be sick.

"The Southern pack...they've been...murdered..."

His words are a staggering punch to my gut. *"No!"*

"Everyone. Men...women...children. They're all dead." He struggles for breath and seems precariously close to falling over. I grab hold of both his arms to steady him.

Brendan lifts his head, his face a mask of grief. "Jarod and Diana's parents... Kendra...my beautiful Iliana." He chokes back a sob. "All of them."

"No," I breathe, horror seizing me.

Brendan looks around blindly, eyes glassy and unfocused. "The Mage Council... They demanded that we cede our territory to Gardneria." He chokes on the words. "We defied them, and they threatened to wipe us out. We...we didn't pay any heed to this. They've threatened us so many times before."

His chest heaves as if he's about to retch, and I keep a tight grip on his arms. "I went out to hunt...and when I returned, I... I found them...all of them...*dead*...our homes turned to blackened ash."

My eyes fill with tears as my gaze drops to Andras's son. "How did Konnor survive?"

"His parents... I found him...under...under their bodies." Brendan breaks down sobbing, his eyes screwed up tight as little Konnor hides his head in Brendan's chest.

"Did the Gardnerians attack the Northern Lupines, too?" I ask, frantic.

Brendan shakes his head. "I don't know. But if they did, then... Jarod, Diana, Konnor and me...we might be the only Lupines left. They killed *everyone*, even the babies." He looks around wildly. "I have to find Jarod and Diana. And Andras." His eyes are imploring. "Where are they?"

My mind is a storm. I struggle to think as panic cyclones through me. "Andras is probably with the horses."

"Take him," he implores, holding Konnor out to me. The child stiffens, as if bracing for a blow, his eyes unblinkingly wide, filled with unimaginable horrors. "Take him to Andras," Brendan says, desperation in his eyes.

"Oh, sweet one," I whisper to Konnor, my heart tearing in two. He presses his little head against my chest as I hug him protectively close. Fiercely close.

I motion to the back kitchen entrance, my voice choked.

"Diana and Jarod...they might be in the dining hall. Through the kitchens. In there."

Brendan makes for the door, and I hurry in behind him, clutching Konnor. Everyone looks up from their labors as we burst inside, their eyes flying wide to see Brendan rushing through, trailed by me, hugging a Lupine child in my arms. Yvan's eyes home in tight on me as he pulls a wooden bread paddle from the oven. Rafe slams the door of a cookstove closed and rises, immediately registering my alarm. Trystan is there with him, as if they've just been conversing. My younger brother searches my face, his hand reflexively sliding to grasp his wand.

"Elloren," Bleddyn says sharply, her hand freezing in the act of stirring a large kettle of porridge. "What happened?" She abandons her task as she, Yvan, my brothers and Fernyllia rush over to me, the rest of the workers instantly on alert.

I pause, a tremble taking hold of me. My eyes flick to Brendan's back as he disappears through the entrance to the dining hall, the door slamming shut behind him.

Olilly has fallen back from where she and Iris were filling muffin tins, terror in her violet eyes. Iris wraps an arm around Olilly, her gaze riddled with fear and confusion.

"What's going on, Ren?" Rafe asks, his strong hand coming to my arm. His face pales as he takes in trauma-stricken Konnor. "Why do you have Andras's son?"

"Jarod and Diana's pack." I'm barely able to get the words out. "They've been murdered. By the Gardnerians."

Rafe's eyes widen. *"What?!"*

A loud, earsplitting scream erupts from the direction of the dining hall. It quickly morphs into a tortured wail of grief.

Rafe, Trystan, Yvan and I all rush through the door at the same time. Diana's in the far corner of the hall, trying to pull away from Brendan, his hands on her shoulders. Jarod is standing next to them, his face chalk white.

"No! No!" Diana screams over and over. She wrenches free of Brendan, almost losing her footing as she does so. Rafe, Trystan and Yvan rush toward them, and I follow close behind in a nightmare daze as I clutch Konnor to my chest and dart around what feels like a sea of people, all turned in the direction of the screaming and murmuring in confusion.

I push past a knot of Gardnerian military apprentices who are watching Diana with shocked interest, craning their necks to see.

They don't know, I realize as I pass them. *They don't know what's happened.*

Ahead of me, Rafe has reached Diana, who's sobbing uncontrollably. Rafe grabs hold of her and pulls her into a fierce embrace as Yvan and Trystan fall in with Jarod and Brendan. Diana pushes away from Rafe and begins to Change, thick hair sprouting all over her skin, her body lengthening in some places, contracting in others, her clothes tearing.

I reach them all as Diana rapidly finishes the Change, her forepaws falling to the floor with a dull thud. I skid to a halt next to Yvan, shocked to witness Diana's transformation. She's the largest wolf I've ever seen, golden-haired and magnificent with wild amber eyes.

Diana gives Rafe a devastated look and bolts into a run. She clears the room, fast as lightning, scholars shrieking with fear in her wake.

"I'll go after her." Brendan peers toward where Diana ran out, a dazed expression on his face.

"I'll go, too," Rafe offers in turn, his face stricken.

"No," Brendan tells him, his eyes darting down the length of Rafe's figure in grim appraisal. "You'll never catch up with her in that form. And you can't scent her like I can. I'll bring her back."

"There's a tower," Rafe tells Brendan with heightened urgency. "On the north end of the grounds...just past the University stables and a broad field. Bring her there."

Brendan nods and runs out, so fast his form is a blur.

Grief whipping through me, my eyes meet Yvan's, his fire giving a hard flare toward me.

"I'll help find her," he tells me, his voice low. I nod, and he glances at Jarod and my brothers for a moment before breaking into a run across the hall that I know is only a fraction of the speed he's capable of.

Jarod is doubled over and looks like he's having trouble breathing. His eyes are wide and uncomprehending, as if he's suddenly trapped in a nightmare with no escape. "My parents..." he chokes out, "my sister...my entire pack." His knees buckle.

Rafe and Trystan catch him before he hits the ground, holding on to him from either side.

"I think I'm going to be sick," Jarod says, his voice constricted.

Rafe glares across the room at the large cluster of Gardnerian military apprentices with barely contained fury. "Come on," he says to Jarod. "We're going to get you out of here."

Jarod regains some of his footing, his face taking on a dazed expression as we lead him through the dining hall, all of us the center of attention while bewildered and mortified conversation buzzes all around.

As we pass by the table of military apprentices, one of them smirks and calls out, "Hey, Rafe!" Then he lets loose with a boisterous wolf howl, the other apprentices breaking into laughter.

Abruptly, Rafe releases Jarod and lunges at the young man, pulls him out of his seat and punches him in the face so hard that a sickening crack reverberates throughout the room. Then Rafe hurls the apprentice onto the dining table, blood gushing from the young man's nose as plates, cups and silverware fly everywhere. The other apprentices jump back to avoid the spray of food and drink and the body being hurled about.

The young man's companions move to pull wands, but Trystan is faster, his wand already pointed at the group.

"Get back," Trystan warns, the Level Five Mage stripes edging his military uniform a silent threat. The other apprentices waver and eye him with extreme trepidation, their hands on unsheathed wands and swords.

Rafe looms over the bleeding young man, fists clenched, cold fury in his eyes. "If I *ever* hear you mocking her like that again," he snarls, "I will *kill* you." Rafe turns back to Jarod and takes his arm once more.

We stride out of the dining hall, Trystan half-turned with his wand pointed behind us, the crowd growing quiet as they watch us go.

As soon as we're outside, Rafe turns to me. "Get Andras. Tell him to get five horses saddled and ready for a long journey. Get him *quickly!*"

CHAPTER FIVE

SHIFTERS

I race toward the long stables where most of the University scholars' horses are kept. Andras is out in the field, examining the back leg of a white-speckled mare as lightning flashes over the distant wilds.

"Andras!" I rasp out, my side painfully cramping as I limp toward him, Konnor in my arms. Andras looks up and rises, his eyes immediately lighting on his son. He breaks into a run toward me.

"The Lupines," I gasp as he reaches me and takes Konnor into his strong arms. "They're *dead*. The Gardnerians. They might have killed them all. Everyone but Brendan and Diana and Jarod and Konnor…"

Andras stares at me with dawning horror as he hugs his son close. He murmurs to Konnor for a moment, kissing his son's dirty head before gently handing the trauma-stricken child back to me.

Thunder rumbles overhead.

"Come, Elloren," Andras says, more an urgent command

than a request. I follow him as he breaks into a run toward the stables, breathlessly telling him everything I know.

Once inside, Andras grabs his rune-marked weapons and deftly fastens them to himself. Then he grows still, closing his eyes and tilting his head up. His black stallion gallops toward us from a far corner of the field. Andras walks out to meet the horse and leaps astride, then holds his arms out for his son.

"Rafe said to bring horses," I say as I hand little Konnor up to him.

"No," he counters, pulling Konnor into a tight, one-armed hug. "We need an army. We need the Vu Trin."

"Why?"

"The Gardnerians are killing Lupines, Elloren. Which means they'll come for Diana and Jarod."

Oh, Holy Ancient One.

"Go back to the North Tower. I'll bring the Vu Trin."

Just as I reach the North Tower, I spot Brendan and Yvan in the distance. They're both emerging from the woods, Brendan carrying Diana in his arms, her limp form wrapped in his cloak. Rafe and Trystan run out from the North Tower, and I break into a sprint up the field, Yvan the first to spot me as I draw near.

"What happened to her?" I ask fearfully. There's a large, bloody welt on the side of Diana's head.

"She hurled herself over a cliff," Brendan says, pain etched hard on his face. "But she's alive."

"Bring her upstairs," I tell them all, steeling my nerves. "Andras has gone to get the Vu Trin."

Rafe sends me a grim look, and I can tell that he's rapidly reaching the same conclusion that Andras did. We have to find a way to keep Jarod and Diana safe, and the Vu Trin might be the only ones who can help them escape.

I follow them all up the stairs and into the North Tower's lantern-lit hallway. A stunned shock washes over me anew at the sight of Jarod sitting on the hallway's stone bench, his eyes unfocused, his body slumped against the wall behind him.

Brendan brings Diana into our lodging and lays her on my bed. Rafe swoops in to her side, his hand caressing her cheek as he murmurs to her with heartbreaking tenderness.

I catch Wynter's eye, desperation rocking me. "She hurled herself off a cliff." I break into tears as I speak. "We don't know how bad it is…"

Wynter's silver eyes darken with grief, and she nods. Ariel is standing beside Wynter, her eyes darting anxiously around at all of us, her wings flapping erratically.

Wynter goes to Diana and kneels down beside her. She places her hands gently on Diana's face, closes her silver eyes and takes a long, slow breath. "She's all right," Wynter assures us, eyes still closed. "She wants to be unconscious."

I cough out a relieved sob as Wynter tends to Diana and gets clothing for her. I look through the open doorway toward Jarod, who's still sitting there with that frighteningly blank expression on his face. Trystan is now down on one knee before him, moving his wand back and forth in front of Jarod's eyes to no response.

"He's in shock," Trystan says.

I look to Yvan, who is standing just inside the doorway, his face tensed with the same anguish I feel, his fire frenzied and volatile.

Boot heels sound on the stairs, and Trystan rises to his feet, drawing his wand. Yvan and I step outside the door just as Aislinn bursts into the hall, her face distraught.

"Aislinn!" I cry, stunned.

She spots Jarod, and her face wrenches with pain. Aislinn rushes over to him and falls on her knees before him, grasping his arms and breaking down at the sight of him. "Ancient One, what have they done to you?"

"Aislinn," I say, my voice rough with tears. "He may not answer you."

"I just heard what happened," Aislinn tells Jarod, her attention only on him. "Jarod, I'm so sorry. I'm here and I love you. I have *always* loved you. Jarod, please, look at me."

Trystan places a kind hand on Aislinn's heaving shoulder. "Aislinn."

She gazes up at Trystan, tears streaming down her face. "Why won't he look at me?"

"He's in shock," Trystan repeats, his voice catching with emotion.

"It's all my fault," Aislinn sobs, shaking her head. "My father kept alluding to something like this... I should have found out exactly what they were planning to do."

"It's not your fault, Aislinn," Trystan insists. "Everyone knew of the threats."

Aislinn keeps shaking her head from side to side. "I knew the Mage Council was planning something...but I never dreamed... How *could* they?" Aislinn falls into Jarod, embracing him tightly, trying in vain to break through his haze. "Jarod, please, it's me. It's Aislinn."

A frantic Ariel stalks out of our lodging, wings flapping, her crow on her shoulder, her two chickens trailing her in a panic as she treads down the hallway. She peers through the hallway window, out over the field.

Ariel turns, her pale green eyes wide. "They're here."

Yvan, Trystan and I rush to the window.

Andras is riding up the field with a large contingent of Vu Trin sorceresses, their black military tunics marked with glowing blue runes, silver stars strapped diagonally across their chests and curved rune-swords at their sides. Commander Vin is riding beside Andras, Ni Vin following close behind. And, to my astonishment, Andras's mother, Professor Volya, rides on his other side, little Konnor held tight in one arm.

As soon as the Vu Trin reach the base of the tower, Commander Vin leaps off her horse and begins yelling out orders in the Noi language. The other sorceresses immediately dismount and fan out around the North Tower.

A heavily armed Andras rushes inside, his weighty steps echoing up the tower's stairs. Trystan opens the hallway door, and Andras bursts inside as Rafe and Wynter join us in the hallway.

"The Gardnerians have taken out both the Northern and Southern packs," Andras says without preamble, his expression steely. "They're all dead. The Vu Trin just received a rune-hawk from the Mage Council. The Council sent hawks out to the Verpacian Council and the Verpacian military, as well—they're demanding that Verpacia cede their land." Andras looks to Rafe. "Vogel is on his way here. The Gardnerian military is coming for Diana and Jarod—they want Gunther Ulrich's children. They're already within the city limits."

Determination fills Rafe's eyes as he abruptly turns and strides back toward our lodging. Andras and the rest of us follow him inside as Rafe lifts Diana up into his arms.

"We're getting them out *now*," Rafe says to Andras. "Are the horses ready?"

"No," comes Andras's succinct reply.

Anger flashes across my brother's face.

"We're not taking Diana and Jarod anywhere," Andras says firmly. "It would be suicide."

Ignoring him, Rafe strides toward the hall, holding an unconscious Diana, but Andras refuses to budge from where he stands in front of the door. Rafe narrows his eyes darkly at him. "Get out of my way, Andras."

"No, Rafe. Normally, I would respect your judgment, but right now it is compromised."

"No, it's *not*."

"Yes," Andras rumbles, "it *is*." He tilts his head toward Diana. "Because you're in love with her. You're not thinking clearly. Where can you go, Rafe? *Think*. The Gardnerians have some kind of weapon that can take out large numbers of Lupines, despite their immunity to magic. They took down two entire packs in one night. And just *look* at them." Andras gestures to Diana and Jarod. "One is unconscious and the other is in shock. They are in no condition to escape, much less fight."

"They could Change us," Rafe insists. "*We* can fight."

"The full moon is more than a week away," Andras counters. "The Gardnerians will find us long before then. They're converging on this city *right now*. They'll capture you before the day is out."

"So, you want us to just leave them here for the Gardnerians to take?" Rafe snarls.

"No," Andras counters. "I want you to leave them here for the Vu Trin to *guard*. They arrived first, so they can seize the higher ground and the advantage on this field."

Rafe glares at Andras. Then he walks back to my bed and lays Diana down with exquisite gentleness. Then Rafe goes over to my empty desk chair and kicks it so violently that its leg cracks, cursing loudly as he does so, causing Wynter and me to jump in alarm. My heart thunders in my chest.

Rafe pauses to rake his fingers through his hair. "They

should have Changed us," he rages to Andras, "back when we had the chance."

"They couldn't have," Andras says. "Not without pack approval."

"Jarod might have."

"No one knew it would come to this."

Rafe's face fills with anguish. "I *can't* lose her!"

"Then listen to me carefully," Andras says firmly. "There will be a time to grieve, but it is *not* now. We must all think, and *fast*."

"You have to get out of here," I tell Rafe, urgency welling. "Trystan, too. You attacked a military apprentice, and Trystan pulled his wand on them. They'll arrest you both."

Rafe blinks at me, his eyes a storm.

"You are no use to her in prison," I doggedly insist, fear rising. "Go get Jules. And Lucretia and Fernyllia."

Rafe holds my stare for a long moment, his jaw rigid. "I'll get them."

"The Icarals have to get out, too," I say, my voice shaking. I turn to Yvan. "Ariel and Wynter have to get out of here before the Gardnerians come."

Yvan nods, his gaze searing. "I'll take them. I can bring them to Naga's cave." He looks to Wynter. "We'll need to find your brother and Rhys."

"I'll find them," Trystan volunteers, wand in hand. "I have an idea of where they might be. I'll bring them to the cave. You get Ariel and Wynter out of here, Yvan."

Wynter and Ariel immediately begin throwing together some of their belongings as Trystan leaves to find Cael and Rhys. Ariel's chickens run frantically around her legs as she throws books and clothing into her ratty travel bag.

Andras crosses the room to stand before Brendan, who's slumped down against a wall. "You need to come with me,"

Andras says, his deep voice imperative as he holds out his hand for Brendan to take. Looking haggard, Brendan grasps onto it and lets himself be pulled up. "The Gardnerians don't know that you and Konnor survived," Andras tells him. "The Vu Trin are going to bring my son and my mother and me east. They're prepared to bring you with us, as well."

The full magnitude of this spears through me. Andras, Brendan and Konnor are leaving, and I'll probably never see them again. Professor Volya, too.

Andras glances over at Diana. "It will all come down to her," he says to Rafe, his face grim. "Everything rests on her shoulders. When she wakes, she needs to keep control of herself."

"I know," Rafe says.

"Rafe," Andras continues, "self-control has never been her strong suit. If Jarod and Diana are going to survive, she will need to rein in her rage and give the Vu Trin time to formulate a plan to get them out."

Rafe glares at him. "She's the daughter of an alpha, Andras."

Andras is unmoved. "Who just hurled herself off a cliff."

"Diana knew that wouldn't kill her," Brendan says, his voice haggard. "She knew it would only give her a few hours of peace. That it would keep her from going completely wild and killing every Gardnerian she could get her hands on."

"Go with Andras, Brendan," Rafe says. "There's no more time." He looks to Andras and pauses, as if his throat is momentarily locked tight. "Be safe, my friend."

Andras holds Rafe's gaze. "You, as well. May we meet again in Noi lands."

Andras and Brendan leave, and pain grips my chest as I watch them go. Wynter follows them out, catching my eye with her mournful gaze before she disappears from sight.

Ariel scoops up her chickens in both arms and gives me a conflicted look as she departs, her raven flapping out behind her.

Yvan pauses before me, a million unspoken things raging through his gaze. I reach out for him at the same time he reaches for me and we hold tight to each other's hands.

"Keep them safe," I say raggedly, his fire streaking through my lines. "And keep yourself safe, too."

"I will," he promises.

My fire lines clamor to hold on to him as he pulls away from me and walks out the door. I'm lost for a moment, overcome by a sense of vertigo and feeling as if the ground is unsteady beneath my feet. I draw in a long, shaky breath and go out to the hallway, rushing down its length to peer out the window.

My pulse ratchets higher.

Over a hundred Vu Trin sorceresses surround the North Tower. More are riding in by the minute, and behind them marches a contingent of Elfhollen archers in the pale gray uniforms of the Verpacian Guard.

And at the very far end of the field, a regiment of mounted Gardnerian soldiers has just reached the base of the long field and is paused there, as if calmly surveying the situation.

"Aislinn," I gasp, and she looks to me, her eyes wide with fear. "They're here," I tell her. "The Gardnerians are here." Her expression of terror gives way, her eyes suddenly blazing with reckless courage.

"Rafe!" I call out, quickly rushing into my lodging room. Once inside, I skid to a halt. Diana's head is moving lazily back and forth as she lets out a low moan, Rafe's hands tight around her arms.

"Rafe," I say again. "The Gardnerians are here."

Rafe's gaze whips toward me. He opens his mouth to respond, but then Diana cries out and opens her eyes. Rafe turns back to her, and she stares at him quietly for a long moment.

Then she begins to scream.

"Oh, Diana," Rafe says brokenly, trying to hold on to her as she twists and writhes in agony.

"My *pack*!" Diana screams. "They *killed* them! I'm going to kill them *all*!" Her voice breaks off into a long, tortured wail that shatters my heart. "My *father*! My *mother*! My *sister*! Oh, Kendra! *Kendra!*" She sobs uncontrollably. "We're all alone! Jarod and I are *all alone*!"

Boot heels sound in the hall, and then Ni Vin appears at the door in full uniform, weapons strapped all over her body. "Everyone but the Lupines must leave," she orders. "The Gardnerians are coming."

Rafe takes Diana's head firmly in both of his hands. "You're *not* alone, Diana."

"Yes, we *are*!" she cries, her eyes tightly shut.

"Diana, look at me!" Rafe says, his voice breaking. "You're not alone. I love you. *I love you.* I'll love you *forever.* Do you understand?"

She opens her eyes to look at him, violently sobbing as he holds on tight to her gaze.

"I know that right now you want to take them down," Rafe says. "That you want to kill as many Gardnerian soldiers as you can before they cut you down. But I need you to *live*, Diana. And if you only live for one thing…live for *me.* Can you do that, Diana? Can you stay alive for me?"

"My *people*!" she wails.

"What would your father want you to do, Diana?"

"He's *dead*!" she snarls.

"I know, love. But what would he want?"

Diana pauses for a moment, looking up at him. "He'd want me to live!" she cries.

"And your mother and your sister? And the rest of your pack?"

"They'd want me to live!"

"What would they do, Diana? What would your father do?"

She's breathing hard, staring intently into Rafe's eyes as if grabbing at a lifeline. "He'd wait," she chokes out.

"And then what?"

"He'd wait and fool them."

"What else?"

"He'd get out. Somehow, he'd get away."

"And then?"

"He'd form a new pack. And once they were strong enough—" her face twists into a mask of hatred "—he'd come after them."

Rafe's hands grasp her shoulders. "That's right, Diana. That's what he'd do. And you're his daughter. You're strong, like him." His voice breaks. "And I love you."

"The Gardnerians are *here*," Ni Vin says urgently. "You must leave. *Now*." She turns, distracted by the sound of more boots thudding up the stairs.

Diana is sobbing, crying out like she's mortally wounded. Rafe kisses the side of her face and clings to her, his expression wildly conflicted.

"Rafe," I prod, panic mushrooming inside of me. "You need to go. Go find Jules and Lucretia and Fernyllia. Tell them what happened." When he doesn't move, I add, "They will *arrest* you. And the Gardnerians know what you and Diana are to each other, especially after what you did back in the dining hall. They'll execute you for a traitor if you stay, and you won't be able to help her if you're *dead*."

Rafe stills, then bends down to kiss Diana's forehead. "You need to be strong," he tells her, his voice distraught. "As much as you want to, *don't* kill anyone...yet. Play the part of the docile prisoner and keep your mind on how much I love you. I *will* be back for you. Don't forget that. No matter what happens, remember that I'll be back for you."

Rafe gets up and looks to me as Diana curls into a grief-racked ball.

"Go, Rafe," I staunchly insist. "Go get the Resistance."

Rafe hesitates, then nods, a storm of emotion in his eyes. He takes one last tortured look at Diana, then leaves.

CHAPTER SIX

BALANCE OF POWER

Moments after Rafe makes his departure, I hear a sharp, commanding voice outside my room.

"Who is *that*?" the voice demands as I rush to the doorway. Commander Vin is standing in the hallway with her sister, her penetrating gaze set on Aislinn. Four more Vu Trin sorceresses are gathered behind them.

"I'm Aislinn Greer," Aislinn bites out, her hand tight around Jarod's. "And I'm staying *right here*."

Commander Vin looks to her sister, fury spiking in her eyes. "Please tell me that this is not the daughter of the Mage Council's ambassador to the Lupines."

Ni Vin shrugs helplessly, and Commander Vin lets out what can only be a string of curses in the Noi language.

"Shall we drag her out, Commander?" a spiky-haired sorceress asks.

Commander Vin looks around like she wants to kill something. "No, there's no time."

Boots sound on the stairs and a gray-skinned Elfhollen

soldier rushes into the hall, the small white star markings of higher rank on his slate uniform, his bow and quiver attached to his back. I realize, with a rush of surprise, that this is the young Elfhollen soldier Lukas was friendly with at the border, when he brought me to Verpacia at the beginning of term.

"Kamitra," he says to Commander Vin, his expression shaken to the core. "What are you doing?"

"We're placing the Lupines under our protection, Orin," she replies, hard as ice.

More boot heels sound, thudding up the stairs. Three more Elfhollen archers filter in behind Orin, looking stunned.

"They've wiped out both the Northern and Southern packs," Orin says to Commander Vin, slightly breathless. "We just got word. They're more powerful than we could have ever imagined, and they're coming for the Ulrich twins. They've sent us ahead to retrieve them."

"Well, they can't have them," Commander Vin counters. "And neither can you." Her sharp gaze tightens on him. "We could use your help, Orin."

Orin shakes his head, stark indecision in his widened eyes. "How can we possibly go up against them, Kamitra? We're part of the Verpacian Guard."

"Break with them."

Her words vibrate on the air.

Orin's eyes cast around, as if searching for a way out. The other Elfhollen soldiers seem to be holding their breath as they wait. "My family… I can't…"

Commander Vin's expression is unyielding. "Verpacia is going to fall to the Gardnerians. What kind of life will the Elfhollen have under Gardnerian rule, Orin? Both the Alfsigr and the Gardnerians revile you as half-breed Elves with Fae blood. How do you think your family will fare?"

She waits for this to sink in. "Join with us, Orin. We'll give your families refuge if you fight with us. We will let the Elfhollen through the pass this very day and give them safe passage to Noi lands if all of your archers join with us." She narrows her gaze. "Or do you expect the Alfsigr Elves will give you refuge?"

Orin's expression shifts from fear to savage resolve. He turns to call out directives to the archers behind him in the Elfhollen language.

The Elfhollen nod, all of their eyes turning just as fierce. They hoist a young soldier up toward the trapdoor in the hallway's ceiling. The young Elfhollen forces the hatch open and climbs through. A moment later, a tattered rope ladder rolls down to the floor. The other two Elfhollen archers climb up the ladder to the lookout tower above, Orin trailing behind.

"Commander Lachlan Grey is here, Commander Vin," a new sorceress says as she pokes her head through the staircase door.

Commander Vin curses to herself. She turns and her eyes bore into me. "Stay here for now," she orders, then follows the other sorceresses out.

I run to the window. There are now even more of the region's Vu Trin ringing the tower, the Elfhollen interspersed among them, arrows set into bows, a steady trickle of new Elfhollen archers coming into the hallway and climbing the ladder to the roof. An additional twenty or so Vu Trin are in tight lines by the North Tower's front door.

And facing them, a short distance away, is a sizable contingent of Gardnerian soldiers riding in, led by Lukas's father, Lachlan Grey, High Commander of the Gardnerian forces. I search for any sign of Lukas, desperate to find one

Gardnerian soldier I might have a chance of influencing. But Lukas is nowhere to be found.

Commander Grey dismounts from his horse and walks toward the tower. He's bracketed by two men whose black garb bears the Mage Council seal—the golden M insignia on the shoulders of their cloaks. My stomach lurches as I recognize Aislinn's father, Pascal Greer.

"Aislinn," I call out, my heart skipping. "Your father's here."

Aislinn's look of defiance only becomes more entrenched. Rattled, I push the window open a crack and peer through. Gray-uniformed Verpacian soldiers stand by Commander Grey, all of them older men who appear to be officers, one with the large white star markings of a Verpacian commander. And all of these Verpacian military men are black-haired, green-eyed Gardnerians.

I strain to hear as Commander Grey strides up to the Vu Trin commander. "Greetings, Commander Vin," he says, his tone filled with triumph. "We have come to take custody of the Lupines."

Commander Vin remains stone-still in front of the door, her hands on the hilts of both curved swords at her sides. "They are University scholars, Commander Grey, and as such are under our jurisdiction."

Lukas's father holds up an official-looking piece of parchment affixed with a gold seal. "I have orders from the Verpacian Guard authorizing you to release them to us."

"Lieutenant Morlyr," the commander of the Verpacian forces calls out, glancing up toward the tower's roof. "Call off the Elfhollen guard."

"No." I hear Orin's voice sounding through the open entrance to the roof, his tone as rigid as iron. "We're breaking with you."

The Verpacian commander's expression becomes one of surprise, then disgust. Aislinn's father leans in toward him. "I warned you, Coram. This is what comes of letting half-breeds into your ranks."

Coram's lips tighten as he looks back up at Orin, furious. "Lieutenant Morlyr, you and all these renegade soldiers are hereby dismissed from the Verpacian Guard, due to your flagrant violation of the laws of our land."

Commander Grey glances at Coram, his expression calm and in control, like he has all the time in the world. "We'll send you soldiers to replace them, Coram."

"Thank you, Commander Grey," Coram says, eyeing Orin with contempt.

"Where are the Lupines?" Lukas's father asks Commander Vin, sounding almost bored.

She jerks her chin up toward where I stand. "In the tower."

Commander Grey makes a small gesture to the soldiers behind him, and they start forward. Commander Vin taps a hand on her sword's hilt in response. In perfect unison, and with a metallic shriek, every Vu Trin circling the tower pulls one curved rune-sword from their sheaths. Through the opening in the roof, I can see the Elfhollen snapping their bows up, arrows nocked.

The Gardnerian soldiers come to an abrupt halt.

Commander Grey narrows his eyes at Commander Vin, clearly taken off guard by the level of resistance he's encountering. He quickly composes himself, relaxes his posture and smiles coldly. "We have no issue with you, Commander Vin, or with your people, for that matter. Our concern lies solely with the Lupines. We received word yesterday that they were planning an attack on our sovereign territory, and we were forced to take the unfortunate steps needed to protect our people. Hand the Lupines over, and we will leave peacefully."

Commander Vin snaps into fighting stance and pulls out her sword, a hum filling the air as blue light flashes from the runes on the blade. "We will not let you have them, Lachlan."

"Be careful, Commander," he warns. "You are a guest force on sovereign territory. Territory that is aligned with the Holy Magedom."

"Aligned with, perhaps. But there has been no Verpacian Council decree regarding who should take custody of the Lupines."

"A technicality that will soon be resolved."

"But not as of yet."

"Kamitra," he counters with cloying pleasantry, "what you are doing could be seen as a blatant act of war."

Commander Vin remains unmoved. "View this as you see fit, Lachlan. We will not let you take them."

Commander Grey's smile creeps wider. "One thing I have never taken you for, Kamitra, is a fool. Things have changed. I think you know that. The balance of power has shifted. It would be best for you and your people if you hand the Lupines over to us and begin adjusting to the new reality you are faced with."

"You have never been shy about pressing your advantage, Lachlan," she calmly rejoins. "If the balance of power is truly as altered as you say it is, you would not be *asking* for my cooperation."

He laughs. "Oh, come now. Does common courtesy need to die along with those who oppose us?"

Commander Vin shakes her head slowly. "No. You have used up whatever advantage you had last night when you moved against the Lupines, and you can't afford an all-out war with us at the moment. Especially when you take into consideration the fact that we are allied with the Amaz, who, last I checked, were not feeling especially friendly toward you."

Commander Grey's smile disappears. He's now glaring at her with barely concealed fury. "Do you think us fools?" he snarls. "Do you honestly think we will allow you custody of the Lupines? To raise an army of shapeshifters that you can use against us?"

Commander Vin tightens her fist around the hilt of her sword. "And we will wage war with you before we let you do the same."

Lukas's father fumes silently for a moment. "It seems, then, that we are at an impasse."

"Indeed."

He regards her for a long moment, a calculating glint in his eyes. "Then I propose the only possible solution."

"And that would be?"

"Joint custody of the Lupines under a combined guard— part Gardnerian and Verpacian, and part Vu Trin, with a doubling of the guard during the full moon, to keep the Lupines from being used to create more shapeshifters. And to keep them from...conveniently disappearing."

"They are scholars, Lachlan, not prisoners."

"They are *weapons*, Kamitra. And very dangerous ones at that. Weapons we will not walk away from."

"Weapons we will not let you have."

He waves away her concerns with his hand. "We can sit down and hammer out the details, but first, we need to see the Lupines. To verify for ourselves that they really are here."

"They are quite distressed at the moment."

"That is no concern of mine."

The air around Commander Vin suddenly seems to vibrate with blue light. "They just found out their entire family was murdered." Her tone is venomous.

Commander Grey steps forward, furious in turn. "Perhaps such unfortunate things would not have come about if the Lupines had simply ceded the land that is rightfully ours. They were given every chance to avoid this fate." He shakes his head at her. "Really, Kamitra, my patience is wearing thin. Show me to the Lupines, or you will force me to take action."

He gives a small nod, and a guard of six Level Five Mages behind him all pull their wands from their sheaths. The Vu Trin, in turn, whip out silver stars ready to throw, their swords raised, ready to deflect all magic.

The two commanders are silent for a long moment, assessing the situation.

Commander Vin steps back, her posture relaxing. "Stand down, Lachlan," she says, "and we will, as well. I will let you see the Lupines, and then we can sit down and talk."

Commander Grey gives a small wave to his soldiers, and they sheathe their wands. The Vu Trin sheathe their star weapons and their swords in turn, although I notice their hands stay firmly on the hilts of their rune-swords.

CHAPTER SEVEN

REBELLION

I watch and listen through the open window as Aislinn's father volunteers to verify the Lupine's presence. Both commanders distractedly wave him through, then go back to hammering out terms.

Panic rearing, I whirl around to face Aislinn. She's on her knees before a blank-faced Jarod, trying to coax a response from him, to no avail.

"Your father," I warn her. "He's coming up."

Aislinn shoots me a white-hot look of defiance. "Elloren," she says, her voice steeled, "if they force me out, don't interfere, because you won't be able to stop them. I want you to promise me you'll stay as long as you can and try to get Jarod out of here."

I've never seen her like this—suddenly a force to be reckoned with.

"I promise," I vow.

Brisk boot heels sound on the stone steps. Aislinn sits

down close beside Jarod and takes his limp hand firmly in hers, ferocity in her gaze.

The door flies open, and Aislinn's father sweeps into the hallway, trailed by Ni Vin and a black-bearded Gardnerian soldier.

Mage Greer's eyes light on Aislinn and Jarod, widening with horror. "Holy Ancient One!" he exclaims. "Aislinn! Get away from the Lupine!"

Aislinn glares at her father rebelliously. "I'm not leaving," she vows, her voice low with resolve. "I'm staying with Jarod."

His eyes catch fire. "What evil is this? Get away from him, Aislinn. *Now.*"

Aislinn doesn't budge.

Mage Greer looks to Ni Vin, his face tight with fury. He points an unforgiving finger at Jarod. "He's mesmerized her somehow. I'm retrieving my daughter. By force, if necessary, which is well within my rights!"

I want to throw myself between Aislinn and her father. I want magical power, so I could whip out the Wand of Myth and blast him clear out the window.

Instead, I look entreatingly to Ni Vin but she ignores me. She gives Mage Greer a curt nod of permission, as another Gardnerian soldier and another Vu Trin sorceress filter into the hall behind everyone.

"Wait!" I cry, throwing my palms up as Aislinn's father advances down the hall toward us.

"Elloren Gardner," Ni Vin cautions, halting me where I stand with a fierce look that's mirrored by Aislinn. The sorceress stares hard at me, as if trying to convey extreme caution.

My mind is an anguished storm. *You can't intervene. You*

can't save Aislinn from this. Not right now. And you promised her that you'd stay and help Jarod.

"Aislinn, come with me *now*," her father commands, looming over her.

"No," she snarls, refusing to look at him, looking only to Jarod, who stares blankly at the wall. "I won't leave him!"

"I said *get up!*"

Aislinn makes no move to comply.

Irate, Aislinn's father steps back and brusquely motions to his guards.

It takes all my willpower not to rush to her defense as the two Gardnerian soldiers sweep toward Aislinn and grab hold of her arms, wrenching her away from Jarod.

"Get away from me!" Aislinn rages as she fights and bucks against their hold, her green eyes wild.

Jarod shivers and blinks repeatedly, as if almost pulled back to reality, as Aislinn is forced to her feet. Then, he lets his head drop into his hands, as if trying to block it all out.

"No!" Aislinn cries at the soldiers, kicking at them. "Let me *go!* I *hate* you! I hate you *all!* You're *murderers!*"

"Have you gone insane?" her father demands as the guards attempt to restrain her.

Aislinn stops fighting, draws back and spits in her father's face.

Mage Greer wipes the spittle off, his stunned expression morphing to one of pure, unadulterated fury. He snaps his hand up and slaps Aislinn hard across the face.

I flinch from the sound of the blow, pulling in a shocked breath.

"You are a *Gardnerian!*" Mage Greer snarls. "Not some Lupine's *bitch!*"

"How *could* you?" Aislinn cries. "How could you *kill*

them? Even the *children*! I *hate* you! I'll hate you forever! You're *murderers*!"

Aislinn's father quickly collects himself and turns to his soldiers, directing them through gritted teeth. "Get her out of here. I don't care if you have to tie her up and gag her to do it. Put her in a carriage to Valgard. *Now*."

I watch through the hallway window as they drag Aislinn off, her father following closely behind. Everything in me rages to do something to stop this, but I'm bound by the promise I just made to Aislinn.

Commander Vin gestures for Commander Grey to enter the tower, then follows him inside. They're trailed by the Verpacian commander and a white-bearded Council Mage, along with several Gardnerian and Vu Trin soldiers.

Heart pounding, I turn and steady myself against the windowsill as Commander Grey ascends the stairs.

"Elloren Gardner," he says as he enters the hall, his cold eyes boring into me.

"Commander Grey," I reply, my voice strangled. Commander Vin and the others filter into the hall, as well.

"What is the granddaughter of Carnissa Gardner doing here?" the bearded Council Mage questions, screwing his face up in shock.

"Vyvian is punishing her for listening to her fool-headed uncle," Lukas's father replies. "Isn't that right, Mage Gardner?"

"That's right," I say, unable to keep the defiance from my voice.

Commander Grey sneers and turns his attention to Jarod. "Attention, boy! Identify yourself! Are you Jarod Ulrich, son of Gunther Ulrich?"

"He can't answer you," Commander Vin says with barely concealed loathing.

"Whyever not?" asks Commander Grey. "Is he dumb?"

Her returning glare is as sharp as her curved swords. "He's in shock, Lachlan."

"Don't believe it for a second, Lachlan," says the Council Mage. "They're full of tricks."

"Jarod Ulrich!" Commander Grey tries again, this time his voice booming so loud that I jump, and so does Jarod.

Jarod's hands drop from his face, and he looks around the room in a stupor, unable to focus on anything, lost in the nightmare his world has become.

I remember the young Selkie girl the Amaz rescued, the one in shock, the one who looked no older than twelve. Her traumatized expression was the same as Jarod's is now.

"That's him," the Council Mage verifies. "I remember him from my visit to their pack."

"Excellent," Commander Grey responds, looking around. His frigid green eyes light on me. "And the sister? Where is the girl?"

I struggle not to glare at him with blistering hatred. My eyes flit toward the lodging door.

"Go on," he orders me, his tone cool. "Go fetch her."

Nausea overtaking me, I cautiously move to the door. Commander Grey and the Council Mage wait, arms crossed, as I peer into our room and search for Diana.

She's not there.

I tentatively make my way through the door and into the room. My eyes dart around as Commander Grey and his Mage Council cohort follow close at my heels, my heart violently pounding in my chest.

Holy Ancient One, where is Diana?

I scan the room. She's nowhere. I turn around to glance behind me, and that's when I see her.

I flinch at the sight of her and take a step back.

She's on Wynter's bed, hidden in the shadows just behind the open door, still as death, her eyes alert and wilder than I've ever seen them.

Full of a frightening level of hate.

Her hands are shifted from the wrists down, transformed into clawed weapons and clutching at the edge of the bed so tightly her nails are sunk deep into the wood of the frame. I've never seen her look so terrifying, as if it's taking every ounce of self-control she possesses to keep from killing everyone she can get her claws and teeth on.

"There she is," the Council Mage says, pointing.

Commander Grey takes in the sight of her. "Wild-looking thing, isn't she?"

"I can tell she's the daughter," the Council Mage says. "She looks quite a bit like the father."

Diana's nails flick into the wood a fraction more, the hair at her wrists creeping up her arm.

No, Diana. Sweet Ancient One, don't do it. There's too many of them...

"Diana Ulrich," Commander Grey says, his tone formal and commanding, "you are hereby placed under the joint custody of the Gardnerian and Vu Trin command, along with your brother, Jarod Ulrich. Do you understand?"

Oh, Diana, please. Please don't kill them. They'll take you down.

I can't breathe. I can't move. All I can do is wait and pray as she surveys them like a cobra ready to strike.

And then her fur starts to recede, fading from her lower arms, her wrists, until her hands are human once again.

There are deep holes under her fingers where her claws gouged the bed.

Only the wild violence in her eyes remains.

"I am prepared to cooperate with you fully," she says, her voice so ice-cold and completely altered that it sends a chill straight down my spine.

"A wise decision, Diana Ulrich," the commander congratulates her.

"The females are more docile than the males, Lachlan," the Council Mage says. "This one's mother was quite submissive."

"That's not surprising," Commander Grey replies. "Females are generally easier to handle."

The Council Mage purses his thin lips. "I would watch the brother carefully, however. The males are very aggressive."

One of the Gardnerian soldiers steps into the room. "Commander, it seems the easiest place to hold the Lupines, at present, is here in this very tower. It's separate from the rest of the University and easily guarded by both forces."

"Very well," Lachlan agrees with a dismissive wave of his hand. "Elloren Gardner, you will come with us now." He eyes me frigidly. "Your aunt has had safer and more appropriate lodging set aside for you for some time now."

Jarod is ushered into our bedroom by two Gardnerian soldiers and roughly pushed onto my bed. He lies down and turns his back to all of us.

As I'm led away, I turn once to look behind me.

Diana has moved inhumanly fast.

She's now perched on the windowsill directly opposite the door, perfectly still, her violent amber eyes fixed on Lachlan Grey.

The Gardnerians seem oblivious, talking among themselves in the hallway, completely ignoring her and unaware of her swift, predatory movement. Her gaze meets mine for just a moment before Commander Grey slams the door shut.

"Kamitra, I want a lock placed on this door," he demands.

As if that could keep her in.

"And I want guards posted in the hallway."

As if they could fight her off.

"Very well, Lachlan," Commander Vin capitulates. "We will post a joint guard."

I'm numb and dazed and want to scream, all at the same time.

But I don't scream. Instead, I follow them outside, through the throngs of Gardnerian, Verpacian, Vu Trin and Elfhollen soldiers.

The number of Gardnerian and Vu Trin soldiers has more than tripled in size and covers the entire field.

Newly arrived Elfhollen guards have brought their families with them, and I catch the eye of a silver-eyed Elfhollen girl in the now steady stream of Elfhollen refugees passing by, many with owls on their shoulders or winging overhead. The little girl and her mother look stressed and like they've quickly pulled together as many of their possessions as they could, each of them wearing multiple sweaters and cloaks. They quickly disappear into a protective throng of both Elfhollen and Vu Trin soldiers.

Thunder cracks and lightning flashes in the sky above.

Both sides are erecting tents all over the field—dark, angular canvas tents on one side for the Gardnerians, and circular, rune-marked tents on the other for the Vu Trin. And in the middle stands the North Tower, where my friends…

No.

Where my sister and brother are now prisoners. Where they're no longer seen as people, but as dangerous weapons.

Two pawns in the middle of a war.

I follow Commander Grey down the center of the field as an overwhelming grief swells in my chest and tears well up in my eyes.

Dead. Almost all of the Lupines are dead, and everyone's hopes and dreams are dead with them. My brother will never take Diana as his mate in front of all her family and friends. He'll never join her pack, his true people. And Andras will never be part of a pack that accepts him as family.

All the Fae children and the Gardnerian families who've rescued them will be discovered by the Gardnerians and killed. And Yvan and his mother, they'll have no place of refuge. Like the other Fae, there will be no safety for them, nowhere to run.

Aislinn will be fasted to Randall and forced to stay in Valgard. And I will no doubt be dragged to Gardneria and fasted against my will to someone I can never love.

No. Now is not the time to think on these things.

I roughly wipe away the tears.

Andras was right.

There's no time to grieve. That will have to come later.

We have to get them out.

CHAPTER
EIGHT

BATHE HALL

I'm met by two Gardnerian soldiers at the edge of the North Tower's field. One is bearded and brawny and glowers at me through flinty eyes. The other is young, smooth-faced and hawkish, with pale green eyes and a level, predatory stare.

"We've been sent to accompany you to your new lodgings, Mage Gardner," the bearded soldier tells me, his stance domineering. "We'll be acting as your personal guard, at the direction of your aunt."

My pulse quickens. Everything about this shouts confinement and control. "I need to find my brothers," I inform them, forcing calm.

"They've been arrested, Mage," the bearded soldier says, his expression stony. "One for assaulting a fellow Mage. The other for pulling his wand on a Mage."

All the blood drains from my face.

Tight-lipped, he hands me a rectangular block of parchment, still folded from its rune-hawk flight. A vein of lightning streaks across the sky as I unfold the letter with trembling hands.

My Dearest Niece,

I received word via rune-hawk of the dangerous situation un-folding at the University's North Tower. As you know, I've been holding lodging for you in Bathe Hall for some time, so I am having you brought there immediately.

I have also been in touch with Lukas Grey. He has agreed to place you directly under his personal protection once he ar-rives. Until then, I have arranged for you to be under the close watch of two guards. They will accompany you everywhere until you are safely reunited with Lukas.

Your Devoted Aunt,

Vyvian

I refold the paper, my mind a cacophony of turmoil.

"You need to come with us now, Mage Gardner," the bearded guard says, more forcefully this time.

Distraught and clearly out of options, I follow my new guards through the winding University streets, toward the very southern edge of the city.

Far away from the North Tower.

My new lodging is sumptuous, and in the newly segre-gated Gardnerian section of the University.

I follow my guards into the lavish Ironwood hall built in the traditional Mage style—no ivory Spine-stone, only wood and sanded trees and forest decor.

The lodging hall is mostly deserted—my guards and I pass only a few harried Gardnerian scholars who are bundled up and lugging travel trunks.

"What's happening?" I ask the bearded guard.

"They've shut down the University, Mage," comes the stern reply.

My guards unlock the door to my lodging and position

themselves on either side of it. My hand trembling, I open the broad door, the dark wood exquisitely carved with flowing vines, and step into a cloakroom.

Velvet cushioned benches are set into the Ironwood walls on either side, and there's a line of brand-new cloaks, each finer than the next, hanging from a row of iron hooks. One is lined with black fox fur. Another is fashioned entirely from ebony mink. A row of new boots sits under a bench, four pairs of new shoes under the other.

I pass under an archway of dark branches and step into a circular parlor with a lit fireplace. The logs crackle and spit up tiny, glittering sparks. More sanded Ironwood trees are set into the walls, with bookshelves placed between their expansive trunks, already stocked with new, leather-bound tomes with gilded lettering on their spines.

An entire apothecary library—one that rivals the selection in the Gardnerian Athenaeum.

Emerald velvet-cushioned chairs and a divan are arranged near the fireplace, as well as a table set with a steaming tea service, a tower of pastries and a vase of bloodred roses.

My aunt's signature flower.

In a grief-muddled haze, I wander into the adjacent glass conservatory, each windowpane edged with a stained-glass Ironflower design. The conservatory looks out over the lodging hall's central gardens, with a grove of Ironwood trees in the center.

Black-lacquered planters line the sills of the conservatory, full of living Ironflowers. The glowing blooms suffuse the storm-darkened conservatory with a sapphire glow, and even the rug beneath my feet is patterned with a torrent of Ironflower blossoms.

I test the locks on the windows, jiggling them as hard as I can as my sense of being under siege bears down on me.

No give.

Two unfamiliar Gardnerian soldiers suddenly appear down the garden path, through the grove of Ironwood trees. One of the soldiers catches my eye, and I can see by the gruff, watchful look he gives me that I have more guards than just the two outside my door.

My claustrophobic alarm mounts. Feeling horribly exposed, I flee the glass room and escape through the parlor into my windowless bedroom. As I cross the threshold, I freeze in astonishment.

On the canopied bed, laid out over its deep green quilt, are a series of brand-new tunic and skirt sets, each more luxurious than the next.

The black silk of one is outrageously awash with scarlet blessing stars embroidered in glistening thread. The stars are splayed over the silk like a ruddy constellation, rubies shimmering around the stars.

The next set is covered in whorls of emeralds, the gems thickening at the edges of the garment and glittering spectacularly. A third is delicately embroidered with deep green leaves, the neckline of the tunic cut scandalously low.

And there's another Ironflower dress.

She knows, I realize. *Somehow, she must know how much Lukas loved the shockingly brazen Ironflower dress I wore to the Yule Dance.*

Because this dress rivals my Yule dress in its sheer flouting of all Gardnerian convention. The elegant black velvet tunic and skirt are embroidered with dark Ironwood trees that root at the base of the skirt and explode into a riot of Ironflowers on the tunic, each blossom sewn with phosphorescent sapphire thread.

Aunt Vyvian's keeping me here in Verpax City for one reason, I realize, stunned and appalled. *To keep me in the path of Lukas Grey.*

I flinch at a pounding knock at the door.

"Rune-hawk message for you, Mage," the bearded guard's rough voice booms through the closed door.

On unsteady legs, I go to the door and open it. His pitiless eyes bore down on me, and I force myself to hold his cold glare. He stiffly hands me another folded letter that's marked with the dragon seal of the Fourth Division Base. I take it from him and shut the door. Then I return to the secluded bedroom, unfold the note and read.

Elloren,
I'll be in Verpacia this eve. I'll send for you when I arrive.
Lukas

Thunder booms overhead.

A blistering rage I can barely contain swells up and crashes through me with devastating force.

The Lupines are *dead*. Almost all of them *murdered*. And now, Lukas and Aunt Vyvian are using the slaughter of an entire people—of Diana and Jarod's entire family—to advance my wandfasting to a member of the military that committed this heinous crime.

All of a sudden, I can't think. I can't breathe. My head pounds along with my pulse, and bright lights crackle in my vision. My knees buckle, and I slide down, bumping against the bed's edge as I make clumsy contact with the lush rug beneath me. My breath comes in uncontrolled, staccato bursts as I throw back my head and cry.

I'm curled up, sobbing in a tight ball on the floor when I hear a door click open and the sound of light footsteps in the entrance foyer, then the parlor.

Alarmed, I lift my head as Tierney's stern face comes into view and emotion blasts through me.

"Tierney," I croak out. "They let you in?"

She falls to her knees before me as her tight, stoic expression collapses. We grasp onto each other, our foreheads pressed together as tears fall between us and mingle on our dark skirts.

After a moment, Tierney sits back and roughly wipes away her tears, her expression shifting from one of profound grief to a mask of grim endurance. We hold each other's gaze, the silence between us weighed with devastation.

"How did you get past my guards?" I ask, bewildered.

Tierney's frown deepens, and she glances distractedly at her white Vogel armband. "My father is active in the Crafters' Guild. I tossed around a few names."

"My brothers have been arrested," I tell her, my voice breaking.

Her grave stare doesn't waver. "I know. They've been taken into military custody. They'll likely be tried for attacking those military apprentices."

"Ancient One." I drop my head into my hands as panic whirls through me.

"The scholar Rafe attacked—he's the son of Mage Nochol Tarkiln, head of the Merchants' Guild."

Fury rises in me, red-hot, cutting clear through my panic. "I'm glad Rafe attacked him," I lash out in a snarl. "I wish he'd torn his head clear off."

My anger rapidly evaporates into a stifling fear for my brothers. I force a long, quavering breath. "I have to help them, Tierney. Where were they taken?"

"The Fourth Division Base." Tierney's eyes are heavy with import. "Lukas's command." She lets this new piece of information sink in, and a look of complicit understanding passes between us.

"Lukas will be summoning me later," I tell her.

She gives a tense nod. "Elloren, everything's changed out there. The entire power structure of the Western Realm has shifted overnight."

I can feel it, too, this new, terrifying world pressing down on us. "I know."

"I've found out as much as I've been able to," she says. "The Gardnerians have given the Verpacian Council two choices—peaceful annexation or military action."

We're silent for a fraught moment.

"The Verpacians will cave," I say, giving her a dark look. "There's no fighting the Gardnerians now."

Tierney returns my jaded expression, her body stiffening as if braced for a blow. "The Verpacian Council has called an emergency session. They're meeting right now."

My skin crawls with gooseflesh. I know what this means for Tierney and her family. What this will mean for everyone I care about.

"Do you think they have their Black Witch?" I whisper. "Could Fallon have wrought this somehow? Lukas told me that he might have been wrong about Fallon and her level of power."

Tierney's brow furrows. "Fallon's abilities are said to be increasing, but this is a stunning level of power at work. And Lupines are immune to wand magic." She shakes her head. "This is beyond anything the Realm has ever seen, Elloren."

Disquiet worms through me as I hold her grim stare.

"I was told that Vogel's coming," Tierney says.

I inwardly recoil from the name, remembering the shadow tree that shudders into my vision whenever I'm around the

Vogel, overcome by the sense of something shadowed about to envelop us all.

"He's to meet with the Vu Trin," she says. "To negotiate what will happen to Jarod and Diana. Both sides want them—"

"To create an army of shapeshifters," I finish for her. "That's what both Lachlan Grey and Kam Vin accused each other of wanting."

Tierney nods, biting nervously at her lip. "Yes. I don't think the Gardnerians want to kill them."

"No," I agree bitingly. "They just want to enslave them."

"Vogel is pulling the Fourth Division soldiers in to guard the North Tower," she tells me. "They'll be here by nightfall." She gives me a weighted look. "You'll need to press your advantage with Lukas when he arrives. And not just to help Diana and Jarod and to get your brothers out of prison. If Verpacia falls to the Gardnerians, Lukas will become a major power here."

She doggedly holds my stare, the unspoken hanging in the air between us.

No, I inwardly protest. *I cannot fast to him. Esptecially not now. Not after what the Gardnerians have done.*

"Have you seen Yvan?" I ask, an edge of cornered defiance in my tone.

Tierney's gaze narrows in, as if she's reading the conflict suddenly raging inside me. "He's guarding the kitchen workers."

"Did he get Ariel and Wynter to safety? They can't be here, Tierney. If the Gardnerians take over Verpacia, they'll round up all the Icarals and throw them in prison."

"They're safe," she assures me. "Yvan brought them to Cael and Rhys, and they've left Verpacia. Cael has an ancestral home in the extreme north of the Alfsigr lands. He's taking them there."

Relief shudders through me. *Thank the Ancient One. At least they got out.*

Tierney eyes me sidelong. "Yvan's a bit desperate to get back to you. He found me. Asked me where you were. But it's not safe for him to seek you out right now."

"No," I say bitterly. "Not with my new guard."

Tierney's even stare doesn't budge. "I think he's in love with you."

Longing for Yvan flashes through me. "I know," I tell her, pained. *And I'm falling for him, too.*

"You need to let him go, Elloren." Her voice is firm, but not without compassion. "He needs to go east. And you need to stay here and secure an alliance with Lukas Grey." She takes in my stricken look and softens slightly. "I'm sorry, Elloren. But they're going to fast you anyway—"

"I can't fast to him," I cut her off, my voice suddenly rough with defiance. "Tierney, the Gardnerian forces *murdered* the Lupines. And I don't even know what side Lukas is really on."

"Then find out," she says, her voice severe, but her eyes conflicted. "Elloren..."

"I know," I say, fighting back the sting of tears. "I know that everything has changed. And I know my lineage puts me in a position with some power."

And I have to get my brothers out of prison and help Jarod and Diana escape from the North Tower.

Tierney's mouth tenses into a grim line. She glances around aimlessly and growls out a curse. "We need that blasted dragon. I hope she's having fun gallivanting around the wilderness."

"Naga said she'd come back."

Tierney scowls. "Yeah, well, her timing could be improved." She gets up and winces as she stretches against the constant pain in her back. Then she holds a hand out to me and nudges me into motion with a determined glare.

I take her hand and rise, pushing back the misery.

Pushing away thoughts of Yvan.

Tierney's eyes flick toward the elegant row of dresses on the bed. "Get cleaned up," she says. "And put on one of those obscenely lavish dresses. Then we'll get you ready to go meet with Commander Lukas Grey."

I pull in a breath as Tierney laces up my opulent tunic and stare into the full-length oval mirror before me.

"This is really more blue than black," I comment, shocked by my reflected image. The dense, glowing Ironflowers dominate the black velvet in a way that doesn't just push against the edges of Gardnerian respectability.

This dress blasts clear through them.

"I'm amazed your aunt can get away with defying convention like this," Tierney says as she fishes through a lacquered Ironwood jewelry chest for just the right pieces. "Our rules about dress are getting stricter. This is risky."

Aunt Vyvian doesn't care, I bitterly consider. *She'll throw caution straight off a cliff to lure in Lukas Grey.*

"Ah, this is perfect," Tierney crows as she lifts up a gleaming necklace. Obsidian branches are linked to a slim silver chain, sapphire Ironflowers lush on the branches. There's a pair of dangling earrings with the same branching design as well, glinting azure in the lamplight.

Tierney fastens the necklace around my neck as I put on the earrings. Then she carefully applies my makeup, rouging my lips and cheeks and lining my eyes with kohl. Scrutinizing me in the mirror, she picks up a gilded brush and styles my hair with braided accents.

When she finally steps back, she frowns into the mirror, dissatisfied. "Wait one moment," she tells me.

Tierney disappears through the door and into the conservatory, then returns a moment later with a fist full of Ironflowers. She pulls off portions of the stems and weaves the glowing flowers into my hair.

Then she picks up her teacup, steps back and sips at it, eyeing me with cool speculation. "Yes, that will do." Her expression hardens, braced and unforgiving. "Go get your brothers out of prison, Elloren."

CHAPTER
NINE

BREAK

Outrage carves out my center and lightning flashes in the sky as I survey the field before me. Both the Gardnerian forces to the right and the Vu Trin on the left seem even more firmly entrenched, a wide aisle cutting up the center to expose the North Tower at its apex.

My home.

I want to run to the North Tower. I want to pull my Wand, harness my power, fly up the stairs and get Jarod and Diana out of there.

"Mage, Commander Grey is expecting you." My bearded guard firmly nudges me, barely hiding his ill humor over how I'm dragging my heels.

There's a sizable black tent on the Gardnerian side of the field now with our new flag, the white bird on black, flapping above it. A large, newly raised circular tent stands on the Vu Trin side, its black canvas covered in glowing blue runes, the flag of the Noi people flying above it—a white dragon emblazoned on blue. Two large, cleared circles are in the center of both fields, ringed by soldiers.

Intimidation carves through me.

Get ahold of yourself, I harshly remind myself. *You have to act like you're Carnissa Gardner.*

I straighten and force a more purposeful stride up the center of the field. As I pass, Gardnerian soldiers on one side of the aisle snap to attention, their eyes flicking over my bold dress and registering my Black Witch looks in obvious appreciation. The Vu Trin standing on the left grow rigid as I walk by, their eyes watchful and wary.

I spot Ni Vin on horseback, just behind the line of Vu Trin, and her gaze briefly lights on me, her expression carefully neutral.

A shriek splits the air.

My heart picks up speed and my eyes dart up, but I can't make anything out in the storm-darkened twilight.

Brusque orders are shouted as both Vu Trin and Gardnerian soldiers crowd into the aisle before me, blocking my ascent.

A great hush falls over the entire field as all of the soldiers, including my guards, look to the sky.

Lightning pulses in thin lines from cloud to cloud, illuminating them with gauzy puffs of light. I squint at the intermittently storm-lit sky, trying to make out what everyone is searching for.

Another screech rends the air, and then a full-bodied roar that resonates through me. This time from the east.

Lightning flashes again, and I suddenly make out a dark, winged silhouette moving in from the east and another from the west, the incoming dragons growing larger and larger as everyone looks to the sky.

The Vu Trin dragon soars in to land, its expansive wings

flapping. It flies down into the cleared circle on the Vu Trin side of the field and hits the ground with a weighty force that reverberates under my feet, the unbroken dragon gleaming sapphire, its eyes flashing silver.

The Vu Trin sorceress on the dragon's back is outfitted in rune-marked black armor. There's a silver circlet around her brow, two curving dragon horns rising from it. She swings off the dragon as Marcus Vogel's opaque-eyed black dragon touches down in the middle of the Gardnerian side of the field with another ground-shaking thud.

All eyes turn to Vogel, the new decider of the Realm.

The new center of power.

Rage flashes through me, and I struggle to contain it as unsettled power kicks up in my affinity lines, burning in fits and starts.

Murderer. You vile murderer.

Vogel dismounts from his broken dragon as the horned Vu Trin sorceress crosses the central aisle and approaches him on the Gardnerian side. She's flanked by Commander Vin, as well as a sizable Vu Trin guard outfitted in rune-marked gray.

Soldiers on the Gardnerian side part, and High Commander Lachlan Grey falls in beside Vogel along with several other high-level Mages.

And just behind them strides Lukas Grey.

Anger spasms inside of me at the sight of Lukas up there, in league with such evil.

How could you be a party to this, Lukas? How?

I struggle to conceal my burning outrage as my eyes slide back to Vogel, and the Wand in my boot starts up a warm thrum against my calf.

Vogel stills and lifts his head, as if he's sniffing the air. He makes a slow turn and glances out over the field in my direction.

The dark shadow tree flashes in the back of my mind, and suddenly I'm pinned by Vogel's unfocused gaze, rendered immobile, panic swiftly overtaking me.

The Wand of Myth hums against my skin, and I've a sense of silvery branches emanating from it, flowing through my affinity lines and twining around Vogel's shadowy tree. The shadow tree explodes into tendriling, dark smoke.

My body slumps in, able to move again.

Vogel abruptly turns away, as if a connection has been broken. He strides off and disappears inside his tent with the horned Vu Trin sorceress.

I pull in a haggard breath, stunned and terrified by Vogel's palpable increase in power.

My eyes suddenly collide with Lukas's.

He starts down the aisle at a fast clip, his focus on me like a raptor focused in on its prey, and my fire lines give a hard flare as he nears, his face a lethal storm.

Lukas barely pauses when he reaches me. He holds out his elbow, and I wordlessly take his arm, an enraged fire whipping through my lines.

"You're dismissed," Lukas tells my guards without looking at them, his voice taut with anger.

I want to scream at Lukas and strike him. I want to take every last Gardnerian soldier down with my bare hands. Instead, I match his long stride down the field.

At the field's base, we veer off toward the forest, the silence between us crackling with an almost unbearable tension. Lukas's hand slides down to grasp my arm as he pulls me through the dark woods, the lights of the military encampments and the University rapidly fading as we move farther in.

The trees' hatred strafes at us from all sides, and Lukas

blasts his fire lines out at the same time I do, the forest abruptly withdrawing.

We come to a small clearing, and he releases me and turns, our eyes locking with savage emotion. All artifice instantly breaks down, the Dryad pull an overpowering wave, overtaking me.

"How could you be part of this?" I snarl at him, teeth gritted. "Did you know the Gardnerians were about to *slaughter* the Lupines?"

"I didn't know." His eyes are incendiary.

"I don't believe you!"

"Can I lie to you?" he asks, his voice daggered.

"No. You can't," I slice back at him. "So, tell me, Lukas. Now that all of you *do* know, is your whole division *celebrating*?"

"Yes," he says. "They're celebrating."

"And what about you, Lukas? Are you celebrating, too?"

Combative fire lights his gaze. "No, Elloren. I am not. Vogel just destabilized the entire Western Realm."

"That's what you care about?" I lash out, my rage blistering and raw. "That the Realm is *destabilized*? Not that large numbers of innocent people have been *murdered*?"

I've a sudden sense of ferocious conflict slashing through his lines. "Is this still just the normal cycle of history, Lukas?" I demand. "Just the way of things?"

He remains infuriatingly silent, but I can feel it building inside him—fire exploding all over his earth affinity lines. I want to harness that fire and throw it at him. To watch him ignite.

I stalk close to him, fists tight, fire raging. "*This* is what it was all leading up to, Lukas. 'Erthia for Gardnerians'. The idea that we are the First Children, and everyone else is an Evil One. The mobs. The burning blessing stars. *This* is what comes of it. Not some shining, blessed Gardnerian paradise. Dead *children*. Dead *families*. And Gardnerians *celebrating* because our cursed book tells us that it's all *just fine*."

I get right up into his face. "I don't care if this is the normal cycle of history. Over and over and over. This needs to be fought *now*. This needs to end *now*."

"Vogel would have to be deposed."

The world tilts. "What did you say?"

Lukas's lip curls into a grimace. "You heard me, Elloren."

My throat pulls in tight, my voice reduced to a scraping whisper. "What are you telling me, Lukas?"

"The truth." He glares heatedly at me. "Because you and I are incapable of anything else." His hard gaze falters. "I wish I could lie to you, Elloren, but I can't."

"Then tell me the truth," I say, my thoughts reeling.

"Vogel's too powerful, and so is our military. He can't be fought from the outside—he'd have to be taken down from within."

"How?"

"The Gardnerian military would need to overthrow him."

Lightning flashes. I pull in air, stunned.

I search Lukas's eyes, but he's giving nothing away. Nothing except the turbulent fire that I can sense raging through his lines.

"Do you think enough of the military would be willing to turn against him?" I'm barely able to take a breath.

"No," he says with terrible finality.

We hold each other's gaze in sudden, grim understanding.

"My brothers have been taken into military custody," I tell him.

"I know."

"I need you to get them out."

He nods, fire roaring through his lines.

"And I don't want a guard," I doggedly press. "My aunt's assigned them to me. I want you to permanently dismiss them."

He nods again.

"What are they going to do with Jarod and Diana?"

"I don't know." His jaw ticks. "Vogel's leaving this evening to fly to the Vu Trin base near the Eastern Pass. He's going to hammer out an agreement with Vang Troi."

I tense my brow in question.

"The woman who rode in on the dragon," Lukas clarifies. "She commands all of the Vu Trin forces. In any case, I'm to accompany them."

We both grow quiet, the darkness pressing in around us.

"Was it the Black Witch, Lukas? Has Fallon's power quickened to such a devastating level?"

Lukas shakes his head. "No. This was something else. Something worse." He eyes me darkly. "But soon, Fallon will be a weapon Vogel can deploy, as well."

I cast about, my mind a storm, searching for solid purchase.

"Fast to me, Elloren," he says.

His tone is so brutally insistent, I'm launched into a deeper turmoil. "Why, Lukas? So you can draw on my power?"

His scalding gaze only intensifies. "In part. Yes." He takes my wand hand into his, and I let him. His green eyes locked on to me, he turns my hand over and slides his palm firmly against mine. A shiver races across my skin, and I've a sense of his branches twining into my hand, fanning out over my earth lines in a heady rush.

I swallow, my heartbeat deepening. Lukas grasps my hand more firmly, and I tremble as a rush of dark flame skids along the branches and all through my lines.

"When we kissed at the Yule Dance," he tells me, "my

fire lines were strengthened for a good week. My earth lines for a full month."

I struggle to think clearly as his overwhelming heat arcs through my body.

He leans in close. "If I can access your power when we kiss," he says, "then I imagine the fasting link would allow me to draw even more." The motion of his fire slows to a seductive caress, stroking down my lines. "Let me pull on your power, Elloren," he murmurs. "You can't access it. But I can."

Alarm overtakes me, abruptly severing his feverish spell. I wrench my hand away from Lukas and step back, breathing heavily as I massage my fingers. An echo of his power pulses through me as I force myself back to coherent thought. I look up at him, defiance suddenly blazing through me.

"Break with Vogel completely." I glare up at him with stiff challenge. "Give me your word that you will fight to overthrow him. No matter the odds."

Lukas's face becomes a storm, his whole body tensed as a silent argument rages between us. Thunder booms overhead, neither one of us relenting.

"I want to lie to you, Elloren," he frustratedly lashes out. "I'd give anything to be able to lie to you right now."

A caustic anger rises, and I look him over with blistering scorn. "Those Level Five stripes are *wasted* on you. If I had access to my power, I'd fight Vogel. With *everything* in me."

Lukas's fire gives off a violent spasm of heat, and he stalks close. "You're making a choice that will end *horrifically*."

I hold his stare, unmoved as my rage implodes, and desolation sweeps through me. "Lukas. *So are you.*"

We hold each other's implacable gazes for a long, tortured moment as our fires race through each other's lines. And then it's abruptly gone—all trace of Lukas's intense fire. Like a wall being slammed down.

I move away from him, and a realization hardens deep inside me with irrevocable conviction. As much as I need his help right now, I can't align with him and risk becoming any part of this *thing*.

"Goodbye, Lukas," I tell him roughly, even as my affinity lines strain toward his. Even as all hope for my brothers' freedom turns to dust. Even as all hope for the future comes unmoored.

I turn on my heels and walk away.

I stride away from the North Tower and onto the cobbled University streets as the wind picks up and the storm finally gives way, lightning cracking overhead and a pelting rain beginning to fall.

I walk as Urisk workers scurry toward the North Tower's field, bringing trays of food to both sides.

I walk, alone and untrailed by guards, increasingly chilled, until I'm clear on the other side of the University, and then past it. I cross over a scrubby side field and head straight into the bordering wilds.

I dully register the forest's hostility, but deftly force it back. The trees are so dense that I can barely feel the rain under the canopy of thick branches.

Soaked through and uncaring, I slow to a stop, my breathing ragged as an overwhelming desolation sweeps over me.

Diana and Jarod. Rafe and Trystan. Tierney and Yvan. And all the others I've come to care about.

There's no one who can save them.

A wave of anger and grief crashes into me, and I'm swept into its undertow. My legs buckle, and I fall onto my hands and knees, vomiting up all the bile from my stomach.

I'm breathing heavily, spit hanging from my mouth as I stare at the wet, dark earth. Lightning flashes, and my gaze snags on a small, arcing stem pushing its way up through the bed of leaves.

I push myself up and grab at a nearby tree for support.

Lightning flashes again with an earsplitting crack, illuminating the tree.

Ironwood.

I lean into the tree, ignoring its silent cry of protest as I rest my head against it. It's cool and rough, and even though I have to force away its revulsion, I can feel life thrumming inside it. Spring forcing itself to be known.

Another crack of lightning and I glance up to catch a momentary glimpse of a translucent bird shuddering to life in the trees—there and gone again so fast that I'm not sure if I can trust my vision.

Newly alert, I glance around, realizing I'm surrounded by a whole grove of Ironwood trees, and the hooks of arcing stems are pushing up between the rotted leaves all through the grove.

Ironflowers.

The only tree that starts out as a flower, the delicate Ironflower blossoms seeding to trees the following year, trees with branches that bloom with a smaller version of the original flower.

The apothecary wheels of my mind start turning as an idea ignites like an explosion.

To make this work, we'll need Ironflowers. A lot of them.

We're many days away from the glowing Ironflowers blossoming on the forest floor.

Where could I get hold of enough Ironflowers…

In a sudden, swooping rush, it all coalesces in my head.

And I know exactly how Tierney and I are going to get them all out.

CHAPTER TEN

CHEMISTRIE

I receive a rune-hawk missive from the Fourth Division Base the next evening.

"What does it say?" Tierney asks from where she sits on the floor of my lodging's conservatory. Delicate thread shears are suspended in her hand, my almost solidly blue Ironflower tunic splayed out over her lap. My Ironflower dress from the Yule Dance is in a crumpled pile beside her.

Rain batters the night-darkened windows around us, thunder resonating through the lodging house's walls as lightning flashes through the sky. I break the wax dragon seal with my thumbnail, unfold the parchment and read.

Astonished, I draw in a hard breath. "My brothers," I tell Tierney. "They're being released."

Tierney's mouth turns up in a calculating smile. Her eyes dart to the Ironflower dress on her lap. "You made good use of this dress, then, didn't you?"

The missive is written by one of Lukas's subordinates in a formal hand—a soldier named Thierren. I feel a pang of disquiet, uncomfortably aware of the conflict raging between Lukas and me, which is glaringly apparent in his use of someone else to write this note.

I read on.

"The apprentice that Rafe punched," I tell Tierney as I read, "he's dropped the charges against both of my brothers." I meet her gaze as a full realization of Lukas's hand in this washes over me. "In return, the apprentice is being promoted from apprentice to the position of second lieutenant under Lukas Grey's command."

"Well, that's done then," Tierney says, her voice resolute. "The rest is up to us."

Tierney and I empty our sacks of Ironflower threads out on to the apothecary worktable, the pile of tangled string wreathed in a soft, sapphire glow in the dim lab.

"You've locked the doors and windows?" I ask.

Tierney absently nods as she writes down notes with a look of intense concentration, papers filled with her mathematical calculations strewn about the table. Shadows cling to the walls around us, the evening's dark digging in, the apothecary workroom chilly and deserted.

A scuffed, leather-bound Apothecary text is open before Tierney. Her pen makes a rapid *scritch scritch* as she finishes jotting down the boiling points of the components of our complicated fabrication.

Satisfied with her list, Tierney gets up and expeditiously begins setting up the glass reflux apparatus. She nods to me, and I place a funnel in the opening of a distillation flask and pour in the River Maple ash I've prepared. Tierney holds her palm over the opening and flows water from her palm into the container's bulbous interior, filling it. The wood ash swirls around the water in a messy spiral before settling.

Then we push the balls of glowing Ironflower thread into the container's opening.

Tierney presses a long, glass condenser into the distillation flask's crystalline mouth and stabilizes the tube with metal clamps. Then she wraps her hand around the condenser and flows water through it.

I slide a large oil lamp beneath the container's base, then look to Tierney. "Light it," she says.

I strike a flint and ignite the flame.

Tierney holds her palm out toward the mixture and brings it to a rapid yet smooth and rolling boil. Wavering sapphire lines of Ironflower essence leach out of the threads and into the water, curling through it in an intricate dance. Soon, the water takes on a faintly blue glow.

Tierney and I wait as the blue glow intensifies and grows incandescent, washing us in its sapphire light.

"It's ready," Tierney says once the threads and wood ash have settled into a black mass at the base of the glass container. She raises her hands to the flask and creates a cooling cloud that swirls around it.

After a few moments, I disassemble the reflux apparatus and filter out the ash and threads. Tierney readies the distillation glassware, and I carefully pour the glowing blue liquid into a new distillation retort. With practiced grace, Tierney waves her hand over the receiving flask and creates another cooling cloud to hover around it.

I set a flame under the retort, then place my hands around the warming flask, coaxing my earth lines to life. Slim, black branches flow through me, winding toward my hands. "Ready," I tell her.

She lays her own hands on top of mine, and I feel my power flowing out of me in a controlled force, branches twining toward the flask, fire sizzling through them.

Steam shoots through the distillery, the glass rattling as we pull our hands away. For a slim second, I fear the glass will crack or perhaps explode. Tierney pushes one hand towards the flask and the rattling stops, the steam coalescing into a smooth stream.

Liquid starts to accumulate in the bottom of the receiving flask—a vivid, phosphorescent blue, deep as twilight.

I breathe in the steam's Ironflower scent. "I can smell the essence purifying." An image of blue Ironflowers unfurls in the back of my mind.

Tierney smiles at me. "It's working, then."

I give her a returning look brimming with resolve.

She grins, a wicked gleam lights her eyes. "We're going to poison them all."

Commander Vin sweeps into the kitchen, disguised in a heavy cloak. She throws back her hood, scanning the room intently. "Is the kitchen secure?" she asks Fernyllia.

Fernyllia nods grimly from where she sits at the table beside me, Tierney on my other side.

"All the doors and windows are locked," Fernyllia says. "And I have a watch out."

Commander Vin gives a curt nod and sits down at the table between Jules and Lucretia Quillen, just across from me. Yvan stands behind them, leaning back against the kitchen counter, Iris and Bleddyn by his side.

I struggle not to look at him, to not be so overwhelmingly aware of his presence. I can sense Yvan's fire loosened from its constraints, questing toward me, but I staunchly hold my own fire back and push down the fierce ache in my chest.

"Tell me this plan of yours," Commander Vin says to Tierney and me.

We exchange a swift look, and Commander Vin motions impatiently with her hand. "Speak," she orders sharply. "We've little time. We're only days away from the full moon, and possibly all-out war."

"We've crafted a poison," Tierney tells her, the words sly on her tongue.

Commander Vin draws back a fraction. "For a diversion?"

"To poison them all," I say, forcing an even tone. "The entire Gardnerian force. And most of the University."

The commander is quiet for a long moment, her eyes flashing condemnation. "You'd kill everyone in Verpax, would you?" She levels her gaze at Fernyllia. "*This* is the plan you'd have me hear?"

"Hear them out," Fernyllia says patiently, her flour-dusted hands clasped and resting on the wooden table before her.

Tierney leans over, fishes a large jar out of her travel sack, and sets it firmly on the table in front of us. The powder inside glows a vibrant, Ironflower blue.

"Not to kill," Tierney states adamantly. "To temporarily render unconscious. For an entire night—and fairly incapacitated throughout the next day. With a full recovery."

I motion toward the glowing blue jar. "There's enough here to poison all the food in all the kitchens in the entire University city. And the soldiers draw almost all of their food from these kitchens. It will give you six solid hours to get the Lupines out of here."

"That's quite enough time to get through the Caledonian pass in the Spine," Fernyllia puts in, a calculating glint in her eyes.

Tierney sits back, her tenacious gaze steady on the commander.

Kam Vin shakes her head dismissively. "The Gardnerians have spells to detect poison, just as we do. All the food is tested. Always."

"We've forced elemental magic into Ironflower essence and combined it with the poison," Tierney explains. "So, now it can suppress magic. There isn't a single spell that *can* detect it, wand-or rune-based."

Jules picks up the jar thoughtfully. He looks to me, his lips curling into an impressed smile. "It seems you've found your calligraphy, Elloren Gardner."

I let out a resigned sigh and nod. "I have."

"It's as we've said." His tone is amused, but his eyes are serious. "If one can't be powerful, it pays to be clever."

Commander Vin is staring at the jar, nodding, and I can see the wheels of her mind turning. She looks to Tierney and me. "You've stipulations?"

I take a deep bolstering breath. "You need to take my brothers to Noi lands along with all the Lupines."

"A Level Five Mage and a tracker," she says, cutting me off impatiently. "Fine. We can make good use of them."

"You need to bring every last kitchen worker who wishes to leave, as well," Tierney says, her tone brooking no argument. "And their families, too—including Fern, Iris, Bleddyn and her mother, plus Olilly and her sister."

Bleddyn's mouth falls open, and Iris's face takes on a look of stunned confusion.

"You ask too much," Commander Vin says coldly.

"No," Tierney shoots back. "We ask for little. We are delivering the Lupines to your military and keeping them out of Gardnerian hands. War is coming, and you know it. An army of Lupines could sway the tide in either direction."

Commander Vin is utterly still as she scrutinizes Tierney. "Go on," she prods.

"Tierney's entire adopted Gardnerian family needs to go with you," I put forth. "And a young mariner named Gareth Keeler should be docked at Saltisle Harbor—you need to find him and bring him with you, as well."

I take a deep breath, a sudden swell of emotion overtaking me, and I stiffen my whole self against it. "Yvan Guriel and his mother need to be brought east, too."

I can feel Yvan's fire blast toward me from across the room, chaotic and overpowering. I can't look at him. I just can't.

"All of the people on Fernyllia's list need to be evacuated," Tierney insists. Fernyllia runs down her long list, and Commander Vin nods in agreement.

"And Fernyllia, too," Bleddyn says emphatically, looking at the kitchen mistress. "You forgot to put yourself on this list."

Fernyllia pauses and grows very still, and Bleddyn's voice tightens with alarm. "Fernyllia. Why are you not on this list?"

I jerk my head toward Fernyllia, all of us looking at her in surprise. She's quiet for a long moment, but her expression has gone stone hard. "I will be the poisoner."

Shock races through me as Bleddyn shakes her head vehemently, outrage lighting in her eyes. "No! Absolutely not. Fernyllia, you can't." She lapses into what sounds like aggressive pleading in Uriskal, her hand slashing the air, as if defending Fernyllia's life in this very moment. Iris starts to cry, her tears rapidly devolving into great, heaving sobs.

"Bleddyn Arterra and Iris Morgaine," Fernyllia says, her voice low and hardened. *"Stop."*

Bleddyn quiets, her face a tortured grimace, the cords of her neck tensing. Iris turns her head away, her eyes shut tight as she continues to cry.

"I am an old thing," Fernyllia says, her voice softer this time, but solid and unmovable. "Bad knees. Bad back. Bad health. I could not make this journey to Noi lands. But all of you *can*. And you can bring my granddaughter east, where she can have a good life. There is *no life* for her here. If you love me, you will stop your grieving, and you will bring my Fern to safety."

Bleddyn is nodding resolutely now, tears streaking down her face. Iris is crying into her hand.

I make no move to wipe away the tears that roll down my own face. "Don't do this," I implore Fernyllia. I look to Commander Vin. "Surely there must be another way. There has to be a way for her to go, too. A way we haven't thought of."

Fernyllia puts her calloused hand on mine. Her eyes rest gently on me with maternal sadness. "Child, you don't know what you're dealing with. You need to trust me. I've been fighting this fight much longer than all of you."

I shake my head, crying, and Fernyllia puts her arm around me. "This is what I want," she says, her voice more insistent now. "Do you understand?"

I nod, overcome with sorrow.

"What of the Icarals?" Lucretia asks, forcing our attention back to the rushed planning. "Now that Verpacia has fallen, it's dangerous for them to be here."

"They've already left," Tierney tells her. "With Wynter's brother, Cael. He owns a piece of ancestral land in Alfsigroth, and he's taking them there."

Everyone leaving. Everyone soon to be gone—eventually only Aislinn and Uncle Edwin left behind in Gardneria with me. My chest tightens with grief at the idea of so much loss.

"And what of you?" Commander Vin asks me.

I look up to find her eyes tight on me. "I need to stay behind to care for my uncle," I tell her, roughly wiping away my tears. "I've no magic or skills past medicinal, and my aunt has made it clear she won't care for him forever. My family can't leave him all alone, and my brothers will be in too much danger if they remain here. So...it makes sense for me to be the one to stay."

The commander sets her implacable gaze on Tierney. "And you?"

Tierney meets her intimidating stare without flinching. "I'm staying for now. There's a chance that the Amaz will be able to remove my glamour, and after it's gone, I've a water route I can use to escape east."

"The Gardnerians are planning to spike every body of water in the Western Realm with iron," Commander Vin puts in flatly.

"They can try," Tierney counters, eyes flashing. "The forest has rerouted some of the water."

Commander Vin considers this, a shrewd gleam edging her gaze. She sits up, military straight, and faces the two of us. "Elloren Gardner and Tierney Calix," she says gravely, "I give you my word. If you supply us with this poison, I will bring your people to Noi lands."

Bleddyn lets out an overwhelmed gasp. Yvan's fire reaches for me again, an intentional flare this time, but I can't look at him.

Instead, I stare down at the table and swallow back the tears.

I stand with my brothers in the hallway of the North Tower. Rafe seems like he's aged several years since I've last seen him, a hard line of tension etched between his brows. "We'll come back for you," he insists, his voice determined. "We'll find you."

I nod, trying to be strong as I turn to my younger brother. Trystan's dressed as he usually is—in his perfectly pressed military apprentice uniform, somber and important-looking, his wand sheathed at his side.

"You've gotten so tall," I tell him with a tremulous smile. I reach up to grasp his shoulder.

Trystan's eyes close tight, and he shakes his head, as if fighting desperately for control. The image of the powerful Gardnerian Mage dissolves into my little brother—the skinny boy I used to carve wooden animal toys for.

Trystan's lips are trembling, tears welling in his eyes. I pull him into an embrace as my own tears fall, and Rafe's arms come up around us both as we all say goodbye.

Yvan's eyes blaze with emotion as we face each other in the circular barn, a single lantern casting the deserted space in a flickering glow.

I can feel his fire power radiating off him in guttering flashes of heat.

The pages ripped from *The Book of the Ancients* are now long weathered and worn beneath our feet. But *The Book* has won. There will be no dancing on its pages.

"I don't want to leave you," Yvan says, his voice rough with passion.

My words are tight when they come, my grief tamped down. "You can't stay. You and your mother have to get to safety."

Ferocity overtakes him. "We're putting off the inevitable, Elloren. At some point, we're going to have to fight them."

"We can't fight them here. It's over, Yvan. The Western Realm has fallen."

The edges of his eyes ignite, like the times he's pulled in fire. Yvan looks around desperately, as if searching for a way out, a way to fight back. His eyes light on the battered leather covering of *The Book of the Ancients* near his feet, about a third of the holy book's pages still clinging to the inside. His expression hardening into savagery, he grabs up *The Book* and closes his fist around the thick leather.

I jolt back as *The Book* catches fire, the flames quickly spreading to the edge of his sleeve.

"Yvan!"

As if abruptly broken from a spell, Yvan blinks hard and looks to his burning sleeve, then at me, a flash of agony on his face. He closes his eyes and breathes deep. The flames slowly pull into him and disappear, and when he opens his eyes again, they glow a fervid gold.

He's so excruciatingly beautiful, he takes my breath away. I try to memorize every aspect of his face so I can hold it deep inside my heart. Forever.

"When are you poisoning them?" he asks, the fire in his eyes surging.

I reach up to wipe away a tear. "Fernyllia's doing it tonight. Tierney and I are going to eat some of the poisoned food, as well." When he opens his mouth to protest, I add, "We have to. Or else the Gardnerians might suspect our involvement."

I hold his heated gaze, and the silence between us deepens, filling with unsated longing.

"Your mother's on her way," I remind him, an ache gathering in my throat. "You need to get her out of here. There's no more time."

He nods stiffly, his eyes blurred with tears. When he speaks, his voice is ragged. "Goodbye, Elloren."

For a split second, we pause, our eyes locked, and then he comes to me. I fall into the warmth of him as he wraps his arms and fire tight around me, kisses my hair and murmurs ardent Lasair that I don't understand and don't need to.

CHAPTER ELEVEN

POISONED

When the next day comes, I feel as if I'm underwater and can't surface.

I hear voices, but it's like they're on a distant shore—muffled and strange and far away. My body is numb, and my mouth feels like it's been stuffed up by cotton. Listening to the unintelligible voices around me, I groggily wonder if this is how we first sounded to Marina.

I try to open my eyes, but they're crusty and pasted shut. After a few false starts, I finally succeed in pulling my lids apart. The light is blinding and knifes into my eyes.

There are people in the room, or at least the shadowy shapes of them. They're talking in a dreamlike, slowed way and loose words float toward me, like so many soap bubbles.

Lupines. Escape. Full Moon.

I struggle to knit the words into a coherent thought with my sluggish brain. The world sloshes when I move my head from side to side, but the people start a slow pull into focus.

Several Gardnerian soldiers.

An older, white-bearded Gardnerian man.

Aunt Vyvian.

I blink repeatedly as the fuzzy outlines became sharper, the voices clearer, but I'm disturbingly unable to fully connect with my own body. I struggle to open my mouth, but it won't budge.

"They left her behind," my aunt is saying to the white-bearded Gardnerian, a stern-faced man with the Physicians' Guild crest on his tunic. "She may not have any knowledge of this. Elloren, *wake up!*"

I try to speak again, my lips like heavy stone.

My aunt leans over to peer at me closely. "Where did your brothers go, Elloren?"

"She can't answer," the white-bearded physician says. "The poison hasn't worn off yet. We'll have to wait."

"There is no *time!*" Aunt Vyvian snipes. The physician withers under her fierce censure.

Slowly, the previous night's events seep back into my mind, each new thought like a fresh wound opening.

"Where did they go, Elloren?" my aunt demands. *"Where?"*

Again and again she interrogates me, not bothering to hide the threatening edge to her tone. My heart begins to beat more strongly, and a sharp fear washes over me. *Danger. There is danger here.*

All at once, reality slams into me with the force of a gale wind.

My head immediately starts to pound as if hit by a hammer over and over and over. I cry out in agony, my hands flying to my head. I force myself up, desperate for a change in orientation to lessen the pain, vertigo overtaking me as the room tilts. I drop my head between my knees and moan in distress.

"Where did you brothers go?" Aunt Vyvian presses.

Slam, slam, slam goes the pounding in my head. I try to hear around the pain, try to respond, but the pain is everywhere.

"My *head*!" I cry, clutching at my sweat-soaked hair, digging my nails into my scalp.

It all rushes back—everything that's happened. And I remember that I have to focus. I have to lie to her.

"What *happened* to me?" I whimper.

"You've been poisoned," the physician states in a carefully calm tone.

"Poisoned?" I ask, faking great disbelief.

"Yes," he gravely affirms.

"By who? Aughh! *Oh, Ancient One!*" I flop down on my side, clutching at my head. They try to talk to me, to interrogate me, but it all fades into background noise again, fighting to be heard around the pain.

I catch snippets of what they're trying to tell me as I grasp at my scalp: Fernyllia Hawthorne responsible, poison in the food, everyone sickened—Gardnerian and Verpacian soldiers, scholars, workers. Lupines gone. Rafe and Trystan gone. Vu Trin sorceresses and Elfhollen and some Urisk gone. Amaz horse-physician and his professor mother gone with stolen horses, all the rest of the University and military horses scattered to the wilds. Gone. All gone.

Fifteen Gardnerian soldiers are dead. The University groundskeeper is dead, viciously decapitated. The ears pulled clear off a group of Third Division Gardnerian military apprentices. All of this havoc wreaked by the savage Lupine female.

Fernyllia, executed this morning. The Eastern Pass shut down. Rafe and Trystan Banished. Never would have happened if they'd been fasted and raised by Aunt Vyvian instead of Uncle Edwin.

"Where are they? Where are they? Where are they, Elloren?"

"I don't know! I don't know!"

And then, silence as I writhe in pain.

Oh, Ancient One, Fernyllia! You saved everyone and they killed you for it...

"Why are you crying?" my aunt snarls.

"The *pain!*" I lie, racked by the staggering loss of Fernyllia, each lie slicing straight through my heart like jagged glass.

"I don't think she knows where her brothers are," the physician says to Aunt Vyvian.

"Of course she doesn't," my aunt snaps. "Rafe and Trystan didn't tell her anything. They were under the thrall of the Lupines. That's why they let their *own sister* be poisoned."

They question me for what seems like an eternity, while my head splits in two along with my heart. And then they leave me alone to wrestle with the pain.

Finally, I give up and pass out.

Hours later, I'm still shaking from the aftereffects of the poison, my skin clammy, my balance off. Lightning flashes in the night sky visible through the windows of my Bathe Hall lodging.

Aunt Vyvian sits before me on another velvet-cushioned chair, a fire crackling in the fireplace beside us. I clutch at the cup of bitter *Borsythian* tonic Aunt Vyvian had an apothecary brew for me, feeling hollowed out and broken.

"I never imagined your brothers would go so terribly wrong," she rages, her green eyes searing.

Trystan. Rafe. Where are you right now?

Her cruel words skewer into my heart. I miss Rafe and Trystan so much already I don't know how I'm going to bear this new Realm without them.

"Rafe was turning out to be a bad one," she seethes,

"running around with that Lupine bitch. But Trystan." A look of wounded betrayal flashes across her features. "I *never* imagined."

She looks to me, uncharacteristically distraught, as if there might be some clue in my gaze as to how things went so horribly wrong.

They're gone. Almost everyone I love—gone.

The finality of it is too much to bear, and I'm not prepared for the force of my grief. I start to cry, letting the tears fall freely, knowing she'll assume I'm crying over my brothers' betrayal.

Aunt Vyvian's face contorts into a hateful grimace. "It's your mother's blood. That's what caused this."

I look up at her, startled, her mention of my mother momentarily halting the flow of tears. Aunt Vyvian shakes her head and glares off into the middle distance, as if a terrible, perfect clarity has descended.

"Tessla Harrow." She hisses my mother's name with such venomous loathing that it stuns me. "That *Downriver* girl. Raised around Kelts... Urisk. You wouldn't *believe* how Keltish she was when she first came to Valgard. And she *never* shook her low-class ways."

She bites out the words. "And Rafe looks *exactly* like her. Trystan... He resembles your father a bit more, but the Downriver blood ruined him in the end." She looks to me, her expression of hatred softening, her eyes glassing over. "But not you, Elloren. You look so much like Vale. And *exactly* like Mother."

She nods to herself, as if affirming her own argument. "You have the blood of our line, not your mother's. That's why you're good and pure, and your brothers are so bad." Her expression turns bitterly rueful. "If only you had our legacy of power. But it's in you, and it will manifest in your children." She nods to herself again as if our salvation is assured. "You'll fast to Lukas and you'll redeem our family name."

I inwardly draw back from her, stunned and outraged, a remembrance of my mother's smiling face filling my mind, my father's kind presence.

You witch, I silently rage. *You cruel, elitist witch.*

"Did you know your father fasted to that Downriver girl out of *pity*?" she snipes, a volcanic fury simmering in her eyes.

"No," I force out in a wavering voice.

"Oh, yes. She was trying to whore herself out to a Kelt. No one else wanted her. So, my brother foolishly stepped in and fasted to her. *That's* the type of blood your brothers have in their veins."

"What...what do you mean?" I'm practically light-headed with confusion.

"Your mother wanted to run off with a Kelt," Aunt Vyvian spits out. "At the same time the Kelts were rounding up Gardnerians for slaughter."

What? No. You're wrong. She loved my father.

"He's a professor here, that Kelt," she grinds out. "Or was." Aunt Vyvian gives a small, hateful laugh. "But not anymore."

"Which professor?" I ask.

Her lip twitches. "Jules Kristian."

Shock blasts through me. *No. That can't be true.*

"None of these heathens should be allowed to teach at a University," she seethes. "You wouldn't believe what our soldiers found in Jules Kristian's office—proof of a web of illegal activity stretching clear across the Realm."

"Where is he?" I ask breathlessly. "What happened to him?"

"They haven't found him yet," she answers, her face clouding with frustration. "But when they do, he'll be arrested. And I'll personally oversee his sentencing."

Vertigo assaults me. *Where are you, Jules? Could any of this be true? Why didn't you ever tell me?*

"I'll never forget that man's name," Aunt Vyvian rages. "And I'll never forget the night Vale fasted to that woman. That's the type of trash your father brought into this family. And now look. Just *look* at what it's wrought."

A mounting anger takes hold.

My mother wasn't trash, you wicked thing.

Aunt Vyvian rises to her feet and picks her black calfskin gloves up from the small table beside her, her eyes full of pent-up fury, her gaze boring down on me as I struggle to keep my face impassive.

"I have to leave for Valgard to try and undo some of the horrific damage your brothers have wreaked," she tells me, her voice tight, barely controlled. "It's going to be up to you, Elloren, to save our family's legacy. You're staying here. And you are to spend as much time as you can with Lukas Grey. I'll be back in two weeks' time, and you will have secured a fasting date and your uncle's permission. No more waiting. No more of your uncle's games." Her gaze hardens with a malice that sends a chill racing down my spine. "You can inform your uncle that if you do not fast to Lukas within three weeks' time, I am cutting you both off completely. What little funds he once had are gone. So, you'll both be on the street if you do not obey me in this. Do you understand?"

I will defy you in every last thing, you monstrous hag.

I force my expression into a mask of somber obedience. "Yes, Aunt Vyvian."

She searches my face, as if scrutinizing for a chink in my deference. Seemingly finding none, she looks me up and down, no doubt taking in my sickly coloring, rumpled hair and miserable expression. A trace of sympathy lights her gaze.

"I'm sorry your brothers did this to you, Elloren. They've been Banished from Gardneria and from this family. We'll speak of them no more."

She sweeps out of the room, and I jump at the sound of the door slamming behind her.

I wait and wait, gripping the edge of my chair as fire sparks along my lines. I wait until I can't hear her confident steps anymore. Wait until I imagine she's in her carriage and pulling away, my breathing constricted and uneven, anger cycloning around and around inside me. My rage rapidly overtakes my frail, poison-hammered body, straining like an avalanche about to give way.

In a heated rush, I spring to my feet, grab the vase of roses beside me and hurl it at the fireplace with a growling cry. The vase explodes into a crystalline shatter, glass and flowers flying everywhere, some of the blooms bursting into flames in the fireplace.

I stand there, fists clenched, not caring about the flaming rose smoldering too near the edge of the rug.

What am I going to do? I agonize, tears streaking down my face.

Gareth is gone, my fasting backup plan gone with him, and the mandatory fasting deadline is only weeks away. But I can't flee while Uncle Edwin is sickly and needs my care.

My mind spins, grasping for a solution.

I'll look at the fasting registry, I desperately consider. *I'll find a young man who isn't in the military. Then I'll get Uncle Edwin's approval, and keep it from Aunt Vyvian somehow...*

How? I argue against myself. *She'd know immediately. The Mage Council offices are overrun with her sycophants.*

Suddenly, it's like the walls are closing in on me, and I can barely breathe. I can't be here anymore, in this stifling

Gardnerian place. I want the North Tower. I want to be inside its familiar stone walls.

Even if only the ghostly imprint of my friends and family remains.

CHAPTER TWELVE

EALAIONTORA

I stumble through the night-darkened University streets toward the North Tower, the poison-wrought anvil in my head reduced to a fuzzy, rhythmic discomfort that keeps time with my heartbeat.

At the base of the long, sloping field, I slow to a stop as lightning flashes in cloud-muted bursts, but still no rain.

The field is empty.

The Vu Trin are gone from Verpacia, and the Gardnerian soldiers have been stationed elsewhere, their scattered detritus littering the muddied earth.

The North Tower's cold, dark silhouette is stark against the night sky—empty and forgotten. On its door is painted a bloodred Gardnerian blessing star.

Sorrow lances through me at the sight of it. And a knife-sharp sense of violation.

I've seen this mark before. On places Gardnerians have marked as spiritually polluted. Places to avoid because of the stain of the Evil Ones.

Outrage pierces through me as I press on up the rocky central path, a chill wind kicking up and cutting into me. I reach the base of the North Tower and push my hand against the door, which is slightly ajar. The hinges squeak in protest at my intrusion.

I step inside, the hallway pitch-dark, with only the occasional flashes of lightning to illuminate the spiraling staircase. Navigating from memory, I'm halfway up the stairs when the sound of murmuring from upstairs catches my attention.

I freeze as fear snaps through my blood.

Who could possibly be here?

I hear the muffled voice again. A male voice. I can just make out the High Alfsigr inflection.

My heart leaps in my chest. *Cael?*

I quietly pad up the stairs and through the upstairs hall, speeding up as I draw near our lodging, becoming overwhelmingly certain that it's Wynter's brother I'm hearing.

I peer inside the room and shock jettisons through me.

Wynter is huddled limply in a corner, her eyes vacant, her wings wrapped tightly around herself. Ariel's raven is perched on the rafter above her, and Ariel is crouched protectively in front of Wynter, hissing at Cael, who stands before them. Slender Rhys hovers nearby, his look of desolation taking me aback.

Everyone turns to look at me as a whirlwind of conflicting emotions explodes inside of me. Overwhelming joy to see them again rapidly gives way to staggering fear.

They can't be here. Verpacia has fallen, and soon it will take on the laws of Gardneria—laws that now mandate the imprisonment of Icarals.

"What happened?" I ask Cael, my heart hammering. "Why in the Ancient One's name are you *here*? Cael, it's not safe."

Cael's expression is ominously bleak. "My sister," he says. "She has been shunned from Alfsigroth. All Icarals have been."

I pull in a hard breath as Cael's words crash home. I know what this means. If Wynter has been banned from Alfsigr lands, then she'll be killed if she sets foot inside their borders.

"Our rulers are calling for a stricter adherence to our sacred texts," Cael tells me. "And our sacred teachings call for the deaths of all *Deargdul*—the Winged Ones. Our High Priestess has always sounded the call for the casting out of my sister, but it was never acted upon until now. But with Realm-wide war on the horizon, our people grow superstitious. They have not only shunned my sister—they have also threatened to shun every Alfsigr who aids her. My parents and the rest of our kin have disowned her. It is like your people's Banishment. I fear there will be a call for her to be hunted down."

I feel myself blanching. "Sweet Ancient One... Cael..."

"If there is a formal call for her death," Cael says, "they will send out the Marfoir."

"The Marfoir?" I haltingly ask.

"Alfsigr assassins," Cael says, stone hard.

My stomach quails as a dread-filled silence falls over the room. Cael looks around aimlessly, then sets his silver gaze back on me. "This is the only place we could think of where an Icaral could safely stay." Cael's brow creases, his words tinged with disgust. "I know your people will avoid coming to this 'polluted' place."

Ariel shoots Cael an eviscerating look, completely missing the bitter sarcasm in his tone.

"Have you and Rhys been shunned, too?" I look toward Cael's pale, quiet second.

"Not yet," Cael says. "But it may come to that."

I glance over at Wynter, who seems to be in a state of shock, staring out into nothing.

"Wynter, I'm so sorry," I say to her, but she doesn't respond. "I've never seen her like this," I tell Cael and Rhys.

"She loves our people," Cael says, his elegant voice breaking. "To the point where I believe she would give her life for them." Sorrow lances through his expression. "She should be an *Ealaiontora*. Yet the Alfsigr turn their backs on her."

I send him a questioning look.

"It is difficult to translate," Cael tells me. "An *Ealaiontora* is...a great artist. And yet...it is even more than this."

"An *Ealaiontora* is a prophet," Rhys says softly, catching me off guard. He's always been so silent, so watchful. His voice is gentle and heavily accented, all the sharp edges of his speech rounded off, like they've been smoothed by flowing water.

"Not like in your sacred texts," Rhys gently explains. "An *Ealaiontora* is a prophet not through words, but through their art and their very life. They are a reflection of the Soul of The People."

"If my sister had been born without wings," Cael says, "she would be revered by all of Elfkin. We have not seen the likes of her...the *talent* she possesses...for generations. Her art should decorate the halls of the Alfsigr monarchs and the steps of the *Ardeaglais*."

"I am not an *Ealaiontora*," Wynter says from where she's slumped against the wall, her voice dulled. "I am one of the Foul Ones. Leave me and return to our people. I accept my fate."

Ariel bolts to her feet, her black wings unfurling, a small ring of fire erupting around Wynter and herself as she glares at us. "Get out," she seethes at us. "Get *out*. *All* of you. You are *poisoning* her mind."

"Ariel, they're trying to help her," I insist.

"Get *out!*" Ariel snarls at me, at Cael and Rhys. *"Leave. Her. Alone."* She kneels back down in front of Wynter. "We don't need them," she tells Wynter as she strokes her hair clumsily, silent tears streaming down her livid face. "We don't need *any* of them. They only want to hurt us. *They're* the Foul Ones. You can't let them *break* you."

"What are you going to do?" I ask Cael, twisted up with anguish.

"We will seek an audience with my aunt, the queen. We will beg her not to send out the Marfoir. And to rescind this decree against the Icarals."

"And if she denies you?"

Cael nods gravely, as if already braced for this possibility. "We will break with my people. Somehow, we will get my sister through the Eastern Pass. We will journey to Noi lands, where Rhys and I will join the Wyvernguard." Cael's cultivated face grows hard as flint. "And then we will take up arms against the Gardnerians and the Alfsigr Elves."

PART FIVE

MAGE COUNCIL
RULING

#340

The peaceful annexation of the territories
formerly and illegally occupied by the Northern and Southern Lupines will commence
immediately, bringing the northern territory
under the protection of Alfsigroth and the
southern territory under the protection of
the Holy Magedom of Gardneria.

VERPACIAN COUNCIL RULING

#73

By unanimous decision, the Verpacian Council has voted to bring Verpacia under the protection of Gardneria. The peaceful transition of power will commence immediately, beginning with the merging of the Gardnerian military with the armed forces of Verpacia. The Verpacian Council will hereby operate under the jurisdiction of the Mage Council of Gardneria.

MAGE COUNCIL RULING

#341

The peaceful annexation of Verpacian lands
will commence immediately, bringing the
formerly independent country of Verpacia
under the protection of the Holy Magedom of
Gardneria.

MAGE COUNCIL
RULING
#342

All diplomatic relations with the Noi people
are hereby severed in response to the egre-
gious and unprovoked actions against both
the Gardnerian and Verpacian militaries.
The Vu Trin forces are hereby barred from
the newly annexed Verpacian province of
Gardneria, and the Holy Magedom has
appropriated the Vu Trin military bases
in eastern and western Verpacia.

Further Vu Trin aggression or trespass onto
the sovereign territory of Gardneria
will be considered an act of war.

PROLOGUE

Damion and Fallon Bane peer through the windows of the glass-enclosed balcony, out over the sea of black-clad Gardnerians in the plaza below, the crowd captivated by the commotion at the apex of the cathedral's grand, sweeping staircase.

A male Icaral is being hauled up for execution, two soldiers grasping its arms, the creature's wing-stumps flapping in panic.

Damion savors the panoramic view of the scene from the fourth story of the Banes' most palatial estate. His gaze sweeps over the crowd toward the mammoth statue of Carnissa Gardner that dominates the plaza's center—the larger-than-life Black Witch leveling her wand at the evil Icaral demon that lays prostrate at her feet.

Movement draws Damion's focus back toward the scene unfolding in front of the cathedral's enormous front doors. Marcus Vogel, Vyvian Damon and the rest of the Mage

Council stand in a semicircle around the bound, kneeling Icaral as three Level Five Mage soldiers stride forward.

Damion watches impassively as the soldiers pull wands and point them at the Icaral demon's head. The creature's wing-stumps continue their agitated flapping, its head hung low. Thunder rumbles in the distance, the dark clouds bundled tight and low as lightning streaks across the sky.

"Did you know Mother was attacked by an Icaral?" Fallon asks, her chair set close to the glass, her eyes pinned on the Icaral. "During the Realm War. The night the Kelts rounded up her entire family." Fallon's eyes flash with outrage.

Damion Bane eyes his sister with careful consideration. She sits in a high-backed, velvet-cushioned chair, her head resting on a silken pillow, tree limbs embroidered along the black pillow's edging in a deeper matte black. Her torso is still wrapped in broad bandages, and an emerald quilt with a tree design has been carefully placed over her lap by her skittish Downriver Gardnerian handmaid.

She's still recuperating, but she's a marvel. Her powerful affinity lines have saved her.

And her magic is growing.

"Mother told me of the Icaral attack," he says. Their eyes meet and hold, a fierce look of solidarity passing between them. Their mother, Genna Bane, rarely speaks about what happened that night, over twenty years ago. When the heathens had power and were slaughtering entire villages of Gardnerian men, women and children.

When the Kelts and Urisk and Icaral-demons came for their mother and her entire family.

Damion looks back at the broken Icaral with renewed hatred and blazing satisfaction. The Reaping Times have only just begun. The scourge of Evil Ones is about to be wiped clean from the Western Realm—and then the Eastern Realm, as well.

The work of the Black Witch taken up and finished, once and for all, by his powerful sister.

Fallon's mouth twists with abhorrence as she watches the scene. "The Icaral threw fireballs at Mother's family as they were being herded into a barn for slaughter. And it *laughed*. It actually *laughed* as it burned the children's feet and set the little girls' skirts alight."

Rage flashes in Fallon's eyes, her fingers curling tight around the Ironwood wand in her lap. The entire room chills, and Damion feels the cold seeping into his bones as frost forms on the windows.

"I know, my sister," Damion says, his voice low.

"Leave just *one* of the Evil Ones on the face of Erthia, and what happened before will happen again," Fallon warns. "The word *Mage* will once again become a slur. Our people, our children will be mocked as 'Crows' and 'Roaches.' Enslaved...beaten down. And then gathered up and murdered." She sets her formidable gaze on her brother. "*That's* where it will end if we do not bring the full might of the Reaping Times down on their heads."

Damion holds his sister's gaze, ignoring the alarming cold. He knows better than to react to her with fear.

"The Icaral demons need to be Reaped, to be sure," he agrees coolly, gesturing toward the Icaral below as Marcus Vogel addresses the crowd. "But this frenzy of executions is just a political move on Vyvian's part."

Some of the chill withdraws.

"Of course it is," Fallon says, seeming placated by their easy agreement. "To secure her seat on the Mage Council." She glances at her brother. "I *do* believe Vyvian Damon is truly with the Magedom. Regardless of how much she and

Mother hate each other." Her beautiful face hardens. "But Vyvian harms the Magedom by not moving aside and accepting where the Black Witch power now lies. With *our* line."

"The Black Witch bloodline rests with Elloren Gardner," Damion gently reminds his sister. "Now that the Gardner brothers are Banished."

The cold rises and bites into him, the frost creeping out over the windows.

"Elloren Gardner is no different from her brothers." Fallon throws her brother an incensed glare. "She's *staen'en*. She consorts with every type of Evil One."

"Fallon," he says with cool reason, "it is widely thought that the Evil Ones are coming after Carnissa Gardner's line because they are still the *true bloodline*. You will have a hard time convincing the Mage Council to mark the Black Witch's own granddaughter as *staen'en*."

"Which is why Elloren Gardner needs to be disciplined. By us."

Damion is well aware of one of the reasons why Fallon hates the Gardner girl.

Lukas Grey.

"Discipline her, then," he idly comments. "You grow stronger every day. Soon, no one will doubt that you are the Black Witch of Prophecy."

"There is no time." Fallon's eyes narrow. "We need to push that entire family *firmly* under our heel, starting with Elloren Gardner, and we need to do it soon."

Before she's fasted to Lukas Grey.

"How would you have me deal with the brothers?" Damion asks, skeptical. "They are likely under the protection of the Vu Trin and well on their way to the Noi lands."

"I will take care of the brothers myself."

Damion cocks a black brow. "The younger one is a Level Five Mage."

Fallon sharpens her glare. Hoarfrost forms on every surface in the room, the frost like bunches of crystalline needles, everything now coated with white, the view across the plaza completely iced over. The temperature takes another alarming dip, and cold worms its way through Damion's body.

Cold that hurts.

"Do you doubt me, Brother?" Fallon asks, her voice low.

Damion gives a short laugh and flexes his stinging fingers. "No, dear sister," he says, glancing around appreciatively. "Beautifully done hoarfrost. How did you come to master it?"

"I've used my bedridden time well." Fallon's lips turn up in the trace of a smile. "And I know how we can crush Elloren Gardner—a way to destroy the little *staen'en* whore and absorb Carnissa Gardner's bloodline of power."

Damion smirks at his sister as he tenses against the painful, full-body chill. "If you freeze me to death, Fallon, I won't be of much use to you."

Fallon considers this.

All the cold in the room abruptly withdraws, and the hoarfrost pulls away as the space warms once more. The blood rushes back into Damion's arms and feet in a painful rush of tingling sparks, the view over the plaza restored.

Damion looks down just in time to see blue light exploding from three wand tips, engulfing the Icaral demon in a torrent of blue fire. The Mages step back as the Icaral collapses into a pile of smoking, charred flesh.

Damion turns back to his sister and matches her look of dark resolve. "So, tell me, Sister. How would you have me destroy Elloren Gardner?"

CHAPTER ONE

WINGS

I peer out the North Tower's huge circular window, perched like Wynter so often is up here. My eyes scan the night-blackened field and the even darker forest beyond, searching for any sign of Cael and Rhys. The moon rides just above the jagged Northern Spine.

A gloomy silence has fallen heavily over Ariel and Wynter, the wait for Cael and Rhys's return an agony. Ariel wears a grim mask of endurance that's new. Her past hostility has shifted into a fierce protectiveness of Wynter, and there's a growing strength to her. A filling in of her wings, the feathers glossing. Her fire slowly returning.

It's the only heartening thing in an increasingly heartless Realm.

Unlike Ariel, Wynter seems crushed, listlessly curled up on her bed for hours at a time, as if her spirit has been irretrievably broken. I glance over to where Ariel is futilely trying to cajole her into eating something, but Wynter won't move. My eyes meet Ariel's, and I can see the same grave worry there that's mounting in me.

Over the past few days, the University has slowly reopened under new Gardnerian leadership. Lucretia and Jules have both fled, their offices taken over by professors loyal to Vogel and the Holy Magedom.

Every evening, Tierney and I visit the newly reopened Gardnerian Archives and pore over the *Mage Council Motions & Rulings* by guttering lamplight.

"The Council has thrown all Icarals who were once in the Sanitorium into the Valgard prison," Tierney gruffly whispers, her finger moving along the lines of text. "And it seems your aunt is making good use of the anti-Icaral fervor that Marcus Vogel has whipped up."

We read, with rising horror, about how my aunt's taken to pulling Icarals from the cells in Valgard's prison and marching them through the city streets, the crowds stirred up into a mob-like frenzy. She hauls the Icarals, one by one, to the Mage Council meetings, demanding that the "demons" be cut down.

So far, she's succeeded in bringing about the public execution of four Icarals on the steps of Valgard Cathedral.

"She's trying to regain her good name," I murmur to Tierney with scathing revulsion. "She's Banished my brothers from the family, and now she's propping up her hold on her Mage Council seat by doing this."

"Ariel and Wynter *have* to get out of here," Tierney says in a low, tense whisper. "Someone will come to the North Tower at some point."

"I know. But Cael and Rhys should be back any day now." I don't like how unsure my own voice sounds when I say this.

Tierney's expression becomes oddly hesitant. "Elloren,"

she whispers haltingly, as if having difficulty forming her thought.

Anxiety rises in me. "What is it?"

She swallows and struggles to meet my eyes. "Valasca sent word..." She scans the broad room, moving closer and lowering her whisper until it's faint as a feather's brush. "The Amaz have figured out how to remove Asrai glamours. They're going to—" she gestures toward her body "—pull this *thing* off of me."

My eyes widen. "Tierney...that's incredible."

"They've figured out how to draw off even layered glamours and trap them in rune-stones. That way they can use them to glamour someone else, if needed."

I stare at her in amazement. "That's a powerful skill."

Tierney's gaze turns somber, her eyes flicking around cautiously. "Yeah, well, the Amaz will need every advantage they can secure in this new Realm."

"So, they'll pull your glamour off...permanently?"

Tierney nods, and the ramifications of this wash over me. What will she look like when she's been stripped of the glamour that's imprisoned her for almost her whole life? What powers will she finally be able to access?

"Elloren," she whispers falteringly, "Valasca and Alder are pulling the glamour off me in six days' time. Once it's removed, I'll be able to morph with water in my true form. So... I'll be leaving for the Eastern Realm."

It stuns me, how hard her news strikes me. I've known for a while now that Tierney would eventually leave—that she *must* leave. But I never realized how catastrophic the imminent loss of my irascible, intellectually fierce friend would actually feel.

I blink hard, suddenly fighting back the tears and abruptly

choked up. I roughly wipe a stray tear away. "I'm sorry, but...
I'll miss you."

Tierney attempts a sardonic look, but her lip trembles at
the edges. "Even though I snarl at you all the time?"

A laugh bursts from me, and I smile waveringly at her
through a sheen of tears. "I'm glad you're leaving," I whisper emphatically. *I'll miss you desperately. I'll be so alone.* "I
want you to go. I'll be so happy just knowing you're safe."

It's going to shatter my heart to have you all gone.

The next night, I'm back in the North Tower, my forehead pressed against the cool glass of the window, the night
clear, the field before me silvered by moonlight.

I wonder where Yvan is right now, and if he's looking at
the same moon. A forlorn sadness washes over me as I let
my eyes slide down the night-grayed peaks of the Spine toward the wilds below.

A shadow bursts from the trees, and I flinch back. At first,
I assume it must be Cael, and I squint to make out exactly
what I'm seeing—a dark figure on horseback, racing toward
the North Tower. But then I notice that the horse has an
odd, flowing quality to its gait, its inky body reflecting the
moonlight in undulating silver lines.

My pulse leaps.

What in the Ancient One's name is Tierney doing? She's risk-
ing everything, riding a Kelpie out in the open.

Her name bursts from my lips. "Tierney!"

I jump down from the sill, meeting Ariel's and Wynter's
looks of surprise, my outburst seeming to have galvanized
Wynter to sudden attention.

"She's on a Kelpie," I hastily tell them as I rush to the
door. "Something's wrong."

I sprint out of the room, race through the hall and down

the spiraling stairs, Ariel's and Wynter's steps thudding close on my heels, Ariel's raven winging in behind us.

I throw open the North Tower door as Tierney rides up to us, positively wild-eyed. I draw back, resisting the urge to shut the door against the dangerous creature, but as Tierney jumps off the Kelpie's back, it swiftly dissolves to the ground in a blackened puddle of water.

"They're here," Tierney rasps out, terror stark on her face. "The Marfoir. In the woods. Es'tryl'lyan and I saw them just north of here. Two Elves, like none I've ever seen before. They've got...*curling* weapons. Wynter, they're coming for you. You have to leave. *Now!*"

No. It can't be. What happened to Cael and Rhys?

Tierney rushes inside the North Tower's circular foyer and slams the door shut behind her.

"Can you fight them?" I ask her fearfully. "With water magic?"

Tierney shakes her head emphatically. "No. Their magic is...twisted, somehow. They have water rune-sorcery—I can sense it on them. But it's all *wrong*. It's not connected to the forest. It's working *against* it. They've got these shadow-runes. Not the normal silver runes of the Alfsigr Elves." She turns to Wynter, savagely decided. "You need to come with me *now*! Es'tryl'lyan and I will get you out of here."

For a brief second, Ariel, Wynter and I are frozen as the horrific situation crushes down on all of us. And then Ariel straightens, her face becoming calmer and steadier than I've ever seen it. She places her hand firmly around Wynter's wrist, her voice low and implacable. "Give me your clothes."

Wynter recoils as she reads Ariel's thoughts. Her eyes widen with horror, and she shakes her head violently from side to side. "No. *No!*"

"Give me your clothes," Ariel insists. "I'll give you mine. I'll lead them away."

"*No!*" Wynter starts to cry.

"They will *kill* you," Ariel insists through gritted teeth, her calm giving way.

"But they'll take *you*," Wynter cries, struggling to pull away as Ariel holds on to her firmly. "They'll throw you in the Valgard prison and cut off your *wings!*"

"If you don't leave with Tierney and let me save you," Ariel spits out harshly, "I'll fight them so hard, they'll have no choice but to kill me." She stares Wynter down as she lets her ultimatum sink in.

Tears streaming down her cheeks, Wynter finally nods and gives in. With shaking hands, she begins to undress, and Tierney springs forward to help her.

"No," I protest, looking to Ariel. "There's got to be another way."

"There is no other way," Ariel says. "If I don't lead them off, there won't be enough time for her to get away." She turns her back to me, her voice steady and sure. "Unlace my tunic, Elloren."

Tears sting at my eyes over her use of my name. My hands tremble as I pull the laces loose and Ariel shrugs out of the long black tunic.

Wynter hands her Elfin garb to Ariel piece by piece, then Tierney helps Wynter into Ariel's black clothes as my heart twists to the point of breaking.

A hard pulse along my affinity lines cracks through my misery. The Wand of Myth buzzes to life against my ankle, and I've a sudden awareness of a tang of menacing power in the air, moving rapidly toward us.

I straighten, instantly alert. "They're almost here," I say in a daze. "I can feel them. They're coming in from the north."

"Bring Wynter to the Amaz," Ariel tells Tierney as she rushes to finish pulling on the rest of the Elfin clothes, grabbing up Wynter's white scarf from a wall peg.

Tierney shoulders open the door, and we all hastily gather outside the North Tower. It's a warm night, the stars bright in the sky.

Ariel is now dressed from head to toe in white, Wynter's scarf wrapped around her head to conceal her dark hair. Wynter has on Ariel's tunic and black pants, a dark cloak fastened around her slim frame with the hood pulled low, hiding both her snow-white hair and her wings.

Wynter is silently weeping, her face so distraught, it's as if she's holding all the grief in the world. Ariel looks north, toward the direction from which the Marfoir are coming, then turns back to Wynter. "I love you," she says flatly, as if stating an irrefutable fact.

"I love you, too, my sister," Wynter says, her voice breaking around her tears.

"No," Ariel says emphatically. "Not as a sister. I *love* you."

Wynter nods in understanding, her eyes full of pain. "I know."

"Goodbye," Ariel says to all of us, and then she turns, without hesitation, and walks straight toward the northern wilds—right into the path of the Marfoir. She flicks her wings, and they fan open to their full size, washed in silver by the moonlight.

I realize, as tears fall from my eyes, that Ariel is the most heroic person I have ever met.

"Get back inside!" Tierney hisses at me as she pulls Wynter in front of her. The Kelpie rises up from under them, and Tierney gives me one last fraught look before she and Wynter take off like a shot toward the northwestern wilds.

No. No. No.

My heart constricts as I watch them disappear into the pitch-black forest.

Stinging pain sizzles along my abdomen, like lines of insects biting, and I pull in a sharp breath, reaching toward my center.

Sage's rune, I realize with burgeoning fright.

Two spectral figures on ivory horses slip out of the northern forest and into view. Ariel halts just before them as a paralyzing terror seizes hold of me.

The Marfoir are taller than Elves should be, their limbs bizarrely stretched out, their eyes too big. Insectile and dark gray. An ancient, slithering malice washes over me as Ariel turns and breaks into a run back to the North Tower, her eyes thrown open wide and locking on to mine.

"Ariel!" The cry bursts from me as I set off at a sprint toward her.

The two Marfoir raise their hands in unison, their palms marked by gray runes. Lines of shadow scythe toward Ariel and twist around her limbs and mouth.

Ariel lets out a strangled cry as she's yanked roughly to the ground.

A flood of outrage surges through me. "Get away from her!"

The eyes of the Marfoir flick to me. They move their palms toward me, and an invisible solid mass slams into my body, knocking the wind from my lungs and hurling me into the air and back several feet to land with a painful thud on my side, my hip and elbow painfully jarred.

I move to get up and realize I'm pinned to the ground by

a web of shadow, like an insect in a spider's clutches. Ariel is trapped as well, her mouth bound closed.

The Marfoir ride close, their cold, malignant eyes a roiling gray in their white faces, focused in on Ariel with deathly intent. And that's when I notice it—they have horns made of shadow emerging from their heads, the dark smoke spiraling up to disappear into a twirling mist at the points.

They dismount from their steeds in one unified motion, as if they're a mirror image of the same being. Together they flick out their long-fingered hands, and curved knives screw out from their palms, glinting in the moonlight.

They stalk toward Ariel, angling their knives toward her neck.

"Leave her alone!" I cry. "She's not Wynter Eirllyn!"

The Marfoir pause. One of them holds a palm out to me, and shadow bindings lash toward me, slapping around my mouth, my head. Gagging me.

The other Marfoir tears the ivory scarf from Ariel's head and wrenches her head back as Ariel hisses and struggles. The thing's mouth jerks into a sudden, gruesome frown as Ariel's spiky black hair is revealed. More shadow lines fly out from its hands, wrapping Ariel in a cocoon of darkness, only her wild, rebellious eyes still exposed.

The Marfoir lifts Ariel onto its horse as if she weighs nothing and hurls her over the animal's back as I fight against my bindings. The other Marfoir throws out shadow lines to secure Ariel to the horse.

I scream against the gag of shadow as the Marfoir ride off with her. When they're halfway across the field, headed toward the western wall of dark forest, all my bindings suddenly give way, tendriling into lines of smoke.

I surge to my feet and run after them as Ariel's raven shoots overhead like a small, black arrow, winging toward them.

"Ariel!" I scream.

But they've already disappeared, along with Ariel's raven.

I slow, then stop as desperation hits me with crippling strength. I know what they're going to do with her.

They'll hand Ariel over to the Gardnerians. And once the Gardnerians get hold of her, they'll throw her into the Valgard prison.

And once she's there, they'll cut off her wings.

The predawn sky is overcast and spitting rain as I watch the young Gardnerian fowler tie my missive onto the leg of a rune-hawk.

The Northern Spine is barely visible through the panoramic windows of the hawkery, shrouded in the morning fog. I watch as the rune-hawk is released into the damp gloom, winging its way north—but not to Lukas this time.

To Valasca, Alder and Tierney.

I feel myself honing into a battle-ready, tempered sword as I watch the bird disappear into the mist.

I trek back to the North Tower, my cloak pulled tight against the now-driving rain. A punishing wind has kicked up, and my steps are hurried against the quickly worsening weather.

I start up the North Tower's rain-drenched field, my heels sinking slightly into the muddied ground.

"Elloren."

I turn at the sound of my name, the voice muffled by the driving rain. A young man is running toward me from the direction of the University city. I squint to try to make out his face in the storm-darkened morning as a sense of powerful fire rushes through my affinity lines.

Heated recognition washes over me, and I set out at a run toward Yvan. His eyes blaze to gold as I throw my arms around him, emotion rushing through me in a powerful wave. "Elloren," he breathes, his heat blazing through my lines. Rain sheets down on us both as we cling tightly to each other.

What he's done cyclones up inside me, in one overpowering whorl, and I draw sharply back from him. "What are you doing here?" I cry. "You can't be here. This is *Gardneria* now."

"I *had* to come back." His voice is low and urgent as he clings to me. "Wynter and Ariel are in terrible danger. Cael and Rhys, too. I spoke to a fleeing Alfsigr diplomat. Their monarchy has ruled to kill Icarals. *All* of them, Elloren. They'll send the Marfoir—"

"They've already come," I tell him, trembling at the memory of those...*things.*

Yvan freezes, shock in his fiery gaze. His face twists with anguish as he steps back, his muscles tensing as he spits out what sounds like a frustrated curse in the Lasair language, and the rain sheets down on us both.

"Wynter escaped," I tell him breathlessly. "She's with Tierney, headed for Amaz lands. But Ariel..." I break off, my voice fracturing with emotion. "Yvan, the Gardnerians are sure to have her."

"*No.*"

I tell him of Ariel's sacrifice. How she impersonated Wynter to save her.

"I'm going after her," I tell him.

Yvan's eyes flare. "Do you know where they've taken her?"

I nod, my rain-soaked lips twitching with outrage. "The Mage Council has ordered that all Icarals be brought to the

Valgard prison, so I'm pretty sure that's where she is. But I have an idea of how I can get her out of there."

Yvan's eyes burn with solidarity. "I'll help you."

"It'll be dangerous," I tell him. "But I don't care. I don't care what it takes. We *can't* let them take her wings."

CHAPTER TWO

GLAMOUR

"Are you ready?" Valasca asks Tierney.

Tierney stands before us, trembling, her eyes a storm of emotion.

"I haven't seen my real self since I was three." Tierney's words come out in a constricted whisper. "I don't... I don't even remember what I looked like."

Yvan, Tierney, Valasca, Alder and I are gathered in the isolated circular barn. Dim lantern light gutters in the space, illuminating Ariel's raven who returned to us this morning, the canny bird perched high in the rafters. The faded pages of *The Book of the Ancients* lie scattered beneath our feet.

Alder grasps a black stone disc marked with a glowing scarlet rune. She holds a slender, streamlined branch in her other glimmering green hand.

Star Maple.

Tierney points to the rune-stone. "So, my glamour will flow into that?"

"Yes," Alder affirms, her posture serene and tall, her voice a melodic lull. She sets unblinking forest green eyes on Yvan and me. "Then we will transfer the glamour to the two of you."

Yvan meets Alder's unnervingly placid stare in that unflinching, intense way of his.

"All right, then," Tierney says, her face rigid with determination even as she trembles. "Let's do this."

Valasca glances toward the ceiling, and I follow her gaze.

Fitful, dark clouds are forming high above Tierney, rapidly spreading out to fill the barn's roof and obscuring the crisscrossing rafters. Threads of lightning pulse from cloud to cloud, eliciting an indignant caw from Ariel's raven.

Valasca looks to Tierney with concern. "We'll be right here," she tells her with steadfast reassurance. "We'll help you through this."

"Just do it," Tierney says roughly.

Alder moves toward her, the motion smooth and spare, as if she's gliding across the floor. She gently lowers her branch to Tierney's quaking shoulder as the clouds grow dense and fitful, so thick that I'm no longer able to see the rafters. Mist envelops us all, along with a cool dew that sets my skin prickling.

My eyes meet Yvan's through the mist as Alder begins a low chant in the flowing Dryad language, and I feel a tremor of surprise. It sounds so much like our Ancient Tongue, the sacred language used during our holy services.

A static energy picks up in the room. Tierney's storm-driven lightning increases, pulsing the mist with flashes of white.

Tierney's form abruptly shudders, and Alder steps back as Tierney's wavering form darkens. My eyes widen as she bulges and stretches, the dark mass of her straining outward, rippling like she's a molting insect.

A face forms in the darkened mass, contorted in pain—her eyes closed, her mouth open in a tortured, soundless circle.

Tierney's scream suddenly tears through the room, and the glamour springs away from her and into the rune-marked stone with a loud snap that reverberates down my spine.

For a split second, I'm aware of several things at once—Tierney collapsing to the ground. The clouds and lightning blinking out of existence, the mist abruptly clearing. The surface of the disc in Alder's hand now swirling gray and black, as if overtaken by a storm.

Tierney cries out in agony, her neck stretched backward, blue hair splayed out all around her, long scraps of cloth wrapped mercilessly tight around her body.

Valasca curses and pulls out a rune-knife. She throws herself onto Tierney, her knife a blur, and slices at what I realize is Tierney's childhood clothing, now much too small for her adult body.

Tierney's whole body loosens as she's freed from the cloth bindings, her chest heaving as she gulps in great lungfuls of air.

Valasca helps Tierney into a sitting position as Tierney gasps for breath and struggles to hold the tattered remains of the child-size dress over herself. I unbutton my cloak, swing it off and swiftly wrap it around her.

Alder's almost supernatural forest calm has been breached. She's staring at Tierney, her green eyes wide, the rune-stone clasped loosely in her hand, as if she's in a slight daze over what she's accomplished.

Stunned, I pick up one of the discarded cloth scraps, realizing that this is the dress Tierney must have been glamoured in—when she was three years old.

The dress has been rendered to glistening, viridian remnants, the fabric decorated with whirls of small, gleaming river-smoothed stones.

Lovingly hand-embroidered.

Tierney's skin is marked by bright red slashes where the too-small clothing tore at her skin.

Lake-blue skin that is not static in color.

Tierney's hair and skin both ripple dark blue, the color a perfect reflection of deep water. She glances up at me, her eyes such a dark blue they're almost black, with the same water-like quality as her skin. My cloak slips off her shoulders as she clutches it tightly against her front.

Her body, so long constricted by her Gardnerian skin, seems loosened and freed. And her features are no longer sharp and hard, but all lovely curves—her nose widened, her lips full and deep-blue, her ears pointed in two long, graceful swoops and her back flowing like a gently winding stream.

"What do I look like?" Tierney breathlessly asks me.

Tears fill my eyes. "You're beautiful. You're *so* beautiful."

Tierney extends an arm and views it in wonderment. Her nails are a gleaming opalescent blue. A laugh bursts from her. "I can breathe," she says, looking around at all of us, her voice breaking. "I can finally breathe freely." She pauses and takes a long breath. "It feels...so *good*." She rolls her shoulders. "I can *move*."

Valasca's gaze lights on a metal bucket nearby. She retrieves it, polishes its gleaming surface with the edge of her tunic, then solemnly brings it over to Tierney.

Tierney takes the bucket, swallowing nervously, her eyes sheened with tears and staunchly averted from the bucket's mirror-like surface. She takes a long, shuddering breath, her eyes meeting mine.

A warm tear rolls down my cheek, a laugh breaking through. "Go ahead. Take a look."

Tierney glances at her reflection and lets out a hard gasp, her hand flying up to cover her mouth. "I look like *her*," she chokes out. Her face twists as she starts to cry, her eyes screwing shut. "I look like my *mother*." She curls up, her arms around her knees, the bucket clattering to the ground and rolling over the pages of *The Book*.

Valasca's eyes fill with tears, her face tightening as she looks away. Yvan kneels down in front of Tierney, his hand coming to her arm. "Let me help you. I can heal where the clothing tore at your skin."

Tierney nods, sobbing, and Yvan gently places his hands over the angry, reddened marks on her body. One by one, the wounds fade under his Lasair touch. When he's done, Valasca hands Tierney a simple brown tunic and black pants, everyone averting their eyes as she rises and throws on the clothing.

When I turn back to look at Tierney, I'm surprised to see how much taller she is now. Tierney shifts her weight and looks down at her feet, as if testing her new legs, her wavy midnight blue hair cascading over her shoulders. Then she glances up at all of us, her smile radiating pure, unbridled joy. She bounces on her heels, seeming finally, *finally* comfortable in her own skin.

"Are you ready?" she asks Yvan and me, bold challenge now in her tone.

An anxious shiver ripples through me as Alder holds out the storming rune-stone. It's warm and fills my palm with a staticky prickle as I take it from her. Small gray-and-black clouds drift over its surface, the central scarlet rune gauzily luminescent through the shifting haze.

"Picture the form you want," Alder directs me. "In detail."

I close my eyes and bring Aunt Vyvian's face to mind. Her

graceful figure. A black tunic, riding skirt and cloak. I build the image, painting it in my mind, detail by detail.

Aunt Vyvian's braided hairstyle, delicate Ironflower earrings, swirling fastmarks, vivid green eyes...

When I'm confident my image of her is clear, I open my eyes and give a start. Aunt Vyvian looks out at me from the disc, the storm clouds hovering around her—so clear, it's as if someone shrank her down to size and tethered her there.

"Is that right?" Alder asks me, touching the disc with her long, green-sheened finger. "Is that her?"

I scrutinize the image. Unsure, I concentrate more fully on the exact line of Aunt Vyvian's jaw, the curve of her ears. Her face sharpens, bit by bit, until the image is finally the very picture of my powerful aunt.

Satisfied, I look to Alder. "That's her."

Alder nods and places her branch lightly on my shoulder. "Hold tight to the rune-stone," she tells me.

I clasp it tight in my hand and close my eyes as Alder chants a flowing spell.

A buzz of unsettled energy courses through me from Alder's wand. My skin tightens painfully, and I give a small cry, my eyes flying open. I'm immediately thrust into a near panic.

There's nothing but darkness before me, and my body is covered with an oily substance, my fingers slick against each other. The oil abruptly solidifies, constricting my body, the breath driven clear from my lungs. I gasp for air and almost lose my footing. Then the dark cloud abruptly breaks up and clears, and I'm able to pull in a long breath.

Alder's shimmering green face is before me. She lifts her chin, looking pleased. Yvan, Tierney and Valasca are regarding me with wide-eyed astonishment.

"I look like her, then?" I question, my pulse thudding.

"Scarily so," Tierney says, her usual sardonic tone seeping back.

I flex my fingers, my toes. Fidget and tense my muscles. It's disturbingly claustrophobic to be in someone else's skin while having a sense of my own body trapped just beneath it. I extend my arm and marvel at the sight of my aunt's shimmering arm, her fastmarked hands, her manicured nails. I reach up to touch my face. It's all smooth lines, the normally sharp bones of my cheeks drastically altered.

"Now hold the stone up and picture your aunt's guard," Alder says, her wand back on my shoulder.

I loosely cradle the rune-stone in my palm as I repeat the process again, calling up an image of Aunt Vyvian's guard, Isan, this time. Black hair, square jaw, broad chest, surly moss green eyes. When the image scried on to the stone seems right, I hand the disc to Yvan.

Yvan grows very still and closes his eyes, as if unfazed and oddly practiced in this. Alder places her branch on his shoulder and sends the glamour over him.

I watch, transfixed, as Yvan's hair flashes from brown to bright red, and then his form blurs and grows inky, sharpening and then coloring into... Isan.

Like Tierney and me, Yvan is completely altered—stocky and a good ten years older in appearance, dressed in Gardnerian military garb.

Yvan lets out a long breath and looks down at his splayed-out hands with apparent curiosity. I catch his eyes, now a darker shade of green, as he flashes me a penetrating, almost guarded look.

I turn to Alder. "How long do we have?"

"A day, perhaps," Alder says evenly. "Possibly less." She points her branch at the rune-stone in my hand. "This glamour is very strong, but it will strain to pull back into the rune-stone more and more as the hours pass. You'll have to be quick."

We all make our way outside into the predawn darkness, Yvan and I mounting the horses Valasca has secured for our journey. Ariel's raven flies out of the barn into the sky.

"Go," Tierney prods me, her looks mind-bendingly altered, but her voice unchanged and hardened with purpose. "Go save Ariel from those monsters."

CHAPTER
THREE

ARIEL

"Open the gates! Make way for Mage Vyvian Damon!" a granite-faced soldier yells at two sentries who are stationed just inside the prison's high, iron-barred gates.

My horse shies in response to the screech of iron as the gate's locks are undone.

The prison looms before us, built in the style of most Gardnerian architecture—gigantic, carved trees forming the walls, their branches coalescing to support the expansive roof. But instead of being fashioned from our sacred Ironwood, the building is crafted from obsidian stone.

A hexagonal wall surrounds the immense prison, edged with rows of iron spikes pointed to the heavens. Each corner of the wall is capped off by a guard tower that houses a single archer. It's a veritable fortress—I don't know how we would have ever gotten in without the glamour.

The gruff soldier helps me dismount while Yvan deftly swings off his horse, handing both sets of reins over to one of the sentries and giving brusque orders regarding the care of the animals.

The other sentry gives a small bow, pushes open the gate and motions me forward. I glance back to find Yvan just behind me, and we share a swift, grimly resolved look. I turn forward once more, take a deep breath and step through the prison gates.

The iron gates clank shut behind us, and I wince inwardly as the screeching lock is thrown back into place.

I gaze up at the towering prison and swallow nervously. The sheer size of the building is daunting, as is the overwhelming number of guards.

And there's iron everywhere.

Iron-tipped arrows. Iron swords propped against the walls. And thick iron planks stripe the surrounding wall from top to bottom.

As if the prison was built to withstand a Fae assault.

I fight the urge to grab Yvan and run away from this malevolent place.

The young, square-jawed sentry wordlessly escorts us toward the prison's main entrance, an imposing pair of wooden doors etched with a giant, leafy tree. We wait as the sentry slips inside the doors to announce our arrival.

A few moments later, the door is opened again by the sentry and a willowy older man stands in its frame. The elderly Mage's green eyes calmly regard us through silver-rimmed spectacles, his demeanor coolly intellectual. His black robes bear the crest of the Gardnerian Surgeons' Guild—a tree made of surgeons' tools. A wand is sheathed at his side, and his garb is marked with Level Three Mage stripes.

"Mage Damon," the surgeon fawns, bowing slightly. "Another surprise visit. But certainly not an unwelcome one."

"Bring me to the Icarals," I say, trying to mimic my aunt's

smoothly domineering tone. "I've come for the one called Ariel Haven."

He nods deferentially, steps back and motions for us to enter with a refined wave of his slender hand.

Heart thudding, I step inside the prison door.

The circular foyer resembles a midnight forest, the carved, obsidian trees dense and leaning in. Stone branches tangle overhead, the tree trunks bracketing several shadowy hallways. Green lumenstone lanterns are set about the space and line the multiple hallways, washing everything in a swampy glow. I glance down at my fastmarked hand, the green glimmer of my skin enhanced by the eerie light.

"You have secured an order of execution this time?" the surgeon inquires lightly, as if treading carefully.

I beat back a tremor of panic. "No. No order. I'll obtain it from the Council and send it to you. We're convening in less than an hour, so I don't have time for technicalities."

The surgeon dips his head, going soft and pliant. "Of course, Mage Damon."

We follow him down a series of obsidian hallways, the heels of my shoes clicking against the black geometric tiles of the perfectly polished floors, Yvan's steps echoing behind me.

At the end of one darkened hall, the surgeon unhitches a ring of keys from his belt and unlocks a heavy wooden door. We trail him through the door and down a spiraling stone staircase, the air around us cooling as we descend.

We reach the bottom of the stairs and enter a tunneling hallway washed in dim green light. Faint groaning and nasal chattering sound up ahead.

I can make out the foul stench of nilantyr long before we reach the arching entrance to the dungeons, the odor triggering a wave of nausea and dark memory.

And there's something else. Something that sends ice knifing down my spine. Somewhere far ahead, hidden in the bowels of this malignant place, a child is screaming.

The surgeon pauses to grab a large brass ring of keys from a hook set in the wall. A series of iron-barred prison cells bracket the hallway just ahead of us.

It's hard to make it all out, the lumenstone more sparsely hung down here, the greenish glow fainter. But I have a strange sense of déjà vu.

A dream I once had. A dream in which I was trying to free Marina and little Fern from a cage. In this exact green-lit dungeon.

My eyes are drawn up to the ceiling of tangling, stone branches as a translucent white bird shimmers into view, then blinks out of sight. Apprehension ripples through me, and the Wand pressed into my boot warms against my ankle.

We pass under an archway of branches into a hallway filled with cavernous, barred cells. I can't make out anything at first, but my eyes soon adjust to the light.

I turn, pausing in front of the first cell, and that's when I see him.

A male Icaral is crouched inside, eyeing me with milky white, soulless eyes, his spindly arms wrapped tight around even spindlier legs. Wingless, ragged stumps jut out where his wings used to be.

The cell is cold and small, empty except for a hard wooden bed without blankets and an iron chamber pot.

And a metal bowl full of nilantyr berries.

The Icaral opens his blackened lips and hisses at me, baring sharp, rotted teeth.

Recognition spasms through me.

I know this Icaral—he's the one who escaped that day I was attacked in Valgard.

Horror and pity rush over me like a wave, forcing me

backward, away from the broken creature, until I collide with the iron bars of another cell.

Clawed hands come from behind and grasp my arms, pinning me to the bars at my back, foul breath at my ear. Terror leaps into my throat as I whip my head around and stare into the empty eyes of another male Icaral. "I will rip its arms off," he hisses at me, hatred burning in his emaciated face. "Like they rip and tear at our wings."

The surgeon jams his wand through the cell's bars and mutters a spell. A bright blue explosion bursts all around me, and the Icaral's piercing grip falls away.

I stumble forward and whirl around to find the Icaral knocked to the ground, a network of glowing blue lines traversing his body as he writhes in agony.

I struggle to catch my breath, trembling with both fear and horror at the surgeon's casual use of torture. My hands rub at my stinging forearms as the surgeon considers me with a slightly perplexed expression.

Like something doesn't quite add up.

"You need to stay away from the Icarals' cells, Mage Damon," he says, his brow creased, as if he's surprised by the need to advise my aunt.

My heart blasting against my rib cage, I struggle to regain my composure. I force myself to take a few deep breaths while the surgeon eyes me with budding suspicion.

You have to be Aunt Vyvian, I chastise myself. *Calm down! You have to get Ariel out of here!*

"Where is she?" I ask, forcing my chin up and assuming a haughty expression.

The surgeon's face relaxes, as if he's more comfortable with my predictably imperious behavior. "The creature is housed at the end of the hallway."

Housed.

What a wildly inappropriate way of describing this nightmarish dungeon.

Horror and acute distress seep into me as we walk down the curved, winding hall and I come face-to-face with the Icarals imprisoned here. I try not to stare, try not to slow my regal, unsympathetic gait, but I can't help but hear them, to see them out of the corner of my eyes.

There's one, a female. She looks to be about thirteen years of age, dressed in rags, her hair pulled out in scabby patches. She's banging her head against the stone wall of her cell again and again as her wing stumps frantically flap behind her, the rhythmic thud echoing after us as my heart begins to fracture in my chest. We pass another female, this one even younger. She's crouched in the corner of her cell, muttering darkly to herself in a high-pitched voice.

Other Icarals cry out strange, twisted things, rattling the bars as we pass them.

"I am filthy, so *filthy*..."

"I will fly at you! They tried to take my wings, but I *hid* them!"

"Look into my eyes! I will turn you into one of us!"

They're all wingless, with the same dead, broken eyes.

A catastrophic outrage pours into me.

My own people, we've made them this way.

They could be whole and unbroken, like Wynter, if the Gardnerians had only left them in peace. Instead, they've been tortured and drugged into insanity.

I realize the Icarals that attacked me months ago were probably tormented like this, perhaps since they were small children.

Like Ariel.

A fierce wave of compassion for all of them, even the ones

who tried to kill me, washes over me along with a staggering, nauseating fury.

We pass by a few vacant cells scattered among the occupied ones—the empty cells that probably once "housed" the Icarals my own aunt methodically hauled before the Mage Council for execution.

Devastated, I turn toward Yvan. He's staring at one of the Icarals, his eyes wide, his face gone sickly pale. I've never seen him so rattled before, and it fills me with deep concern.

"Do not look directly at the Icarals," the surgeon instructs Yvan and me, his tone clinical. "It's polluting to the soul, bad for the spiritual health of a Mage."

"I assure you," I reply, wanting to cut him down and free every last Icaral imprisoned in this evil place, "I have no desire to stare at the vile creatures."

The surgeon seems pleased with my response and turns to lead us farther down the nightmare hallway.

The child's screams split the dank air, cutting through the Icarals' ceaseless moaning and dark mutterings.

"I apologize for the disturbance." The surgeon half turns toward me as we walk. "We apprehended a young one only yesterday. I'll be removing the creature's wings later on today. That should quiet it down a bit. Although, as you can see—" he waves his hand dismissively toward the noisy cells that surround us "—not *nearly* enough."

"Apprehended?" I'm stunned by the use of such a term to refer to a child.

The surgeon presses his lips into a thin, disapproving line. "*Never* underestimate the ability of these Evil Ones to disguise their true natures, Mage Damon. Even a very young one. The mother of this one was completely under this creature's thrall, convinced it's not a demon, but a harmless child.

Thank goodness her neighbor alerted us to the Icaral's existence. Who knows what future evil could have come of it?"

"And the mother?" I ask, thinking of Sage and little Fyn'ir, wanting to retch. "Where is she now?"

His expression tightens. "Dwelling with the Evil Ones, no doubt. Her soul was so polluted by the evil being she created, that after we took it from her, she killed herself rather than live without its vile presence."

A wave of dizziness threatens to overtake me, and I bite down hard on my cheek to steady myself.

"There it is," he says, a look of disgust on his face as he gestures toward an open cell.

There's a woman inside, dressed in dark apothecary garb marked with Level Two Mage stripes, a wand sheathed at her side. She has a pinched face and gray hair pulled back into a tight bun, and she's struggling with a child of about three. A little girl.

The woman appears to be trying to force-feed nilantyr to the child, the little one's white tunic stained down the front with black vomit as she whips her head from side to side, her eyes wide and bulging, her mouth closed defiantly tight.

Seeing us, the apothecary abandons her task and rises, the child fleeing from her with desperation and launching back into her panicked screaming. She flaps her black wings rapidly and futilely, only able to lift herself slightly off the ground. She falls back onto the stone floor, restrained by an iron shackle locked around her ankle. The shackle is attached to the wall by a short metal chain that rattles against the floor as the child pulls at it as far as it will stretch.

Horrified, I glance back at Yvan, whose shocked, pale expression has morphed into one of undisguised rage. Hectic red colors his cheeks, and his hand clutches the hilt of his broadsword so tightly that his knuckles have turned white.

"Do not look directly into its eyes," our guide cautions the apothecary, who's resumed her attempts to drug the child.

"I will not, you can be sure," she replies, flustered and sweating from the effort. She gives up again for a moment, stands and smooths her skirts as the little girl shrieks and pulls desperately at her chain. "I'm finding it particularly difficult to sedate this one."

"Well, tie it down if need be," he counters with cool efficiency, stepping into the cell and handing the apothecary a coil of twine from a nearby table. He looks to me apologetically. "I'm sorry that you have to witness this, Mage Damon. You can see that dealing with these creatures is no easy task."

"Quite," I reply, bile rising in my throat.

"We are of your same mind, Mage Damon," he cloyingly simpers. "It's a wonder that the Mage Council has insisted on keeping them alive for so long." He shakes his head and clicks his tongue disapprovingly. "That will soon change, with blessed Vogel at the helm of our great Magedom, and with your courageous intervention. The Council needs to realize that killing Icarals is an act of kindness. There are those who have become squeamish about the idea of putting them out of their misery, full of romantic notions that their souls can yet be saved if their wings are removed. If they could labor but one day with these creatures, they would not hesitate to take a much harder line."

"No doubt." My heart beats high in my chest.

He smiles obsequiously. "You came here with a task at hand, and I digress into politics. My apologies."

The little girl is screaming even louder as the woman goes about tying her up with the heavy twine, having to practically sit on her to do it.

"Where is Ariel Haven?" I ask, struggling to keep my voice icy calm.

He motions across the hallway. "There."

I turn, and my heart leaps in my chest.

Ariel. Right in the cell behind me all this time.

Ariel is slumped down in the shadows of her cell, sitting listlessly on a hard wooden bed, her head resting against the stone wall.

It's only been a few days, but she's shockingly emaciated, her half-closed eyes recessed into hollowed-out sockets. Her gaze is unfocused, her mouth curled up at the edges into a numb, blissful grin.

A bowl half full of nilantyr berries is cradled under her arm.

Grief rocks through me. *Ariel had won. She had broken free of the nightmare bonds of the drug.*

And now they've destroyed her all over again.

An overpowering, volcanic rage flashes through me.

"I don't think you'll have any difficulty bringing it to the Council," the surgeon idly comments. "Unlike the Icaral child, this one is more than happy to consume as much nilantyr as we're willing to give it. In fact, I believe this one would kill itself if we simply gave it enough of the drug, thus saving the Council the trouble of having to execute it."

My chest constricts, the rage mounting.

Ariel isn't just sedated. She's practically comatose. And, by the looks of things, the soldiers here had one hell of a time getting her to this point. She's covered in bruises and lacerations, and one of her wings appears to be hanging at an odd angle, as if it's been partially torn off, a trail of dark blood seeping from it. She's wearing the same Elfin clothes she was dressed in when the Marfoir seized her, and they're filthy and torn.

A crash sounds behind me, and the woman shrieks.

I wheel around. Yvan is standing over the surgeon and the

apothecary, who are now cowering on the floor, their arms held up protectively in front of themselves. Yvan is grasping their wands in one fist, his other hand pointing his broadsword at them, his teeth bared.

"What are you doing?" I cry, frozen to the spot.

Yvan ignores me, keeping his eyes pinned on the surgeon and the apothecary. The little girl continues to scream her lungs out as she lies tied up on the floor, rolling back and forth in desperation.

"Eat the nilantyr!" Yvan orders the surgeon and the apothecary, gesturing sharply toward the bowl.

They nod compliantly, all color drained from their faces. The surgeon reaches for the bowl with a shaking hand. He grabs a handful of the berries and stuffs them into his mouth, then offers the bowl to the apothecary who fearfully does the same.

"Keep eating!" Yvan snarls at them. "Eat until you pass out, or I will kill you both!" He glances over his shoulder at me, a rigid set to his jaw. "We're taking the child with us."

I look to the terrified little girl who's tied up and rolling around on the floor, screaming. Of course we're getting her out of here. We can't leave her here with these monsters.

"I want to save all of them," Yvan says fiercely, "but we can't. But we *can* save her."

I nod, my body breaking out into a cold sweat.

The surgeon and the apothecary have grown limp, their bodies slumping down against the stone wall and eventually falling over onto the floor, their limbs awkwardly draped over each other.

Yvan sheathes his sword, breaks their wands in his fist and throws the pieces off to the side. He kneels to check inside their mouths. Confident they've swallowed the nilantyr, Yvan grabs the twine the apothecary trussed the little girl up with and ties both the surgeon and the apothecary up in a similar way. Then he retrieves the surgeon's ring of keys, takes hold of the little girl's foot and unlocks her shackle. He tosses the brass keys to me and turns his attention back to the the child.

She's screaming at an even louder volume, her green eyes huge in her face.

"Give me your cloak," Yvan orders, his tone relentless and stiff.

I unfasten and shrug off my cloak, then toss it to Yvan, and he immediately begins tearing long strips from it.

Yvan tries to gently coax the child to calm down, but she's completely hysterical.

"I'm sorry," he murmurs to her as he uses one strip to blindfold the girl and ties another around her mouth, cinching it tight behind her head, her cries now low and muffled. He wraps her whole body in a larger swath of fabric until she's completely immobilized. Then he grabs the twine, picks the child up, stands and turns to me.

Every muscle in his body is tense and ready for a fight, his eyes blazing, as if he's ready to take on an army to deliver all of us to safety.

"Tie her to my back." He tosses me the twine and holds the little girl firmly against his back. I wrap the twine around his chest and shoulders and over the child again and again until the little girl, who is violently straining against her bonds, seems relatively secure.

"Now get Ariel," Yvan orders.

Key ring in hand, I go to Ariel's cell and unlock the door. It swings open with a rusty creak.

"Ariel," I croon as I enter the cell. I place a hand on her thin shoulder, despairing for her. "You need to come with me, love."

Her barely conscious head lazily turns to face me, her blackened smile widening. I wrap an arm around her frail body and help her rise from the bed.

Ariel looks over at the surgeon and the apothecary and starts to laugh, high and manic, as if she finds the sight of them funny. She turns back to me and gives me another wide, twisted grin.

"Elloren," Yvan says, his voice harsh. "I'm going to pretend to take you hostage. I'm a traitorous guard you thought you could trust, but I'm really in league with the Evil Ones, hell-bent on rescuing Icarals. I'm going to be rough with you. If they don't believe this, they'll kill us."

I struggle to calm my breathing, my emotions reeling but my mind grasping the details of his new plan.

"Hold tight to Ariel," Yvan orders. "We're getting out of here."

"I order every one of you to stand down!" Yvan bellows as we burst out the front doors of the prison.

Yvan's arms are rough around me as he holds his knife to my throat. I grasp Ariel's bony arm while she giggles dazedly.

Initially, the guards do exactly the opposite of standing down. The archers in the towers nock arrows, and the sentries on the ground draw their broadswords—until it dawns on them who I am, and their weapons fall away.

"Make one move," Yvan threatens, tightening his hold on me, "and I will kill her."

The guards remain motionless, and Yvan wastes no time deliberating.

We hurry toward the exit gate, one guard yelling for it to be opened immediately.

"Stop!" a deep voice commands just as we reach the gate,

the man's voice so thick with authority that everyone freezes and turns.

A burly man in a lieutenant's uniform with Level Four Mage stripes strides toward us, pointing accusingly. "They are *not* who they appear to be!"

Oh, sweet Ancient One, help us.

The other guards seem bewildered, their eyes flicking back and forth from us to the lieutenant, as if unsure what to do.

"Stay back!" Yvan yells, yanking my head back, his fist knotted in my hair, the sharp edge of his knife pressed to the skin of my throat.

"You are an impostor!" the lieutenant bellows at Yvan. He halts a few feet away from us and draws his wand. "I just received a missive from Mage Vyvian Damon. She's on her way here as we speak to bring the Icaral, Ariel Haven, before the Mage Council for immediate execution."

He points his sword at me. "*You* are not Vyvian Damon." His eyes track to Yvan. "And I'm willing to bet that *you* are not her chief guard, Isan Browen. Gardnerians, draw iron arrows!"

The archers raise their bows and point iron-tipped arrows straight at us.

"But, Lieutenant," one of the men ventures, "I know Isan, and he looks—"

"I don't *care* how he looks!" the lieutenant snaps. "It's an illusion! A glamour!" He turns back to face me. "You're Sidhe Fae, aren't you? Out to steal Icaral demons? What's hiding under that glamour of yours?" He pokes me in the side with his sword.

Quick as a blur, Yvan drops the knife and wrests the sword from the lieutenant in one smooth motion. The little girl on Yvan's back screams, the sound muffled through the strip of fabric.

"Easy, Fae," the lieutenant says as he backs away from Yvan. He glances around at the growing number of archers surrounding us, a triumphant smile forming on his lips. "Planning on taking us all on? Making a run for it? You're in the middle of Gardneria. How exactly are you going to get out?" He gestures toward the impossibly high stone walls. "There are iron spikes lining the top of these walls. And all our arrow tips are made of iron."

Yvan's jaw flexes as he continues to point the sword at the lieutenant, his face tight, his body rigid.

"Sidhe Fae rescuing two winged Icarals," the lieutenant observes with a trace of sly amusement, shaking his head from side to side. "What could you be using them for? This *is* a puzzle." He angles his head toward one soldier. "Malik, send word to High Mage Vogel that we've apprehended two Sidhe. In the meantime, we'll just wait for Mage Damon to arrive."

Soldiers encircle us but keep a wary distance as the lieutenant discusses plans with three of his subordinates in tones too low to make out.

The sun has newly set, the otherworldly light of the lumenstone casting everything around us in a greenish glow. I touch Yvan's shoulder with a trembling hand, and he inclines his head toward me in response, his eyes darting from soldier to soldier.

"What are we going to do?" I ask, panic mounting.

He doesn't answer, and I hear him swallow hard. "I don't know," he finally admits.

Panic rushes over me and consumes me with debilitating fear.

And that's when I cave. Grasping Ariel tight, I bow my head and begin to pray. Repetitive, familiar prayers for mercy, for protection, for a miracle.

THE IRON FLOWER

"What are you doing?" Yvan snarls.

"Praying," I answer, tears streaming down my face.

He makes a noise of disgust. "In the words of a religion that hates Ariel and me?" he asks in a seething whisper. "That hates the child strapped to my back?"

"They're the *only words I know*!" I cry, my body starting to shake. "We need a *miracle,* and that's what I'm praying for!"

I go back to desperately chanting the prayer for the Ancient One to bring about a miracle in the middle of the Realm of Death, the hope-filled words keeping me from completely falling apart.

"There are no miracles," Yvan hisses.

A thunderous whoosh passes over us, high above.

My head jerks up along with Yvan's as flames burst into the sky and roar down, lighting the world orange. Yvan throws Ariel and me behind himself as he thrusts out one palm, holding the fire at bay. A punishing heat presses down on us, everything around us suddenly alight in a deafening explosion of fire.

Incoherent yelling and screams sound from every direction. The gold and orange and bright white of the flames leap everywhere, sparks flying above like a million shooting stars, the heat searing. More long jets of fire blast down from the heavens as iron-tipped arrows whiz overhead.

And then a large, ground-shaking crash directly behind us. As if the Ancient One himself has heard my prayer and descended from the heavens.

Yvan loosens his hold on me, and we turn.

Naga.

The dragon jerks her head back as she catches sight of Ariel, fury blazing in her eyes. Her gaze slides to Yvan, her serpentine head flowing down until her firelit eyes are only inches away from his.

"Oh, Naga," Yvan tells her, his voice strangled with emotion, "you have *very* good timing."

Ariel's raven lights on Naga's scaled head, the bird's black eyes darting over us.

You blessedly ingenious bird. You found Naga.

Yvan places his hand on the dragon's neck, and they stare at each other for a protracted moment. Then Yvan turns to me, new purpose to his movements. "Get Ariel on Naga's back! You, too! We've got to go! *Now!*"

It's hard to hear Yvan over the roar of the fire, but his hand gestures make his meaning clear. Not wasting a second, Naga flattens herself to the ground.

I climb on to her back and pull Ariel up in front of me, throwing my arms on either side of Ariel's frail body and grasping onto the two horns that protrude from Naga's shoulders. Yvan swings on behind us, his hands grasping the horns just above mine.

Naga springs up, spreads her wings and leaps into the air. Her wings whoosh down, and we rise and rise in rhythmic jolts as I struggle to hold on. Yvan's arms hold steady around both me and Ariel as men yell and arrows fly overhead and past our sides. One arrow nicks Naga's remaining ear, and she gives a roar of outrage. She whips her head around and breathes out several more columns of fire, expeditiously taking out the remaining guard towers, then swoops up, racing away from the prison.

I drape myself low over Ariel's frail, semiconscious body, the dragon's warm back cutting down on the chilling wind, the air growing colder and colder as we rise. Yvan presses his warm chest against my back, effectively cutting the chill behind me.

Before I know it, the prison is a firelit, smoking nightmare fading into the distance behind us, the glittering center of Valgard just beyond it.

Yvan reaches around me to clasp Ariel's torn wing. I hold her wing steady as Yvan places his hand over the bloodied tear, his fire rippling through me toward Ariel.

A few moments later, when he removes his hand, Ariel's wing is reattached, hanging straight once more.

"Can you help her regain consciousness?" I ask him anxiously.

"No," he says ruefully. "She's taken too much of the nilantyr—purging it is beyond my abilities. She needs a healer with more training than I have."

Soon we're flying over farmland, then black wilderness at a steady pace, the moon lighting our way, gray clouds drifting lazily across the starlit sky. I let out a long, shuddering breath.

For a long while, we fly on, Naga shooting through the sky like our own powerful arrow, Ariel's raven winging just below us. We fly over broad expanses of forest, the white peaks of the Northern and Southern Spines growing closer up ahead. And then we're flying over the gigantic spikes of the Northern Spine, the view breathtaking and familiar and terrifying all at once.

"Your glamour's fading," Yvan tells me after a time, his breath warm on my neck. I glance down at my hands in the bright moonlight—my *own* hands, with chipped nails and shimmering skin blessedly free of fastmarks, and I'm surprised by the glamour's imperceptible release. I turn to find Yvan looking like Yvan again, blessedly back in his own skin.

It's so quiet up here after all the chaos and noise of Valgard, the only sounds the heavy whooshing of Naga's huge wings and the muffled whimpers of the little girl strapped to Yvan's back.

"Where's Naga taking us?" I wonder as cold air rushes over us.

"To the Amaz." Yvan's voice has turned grimly decisive.

I whip my head toward him. "No. You can't go there. They'll *kill* you."

His gaze is resolute. "Ariel needs their care," he says. "And it's the only place we can bring the child. The only place she'll be safe. They'll shelter her, you know they will. They'll protect her."

"Land near the border," I insist. "You *can't* land in the middle of Amaz territory."

"We have to!" he counters, suddenly fierce. "There's no time to lose. They'll have rune-healers, and Ariel needs immediate care. We don't know how much nilantyr she took—she could *die*!"

My hands tighten around Naga's horns as my thoughts reel into panic. We can't do this—it will be suicide for him. Maybe suicide for us all. You don't just land what appears to be a Gardnerian military dragon in the middle of Amaz territory with a male on its back and live to tell the tale.

But it's too late to argue.

We crest the Spine, and the rune-light of Cyme comes into view just as Naga begins her rapid descent.

CHAPTER FOUR

BATTLE CRY

Naga flies us right over the Amaz city as she descends at breakneck speed.

Holy Ancient One. Holy Ancient One. Holy Ancient One.

I thrust out my rune-marked forearm, desperately hoping the rune Sage placed on my forearm will spare us from an explosive death.

Pain bursts through my arm as my rune-mark makes contact with the city's translucent dome, the dome flashing scarlet as the rune on my arm blasts out rays of emerald light.

We hurtle through the shield, the air instantly warming as Naga begins a series of complicated wing maneuvers in an attempt to slow our speed.

Chaos breaks out underneath us.

Women and children cry out in alarm and rush into nearby dwellings. Small deer scatter away from the wide central plaza as Amaz soldiers on horseback gallop in from every direction. The soldiers rapidly fill the plaza and send up a rune-amplified sound that's so terrifying, I hope to never hear it again.

The Amaz battle cry.

It's extreme, horrific violence, rivers of blood, bone-crushing blows and every fear that lurks inside your mind wrought into one, bloodcurdling sound.

As their unified cry grows louder, scores of rune-marked blades, axes, swords and scythes are hastily pulled out as row upon row of glowing rune-arrows are drawn back, all pointed at a single, enormous target.

Us.

That's when I start yelling at the top of my lungs.

"Valasca! Alder! Freyja! Queen Alkaia! It's me! Elloren Gardner! *Don't shoot!*"

Vertigo assaults me as the torchlit plaza and central Goddess statue rise up to meet us, far too fast.

We're going to crash.

I close my eyes, the Amaz battle cry searing through me as Naga hits the ground with bone-jarring force. I cry out in primal terror as I'm thrown from her back and hit the stone of the plaza hard.

Soldiers swarm around us, yelling orders to each other. I scramble toward Ariel, who is sprawled on the ground, passed out.

"She needs a healer!" I cry out as soldiers surround us, yelling out orders.

I whip my head around to find Yvan on his knees, his palms held up in surrender, blood trickling down the side of his face. Three rune-archers have closed in, their scarlet-tipped arrows drawn and inches away from his head. Alcippe is looming over him, her rune-axe raised in her fists.

Their battle cry fades, and all movement stills, as if everyone has suddenly been turned to stone. The only distinct sound left is the muffled moaning of the Icaral child.

Surrounding us are ring upon ring of Amaz soldiers, many

on horseback, all with weapons drawn. Naga lays flattened on the ground with six soldiers surrounding her, rune-spears pointed directly at her neck. Her eyes are shut, her wings folded in, her posture deliberately passive.

"She needs a *healer*!" I cry again, cradling Ariel's head in my hands, my voice rough with desperation. "We just rescued her from the Valgard prison!"

"What is on your back?" Alcippe demands of Yvan, her face twisted with hatred.

Yvan keeps his head cautiously down. "An Icaral child."

Murmurs of shock go up as Alcippe jerks her chin at two soldiers. The young women draw rune-blades and sever the bindings that secure the little girl to Yvan's back. Then they lift her off Yvan's back and carefully cut through the twine that restrains her, the child's untethered wings now flapping frantically. The minute the soldiers remove the cloth around her mouth, she breaks into a high-pitched, terrified scream.

The soldiers finish freeing the child, both of the women talking gently to her, trying to calm her down, but she takes one terrified look at Yvan, breaks free of the soldiers' grip and attempts to fly away. She only manages to lift a few feet off the ground before she hurtles back down, hampered by her uncontrolled panic and tears, the soldiers rushing in to help her.

Alcippe takes in the child's incapacitating fear of Yvan with narrowed eyes. Her expression turns lethal, the veins on her temples and neck bulging. She hoists her rune-axe higher.

"No!" I cry out in protest just as Freyja bursts through the ranks of soldiers on horseback.

"Stand down!" she commands.

Alcippe hesitates, axe still raised, her breathing heavy with rage. Yvan has moved into a crouch, his eyes pinned on Alcippe with predatory stillness.

"Freyja!" I beg. "I need to speak to Queen Alkaia. I swear to you, Naga and Yvan mean you no harm! They rescued the Icarals. Please...*help us.*" I incline my head toward Ariel. "She needs a healer. *Please!*"

"This male has defiled the Goddess's own sacred ground!" Alcippe spits out at Freyja, refusing to lower her rune-axe. "He is an abomination! Look how the child flees from him! He *must* be killed!"

The two young soldiers are struggling to both comfort and keep hold of the screaming, panicked Icaral child. Freyja's face is tense and undecided as Alcippe silently entreats her for permission to kill Yvan.

"You will all stand down," a dominating voice calls out as hooves sound on the plaza's stone.

Valasca rides in on her red-maned black horse, Queen Alkaia mounted behind her, Alder riding in beside them.

"Ariel needs a healer," I cry out to Valasca, growing frantic. Valasca nods and calls out over the crowd.

"Lower your weapon, Alcippe," Queen Alkaia says, so calmly she almost sounds blasé. "Stand down, all of you."

Weapons are lowered as Valasca slides off the horse and helps Queen Alkaia dismount, supporting the queen as she makes her way toward us.

"But... My Queen..." Alcippe protests, her face twisted with rage.

"Patience, Alcippe." Queen Alkaia holds up a hand. "We will deal with the male in a moment."

Two older women with elaborate facial tattoos shoulder past the soldiers and make for Ariel, lowering themselves beside her. I move aside as the women quickly assess Ariel, then hastily pull small rune-stones from shoulder sacks to place on Ariel's forehead, her throat, her shoulders. A scarlet glow forms, then radiates out from stone to stone, rapidly encompassing Ariel in a luminous web of light. Naga carefully slinks toward us, fierce concern in her slit-pupiled eyes.

"Ariel!" a familiar voice cries out.

Naga lifts her head as Wynter's slim figure breaks through the crowd, her thin black wings flapping in distress. She's garbed in a purple tunic and pants, the tunic modified slightly for her wings.

The crimson rune-web encompassing Ariel grows patchy and faded. The rune-healers mutter to each other, their brows tightly creased, one of the women shaking her head in dismay. Anguish tightens Naga's fiery eyes as the rune-web's light blinks out.

"I'm sorry," one of the healers says to me, her eyes grave. "She is poisoned beyond help. There is nothing we can do."

Naga flows in around the healers. She gently picks up Ariel, hugging her close to her shimmering, black-scaled breast, cradling Ariel's head in one dangerously taloned hand. She draws back and looks deeply into Ariel's emaciated face.

The dragon's face fills with unbearable pain as she glances wildly around at all of us. She cranes her neck toward the heavens and lets loose a heartbreaking roar.

"Is she dead?" I cry to Wynter. A sob tears from my throat. "She can't be dead!"

Wynter goes to Naga, who is now nuzzling Ariel's filthy hair with her sharp snout. She places a slender hand on Naga's scaled shoulder.

"'She is not dead,'" Wynter says with effort, speaking for Naga, her own silent tears slipping down her cheeks. "'But her life force is ebbing. She feels no pain, she is so drugged.'"

Anger flashes hot in Naga's green eyes. Then, just as quickly, her expression morphs from rage to one of pure misery.

"Naga says," Wynter continues, "'I am leaving, and I am taking her with me.'"

"This is a Gardnerian military dragon," Alcippe rages to Queen Alkaia, gesturing to the Mage Council brand on Naga's side with her rune-axe. "It needs to be killed!"

Naga's head whips around to face Alcippe. A deep growl rumbles at the base of her long throat.

Wynter turns to Alcippe, her hand still firmly on Naga's shoulder. "Naga says, 'I am *not* a Gardnerian military dragon. I am Naga, Free Dragon of Wyvernkin. And I could scorch this entire city if I so chose. I have no quarrel with you, Free People. I am taking Ariel Haven to draw her last breath where she belongs, among Wyvernkin, her true kin. I have heard tales of wyverns surviving high in the mountains of the east. I will seek them there. The people who birthed Ariel Haven never loved her, never saw her for what she truly is. They crushed her spirit, abused her, drugged her, told her she was foul and filthy and wicked. She does not belong here among any of you. She belongs with the winged ones.'"

"Alcippe Feyir," Queen Alkaia says after a long moment, keeping her sharp eyes on Naga. "Hand me your rune-axe."

Alcippe complies without question, her jaw set tight. Then she strides over to where the Icaral child is curled up, weeping. She scoops the little girl up into a tight, one-armed hug and grimly walks away, cradling the whimpering child against her broad chest.

Queen Alkaia looks at Naga appraisingly. "We, the Free People of the Caledonian Lands, wish you safe travel, Winged One. Take this with you, Free Dragon." She hands the rune-axe to Valasca, and Valasca solemnly brings it to Naga. "Bury Ariel Haven with it so that she will have it in the next life," Queen Alkaia says with great reverence, "where she will rise in the Goddesshaven as a fierce, proud soldier."

Naga accepts the rune-axe from Valasca as she cradles Ariel, then looks to Wynter.

Wynter sets her gaze on Queen Alkaia. "Naga says, 'Thank you, Queen Mother. I wish Ariel Haven had been welcomed into your lands as a child. She would have been a great warrior.'"

Then both Naga and Wynter turn to me as Wynter continues to voice her words. "'Elloren Gardner, I wanted to kill you on first sight, but you have proven yourself a friend to me.'"

Both Naga and Wynter look to where Yvan is still crouched on the ground. "'Yvan Guriel, I owe my freedom to you, and you are my friend. The Gardnerians grow stronger, and war is coming. You must rise up to meet your destiny. You cannot fight who you are meant to be.'"

Yvan's eyes are riveted on her, his face full of wild conflict and pain. Naga then turns to Wynter and looks deeply into her eyes.

Wynter nods, tears streaming down her cheeks. She throws her arms around Naga, clinging tightly to her for a moment, then steps back and faces all of us, her slender hand still on Naga's side.

Naga's wings begin to flap, and she lifts slowly into the air, Wynter's hand skimming along her body as she rises.

"Naga says to all of you," Wynter says, her voice choked, "'Amazakaran, war is coming. You must fight the Gardnerians and the Alfsigr, but you cannot do it alone. You underestimate their evil. You underestimate the shadows claiming this land. Wake up now, Free People, before it is too late. In the name of Ariel Haven, who was raised in captivity, yet remained unbroken, I will return to fight with you!'"

With those final words, the tip of Naga's tail slips from

Wynter's hand, and she flies east into the night sky, Ariel cradled against her breast, Ariel's raven winging alongside them.

Ariel! I scream her name out in my mind, stretching it across the vast sky, my heart twisting with unbearable pain.

Ariel is gone.

Ariel, who gave her life for Wynter.

How could I have ever thought she was evil? How could I have not known the truth? Not understood? How could I have ever believed all the lies about her?

Wynter is crying softly next to me, her wings wrapped tightly around herself as we all mourn under the cold, apathetic moon.

As Naga's form disappears into the distance, Queen Alkaia turns her attention to me. I'm sitting on the ground next to Wynter, quietly weeping, the crimson lights of the plaza's torches casting fitful illumination over all of us.

"The male must go," Queen Alkaia says definitively, gesturing toward Yvan, who raises his grief-stricken gaze to her.

"No." I stand and move toward him. As if I could protect him against *them.*

Queen Alkaia raises her palm and gives me a fierce, narrow look. "We will spare the male's life," she says evenly, not deigning to look at Yvan. *"This time."* She glares at me, and there's serious warning in her gaze. Then she calls out for three of her guards. "Bring the male to the edge of our territory. Stand guard over him while I speak with Elloren Gardner. When I am done, if she so chooses, she may join him there."

Two soldiers on horseback, one an archer, the other carrying a rune-sword, ride up to Yvan and prod him to stand up. Another older, muscular woman with a large rune-spear in hand strides toward him, as well.

Yvan turns to the queen, his green eyes blazing with emotion. "Thank you," he says to Queen Alkaia. "For taking in Wynter and the child."

Queen Alkaia's face tenses, but she stolidly refuses to look at him. The soldier beside Yvan makes a jabbing motion with her rune-spear, urging him into motion.

I want to wrest that cursed spear from her hands and crack it in two.

But they're letting him live.

It seems an extraordinarily delicate and dangerous situation.

As Yvan is roughly ushered away, I turn to Queen Alkaia, anger getting the better of me. "He saved the child, you know. Naga, too. And he tried to save Ariel."

The queen's guards bristle, hands tightening on weapons.

Queen Alkaia holds up a hand to calm her guard. "I know," she says, an edge of danger to her tone, her piercing gaze unwavering on me. "That is why he is one of the only males ever to have strayed inside our borders who will live to tell the tale."

I glare at her, anger spiking over their inflexible mores.

"You find our ways harsh, Elloren Gardner?" the queen asks with a note of challenge.

"There's not a lot of gray area, no."

"Perhaps," she agrees, her eyes probing, "but this is also the *only* safe place on Erthia you could think of to bring the Icarals."

She has a point. But only half of one. What if the child had been a male with wings, instead of female?

But I realize I've said enough. Challenging the queen further would be foolhardy and might even jeopardize Yvan's life.

Queen Alkaia motions for people to leave, and the soldiers

depart, one by one, until only the queen, Valasca, Wynter and some of the queen's guards remain. Wynter quietly rises and comes over to stand beside me, her face slick with tears.

"Wynter Eirllyn told us much about Ariel Haven," Queen Alkaia tells me, her expression grave.

I nod mutely, unable to speak about Ariel and keep any semblance of composure.

A voice rising in song catches my attention, and I look past the queen and spot Alcippe at the far end of the plaza, just before a dense grove of trees. The Icaral child is in her muscular arms, the child's screams having subsided. A new sound rises from the little girl—a low, keening sound of despair.

Alcippe continues singing, her deep voice resonating on the rune-warmed air. It's a song in a language I don't recognize, some Urisk dialect perhaps, and it's soothing, but sad.

As we all listen to the calming melody, the child grows quieter and quieter, then completely silent. Alcippe stands for a moment longer, rocking the little girl gently, then slowly walks across the plaza and up to the queen, kneeling down on one knee before her.

Queen Alkaia sets her gaze favorably on Alcippe.

"I have named the child Pyrgomanche, My Queen," Alcippe announces with some formality. "Pyrgo for short."

"Ah, yes." The queen nods approvingly. "It suits her well. 'Fiery Warrior.' A good choice, Alcippe. A strong name for a strong child. She will be a great warrior someday. She will make us all proud."

"I will take this child under my protection," Alcippe goes on to say with firm resolve.

The queen tilts her head in respectful acknowledgment, and Alcippe rises and carries the child off across the plaza and toward the Queenhall.

I look to Queen Alkaia, full of conflict over having argued with her. "Thank you," I say to her, my voice catching. "Thank you for helping the child. And for sheltering my friend, Wynter Eirllyn...and for freeing all of the Selkies."

The queen's mouth twitches as if she's fighting off a smile, amusement twinkling in her savvy green eyes. "I will not say goodbye to you, Elloren Gardner. For I feel certain you will be back in a few weeks, perhaps, with a few rescued Kelpies or even a couple of liberated pit dragons."

Her smile fades, and she fixes me with an expression touched with what looks like affection. "Or, perhaps," she goes on, more seriously, "you will let go of your attachment to the male and join us. We would welcome you gladly."

I'm shocked by her offer.

What would it be like to learn to be a warrior? To be the strong one for once, perpetually backed up by a whole army of female warriors? To learn to use weapons? To wear clothing I could move more freely in? To be free of all the Gardnerian rules?

It's an astonishing, mind-altering idea.

But I wouldn't be allowed to be with Uncle Edwin. Or Yvan, or my brothers or Gareth...or any of the other good and kind men in my life.

No, I think to myself, with a twinge of regret. *I could never leave them behind forever.*

Queen Alkaia seems to read my mind. She frowns at me, but then her expression becomes resigned, and she waves her hand dismissively. "Go, then, Elloren Gardner. Go back to your male. And may the Goddess protect you. Ride with Valasca." She waves the commander of her Queen's Guard forward, and Valasca flashes me a look of solidarity. "She will bring you to him."

Valasca grabs her horse's mane and leaps astride. She rides over to me and holds out her hand. I grab hold of it and pull myself up behind her, sliding my arms around her waist. She squeezes my hand warmly.

"Goodbye, Wynter," I say, looking down at my friend. Wynter's wings are drawn in tight around herself, her eyes full of sorrow. "I'll visit you when I can."

Wynter nods, and before I can say anything more, Valasca and I are off, riding toward the border.

We find Yvan just where they said he'd be, near the edge of Amaz territory, just past the border's rune-wall. His guards nod to Valasca as we approach, and she helps me dismount.

"I'll be in touch," I tell Valasca before I release her hand.

"I will, as well," she promises, her expression grave.

The Amaz take their leave, and Valasca shoots me one last look before she disappears into the forest, the crimson border runes fading as they depart.

Yvan and I stand alone in the darkness.

I don't know what to say, so I just remain there facing him, Ariel's face stark in my mind. Yvan looks haggard and drawn as he leans back against a tree, his expression devastated.

"Yvan," I breathe out, shaking my head in sorrow.

It's all there is to say. How can anyone put into words all that's happened, the immensity of the evil we're up against?

"We failed her," he says in a rough whisper.

We were too slow. Too powerless. Too late.

I can't speak, so I just nod in response, tears stinging at my swollen eyes.

"I'm sorry," he goes on. "I'm so sorry." The words come out in a rush, his tone desperate.

"Yvan," I say, grief overtaking me, "you did everything you could. You risked your life to get her to safety. There was nothing more you could have done. *Nothing.*"

Yvan nods brusquely, his face tight, like he's holding back a wave of such strong emotion it threatens to breach every gate.

"How is she? The child?" he asks, his voice choked. "Did she stop screaming?"

I nod. I imagine that, like me, he's hearing the echo of the little girl's screams reverberating in his mind, feeling the weight of her terror. "She passed out from exhaustion. They're taking her in. They're taking Wynter in, as well."

He swallows and nods, seeming momentarily unable to speak, his breathing becoming labored as his face dissolves into a mask of grief. Yvan clamps his eyes shut and turns away from me, toward the tree he's leaning on, one hand clutching at the bark for support, the other flying up to cover his eyes as he lets out a harsh, choking sound.

"Yvan." I step toward him.

He's sobbing now, the sound of it like sharp, rasping cough, his shoulders convulsing, as if he's having trouble catching his breath.

My own tears run down my face as I go to him. I hug his rigid shoulder while he struggles to stop crying, failing as grief overwhelms him.

He lowers the hand covering his face and turns to me, his eyes full of unguarded despair. He pulls away from the tree and falls into my arms, crying into my shoulder.

I embrace him tightly, his tears damp on my neck, his whole body racked by sobbing.

"I'm sorry," Yvan cries again, his voice muffled on my shoulder as he shakes his head from side to side.

"Yvan," I say, my own voice breaking. "It's not your fault." I hug him tightly, his arms gripping me like I'm a lifeline.

We hold each other for a long time, lost in sorrow.

His sobbing finally subsides, and he pulls away, wiping

his eyes roughly with the back of his hand. Then he looks at me, his eyes rapidly blazing to gold. "I love you, Elloren."

My breath catches in my throat.

We both know what this means. What this declaration, this path will cost him. Will cost both of us.

My tears are cool on my skin as they slide down my face. I blink them away, so I can see him clearly. We're completely star-crossed in every way possible, but there's no way to fight it anymore.

"I love you, too," I whisper through salty, tear-soaked lips.

Yvan takes my face in his warm hands and looks at me intently as my heartbeat quickens.

"I want to kiss you, Elloren," he says, the words weighted with import, "but...it will bind us."

"I don't care," I tell him, impassioned. "I want you to kiss me."

And then he brings his lips to mine.

His lips are warm and full and salty from his tears, his kiss tentative as a surprising warmth blooms from where his mouth touches mine, his heat sliding through my affinity lines in a tingling rush.

His kiss is like the sweetest honey, like something I could gladly drown in forever.

And then the warmth builds, growing heated where his lips move against mine, my sense of his fire rapidly escalating until his heat is shuddering through my entire body, flames coursing through my lines and around us both.

I gasp, pulling back a fraction, my breathing gone deep and uneven. "Your fire..."

Yvan stares at me through wild, glowing eyes, his voice ragged. "Is it too much?"

"Oh, no," I breathe out, bringing my lips back to his.

Yvan's hot mouth claims mine, his hands fanning out over

my back, holding me tight against him as his incredible fire courses through me. It's better than anything I've ever felt. Better than the first warm sun of spring, better than the feel of the woodstove after coming in from the frigid cold. The fire burns away every tragic, heartbreaking thing.

"I've been alone for so long," he whispers, his lips a fraction from mine, his heat racing through me.

"Not anymore," I whisper back.

He nods and reaches up to tenderly stroke my hair as his fire envelopes me, and I smile at him through my sadness, because even in the midst of so much horror, it's wonderful to finally find each other.

"Can I stay with you tonight?" he asks. "I don't mean..." He pauses for a moment, his hand stilling in my hair as he visibly attempts to collect his thoughts. "I just want to be with you."

I nod in assent.

He takes a deep breath and presses his forehead lightly against mine. "We should get back. We have a long walk."

"All right," I agree.

He leans down to kiss me softly, his heat shivering through me. Then he takes my hand firmly in his, and we set off in the direction of the North Tower.

CHAPTER FIVE

BOUNDARIES

As the woods open up before us, my heart leaps at the familiar sight of the North Tower—a welcome refuge from the harsh world surrounding us.

My hand clasped firmly in Yvan's, we walk silently across the moonlit field until we reach the stone structure.

Yvan takes the lantern by the door down from its hook, lights it with a wave of his hand and opens the door. He trails me wordlessly up the winding staircase, long shadows bouncing off the walls as the lamp sways back and forth in his hand.

I'm deeply aware of his presence, the sound of his footsteps, his breathing. I have so many conflicting emotions at this moment, it's difficult to sort them all out. The faces of Ariel, the little Icaral girl, the broken Icarals stripped of their wings—all these things devastate my heart.

But it's not all darkness.

Yvan loves me.

I've sensed it for a long time, but now he's fully surrendered to it, and so have I. And the completely unexpected, all-encompassing fire of Yvan's kiss—just the thought of it makes my feet unsteady.

We enter my cold, silent room, so empty now of life—the birds gone; Wynter, Ariel, Marina and Diana gone. Only Wynter's artwork provides a lingering, bittersweet memory of what was.

Yvan stalks toward the fireplace and throws out his hand. A ball of flames explodes in the hearth and lights up the haphazard pile of logs. The fire rapidly warms the room and casts a flickering orange glow over everything.

Yvan looks distractedly around, as if not quite sure what he should do next. "Which bed is yours?" he asks.

"That one," I say, pointing to it. Grief stabs at me as I look around at the other empty beds. "Not that it matters now."

He sits down on the bed, looking pale and traumatized.

"Your face... There's some blood on it," I say, my voice low.

Yvan reaches up absently to touch the small wound on his cheek, then briefly examines the blood on his fingers before looking back at me, stricken.

I fetch a cloth and a basin of water from the washroom and bring it over to my bedside table. Standing before Yvan, I place one hand on his shoulder and bring the washcloth up to gently clean the gash on his cheek.

Yvan's lip twitches as I make contact with the wound. He brings one hand up to rest on my hip, closes his eyes and takes a deep breath as I continue to dab the blood away from his face and neck, dipping the cloth back in the basin every so often.

I notice the smear of blood flows under his shirt. His eyes are still closed as I reach down and unfasten the top button of his shirt to allow better access. I'm gently pulling the edge of his shirt open toward his shoulder when his eyes fly open.

His movement a blur, he grabs my hand away from his shirt, his face taking on a wildly fierce expression.

My heart speeds up, my face coloring until it's uncomfortably hot, ashamed to have overstepped the boundaries between us.

"I'm... I'm sorry," I blurt out, stumbling over the words. "I was just going to clean up the blood that got under your shirt..."

His grip on my hand is still hard—too hard.

I'm deeply embarassed, not understanding what I've done. Not knowing enough about men to figure out my error.

Yvan's grip on my hand loosens, and his fierce expression falls away, quickly replaced by a look of mortification. "I'm sorry, Elloren," he says, his voice strained. He holds on to my hand, gentle now, the sadness and conflict in his eyes deepening. "I just want to lie down...with you."

I nod, and Yvan releases my hand, refastens the top button of his shirt and reaches down to pull off his boots.

I glance down at my clothes. Like his, they're mussed and smell of sweat and blood.

Ariel's blood. The blood from her wing.

It all crashes back into me. That horrible place. What they did to Ariel. How we were too late.

Too distraught to care about modesty, I pull my tunic off over my head, then unfasten my long skirt. I throw the clothing roughly into the corner, wanting to burn the bloodstained garb to ashes. I kick off my boots and slide the Wand into one of them, now clad only in a thin camisole, pantalettes and stockings.

I blow out the lamp on the table, wishing I could snuff out every horrible thing in this world as easily.

When I turn back to Yvan, he's sitting on the edge of the bed, quietly watching me as firelight flickers over the room. I walk over to the bed and slide around him on it, lying down and getting under the covers. I settle in, staring at his back as sadness and grief overtake me.

Ariel. I want her back. I want everyone back.

Yvan turns and places his hand gently on my arm.

We remain like that for a long while, lost in thought and mutual sorrow. My eyes grow heavy, and I've just surrendered to letting them fall shut when I feel Yvan sliding under the blankets facing me, his hand finding my waist.

I reach up to caress the edge of his face, careful to avoid the gash, and can make out his eyes closing in the firelight. I stroke my hand through his silken hair, and his breathing deepens.

He pulls me close and brings his lips to mine, kissing me gently, his fire sparking as he traces a slow line down my back with his fingertips, his warmth shivering through my lines and setting off an ache deep inside me. I can sense him holding himself back and giving in to something powerful all at the same time, as his fire quickly rouses to a ravenous stream.

Yvan's grasps hold of my waist as our kisses rapidly deepen in hunger, his fire and my fire lines surging around each other.

"I love you, Elloren," he breathes against my mouth before bringing his full lips insistently back to mine. My body arches toward his as he grips me close, and I lose myself to the feel of his fire coursing through my affinity lines and his long, hot body pressed against mine.

Yvan's breathing quickens as I twine my tongue around his, his fire pulsing through me in a decadent rush as he takes his time kissing me, his deft hands trailing along the length of my back.

We kiss for a long time, caressing each other, losing ourselves to the mounting fire.

Then I slide my leg over his, and Yvan's breath hitches. He slips his hand just behind my knee, groaning into his kiss as he pulls me even closer. His seductive heat whips through me, filling me with the irresistible desire to merge with him completely.

Both of us are breathing heavily when Yvan slowly slides on top of me, still kissing me passionately, both of us completely lost in this unexpected heaven in the middle of hell.

As Yvan moves against me, I can feel how much he wants me. I wrap my legs tightly around him, and he gasps, his fire giving a hard flare as he kisses me deeply, his fire and his body making me as dizzy as the Tirag.

He draws back a fraction, his breathing ragged. His eyes are molten as he looks down at me, my skin glittering green in the firelight.

"You're so beautiful," Yvan breathes. He traces his finger along the neckline of my camisole, fingering the top button. He glances back up at me as if silently asking for permission, gauging my reaction to his brazen touch.

My breathing quickens as he traces a line down the buttons until he reaches the sliver of naked skin just below, his graceful fingers sliding under the fabric of my camisole.

I gasp at the sensation his touch creates on my bare skin, a trail of delicious sparks. Yvan slides his hand higher until he reaches just under my breast, hesitating, his eyes flicking back toward mine.

I reach up, curl my arm around him and pull his lips insistently back to mine, kissing him as his hands explore my body, working their way under my clothes. His fire surges as I caress his back and feel along his taut muscles, his sharp shoulder blades. Wanting to feel more of his skin, I tug at his brown woolen shirt, freeing it from his pants.

I've just pulled his shirt free when he abruptly pushes himself off me and rolls onto his back, his breathing hard and ragged.

"We can't…" he says, shaking his head firmly side to side, as if attempting to wake himself from a dream, his hand coming up to clutch at his head. "We can't do this."

I lie there, my heart thudding, a heated longing for him pulsing through me.

He's right. We're literally playing with fire. We aren't thinking. We're both traumatized by the day's events, looking for escape, for comfort.

Yvan turns back to me. "I love you, Elloren, but we can't do this. Not right now."

Of course we can't. We can't just forget about everything that's happening. We can't afford to act on every impulse. What if I got pregnant, with the world around us spiraling into disaster?

Yvan finds my hand and wraps his around it, holding my gaze with his fiery eyes.

"You're right," I say as my breathing gradually evens out, and we lie there, holding on to each other, until my eyes grow heavy with fatigue.

Just as I've let my lids fall shut, I feel Yvan roll toward me. His arm encircles me as he brings his lips to my forehead. "Good night, Elloren," he whispers, and I reach around to hug him back.

And then we fall asleep, wrapped up in the warm safety of each other's arms.

"Elloren."

The sound of his voice comes from far away as I float in the darkness of a dreamless sleep.

"Hmm," I murmur, slowly regaining consciousness, Yvan's lovely voice filling me with a delicious warmth. I stretch languidly, like a contented cat, wanting to wrap myself around him.

"Elloren."

There's a strange urgency in his voice.

Something's wrong.

The peaceful, floating feeling disappears, replaced by a spike of nervous tension, and I struggle to wake up quickly. I jerk my head side to side, the movement forcing me fully into reality.

Yvan is lying next to me, propped up rigidly on one elbow. He's not looking at me, but at something just past me with deep concern. I turn to follow the direction of his gaze.

Aunt Vyvian stands in the doorway, her eyes narrowed to tight, livid slits as she takes in the scene before her.

"Hello, my niece."

"Aunt Vyvian!" I exclaim in mortified surprise, bolting up and quickly remembering that I'm half-clad in my underwear. "I... We..."

"Why are you in bed with a Kelt, my dear?" she asks me slowly, smoothly.

"We didn't..." I defend myself breathlessly, shaking my head to refute her conclusions. "We haven't... It's not what it looks like..."

"What it *does* look like, Elloren, dear, is that you're in your underwear, in bed with a Kelt." Her cool gaze flickers back and forth from Yvan to myself.

I look over at Yvan, panicked. He's watching my aunt carefully, eyes narrowed, sizing her up and, if his body language is any indication, finding her to be dangerous. His hand slides protectively over mine.

Aunt Vyvian stares back at him, and the side of her lip twitches. "Aren't you going to introduce me to your friend, Elloren?"

Yvan glances over at me, his expression guarded. He releases my hand and stands up to face my aunt. "My name is Yvan Guriel."

My aunt eyes him up and down with a look of contempt that's scathing.

Fear seizes hold of me.

Does she suspect our involvement in what happened at the prison?

Aunt Vyvian turns to me, her brow tensing. "Your uncle is very ill, Elloren."

The world tilts.

Oh, Ancient One, no. Not this. Not now.

"What's happened?" I ask shakily, my voice high with worry.

"It's his heart, Elloren," she says. "I'm sorry. There may not be much time. He's back in Valgard, with my personal physician."

The room recedes into a blur, and I'm only half-aware of Yvan's hand on my shoulder, steadying me.

"You need to come with me at once," she says stiffly.

I nod mutely at her.

"Why don't you leave, *Yvan*," my aunt says to him, grimacing as she says his name, as if it leaves an unpleasant taste on her tongue. "My niece needs to get dressed."

Yvan looks intently at me, and I can see him trying to convey a million things silently. He takes my hand in his, and I hold tight to him, wishing we could speak to each other through our minds, like he can speak to Naga.

"I'll see you when you get back, Elloren," he says, his voice warm with affection. He shoots my aunt a look of distrust, wishes us a safe journey and leaves.

CHAPTER SIX

GUARDIAN

It's during the carriage ride to Valgard, forced to endure such close quarters with Aunt Vyvian, that I start to realize I'm in serious trouble.

Her response to every question I venture is terse. She can barely bring herself to look at me, and her tense disapproval from before has given way to an almost barely concealed loathing.

My overwhelming sense of dark trepidation grows, sucking up all the air around me as we pass through large swaths of wilderness, farmland and small towns. Then the carriage takes an unexpected turn into the forest, trundling beneath the trees until we reach an isolated military outpost.

I'm thrust into vast confusion as I take in the Ironwood structure, two Level Five Mage guards stationed outside it.

Where are we?

"Get out," Aunt Vyvian brusquely orders as the carriage comes to a stop and the guards stride toward it.

I blink at her for a moment, alarmed by her harsh tone.

She leans forward and fixes me with a chilling stare. "I said, *get out.*"

Ancient One, she knows. She must know about everything.

I step out of the carriage and am immediately flanked by the guards, feeling as if I'm locked in a nightmare. Their expressions are rigidly neutral as they prod me forward, but I can feel the contempt radiating off them.

I nervously glance back at the carriage. My aunt is standing there, watching me, slowly removing her black calfskin gloves. She makes no move to accompany me into the outpost.

One of the guards expressionlessly opens the door for me, motioning for me to enter.

Another stony-faced Level Five guard meets us inside and ushers me down a spare hallway with Ironwood tree trunks and branches worked into the dark walls. The other two guards fall in behind me.

The guard ahead of me unlocks a cell door with a small, iron-barred window cut near the top. He opens it and motions brusquely for me to get inside.

I hesitate. "Where's my uncle?" I ask the guard to no answer, really scared now.

I'm shoved from behind, and I cry out, almost stumbling, as fear leaps inside me. Powerless to fight them or flee, I haltingly move forward.

An explosion of shock overtakes me as soon as I reach the cell's door.

Uncle Edwin is inside, crumpled against the far wall. He's clutching at his chest, his breathing labored, and there are bruises all over one side of his face.

I gasp and run to him, falling to my knees at his side. "Uncle Edwin! What happened? What did they do to you?"

He opens his mouth as if to speak, but then his eyes go wide as he stares at something just past me.

I turn to find my aunt framed in the doorway.

"Did you do this to him?" I croak out in disbelief.

"You are a disgrace to this family," she snarls with disgust. "*Both* of you. I was a fool to let you raise these children, Edwin. A fool in so many ways. But I will *not* make the same mistake again. Elloren fasts *today*. Give me permission, or I will have it beaten out of you."

"Fasting?" I cry. "What's going on?!"

"The fasting spell," my aunt says. "It won't work without your guardian speaking the words of consent." She points at my uncle. "You will speak them, Edwin. *Today*."

"Leave him alone!" I cry, protectively shielding him with my own body as Uncle Edwin wheezes for breath. "You're hurting him!"

"All he has to do is speak the words," my aunt hisses.

"No," my uncle chokes out, the word barely audible.

I wheel on him, imploring. "Say whatever she wants," I beg him.

He tries to speak, but his voice is too weak. He can only stubbornly shake his head at me, his expression anguished.

"Please, do what she says," I implore him, tears running down my cheeks as I take one of his hands in mine. I rack my brain, panicked and desperate to find some way to save him.

I turn to my aunt, fury rising. "If he dies," I spit out through my tears, "Rafe becomes eldest male in the family, and he'll *never* give in to what you want. Uncle Edwin *might*, if you give him some time. If you let me nurse him back to health, I'll talk to him. I'll get him to agree to my fasting."

My aunt runs her fingers over the silken gloves in her hand, a dark smile twitching at her lips. "You forget, my niece. Rafe doesn't turn twenty for three more days. If something happens to your uncle, *I* become your guardian for those three days. So, it's in his best interest to cooperate. I will give him ten minutes to decide."

She leaves and shuts the door.

Fear slices through me, its taste cold and metallic in my mouth. "Please tell her what she wants," I beg my uncle, hugging him, crying into his shoulder. "Please, Uncle Edwin. I can't lose you."

"Elloren," he says with incredible effort, still wheezing and clutching at his chest. "I've failed you. I was wrong..." He stops, his breathing increasingly labored.

"I don't understand," I cry. "Wrong about *what*? You've never failed me. Not ever."

"I raised you—" the weak breath in his chest rattles like bones "—to think you are weak... I didn't want them...to *use* you...you are *not* weak...you must *fight* them... I was wrong... Your power..." He stops, his eyes going wide as he gasps for breath.

His shaking hand finds mine, and then he slumps back, his head lolling, his eyes glazing over.

And I know he's gone.

I fall into him, sobbing, hugging him tight to me.

For ten minutes.

Then the door opens behind me, and I hear the click of her heels on the floor.

"Get up," my aunt orders.

I whirl around to face her. *"You evil witch!"* I scream, launching myself at her.

Her guards jump to her side, roughly pushing me back and restraining me.

Aunt Vyvian looms overhead as I struggle like a feral animal to break free of the guards' rough hold.

"I suggest you calm yourself down," she says coolly. "Or

I shall have to pay a visit to the Kelt boy you were in bed with. Yvan Guriel, was it?"

Go ahead, I seethe. *Go ahead and pay him a visit, you witch. Go seek out Yvan Guriel. He'll set you on fire, and I'll dance on your ashes.*

Wild with grief, I look back at my uncle, lying dead on the floor behind me.

And that's when I buckle.

I let loose with a terrible wail and go limp, letting them drag me out as I shatter.

Into the carriage, out of the carriage, through the ornate halls of some town's council magistrate hall.

There are high-level soldiers everywhere. A white-bearded priest dressed in sacred robes stands in front of a small altar, his wand in hand, the white bird symbol of the Ancient One embroidered on his chest.

I'm pushed roughly forward, and I fall to the ground in front of the priest.

The click of my aunt's heels sounds on the tile floor as she walks up beside me and comes to a stop.

Her voice is glacially calm when it comes. "Though it makes me question his sanity, there is one young man who, miraculously, is still willing to fast to you. That is, if you can be fasted *at all* at this point."

"I didn't do anything with Yvan!" I cry, terrified of what they might to do to him. To his mother. *"Nothing happened!"*

"We shall see about that soon enough," Aunt Vyvian snipes. "I am going outside to await your fastmate's arrival." She lowers herself down and brings her elegant face close to mine. "I trust you will not be foolish enough to follow Sage Gaffney's path once you are fasted. They say the pain of a broken fasting is ten times worse than being branded by hot irons. And it lasts *forever.*"

THE IRON FLOWER

★ ★ ★

I'm slumped on the floor, sobbing, snot running from my nose, when the door to the room opens again with a loud bang.

Lukas strides in, trailed by several soldiers, his black cloak billowing out behind him, his gleaming sword and wand sheathed at his sides.

He barely glances at me as he passes, exuding only dominance and anger. "Let's get this over with, shall we?" he says to the priest, but it's more of an order than a request. The priest bows his head to Lukas repeatedly as he readies his wand and opens up *The Book of the Ancients* on the altar before him.

Two guards roughly pull me up from the floor, and I struggle against them as they drag me over to where Lukas and the priest are waiting. They force my hands out in front of me, and Lukas reaches over to clasp his hands over mine.

"I hate you for doing this!" I snarl at him, tears falling from my eyes, one of the guard's nails digging into my wrist.

"They're going to wandfast you today, Elloren," Lukas spits back. "It can either be to me, or to someone far worse."

"How can you do this?" I cry. "You said you were my *friend*!"

"If I walk out of this room right now," he says through clenched teeth, his voice so low it's almost a whisper, "your aunt will still be fasting you to someone who, in her exact words, will 'beat some sense into you.' I'm here because I *am* your friend, whether you think I am or not. Believe me, I'm not thrilled about someone fasting to me only because she's being held down by two armed guards."

"Then don't do it!"

"Maybe if you don't want to be placed in a situation like this," Lukas snipes, his face furious, "you should avoid spending the night half-naked with a *Kelt*. Oh, yes, Elloren, your aunt told me all about your night with Yvan Guriel. We'll see just how innocent it was in a moment, won't we?"

"What do you care?" I snarl back at him. "You don't even love me."

Lukas's face takes on an expression so dark that for a moment, I fear he'll strike me. He looks away, his mouth pressed into a hard line, like he's at war with himself, then he glances back down at me again with intense frustration. "I'm trying to *help* you!" he grinds out.

"I will hate you *forever*!" I seethe, straining against the guards, against Lukas's hands on mine.

Lukas's neck tenses, and his face clouds over with disgust. He quickly composes himself and turns to the priest. "Just do it. Fast her to me. Then seal it."

"No!" I cry as they hold my hands in place, the priest reciting the fasting spell, his voice a nightmarish, monotonous drone.

The priest waves his wand above our hands, and I flinch as a slight sting races over my hands and branches out, thin black lines flowing out from the wand's tip and around my hands and Lukas's. I cry out in futile protest as the fasting lines curl and spiral, then darken as the sealing spell takes hold, like a spider's web wrapping me up.

And then it's done, and I'm released.

I fall backward and splay my hands out in front of me, horrified by the black lines now permanently branded on my skin.

Lukas is in charge of me now. He *owns* me.

"Where should we take her, Commander Grey?" one of the guards asks him.

"She has my permission to go wherever she chooses," Lukas snarls before storming out of the room.

CHAPTER
SEVEN

REVENGE

Yvan is there when I stumble back to the North Tower.

The night is inky black, thunder rumbling in the distance. A weak flash of lightning pulses.

"Your uncle. How is he?" he asks, clearly thrown by my expression as I enter the bedroom. "Why are you back so soon?"

"He's dead," I reply, my voice flat and lifeless.

"Oh, Elloren...oh, no..."

"She killed him. My aunt good as killed him. Your mother's right. My family is evil. You should stay far away from all of us. I'll ruin your life."

Yvan slides off the windowsill and comes to me, his face tensing with confusion. "I don't understand."

"Uncle Edwin's heart gave out. He's been sick for a long time. My aunt knew he couldn't handle stress." I stop. I can't say any more.

Yvan wraps his arms around me as I stand there, limp and unresponsive.

My hands. How can I tell him about the fasting?

Grief and dark rebellion rear up within me like a vicious tide, and an even darker idea springs from it.

I'll break the fasting.

Even though my body is numb from grief, unfeeling, uncaring, I reach up and twine my arms around Yvan. And then I bring my lips to his, my kiss soft and then deliberately teasing.

Yvan kisses me back at first, his fire rousing, but then he pulls away to look closely at me, seeming deeply confused by the dramatic change in my demeanor.

I ignore his hesitation, caressing his cheek. "Just kiss me," I beg of him, my voice husky. "I need you to kiss me." I bring my lips back to his, my fingers tracing up his warm neck, and as we kiss, I can feel him slowly giving up on his confusion, giving in to me.

Yvan's breathing deepens, his body tensing in response to my suggestive embrace, his fire quickening and then shuddering into a blaze.

I skim my fingers languidly along his back, down and around his waist in a supple caress. Then still lower, my hands sliding over his hips, his fire coursing clear through me now, his hands gripping at my tunic.

Yvan's fire intensifies as I kiss him more provocatively, his increasingly unbridled heat racing through my lines, his hands beginning to touch me boldly as he senses all the boundaries between us suddenly erased. A small groan escapes his lips as I pull his body aggressively toward mine.

Abruptly, Yvan's body goes rigid, and he reaches around to grab my wrists, pushing away from me. "Elloren..." His eyes are on fire with equal parts desire and dawning suspicion. "What are you doing?"

I flash a sultry smile and move toward him. "Take me to bed."

His hands reflexively tighten around my wrists as he maintains the distance between us, searching my face intently.

Then his gaze drops down, and he sees them. *My hands.*

He pulls in a hard breath, outrage flaring to a golden blaze in his eyes. "It's Lukas Grey, isn't it? They forced you to fast to him."

"Please, Yvan," I beg, desperate. "I want to break the fasting. Please, help me do it."

His hands are tight on my arms, holding me back. "No, Elloren."

I glare at him, suddenly furious. We stare at each other for a long, tortured moment.

And then my fury collapses in on itself. An abyss opens up under me, and I feel my center drop down into it, despair rushing in to fill the void.

An overwhelming sense of loss sweeps over me with the force of a killing wave, knocking the wind out of me as I begin to completely fall apart.

"You don't want me anymore." My voice is a strangled whisper, my throat gone rigid. My eyes lose their focus, and I stare out into nothing.

"Is that what you think?" he asks, incredulous.

I hear his voice from somewhere in front of me, like we're both underwater. I'm vaguely aware of him, of his face in front of me, his eyes fervently trying to find mine.

But it's all too much. Too horrible. No one left to be a parent to me. Bound to Lukas Grey forever. And now Yvan will leave me, too.

I'm all alone.

I stare out into nothingness as tears stream out of my eyes, like a dam opening, my face unmoving, blank and numb with grief as I begin to fall apart.

Yvan's hands hold tight to my arms, willing me to listen.

I look into his fierce eyes, my vision blurred by a curtain of tears.

"You think I don't want you now?" he asks, impassioned. "Because you're fasted to Lukas? That doesn't change *anything*. I *love* you."

I search his eyes, looking for some chink in his armor, for a speck of doubt to confirm my worst fears...and find none. His gaze is strong and steady, wide-open and full of love.

"Listen to me, Elloren," he tells me, his grip loosening to a caress. "Our being together *can't* be about revenge. That's why I'm refusing you. I love you. *That's* why I want to wait."

I suddenly feel like someone who's almost drowned, who's stopped breathing, only to be resuscitated at the last minute. The air rushes back into my lungs as I fall into him, his arms wrapping tightly around me, holding me up, keeping me from collapsing. I find my voice and cry out in sorrow, sobbing uncontrollably, a keening wail of despair.

I don't know how long we stand like this, but his loving hold on me never loosens as I cry and cry for my uncle, my brothers, for Ariel and the Lupines, for my friends...for myself.

He stays, holding me, keeping my head just barely above the surface.

Keeping me from drowning.

CHAPTER
EIGHT

REVELATIONS

The next two days are a murky haze.

I spend them mostly in bed, drifting in and out of sleep, half aware of Yvan trying to get me to eat and drink, of Tierney arriving at one point, bits and pieces of their hushed conversation piercing through my fog of grief.

She looks so different now. Her blue hair in twisted, knotty coils, her eyes a deep-lake blue, a sack slung over her shoulder.

"I'm setting off for Noi lands tonight," Tierney tells him. "The Gardnerians are spiking more of the waterways with iron. My Kelpies and I have an ever-narrowing corridor to travel through, and we have to get through the Eastern Pass now, before the Gardnerians completely choke it off."

Tierney pads over to me, her hand cool on my arm, and I feel a gentle pull on my slim water lines. She leans in close. "I'll see you in the Noi lands, Elloren. I know you'll find your way to us someday."

I stare up at her, hopeless. "Nothing can stop the Gardnerians. They're going to win."

A spark of defiance wells in Tierney's deep blue eyes. "Then I'll go down fighting in the waters of the Eastern Realm. And you'll be there to fight with me."

I turn away from her and shake my head listlessly. "No, Tierney. It's all lost. Everything."

I can sense the defiance rippling through her. "Goodbye, Elloren," she says as she rises. "You've been a good friend to me." Her voice breaks and she's silent for a moment. When she speaks again, her tone is full of sharp, implacable resolve. "I *will* see you in the Noi lands."

On the third day, I wake and hold up my hands and wait for the fierce wave of grief to wash over me at the sight of the spidery lines, but I'm not overcome this time. My despair is muted, beaten back by the feel of Yvan's arms tight around me. My eyes are sticky and swollen from crying, and I can't breathe out my nose. I haven't bathed in days, and imagine I must smell like sweat, but still, he holds on to me.

I turn to look at him. His eyes are open, his gaze level and kind. He reaches up to stroke my head, my dirty tangled hair, and leans in to kiss my forehead. "Good morning," he says gently.

Later, when he offers me food, I eat it.

I awaken on the fourth day to the sight of warm spring sunlight streaming in through the window. Yvan is standing by the window, looking out toward the wilds. "I'll be back later," he promises, and I watch him leave.

I get up and go to the window, spotting him as he makes his way across the green field, into the wilds.

I remember how he used to disappear all the time to visit Naga. How curious I was about where he was going. I glance up at the sky, the sun high, and realize I've slept most of the morning away. I look back down at the spot where Yvan entered the trees and give a start.

A white bird.

Sitting on a tree limb among the delicate new leaves and looking at me with expectant eyes. Like the first time I saw one of the Watchers, the day Sage gave me the Wand of Myth.

My heart picks up speed.

I spring out of bed, throw on my boots, press my Wand into the side of one of them and run through the hall, down the spiraling staircase and out the door, the leafy spring air filling my lungs.

There it is—the Watcher. Still sitting on the branch as golden-green leaves dance in the gentle breeze around it.

I rush across the grassy field, the bird winking out of sight when I reach it and reappearing inside the forest on a sun-dappled tree limb.

Spring is everywhere, golden-green flashing.

And when I step into the wilds, the forest's usual flare of hatred doesn't come. It's as if the hostility has been thrown off to the edges, as if the bird is clearing a path for me. My heart fills with an amorphous sense of anticipation as I take in the sight of greenery everywhere, bursting up from the forest floor, climbing up through the rotted soil.

The bird plays hide-and-seek with me for over an hour as I follow it blindly, sunlight spearing through the shadows, falling down in shimmering rays like cascading water. I watch the bird disappear, only to reappear in another tree far ahead, then disappearing again. Over and over, until I can finally make out a clearing in the distance, the light shining stronger through the trees. Glimpses of water sparkling in the sunlight appear through the branches, just past the trees' broad trunks.

I look up at the Watcher and wait for it to take flight

again, but the iridescent bird simply wraps its wings around itself and vanishes.

I set my gaze ahead and start toward the clearing, moving quietly. Returning geese are flying high above, honking in formation in the vivid azure sky. I reach the edge of the wilds and look out over a beautiful blue, shimmering lake.

Yvan is there, right at the water's edge.

I watch as he unbuttons his shirt, pulls it off and throws it over a log near his boots.

I hold my breath to keep from gasping at the sight of him in the brilliant sunlight. His lean, sculpted chest. His broad shoulders and strong arms.

Then he reaches down to remove his belt.

Oh, sweet Ancient One. He's going for a swim, perhaps, or to bathe in the lake. And he's going to undress completely.

Heat suffuses my face, my neck. I know I should go, but I'm so curious to see him. Spring's restless energy wells up inside me, feeding a warm spark of desire.

He's so beautiful...

Some geese fly down toward the lake, their wings spread wide as they maneuver to the water with a loud splash. Yvan pauses his undressing to turn and look at them.

I draw back in surprise. He has an elaborate tattoo on his back, like someone has inked giant, black wings over its entire surface. Incredibly detailed wings, every feather carefully wrought.

Yvan stands up straight, his hands on his hips. He looks out over the lake, his head tipped up to the sun, as if drinking it in. Then, unexpectedly, his hair brightens to a dazzling red, his ears elongate to lithe points and the tattoo on his back comes to life, like a fan slowly opening.

Shock blasts through me as the wings grow and unfurl,

spreading out magestically. Like he's a giant hawk in its prime, his wings flexing, strong and sure.

They're nothing like Ariel's ragged, half-healed wings.

Nothing like Wynter's dark, thin ones.

They're stunningly beautiful, the feathers glittering like opals, a rainbow of colors rippling and shining off their edges.

I gasp and fall back and a branch snaps under my foot.

Yvan's head whips around, his eyes instantly fierce, searching the woods for the source of the sound. He starts for the forest, slightly crouched, his eyes feral as his wings fan out impressively behind him.

He falls back with a start when he spots me. "Elloren," he says, his angular face constricting.

My eyes are wide as I stare at him. "You're an Icaral," I breathe out.

His face clouds over with fierce anguish.

Suddenly, everything falls into place. All of it.

My world rocks alarmingly.

"Yvan...how did your father die?" I ask, my voice strangled, knowing what the answer will be even before he says it.

His black wings flex. "He was the Icaral killed by your grandmother, Elloren."

I wince and grab onto a nearby tree to steady myself.

It all makes sense now. The horror in his mother's face when she saw me. It wasn't only because she's yet another Kelt who hates the Gardnerians, who hated my grandmother. It's because I look *exactly* like the woman who killed her husband—the Icaral shown in the statue in front of the Valgard Cathedral.

Yvan's father.

I cling to the tree as my knees start to buckle.

"Elloren," Yvan says as he quickly strides toward me, his hand coming to rest on my arm.

I glance down at his hand, the ground beneath me feeling unstable. Has he been able to read my mind all this time? I look up at him. "Are you an empath, too? Like Wynter?"

"Only partially," he says, his brow tensing. "I can read emotions, but not memories or specific thoughts. And I can only mentally communicate with other dragons."

"*Other* dragons?"

"That's what being an Icaral is, Elloren. You know that. I'm part dragon."

A light-headed rush sweeps over me. "If the Gardnerians find out about you..."

"I know."

We hold each other's gaze, the full ramifications bearing down on us both. "Naga knows, doesn't she?" I realize. "And Wynter, too. She's touched you. She must know."

He swallows and nods stiffly.

"Why didn't you tell me?" I ask, my voice unsteady. "You know you can be honest with me."

"I promised my mother I wouldn't tell anyone," he explains haltingly. "I *wanted* to tell you. But, Elloren...even just knowing this puts you in danger."

He's right. The mere fact of his existence is extraordinarily dangerous information.

I take his warm hand in mine, my fingers twining through his. "Yvan, this is much too big for you to deal with alone."

His eyes blaze, the line of his mouth hardening.

More memories flood into my mind, the pieces of so many puzzles falling into place. "That night we spent together," I say, "I tried to unbutton your shirt, and you stopped me. You didn't want me to find the imprint of your wings."

A stricken look crosses his face. "That's right."

"And later, when we..." I pause awkwardly. "I thought

you stopped because you didn't want to...put me in a difficult situation. But it was the wings all along."

"It was," he admits. "But I meant what I said that night. I want to be with you in that way, more than anything, but I don't want you hurt because of it."

I hold up my marked hand and consider it despairingly. "But now...that can never happen for us." My despair rapidly starts a spiral down into panic. If the Gardnerians or the Alfsigr discover his existence, they'll do everything in their power to find him. And they'll be bent on killing him.

"What abilities do you have?" I ask, desperately hoping he's far more powerful than I can imagine.

He takes a deep breath. "I can throw fire from my hands. *A lot* of fire. More than you've seen. I'm incredibly strong and fast. I can heal people, which you already know. And I'm impervious to fire."

"Could there be more?"

"Yes. But my father died before he could teach me anything about myself."

The horrible truth rears its head—his father cut down by my own grandmother. "Does your mother know the extent of your power?" I ask, my thoughts careening.

"I think so, but she won't tell me anything. She wants me to stay in hiding so that history doesn't repeat itself. She's tired of everyone she loves dying. And she doesn't want me used as a weapon."

I close my eyes and bring a hand to my face, my head starting to throb mercilessly, distress rising.

Everyone I love will be slaughtered in the coming war, and there's *nothing* I can do to stop it. My brothers and the Lupines, along with everyone else they've escaped with, will probably be hunted down by the Gardnerians and killed. The Kelts and the Urisk and the Smaragdalfar Elves will be enslaved by the Gardnerians and the Alfsigr. All the Fae in hiding, everyone who sheltered them, Tierney and her family—they'll be discovered and murdered. Wynter, Fyn'ir, the little girl Pyrgo—they'll all be cut down.

And Yvan will suffer the same fate—maybe worse, because he doesn't know the full extent of his powers or how to use them.

And because I'm power*less*, there will be absolutely nothing I can do to stop any of it. Because all I possess is a cursedly inaccessible echo of my grandmother's abilities.

"I wish I had power," I bitterly rage. "I'm the granddaughter of the Black Witch, and I'm *worthless* when it comes to helping you or anyone else I love."

"You're not worthless," Yvan vehemently insists, his wings folding rigidly in.

"You're wrong." I pick up a stick lying at my feet and rip the small diverging branches off it as I step into the clearing. "I'll show you *exactly* what happened when they wandtested me."

"You don't even have a real wand in your hand, Elloren," he points out gently.

I don't care. I want him to see just how powerless I am—how I can't even perform the simplest spell of all.

I lift the makeshift wand, point it at some trees in the distance and focus on the image of a candle lighting, searching my mind for the words to the lighting spell.

"Illumin…" I begin, the words of the spell coming together seamlessly from memory.

Power rumbles against the balls of my feet, just like on the day of my wandtesting so many months ago. Power pulled straight from Erthia's core.

Power pulled from the trees.

It works its way slowly up my legs, coiling like an enormous snake ready to strike as I sound out the words to the spell.

The swirling, pulsating power catches on to my affinity lines like fire on dry brush. But this time, the power doesn't meet with resistance, and the pain doesn't come in its wake.

Instead, the power rushes out into every part of me, through every affinity line, flying straight toward the branch. As the power reaches my arm, it coalesces like lightning and explodes out from my wand hand and through the branch in a violent blast toward the trees.

A loud explosion assaults my ears as the trees before me are engulfed in flames that rise as high as the Valgard Cathedral. I fall back, slamming into the ground, the branch flying from my hand as birds and animals flee from all sides, the roar of the fire deafening, the trees screaming in my head.

I scuttle away from the flames as fear washes over me, my heart pounding against my chest. Yvan's hand grabs my shoulder, and I jerk my head toward him.

He's staring at the inferno I've created, his mouth agape as he crouches protectively over me, his large, black wings arcing around us.

"Holy Ancient One," I cry, terrified.

His eyes are fixated on the swirling flames, riveted.

"But they tested me," I stammer out. "Nothing happened. They told me I was powerless."

"Whose wand did you use?" he asks with dawning suspicion as he stares into the fire with great concentration, as if he's struggling to put everything together.

"Commander Vin's."

Yvan turns to me, a look of fear on his face. "Are you sure?" His hand tightens on my shoulder. "Are you sure it wasn't the Gardnerian military's?"

"Yes," I insist as the flames in front of us engulf another tree, the sound of the destruction deafening.

He turns back to the fire, eyes widening with deepening realization. "She gave you a rune-blocked wand."

"I don't understand," I say, scared of what this could mean.

"She didn't want the Gardnerians to know," he breathes, and I brace myself, knowing what he's going to say before he says it.

Yvan's eyes meet mine, full of utter certainty. "Elloren, *you're* the Black Witch."

I sit, stunned, as we watch the trees crackle and burn, Yvan's arms and wings tight around me.

After a long while, the flames die down and the deafening roar calms to the crackle of a huge bonfire.

"So," I finally venture in a slow, horrified whisper, "you're the Icaral who's supposed to destroy Gardneria, and I'm the Black Witch who's supposed to kill you. *We're* the two points of the Prophecy."

Yvan swallows hard, studying the flames in front of us. "I don't believe in prophecies," he says, his jaw going rigid.

"Everyone else does."

He turns to me with a jaded look. "Yes, they do."

"And I wasn't even using a real wand."

"I know."

"So, if I use a real wand…" I think back to Ni Vin's stories about the fireballs my grandmother created, the ones she used to destroy entire villages, to terrorize entire countries.

I have that terrible power. Like my grandmother, I'm something potentially horrific to behold.

"Kam Vin knows," Yvan says darkly.

"Why didn't she tell me?"

Yvan shakes his head. "I don't know."

His wing brushes against my cheek. It's soft and silky against my skin. "Can you fly?" I ask abruptly, feeling like I've fallen into a surreal dream.

He hesitates, then nods.

I stare at him, stunned by this revelation. "Ariel and Wynter can't fly."

"Ariel and Wynter were raised to believe that they're foul and evil. Their wings are weak."

"I don't understand."

He shrugs. "I don't completely, either. It's just the way it works with Icarals."

I take a deep, shuddering breath. "I was raised to believe that you're the most evil monster on all of Erthia."

"I was raised to believe the same thing about you."

An involuntary laugh escapes me. "At least we have that in common." I pause, growing serious and remembering Uncle Edwin's final words to me. "My uncle knew. I think he was hoping I'd live my entire life not knowing. And I probably would have, if I'd never come here."

"He wanted to protect you."

"Like your mother wants to protect *you*."

"Another thing we have in common." He flashes me a small, kind smile, but his eyes remain grave.

"So, we're potentially the two most powerful beings on Erthia."

"Who have no clear idea of how to use our powers," he adds.

My head is throbbing mercilessly now. I let it fall into my hands and close my eyes tight.

"Are you all right?" he asks, concerned.

Of course I'm not. This is an unparalleled disaster.

"I get stress headaches," I tell him, pressing my forehead against my balled fists.

Yvan shifts around until he's in front of me and places his warm hands on either side of my aching head. I open my eyes to find him deep in concentration, focused on a point just above my eyes. Heat radiates from his hands, vibrating outward, and the ache in my head begins to diminish little by little as he holds me, until it's completely gone.

He drops his hands down from my head, keeping one on my shoulder.

"Thank you," I say, amazed.

He nods, his lip lifting.

"That's quite the skill you have there."

He reaches up to gently push a stray piece of my hair back behind my ear. It's such a tender gesture, it brings tears to my eyes.

"Before my uncle died," I tell him, my voice breaking, "he told me I should fight the Gardnerians. That he was wrong to think otherwise. He tried to tell me everything. And then he was gone, before he could finish what he was trying to say."

I stop for a moment, afraid I'll come undone. "Do you think they were right?" I finally ask him. "To shelter us like they did?"

Yvan looks briefly at the bonfire before us. When he turns back to me his expression is as hard as forged steel. "No."

My head spins from the sheer vertigo of it all. Everything has been turned upside down and inside out.

"This can't be happening," I protest, suddenly overcome. "It shouldn't be me. I don't know how to wield this kind of power."

He glances over at the fire again, looking impressed. "You can learn."

I remember Marina's words the day we found her skin.
Power changes everything.

"This is bigger than just us," Yvan says. "If no one steps forward to fight, they'll win."

But could we actually do it? Could we harness our power and help take down the Gardnerians and the Alfsigr and any and all of their allies?

Yvan holds on to me for a long moment, the fire crackling in the distance as I wrestle with this new fate.

"Maybe we'll win," he finally says.

"It's a *really* long shot, Yvan."

"Stranger things have happened."

I look up at him. "We did rescue Naga from a Gardnerian military base," I say, as bold defiance starts to rise within me.

"And destroyed half the base," he adds thoughtfully.

"And the Selkies. They're free."

"That was a long shot, as well."

"As is you turning out to be half dragon."

The edge of his mouth lifts in a smile. "And then there's you...being, of all things, the Black Witch."

I nod, a bit dazed as I glance at the flaming trees. "That is *definitely* unexpected."

Yvan gives my arm a warm squeeze, gets up and walks down to the lake to gather his things. When he reaches the shore, he goes very still. Then he pulls his wings in tight behind him, folding them flat against his back, until only their imprint remains. His hair morphs from vibrant red back to its glamoured brown, and his ears shift to a rounded shape once more.

When he's done, Yvan lets out a long breath, as if it's taken quite a bit of effort. Then he quickly throws on his shirt, his belt, his socks and boots.

He offers me his hand as he approaches. "Let's go to Kam Vin," he says. I take his hand and let him pull me up. "It's time for her to know we're ready to fight with them."

"How did you learn how to hide your wings?" I wonder, amazed at what I've just witnessed.

"I'm Lasair, Elloren" he says matter-of-factly. "We can form weak glamours."

"Oh."

For a moment I just stand there, feeling dazed.

"Elloren," Yvan says softly as he pulls me into a warm embrace, his lips soft on my temple.

"I still can't believe you can fly," I say, surreptitiously feeling along the hard planes of his back for some hint I might have missed. But I can't feel any trace of his wings.

He lets out an incredulous laugh and leans down to lightly kiss me, his lips enticingly warm. "And I can't believe I've fallen in love with the Black Witch."

"It certainly seems that way."

Yvan pulls away a fraction, his gaze ardent and firing up to gold. "It *is* that way." And then he kisses me again, his lips growing heated, his fire building and then flashing through my lines with a feverish urgency that makes me shudder against him.

"I'll bet no one imagined this when they wrote that Prophecy," I whisper as he brushes his mouth along the edge of my lips.

"I imagine not," he breathes. Then he brings his lips back to mine and kisses me ravenously.

He feels so good, so deliriously warm, that my thoughts tangle in on themselves and I almost forget about the fasting marks on my hands, about the huge forest fire still burning, about every impossible, world-shattering thing going on around us.

"So," I breathe, completely under his spell, "this is what it's like to kiss a dragon."

He smiles suggestively, his eyes blazing to gold. Then

he leans in and kisses me again, his tongue twining around mine, his movements slow and serpentine as his fire curls in a slow caress down my lines, trailing sparks all the way to my toes.

The sensation startles me, all the more heightened by the way he's pulling me against his long, hard body, and a tight desire takes hold.

"That's...interesting," I say, overwhelmed by my reaction to his touch, to his unbridled fire.

"I love kissing you," he says. "Sharing this fire with someone... It's *incredible*."

"What did you mean when you said that kissing would bind us?" I ask as he threads his fingers back through my hair, brushing his lips along my neck.

He hesitates, his breath hot on my skin. "A dragon's kiss binds him to his mate."

I pull back to meet his molten gaze. "So...now we're bound?"

He shakes his head, a ruddy flush on his cheeks. "No. You're not a dragon. In our case...it only goes one way. I'm bound to you."

"Like fasting?" I ask haltingly.

He tilts his head, considering. "No. It's more of a bond of fealty. I'll know when you're in danger. I'll sense any pain you experience."

A troubling thought occurs to me. "And if I die?"

Yvan's face tenses at the idea. "For a time, I'd be stripped of my fire, my power."

"Oh, Yvan." I pull in a long breath. "Maybe you should have held off on kissing me." I reach up to touch his face, running my thumb along his angular cheekbone.

A large branch crackles and falls to the ground, making both of us jump. I glance at the fire, trepidation rising. "We should go. We need to find the Vu Trin and tell them what we are." I lift up my wand hand. "And I need to learn how to use this…this *power.*"

If we're going to fight, we're going to have to learn how to fight well.

"Commander Vin will bring us east," Yvan says with certainty, watching the fire.

I reach down and pull the Wand of Myth from my boot, my affinity lines lurching toward its spiraling wood. I tighten my fist around it and test the weight of it in my hand.

Weakness is no longer an option.

"I'm going to learn how to use this." I look up into Yvan's fiery eyes. "I'm going to harness every last bit of power inside me, and I'm going to learn every spell in every grimoire. And then I'm going to come back for Marcus Vogel."

CHAPTER NINE

RESISTANCE

Yvan and I set out for the eastern outskirts of Verpax City that evening, the two of us heavily cloaked and riding on the same horse. We pass through the city, then farmland and into the starlit wilds, our path lit by the lumenstone lantern I'm clutching in my hand.

I cling to Yvan, drawing some comfort from the warm solidity of him, but still, trepidation swells in me, threatening to overwhelm. Yvan's palm slides over my hand, as if sensing my disquiet, his fire reaching out to me and enfolding me in warmth.

After a time, Yvan abruptly veers off onto a slim road that passes through the dense forest and comes to a stop before a small clearing.

Silence fills the air around us, save for the spring peepers sounding their chirping call. I take in our surroundings as we dismount, and Yvan secures our horse. There's a short, sloping hill before us, a hillock at its crest with a large, flat stone face.

"Elloren."

I turn to find Yvan by my side. He takes my hand in his, our fingers lacing, and we start up the hill.

We're not more than halfway up when emerald runes abruptly burst to life in a circle around us. We both freeze, the plate-sized runes glowing brightly and floating in the air.

A tall, slender man strides toward us from the shadows near the hillock, runic-illumination washing over him as he nears. He's a Smaragdalfar Elf, the emerald pattern of his skin enhanced by the green light. His silver eyes bore into us, then widen as recognition spreads across his face.

"Professor Hawkkyn?" I ask, surprised.

"Elloren Gardner," my former Metallurgie professor says, his voice riddled with confusion. He looks to Yvan, as if searching for some explanation.

"We need to see Commander Vin," Yvan says, his hard tone brooking no contradiction.

Professor Hawkkyn eyes him with incredulity, his gaze flicking to me. "She cannot go in there."

"She has power," Yvan states.

He shakes his head, unmoved. "I don't care if she has some wand-power, she can't—"

"No," Yvan says, his voice sharpening. "She has *power.* And I have wings."

Professor Hawkkyn blinks at us, as if suddenly readjusting his entire view of the world, fierce astonishment in his silver gaze. His eyes don't budge from us as he lifts his fist, palm out, and splays open his fingers.

The runes blink out of existence.

I pull in a deep, shuddering breath as he angles his head toward the hillock, indicating for us to follow, then turns and strides up the hill. Apprehension kindles my nerves as Yvan and I trail him up, our hands clasped tightly together.

THE IRON FLOWER

When Professor Hawkkyn reaches the hillock's stone face, he wordlessly pulls a small stone marked with an emerald rune from his tunic pocket and presses it to the rock wall.

I watch, transfixed, as circular emerald runes burst to life all over the stone. A portion of the wall shudders, like the surface of an agitated lake, then dissolves to verdant mist, revealing a rune-marked double door.

Professor Hawkkyn pulls the doors open, and blue light floods over us. Inside, two young Vu Trin sorceresses spring to attention and unsheathe curved rune-swords.

Professor Hawkkyn steps inside and speaks to them in what sounds like the staccato notes of the Noi language. Both sorceresses' eyes light with surprise as their gazes fly toward Yvan and then me with no small amount of alarm, and I notice that they keep their swords unsheathed.

My heart thuds against my chest as Professor Hawkkyn motions Yvan and me forward. The sorceresses fall in behind us as we follow him into a narrow, tunneling corridor that slopes sharply down, and I can sense their eyes on my back. The air cools as we descend, and I breathe in the chalky smell of clean, water-washed stone.

The clank of metal on metal sounds up ahead, as well as the sound of men's voices, and we soon approach a smithy that's been built right into the cave. A blast of heat washes over me as I spot two muscular Smaragdalfar Elves busily pounding rune-swords into shape. The two smiths pause in their work as they catch sight of us, eyeing me with open astonishment mixed with a troubling edge of hostility.

There are runes everywhere in the network of caves, suspended in the air and glowing both Smaragdalfar green and Noi blue. Some are motionless, while others rotate lazily, and a few spin so fast, they look like solid discs of light.

We pass multiple weapons caches—swords and every type

of bladed weapon jammed into large vaults hewn into the cave's walls. Enough weapons to supply a sizable army.

The sheer scale of what's happening here starts to dawn on me. *The Resistance never left Verpacia. They simply brought it underground.*

Yvan and I follow Professor Hawkkyn through another winding, narrow corridor, the repetitive clacking of wood against wood echoing off the stone walls. An expansive cavern comes into view up ahead, a wide variety of rune-weapons hang all over the stone walls. Commander Vin and her sister are sparring with rune-staffs, bursts of blue light flashing off the staffs with each parried blow, a sizable number of Vu Trin sorceresses intently watching their engagement.

We step out into a large, circular cavern and everything stops.

Commander Vin swings around to face us, her battle staff clutched in her fist. She brings one end of it to the stone ground with a decided *thud* as her eyes narrow on me with potent focus. Close to twenty other sorceresses dressed in military garb stand around the cavern, lines of silver stars secured diagonally across their chests. Four of the sorceresses wear the dark gray uniforms and black head wrappings of their elite Kin Hoang fighting force.

Shock scythes through me as I catch sight of Jules and Lucretia hovering around a wooden table set by the wall, the table's broad surface covered in maps and a pile of documents. I do a double take as my gaze takes in bespectacled Lucretia, her Gardnerian clothing gone and replaced by a black Noi military tunic and pants. There's a sprig of glowing Ironflowers in her upswept hair.

"Elloren," Jules says, blinking in obvious astonishment. Lucretia straightens, her eyes moon-wide.

They don't know what I am, I realize. I look to Commander Vin, who's watching me closely.

But you've known all along, haven't you?

My composure snaps. I release Yvan's hand and step toward her, a reckless outrage overtaking me.

"How long have you known what I am?" I demand of Commander Vin.

Murmurs of confusion fill the cavern.

"I didn't know. I only suspected," she says grimly.

"Know what?" Jules asks, stepping forward.

"Kamitra, what's this?" Lucretia asks, seeming deeply thrown.

"I have power," I tell them, not taking my eyes off Commander Vin. "Quite a lot of it, actually. And I can access it. Isn't that right, Kamitra?"

More agitated murmuring.

"I gave you a blocked wand for your wandtesting," Commander Vin tells me evenly. "When you dropped it, I suspected that you were powerful. Only a Mage of great power could summon enough magic to cause pain."

Sounds of uneasy surprise ripple across the room as a feeling of unreality washes over me.

"You should have told me," I challenge her, a bitter frustration rising in my throat, my voice becoming rough with emotion. "I could have helped my uncle. He's dead now, at the hands of my aunt. Did you know that?"

Commander Vin's face tenses. "No, I did not. I'm sorry."

"All the others," I press, caught up in a sudden clutch of anguish. *Ariel. All the refugees now trapped in the Western Realm.* "I could have done something."

Her mouth becomes one tight line. "I could not be sure of your intentions or of your character. Only the Wand of Myth choosing you gave me pause..."

"Pause in what?"

She eyes me with stark focus. "Pause in cutting you down."

My thoughts cyclone, her words hanging in the air with terrible resonance.

"Once your power quickened," Commander Vin says, "you needed to prove yourself by coming to *us*. And I needed to watch you for a time—to see what direction you chose. You are a dangerous weapon, Elloren Gardner. And every seer of every land has scried the same Prophecy."

"Of the Black Witch and the Icaral she's supposed to defeat," I offer up stiffly.

"Yes," Lucretia says with a slight nod. "Possibly you. And Sage Gaffney's child—the only male Icaral in the Western Realm with intact wings."

I turn to Yvan with a meaningful look. His eyes flash to mine, flaming gold at the edges. He reaches up and starts unbuttoning his shirt.

Commander Vin cocks her head to one side as everyone in the room eyes Yvan with confusion. He shrugs off his shirt and lets it drop to the floor. Then he leans his head down and closes his eyes.

His hair brightens to flame red, like fire catching on a candle's wick, his ears forming Fae points, his black wings coming to life and unfurling.

Shocked gasps echo throughout the circular room as Commander Vin's eyes widen.

Yvan takes my hand firmly in his as his wings fan out and flap once, a defiant look flashing across his face as we hold on tight to each other.

"Well, now," Commander Vin says, quickly regaining her rock-solid composure. She slowly walks around us, her eyes riveted on Yvan's wings. "This is a particularly interesting turn of events. The two points of the Great Prophecy are allies. Lovers, by the look of things." She pauses in front of Yvan. "What do you know of your powers, Yvan Guriel?"

"Very little." Yvan describes what he can do, the faces of everyone surrounding us becoming impressed and heartened. But I notice another undercurrent at work here, the sorceresses' eyes narrowing with apprehension as they glance toward me.

And fear.

Commander Vin shakes her head incredulously. "The two most powerful beings on Erthia, ignorant of how to harness or use their full powers. Incredible."

Her eyes flick over to the other sorceresses, then back to me. "Are you ready to fight both the Gardnerians and the Alfsigr, Elloren Gardner?"

"Yes," I say adamantly, unease spiking as I note the dubious looks on so many faces, and the fact that she leveled this question *only* at me. "We're *both* ready to fight the Gardnerians and the Alfsigr."

"In that case," Commander Vin says, "it is high time you were both well trained. Elloren Gardner, you will come with me and a portion of my guard." She looks at Yvan. "Yvan Guriel, you will travel east with our Kin Hoang division."

Panic rears inside me, and my eyes fly to Yvan's, our hands tightening protectively around each other's.

"We're staying together," Yvan stolidly insists, rebellion firing in his eyes.

"You cannot," Commander Vin counters. "You must see that. We have to separate you."

I glance around, feeling suddenly cornered as I realize what they're trying to do.

They want to make it harder for the Gardnerians to kill us both. But they also want to protect Yvan, the blessed point of the Prophecy, from me.

In case I turn into the Black Witch of their nightmares.

I inwardly rail against Commander Vin's cold, unflinching logic, even as I grapple with the fact that, in part, she's probably right.

"I won't leave you," Yvan protests, his eyes burning gold.

You need to. For your own safety. "Yvan, this is bigger than us."

The Western Realm has fallen. Everything has shifted to the East—both the flow of refugees and the coming war. And Yvan and I are potentially the head of the spear in that war.

We are the front lines.

A tear slides down my cheek even as something tough and jagged as the Spine rises within me. Yvan reaches up to gently wipe the tear away with his thumb, his eyes blazing.

"I love you," I tell him as the rest of the room falls away into insignificance.

He pushes his fingers back through my hair and cups my head in a way that speaks of a sudden, covetous fervor. "I love you, too." He pulls me close and encircles me with both his arms and his wings.

We cling to each other, his heartbeat sounding against mine. I close my eyes, and for a brief, blessed moment, we're the only two people in the room.

"Wait for me," he whispers.

I nod against his tear-slicked cheek, and it's impossible to tell which tears are his and which are my own.

"Yvan Guriel," Commander Vin says, her tone filled with urgency. We both turn to her. "We need to remove you from the Western Realm. *Now.*"

Two gray-clad Kin Hoang sorceresses step forward, and my heart pounds against my chest. Yvan and I cling to each other.

"Where will you take him?" I ask, imploring.

"Somewhere safe," Commander Vin assures me. "Somewhere isolated, where he can train. We cannot tell you where that is, Elloren Gardner. You must understand."

In case the Gardnerians find me. In case I'm the wrong point of the Prophecy after all.

I look to Yvan, tears falling. "So, this is goodbye, then."

He reaches out to stroke my hair and looks at me intently, as if he's trying to memorize my face. "Be strong," he says, both of his warm hands on my face now.

"I will," I promise through my tears.

And then Yvan brings his lips to mine one last time and sends his fire through me with such force that the heat still blazes through me even after he breaks the kiss.

He gives me one last impassioned look, then gently pulls away and turns to the Vu Trin. "I'm ready," he says.

The Kin Hoang fall in around him, and I watch him leave through a sheen of tears, his back decidedly straight, his wings freed, as he strides into the glowing blue haze of one of the cavern's many exit tunnels, the Kin Hoang following close behind.

And then he's gone.

I'm crying in earnest now, hollowed out.

Jules Kristian's arm comes around me, and I fall into him.

"Did you know?" I cry into his tunic.

"No."

I shake my head back and forth against the rough wool on his shoulder, then look up at him with disbelief. "I don't know if I'm equal to this."

Jules meets the gravity of my stare. "You will be. In time." He smiles ruefully. "You did wish to be clever *and* powerful."

I bark out a futilistic laugh at the absurdity of it all.

"You have to be careful what you wish for, eh?" he says.

I nod, drawing comfort from his kind words and gentle humor in the face of all this.

"What a startling turn of events," he says, shaking his head. "I am glad it's you, Elloren."

Me, of all people.

The Black Witch.

Jules reaches into his shirt pocket and pulls out a small bouquet of Ironflowers, the glowing blue blossoms a match for the sapphire Noi runes glowing around the room.

"Lucretia wanted you to have these," he says, growing reflective, eyeing the blooms. "The Ironwood tree has an interesting life cycle. It spends one long year on the forest floor as a delicate, fragile flower. Easily broken. Easily destroyed." His eyes meet mine. "But if it survives, it seeds to become a strong, deeply rooted tree."

I take the flowers, their glow washing over my hand like a splash of paint. "These flowers," I tell him, eyeing the luminous blossoms, "they were used to fight demons in our myths."

When I look up at him, his expression has grown serious. "The true demons of this world come in many guises, Elloren Gardner. Go find them," he says, his tone unyielding. "And go fight them."

Bolstered, I take one last look at Jules, then straighten and turn to face Commander Vin. "Let's go."

EPILOGUE

Hours later, I'm dressed in Noi battle armor and being silently led through a series of descending, tunneling passageways, the Wand of Myth sheathed at my side.

I follow the long line of Vu Trin sorceresses, my eyes set on the straight back of the young sorceress before me as I try to beat back the claustrophobic sense that we're inescapably burrowing down toward the very center of Erthia.

Eventually, the corridor spills out into an enormous cave that I take in with no small amount of awe.

Crystalline stalagmites and stalactites rise and fall all around us, their translucent surfaces glinting blue in the Noi rune-light. The mineral formations have been cleared away in the center of the cave, the hard floor a flattened swirl of crystal.

A throng of Vu Trin sorceresses and a smattering of young Smaragdalfar men and women mill about, stacking crates of weapons. Off to the side, a line of horses is saddled and tethered, most of them weighted down with the heavy packs needed for a long journey.

But none of this is what draws my eye like a moth to lantern light, my breath catching tight in my throat.

In the center of the cavern stands an arc of rotating Noi runes forming the outline of a passageway. A line of blue light scythes from rune to rune, spitting out slim veins of sparking lightning over the expanse of the rune-portal's frame. The center of the portal is wavy and rippling, like the surface of a golden lake.

Two white-haired, elderly Vu Trin soldiers stand at the portal's sides. One of the women supports herself on a long rune-staff and is tapping what seems like a series of codes into the portal with a flat, rune-marked stone.

A pat on my arm pulls my attention away from the huge portal and toward a serious young sorceress, the reins of a horse tightly gripped in her hand. She motions curtly for me to mount, the other soldiers in our party already pulling themselves astride horses.

I climb on top of the ebony mare and ride toward the looming portal with Commander Vin and our party's small contingent of soldiers.

I slow my horse to a stop before the looming portal and look toward it with mounting apprehension.

I've no idea where it leads.

Commander Vin rides up beside me and turns to look at me. The motion crinkles the neckline of her tunic, revealing a small tattoo just below her collarbone.

A white bird.

"Are you ready, Elloren Gardner?" she asks.

I reflexively reach for the comfort of the Wand of Myth as I take in the shimmering portal before me.

I think of Uncle Edwin and my brothers. Of Fernyllia

and Fern. Bleddyn and Olilly and all the kitchen workers. I think of Wynter and Ariel, Cael and Rhys and Andras. The Lupines, Tierney, Aislinn...

Everyone I love.

And Yvan.

I grasp the Wand firmly and turn to Commander Vin. "I'm ready," I say with conviction.

She glances down at my fastmarked hand clenched around the Wand's handle. A satisfied smile turns up the corners of her lips. She straightens on her horse and motions toward the portal before us.

"Then enter, Elloren Gardner."

I tighten my grip on the Wand, drawing comfort from the feel of the spiraling wood. My affinity lines flare—earth, fire, air and a slim trace of water.

Full of resolve, I prod my horse forward, the Ironflowers Jules gave me tucked into the collar of my tunic. The portal's wall of shimmering gold ripples as I approach, flashing silver as I ride into it.

I'll be different from you, Grandmother, I inwardly vow as the Western Realm fades away behind me. *And I'll be back for Marcus Vogel.*

I'm going to take him down.

★ ★ ★ ★ ★

Will Elloren's fire be enough to hold back the forces of darkness bent on consuming Erthia?

Find out in
The Shadow Wand
book three of The Black Witch Chronicles,
only from Laurie Forest and Inkyard Press!

MAGE COUNCIL
RULING
#366

All Icarals in the Western and Eastern
Realms of Erthia are to be hunted down and
executed.
Assisting in the concealment or escape of
Icarals is hereby declared one of the worst
possible crimes against the Holy Magedom of
Gardneria.

It shall be punished without mercy.

ACKNOWLEDGMENTS

First of all, thank you to my husband, Walter, for his unflinching and enthusiastic support. I love you.

To my epic daughters—Alex, Willow, Taylor and Schuyler—thank you for supporting me in this author thing and being so all-around great. I love you.

Love going out to my late mother, Mary Jane Sexton, and to my late close friend, Diane Dexter. In the moments that seemed most daunting, I remembered how much you both believed in me and this series. Your feisty legacy continues to inspire me.

Thank you to my mother-in-law, Gail Kamaras; my sister-in-law, Jessica Bowers; and Keith Marcum, for all your support. I love you guys.

A shout-out to my brilliant author brother, Mr. Beanbag, for always being awesome and always being supportive of me. Love you.

Thanks also go out to my nephew, Noah, for your support and humor. You rock!

To authors Cam M. Sato and Kimberly Ann Hunt, my international writing group cohorts—thank you for sharing your incredible talent and friendship with me week after week. I feel privileged to be on this writing journey with you both.

Thank you to author/editor Dian Parker for sharing your incredible talent with me, and to author Eva Gumprecht for being an inspiration.

Thank you to Liz Zundel for sharing your writing talent and for your friendship. Love you, Liz. And thank you, Betty—much love going out to you.

Thank you, Suzanne. Your support this past year has been everything.

A million thanks to my fellow authors at Harlequin TEEN. I'm not only starstruck by all of you and your talent, I'm also so grateful for your support and friendship.

To the authors of Utah (a new favorite place) and the librarians of Texas (I was told you all rock, and now know the praise is spot-on)—I am so happy to know all of you. Thank you for all the support.

To YALSA and all the librarians who have supported me and my series—you are the definition of awesome.

Thank you to Jessie. And thank you to authors Ileana, Shaila, Jennifer, Summer, Ira, Erin, Stephanie, Keira, G., Abby, McCall, Liz, Lia, P., Joel, Laura, R., C., Meg, Sierra, Jon, J. and V. and thank you to all the other authors who have supported me throughout the past year. I feel so lucky to know you and to have the privilege of reading your phenomenal books!

Thanks going out to Lorraine for so much positive support. Love you, college roomie :)

Thank you to the Burlington Writers' Workshop and the

2017 debut group for all the support, and for sharing your endless talent and creativity with me.

Thank you, Mike Marcotte, for all the tech support with my website.

A shout-out to Seth H. Frisbie, PhD, for being the coolest scientist out there and helping me bring real-world chemistry into my fantasy Chemistrie chapters.

Thank you to local authors Rickey, Kane and Ryan, and to all the other Vermont authors (you are legion) who were so supportive of me and my series throughout the last year. I'm so grateful to you all. Also, thank you to the Vermont College of Fine Arts for all the support throughout the year. You are a magical place of inspiration. And thank you to the League of Vermont Writers for being awesome.

Thank you to Dan and Bronwyn (I love you guys), and thank you, John G., for your support and friendship.

To all the librarians at the Kellogg Hubbard Library for being so enthusiastic and supportive of my series—a giant thank you. And thank you to librarian Loona for all the support.

Ashley and Milinda—thank you for all the equestrian information (and for not laughing too hard at my supreme horse ignorance).

Thank you to all the bookstores that have been so enthusiastic about this series, including Phoenix Books in Burlington, Vermont; Bear Pond Books in Montpelier, Vermont; and Next Chapter Bookstore in Barre, Vermont. Also, thank you to the booksellers working in the YA section at the Burlington, Vermont, Barnes & Noble, for your boundless enthusiasm.

To all the bloggers and readers who have been so supportive of me online—you are all so fun and great. I'm enjoying being on this series journey with you all. Thank you for all the notes and letters and great ideas!

To my sensitivity readers: Thank you for making this book so much better with your insightful suggestions and inclusive vision. Any flaws that remain are completely my own.

Thank you to two of my favorite authors, Tamora Pierce and Robin Hobb, for your support and praise. I'll never be able to thank you enough.

Thank you to my phenomenally talented audio readers for the series—Julia Whelan, Jesse Vilinsky and Amy McFadden.

And a huge thank you to everyone at Harlequin TEEN and HarperCollins who have supported both me and this series. I can't believe I get to work with people of your caliber.

Thank you to Natashya Wilson, editorial director at Harlequin TEEN and Gabrielle Vicedomini, editorial assistant, for everything. And thank you to my phenomenal editor, Lauren Smulski, for making every one of my books miles better.

Thank you to Reka Rubin and Christine Tsai on the Harlequin subrights team, for being such huge fans of The Black Witch Chronicles, and for your efforts to bring my books to readers all over the world.

Thank you to Shara Alexander, Laura Gianino, Siena Koncsol, Megan Beatie, Linette Kim, Evan Brown, Amy Jones, Bryn Collier, Aurora Ruiz, Krista Mitchell and everyone else in marketing and publicity who helped to promote this series.

To Kathleen Oudit and Mary Luna of Harlequin's talented art department—I can never thank you enough for my spectacular covers and map.

Many thanks to the sales team for their support—and especially Gillian Wise, for your boundless enthusiasm for The Black Witch Chronicles.

A big thank you to Harlequin TEEN's digital promoters/ social media team: Eleanor Elliott, Larissa Walker, Monika Rola and Olivia Gissing.

And lastly, thank you to my wonderful agent, Carrie Hannigan, and to everyone else at the HSG Agency, for all your support and for believing in The Black Witch Chronicles for so many years. Much love going out to all of you.